DUNCTON TALES

Moledom

WHERN

Wharfe

SIABOD

Beechenhill

Dark Peak

Cannock

Rollright

Caer Caradoc

THE WEN

Severn

DUNCTON WOOD

Thames

Fyfield

Avebury

Buckland

UFFINGTON

The Stones of Seven Barrows

Based on Mayweed's map found in Seven Barrows

DUNCTON TALES

WILLIAM HORWOOD

HarperCollins
An Imprint of HarperCollins*Publishers*

First published in 1991
by HarperCollins*Publishers*,
77–85 Fulham Palace Road,
Hammersmith, London W6 8JB

9 8 7 6 5 4 3 2 1

A catalogue record for this book is available
from the British Library

ISBN 0 00 223676 1

Typeset in Linotron Caledonia by
Rowland Phototypesetting Ltd
Bury St Edmunds, Suffolk

Printed and bound in Great Britain by
HarperCollins Book Manufacturing, Glasgow

CONTENTS

	Prologue	1
Part I	*A Pilgrim in Winter*	5
Part II	*Darkness Newborn*	83
Part III	*Rooster*	189
Part IV	*The Sound of Silence*	401
	Epilogue	451

PROLOGUE

Greetings mole, and welcome.

Today, when moledom has its liberty, and all systems allow moles to speak their minds without fear of retribution or attack, and to worship as they will, only pilgrims like yourself visit sleepy Duncton Wood.

Moles reared to a sense of history, who can never quite forget that their present freedoms were won by Duncton moles, and who, if only once in their lives, wish to visit this old place of ours, and see the tunnels and trek the surface where our great forebears lived.

All moledom knows that it was they who a century ago, in those dark days when disciples of the cruel Word spread down from the north with their tyranny of dogma and destruction, had the courage to raise their talons in defence of faith in the Stone, and risked – and sometimes lost – their lives that future generations might be free.

The inspiring story of that generation of Duncton moles has often been told, most notably by Woodruff of Arbor Low, whose Duncton Chronicles is as good and true account of the war of Word on Stone as is ever likely to be scribed.

Yet you have asked for a different tale, which makes you rare, and doubly welcome. You've asked to be told the subsequent history of Duncton Wood, from the time of the arrival of a certain female scribe called Privet, and a modest little text she brought which is generally called the Book of Tales.

How very interesting! What an acute mole you are! Most moles who come here as you have done, with the look of the hungry scholar in their eyes and their scribing paw at the ready, are not in the slightest bit interested in the Book of Tales. Oh no, they hurry old tale-tellers like me past such things, and try to get us to tell them about the lost Book of Silence, which is the greatest of the Seven Books of Moledom.

But not you! You keep asking about Privet and the Book of Tales, and you evidently know something about it too, because you've been seeking information about certain other moles, like Cobbett and Husk,

1

whose names are, to those who know about such things, also associated with Tales.

So they've sent you to me, for they know I'm one of the last of the generation whose kin were living at the time and remember something of the facts, even though they know I vowed I'd never talk about such things again.

But old moles can change their minds, and there's something about you I recognize in myself when I was young, and, like you, just a little bit too earnest. But your heart's in the right place, and you've understood something which few others have ever seemed to: there would have been no Book of Silence, no saving and redemption of moledom, without the 'little matter of Tales' (to quote one of your more impatient predecessors on the scholarly trail) in the first place. Aye, in its beginning is its ending, in its ending is its beginning.

Mole, I'll talk to you because you're willing to listen to things others deem unimportant and you're willing to indulge an old mole to get at the truth.

Now, you've asked if you might scribe my words down, and so you may. But I've brought you here to the Stone Clearing in the High Wood so that if exaggeration or romance or an untoward love of horror, drama, thrills or even sensuality should begin to affect your scribing paw, you may glance up at the Stone and be reminded to scribe only as truly as I shall seek to tell . . .

No, no, tell me not your name. It is easier if I know it not until I have done, for I've a feeling this is the last time I shall ever tell this tale, and I have an old mole's fancy to tell it, as it were, to allmole, not just one. And anyway, as you'll see, there's subtlety in Duncton Wood and subtlety in this: anonymity is of the very essence of what I have to say.

As for your questions, there was a time in the decades after the conclusion of the war of Word upon Stone when many moles asked as you have also done: 'What of the Book of Silence? Where is it? What is its significance?'

To which the answers were once many and the controversies varied, but it may be said that most moles at that time believed that this last Book had not been scribed *and would never be.* Its nature, even wise moles said, was unscribable. Yet in all generations there rise up a few exceptional moles who question, and who doubt, and in whom the spirit of enquiry and desire for truth is so powerful that they sacrifice much to wander moledom all their lives in a search for satisfaction of it.

2

Such moles as these moles were known in the decades after the events described in the Chronicles as wandering scribes, and sometimes as wandering scholars. Moles of open heart and open spirit, who travelled out into moledom to learn things for themselves and who often ended their days teaching other moles what they had found.

Most were scribemoles like yourself, obsessed by some question they had asked when young to which the answers they received seemed less than satisfactory. In time most found their answers, or having learnt enough, lost interest or belief in the pursuit of final answers and settled down in some niche of their own, to leave another generation to take forward once more the spirit of enquiry.

The tale, or rather tales, that I shall tell you concern the greatest of the wandering scholars of that time. Her name was Privet and she was born in a place to the north called Bleaklow Moor. Her greatness lay not only in asking the right question, but in pursuing its answer to its very end, even at the risk of faith, of love, of life itself.

After suffering certain trials and tribulations, and a sojourn at holy Beechenhill, shy Privet, as moles called her, finally set off to Duncton Wood as you have done, bringing with her as her only offering a modest text.

Few can have expected her to solve the mystery of the Book of Silence; none to have found a way to complete that circle of seven hallowed Books and Stillstones that lies within the eternal protection of the Chamber of Roots beneath the Duncton Stone.

The tales you seek to scribe down from me make up something of Privet's story, and tell of many moles whose destinies touched hers. Moles she learned to love, and who learned love from her.

Some have called these tales the last of Duncton Wood. Others, whose understanding runs deep indeed, have said they really are the first. For after them, and after Privet's extraordinary quest was done, Duncton slipped away into the mists of time and legend, its noisy moment in the pageant of history seen at last as but the preface to a time of renewal and peace.

In that beginning, wise moles have said, was our ending; yet perhaps it is more true to say that in that ending was our true beginning . . . and some would add that if moles first knew these tales, they could the better ken the deeper meaning of the Duncton Chronicles.

Therefore, mole, from my heart to your heart I now tell these tales, my words spoken in the presence of the Stone I love, which has given my life meaning and faith.

3

Yet I am weak, and sometimes the Silence calls me now, and all my tales begin to fade . . .

Therefore fetch me food!

Encourage me!

And scribe well, for I'll not repeat myself!

As for this sun which warms my patchy fur, and the pleasant rustle of leaves about us, and that blue sky far above our pates, forget them all, mole!

Imagine instead that you shiver with cold, and that your snout is freezing, and you've fluffed out your fur for warmth: for it is with a pilgrim in harsh winter that I must begin . . .

PART I

A Pilgrim in Winter

Chapter One

December, deep December, and the trees of Duncton Wood were restless with cutting winter winds. Then, somewhere high above, a dead branch cracked and swung dangerous and ready to fall, while far below, upon the surface of the wood, dead leaves swirled and gyred on themselves.

The wind blew on, and brought a solitary traveller up the south-eastern pasture slopes to the edge of the oldest and highest part of the Wood, where she was halted by the sound of that branch finally crashing down. Anxiously she peered in among the trees. Her paws were muddy and torn from the long trek she had made that day to reach the safety of moledom's most famous system before worse weather came.

As she stanced and stared her fur blew this way and that, as if the wind were cruelly trying to make one last desperate effort to tear her away within the very sight of the place she had striven so long to reach. Indeed, she seemed to remain on the ground more from strength of spirit than of body, for she was slight, her flanks thin, and her face that of a thinker and scribemole, and not a normal venturing traveller. Yet, in truth, she did not even look as if she had much spirit left, or strength of any kind at all. She was of middle age, and seemed like a mole who had been hurt so terribly and lost so long that she had no faith any more in what lay ahead.

So she stanced in the wild wind, before the great Wood, and stared into the darker light among the trees. Only an observant mole would have noticed that she had carefully placed the battered text she had been carrying on a dry root near where she stanced and occasionally glanced towards it, to make sure it was still there, and safe. She did not look like one who has ever pupped, or one with any friends, or one who has any expectation of love or comfort, or of ever finding a home to which she might be welcomed back by those who have long missed her. A mole alone; driven, it seemed, to make a long and dangerous journey by some urge far stronger than herself. But a journey that seemed almost at an end, judging by the curious combination of fatigue and excitement with which she seemed filled.

For as she stared, once she had rested a little and seemed reassured by where she was, her timid eyes grew bright and she looked ready to venture on. But before she did she turned back to look behind her one last time, and paused for a long moment, like a mole who was saying goodbye, for good or ill, to all her past life.

Then, talking to the Stone as if it were her only friend, putting a paw on the text she had placed down, she whispered, 'Stone, I vowed I would bring this safely to Duncton Wood and I have. As you have guided me this far, may you direct my paws onward, to serve you and moles who have faith in you, as best I may! Help me know truth, help me to learn the truth of the mystery of all things, even of thy Books, and the Book of Silence. But Stone . . .'

She fell silent, and how long she stared, how sadly!

'Stone, wherever he is, whatever he does, give him strength all his days. Bless him Stone, keep him, guard him. Love him as I once loved him, and help him know thy love. Stone, my task is with this Book of Tales, that Duncton's great Library may accept it, and in time send copies to other great libraries that it may be for ever preserved. Ask no other task of me, for I have strength for no more.'

But more she could not say. But stanced in all the wind and bluster of the world with snout low, thinking of her precious text, and one final time of a mole to whom she was saying her last goodbye but whose name, even at such a moment, she seemed unwilling or unable to speak.

Yet any wise mole who had seen her then would have known that had the one of whom she spoke appeared trekking up that slope after her, joy would have been at Duncton's edge that day, and a whole life's recovered happiness. But such dreams are not to be. She stared alone, and nomole appeared upon the wintry slopes below. Nor was there shape or form in landscape or cloud that might have been construed to be even the hint or shadow of the mole she had evidently loved and lost.

The wind doubled upon itself, and a wall of grey hail swept across the pasture slopes below; she turned back to the Wood again, summoned up what little strength she had, bravely sought to seem a most courageous mole, and thrusting her snout forward, plunged in among the great beech trees of the highest part of Duncton Wood.

Then, with the strongest winds roaring impotently among the branches high above, she peered this way and that, wrinkling her snout and scenting the gusting air in the hope that some instinct would guide her to where she wished to go. But none seemed to, and after a few steps forward she paused again and looked about the gloomy place.

Gnarled and ancient beech trees were the only life, their grey-green trunks rising majestically through the surface covering of russet fallen leaves. The only bright thing she could see was a holly tree downslope to her right, whose green leaves and red berries gave some cheer to the sombre scene. It stood stiffly in the wind, shining leaves shaking slightly, and alone. She took up her text and made her way cautiously down towards it picking her path among dead leaves and fallen twigs and then past what must have been the great dead branch she had heard crash down earlier, soon finding that there was a track to follow which seemed to head towards the tree.

The track took her out of the wind and soon afterwards, though with her ears still thundering with its sound, she reached the tree and paused for breath and to consider what to do next. She sniffed her snout, wiped her eyes on the back of a paw, looked up, and saw with a start, staring at her from among the shadows at the tree's base, another mole, and a female at that.

'Cutting it a bit fine, aren't you?' said the mole by way of greeting. 'A bit longer and you'd have been benighted and not known where to go, for even if they can find them moles don't generally use the tunnels hereabout, least of all in weather like this. Dangerous, ruinous, haunted tunnels *they* are.

'Anyway, my name's Fieldfare and I'm Duncton-born, and seeing as I'm the only one daft enough to be here I'll be the one to welcome you to our system and wish you well.'

Fieldfare paused expectantly. She was a plump mole only a little older than the visitor, but with warm motherly eyes and pleasant grey fur. Either life had treated her well, or she had known how to get the best from it, for she radiated busy content.

'My name's Privet,' said the new arrival, 'and I . . . I'm very glad to see you. I *was* wondering where to go. But . . .' Her voice was as timid as her appearance, and she seemed anxious to please.

'If you're wondering why I'm here,' said Fieldfare, 'I'll tell you. It's because I'm a fool, that's why. A fool that hopes a certain mole might get himself back to Duncton in time for Longest Night.'

Privet nodded sympathetically, for Longest Night, the holiest night in all the cycle of the seasons, was but three days off. Most systems had a mole or two waiting at the main route around the time of Longest

Night, hoping that their heart's desire would return. Longest Night is not a time to be alone.

'What's his name?' asked Privet politely.

'Chater,' replied Fieldfare very willingly. 'He's a journeymole and *promised* me he'd be back. Swore till his snout was blue. Said there was nomole else and he'd die of loneliness if he wasn't with me on Longest Night. But . . . you know males, especially journey*males*!'

She laughed at her pun and Privet tried to laugh with her, though it was not in her nature to laugh quite so freely as Fieldfare seemed to, nor was this the moment. Yet, though she might not know much about males, she knew enough to know that journeymoles, whose job it was to carry copied texts from one library to another, had a reputation for fickleness and broken promises. A mole in every system, that seemed to be their way.

'You got a beau?' said Fieldfare, coming closer in a conspiratorial way.

Privet shook her head.

'Just now, or never?'

Privet said nothing and Fieldfare studied her.

'Had one once, eh?'

Reluctantly Privet nodded, plainly unsure whether to smile or cry. 'I came here . . .'

'. . . to forget,' said Fieldfare knowingly and with a sudden warmth, sensing she had touched on something the visitor was unhappy to talk about. As yet!

'Have a bite of this worm, my love, and take a tip from long-suffering me: the more you try to forget the more you fail to. So tell the world, and its boredom about your troubles will heal you. Mind you, I must admit that having followed my own advice it's so far failed. But then Chater, bless him, is something else again. So here *I* have been, day after day, hoping he'd show up and wishing to be on the spot to welcome him. But now 'tis getting dark and Chater may be lots of things but he's not a fool. He'll not trek up the slopes at night. There's always rooks, and even in this weather owls can fly, *and* take prey. So failing him, perhaps you'll keep me company?'

'Well, I don't know . . .' began Privet, 'I mean I was thinking I'd go straight to report to the Master Librarian when I got here, or perhaps if I was too late for that to the Stone to give thanks. And I don't want to cause you trouble. I have a text I wish to deliver to the Master Librarian. When I've done that I'll feel more . . . comfortable.'

'Master Librarian? The Stone? Cause me trouble? Comfortable?

For goodness' sake, mole! The one's been in retreat since October and nomole seen him since, and the Stone will still be there tomorrow and the next day after as well. As for troubling me, you look tired and in need of a rest and you can go through all the courtesies and rituals you like when you're more up to it. No need to put on a show for me, or be anything but yourself. I'd suggest Barrow Vale, but it's a fair way off and I'm cold and tired so I won't offer to take you.

'No, you come with me to my tunnels and relax, my dear, and tell me where you're from and why you're here. We like to know these things in Duncton, being an inquisitive lot. Your text will be safe enough in my tunnels for the night.'

'Well . . .' began Privet doubtfully.

'But then again, if you want to preserve your anonymity as they say, I will be only too pleased to tell you all about myself and about Duncton, and whatever else you may be pleased to know. In short, Privet, I'm fed up with being alone and I fancy a natter. What do you say?'

'Well, I don't know . . . I'm not sure . . . I mean . . . yes, please, I *would* like that!' said Privet with resolution, suddenly very tired indeed, and with a tremor to her voice which suggested that tears she did not wish to shed in front of a stranger were imminent.

The kindly Fieldfare stared at her, silent and thinking, reached out a paw, and said, 'There, you've arrived now and there's no need to struggle more. Duncton's a place that heals moles. Always was and always will be. You're *welcome*, mole.'

'Am I?' said Privet staring, her eyes full of tears.

Fieldfare seemed to know it was a question asked not of her but of all moledom. 'Yes,' she said, 'I'm sure you are.'

In truth, Privet felt happy to be so warmly welcomed at the end of her long journey, happier than her reserved nature could easily allow her to admit. It seemed that Duncton moles were as friendly and as direct as moles had always said they were. It seemed . . .

'Come on then,' said Fieldfare firmly, stancing up and thinking perhaps that if they carried on like that *she* would be in tears as well, and for what? She had absolutely no idea. 'Follow me and we'll be there before darkness falls, and snug and replete before you can say "lobworm"!'

'Thank you,' said Privet, tiredness, gratitude, and relief flooding into her with each step she took, as she followed Fieldfare downslope through the wood.

11

Chapter Two

'Now,' said Fieldfare, as soon as had they settled down in her homely if untidy burrow, 'I've not brought you far from where you want to go, for the Library's not far off from here. If the weather eases off a bit overnight I'll show you the way there in the morning when I go back to do my stint of waiting for Chater once again. Meanwhile let's forget duty and good intentions, and talk! But put that text of yours over there, it makes me nervous the way you clutch it. Now, tell me about your journey getting here, and what bits of moledom you've seen.'

'What parts do you know?' asked Privet.

'Me? Oh, none at all. I'm Duncton born and bred. I've never been out of the system in my life. Never seen the need so far – too busy having pups and pushing them out of my tunnels and into the world. I doubt if even Chater could get me to leave now. But I've heard lots because when he's home Chater tells me, and down in Barrow Vale the visitors tell us what they've seen and all the news.'

Privet listened to the howling wind outside, snuggled into the comfortable nesting material Fieldfare had spread about her burrows, and began to think she had never felt better in her life.

'What news have you heard lately?' she asked.

'Nothing much. Rollright's got a new lot of elders, and about time too. Cannock's finally been re-populated after the nasty goings on at the time of the Word. The so-called Newborns are making a nuisance of themselves even here with their preaching, and moles generally are getting worried about them. That's about it really.'

She looked hopefully at Privet and said, 'Tell me something *juicy*.'

Privet smiled and looked apologetic. 'I think I know what you mean,' she said, 'but really I'm not that kind of mole. You're the first mole I've talked to for days and the last was just a youngster. But . . .'

She frowned, and Fieldfare looked at her with concerned interest.

'What I've seen of the Newborn moles *is* a bit worrying,' said Privet finally.

'Tell me about them if you like,' said Fieldfare, 'and when you've done I'll tell you about Duncton Wood.'

'Agreed!' said Privet.

Each mole was as good as her word, and they talked in the way that moles who know they are going to become friends talk, deep into the night, with never a pause or break, except for food, and to listen to the changes in the wind.

Privet told all she knew of how the Newborn sect had started and developed at Caer Caradoc, one of the seven ancient systems, lying far to the west of Duncton in the Welsh borderland. Caradoc had played a heroic role in the days of the defence of the Stone against the Word a century ago, but it was a high wild place which attracted strange moles and extremists, and after peace had been restored to moledom, the moles there had reverted to old ascetic ways of worshipping the Stone. However that mattered little, for if moles wish to plague themselves with guilt and self-inflicted punishments of body and mind, and deprive themselves of worms, let them do so. They'll see their foolishness in time.

But *this* sect not only believed its Newborn way was right, but, more sinisterly, that other moles who did not follow its beliefs were blasphemously wrong. Perhaps punishably so. Here then was the making of a new war, different from that of Word on Stone: a war in the name of the Stone upon moles who already believed in the Stone; a sectarian war, than which none can be more bitter nor more cruel.

It seemed that in recent years the long-lived Elder Senior Brother (as Cadarocian moles called their leader) had come under the influence of a much younger and more aggressive mole who had begun to send out young male missionaries to convert neighbouring systems to the Newborn way. Latterly these groups had gone further afield, and especially to the other ancient systems, including Duncton Wood itself, where they were tolerated but disliked.

'I mean,' declared Fieldfare, 'we may not seem to be ardent worshippers of the Stone, being a quiet lot that way and leaving much unspoken when it comes to faith, but we're followers through and through. What we don't need and don't like is those Newborns coming up from the grubby Marsh End and singing their stupid songs about love and the Stone's light being in the dew-drops, and the sinners among us blowing away before the Stone's anger like leaves from a dead tree. Nor do we want those preachers of theirs rabbiting on about Silence only being for those who follow the true way, which so far as I can see involves singing those songs and listening to those preachers – all male, I might say, every one of them – with adoration in our eyes like they was the Stone itself!'

Fieldfare was breathing heavily by the time she reached the end of this outburst, and briefly glared at Privet as if *she* might be a Newborn.

Then, calming down again, she said in a very different voice, 'Have you come across any of the Newborn moles then? And what about this mole who leads them by the snout?'

Privet nodded seriously. 'You mean Thripp of Blagrove Slide?'

'If that's his name, he's the one I mean. They call him Head of Missions or some such nonsense. Titles! Duncton moles don't go in for them, except in the Library, though even there they're a bit over the top. Cause more trouble than they're worth!'

'I don't know much about Thripp apart from his name, except that the Newborns seem to fear and respect him. These days they keep themselves to themselves in the systems I've visited where they have a presence, because they came up against the kind of resistance they obviously found here. Some say they're biding their time before becoming more aggressive again. In fact, I did meet a few of them in Rollright, where they tried to persuade me of the error of my ways!'

Privet smiled the tight smile of a mole who knows her mind and does not appreciate being evangelized by self-righteous moles convinced that they know best. Rollright was the nearest of the seven Ancient Systems to Duncton Wood itself, being but a few days' journey to the north.

'You're of the Stone then?' said Fieldfare, more interested now in Privet than the Newborns.

'I am,' said Privet briefly.

'Brought up in a system with a Stone, were you?' asked Fieldfare hopefully. But not for the first time in their conversation Privet proved unwilling to talk about her background and past, and fell silent.

'Yes, well, there we are,' said Fieldfare.

But she was a mole not easily put out, and she changed the conversation back to Newborns by asking if they had tried to persuade Privet from her beliefs.

'Once they realized I was not prepared to "open my heart", as they put it, they were courteous enough to me,' said Privet, 'but then moles usually are. I seem rather dull and harmless, I suppose, and not much use to anymole!'

'And aren't you?' said Fieldfare with a grin.

'I hope not, but then I've always been interested in scribing and

14

texts and know nothing else as yet. One day perhaps . . .' She looked coyly at Privet.

'No two ways about it,' said Fieldfare firmly, 'if a mole wants something badly enough she shall have it in time! Be it a worm, a friend, or an attractive male! It's deciding to get on with it that's the difficult bit. So you'd be a scholar then, or a journeymole perhaps, seeing as you've brought a text for the Library?'

'A scribemole really, scholar perhaps,' replied Privet. 'This text is just a few tales scribed with the help of a friend whose dying wish was that I bring them to Duncton Wood and continue my researches here. I really don't want to do anything more than that – it's enough to have got here, let alone try to do more!' She said this last quite vehemently, concerned, it seemed, with something Fieldfare had not even asked.

'Well, I'm sure nomole in Duncton will ask you to do what you don't want to,' Fieldfare felt obliged to say.

'If they do I'll not answer them, and I might even leave!' declared Privet. 'All I ask is to be left alone and given a chance to begin again!'

In the face of such an outburst Fieldfare felt it best to say no more.

The wind suddenly shook the roof above their heads and sent bits of chalky earth down on them. Fieldfare dusted herself off, looked up, and said, 'Oh Chater my love. I hope you're safe and sound and snug. I want you back in one piece!'

'Tell me about Duncton Wood,' said Privet, hoping to take her new friend's mind off her worries, 'and about the Library, and Stour, and any other mole you think I ought to know about!'

'I will, I will,' said Fieldfare, crunching at a worm and wondering where to start. 'I will!'

At the time this tale begins, no system in all of moledom attracted more interest, more pilgrimages, nor more anecdotes than Duncton Wood. For all moles knew that of all the seven Ancient Systems it was the one with the longest and proudest history of protecting Moledom's freedom against those incursions of body and spirit that from time to time evil moles seek to impose upon it. Indeed, Duncton had been at the forefront of the struggle of followers of the Stone against the cruel Word, a bitter fight that had ended seven Longest Nights of nearly a century before, but whose livid scars remained to that day in many of moledom's systems.

True, places to the north like Beechenhill, where the Stone Mole served his final ministry, and found his greatest trial, were for a time a greater focus of reverence and quiet journeying; while the dread system of Whern, for those travellers whose natures bent darkly to visiting the terrible and odd, undeniably held a morbid fascination. Then, too, Siabod to the far west in Wales, and ruined Uffington to the south, had their share of legend and story for a generation that had been too young to remember the cruel war wreaked by disciples of the Word upon the followers of the Stone.

But Duncton was the system moles most liked to hear their elders tell about, and no Longest Night could pass by and be *called* Longest Night, without a tale or two of the heroic deeds and doings of the moles who in the days of Bracken and his son Tryfan, kept their faith with the Stone and struggled to vanquish the vile terror that had been the Word, and whose full history was first chronicled by Woodruff of Arbor Low.

It had been most wisely decreed at the great Conclave of Cannock, when the last followers of the Word were arraigned and their crimes finally punished or absolved, that copies of Woodruff's great work should be made and distributed to all the seven Ancient Systems, and five systems beside including Beechenhill, so that allmole might have access to the sobering history therein.

In the period when there were moles still alive who had stanced flank to flank with Tryfan himself, or had heard the teachings of the Stone Mole with their own ears, much else had been scribed down, and there had begun a tradition that the texts from Duncton (and other places too) should be spread far and wide, and not be confined and held secretly as such texts had been in the not-so-distant days when only the holy system of Uffington had been allowed to train scribemoles. Added to which, those twelve systems mandated at Cannock to hold copies of the great mole texts were likewise told to encourage the teaching of scribing, so that the office of scribemole should be free to all willing to strive for it, a freedom first dreamed of by Tryfan himself.

So it was that in the moleyears and decades following the coming of the Stone Mole and the mystery of his passing, words of scribe and storyteller served not only to consolidate moles' faith in the Stone once more, but also to emphasize that pre-eminent among all the systems of moledom as a place of faith, community and love of mole for mole, was Duncton Wood.

These surely were glorious years, and ones which would have warmed the heart of the great Duncton-born scribemole Tryfan, a mole who, though he said of himself that he made mistakes aplenty, yet led moles forward through the affliction of the Word, and scribed as his last gift to moledom the Rule of Duncton, which had become the Rule many other systems chose to follow for the proper conduct of their community life.

A Rule which despite its name was remarkable, not for its rules and strictures on how moles should live, but for its insistence that communities should never exclude dissidence, never cease to listen to follies of youth, of age and of obsession, never cease to learn to change; for in constraint, in judgement, in unthinking regulation and law, is communal death and not, as the proponents of such laws so often argue, the true maintenance of ordered life. At the centre of Tryfan's Rule was this: an open faith in the Stone, but with a tolerance and trust for everymole's right to reject the Stone if they wished. This freedom of faith was Tryfan's greatest gift to the generations that followed him.

But by the time Privet came to Duncton Wood these recent glories and new traditions of tolerance were under threat once more, not from outside, but from within. The war of Word and Stone had created successive generations of moles who were tired of fighting and reluctant to raise their talons once again. Worse, they were reluctant even to see that they might need to do so.

In such a situation dangerous sects like the Newborns easily thrive, and moles may come to see too late that they are on the way to losing their liberty once more . . .

But first, and before we take up our journey at Privet's flank, for moles who know not the system on which the Duncton Chronicles was centred and in which so much recent history was made, and for those who wonder what happened to it in the years following the events described in the Chronicles, we must learn something more of Duncton Wood itself.

Moles familiar with Duncton's history will readily appreciate that the wormful soils of its Westside attracted many of the moles who recolonized the system after the wars of the Word were over, and that from the conflicts for space and territory that inevitably ensued, the bigger and more enterprising moles tended once more to adopt that part of the Wood as their own.

But while in Bracken's day these more aggressive moles had extended their power on into the Wood beyond their natural territory, such was the spiritual strength of the whole Duncton community since Tryfan's day that this had not happened again. So far as there was expansion from the Westside it was out on to the Pastures, which in

17

former times was a separate and disliked community. Now it was cheerfully occupied by moles of the new Duncton stock, and communal tunnels between the Wood and Pastures ensured a ready and frequent interchange of moles. Indeed, if anything, this expansion of Duncton's traditional boundary had made Barrow Vale, which lies in-wood of the Westside, even more central to the system as a whole.

Barrow Vale itself, with its extensive communal chamber supported by the roots of trees which twisted and turned into a myriad of antechambers, nooks, and side burrows, remained the natural place for moles to meet and chatter, debate and fall in love. The runs and burrows around it formed an area that was the second most occupied part of the wood, and here older, more experienced moles had settled, and there was an air of sociable content about the place. It was to this part all visitors came or were soon directed, and here, adopting a tradition from Uffington's greatest days, several burrows were set aside for visitors, each with its own entrance, and all wormful enough to permit visitors and pilgrims to stay awhile in peaceful comfort.

Over on the less productive Eastside, where the trees and undergrowth thinned out above the poor soil, the more austere and reverent chose to live. Some of these found tasks in the Library under the direction of Stour (who himself lived in those parts), but others were there simply because they were wanderers by nature who liked a location near the cross-under below the south-east slopes so that they could come and go as they pleased without being observed, and live quietly undisturbed.

We have already seen that tunnels at the northern edge of the High Wood were used as the Library of the system. Of how this came about we shall have more to learn, but for now it is only necessary to say that the chambers and tunnels taken up with these texts (which also gave room to the copiers who serviced other systems and who formed an important daily function of the place), vast though they always seemed to newcomers, were in fact only a small part of the Ancient System as a whole.

The rest of it, the greater part covered by the High Wood, consisted of the unknown and long-deserted tunnels which once, before scribed history began, must have been a great system indeed. Of how it came to be deserted moles were, are, and always will be told fanciful tales. But we may guess that the real explanation for its desertion lay in some change of climate and soil that had robbed the area of its worms. For there were few of them about, and those thin and sour of taste, and even hungry moles avoided them.

So apart from the chambers and tunnels of the Library, the Ancient System remained barren and deserted of mole, and its tunnels, filled as they were with the sinister carvings which generated Dark Sound to confuse moles who ventured there, were visited by no sensible mole.

Although in Bracken's and Tryfan's day there had been some venturing down into these old tunnels, in the decades of peaceable content, since then they had become forgotten and feared once more. The very existence of the famous Chamber of Roots which protected the Stone's base, and into which nomole but those with a true heart and absolute faith dared venture, was known to none but a very few, except as legend, and a place that once was great. But there was something fitting in the fact that the Stone rose through tunnels now empty of mole, and silent of daily busyness, toil and strife. Ghosts there were, and shadows to frighten a mole, and strange sounds from the few entrances that still remained.

Moles chose to travel only the surface of the Ancient System, and that in awe, and they reached the Stone Clearing with gratitude, properly reminded that life is but short when set against a mole history in which whole systems of moles could be lost and forgotten.

Another area that was much as it had been in Bracken's youth, when the Chronicles began, was the low-lying Marsh End to the north. For such grubby and worm-poor ground, the Marsh End attracted extraordinary loyalty in its moles. The present occupants indeed were mostly descended from moles in whose hearts the memory of Duncton had been kept alive by those who succeeded in escaping the scourge of Henbane and her grikes in Tryfan's day, and who had come back to their ancestral home.

Thus far, then, was Duncton as it had been at the time of Bracken and his kin. But there were differences. In those days of which the Chronicles tell, the tunnels of Duncton were heavy with the threat of Mandrake and Rune, and loud with the rude laughter and mocking jeers of their henchmoles. Such debates as there were then were conducted in a Barrow Vale ruled by fear, for blood was ever on the paws of those that had ascendancy, and behind the chilling smiles of Rune and others of his kind (though thank the Stone there never was another *quite* like him) were eyes that saw innocent pups as things to kill, and they killed them even at their mothers' teats.

How different Duncton had become in the decades since those fateful days! Laughter and merriment had been the way since then, of moles whose lives were lived with respect for others' space and wish. Moles reared in a tradition of listening; moles who knew that whatever task they have, whatever skills or weaknesses the Stone and their own endeavours give them, they may find a worthy place in their community.

Through those great decades Duncton honoured its inhabitants, and opened its paws to any who came, giving them a welcome and a place, asking only that they were tolerant of others, whatever their faith or inclination might be. For make no mistake, there was many a mole who came to Duncton Wood (and some reared in its tunnels too) who were not especially of the Stone, and were willing to argue the night away with moles of faith, and prove what points they could.

Such is true freedom, and everymole in moledom knew that Duncton moles would hear another out and argue and share as hard as they could without bearing grudges or making judgements and condemnations.

Another way in which Duncton had changed somewhat since former times was that it no longer had the traditional system of elders which even now many systems have, by force of habit and molish inclination, despite the fact that such a system was not part of Tryfan's famed Rule.

Indeed, the absence of official elders was a source of wonder to visitors from systems run by a selected few. It was precisely that abrogation of communal responsibility that Tryfan was so much against in formulating his Rule, since in it he saw the beginnings of the very corruption of power that had so dominated his life.

Certainly it was plain to outsiders that Duncton ruled itself successfully without the help of elders. There was no council, no assize, nor any formal routine regular meeting of a minority whose task was, to put it at its simplest, the ordering of the majority. What the system did have was an irregular Meeting down in Barrow Vale, held when moles felt moved to call one, and attended by as many moles as wished to come, but presided over by nomole. Such was Duncton's unique government, and it was the wonder of moledom.

But naturally, at any particular time there were moles in the system who by virtue of their intelligence or persistence, cunning or good diplomacy, were recognized by others as having something more than average to contribute and so were elders in all but name. Sometimes an individual emerged who combined the right qualities in such balance and good measure that he or she adopted a role that was near to being the very thing Tryfan so disliked: the role of leader.

Such a mole was the great and wise Drubbins, about whom many a tale has been told, and will continue to be told so long as moles enjoy accounts of moles who know how to be both decisive and judicious in a crisis. Drubbins was a large rough-voiced Westsider, with a liking for lobworms and a legendary and abiding loyalty to his gentle mate Lavender for whom he would have moved the earth (and often did!). At the time Privet came to Duncton Wood, though Lavender was already infirm with age and Drubbins was beginning to lose his former energy, this pair was regarded as the first and most important in the system.

But if Drubbins was still first among equals there were other moles in Duncton at this same time whose special qualities put them amongst those to whom others willingly turned in times of doubt or argument, or for leadership. And since these moles shall have their part to play in the story of Privet's quest, their names and characters should be swiftly scribed down.

There was, for example, Drubbins' younger brother, Chamfer, who had the same gravelly voice as his sibling, and the same large, rough, companionable frame, though not, it must be said, the same acuity. But what he lacked in perception he more than made up for in good intent and strength when strength was needed, which it was all those times when moles are inclined to fight, which is mainly in the spring over mates, and in the autumn over winter territories. Chamfer's easy confidence, and benign but firm manner, had often kept the peace in the Westside and Barrow Vale.

The Marsh End at that time had at least two moles who held sway in their different ways over moles of their generation. One of these was the forceful Bantam, pre-eminent among the fecund Marshend females. For a small mole Bantam was remarkably overbearing, interfering, and unlikeable, but she had a way of making moles defer to her and thus had a following. She had in recent moleyears, and following the arrival in Duncton Wood of missionaries from Caradoc, become Newborn, and helped the Caradocians establish the only paw-hold they had in Duncton, which was down in the Marsh End.

The second well-known mole from those parts was Snyde, a clever mole with sharp eyes and a head bent unnaturally low by a slight crook-back, which made him always look as if he were peering and prying about. He had the quick malevolent wit of one whom life has made bitter, but who knows how to make the majority laugh at the minority's expense. He studied others as an owl studies its prey before it strikes, and had a voice that was thin, high and snoutish. He was the kind of mole who, in a system of elders and factions, would have known how to rise far and fast, playing one off against another and emerging not as leader but as the power and malign intelligence behind a more physically charismatic mole – though only one himself malign would have given Snyde much time.

Since Duncton lacked any hierarchy culminating in a system of elders up which Snyde could climb, he early chose to enter the one institution in the system in which such an opportunity existed: the Library. Here was a hierarchy of aides, scriveners, scribes and Keepers that an ambitious mole could exploit, and that is what this most ambitious Marshender of his generation had successfully done. By dint of hard work, manipulation, and sheer persistence, Snyde had risen to his present position as Deputy Master, second only to Stour, and was in line to succeed as Master when the time came; which, since Stour, like his good friend Drubbins, was ageing, seemed likely to be sooner than later.

Snyde's work prevented him living any longer in the Marsh End, for the daily trek would have been too great, and he had taken burrows on the slopes below the High Wood and uncomfortably near (from her point of view) those of Fieldfare, who though not a mole who easily disliked others, disliked Snyde.

'He has a sneezley, snoately, insinuating way has Snyde, and when Chater's away he comes avisiting, and prying, and touching,' she told Privet.

Privet had wriggled in discomfort at this description and asked what special expertise Snyde had in the Library, a question Fieldfare could not answer. But the truth was he had chosen the academic study of modern history and, later, the arcane world of Word, Sect and Schism, because he believed these would serve him better in his insatiable ambition to reach the pinnacle he desired. To this end Snyde, unlike Privet, was an indefatigable creator of monograph studies on the fields in which he specialized, including the only recent work on that traditionally dangerous and controversial subject, Dark Sound.

But while Fieldfare had nothing good to say about Snyde, she had nothing but praise for a younger mole called Maple, who came from burrows near Barrow Vale itself. He had all the best attributes of a mole who would in the old days before peace came have been a fighter for justice and right causes: physical strength, common sense, and decisiveness. His manner was open and easy, his form fairer than most of his generation, and his fighting ability – so far only for territorial skirmishes and the occasional settling of disputes between others –

had developed into something widely respected. Moles said of Maple, who was a nephew of Lavender and a mole Drubbins had taken to his heart, that it was a pity that the system had no need for warriors, for he seemed wasted where he was.

Since he had no opportunity to fight, or lead others in battle, Maple had made it his interest to study such matters in Library texts and had kenned every text on warfare ever scribed. Drubbins said of him that if ever the need for battle or war arose – and Stone forfend that it should – Duncton would be well served by Maple's leadership.

These, then, were the moles who in their different ways, and different areas, held sway in Duncton Wood at the time of Privet's coming. Most, indubitably, were moles whose nature and background led them to thoughts and actions for the good of the community and towards the light of the Stone, but a few, like the infuriating and powerful Bantam and the cunning Snyde, seemed turned towards darkness and trouble.

We have one more mole to describe, though his domain was not the Wood itself, where, though he was known, he was very rarely seen, but the great Library. This was old Stour, Master Librarian, and arguably the best-known Duncton mole in moledom. In his younger days he had been fierce and fearsome, equalled in reputation and respect within the Wood only by Drubbins himself, and un-equalled outside it, where his reputation as the mole who had pro-moted scribing and books far and wide was unrivalled.

But those days were long gone, and Stour had not set paw outside the system for nearly two decades. Now he was old, and in recent moleyears, since October, had gone into retreat in the Library itself, and even there he was almost never seen.

This was the mole that shy Privet – perhaps naïve Privet! – was most eager and most excited to meet once she had slept off her long night's chatter with Fieldfare, and felt ready at last to begin the first day of what she hoped, for unspoken reasons of her own, would be a new and very different life.

Chapter Three

'The Master? You want to see him? *Every* new visitor who fancies themselves half a scribe wants to see him, but very few succeed!'

With these unpromising words Privet learned from the first aide that she met in the Duncton Library who was not too busy to talk that it might not be as easy as she had hoped to meet Master Librarian Stour. Since the prospect of such a meeting had borne her onward for so long through the moleyears of her trek to Duncton Wood, she could not hide her disappointment.

'But I have a text to give him I have brought all the way from Beechenhill.'

The aide, a mild and elderly male, was sympathetic, and added in a gentler way, 'You're not the only one, believe me, looking for tasks in the Library, who brings some text or other in the hope it will win them favour. It's been near impossible for anymole to see him since November, when he went into retreat. He never seems to come out of his study cell these days and some even say he's dead, or languishing. So I very much regret to tell you that it's Deputy Master Snyde you'll have to see, may the Stone help you. No doubt he'll put you to work on some mundane task to see what you're worth.'

It seemed that enthusiasm and knowledge were not enough, nor even a burning mission to find out about the Book of Silence: persistence was needed too.

Though a good deal older than Privet the mole gave the impression of vigour and intelligence, talking quickly, and seeming restless. He had short grey fur, and a lean wiry body gained through years of moving texts about, one of which he carried as they talked.

'My name's Pumpkin, and if you need help in the future don't hesitate to ask. I presume you will be over-wintering with us? This place is run peculiarly, and there are books and texts here that nomole would ever find if he or she didn't know where to look in the first place! What's your speciality?'

'Mediaeval and Whernish work,' said Privet.

'Really? Oh!' said Pumpkin doubtfully. 'You can scriven then?'

Privet nodded. She knew that down here in southern moledom, scrivening, as the ancient scribing of moles of the Word centred on grim Whern was called, was little known, and she had hoped that it might be a useful skill in Duncton. But what Pumpkin said next dashed her hopes about that as well.

'At least you'll not pose a threat to Snyde, who has not the least interest in scrivening. Just as well – he doesn't like moles who know more than he does about something he thinks important. You should have been here when Old Duckett of Cannock turned up last October. He's the one did the work on the modern role of elders in the Midlands which Snyde had ripped to bits and said was a load of old rubbish, to put it somewhat inelegantly. Well! Right to-do that was! Duckett accused Snyde of withholding important texts and the Master had to intervene. Dear me! What academic moles do in the name of truth! Ha ha ha! I wouldn't give this job up for all the worms in the Westside! No, it's a laugh a minute down here. You can rely on Pumpkin here never being anything other than an aide, Miss Privet.'

'Well, as you say, my own interests are hardly likely to conflict with those of scholars like Snyde,' said Privet a little ruefully.

'I'd call him *Deputy Master* Snyde if I were you,' said Pumpkin with a wink. 'He likes moles to respect his rank. You'll find him down there somewhere in Modern, through this part which is called the Small Chamber, to the Main Chamber itself. No, down there . . . As for mediaeval and Whernish work I'll tell you what I'll do. I'll ask about and see if I can't find some texts that have not been looked at in a while that might interest you. Anything you're thinking of in particular?'

Privet hesitated and then said, 'The Books of Moledom, where are they kept?' Her voice fell to a hush at the mention of these awesome texts, copies of which were in all the main libraries of moledom, but the originals of which were held somewhere in Duncton Wood. Of the seven Books only six existed, for nomole had ever proved the existence of the Book of Silence, the last of these mysterious Books.

'Them? *Everymole* asks about *them*! They're kept in deep-delved chambers beyond the Master's study cell into which nomole but the living Master may go – daren't go, because the place is protected by Dark Sound. Mind you, once in a while the Master will bring one of the Books out for study, and I've seen them then myself, even had to carry one once. The Book of Healing it was, and I felt queer for days afterwards. Put the fear of the Stone in me I can tell you!

'But fat chance you've got of seeing the Books at the moment. Best

25

to wait until the Master dies, get on the right flank of Snyde, and hope for the best. Of course there *are* copies, and he'll expect you to study those first.'

'I've studied all of them,' said Privet.

'Have you now,' said Pumpkin with renewed respect, for it was a well-known fact that moles *said* they were going to study them but few ever did. There was something about the Books of Moledom that burdened moles not yet ready for them. But a mole who claimed she *had* studied them was probably telling the truth, and anyway there was the ring of sincerity about all that Privet said and did.

'Well then perhaps if you're lucky –'

'Pumpkin!' called a voice from a nearby chamber, 'stop chattering and bring that text to me!'

'I must get on, Miss,' said the aide, lowering his voice and giving her another wink.

Pumpkin shifted the text he had been clutching throughout this exchange from one paw to the other, pointed a talon down the length of a crowded, high, dark chamber, to indicate again the way she should go, and went on his way, leaving Privet to pause and take in the extraordinary scene.

Even the approach down into the Library from the surface above had awed her, so hugely delved were the tunnels, so impressive the high arches where the main tunnel joined what they modestly called the Small Chamber.

This great place, which was bigger by far than any library Privet had been in before, was lit from fissures in the murky roof high above, and held more texts than she had ever seen in one place. It was obvious from the hushed comings and goings of aides and librarians that the chambers that ran off it, some large, others narrow and confined, all held more material. The texts themselves were in shelves arranged in stacks, and the librarians had study places all higgledy-piggledy among them. At the far end the chamber narrowed into a curious soaring fissure at the base of which, like ants hurrying to service a nest that lay beyond, moles came and went, their paws echoing, and their voices muffled and subdued.

Nomole noticed Privet as she diffidently made her way among the stacks down the length of the Chamber, staring at texts when she could, but catching sight of few she knew. Why, where she came from . . . But she banished such thoughts. Her past was over and done with. Her life was beginning again now in the present, and her future was what she could make of it.

For a shy mole, with little confidence left beyond matters textual, she felt she was doing well.

'Can you tell me where Sny . . . I mean Deputy Master Snyde is please?' she asked one of the less busy, more friendly-looking moles.

'No idea,' replied the mole, not looking up from the text he was working at. Abashed, Privet travelled on, arrived at the fissure that led to the Main Chamber, gulped, and followed a mole carrying a text through it.

She emerged into a cavernous space, most beautifully lit about its high roof, where the tendrils of plants and white fibrous roots of trees carried light from without, and reflected light from surface fissures. Beneath this grand, arching roof what was surely the main part of the Library stretched away, so huge that she realized that it made the 'Small' Chamber she had just come from seem small indeed. The Main Chamber was hushed, organized, busy, a place to inspire a mole to work and study, and to subdue the uninitiated into awed silence. Moles of both sexes and all ages worked here, and though it seemed at first to Privet that they were scholars studying texts it was soon very plain to her that they were, for the most part, only copyists.

'This is where . . .' she whispered to herself.

So! This was where the great work of copying moledom's classic texts was done, the texts which by an ordinance of the Conclave of Cannock over thirty moleyears before must be disseminated through-out moledom. It had been initiated by a small group of scholar scribe-moles led by Stour himself, driven by memories of the war of Word and Stone, when the light of Stone was so nearly lost for ever. What the decision at Cannock meant was that this great Library, the greatest in moledom, would eventually be replicated in the eleven other chosen sites, which included the Ancient Seven.

Most of these copies would be taken forth in the spring and summer years to the other libraries by journeymoles like Fieldfare's Chater. It was a great enterprise, one that would take several more generations of moles to complete, but when it was completed it would mean that all moles, wherever they lived, might have access to all the scribed knowledge, history, thoughts and traditions of moles gone by. In such an enterprise, Stour had successfully argued, lay the way to the creation and preservation of freedom in moledom for evermore.

Stancing there, with so many copyists about her, and with so many more texts in the stacks all about, Privet saw both the grandness of the conception, and the enormity of the task, and felt a renewed determination eventually to meet the Master Librarian himself.

'Excuse me,' said Privet, plucking up courage to speak to another mole, 'can you tell me where I might find Deputy Master Snyde?'

'Seen him round, seen him *there*,' said the mole, pointing to a narrow gap between stacks, and scarcely looking up from the copying he was doing.

Privet went that way, turned a corner, went on a bit towards a smaller chamber, turned to the right and realized she was lost.

'Yes, mole?'

The voice was quick and nasal, the mole that spoke it crook-backed, with a head laid low by his deformity, which gave him the look of one who was perpetually peering at others to find them out. He was amongst shadows, and at his flanks were a couple of moles, one male, one female, both wearing the smiles of moles doing their best to please a mole they fear and dislike.

'I'm looking for –'

'Me. You're looking for me.'

'Deputy Master Snyde?' she said carefully.

A brief complacent smile lightened his face and he licked his mouth. He looked proprietorially at the two moles with him.

'It seems so, doesn't it? They sent you to me. Yes. Good. And you're from?'

'Rollright.'

'You'll be badly trained then. *They*'ve never got it right.'

'I wasn't raised there,' said Privet, as affronted as Snyde had intended her to be, 'but I was there for a time. Before that –'

To her relief Snyde waved her into silence.

'You can scribe?'

'Yes, of course.'

'Of course,' said Snyde with a slight sneer, smiling again, this time coldly. 'Anything else?'

'I'm a mediaevalist, I think.'

'Oh, she thinks she's a mediaevalist,' said Snyde to his acolytes. They sneered dutifully, though the male less than the other. 'Frankly mole, we have no use in Duncton these days for mediaevalists since the demand is for our modern texts and for copying. Must keep on with the copying, of course, and we do, we do. But as for scholarship, well, the past is dead, long live the present.'

'The present will become the past,' said Privet, much provoked and unable to prevent herself from arguing. It was the first time since she had been in Duncton that the tougher side of Privet, the part that must have given her the strength to get there at all, had shown itself.

28

The male aide grinned to himself, while the female looked at Snyde to see what he would do.

What he did was to thrust his thin and wrinkled snout out into the light towards Privet, peer at her through narrowed eyes, and say, 'Of course it will! How right you are, very clever, very . . . disputatious.' He was smiling in a most unpleasant way and his talons were kneading the ground with an almost sensual pleasure at the sudden prospect of intellectual argument.

'And when,' he said, 'does our mediaeval visitor maintain the past begins?'

'I . . . I'm not sure,' said Privet slowly, unable to take her eyes off Snyde's, which had a curious and hypnotic weasel-like quality. 'I only know it ends in myth.'

'Myth?' said Snyde, evidently surprised at this answer, and somewhat disconcerted by it.

'The final truth of history is myth,' said Privet. 'Until then it is but surmise. I feel more comfortable with the distant past but that is my failing, Deputy Master, and I know from your work that you have the breadth of vision to feel comfortable with Modern.' She was careful to allow no hint of flattery or unctuousness to enter into her voice, and she ended what she said with a short, brief, apologetic smile.

'Ah! Good! Very good or very clever,' said Snyde. 'More on this later one day. Meanwhile, we must welcome copyists, whatever their quality, for once winter sets in the supply will end. One big task to complete for Avebury, and another for the aforesaid and mediocre Rollright. What was your name?'

'Privet.'

'Not a name I know. Not a very nice name really.'

'I have scribed nothing that you would have seen, Deputy Master.'

'But something?'

Privet shrugged. 'A monograph on Whernish texts at Beechenhill, and a study of scrivening styles, and an account of the lost tales of Bleaklow. Tales has become my speciality and I have a text . . .'

'Bleaklow? Well . . . Yes . . .' said Snyde, clearly uninterested in these offerings. 'Perhaps if you prove yourself a worthy copier you can be given a little time for your own private researches, but I stress we are rather busy with more important things . . . Since you appear to show neither interest nor belief in Modern I fear I cannot offer you a task in my own specialist department.' She did not choose to press her Book of Tales on him.

He turned to the male and said, 'Avens, you can show her the

Library and ask the Copy Master to set her a task within her capabilities.' He smiled in a cloyingly possessive way at this weak-looking youngster and then turned to the female and said, 'You can come with me now . . .' and low, and sneaky-seeming, Snyde slid away.

The mole Avens turned without much interest to Privet, who saw that the moment the Deputy Master was out of sight he assumed a cocky stance as if all moledom were a bore and his great talents were wasted upon it.

'Just arrived?' he said carelessly.

She nodded again.

'Well, showing you round will be a pleasant break for me, I suppose, so we might as well take our time.'

Privet did not at first much like Avens, for she soon found he had no real interest in scribing or in texts, or any great ambitions. He had come with a journeymole from Avebury and was 'putting in a few moleyears of study', as he put it, before returning home.

But at least he told Privet a good deal more about the Library, and its organization, than Fieldfare had been able to. She learned that each separate Collection in the Library had its Keeper, of whom there were nine, or ten if a mole counted the odd one out, which was Rolls, Rhymes and Tales, 'of which none of us knows much since it's separate from the main library, and its Keeper, a mole called Husk, never comes here at all, nor welcomes visitors there.'

'I have heard much of him,' said Privet with some excitement. 'I have a text of tales with me – perhaps I should give it to him?'

'I wouldn't bother Snyde with it, that's for sure,' said Avens. 'Husk might take it, but be warned,' he went on in an outraged kind of way, 'I myself tried to offer Keeper Husk my help and advice, after the Master had suggested I might usefully adopt the task of ordering his Collection, but the old fool was abusive and rude and told me I was a fool and suchlike.'

Privet did her best to keep a straight face at this, and rather liked the idea of a crusty old Keeper of ancient texts sending young Avens packing. She might have been tempted to do the same herself.

'No, the most important Collection is Modern, of which Deputy Master Snyde has been Keeper since his predecessor died in mid-September. He's not an easy mole of course, but he seems to have found old Stour's favour, and certainly knows his job. I'm told Modern's become very well organized since he took over. Now Snyde's about to take over the control of copying and the Copy Master is upset about it. But of course he's another old mole and Snyde seems to know how to drive his older superiors towards an early demise and so gain promotion. But you began well with him!' There was admiration in his voice.

'Me?' said Privet, surprised.

'By arguing with him, about history and that. He likes an argument does our Deputy Master. Have you really researched and scribed texts on Whernish?'

'Yes,' said Privet.

'Well, that's a bit different then,' said Avens vacuously. 'Now, let's find you a task . . . Frankly, with Longest Night just two days off, you've timed it well. There may be the appearance of busyness about the place, but this is calm compared to what it's normally like. Once Longest Night is over and January begun then it'll be all snouts down to get texts ready for the journeymoles in spring. I'm going to find myself an easy studying task and keep *well* out of it!'

With this complacent comment, Avens led her back into the Main Chamber where Firkin, the doddery old Copy Master, found a librarian who needed a copier.

'What's *that*?' asked Privet of Avens before he left her to her task. She pointed up at a great dark gallery that ran high across the narrower end of the Main Chamber. A slipway went up to it, at the bottom of which a large and corpulent mole stanced quiet and half asleep.

'That's where the Master is. He watches us from there. His study cell is at the top of the slipway, and beyond it . . .' he gesticulated in a vague and bored way.

'Beyond it are the Books of Moledom,' said Privet.

'Yes, I suppose they are,' said Avens without any interest at all.

Privet looked up at the enshadowed gallery, fancying she could see movement there. A snout? Eyes? She knew not.

'Master Librarian Stour!' she whispered to herself in awe, the greatest scholar and librarian in moledom. She had come far to get here, and if for a time she must revert to being merely copier, so must it be. One day, one day . . . she hardly listened as old Firkin presented her with a text and told her how she must copy it. But as she turned to begin her tedious task, her eyes looked back briefly at the high gallery, and lit up with a dream.

In the winter months that followed into January Privet slowly began to build a niche for herself in both the Library and the system.

She continued her copying tasks, content to adopt a low snout and avoid notice, as she thought, by anymole of importance. Pumpkin became a friend, happy to find her texts now and then when she had time to begin to get to know the vast resources of the Library. Avens, too, a witless inconsequential mole, began to see the depth of her knowledge of older texts and was happy to ask for her help in some of the work he was doing and lazy though he was, she was glad to have a mole with whom to share a worm in moments of rest from her work.

In this way, to a small circle of less important moles in the Library, she became known as a mole who knew both scribing and scrivening, and one dedicated to her work. Her determination to copy well and accurately worked, if anything, against her ambitions, for libraries such as Duncton are often reluctant to let copyists move on to less productive research, especially of an out-of-fashion mediaeval kind. But Privet was content to be patient for a time, hoping that eventually the Stone, or luck, would bring her more interesting work.

She grew to know and like Copy Master Firkin, too, a knowledgeable mole growing too old for his task, for he was much harried on all flanks, not least by Deputy Master Snyde. Firkin was one of the few who seemed to have any contact with the Master Librarian himself, up into whose study cell he would sometimes go for 'consultations'. But he never said, nor ever would say, a word about these meetings, though many moles tried to get something out of him about them, and Privet much respected this discretion and loyalty towards Stour, and thought to herself that there might be more to the old mole than there seemed.

The other Keepers she rarely met, not even Sturne in mediaeval who was a taciturn severe mole who said little to anymole.

Her life outside the library was quiet, and often in the gloomy months of January she wondered what she would have done without the friendship of Fieldfare who, from the time they had first met, she had liked and trusted, and who had felt the same about her.

Longest Night had passed by without incident, and Chater had not returned until mid-January. For a time after that the two females saw less of each other, for Fieldfare was a mole who liked to give time to her mate, and, in truth, Chater was not a sociable mole in winter, least of all with librarians, whose texts he was happy to carry from system to system, but whose company he was disinclined to keep. Despite Fieldfare's best efforts he steered clear of Privet, and Privet, sensing this, kept clear of him.

She had found some deserted tunnels on the eastern slopes near Fieldfare's and made them comfortable enough in her austere and simple way. Then, quietly, she had begun to get to know other Duncton moles. Their tradition of acceptance of others, and their willingness to let others be themselves, suited her well, and since she was an unassuming mole and a little reserved, nomole troubled her.

Occasionally she went down to Barrow Vale with Fieldfare, and stanced down to listen to the chatter and backchat of other moles. From time to time they would try to engage her in conversation, but since she would give little away about her past, and since Duncton moles liked to know such things, she was seen as reserved and, after a time, came to be considered a dull mole with little to say for herself.

Fieldfare, ever curious about her, tried to find out what she could, but after a time gave up trying, believing that if a mole wanted to say nothing there was good reason for it and another shouldn't pry.

Ironically, it was this reticence which first interested Chater in the new mole, for he knew how persistent Duncton moles could be in general (and his mate in particular) about getting information out of others and thought that anymole who could maintain her silence must have something about her.

'It's not that I'm not interested, Chater my love, but just that she doesn't want to talk yet.'

'Yet? You mean never!'

'I don't agree with you there, not I. A female crossed in love will always talk about it in the end, unless they wither up inside.'

'Ah, it's unrequited love has brought her here, is it?' he said. 'Love my arse! From what I've seen of Librarian Privet she looks too withered up for love to me. The passion that's brought her here, my dear, is *texts*. Believe me, it gets to them. I heard from that daft Avens that she scribed in Beechenhill and you can bet your life she's here to research some tedious bloody subject or another, not simply to scribe another text to be copied. Texts breed like rabbits. Never be a stop to them. Not ever.'

'My dear,' said Fieldfare stoutly, 'I will only say that in all my years I have never met a mole I felt more certain was and is heartbroken and thwarted in love as Privet. And you've not seen it because you're so prejudiced against scholars and the rest – execpt the Master himself of course – that you don't give them the time of day or believe they can have hearts and feelings like the rest of us. Also, beloved, I can only say that if you had bothered to learn to scribe you wouldn't be a mere journeymole and forced to wander mole knows where and deprive me of my proper rights to a mate.'

'Hang on a bit, angel-snout!' protested Chater, taken aback by this outburst, 'I only –'

'I shall not, precious one, I shall speak my mind. We have good times together, Privet and I, and I believe that if she would only let others see her as I do then there's many would be glad to know her more. She's very knowledgeable.'

'About what, for instance?'

'About texts.'

'All librarians give that impression, my love, but most of them don't know their arse from their lughole –'

'Chater!'

'It's true. They talk a lot but when it comes to it they know bugger-all. I mean I've travelled here, there and everywhere and know the routes well, and has a single librarian ever consulted me about mole-dom, about which they scribe their monographs and histories and texts? Not one, my dear, not a single solitary one. Oh yes, they're very good at theory but no bloody good at getting off their bums and looking for themselves! Take for example –'

'Chater! You know I get upset when you talk like this. Perhaps you ought to consider, my own sweet love, whether or not *you* get off *your* bum and really *listen* to other moles – like my friend Privet, for example. Now when I say she's knowledgeable I don't mean she goes on about what she doesn't know about, like some moles I could mention. I mean that when I ask a question about something she might know about then if she doesn't she says so, and if she does she tells me a little until I ask for more. Then when I ask for more she tells me still more. Until by the end of it I know a lot and she's made it easy for me. That's being knowledgeable.'

'No it's not, beloved, that's being a good tutor, which is different altogether.'

'Well maybe, maybe not,' said Fieldfare huffily. 'I still say she's more knowledgeable than some I could think of.'

Chater sighed, and grinned. 'You're probably right there. Next time she tells you something helpful, you pass it on and improve me too. I definitely need improvement, my delightful one.'

'You do,' said Fieldfare softly, bringing her ample body close to Chater's.

'I do,' he agreed, 'so show me.'

'Now?'

'As good a time now is, as any.'

She giggled and sighed.

34

'I wish Privet had a mate,' she said as she showed him . . . 'I'm sure she did have once. If she's withered, as you put it, it's not from studying but because she misses him.'

But Chater was not interested any more that day in Privet's mate but in his own, and it was not long before his mate was interested only in *her* own as well . . .

So it was that Duncton Wood carried on as it always had, its true history more that of harmless moles like Fieldfare and Chater, living their lives out, loving and respecting each other, safe in a system whose freedom had been won for them by moles long dead.

Duncton absorbed Privet into its tunnels, as it had so many others in the past. Unremarkable and unremarked but by a few like Fieldfare, Privet found her niche and had her dreams, and kept her past to herself. But, as she herself had said to Snyde, the present will become the past as well, and out of that past with its little and its great events, history will be made. And history, at that time, was stalking towards Duncton Wood once more and had in its unremitting sight the shy, the modest, and the unremarkable Privet.

'Me?' she might have said, shocked at such a suggestion.

'Yes, you,' sighed the trees of old Duncton Wood, whose voice moles there have always heard, but rarely understood it was the voice of history.

'One last time we shall need the moles of Duncton Wood, and you, Privet, are of their number now. But more than that, you carry a dream, and moles with dreams, however modest the moles themselves may seem, must discover for good and for ill that the past and the present are inextricable, and unavoidable, however far a mole may run.'

Chapter Four

Privet's curiosity about Stour, the Master Librarian, had naturally increased the more the molemonths went by in which she did not meet him. She knew where his study cell was for even if Avens had not pointed it out during her first day there, its location was obvious from the way moles in the Main Chamber were inclined to glance up towards the mysterious shadowed gallery from which the Master was supposed to watch them all.

Occasionally Snyde or Firkin, or other Keepers like Sturne went up the slipway and disappeared from sight, and once Privet caught a glimpse of one of these talking into the shadows to a mole she could not quite see who must have been there. This was the nearest she ever got to Stour. The corpulent guard disappeared in late January and nomole was left there at all, yet he might as well have been there for all the likelihood there was of anymole daring to set paw upon the slipway.

Sometimes, when she worked into the dark afternoons, she heard strange wind-sounds reverberating from the galleried heights, and knew from her own studies that this was Dark Sound, though of a benign and gentle kind. Dark Sound of the Whernish kind she knew was a killer of moles, unless they were of extraordinary spiritual strength.

As she got to know the more obscure parts of the Library which lay to the west in the direction of the Stone, mainly with Pumpkin's help, she discovered tunnels in which the stacks of texts petered out, and where most dark, most mysterious, and most dangerous, the tunnels ran on, blocked only half-heartedly it seemed by seals delved a long time since, and now in a ruinous state and choked with rubble, flints and broken soil through which roots twined.

But so afraid were the Duncton librarians of what lay beyond – a fear bolstered by the Dark Sounds that emanated from these tunnels too, especially on days when the wind was gusting northerly – that nomole had been willing, or felt it necessary, to clear these partial obstructions and rebuild the seals properly.

'If I have to get texts from those parts,' said Pumpkin once, 'I make sure to do it in the middle of the day when the light is good, and if I possibly can I choose a day when the winds are light. Never go anywhere near there if you can help it when the wind blows from the north,' he added, as if he expected that Privet might, 'for it's then the Dark Sound eats into you and muddles your head. I've heard screams from those tunnels, and the sound of moles running, and of talons, cruel talons, scraping on flint, and things I'll never talk about not ever. Some say Dark Sound is just fancy, but I think it's real.'

Poor Pumpkin's eyes were wide with fear and Privet nodded sympathetically.

'I know it's real,' she said flatly.

'You've heard it near-to?' he asked incredulously.

She closed her mouth, looked away, and vaguely shook her head. Pumpkin said no more: like most others who had got to know Privet, he knew there were things in her past she did not talk about.

'Tell me,' she said to change the subject, 'doesn't Master Stour ever come down into the Main Library?'

'He used to regularly when I first came to work here three Longest Nights ago. He was in his prime then and moles trembled at his approach. Sharp as blackthorn his mind was, and he looked like thunder in a mean sky if he was crossed. Of course that Snyde was just a starter then and Stour didn't give him the time of day. But the years passed, seasons came and went. The copying became the main part of the Library's work and gradually Stour grew older, and we began to see him less and less.'

'You said that copying became the main task – what was important before then?'

'Well, the Conclave of Cannock that he inspired and which led to all this copying was years before my time. But before that this place was all collecting and scholarship. These days moles don't bring discovered texts here like they used to, preferring to keep the originals in their own systems and send copies instead. Except we rarely see even those. As for scholarship, why there's hardly a mole here worthy of the name scholar – they're all like that cluck-headed Avens from Avebury, though he means well enough. No, Miss Privet, I hope it's not out of turn my saying that you're the first real scholar we've had in Duncton in a very long time.'

Privet's snout turned a darker shade of pink at this compliment and she looked away, much touched.

Then, 'What about the Master's present retreat? What's the explanation of that?'

Pumpkin shrugged, and scratched his head. 'Makes no real sense to me. In fact if anything he had been getting more mellow. I even saw him smile once or twice – even at me! I don't know . . .'

Privet looked at him quizzically, for he obviously *did* know.

'You're not half bad at getting others to talk, Miss, even if you give nothing away about yourself!' declared Pumpkin, with a cheerful combination of ruefulness and respect. 'I suppose what I was thinking was that last October two of those Newborns came up from the Marsh End and asked to see the Master. Of course they got short shrift from Snyde but old Stour must have been watching up there in his gallery and bless me but he appears all of a sudden and says it's all right, he'll see them. Well, they talked for a whole afternoon and eventually those of us who were watching and listening out for what was going on – which included myself, needless to say! – saw the Master more or less driving those Newborns out of the place and saying he was outraged and trust was trust and they would not be welcome back and so on. Stone knows what it was about because I didn't then and never found out since. But shortly afterwards Drubbins was sent for and he spent a long time with the Master and came out looking grim and it was after *that* – though I only put two and two together later – the Master began his retreat. Don't ask me what he does up there all alone, but there it is. Now he issues orders for texts only through Deputy Master Snyde.'

'But surely a librarian needs to know his texts and folios?'

'He does, better than anymole alive. They say he wanders about the library at night, feeling the texts, and sometimes you'll catch sight of a shadow among the stacks at dawn, if you come that early. That'll be Stour. But these days he may not have need of coming here so much.'

'Why not?'

'Well, they say he has his own private library up there among the galleries, and that his work now uses only those few texts and . . . well, and himself.'

'Himself, Pumpkin?'

Pumpkin shrugged. 'It's only what I've heard others talk of, which means to say Snyde because of course old Firkin never breaks the Master's confidence and Sturne says nothing at all. Doesn't mean much to me but I heard the Deputy Master talk about the very self-same thing, and not to a librarian either. He was saying that

Stour's work these days concerns the Silence, and that he, Stour, had said the very last thing a mole needs for that is texts. Quote: "Texts get in the way" unquote. Sounds daft to me, and he wouldn't be the first Master who ends his days mad. It's the isolation of the job and responsibility, you see. Of course the fancy name they give it is a "retreat" but there's nothing normal or healthy about secluding yourself from others, is there?'

'Has he never had a mate?'

'Never to anymole's knowledge. No, never. Fell in love once they say, but now the only mole who's old enough to remember the truth, and sensible enough not to exaggerate, is Drubbins.'

The two moles fell into one of those companionable silences, thinking about all they had talked of until Pumpkin repeated suddenly, '"Texts get in the way". Odd that.'

'Yes . . .' said Privet softly. 'But not perhaps if it's the Silence that you're trying to understand. In fact . . .'

It was Pumpkin's turn to look at her quizzically.

'I was just thinking, Pumpkin, that it's the most sensible thing I've ever heard said about searching for the Silence. "Texts get in the way". Yes . . .'

'Miss, why *did* you come to Duncton? When you first came you asked about the Books of Moledom. I notice that you've not mentioned them since, but several times I've seen you looking through the copies in the stacks.'

'I came . . . I came because . . .'

Pumpkin was suddenly very still, sensing that Privet was about to speak personally for once.

'I came to discover more of Silence. But I thought knowledge of it might be here in Duncton. Does that seem ridiculous to you?'

'No, Miss.'

'I think it *does* exist but we don't know what it looks like. I think it's waiting for us to find it and that we *shall* find it . . .'

'Maybe we shall find it when we need to.'

'Do you really think that, Pumpkin?'

Pumpkin looked around at the stacks in the Chamber they were in, and at the tunnels leading off it. He cocked his head and seemed to listen for a moment to the endless mutter and patter of working moles.

'All this copying,' he said in a low voice. 'All this so-called scholarship. All this *busyness*. I watch it and I do as I'm told but I never forget that it will be the Silence that matters in the end and how we reach it. The way I see the Book of Silence is this. There's six Books so far – I know that for sure. And six is nomole's number. Seven's the thing and a Seventh Book there'll be. You can have all of this, Miss Privet, every last text, because it won't be anything in the end. But the Book of Silence, *that's* the one.'

The normal look of good-natured cynicism on Pumpkin's face had been replaced by a look of awed excitement as he imagined seeing in reality the thing of which he spoke.

'It's somewhere, as you said, or perhaps waiting to be scribed, but it's near, it's near. I would give my whole life for the honour of touching that last Book just for a moment. I mean it! Do you know. I thought there was something more about you than met the eye; a lot more. You're a bit of a one, Miss Privet, aren't you!'

'Am I?' she said, a little coyly.

'And I suppose I'd be pushing my luck if I asked you what made you interested in the Book of Silence in the first place?'

'You would, Pumpkin, yes, you would,' said Privet, retreating to her old self.

Pumpkin grinned, so good-naturedly that Privet could not help smiling back. Somehow both of them sensed that they had formed a bond that day, or perhaps more accurately a pact, and that it concerned the Book of Silence, and that if ever the Stone honoured either of them with the task of fulfilling it they would not hesitate to do so, whatever it might cost.

'Miss . . .' began Pumpkin, suddenly nervous. A whisper of Dark Sound had come into the tunnel where they stanced. Moles desperate. Moles in fear.

'Miss . . .' he said again.

'It's all right,' said Privet, suddenly strong, 'Dark Sound will not hurt you if you have faith in the Stone, or not at this distance. It's all right, Pumpkin – if ever the Stone asks that of you it will give you the strength you need.'

'Will it?' he whispered, shaking his head. 'I'm just an aide, Miss Privet, nothing more and nothing less.'

It was her turn to grin.

'There's something more about *you* than meets the eye too,' she said. And Pumpkin laughed, and the moment passed, but not the memory of their tacit exchange which had to do with the discovery of the Book of Silence.

*

January passed into February with Stour still a mystery, and, as she got to know the library and the Duncton system better, other mysteries began making their presence felt as well.

One of these was the curious fact that there were far fewer ancient texts in the stacks than she might have expected, and she realized that if what Pumpkin had said was true then these probably now formed part of Stour's personal library. But why would he who was so committed to seeing that other moles had texts made available to them, want to make ancient texts unavailable in the Library of which he was Master? It did not make sense. Meanwhile, however, she must continue to make her way in the Library as best she could, getting on with the tedious task of copying texts from Modern which held no interest for her at all, whilst hoping change would come.

But at least in mid-February, when the task of copying for springtime distribution was nearly over, her real skills began to emerge. A question concerning a partially scrivened script came up, to which she was able to provide an answer, and it became apparent that her knowledge of older scripts, particularly those emanating from the north, was thorough and sound.

She began to work as a librarian-aide to Sturne, then the Keeper of Rules, and in that capacity was able to help clear up some problems with the much-copied and corrupted text of the Prendine Rule which, with careful scholarship, she was able to show was a merging of two Rules of different dates, and widely different places.

Obscure though such work was, and unimportant to the main thrust of Modern research in the Library, it established for Privet a reputation for accuracy and dedication, and led her to be chosen to work on the much bigger task of the elucidation of the Farndon Forgery, that brilliant but notorious early Modern attempt to fool scribemoles in Uffington into thinking a contemporary text concerning Stone liturgies was of late mediaeval origin. Unfortunately this work brought Privet into direct conflict with Deputy Master Snyde, whom she had managed to keep clear of since their initial meetings.

The problem was that Rules needed extra aides to help with work generated by Privet's researches, and Snyde objected to this channelling of resources towards something he saw as irrelevant to the Library's main work, and in this matter he won – for all but Privet were removed from the task, which left her working on something that most regarded as a waste of time.

Yet she rose to the occasion, working longer hours and arriving near a solution to the problem in late February, when spring was almost come, and even librarians' inclinations were turning to matters of the heart, and stirrings of the body, rather than dry textual interpretations.

With the coming of March, the days began to lighten, and the soil and undergrowth of Duncton Wood began to stir with new life.

One morning, arriving even earlier than usual, she came upon a thin, gaunt old mole ahead of her among the stacks. He moved quickly, like a weasel investigating an alien creature's run, and his fur had the thin lack-lustre look of one who has been too long physically inactive and out of the fresh air. Yet old though he seemed, he had a certain vigour, and when he turned to look at her his eyes were sharp and penetrating.

'Ah! Yes! The mole Privet, I think.'

'I am,' said Privet, suddenly in awe, for she sensed that this might well be Stour.

'And you . . . ?' she began, feeling that if she did not ask she might regret it for ever.

'Yes, yes, I am the Master. "Old Stour" as they call me.'

To her surprise he laughed in a thin kind of way, though as he did so she was aware that his eyes continued to appraise her.

Then he said, 'I am well pleased with your work, Librarian Privet. The Frandon matter has been one of some embarrassment and I am glad it has been resolved, though the ambiguity remains. You have showed . . . tenacity.'

'It *is* a forgery, Master, and I think I can say which of the Uffington scribemoles perpetrated it, though why I'm not sure.'

'Boredom I expect. A bigger fact in history than so-called historians give credit for. Been tempted towards forgery myself! In fact . . .' he permitted himself the briefest of smiles. She knew suddenly she was not afraid of him. But more than that, she saw he was a mole alone. In that momentary smile was a weariness that came from a remembered life when he had not been Master . . . and not thereby been alone. In that there was something that they shared.

'Master,' she began, daring to take her opportunity.

The smile fled, and he raised a paw to silence her.

'I know,' he said. 'You are a mediaevalist and wish for other and more appropriate work. Scribes and scholars always come here expecting something other than I can at first give them. But you shall have what you desire in time. Now, tell me where you were trained.'

She hesitated. She had hoped that after so long here nomole would ever feel the need to ask her.

'Tell me, mole. I shall tell no other. From what I have heard of you it is plain enough you have fled from somewhere. If I am to trust those that work for me I must know they will answer truthfully what I ask of them, and fully if I request it. We live in strange and changing times and a mole must be cautious. You have more than the makings of a scholar, you are one already. But without a history. We know most moles that come here. Now, whatmole taught you to scribe, and where?'

Even after this Privet hesitated, her face contorted with distress and worry, her mouth open to reply but no words coming.

'Well, mole?' said Stour, coming closer.

She looked into his eyes, and at his austere face, and down at his thin paws, and felt herself in the presence of a mole more clear-thinking, and more dedicated to truth, than anymole she had ever known. If she was wrong in her judgement about this mole, she would be wrong about life itself and in that moment, when Privet trusted her judgement and herself, she turned a corner and began a long journey back towards lost light and love.

'I am of Bleaklow,' she whispered, naming an obscure and outcast system to the north.

'And you learnt scribing *there*?' said Stour, astonished.

She nodded.

'And your teacher?'

'You would not know her, Master,' Privet dared to say.

'Mole . . . ' there was ice in Stour's voice, and warning. This was a mole who demanded the truth.

'Her name was Shire of Bleaklow Moor.'

'Whatmole was she? How came she knew scribing?' His eyes were sharp bright points of black, his body tense. She knew what he was thinking.

'She was daughter of the Eldrene Wort who was my grandmother.'

There was a sharp intake of breath from Stour and utter silence. The Eldrene Wort – but words were not needed. She was the most reviled mole in modern history. She was . . . and then, in the distance, beyond the main chamber where the entrances were, the sound of early arrivals began.

'Come,' said Stour impulsively, 'follow me up to my study cell, for there we can continue undisturbed.'

Without more ado he led her through the stacks and up the slipway to the forbidden gallery above, through an arch where formerly she thought she had seen him talking to one of the Keepers, and there she was in his study cell.

43

How small it seemed, how spartan, and not a text in sight. But beyond it, through another arch, she caught a glimpse of a few texts neatly arranged, whilst to her right she saw a second arch which led to the gallery from which their Master was said to be able to watch them all unseen. He turned to her and bade her stance down.

'Now, is this connection with the Eldrene Wort the reason why you have stayed silent about yourself? You fear that others might not accept you?'

'They never accepted my mother, Master, when she strove to flee from Bleaklow. Yet she did not commit the crime of *her* mother.'

'This Shire, did she only teach you scribing?'

'I can scriven, Master Librarian. I can transcribe mediaeval scrivening, and scribing too. I . . . I know most of the common dialects of the north.'

'But what of your other knowledge? There are surely not so many texts in Bleaklow.'

She nodded her head.

'I . . . I did escape from Bleaklow. At a time of trouble I managed to escape and I fled to Beechenhill.'

She had named the system where the Stone Mole was martyred, and which, though one of the twelve systems mandated at Cannock to be a library, was surely no real library yet. For it had stayed more or less deserted after the martyrdom, and no moles of scholarship had ever come from there. It was thought to have but few texts.

'Although moles say Beechenhill is not a true library, and in a way they're right, yet there *are* worthy scribemoles there, Master. I studied under a mole called Cobbett . . .'

'So . . .' said Stour, a strange look crossing his face as if, in some way, he had half expected her to say that. Privet paused, puzzled by his look, and aware that he knew more about what she said than he had yet revealed.

'. . . I studied, and learnt much. And one day near the Beechenhill Stone, where . . . where . . .'

Again she paused, for the story of what happened there was known to allmole and Stour had nodded briefly as if to say that it did not need repeating.

'. . . Well, one day when I was wondering about something Cobbett had said about what I should study next, it seemed that there was light about the Stone, and a moment of Silence, and I had the sense that there was a task I must seek out and fulfil. After moleyears of wandering with no task at all it felt that I was coming home to the Stone itself. But I did not know quite what it was that I must do . . .'

Then she was in tears at the memory of a sense of Silence few moles ever experience. Stour reached forward a thin paw and touched her gently.

'Continue, mole. I know that you have not spoken of this for a long time. The memory must be . . . difficult.'

'I have spoken of it only once before, Master, and that was to Cobbett. He said . . .' Again there was that strange look on Stour's face, a wistful, loving look.

'. . . He said that he had long thought that my destiny lay in the direction of Duncton Wood, and that it might be there that I would find a task worthy of the Stone. He said that perhaps it had to do with tales, for that was an interest he had in which I had helped him.'

'Did he say more? Did he speak my name?'

'No, Master,' said Privet.

'Did you know he was of Duncton born?'

'I did not, Master,' she said in surprise and wonder. 'He never spoke of that at all.'

Stour looked deep into her.

'How was he, mole, when you saw him last?'

'Master, I was coming to that . . .' she said diffidently, as if she sensed that Stour had once known Cobbett and might take hard the news she now had to tell him. 'I said he had suggested I go to Duncton Wood, but I asked that I might stay with him for a time, to learn more of tales, and to help him as I could. Which I duly did until . . . until Cobbett ailed and I found that the only help I could give, for he would accept it from no other, was to look after him and ease his passage towards the Silence of the Stone. At the end he told me that when he was gone I must travel to Duncton Wood, taking with me the text of tales he had himself been working on, and to which I had contributed. This I have done, though since Deputy Master Snyde appeared uninterested in it I have kept it in my own tunnels . . .'

'You watched over him until the end?'

'Yes, Master. He died peacefully, grateful that at last he was coming near to Silence, which was, he said, the greatest mystery and perhaps the greatest tale in all moledom . . .'

'I am glad it was you who were with Cobbett,' said Stour quietly. 'As for the text you have brought with you, one day I would like to

45

see it but for now, keep it safe in your own tunnels. There is a mole in Duncton who would be interested in it, and his name is not Snyde! The time for that will come, and *must* come, for tales have been much neglected in favour of other work and scholarship. My failing I fear – I never appreciated them enough – though Cobbett always said . . . no matter. I am glad it was *you* he was with, mole.'

Privet was about to ask him what Cobbett was to him, for it seemed Stour knew him of old, but there came again the sound of approaching mole. The Master went to the archway and looked down into the Main Library, Privet at his flank. Full morning light had come, and the librarians were coming in to work. The sound of them seemed so near below that they could hear moles laughing, and then the sharp nasal voice of one of them – Snyde. A look of dislike and urgency came over the Master's face.

'Mole, I know not yet to trust you,' he said. 'But I shall watch, and I shall listen, and when I have decided I shall act. A mole like you shall have a task, and we must trust the Stone to direct us towards it. You however must trust me, you have no other choice. Meanwhile, there *is* a task concerning Tales . . . a task that may prove more important than any we do here. But . . . before that, mole, the Stone will guide me to test you. Work hard at whatever you do, and do *whatever* I may ask you to do.

'And mole, be of cheer. Nomole can flee for ever. This day with me, here, you have turned back to face your past. That must be your struggle, not mine. But the Stone finds ways and means of revealing the truth to guide moles forward. Know this, Privet of Bleaklow Moor, we live in dangerous times. Be warned, be ready, and be watchful. As for what we have spoken of, you shall repeat it to nomole, nomole at all. The texts you learned your scrivening from, this mole Shire's texts . . .'

'None knows of them but I, Master. Nomole in all of moledom beyond the Moors where I was raised. Nor of the many scribings with them. They –'

He raised a paw to silence her.

'For now I would rather nomole but thee knows what they are, where they are and where they came from. It is well it is so.' His eyes grew suddenly intense and he leaned closer still and said, 'This is not the only reason why you have kept your silence, this connection with the Eldrene Wort.'

'I loved a mole, Master, with all my heart. He . . .'

Stour smiled the gentlest smile. 'And I once, mole, I too. Life gave

46

me no second chance, and I have lost much thereby. I shall pray, mole, that you have your second chance with the mole you love, and if you do, that you take it with both paws.'

'That can never be, Master, it is too late. Even if the chance comes, I would not have courage to take it.'

'No, you might not,' he said matter-of-factly. '*I* did not.' Then his voice changed once more; he stanced back and looked severe, and said, 'Now, to your work, and be ready, mole, the test I give may be other than either of us can now predict. The Stone's Light may be in all of this. I pray that it is so!'

He spoke these extraordinary things quietly and urgently, and with a terrible intensity that held Privet transfixed after he turned from her and was gone into the inner chamber where she had seen the texts. For her part she felt . . . recognized. Here, in the most powerful position in the greatest Library in moledom, was a mole she sensed was utterly incorruptible. The burden that she bore, and of which until then she had never spoken except so briefly and so strangely to Pumpkin in January, was no longer only hers to bear. Whatever test he set her, however hard it might be, she knew she would seek to achieve it with all her heart. In one short interview Stour had won her loyalty and her trust.

She turned out through the archway on to the slipway, and hoping that nomole would see her leave, hurried down into the Main Chamber.

'Well, well, well!' said the nasally voice of Snyde, who appeared from among some shadows by a stack. 'The mediaevalist and the Master meet! And what did he wish to speak of, mole?'

'I . . . it is . . . best I speak not of it,' she replied, floundering.

'Best, is it? Best for whom?'

He thrust his snout up at her, and peered in the crooked way he had, narrowing his eyes, not liking her.

Suddenly she smiled – not weakly, but strongly, the smile of one who trusts herself.

'Why do you look at me like *that*?' said Snyde, affronted by her naturalness.

'I feel that winter is nearly over,' she said, staring him out, 'and that spring is come at last.'

He glanced up at the Master's gallery, and then at her.

'Tell me what he spoke to you about,' said Snyde.

She said nothing and he peered at her unpleasantly, and then turned away, smiling in his turn, but coldly, bitterly.

47

From that moment, just as she knew she had found an ally in old Stour, she sensed she had made an enemy of Snyde for life.

Yet she had been right: winter was nearly done, and spring was in the air. Except for Fieldfare, females she had got to know were suddenly friends no more, but rivals for the males. The system went strange, and difficult, as it often does at mating time, and Privet suffered that loneliness that pupless females, desired by few, often suffer when the world about them is in love, or lust. Only Avens made a pass at her, and when she made plain what her answer was he grew cold and distant. Of all the males she knew only Pumpkin stayed as friendly as he had ever been.

'Used to be interested in mating and suchlike, and even did it twice, but . . . I don't know, it's a lot of fuss about nothing which takes a mole's attention from the good things of life.'

'Which are what?' she laughed.

'Spring, of course. New-found warmth. Wood anemones. Trees leafing. Birds twittering. *Those* are the things that matter!'

But to Fieldfare, who was very interested in matters of mating, though her pupping days were done, Privet was something of a mystery and a disappointment.

'You don't even seem interested,' she said one day when, rightly, she sensed that Privet felt lonely. For while Pumpkin's philosophy might work for a mole as old as him, who has had a mate in the past, there were days, and then weeks, when the system tunnels were abuzz with new love and a new life, and a mole might well feel bereft if she had no mate at all.

'I *said*, you don't seem interested.'

'I . . .' began Privet miserably.

'You're pining for a mole who isn't here!'

'I'm not!' Privet replied sharply.

'Yes you are!' said Fieldfare, relieved to have analysed the problem correctly. 'What's his name? It's very frustrating not knowing!'

'It's all long ago . . .'

'So, I'm right, something did happen. I was not quite certain until now.'

'What? Like that? Well I was – once. And once is enough.'

'You still love him!'

'Yes,' said Privet, snout low, 'yes, I do.'

'Won't you tell me about it? You might feel better.'

But Privet shook her head, and Fieldfare, who knew her well by then, did not say more, except to add kindly, 'If you ever want to talk about it, Privet, you can talk to me. Do you miss him badly?'

Privet nodded silently.

'Is there no hope that you could be with him again?'

'No hope at all,' said Privet finally. 'It was over long ago . . . when he went with another mole than me. It was impossible and I know I shall never see him again . . .'

She stared at Fieldfare, unable to go on, for her eyes had filled with tears and her mouth trembled and . . . and Fieldfare embraced her and whispered, 'No my dear, don't say that, for it's not over yet. If you deny it even to yourself it festers inside. You can tell me, my love, for I'll tell nomole.'

And Privet cried but said no more.

The trees leafed more, the wood anemones bloomed, and as the days advanced towards April the system was full of the cries of pups, and the self-absorption of mothers.

Privet, unhappy still and yearning for the longer, warmer days of May, immersed herself in work, the one place where she could forget herself, and all her past, the one place she was safe. The one place in which nomole could have predicted the nature of the test, deep and terrible, life-changing and at first almost cruel, that Stour imposed upon her. A test that changed her life.

A test whose name was Whillan, whose form was puppish, and whose need was as sudden as it was absolute.

Chapter Five

It was during one of the later, milder days of April that Stour finally emerged from his long winter retreat. He came out into the Library suddenly and unexpectedly and went about and talked with moles who had not seen him since the previous autumn years, just as if he had done it every day previously for the winter years past, and intended to do it for ever more into the future.

Even Pumpkin, who regarded himself as too unimportant for such things, found himself snout to snout with the suddenly affable Master, and obliged to overcome his nerves and make conversation.

A buzz of excitement accompanied Stour wherever he went, and in a matter of hours the oppressive winter atmosphere that had occupied the Library for so long was all gone, and the sense of spring, and renewed life, had come. And the sun began once more to light up the entrances of the Library, and send its shafts down through the fissures in the ceilings of the bigger chambers, and catch the dust and busy librarians in its warm rays.

'You've done well through a difficult winter,' said Stour to one and all, smiling upon them, and engendering an excitement at the prospect of the journeymoles beginning soon the great and important task of taking copied manuscripts out beyond the system's boundaries, to the distant libraries that were their destinations.

As the days passed this new mood continued and deepened, and the Master went his rounds each day, and up to the surface too, so that early rumours that his appearance was merely that of a mole making one last show before going into final retreat were proved quite wrong; a fact confirmed by his decision to vacate the temporary burrows associated with his study cell in the Library and return once more to his tunnels on the Eastside.

Meanwhile, many of those to whom Stour talked, especially those who had come to the Library the previous autumn and had never seen the Master, were astonished to discover that he knew not only of their existence, but of their work as well, showing both interest and knowledge.

But though he was friendly enough, the fearsome and sometimes chilly intelligence was still there too: he was still impatient with moles who did not think quickly and respond intelligently, and plainly unsympathetic to the sometimes egocentric concerns of the younger moles in the library. Their growing up, he seemed to think, they had better do elsewhere. As for pups . . . but then it is with a pup we are now concerned.

For it was not long after Stour's emergence into the light of spring that a pup appeared suddenly and unexpectedly upon the scene, in circumstances nomole could have predicted and which would change for ever Privet's life, and Stour's too.

It was the kind of pleasant spring day that hints at summer warmth and pleasures to come, when older and pupless males wish for nothing more than to find some place out on the surface to escape the irritating bleats and cries, mischief and growing clamour of the youngsters who are by then out and about in the communal tunnels and causing pandemonium.

Stour himself had always been restless and discontented at such times, for he did not like or understand the young, and yet felt a nagging, despairing ache when he saw young parents' pride and busy activity around their irritating offspring.

When he was younger, and less wise, Stour had sometimes expressed such irritations and displeasure too bluntly, cuffing the innocent young out of his path, and shouting at them to go away. This had provoked hostility in some quarters towards him – a hostility that lingered still in the family-orientated Marsh End. But he had grown milder, and had come to believe that the best thing was to make himself scarce when late spring came and youngsters started to invade the system once again.

This was one reason why he had long since chosen to live on the sparser Eastside, where most of the pupless solitaries like him lived, but even then the infant invasions took place, and so Stour, unable for those weeks to concentrate much on work, and rather enjoying the solitary pleasures of late spring flowers, and the return of birds and bird-song absent all winter, would take himself down the pasture slopes to east and south adjacent to the roaring owl way where parents, always fearful of owls and other predators, did not allow their young to go. It was the nearest Stour ever got to taking respite from his work.

In fact, though it was not generally known, Stour had from time to time steered errant youngsters back from these exposed parts to where they should be, for even he, faced by a single lost pup, could not be utterly cold and indifferent. And if over the years moles had come to tolerate his awkwardness with the young it was, surely, because they came to see that when given the chance, and when unseen, he could show warmth. But that said, it was more often to adult moles, for the young remained incomprehensible to him, and they feared him as much as he did them.

Yet how gently, how mysteriously, does the Stone watch over all moles, for time and again when they least expect it, when indeed they are quite unaware that its Light shines upon them and they unknowingly hear its Silence, it seems to put them in the way of change, and growth, and almost despite themselves give them the chance to find a way through the loneliness they feel. Perhaps in Stour's long and mysterious retreat, the Stone gave him pause to think about such things, and having made him think, decided to put him to the test.

The day in question occurred in late April, some moleweeks after Stour's emergence from retreat, when, muttering as usual about being dispossessed of peace and quiet by the young, he deserted the Library for a few hours and went wandering as he had in his younger days down by the concrete cross-under below the south-east slopes, which takes a mole under the roaring owl way, and out of Duncton's territory. A place beyond which he himself had only once been, but now never intended to go so long as the Library needed him.

An echoing place, and dank and smelly too if cattle have sheltered there lately and left their spoor; or if foxes have hidden for a time, and watched for prey on the embankment nearby. For Duncton moles it held history enough for here had been the scene of battle and brave death when moles of the Word invaded Duncton Wood; and here too from time immemorial had moles awaited the return of loved ones.

But travellers traverse the cross-under quickly, and with a shudder, glad to get through its puddled, dripping, dark way and into the light of the sky once more: to leave Duncton for the world outside, or, the other way, to see the rising slopes of the pastures that lead up to the fabled destination they have dreamed of for so long.

It was from this dull place of passage, as he passed nearby that April day, that old Stour saw the ominous sight of a rook flap out, with something pale and limp dangling from its cruel white bill. The corvid circled up and settled on the dirty grass edge of the roaring owl way above. Its black wing angled and flapped to balance its body, its head

52

was cocked and still, staring at the food it had found, and then its head and bill darted forward, and whatever it had found was torn apart, and swallowed.

Stour shook his head at the sickening sight, and had started to pass on by when he heard the weak cry of an adult female come from out of the cross-under, and worse, the pathetic bleat of young. Out of the sky another rook flew and wheeled and then landed at the entrance to the place. It stalked vilely forward into the dark, its head sheening, its beak sharp, and Stour heard a renewal of the frightened cries.

He was not a fighting mole, but something in him made him change his course and start suddenly after the rook. He knew enough to know that corvids have not much nerve: they are not brave with living things, being braver with the dying, and bravest with the dead. Aye, a rook is brave indeed when worrying a corpse.

So Stour went quickly into the cross-under's murk, giving a wary glance towards the rook that hunched and gulped on the parapet above, which shot up in alarm into the air on seeing him. Then, shouting as loudly as he could he ran towards the second rook which, predictably, flew up and forward and straight over the prey it had been about to attack once more. The adult cry he had heard before came forth again, weaker now, and then a bleat as well, at which Stour, without fear or hesitation, went forward to where the cries came from.

He found a female prone and helpless, whose present situation, and how she had got into it, was easily deduced. A trail of blood along the concrete floor suggested what her mutilated right paw confirmed: that she had been attempting to cross the way above and had been crushed by a roaring owl.

What drove her to crawl through her pain and mortal distress down the embankment, and from thence into the only cover she could find, was all too plain. For she was, or rather had been, pregnant. Two of the young lay dead and torn to one side of her, where they had been thrown in the attacks she must have endured from the beaks and claws of the rooks. A third pup must have been that limp thing that Stour had seen one of the rooks carry out on to the embankment above.

While a fourth, still alive and protected by the mole's one good front paw, huddled blind and bleating, its flanks shivering with cold, its body blotched red with its mother's and its dead siblings' blood.

'Mole,' began Stour before some instinct made him turn and strike upwards at a raucous rush of black feathered death as one of the rooks returned to the attack. 'Mole . . .'

53

But what was there to say?

The female's eyes were closed and it was plain she was near death. Her good paw feebly sought her one remaining young, her head half turned, her eyes opened as Stour, not knowing what to do at all, stared and did nothing, not even speak.

Yet she saw him there, her eyes widening in fear for a moment before she saw that he was mole, and not attacking her.

'Duncton . . .' she whispered, 'is this Duncton Wood?'

'It is,' he said, adding in his correct librarian's way, even at such a moment, 'or it almost is.'

A very faint smile came to her eyes and she looked at him, or into him, in a way that was open and deep and held him quite still.

'What is thy name?' she asked in the old way, though weakening before his eyes.

'Stour,' he said.

'Yes,' she said, as if she had expected him. 'Oh Stour, the Stone sent you in time.'

'What mole are you?' he asked in surprise.

She smiled again and said, 'He promised you would be here. Now Stour, take up my pup and look after him as you would look after the most precious text in your library. No, say nothing, there is no time. Let me see you take him into Duncton Wood.'

'Mole . . .' said Stour, who hesitated to pick up a thing so tiny and frail as that unfamiliar, bloody, bleating thing.

'Do it for us all, and now, for there is no time,' she whispered. 'And let me see you go.'

Then as he stared at the pup helplessly she said, 'Mole, you take him up by the scruff of the neck, that's how you carry young.' Again her eyes smiled as if she understood his doubt and fear.

So he blankly picked up the pup, she nodded almost imperceptibly, and he turned back towards the light carrying the pup. The pup hung limp, and what Stour did next shows how far he was removed from the nurturing and natural instincts of mole, and how much of a scholar and bookish mole he was. And yet what mole, knowing the outcome of what he did next, would have told him not to do it?

For he lay the limp thing down on the filthy concrete where it was exposed to crippling draught and searching rook and turned back towards its mother.

'What mole are you?' he asked, for all his life's training over texts had taught him that to understand the present a mole must know something of the past. So, surely, he thought, if the pup survived it would one day be glad that he had asked.

'You are . . . Stour?'

He nodded.

'And Privet of Bleaklow is here?'

He nodded again.

'Tell her . . . Oh, mole, tell her not. Not yet . . .' For a moment Stour thought she had gone, for she closed her eyes and gasped. But then, drawn back from death it seemed by a mother's instinct, she opened her eyes, looked at her last living young and said urgently, 'Now, now, take him. Quick now, mole, take him that I may see it . . .'

'But . . .' said Stour doubtfully, before he turned and took his burden once more. 'But . . .'

'Go, mole. Give him what life you can, he was made with love, and borne here in faith, and this *should* be his home and Privet his just mother!' Then as he turned away from her, he heard her whisper hoarsely. 'Name him Whillan and know that he is blessed. This was ordained and meant to be. And you Stour, and Privet, and all of it . . . it was ordained. Stone, help Stour protect our pup that was made in hopeless love . . . yet born here to the distant sound of Silence.'

Then there was silence, deep silence, and Stour knew the poor mole was dead and that in the shadows where she lay was a void whose name was Silence of which he was much afraid. He turned back gratefully to the here and now, suddenly aware of the need to get the pup to safety. Stour gathered all his strength together, and taking up the pup, rushed out from that wretched place and into the light of day, with the rooks wheeling and cawing greedily above him.

He heard the rooks, but once only did he stop and look back. They were not after him yet, but were clustering, fighting, flapping over the carrion that had been a mother and this pup's siblings. So in death, by delaying the rooks, mother and siblings helped save the new pup's life. Then the pup bleated, and blankly Stour struggled on up the slope with his unfamiliar burden, his eyes filled with unwonted tears for what he had left behind.

In which state of grief and shock, his instinct was to take the pup to the place where he felt most secure, irrespective of the pup's distress and immediate needs: the Library.

It was there, that same until-then-pleasant morning, to the astonishment of all the workers in the Library, that Stour stumbled into the

Great Chamber and laid his burden down. It breathed, and its little mouth opened wide and bleated, and for all the weakness of the sound, how it carried about that great and bookish place, and turned the heads of the unsuspecting clerics, librarians and Keepers.

Had a mole searched every system in moledom, it would have been hard to have found such a large collection of moles more unsuited to the mundane and thankless task of fostering a pup, as Duncton's bookish librarians and workers. But there they were, and to them the Stone (for so it must have been) had guided Stour in his wondering distress.

Breathless, speechless, near breaking-point and not his normal self at all, he stared at the unprepossessing sight of the pup without expression; or rather, with an expression that seemed to see only the horror that had been in the cross-under and surprise that he had been involved in such an outcome.

The clerics clustered and whispered uselessly, 'It's a pup! The Master's brought a pup!' And some in that quirky awkward lot even tittered and made comments, unable to comprehend that what lay before them was new life, but life that was failing and slowing, and growing dangerously chilled.

Eventually one of the females asked, 'Where did you find it, Master Librarian?'

Stour's reply was faltering and strange, and so much unlike himself that some there, embarrassed at the sight of the pup, and not liking to see their awesome Stour vulnerable and close to shock and tears, drifted away.

Others whispered, and one said, 'It's dying of cold and lack of mother's sup. Poor thing.'

The 'poor thing' raised its tiny naked head and turned its blind eyes towards the only comfort it knew, which was the austere flank of Stour, and bleated once more. At which Stour realized suddenly that *he* was the one who must act, and fast. The pup's mother had said . . . so much, and yet so little. But she *had* said . . .'

'Fetch Keeper Privet. NOW!' said Stour. '*Now!* Does nomole know where she is?'

'I shall find her, Master!' It was Pumpkin who spoke, his eyes tear-filled to see the pup, his heart full; he had a strange sense that here and now it was he who must fetch Privet, for in this was the Stone's Light. So off he went, not *knowing* where she was, but a certainty guiding his pawsteps through the tunnels until he found her, huddled silent and afraid, at the very furthest point in the Library, where the ruins of the older, mysterious tunnels of the Ancient System began.

'Pumpkin . . .' she said, staring at the dark depths into which no mole dared go, 'I thought I heard a pup's cry. I thought . . .'

'Come, Miss Privet, come with me. You're needed now, Miss, more than you've ever been . . .' And meekly, and staring back again and again at the ancient tunnels before whose Dark Sound she had been much afraid, she followed him.

'It is a pup?' was all she managed to say when she reached the extraordinary sight. 'A pup!' She stared at the gasping thing in utter alarm, and then at Stour.

'Yes, Keeper Privet, it *is* a pup,' said Stour brusquely, his old self coming back more strongly now his decision had been made.

'Quite so, Master,' said Privet uneasily.

'Well, mole, don't just stance there. Care for it.'

'Master?' said Privet again, in disbelief.

'The pup, Privet, the pup,' said Stour more gently. 'The Stone has sent it to the Library's care, and we *shall* care for it, as if it were more precious than any text in this great place. But somemole here has to *raise* it. It will be your task.'

'But Master, I . . .'

'The Master Librarian has put it plainly, mole, so get on with it,' said Snyde, who had appeared round a corner.

'But I have much work. I cannot do it. I have not had pups. I . . .' she said, Snyde revelling in her panic.

'Now's your chance!' he said with a laugh, grinning around at the fascinated crowd of aides.

'Silence, Snyde,' said Stour shortly. 'And you others, get to work. Librarian Privet, I am I think a reasonable mole. Today you must accept that there is reason in my unreasonableness. I ask you again to accept this task.'

'But there is other work . . .' she said despairingly, staring at the pup which had now laid its head along the library floor and was shivering and gasping for breath.

'There is no work more important than this,' said Stour softly, going forward and picking up the pup and taking it over to her. 'I shall appoint you an aide to help you with the raising of . . . of . . .'

The pup bleated weakly, and Privet dared at last to look at it.

'It is a female's work,' said Stour.

'But why *me*?' whispered Privet, sniffling at the pup. At her touch it raised its tiny snout again, quested here and there, and then found hers.

'Because,' said Stour, fixing her with such a look that she had experienced only one like it before, and that from Stour on the first day that they met. It was then she knew his test of her had begun, and knew too that he had not expected this any more than she had. The Stone's Light was in it all.

'Poor thing,' Privet found herself saying in wonder, her voice weakening as that deep urge that lies in moles waiting for its moment to find life, found life in Privet: the urge to save life, to nurture, to make the frightened safe, to help the lost feel secure.

Timid, uncertain, frightened though she was herself, yet she sensed a crucial moment in her life had come. Was it her deep faith in the Stone that helped her see the Light? For surely simple obedience to her Keeper and the Master was not sufficient to give her such strength as she needed to go forward, as she then did, and snout down at the pup, and half lick it, and begin that act of uncritical acceptance from which parental love is born.

Yet doubt still remained and Privet said, 'I don't know his name,' hoping perhaps that in his anonymity would be a way out of the responsibility that faced her.

'His name is . . . Whillan,' said Stour, and there was some wonder in his voice as he said it, and unaccustomed gentleness, and somewhere in his heart, though then denied, he knew that in this strange happening something more powerful than anything he had experience of was speaking to him, and speaking true. In this event lay the beginnings of an answer to troubles that had been building up so long and which were not yet at their worst. In *this* shared act of faith answers to future problems not yet even guessed-at lay.

'Whillan . . . ?' said Privet, frowning and puzzled, as if she knew the name. 'Oh, Whillan . . .' And she snouted down at the pup once more, licking with a sudden and whole-hearted gentleness.

'Whillan, my love!' she whispered, and she and the pup might as well have been alone, for all she cared, or seemed to see of all the world about.

Then she took him up by the scruff of the neck as Stour had done, and accompanied by younger, eager aides, who cooed and chirruped and chattered along behind them both, turned back out of the Library and from thence to her modest quarters down towards the Eastside.

'Well, get on, get on!' said Stour sourly to those many who still stared. 'To your work, the drama's over.' His aides noticed however that *he* could not work, but dithered about all day, snapping at moles to right and left, until, when evening came he who was normally last to leave was first away and off to the Eastside, to Privet's place.

That same evening, gentle Pumpkin, who had been much shaken by the coming of the pup and his part in finding Privet, turned from the Library exit and slowly crossed the Wood westward to the Stone. It was not a place he often went, nor was praying a thing he often did, or felt he knew much about. Yet pray he felt he must.

So into the Stone Clearing he went, across its open space, and stanced down humbly before moledom's greatest Stone.

'Don't know what words to say, Stone,' he said, 'but somemole must make a prayer to welcome that pup Whillan to our Wood. And wish him well. There'll be reasons why he's come to us, and why it's as an orphan he was born and will not know his mother, or father, or much about himself. Well . . . you know best, Stone. You know everything. Grant the pup life, and Miss Privet the patience and the love to nurture him. Watch over her as well, Stone, for she's a mole I think has suffered much and yet finds love to give.'

Pumpkin said nothing for a while, but stared for a long time at the Stone, and shed tears which were neither sad nor happy ones, but tears acknowledging that sometimes life is hard for moles and must be borne.

'Feel better now,' he said at last, 'for good has come this day to Duncton Wood. Grant that I may play my part in it, Stone, and be worthy of what tasks you choose to give me.'

Then he turned and left, and where he had been the Stone was awesome in its Silence, and about it was a Light that seemed to touch all the trees of the clearing, and shine beyond them into the wood to where old Pumpkin went on his solitary way.

Chapter Six

For Privet, who since the mating season had begun had felt so cast down by her unspoken memories of the past, the days that followed the pup's arrival were so far the most extraordinary, most trying, and yet most exhilarating of her life.

Poor Privet. Whatever the burdens she already carried, life had now thrust another upon her, and its shape was puppish, and its sound was puppish, and its effect was puppish: which is to say it offered no possibility of escape.

Twisting, turning, bleating, feeding, excreting, waking, always waking, crying, scrabbling, sniffling, there was not one single troublesome wakesome '–ing' that the pup Whillan did not do, and many that Privet had never dreamed a mole *might* do.

The first day or two was one long frantic worry over keeping him alive, for he seemed limp and desperate, his little furless chest heaving in and out as if breath was in short supply and he had best get it while he may, his mouth sucking for milk she could not give. It seemed certain that death was lurking just beyond the portal of her sparse and modest burrow on the slopes, awaiting the slightest excuse to enter and take the pup away.

But like so many moles who must care for young they have not borne, instinct and necessity found a form of nourishment in chewed worm and spittle. As Privet made it, Whillan took it, and did not die. Worse, he wanted more, and more, and more again, and left Privet more exhausted than if she had been feeding a whole community of moles.

Nor was Privet's most obvious source of help – Fieldfare – available to offer it. She had, for reasons of her own, made herself scarce the moment she had heard of Stour's appointment of Privet as foster-mother to the pup. In this Fieldfare was acting most wisely, and with the thoughtfulness for her friend she so often showed, understanding well that at such a moment a mole must be allowed to sink or swim on her own, and that her presence would have robbed Privet of something of the discoveries she must make for herself in rearing the youngster.

Fieldfare was well aware that this was not something that Privet herself would readily appreciate or immediately understand, but trusted that in time she would come to do so. Nevertheless, the good mole felt obliged to seek Stour out and explain why she was disappearing off to the Westside for a time, and ask him to keep an eye on Privet in the first days and weeks.

Rightly or wrongly he had, against Fieldfare's advice, sent one of his female aides to help Privet, and she was the eventual cause of the first real upset for the new 'mother'. For the crisis of the first days over, and the pup viable, another crisis formed itself in the shape of the female aide Stour had sent. Do this, she said: do that, she nagged.

'Don't go to him, Privet, he's bleating because he knows you'll come. Let him lie in his own mess, Privet, for that way he'll learn. No, Privet, you must you cannot he's looking strange he's an ugly thing you're tired it's no—'

'Shut up!' said Privet sharply, speaking words she had never in her whole life spoken.

The mole's eyes widened and Privet, discovering a strange sense of purpose which felt very right indeed, went on to say, though more gently, that she was very grateful for the help the mole had given and it had got her through the worst but now she thought she could cope, and would cope and would the mole *please leave*.

Well, really! That Privet!

'"Shut up" she told me and "Get out at once" she said,' the outraged mole was reporting in the Library as soon as she could, adding that 'Privet has no idea how to look after and raise a pup at all and in my view it was a *most* unsuitable choice the Master made.'

'Really?'

'Yes. The burrow's disorganized and she spoils the pup and does everything for him and never sleeps herself and everything is a mess, an utter mess. I really think . . .'

Hearing this gossip Stour went visiting, but it did not take him long to see beyond the 'mess' and observe the touching bond between foster-mother and adoptive pup: nor was he wrong in his guess that a softer, gentler look was on its way to displace for ever that loss and withering which had beset poor Privet's face for so long. Stour smiled to himself, thinking that perhaps the Stone knew a thing or two about fostering, and had guided him well to give Privet the task. But then . . .

61

For naturally in the days that followed, as Stour became sure the pup would survive, he began to think again of the extraordinary circumstances of Whillan's birth and rescue, and of the mother who had seemed to expect him to be there, and spoke the name of Privet as if she herself knew what would be best for the pup. Who had she been, and why did she call the pup Whillan? It was not a name he had ever heard before.

Yet Privet had seemed to recognize something about it, and he believed that it was from the moment she heard the name 'Whillan' spoken that her doubts fled, and she decided she would take up the task. It worried Stour that he did not know, nor was able even to surmise, to whom the dying mother had referred when she spoke of 'us' as parents, and who the father might be and what had happened to him, or how it was that the mother felt it was all ordained, and that Privet was the 'just' mother, and that somehow, sooner perhaps than any of them knew, the Stone's Silence, and its Light, waited upon these strange events.

One thing at least was certain in what the mother had said before she died: she had not wished Privet to know much of anything. Long did Stour ponder the meaning of this, concluding that the arrival of the mole, and the so-far unknown tale of its parents, had something to do with that past life that Librarian Privet wished to deny had ever been.

Well, Stour was not the one to interfere with a mole's wishes, or break her confidence, not as *Stour*; yet the scholar in him said that truth was all that mattered, and since he was dedicated to wresting it from the lies or secrets that scribemoles of the past perpetrated through their work, he had no wish to contribute more mystery to the future. If one day he must tell what he knew of Whillan's birth to make the truth known, then tell he would. Until then, silence about the circumstances seemed best.

The drama of Whillan's coming was, for most moles, a thing of a passing moment, and as the weeks lengthened into molemonths, and summer came, and moles saw that Privet could cope, their interest moved to other things.

Yet for those few moles like Fieldfare and Stour, who were concerned, the changes in Privet as young Whillan grew and she suffered and enjoyed all the pangs and delights of rearing a pup, were touching to see. The mole that had come to Duncton Wood as a scholar, her face lined with doubt, her shoulders bowed under an unspoken burden of a past she wished to leave behind, now began to blossom forth in concert with the youngster whom she reared.

Late in coming he may have been, nearly the last pup born to the system that spring, but he grew well and fast. His eyes were clear, his body well formed if perhaps a little thin, his nature curious yet a little timid, as only pups often are.

It was a good, warm, early summer, and through the molemonths of May Privet and young Whillan became a familiar sight on the otherwise pupless slopes of the high Eastside. Moles sensed that a pup without siblings needed company of some kind, and so began to drop by Privet's modest place. Good Drubbins came, and took the pup off her paws for a time; and Maple too, who until then Privet had barely known, brought older pups tendered to his care for exploring through the Wood, who though bigger than Whillan played with him, and let him play with them.

'What's his name?' they said.

'Whillan,' replied Maple, in his deep voice, 'and you look after him.'

'Can we explore with him as far as . . . there!' they said, pointing their young talons at a clump of dog's-mercury.

'Aye, but watch him well, he's only young.'

So does a new generation begin its long and stumbling journey towards adulthood, and the distant day when it must take up the responsibilities its parents seem to carry so lightly, but which, in reality, are sometimes so hard.

Privet and Maple watched the young play their games, and in that sharing Privet found she came to know and like another mole of Duncton Wood.

Others visited her too, among them gentle Pumpkin, and since there was something of the pup in him, despite his age, Whillan liked him, and happily played in the tunnels and on the surface with him as well.

If it was from his 'mother' Privet that he first unconsciously learned not to fear texts or libraries or words, it was Pumpkin who affirmed it, for the aide told the youngster many a tale of the mysterious doings down in the stacks, where texts got lost, and wind-sound was, and what seemed dead to those who could not scribe became alive and rich to those who could.

Then, too, Drubbins, concerned to meet all pups in the system before he conducted the Midsummer Ritual which formally blessed and welcomed them to the adult world beyond their home burrows, called in many times, and Whillan, timid before this most respected of moles, stared in awe, and listened as the old mole talked to Privet for a time of things the youngster could not understand.

All this attention was new to Privet and, in her quiet retiring way, she enjoyed it, though as the time went by she began to miss her Library work, and wished sometimes she could go back to it, feeling guilty that she looked forward to the day when Whillan would grow a bit more and give her freedom to return. Yet she trusted Stour and knew that in good time he would send to let her know when she was needed and perhaps tell her at last what task it was he wanted her to undertake – apart from raising pups!

In fact she had already heard from Pumpkin that Stour seemed to have come out of himself even more since April, and had been seen much more in the Library, and had even talked of the pup Whillan with something like paternalistic pride, as if – or almost as if – the pup were his!

Certainly, when he came to visit her and to see how the youngster was getting on, his thin face managed to beam contentedly, and he seemed not to mind when the pup, not appreciating the importance of the mole who had come, climbed over him and buffeted his face.

'Whillan!' said Privet, embarrassed. But old Stour did not mind, content to see the pup was well and lively. Perhaps, after all, pups were not so bad . . .

'I would like to start my work again,' said Privet during a visit he made soon after Midsummer, feeling now somehow closer to Stour than she had felt before. There was a growing but unspoken trust between them.

'I know, my dear, and so you shall. But if I remember my young days right these are precious months, when the pup stores memories. Well, then, spend time with Whillan while you can, and while he wants to. He'll become independent of you sooner than you think. There's time yet to find you a new task in the Library, and be assured I have one for you in mind.'

So Privet did as he advised, enjoying the easy days of June, when the sun was warm but gentle, and the wood still rich with flowers before the fuller canopy of the trees subdued the light and they died away. Days of wandering at Whillan's pace, and watching him run from her and then, alarmed, run back to the safe encirclement of her paws, and the loving snuffles of her snout. Days when she felt slide from her the prickles and briars of the past, which had made her closed and afraid of life. Austere she might still be, for there was something of that in her nature, but she felt a softening come over her, an easing, and believed that the Stone had sent Whillan to her, to heal her through rearing him.

There were days when they lazed, and she told him stories of the past, tales she had heard when she was young and then later from Cobbett when living in Beechenhill, a system rich in recent history, where there was a Stone as well, in whose shadow the very saving of moledom in modern times had taken place.

Those tales she told him, giving more away of herself than she ever had before, though safe in the knowledge that the youngster would not really know what it was he heard. This freedom helped her begin to come to terms with whatever it was she had left behind at the Wood's edge when she had first come to Duncton.

Then too, she spoke in her precise but vivid way of older tales that all moles learn from their parents, or from other adults, for they are the history out of which the present has grown. Of Whern she spoke, and the dreadful moles who once lived there. Of Bleaklow, where she herself was raised before she was taken into Beechenhill. These were the dark places she unknowingly delved and built in Whillan's imagination, such as all moles have, though their names be different. Immutable places, repositories for doubts and fears just as other places similarly created by myth and story hold a mole's most secret, and most needed, stock of trust, or faith, and of love.

Just such a place for Whillan was Beechenhill, of which Privet sometimes spoke, telling with remembered love of the untidy and disreputable ways of scribemole Cobbett who had been her tutor once. In his character the youngster found more fun than in his reported tales. So when Privet told him of how Cobbett might begin one tale and absent-mindedly end it with the second half of another, the young Whillan was fascinated and begged his 'mother' to tell such a semi-tale to him.

'Oh, I'm not much good at telling tales my dear,' she said, 'or not made-up tales at any rate. My skill was recording them.'

'But Cobbett was?'

'He knows more tales than anymole in moledom, I should think. But he didn't make them up you know, just collected them.'

'What are they about?'

'Anything and everything,' she replied.

'What's old Cobbett *look* like,' asked Whillan persistently.

'Old, I suppose, with untidy, patchy fur which he never bothered to groom, and rather grubby talons. Half the time he could not remember what he was talking about a moment before, and he was restless, so restless, as if he expected something to come round the corner any moment.'

'I'd like to meet him,' said Whillan.

'Oh you can't do that, my love,' she replied. 'That was all long ago when I was a different mole. I'm afraid he's long gone by now into the Stone's Silence.'

Whillan stared at her, his eyes wide and serious.

'Was Cobbett your mate?' he said at last.

Privet laughed freely, in a way she never did with anymole-else.

'No, my love,' she said at last, 'it wasn't Cobbett.'

Such secret moments with Whillan, when he was snuggled up against her flank and she could touch on things nomole else could know, were precious and irreplaceable. When the summer sun was at her tunnel entrances, and the trees of Duncton riffled and shone all green and grey in the warm breeze, she knew she was living at last as she never had before.

So it was that with Whillan's coming, and his growth into a mole in his own right, who asked questions and wanted to know things and whose eyes shone at her words and whose mind travelled in imagination with hers, something of the scars of Privet's past had healed, and their pain lifted from her.

Sometimes during those June days Fieldfare joined them, rightly feeling that Privet had had enough time alone with her pup without interference, to bond to him in a way that could now never change.

So Fieldfare came, and added to Privet's tales stories of her own, and gave to Whillan that heritage of memory of Duncton Wood that Privet herself could not give. In her own maternal way Fieldfare gave her account of the role Duncton had played in the defence of the Stone against the disciples of the Word and even took the youngster off to look at one or two places in the system that had played a part – or so moles said, for none now lived who had actually been there at the time – in the unfolding story of those days.

Perhaps it was with Fieldfare's stories, and in her company, that to those dark places in Whillan's deepest imagination was added another – the Ancient System of Duncton Wood. For Fieldfare feared it, and spoke of it, and at night Whillan would sometimes fancy that he heard strange sounds from the High Wood, and that dark moles were there who lurked at forgotten tunnel entrances, inviting him down with alluring but treacherous smiles. Sometimes Whillan woke with nightmare thoughts, and Privet comforted him, as all parents must comfort their young as they grow and struggle with their fears, until they grow beyond them and the fears go deeper down, and linger, and wait.

For her part Privet was able to tell Whillan of some of the places beyond the system of which Fieldfare knew only the names, and where neither had much of consequence to say Fieldfare would conclude, 'Well then, that's one for Chater when *he* returns! He'll tell you all about *that*, Whillan!'

'Will he come soon?' said Whillan, unconsciously pushing himself closer into Privet's thin flank, for he had not yet seen Chater, since the journeymole had gone off with a text for Avebury before he was aware of much more than Privet's burrows. He was a little nervous of Chater, who sounded big and mysterious and not an easy mole.

'He better!' declared Fieldfare. 'For I miss him and he said he'd not be back much later than June and it's nearly July.'

Yet Whillan was not lacking in male company, or example. Apart from the great Stour himself, Drubbins visited from time to time, as he liked to visit all the new youngsters, and chatted about big things and small. There was growing trust between Drubbins and Privet, for he saw now – as others were beginning to – that there was a good deal more to Privet than a mole first thought, and certainly she had acquitted herself well where Whillan was concerned.

Pumpkin, too, was now a frequent visitor, and it was to that much-liked mole that Privet entrusted Whillan's first venturing into the Library, feeling that it was better that another mole than her introduced him to the realities of books and scribing. The harder, learning part could come later, and no doubt she would have to see that he learnt scribing, but she felt it likely that good Pumpkin could enthuse the youngster better than she herself could. And anyway, as she told Fieldfare a little guiltily, 'It is good to get away from him occasionally.'

When July came Whillan began to wander off by himself, and Privet at last returned for short times to the Library. By then Whillan's character was beginning to form, and his looks too. He was if anything big for his age, but in length rather than muscle, for he was lanky and thin. Time no doubt would put muscle on him, but thus far his physical appearance, combined with a studious and enquiring nature learned from Privet, as well as an ability to stance quietly and listen, gave him the character for a scribemole or librarian, if a somewhat clumsy one.

Certainly, when Privet returned to the Library in July, for brief periods at first, she saw how willingly he went about with Pumpkin, who taught him more than any librarian or Keeper ever could. The youngster wandered here and there with him, helping him by carrying texts, and became a favourite among older, lesser moles who were glad to see some youth in the place, and occasional high spirits. For he had a sense of humour, and enjoyed hearing others tell their tales, knowing how and when to laugh and enjoy their jokes. But . . .

'What's so funny, mole?' a nasal voice snarled one day from the shadows.

It was Deputy Master Snyde, patrolling, looking for something to complain about, or make mock of. The aides who had been laughing with Whillan slid away immediately and unfortunately Pumpkin was not there, so that Whillan was left alone with Snyde.

'It was just a joke,' he said, snout low. He had only ever seen Snyde in the distance, but knew his reputation.

'I know it was a joke because I heard your idiot laughter, mole, but I was wondering if it was funny or not.'

Before Snyde's mocking, withering gaze the youngster stumblingly explained what they had been laughing about.

'And that's it?'

'Um, yes,' said poor Whillan.

Snyde laughed loudly in a terrible way and then his face reverted to deadly seriousness.

'Mole, keep your silly jokes out of here.'

'Yes, Snyde,' said Whillan.

Yes, *Snyde*? The very walls of the Library might tremble at such insolence. But Snyde only smiled, and came close, and caressed Whillan's face in a way that made the youngster want to retch, and said, 'You shall come to me for your tutoring in scribing, mole, for I understand you like texts.'

'I do,' said Whillan, wondering when the dried-up Snyde would take his paw away and trying to look him in the eyes without faltering, not daring to move away.

'That's settled then.'

'But I think my mother is going to teach me.'

'She's your foster-mother, mole. You were found by the Master. In a way the Library itself is your father. In such matters as learning how to scribe don't you think the Deputy Master might know a little more than a mere librarian and foster-mother? Eh?'

Whillan stared, confused and not knowing what to say. Snyde came closer, reached out a paw and touched Whillan's flank strangely, casting a lingering look at it. Whillan dared at last back off a little and Snyde as quickly withdrew his paw.

'Just my little joke, mole, just my own,' he whispered confidentially.

Whillan could scent his dryness, and see the flick of a grey-pink tongue.

'Ha ha . . .' chuckled Snyde.

And Whillan tried to laugh.

But such moments of darkness, which are a part of a youngster's education in learning how to cope with the world beyond his tunnels and home system, were rare and soon forgotten. There was always the surface to explore, and the warm summer sun to enjoy, and when he grew bored, or the light and sun in groves of trees ahead attracted him, he went off by himself to Fieldfare's place, and she would fuss him, and try to fatten him, and say he was the spitting image of his mother, which was strange, since she was *not* his mother. But when she heard such things, Privet took it as a compliment.

None of them kept from him his orphan origin, but so secure was his life among them all that that terrible history seemed to mean nothing to him, and he never spoke of it. But sometimes he seemed older than his years, and only when night came, and the shadows gathered in the chambers, and wind-sound travelled its dark and mysterious way, did he seem younger again, nervous of the dark, afraid to be too much alone.

Yet by mid-July he was willing to go off by himself to places he had not been taken by anymole, exploring the tunnels and the Wood, and meeting up with moles like Drubbins, who was often about. Although he had been to Barrow Vale already in Privet's company, he began now to visit it alone, and in truth began to make more friends than shy Privet ever had, coming back to the home burrow and telling her about them and all they said.

It was sometime then that he came back one day and told of an old mole he had met over on the slopes nearby the Stone.

'What was his name?' Privet asked, tired after a day's work and only half interested.

'Don't know,' said Whillan.

'Must be Husk of Rolls, Rhymes and Tales,' said Privet carefully. 'He's not a mole I've ever met.'

'Talked a lot,' said Whillan, brief as youngsters often are about the adventures they have had.

'And . . . ?' said Privet, very curious.

'And . . . nothing much. Told me a tale and that was good.'

'What tale?'

''Bout Balagan. You *know*. Told it me yourself once. His version was different . . .'

'How?'

'Just different.'

This was the tantalizing first report that Privet ever had directly about Husk, and perhaps wisely she did not press the matter more, trusting that if something more was to be Whillan would tell her of it in good time. Which he did.

A few days later: 'Spent the day at Keeper Husk's. It was *amazing*, much better than the Library!' Whillan's eyes were bright.

'Yes?' said Privet evenly.

'You know, all those texts he's got, *hundreds* of them. He knows every one he said, *every* one. Amazing! Asked me about you. Said you must come from the Dark Peak. What is the Dark Peak?'

Privet was astonished. 'It's the name of the area where I was born. But how did he know?'

'Husk knows lots and lots. I'll go again. *Can* I go again?' He seemed suddenly concerned by the look on Privet's face, thinking her surprise and puzzlement was alarm.

'Of course you can, my love. He probably likes to see you. He's a bit of a recluse.'

'Oh,' said Whillan, uninterested. 'Well, I will then.'

So Whillan began to visit Husk, innocent of the fact that he was the first mole in many years to do so, and as those hot July days passed by he stopped going to the Library altogether, as if it was part of his puphood that he had grown out of. Instead he spent his time in the obscure tunnels of Rolls and Rhymes listening, learning, and helping.

Sometimes he would speak of it, sometimes not, and Privet was content that it should be so. She felt it wisest if she let things be, and curious though she was, did not try to interfere, or visit Husk herself.

That summer the Stone had seemed to cast its Light over their part of the wood, and over her life, and Privet was happy to let life be what it was, and let Whillan grow now as he would. But sometimes she found time dragging, and wondered where life would take her next, for she knew much had changed for ever with Whillan's coming. Yet not everything, and sometimes too, in the shadows of dusk, or in the fastness of the night, she thought she saw a mole, a great mole, and she started forward, unafraid. For he was . . . but a shadow, but a memory from which she had not yet escaped.

'Is it normal to get bored with them?' she asked Fieldfare one August day, though that was not what was really on her mind.

Fieldfare laughed.

'Normal and healthy, my dear. A sign that the time's coming when they'll be leaving the home burrow, though bless me but you'll have a few rough passages before that. They don't leave easily you see. Sometimes they don't want to leave at all. "Bored", as you put, is mild compared to what you may feel by the time winter comes!'

Privet looked at her doubtfully. 'I wouldn't really want him to leave. I mean, what will I do when he does?'

'Be yourself again, and discover that you've become different too. Why, Privet, you've softened, you're *different*, and Chater says . . .'

Fieldfare giggled.

'Well?' said Privet.

'I couldn't! I shouldn't! I will! He says that since Whillan came into your life you've become, as he puts it in his crude male way, *fanciable*.'

Privet's snout went red. Fanciable!

'Well!' she said rhetorically. 'Really?'

Fieldfare nodded. 'The thoughts of males make no sense to me at all, but I think it is time for you to forget the past, my dear. This is where your life is now.'

But Privet's smile faded and she looked away.

'Oh Fieldfare, I've tried, and I thought I had. But sometimes lately in the night . . . I wish I could forget the past. I wish I could. I thought rearing Whillan would make me forget, but somehow it's only seemed to make the past come near to again. Fieldfare, I'm sometimes so afraid, and sad, and lonely for what has been . . .'

'Tell me, my dear,' said Fieldfare.

'One day with your help I may be able to. But not yet, Fieldfare, not quite yet.'

Chapter Seven

September came and subtly the trees began to turn, their leaves becoming drier and more rustly in the wind as the rich greens of summer changed to russet-browns and reds, in a gentle wave across the Wood.

Change was in the very air, and that strange and troublesome time had come to Duncton's tunnels, when young begin to leave the home burrow, some quietly, some with argument, and some with restless bewilderment.

But absorbing though the burgeoning needs of these youngsters were, most especially to themselves, it was in fact an important time for parents too, freed as they now were from the onerous tasks of providing and nurturing. On the days when summer sun briefly displaced the autumn bluster, the Wood seemed especially peaceful, and such moles could ponder the pleasures of knowing that their individuality had survived after all, and could be explored once more, and that with parental responsibilities lifted, all kinds of plans and preparations could begin at last.

Just such a hopeful mood overtook Privet, who, now that Whillan was off and about by himself and seeming to survive well enough, was beginning to raise her snout, look up at the trees and sky, and realize with a jolt that she was in a system that she had grown to love, and that there was much of it still to see, moles to meet, and many a thing to do.

Her work in the Library had grown slowly but steadily since Whillan had been old enough to go there with her, and though she was still formally attached to Sturne, the Keeper of Rules, in practice she was now consulted by moles from all departments of the Library, for she was recognized as having something of an expertise in matters mediaeval.

But for all that she found herself less willing to spend long hours in the Library than she had been before she had taken charge of Whillan's rearing, for she saw that there was more to life than bookish things, and to get to know about them a mole must get off her rump and go and say hello to the world. But to what part of the world, and to which moles to say hello, Privet was unsure, for along with the new sense of freedom she felt had come a uneasy restlessness – uneasy because it seemed to have no obvious outlet or objective.

Meanwhile, Whillan, already inclined to wander off during the day, began to delve tunnels of his own for use at night, and as in other families in the system began the sweet sad parting of the ways which, hard though it may sometimes be, is essential if youngsters are to be independent adults with a mind and nature of their own.

Whillan chose the slopes above Barrow Vale for his tunnels, which though not rich in food, were serviceable enough, and put him nearer the social centre of the system than Privet's austere burrows in the high Eastside. Whillan's interests had moved on from Rolls, Rhymes and Tales, and he now affected complete boredom with anything that old Husk might have to offer him.

Yet though he was nearer other and younger moles, a certain unsociable melancholy of mood had overtaken him and he seemed disinclined to mix and make new friends. About the only positive thing he seemed to do was drift – for that was the only way of describing the lassitude and indifference of his manner at that time – into the Library and wander among the stacks, giving his brief attention to all manner of texts, and scribing thoughts and observations about life on whatever scraps of bark came to paw.

'Life?' repeated Fieldfare with a laugh, when she heard of it.

'"Incantations of Autumn" is the text he's working on,' confirmed Pumpkin, her informant on this occasion. They were having a lazy conversation with Privet out on the surface, enjoying one of the finest days of autumn.

'Incant what?' said Fieldfare.

'"ations,' said Pumpkin, with a twinkle in his eye.

'Incant-nonsense,' declared Fieldfare.

'But I'm sure he has reasons of his own . . .' said Privet, always uneasy discussing Whillan in this disloyal way, yet glad to have friends with whom, even if guiltily, she could do so. He *could*, she conceded to herself, be trying.

'They all go through it, dear,' said Fieldfare, knowingly. 'At least *yours* is taking out his feelings on *bark*. That's better than . . . did I tell you about the time when one of ours got so upset when I wouldn't agree to something that he nearly hit me? Yes, it's true! Luckily for *him* Chater was there so he only got cuffed. If it had been me alone he might have got . . . hurt!'

73

'Fieldfare! You're not like that at all.'

'You've only ever seen the best in me, my love. Never the worst. I can wield a mean talon if I want, and if I ever have to I will. Can't I, Pumpkin?'

Pumpkin, who did not look as if he knew what a mean talon was, nodded in an unconvincing way and Privet smiled to herself as she looked at her two friends – for friends they truly were by now – and thought that neither would be a judge of a mean anything. That was why she . . . loved them.

Love them? she said to herself with wonder. She did! And Duncton too! How much her life had changed. And yet . . . and . . . so . . .

'*Why* do I feel restless and dissatisfied?' she said aloud, starting up from where they had been comfortably stanced as if she there and then intended to do something.

'I expect it's because your mind's too active, Privet. I'm not cursed with your kind of restless curiosity. I'm just pleased if things are all right, and when they're not I do something about it until they are. It's the same with you, Pumpkin, isn't it?'

Pumpkin nodded mildly. 'That's why I never wanted to be more than an aide, you see. If I was a scribemole I'd worry myself to death. Let the others do the worrying!'

'Like me, you mean?' said Privet.

'Seems so, Miss Privet. I can't think what you've got to worry about, you've reared Whillan really well . . .'

'But he's –'

'*Normal*,' interjected Fieldfare. 'More a mole cannot expect. You see . . .' She went on to sensibly point out that there was nothing unusual about a mole teetering at the portal of adulthood scribing incantations and indulging himself in moods, especially if he thought he had good reason to do so. 'And he has, my dear, he has! He's probably worrying about his parentage and that.'

'More than probably I would say, Miss Privet.'

'Hmmph!' said Privet. 'Neither Stour nor I ever kept anything secret from him that I know of, and we answered all his questions frankly.'

'Well, you'll just have to let him carry on asking them until he's bored with it and goes on to more useful things,' said Fieldfare equably. 'Patience, my dear, and a task – that's the way to stop fretting about a thing. Find yourself a task – or better still find Whillan one!'

Privet grumbled some more, but then the air stilled and evening came on, and Pumpkin told them he knew a place which caught the last of the sun where the worms were good, and they drifted off to find it and talk of other things.

The September days went by. Sometimes Privet would spend time by herself, but for the most part she and Fieldfare would join or be joined by moles like Pumpkin, and young Avens (as he still seemed to them), and, once in a while, others like Maple and Drubbins, to talk, and joke, and share. As the evenings began to draw in they became inclined like others to make their way down to Barrow Vale, and gather there in community, to meet old friends and hear how others' offspring were doing, or hear what news of moledom the latest visitors had brought.

Fieldfare noticed that at such times Privet fell silent and did not contribute. She suspected that such talk revived old memories that Privet did not wish to think about, though nothing ever had, nor now seemed likely to induce Privet to break her silence about her past.

But in any case the news was more of current things, and in particular of something that much concerned the easy-going and freedom-loving Duncton moles – the latest doings of the Newborns. Once more, it seemed, with the coming of summer missions had been sent forth from Caradoc and had strengthened their position in those systems where they were already established while sending out what they called pioneer cells to lesser systems. Chater was only one of several journeymoles who had confirmed visitors' reports, in his case after taking a text to Avebury where he found the Newborns now solidly entrenched in important positions in its Library.

Just now Chater himself was away again, but since it was only to nearby Cuddesdon, he would soon be back. Meanwhile September advanced and new visitors confirmed the Newborn expansion, saying the moles in Rollright looked ominously close to going over to the Newborn way.

'The wonder of it is that they haven't sent a new lot of missionaries to join the raggle-taggle Newborns down in the Marsh End,' declared Fieldfare when she heard this. Other moles in Barrow Vale stopped their chatter and listened, for Fieldfare had a way of putting into words what many felt.

'I mean,' she continued, 'Duncton Wood *is* a major system and you'd think they'd send their blessed pioneers or do-gooders or what-ever along to us to convert us lot to their way!'

'No chance,' said one of her friends. 'They know we don't go in for rules and regulations here, and they're too intelligent to try to make us. So they're content to have fuss and feud in the Marsh End.'

'Or too well informed,' growled Maple, whose solid presence always added a certain seriousness to the proceedings. 'From what Chater told me before he went off to Cuddesdon, it strikes me that the Newborns are merely biding their time because they know we'd resist any attempts at coercing us into anything. They're waiting, hoping something happens that will make their task easier, though what that could be I don't know. They'll get short shrift from me . . .'

He loomed forward among them, powerful and clear-eyed, a mole in his prime – but born, it seemed, into the wrong age.

'No, Maple,' said old Drubbins the healer, eyeing Maple's flexing talons, 'persuasion's our way, not force. I doubt if they'd ever find moles able to persuade us to do anything we didn't want.'

'It seems they "persuaded" the Avebury moles without difficulty,' said Maple shortly. 'Moles can talk all they like, but a show of force at the right time and in the right way may be the best defence. The Chronicles show how true that is, and how it's happened often enough in this very system in the past.'

Light had come to Maple's eyes, and an impressive stressing to his talons.

'You missed your vocation, Maple!' said Fieldfare. 'You should have gone from Duncton years ago to find a system that needed a warrior . . .'

A shadowed look crossed Maple's face and he said passionately, 'Moles in former times interfered too much in other systems' affairs. Duncton's my system and here I'll stay until the day comes that it needs me to defend it. And if I die without that ever happening there'll be no happier mole than me. But by the Stone, if I'm ever needed I'll be here and in no other place!'

'We know that, Maple, all of us know it,' said Fieldfare gently. She had watched Maple grow into the great and good mole he was, she had seen Drubbins' brother Chamfer train him in the ways of fighting, and she had even adjudicated between Maple and her own Chater when, for fun, they had tussled about. Why, she remembered the day well when Maple had succeeded at last in forcing Chater to yield and how her beloved, who knew well how to look after himself, had said, 'I swear I've never had the honour of fighting a stronger mole than young Maple. It's not his size, though that's impressive enough, but the way it's combined with speed and aggression. Yet he's the kindest, gentlest mole I know when he's not fighting. Mark my words, Fieldfare, there'll come a day the Stone will call him to its aid, for it does not make such a mole for nothing. You'll see!'

Maple had indeed grown to be indomitable, and looking at him now, with trust and affection, Fieldfare remembered Chater's words, and wondered if a day *would* ever come when Maple's strength was needed, and whether, perhaps, it was better that it never did.

Though Privet said little at such communal gatherings, they invariably stirred something up in her, and returning back to the Eastside with Fieldfare after them she would be taciturn and morose, and her parting for her own burrows would be of the briefest sort.

'If you don't mind my saying so, my dear,' Fieldfare would say to her after yet another vain attempt to get her to talk and unburden herself at last, 'get yourself busy, or find some task or other for yourself in the Library. I can *see* you're not happy at the moment, all restless and bothered. It's very exasperating for your friends!'

'Well! That's how it is, isn't it?' said Privet shortly, turning away. 'I can't help being what I am, or feeling what I do, and friends should be able to put up with it. I mean . . . oh I'm *sorry*, Fieldfare, I didn't mean . . .'

But Fieldfare didn't mind, and understood. She was inclined to be irritable herself when Chater was away too long, and in all the circumstances, mysterious though they were, it must be much worse for poor Privet.

Later, back at her burrows, Privet would be unable to sleep but would lie at one of her tunnel entrances with her snout extended along her paws, watching the night sky deepen, thinking that her past seemed a very long way away indeed and would not, could not, come back now. Yet there was the restlessness, and memories and images of moles and places she thought she had succeeded in forgetting.

'Yes!' she whispered to herself. 'Fieldfare's right, I need a task and now that Whillan's off my paws I'll go to Stour and ask him for one! Yes, I will!'

Yet there was a lack of conviction about these secret determinations, as if Privet felt that whatever task she must next take up, it would find her rather than she actively go and find it.

But, however that might be, it was Stour who sought her out soon afterwards, and not she who went to him. The Master Librarian had every reason to consult with Privet for lately he had been much troubled by Whillan, and not known quite what to do.

For Whillan, now more adult than youngster and almost daily thickening out in that awkward changeling way that such moles have of shedding off their youth in stops and starts and deepening voices, was now more than ever inclined to moodiness.

The reason that he himself gave for this – for he retained a pleasing and charming honesty, even when at his worst – was to do with the tragedy of his birth and the death of his mother and other siblings in the cross-under as witnessed by Stour alone. Though he had been told the nature of his birth when younger, both by Privet and by Stour himself, it now seemed he wanted to go over it again and again, and had even asked Stour himself to take him to the spot in the cross-under where he had been born, and his mother had died.

Few things had ever moved Stour so much as the sight of the young adult crying for a mother he had never known, and a father he would never see, as patiently he told and re-told Whillan the story of his birth. Though because he felt obliged still to abide by the wishes of the dead mother not to tell everything until the time seemed right, which it did not yet seem to Stour, who had to think of Privet as well, he repeated only some of what his mother had said.

'But what does "Whillan" mean?' cried Whillan, anger and frustration mixing with the sadness on his face. 'If she knew your name, Stour, and Privet's, then she must have known a Duncton mole. She *must* have! Why didn't you ask her more?'

'Mole . . .' began Stour, remembering how hard it had been to ask anything that dreadful day the previous spring.

'You could have asked more!' shouted Whillan. 'You could!'

'Mole –' tried Stour again.

'You could!' cried out Whillan, rushing off upslope before Stour could adequately reply.

Later, the Master Librarian wearily reported this encounter to Privet, concluding, 'If I were him I think I too would be angry, and perhaps it is the only thing for him. I have no doubt that eventually he will leave the system for a time in an attempt to resolve the mystery of his beginning, and there may be comfort for you in knowing that just such concerns caused Woodruff of Arbor Low, scribemole of the Chronicles, to wander moledom asking questions until he found answers that satisfied him. You too seem still to have your secrets and you may be thankful they have nothing to do with Whillan, for believe me he would wrest them from you if he thought they had!'

He looked sharply at Privet as he said this, leaving little doubt that whatever he had said to Whillan, he too thought it strange that the mole's mother had known Privet's name, and virtually identified her as the one who should foster the pup. Nor, it seemed, did he doubt that Privet herself knew what the name 'Whillan' signified, for of course he had noticed that only when the name was first mentioned had Privet been willing to accept the task of rearing the pup.

Yet Stour was too wise a mole to force the issue, recognizing even more than Fieldfare that Privet must choose her own time for telling what she wished to of her past, assuming that such a time ever came, which it might well never do.

As usual Privet gave nothing away, but observed with a slight smile, 'For moles who've never had pups of our own, Master, we seem wise in matters of rearing!'

'You more than me I think,' replied Stour. 'But perhaps decades in the Library as Master is not so different as a few moleyears as a parent.'

Privet looked at him for a time and resolved that the moment had come to ask him to give her what he had once promised.

'You were going to give me a task . . . Well, Master, I submitted without complaint to the test of raising Whillan and now I wish to develop other talents in myself. I am ready for a task that will stretch me. I have had enough of copying, and the matters I am asked by others to research are usually of but small consequence.'

'Yes, indeed, Privet, I understand. That is the other reason I came today, for there is a task I have in mind. But for you to understand it I must ask you to join a few of us at a meeting in Drubbins' place this afternoon. I would prefer that you did not mention the fact of such a meeting to anymole . . . Is that understood?'

He seemed severe, and concerned, and she was much mystified.

'What is the meeting about, Master? It might be easier for me . . .'

'I think it best to say no more now, mole. Saying nothing to anymole, come to Drubbins', and once you have heard what needs to be said you shall have your task.'

'Yes Master,' she said obediently, for Stour was at his most magisterial.

'As for Whillan and worries of *his* past, I think it might be better if we found a task for him as well. It would help if he was busy and indeed I have something in mind for him.'

'Yes Master,' agreed Privet, smiling at this repetition of the advice that Fieldfare had often given *her*.

Privet was both puzzled and excited at the Master Librarian's visit and invitation, and she busied herself inconsequentially through the morning and early afternoon until it was time to set off for the low Eastside where Drubbins' tunnels were.

Just as she left she was very surprised to be visited by Avens, whose stay at Duncton had extended longer than he had originally intended, not from any newly-discovered zeal in scribing and scholarship, but from the comfort of his life there and the difficulty he had in summoning the energy and enterprise to set off back to Avebury, from whence he had originally come. He had in any case found himself a niche in the Library as something rather better than a librarian and yet not quite a scholar – a mole willing to help others out with work they were doing and even on occasion to work as little more than a humble aide, and one too who always seemed to know what others were about.

'Have you heard, Privet? There's to be a Meeting at Barrow Vale, summoned by the Master Librarian himself, and as I'm going down that way I thought you'd like to come with me. It'll be the first for a long time.'

Privet was greatly surprised at this news, considering that she herself was attending a meeting also called by Stour, but remembering the Master's request for secrecy she gave nothing away and simply said that she would probably come to Barrow Vale later on. But several times on her journey through the Eastside she met moles who repeated Avens' claim, and she began to think that it was she who was wrong about the time or day, not them.

So she approached Drubbins' tunnels with some uncertainty in the late afternoon, half expecting to find nomole there at all, to find instead that several moles were there already, all quiet, all waiting, all expectant.

There was Drubbins himself, as peaceful and cheerful as ever; and Maple too, restless and serious, his greeting brief and formal. To Privet's surprise Fieldfare was there as well, but when Privet whispered, 'Do you know what this is about?' her friend only shook her head and replied quietly, 'Not really, my dear. I only know that it concerns news of Chater, but that he's all right, thank the Stone. I think . . .'

'I do not think they will be long,' said Drubbins suddenly, 'but they will not wish to be seen, you see.'

But who 'they' might be, Privet could only whisper to Fieldfare, 'Do you know who else is coming?'

But Fieldfare could only shrug and shake her head. She was as much in the dark as Privet herself, and perhaps the others were the same.

But soon after this there came the sound of two more moles approaching, and in at last they came – Master Librarian Stour in the company of none other than . . .

'Bless me alive!' declared Fieldfare utterly astonished, ''tis my love Chater!' But while this loud announcement served to lighten the mood in the chamber, as did her eager rush to him despite so many others being thereabout, her joy was quickly displaced by dismay and concern. For Chater was badly cut about the face, and wounded in the shoulder.

''Tis nothing now, my duck,' he said gruffly, 'for Drubbins saw to it yesterday and 'tis better than it was.'

'Yesterday? You were here yesterday?' said Fieldfare, mildly affronted by this discovery.

'Yes, well, there was a nasty to-do in Cuddesdon, and important things to tell the Master, so when I got back I went straight to him and found him, thank the Stone, before others saw me.'

'I thought it best, Fieldfare, I didn't want others in the system knowing, or rather *certain* others,' said Stour, coming forward and taking charge of the proceedings once Fieldfare and Chater had exchanged their natural and warm embraces, and Chater, to some extent at least, had calmed and reassured his love.

'I will come straight to the point,' Stour said, looking round at each of them in turn. 'You will be wondering why you are here and quite what it is you have in common. Well, of that latter, that is easily said: I trust each one of you. Each of you has different qualities and skills, which I have had time to appreciate and trust. Some . . .' and here he nodded towards Drubbins, 'I have known all my life, and others . . .' and here it seemed to be Maple that he looked at, 'I have known since you were born or, in your case, Chater, since you came to the system. As for you, Privet, I have known you for the least length of time, but everything you have done causes me to trust you, and I know that you are trusted by others here.'

He meant Fieldfare most of all, but touchingly it was Chater who smiled and muttered, 'Aye! She's as worthy as they come of anymole's trust.' At which all the others looked at Privet, and affirmed it in their different ways with nods, and smiles, and in the case of Drubbins, with a touch. It was for Privet a touching moment indeed, to know that these five moles so respected her.

Then Stour said with great seriousness, 'I now believe the day has come that I, and Drubbins here as well, have long feared might one day be. Duncton and its Library are under threat from the Newborn moles. A threat that runs deeper and is more serious than any faced in my lifetime, or that faced by any Duncton mole since the days of the defence of the Stone against the Word – a fact confirmed by news that Chater here has brought back to the system yesterday, at considerable risk to himself.'

'My love!' exclaimed Fieldfare involuntarily, but Chater merely smiled and nodded at her, and reached out a strong paw to shush her. There were, it seemed, more important things to discuss than any risks he might recently have taken.

'For this reason have I summoned this meeting,' continued Stour, 'to warn it of what might soon begin, to seek its counsel and approval of defensive preparations we must make, and to ensure that moles within the system, who can be relied on to act on their own initiative if they need to, know what the consensus is. If there are any here who wish not to accept responsibility for such deliberations let them leave now.'

'But what of the Meeting I was told you had summoned in Barrow Vale?' asked Privet.

'A ruse, I'm afraid, to ensure that nomole stumbled on us here. None will come to Drubbins' place if they think there's half a chance of a good discussion down at Barrow Vale.'

'But won't they miss us and put two and two together?' asked Maple, who must have been similarly fooled as Privet was.

'The Meeting is not starting until this evening,' said Drubbins, who seemed to have been party to the ruse, 'and by then, subject to what we decide here of course, I assume we will most of us have gone on down to Barrow Vale.'

Stour nodded, looked around, and waited for any other comments. But there were none.

'May the Stone bless this meeting, and guide us forward in its Light,' he said quietly. For a long time then he paused, his eyes open and clear and staring nomole knew where, but as he continued the silence among them deepened, and each felt that the Stone was with them.

Then, when he was ready, Master Librarian Stour said, 'Now, we must begin . . .'

PART II

Darkness Newborn

Chapter Eight

'What we must discuss is the expansion of the Newborns, and in particular their long declared intention of ensuring that the libraries of moledom are "fit" for Stone followers to study in,' began Stour. 'In short, I believe they wish to censor and control the contents of the libraries of moledom, great and small. Now, this may not at first sight seem a great danger or problem to us in Duncton Wood, nor one which, as I put it earlier, seems like the greatest threat to moledom's liberty since the coming of the Word.

'So before I ask Chater to tell us what he has so grimly found in Cuddesdon, I want to say something about the reasons for my retreat, recently ended, which started a full cycle of seasons ago . . .'

He spoke slowly and deliberately, and although it was his disconcerting habit to look moles he spoke to straight in the eye, occasionally he shifted his gaze from whichever he then happened to be looking at, to somewhere a little above their heads, as if pondering carefully what to say next. This gave them all the feeling that they were sharing in the process of the Master's deepest thinking, a notion enhanced by the fact that he made no attempt to shorten or make easy his words, or simplify his ideas, but spoke to them as if each were a scholar and his equal, used to being treated as a colleague in a common cause.

'It is important that each of you fully understands why I have summoned this meeting, because there may come a time, sooner than later, when each and all of us will be isolated and under pressure, and will need to know how to act in the knowledge that what we do is in agreement with what we would all do if we were together. Now, about my retreat . . .'

He looked briefly at where his pale talons rested on the ground, and for an instant Privet saw, or imagined she saw, a tremor of trial and weariness cross his body as he turned his attention back to that long time of retreat. Then he looked up at them and smiled a gentle smile, of the same kind that he had given her when they had first met back in February.

'You, Privet, were not yet in Duncton when I went into retreat, but no doubt others have told you that it seemed connected with a visit made to the Library by two of the Newborn moles from the Marsh End. That visit was the first real intimation that I had that for all their appearance of reasonableness and concern with the Stone, the Newborns had a fell intent. Namely, to commandeer our Library, and any other library they could gain control of, to their false and biased intent.

'This worried me, for the whole ethos of a library is anti-censorship. It is to provide a resource of text and learning from every sphere which moles may freely consult, and from which they may freely learn, *without restraint*. Its very essence is that texts and folios are collected for their interest, for the range and shades of opinions and feeling that they represent.

'It was my knowledge that we in Duncton, through historical circumstances and the chance of attracting exceptional moles to our system, had gathered together a unique collection which, by definition, was unavailable except to moles who travelled here to study it, that made me determined that through copying, other systems might in time build libraries as complete as ours and so be free to study as they wished. Our responsibility has always been to create a library that is open to all – as open for textual matters as the community that great Tryfan re-established here in Duncton Wood was to be open to all in matters of the heart and spirit.

'I was greatly concerned therefore when I spoke to the Newborn moles, and realized that they were as dedicated to a closed system of censorship for our great Library as we were dedicated to the opposite.

'Yet, my friends, that was not my only worry after that meeting, nor reason enough to go into retreat. For what concerned me was the *calibre* of one of the moles who came to see me that day. His name, you will know, is Wesley, but I'll warrant that none of you have seen him for a long time.'

'The story is he's dead,' said Chamfer. 'He's not been seen since I don't know when.'

'In fact I'd guess he's not been seen, Chamfer, since he came to see me in the Library, or rather, since I went into retreat. Aye, moles, there is a connection. For know this: when I talked to Wesley that day, and toured the Library with him, I was astonished to find the range of his learning, the quality of his thinking, and the depth of his reverence for the Stone . . .'

'Reverence my arse!' exclaimed Chater.

'Aye, Chater, reverence, though reverence that is in my judgement most gravely flawed. For one thing, he made me well aware of the fact that he felt that many of the texts in the Library were either dangerous for moles to see, or positively blasphemous, to quote the word he used. The texts on Dark Sound, and on fighting, fell into the former category, while Spindle's accounts of Tryfan's doings and certain of the Cuddesdon texts he felt to be blasphemous.'

'Spindle, Tryfan, Cuddesdon . . . blasphemous!' said Maple. 'I may not be a scholar myself, but I've heard the stories many times since I was a pup and if those moles' deeds were not of the Stone then I'm not Maple of Duncton Wood!'

'Ah, but you must understand the way such moles inclined to censorship think. They are of two kinds. First are those who censor the truth knowingly, to aid their cause. Such moles are easiest to deal with because they have no faith but lies, and truth will always outlive them. But secondly are those like the Caradocians, who sincerely believe all they say and do, and believe it right to censor out all ideas, or thoughts, or reports, which conflict with their flawed idea of what is good and just. They believe that any text that contradicts them is evilly inspired and that it, and anyone who defends it, should be destroyed.

'Now, the truth of Tryfan was that he was *but* mole – he was prone to violence in his younger days, he allowed himself to follow his heart, he was impetuous, he made mistakes. Whilst Spindle, as good a mole as ever lived, *was* inclined to scribe down inconsequential things or, when he felt inclined, to report the flaws he saw in Tryfan as well as the virtues. The reverent Cuddesdon too was not without fault, and in his later scribings expressed his deep doubts about his faith in the Stone openly – a fact which to many moles since who have sought to find a way towards the Silence has been a comfort and solace at their darkest times of trial, for if such a holy mole as he had doubts, then their own doubts did not seem quite as bad . . .'

Stour smiled wryly, and Privet, who listened so closely to all he said, felt sure that in what he had just said of doubts, he described himself, and that he had found Cuddesdon's scribings a special comfort during his recent retreat.

'Now, to moles like the Carodocians, bound as they are to a simple and rigorous faith that sees only the black night of evil and the white light of good, anything between, especially if it makes moles they revere – such as the three I have mentioned – seem less than perfect, is an embarrassment. It puts doubts into the minds of their followers. And there must be no doubts . . . And so, they justify censorship in the very name of the truth and mature faith which it denies; and they finally go the fatal way into calling moles who admit their doubts, and seek through learning, scholarship, or thought, to expose those healthy doubts to the light of day, *evil* moles.

'And, my friends, the worst is this: these censoring moles believe they are right in what they do, and that it is just to punish through deprivation or even death those moles who simply dare to question them. When I pointed out to Wesley that moles study to be scholars that they may learn to discern truth, and that truth is not achieved by denying that even the great moles of the past made mistakes or themselves had doubts, he replied in all seriousness that not all moles were capable of such training, and these lesser moles needed protecting for their own good. By "protecting" he meant that libraries should be censored and, in certain circumstances, texts should be destroyed.

'Yet even this was not quite all that concerned me. I had no doubt that Wesley was a great, if flawed, scholar and I wondered why he had chosen to live in the Marsh End where, to my knowledge, there were no texts.

'His reply astonished me, and changed my life. For he said he had gone to the Marsh End expressly to be away from texts, and all but a few moles who might minister to his needs. In effect, he said, he was in retreat and thinking about moledom's future. Naturally I assumed that what he was doing was of his own volition, and one must respect a mole who denies himself so much. But I became alarmed when he went on to tell me that it was not *his* decision to go into retreat in Duncton's Marsh End, but that of the then new Head of Missions at Caradoc, Thripp of Blagrove Slide. It was *he* who had decreed Wesley's retreat, and what was more sinister, the retreat of other such Senior Brothers (as I understand they are called) in ten of the other systems with libraries, making eleven in all. The twelfth of course is Caer Caradoc itself.

'But though greatly alarmed, I was impressed as well, perhaps because in days of old scribemoles went into periodic retreats and always learned much from them. There is something about silence, clearing the mind, and ending one's preoccupation with daily things, that focuses a mole's attention on the essentials of life and death. Perhaps all moles cannot do it, but some surely must. The fact that the Newborns were being led by moles who believed in contemplation and retreat, and had sent out moles of Wesley's character to retreat in our system, suggested that this was a force to reckon with even with – or perhaps because of – their belief in censorship.

'Wesley made his points, I rejected them, and more or less in violent disagreement we parted – he to return to the Marsh End to begin his retreat and I to . . . what? His visit made me decide to do what I had long thought I should do as a scribemole, go into retreat myself and ponder the very points his discussion with me had raised. There was one particular issue that I had long wished to contemplate, and again it was underscored by the meeting with Wesley. You see, I became more aware the more I talked to him that when the day came for him and those others like him to emerge from their retreats back into the day-by-day world of communal living, they would be ready and all too willing to enforce their belief in censorship, and all the grim things it implies, throughout moledom.

'And now,' continued Stour, hunching forward towards them and fixing each of them in turn with his clear intense gaze, 'we come to the central issue this brought into my mind, and one which has concerned many moles through time. Regarding the Newborn moles it was this: do we or do we not personally resist with force a forceful takeover of our Library?'

'You'd have to!' declared Chamfer immediately. 'Couldn't let them get away with that!'

Stour remained silent, waiting for other responses.

'We may be peaceably minded in this system, Stour, but I don't think I could allow the Library simply to be invaded by Newborn strangers because of some scruple you have about violence,' said Drubbins.

'Anyway,' said Maple in a conciliatory way, 'there'd be moles enough would fight the battle for you, Master, you'd not be expected to sully your own paws with blood!'

Stour nodded his understanding of what they said, but not his agreement with it.

'Any other views?' he said eventually. 'Chater, for example?'

'I'd stance at Maple's flank any day, Master, but more to defend your life than your texts and folios!'

'And I'd stance at *his* side,' said Fieldfare, stoutly, 'because where he goes now I go. If there's danger in the system I'll not let him out of my sight any more. Chater, my dear, your days as a journeymole are over!'

Chater growled a grumbly kind of sound, but his eyes softened in appreciation of Fieldfare's passionate concern.

'Drubbins?' said Stour. 'You have more to say?'

'In my younger days I was as tough as any mole, but I'm older now and wiser. I'd never raise my talons to another mole now, whatever the circumstances,' he said quietly. 'I'm a peace-maker, not a destroyer. Fighting will never be my way.'

There was silence after this so-far solitary dissent from the violent way, until Stour turned to Privet.

'And finally, you, Privet. What do you say?'

It was very plain that Privet not only did not know quite what to say, but also was troubled by the question Stour had posed.

'I'm not sure, Master . . . I think, I'm sure, I would fight to protect the lives of moles I love. Of Whillan for example, and . . . and Field-fare here. And others I might name. But to defend texts . . . I don't know. You see . . .'

'Yes, Privet?' Stour's voice was very quiet.

'I saw terrible fighting once, terrible deaths. The cause was just but the results were so bitter, so terrible, that I thought then as I think now, that there must be another way.'

What fighting she had seen she did not say, but surely all of them guessed that in describing it so briefly she had come a little nearer to talking of her past.

Stour nodded appreciatively and repeated quietly the last thing she had said, '"there must be another way . . ." Exactly. And I am sure there is. It was over this problem, this paradox, that I went into retreat and sought the Stone's guidance. Only when I felt I had resolved the paradox did I come out of it again, as, I dare say, a much happier mole. It seems that good Drubbins here has come to the same conclusion as I but without the stress and strain a retreat involves!'

Drubbins smiled and shrugged self-deprecatingly.

'But most of you, for reasons that not only *seem* laudable, but *are* laudable, would fight to save our Library. And all but Drubbins it seems would fight to save the lives of moles you love.'

All but Drubbins nodded their agreement with this.

'Well now, I believe that the issue I have raised is one so central to our lives, and to the furtherance towards Silence of our faith in the Stone, that I ask for your patience while I explain why I have come to the conclusion that I have, and why I hope you will come to see that as the threat of the Newborns now begins to grow, a few of us here today must begin to seek a consensus among ourselves about what we shall do in the event of a Newborn attack or attempted takeover.

'But before I do that I want Chater to tell you of his recent experi-ence in Cuddesdon. What you will hear will shock you, and in the normal course of events would strengthen your stated resolve to fight back. Indeed you might, once you have heard what Chater has to say, feel that to the simple will to resist might legitimately be added the right of revenge. But I pray each one of you, keep an open mind about the best course to take until after you have heard Chater's account, and my own conclusions.'

The chamber grew hushed and the light of the afternoon a little faded. Somewhere nearby wind rustled at dried leaves, and flurried, and leaves scuttered across the surface of the Wood over their heads. Finally all eyes were on Chater, who cleared his throat and looked about a bit, smiling in a consoling way at Fieldfare.

'Could make it long, could make it short, but I'll make it middling,' he said, one paw rising momentarily to his injuries as if he were unconsciously preparing to remind himself of the circumstances in which they had been suffered. 'You all know that the religious community of Cuddesdon was founded there by a mole of the same name at the end of the war of Word on Stone. It was a place of worship, study and refuge for moles who have a preference for celibacy and the life of worship.

'We journeymoles go there from time to time, as much to collect texts originated there as to take copies, for it is not a main or even minor library; but unlike most its moles are inclined to scribe of matters religious and spiritual and the Master here feels that such texts should be disseminated. 'Tis not more than three days' journey from here, on a rise above the vales to the east, a good warm spot as ever was, but not one much visited.

'The last time I was there was a full Longest Night ago when I was a bit younger than I am today. There were no more than thirty moles there then, mainly males, and from all I'd heard, and all I've learnt since, I'd say that until a few weeks back the number had not changed much at all. When I first went they welcomed me and kept me there longer than I should have allowed . . .' he smiled wryly at the Master and then at Fieldfare.

'No matter. The moles were kindly moles, generous, peaceful, and harmed nomole. Studious they were, and scribed most beautifully, even I could see that! They made texts it was an honour for a journeymole to carry. But that's all done, all over, isn't it? Aye. Cuddesdon's finished now.'

There was a stir of alarm and dismay among Chater's listeners before they looked uneasily at each other, and then back at him to continue.

'I'll make what I've got to say next brief, for it's not a matter gives me any pleasure to talk on. Now, it's my habit to get near a destination the evening before I visit it, have a good night's sleep, and then start off at dawn fresh and ready for anything, for a journeymole never knows what he's going to find when he gets where he's going. Cautious buggers we are, and just as well sometimes. Like at Cuddesdon a few days back . . .

'As I said, the place is on a rise and I had stopped down in the vale overnight, and climbed up the westerly slopes as dawn broke. It's a hard climb and autumn dew doesn't help, so I took it nice and slow. First thing I noticed when I reached the flatter part at the top was there was neither sight nor sound of mole, which was a change from my last visit. The Cuddesdon moles are – or were – in the habit of wandering about of a morning doing their contemplations and prayers but there was not a mole in sight. "Something's up," I thought to myself. "Something important that's keeping them all out of sight." But being cautious I hid the text I was carrying somewhere safe, just as I was trained to do when I was no more than a youngster, before I went to find a mole to tell me what was going on. It was just as well I did.

'Down into the tunnels that Cuddesdon himself delved a hundred years ago I went, and snouted about, and scented a dry, miserable, mean-spirited kind of scent that I thought was trouble. But I was too late to get out and away to somewhere I could observe without being seen, for I had been heard. I'd no sooner turned than I heard the faint thumping of signals above, and the patter of snurtish paws of sneaking moles. Ominous, heavy patterings.

'"Chater, my lad," I said to myself, "there's trouble apaw in this system. Better ready yourself to face it out." Just then a couple of moles came down a side tunnel and cut off my retreat, and two more down the tunnel up which I had been heading. I looked them up and down and did not like what I saw. Sleek, glossy, young, male, and all smiling the same way and enough to make you sick. Smile smile smile, from eyes that looked all dead.

'"Hello!" says I, as cheerful as I could make it.

'"Welcome Brother," says they, and I swear they all said it together like they were one mole split into four copies of each other. Welcome my arse. They were as welcoming as an owl's talons in May.

'Then one of them, or all four of them, said, "Brother, why are you here?"

'"To visit the Cuddesdon moles," I replied. They approached me as one, so that if I turned to face two of them the other two were looming behind, if I turned the other way then the others were at my back. Not one of them was bigger than me but all four seemed more than four times as big. Now whilst Chater does not appreciate intimidation, Chater is not a fool.

'"We *are* the Cuddesdon moles now," they said.

'"But –"

'"But what, Brother?" says they, smiling and arrogant.

'But nothing, but bugger off out of there. Chater's not a bloody army. But then, I said to myself, if the Cuddesdon moles are in trouble Chater can at least find out about it, so I smiled back.

'Well, they asked me some questions as to why I had come and I told them, lying through my teeth, that I had lost the text in the vale below crossing a stream and I had come to beg the pardon of the Cuddesdon moles et cetera and so forth.

'"We have no need of texts unless we ask for them," they said. Then: "Are you truly of the Stone, mole?"

'I told them I was worshipful, yes, and went to the Stone at times of ritual and said my bit, but no, I wouldn't say I was exactly *ardent*. So they warned me that a mole is nothing without sincere fear of the Stone and wittered on without even the ghost of a smile for half a day, not letting me eat or sleep and staying that close that I swear there wasn't a moment in all that long time when one or other of them wasn't touching me, and pressurizing me, until even my mind was beginning to go rough at the edges with their talk. I adopted the old trick of acting dim, and it finally worked because they got fed up with me and let me go in the mid-afternoon, with the warning to get back across the vale as quick as I could and not dally on the way.

'They didn't give me any chance to look about the system and see if they had the real Cuddesdon moles sealed up somewhere in the place, but I thought as I traipsed off downslope, "Sod this for a lark, the Master would not wish me to return to Duncton without some idea of what's going on." Then there was the undelivered text to recover before they found it. Then there was my pride. All in all I decided a short sleep in the vale followed by a little nocturnal investigation would not go amiss. After all, thirty moles just don't go missing without something being seriously wrong.'

'Chater, my love!' interrupted Fieldfare. 'You never said you were like this, taking risks and all.'

Chater grinned mischievously.

'My own angel,' he said in reply, 'if I had told you over the years one quarter of what a journeymole does delivering texts you'd have died a thousand deaths.'

'Not any more he doesn't, dear one,' said Fieldfare firmly in reply. 'Not ever!'

Chater grinned again, and looked roguishly charming.

'Well,' said Fieldfare, 'not without me.'

'Fat lot of good you would be,' said Chater cheerfully.

'Not *never!*' said Fieldfare.

'Get on with it, Chater,' growled Drubbins.

'To cut a long story short . . .'

'Not for the first time,' muttered Maple with a grin, and with evident respect for his old friend.

'. . . I went back and was caught.'

'Oh!' said Fieldfare, nonplussed.

'But not before I got round a lot of the tunnels and confirmed there were no other moles there, whether Cuddesdon moles, or the Newborn lot. I also discovered that the Library, not a large one when I saw it previously, was depleted. That was evident because there were gaps in the stacks. Some moles, and I could guess which ones, had gone through the shelves removing texts. Where to and what for? I soon found out, and discovered too the likely explanation of what happened to the Cuddesdon moles. I got caught, as I say, and the smiles on their faces were quick in disappearing when they saw who it was ferreting about "their" tunnels.

'I was accused of disloyalty, abuse of trust, and affronting the Stone – yes, plenty of affront in Chater, brothers and sisters! And then . . . when I protested and said I was only doing what anymole would have done who had half a care for the good moles of Cuddesdon as once was, they asked if I dared question their Stone-given right to judge me. When I said nomole is judge, only the Stone, they talked about appointees, rights, arraignments, and Stone knows what. But late at night or early in the morning is no time for arguments about lore and language.

'"Eff off," I said eventually, driven to crudeness, and it was the best thing I could have said. It provoked them into revealing that beneath their smiles and words, they're violent. They called it blasphemy, swearing like that to the true-born representatives of the Stone and then as sudden as a talon thrust a *fifth* mole appears, a bit older than the rest.

'If the others seemed cold he gave off a chill like ice. When I saw him I *was* frightened. He stared, solid and dark, eyes like tunnels a mole doesn't want to go down, and powerful, like few moles *I've* ever seen.

'"Get him out of here and off the hill. Stretten him!"

'"Stretten him?" I said to myself. "I don't like the sound of that!"

'"Yes. Senior Brother Inquisitor Fetter, anything you say!" they says as one. Fetter, that was his name. Then before I knew it I was harried down the eastward slopes out of Cuddesdon, through brambles and briars, over pasture, over stony ground, pushed bodily down a ledge, and as I went and began to lose consciousness I noticed that they didn't hit me so much as push me in the direction of obstacles enough to maim a mole, or wound him. But I wasn't so far gone as I didn't hear one of those self-righteous bastards –'

'Chater!' expostulated Fieldfare. 'Not in front of the Master!'

'. . . say, "He's tougher than most of those Cuddesdon moles we . . ." but more I didn't hear. Too busy avoiding being blinded in the hawthorns and spear-thistle they were shoving me through. It was enough to make me realize what "strettening" was, and is, and what moles suffered it before me. The Cuddesdon moles, that's who. "Strettening" is the Newborns' word for roughing up a mole to death.

'In that nightmare journey down the hill, I saw not one, not two, but *three* bodies of moles, or rook-torn parts of bodies. Aye, the Cuddesdon moles were murdered down that hill or, if they were not murdered there they were finished off by the same moles who greeted me with thick snouts and narrow eyes and treacherous talons.

'"He has blasphemed and was arraigned," said one of the Newborns when they tumbled me into a miserable group of Garsington moles waiting near the River Thame that runs along there. "Let the Stone judge him."

'With that they left me surrounded by that group of moles, and without looking back headed up the hill again, to their gentle meditations, and worthy worshipping of the Stone, and contemplations on peace and the true way.

'I was in no condition to fight, and didn't try to. Escape was going to be my only way. If my treatment had been rough so far, it immediately got worse, for they shoved me downslope some more to the river.

'"It's to be a drowning then," says I to myself, "or a swim!"'

'You're a good swimmer!' said Fieldfare suddenly, stanced up in alarm and staring blankly at the far side of the silent chamber as if she could see it all as it happened and had forgotten that it was a tale she

95

was being told, and by Chater himself. 'Oh, beloved, I hope you escape!'

'I wouldn't be telling this story if I hadn't, you daft old thing,' said Chater. 'They got me to the river, or rather to its muddy foreshore, and I knew it was now or never. So I turned and in a quavering voice begged to be allowed to live. Just to get them off their guard. Moles like others begging them to do things and they relax. The Garsington moles fell for it and smirked at each other, obviously thinking they could have a bit of fun with me. I did not give them time, but talon-thrust the nearest as hard as I could in the snout, and lashed out with a back paw at another one's groin. Squelch and yelp. Bastards! A third roared so I thrust him in the eyes for good measure and then I turned towards the river, floundered through the mud for dear life, thinking of my Fieldfare here to urge me on, and dived into the river. And guess what I saw just before I dived? Guess what gave me a firm paw-hold to dive from?'

'Not bodies?' whispered Privet, appalled.

'Aye, bodies,' said Chater heavily. 'The rotting, stinking, corpses of the poor Cuddesdon moles. Well, that gave me strength, that did, for I wasn't going to let myself be killed and nomole ever know what had happened to the others. You'll never guess what came to my aid just in time? Texts! Aye, *texts*. The Newborns must have brought them down the hill just like they dragged the Cuddesdon moles, and dumped them in the river to destroy them.

'Well, they saved me by being there. Gave me something firm to put my paws on, which I did, pushed hard, and dived clean into the river. One dived in after me and lunged to hurt me and that's where I got this injury to my face. But as my Fieldfare rightly says, I can swim. Journeymoles have to be able to. And swim I did until I was well clear of Garsington, and clearer in the head as well. After that I laid low a bit and then, keeping clear of any system and with the help of a vagrant mole I met who knew the area well, I made my way back to Duncton and straight to the Master. That's the long and short of it, and that's what the Newborns are up to in Cuddesdon, and probably other systems as well. And if we're not careful it will be what they'll be up to in Duncton before long.'

There was a long silence at the end of this account which, though Chater's basic indomitable nature had made it at times seem jocular, became a silence of dread and horror as the moles contemplated the realities of all he had told them.

Chapter Nine

'Before we consider the implications of Chater's report,' began Master Stour once more, 'let me now tell you the outcome of my own contemplation for so long on whether or not moles should fight. It would be easy to conclude from what we have heard that since Chater would probably not be with us had he *not* fought back then there are some situations at least – the defence of life for example, whether one's own or another mole's – where fighting is justified.'

Stour let this thought sink in before he stanced forward towards them all and said quietly, 'But I think not. Finally, I must think not. Perhaps no community in moledom has in recent history been so involved in what I might call just struggles as our own. Few who know the Chronicles ever doubt that the Stone followers were right to fight and kill in defence of their cause. I do not say that at that time, in those circumstances, those moles were not right. I *do* believe that now we are in different circumstances and we must each ask ourselves in the privacy of our tunnels, and thoughts, what the consequence of "just" fighting is. For myself, I believe that its inevitable consequence is more fighting. One mole's just war provokes another mole's just revenge. War makes war. Like youngsters who tussle and tumble together, and eventually fight, the fighting continues until one wins. Yet resentment always remains with the other side. One day that resentment erupts like a poisoned talon wound, and war starts again.

'This was not the Stone Mole's way, and we should never forget that it was in his name that finally the defence of the Stone against the Word was made. It was in his name that the war was ended. But he never, not once in his life, hurt or struck another mole. He was a mole at peace with moledom. It was moledom that waged a war on him. Yet never did he raise his talons to strike back.

'My friends, I think the time is coming now when Duncton moles must show others that the bravest and most courageous way is to do as he did and not to strike back; not strike at all. To lower the snout before the foe.'

Stour paused again, and the others stared at him, quite still. All but

Drubbins, who nodded his head slightly and whispered, 'Aye!' But his view seemed to be a minority of one, for others, Maple and Chater especially, shook their heads.

'We, who are the inheritors and beneficiaries of the courage of our recent ancestors in Duncton, should now remember that it was not given only to the Stone Mole to be at peace with others. It was Tryfan's way too, in the end – his final pacifism a hard-won discipline for so great a warrior. And others too took his view to its ultimate and chose death rather than resistance. It has greatly concerned me that these lessons of the past have been forgotten. In the aftermath of war was a numbness about this recent past, a forgetting, and moles have been slow and idle about trying to understand what the Stone Mole taught us. Now because of this absence of leadership and thought by any others, moles like those of Caradoc have emerged unchallenged, with their false interpretation of what the ministry of the Stone Mole means for us all. If we disagree with it, and I do, then if we simply fight against what they say we do no more than unthinking moles who strike out when a foe strikes them, but ask not the reason why, nor offer something better instead. In short, if we simply fight we are no better than what *mole* we fight, and in some ways rather worse.

'We need therefore to have a view of what the meaning of the war of Stone and Word was, and what the Stone Mole would have us do. We need to have the purpose and courage to think for ourselves at last – just as great Tryfan taught we should, and just as we are so eager, and so proud, to claim we do in Duncton Wood. I believe that part, perhaps the central part, of any statement of our purpose and faith should be that we will never fight with the talons of our paws again. Instead we must begin to dare to fight with the talons of our minds, and the talons of our resolve, and the talons of our faith.

'This will need great example, and great leadership. The example must begin with ordinary moles, moles like ourselves, who must resolve to "fight" only in the peaceful moral way I have described. Great must be our courage to do it, and perhaps great our sacrifice.

'As for the leadership I mentioned, of that I am not so certain. It will not, it cannot, come from me or moles like me. I, like Drubbins here, am of a dying generation. It must be from among younger moles that leadership will come. Somewhere, some day, a mole will emerge who will have the youth, and energy, intelligence and love, to lead all moledom forward in an interpretation of the Stone Mole's ministry and life. It is nearly a century now since that time, and moledom is ready now for this new direction. But I say this to you: that leader will not come out of nothing. He will learn from and be conditioned by the example of peace and love which it is now our task to demonstrate. My sense is that this is the last and greatest task facing the moles of Duncton Wood, whose heritage is great and whose tasks and responsibilities are ours now.

'I ask not today that any of you should agree with me, or even state that you disagree. I ask that you do as the Newborn mole Wesley inspired me to do: think, live in yourself a little, dare to ask the hardest questions, dare to wonder why it makes a mole feel so afraid and so alone to contemplate raising only the talons of peace in his own defence. Dare to turn to the great Stone, and listen to its Silence, and seek an answer to these questions there. Talk to others.'

'Master, we have had such conversations already in Barrow Vale. You are not alone in your thoughts, though there may be few there, or even here, who seemed to agree with you.' It was Privet who spoke, but others nodded their heads at what she said.

'Then it is well,' said Stour, 'for all I ever wished to be was a librarian, neither more nor less. But what I have found is that I must be mole as well!

'Now, what of Chater's fight against the Newborns at Cuddesdon? It would have been well that he could have escaped without raising his talons. But supposing he could not, and the choice was kill or be killed? We are his friends, he knows that I love him and respect him. I believe he loves and respects me. I can ask only this . . .' Here Stour placed his old paw on Chater's bigger, stronger one. 'I ask only that you and he ponder why it might be that he should not have killed, or maimed, or struck another, even if it meant he died. Because if enough of us show such courage, and a fearlessness of death, then I believe we come nearer to the Stone Mole's way than any dogma or bullying or fanaticism that the moles of Caradoc might try, and that finally the day will come when such evils will wither before our fearlessness.

'Like the Stone Mole, wise Tryfan called such courage "love". We must learn to raise the talons of love at last, and put away for ever the talons of fear. This is the challenge we now face in Duncton Wood, and it is hard and grave and terrible.

'But of one more thing must I briefly speak, for it will help you understand one of the courses of action that I, in consultation with Drubbins here, have already taken. When that fateful conversation with Wesley took place, he was eager, too eager, to know the "truth", as he called it, of one of the Books of Moledom, namely the lost and last book called the Book of Silence.

'It is in the nature of such moles who profess a love of truth, that they have so little faith in other moles to tell it that they do not recognize it when it is spoken to them. Wesley did not believe me when I told him that of the seven Books of Moledom only six exist. All are in our custody, but as for the seventh, that of Silence, I know no more than anymole . . .

'Not only did he not believe me, but it was obvious that his view was that such a mole as I, not of the true faith, was not the proper custodian of the great Books, nor of the other sacred texts, ancient and modern, of moledom. So it seems that their desire is not just censorship, but custody as well.

'But why should custody matter? For you might say that there are copies of the six Books already in most of the main Libraries and it's the words that matter not the actual texts themselves . . .'

'Oh, but Master, the real Books are what matter, aren't they?'

'Why so, Fieldfare?' asked Stour quietly.

'Well, for one thing, they are the actual texts moles strived over, and which came here to our free system because the Stone wanted them too. Their being here tells moles all over moledom that something they treasure is safe in the paws of good moles. . . .'

'But Brother Wesley would argue that if they were safe in *his* paws they would be in the control of good moles too.'

'Aye, and no doubt argue that the fact they were in his paws was ordained by the Stone and therefore he was in the right.'

'Let's get this right,' said Maple as patiently as he could. 'You're saying, Master, that if the Newborns gained control of the six Books they would also gain some kind of authority they would use to impose their dogma on others?'

'Exactly that! The Books legitimize whichever moles have possession of them. Now, as it happens, the kind of faith we've always had and fought for in Duncton Wood is free thinking, and moledom knows that well. We don't use the Books for anything, they simply *are*, and moles rarely see them. By tradition they are looked after by the Master against the day when the Book of Silence is found and all the seven Books can then be placed by some holy mole of the future under the Duncton Stone itself – a dangerous and probably fatal exercise. But we know that already the Seven Stillstones are there awaiting, as it were, the coming of the Books.

'Until the Newborns came along such matters were simple enough

– we had a faith that one day things would be made aright, but none of us was arrogant enough to think we were the moles to see matters to a conclusion: our task was simply to watch over the Books, and the system of free faith of which they are a part, and I, as Master Librarian, have been honoured with, as it were, the day-by-day ordering of things, and dissemination of texts and knowledge as laid down by the Conclave of Caradoc so many moleyears ago.'

'All moledom knows you instigated that,' said Drubbins, 'and honours you for it. None begrudges you the "honour" of being the Keeper of the Six Books.'

Stour was quiet for a moment, as if to remind his friends that this signal honour was a burden too, one which right there and then he was in some way trying to share a little, and gain counsel about.

'Thus far,' he continued, 'I have concentrated on Brother Wesley, and have avoided saying what perhaps is rather obvious, that he finally matters less than the mole who inspired and appointed him – the Elder Senior Brother Thripp of Blagrove Slide.

'I would dearly like to know more about this mole, or to meet somemole who has actually met him – apart that is from Brother Wesley – but that is not possible for a mole like me, though I had considered going on a formal visit to meet him. However, I can reveal that Wesley said certain things about his Elder Senior Brother that interested me, and made me realize that perhaps we should not be as passive about the six books, or even the absent Book of Silence, as we have been.

'I therefore decided to send a mole out under cover as it were, to find out what he or she could – I prefer not to identify the mole concerned, though you may rest assured that that mole is not in this Chamber today, so stop looking suspiciously at each other . . .

'The results of this investigation were most interesting, and thought-provoking. For one thing it seems that Thripp is not as old a mole as his title 'Elder Senior Brother' would imply. For another he is not the oppressive authoritarian mole his Caradocian movement and its representatives would now seem to imply. He is inspirational, he is intelligent, he is the kind of charismatic leader whom others follow.

'Next, I discovered through my sources, that he himself is not pleased with the way in which the Newborns have recently developed, which they have done, as Chater so brutally found out, through a body of zealot moles called Senior Brother Inquisitors, of whom the mole "Fetter" is the first I have ever heard named. I have reason to think that there is a mole senior Inquisitor, we do not know his name,

101

who is behind this new, more aggressive, stance the Newborns are taking. We are faced, in short, by a Caradocian Order which, like all such movements, is suffering a struggle for power which may, in the end, affect us. Indeed it almost did: our good friend Chater might easily not be here today . . .'

'Oh don't say that, Master, *please!*' said Fieldfare, putting her paws around her beloved and drawing him protesting towards her as if it was the Master himself who was the enemy.

'But the mole I sent forth discovered even more . . . We talked earlier about how it could be that the moles, or the order, which controls the Books of Moledom, has a power invested in it by virtue of the fact of possession. It is general knowledge that when Brother Wesley visited the Library here he and I fell out somewhat roughly – indeed, in the end I had to eject him. This was because he not only wanted to see the six Books – I allowed him to see some of them – but also to have the right to take one or other of them away that others of his Order might see and consult them. This he claimed as a legitimate Stone-given right, using some nonsensical reference to other texts to support his claim. When I rejected this he then advanced the not altogether unreasonable argument that we had no more right to hold the Books than any other group of moles, except a historic one.

'When I asked why it did not satisfy him simply to see them where they were – and I invited him to send other scholars if he wished – he said that it was not the Elder Senior Brother Thripp's opinion that the Books were merely for scholars to gloat over – as he put it. They were, he said, "living things that should be freely available to mole".'

When I pressed him on the point, saying they were available to moles who took the trouble to come and ask, and why risk taking them out of the Library he revealed that one reason was that then they might one day "join with the Book of Silence". When I asked him what that meant, and by now I was beginning to think that while Wesley was a great scholar he might also be a slightly insane one, he said it was Thripp's view that the Book of Silence would come to light in this generation. *This*, it seemed, was Thripp's mission, though it is not something the more brutal members of his Order are much concerned with. Indeed, Thripp does not want them to be, fearing that if they gained control over the Book of Silence then it would do no mole any good.'

'But the Book of Silence either does not exist, or if it does its whereabouts is unknown,' said Privet. 'These, surely, are the dreams and desires of a mole who wants to be made legitimate before the Stone, just as obsessive leaders of the past have looked for evidence that their leadership is Stone-given.'

'That I am sure is true,' said the Master Stour. 'Yet there *is* something appealing about the idea of the Book of Silence, and something dangerous in our remaining too passive about it. When Brother Wesley left the Library *I* was left with the abiding impression that one day he or his like would be back in force to try to gain possession of the six Books, as if that might help them begin to realize Thripp's dream of discovering, or rediscovering, the Book of Silence.

'Yet there is one more element in all of this, one about which I so far know too little and intend after our meeting today to discover more from certain mediaeval texts in the Library. It concerns the lost delving arts. You see, it is Thripp's opinion that the coming of the Book of Silence has to do with the rediscovery of the delving arts . . . namely, those arts long since lost by which certain Masters were able to create the kind of great chambers and tunnels of which, sadly, the chambers wherein our Library exists are but remnants. Of course the Ancient System beneath the High Wood was delved by a Master or Masters of those arts in the long distant past, and I have no doubt that the Dark Sound that protects the place – and which I often have cause to hear since my study cell is in peripheral tunnels of the ancient system – was delved by them.

'On this matter I shall have more to say. I will only observe, regarding Thripp, one more, or rather two related things. One is, that he, like me, appears to have gone into retreat for a time and none have seen him. This I take as possibly ominous, for it may signal a change of policy or attitude that will affect us all in time. Possibly for the good, but probably for the bad. Secondly, I have good reason to think that even now there is, or there is coming, a mole to join the Newborn cell in the Marsh End who is none other than Thripp's son, and legitimate spiritual heir. This mole's name is Brother Chervil. Why he should come here, and what it might mean for us, I cannot think, but we must be most wary now . . .

'As for the Book of Silence, my belief is that its time for moledom is near. This last great struggle as I have described it has to do with such a Book, and so far as moles may succeed in setting an example for peace as the Stone Mole did, and find leadership for the way of the great teachings of his ministry, so will the Book of Silence come nearer to us, and perhaps at last be known to us.

'Aye, the "seven Books will come to ground" as a wise mole of the past scribed it, and in our time perhaps, my friends, and in our system. I sense that these things are near, and with us, and that the Stone shall entrust us with much . . .'

Old Stour's voice had grown quiet, and his body still, so that it seemed that it was not he who spoke but something more than him, something like the wind-sound of the tunnel, or the whisper of the trees above, something out of the long decades of trial and faith in Duncton Wood.

'Moles, we are near the end of a long and terrible struggle. Perhaps its hardest phase has already begun. Perhaps this is why the trial of the Newborns is on us. We few must seek a way to break for ever the roundel of violence provoking violence. We who are but ordinary moles must show by example what all moles can do. Somewhere at the end of this unknown and treacherous way we shall find the Book of Silence, and somehow it *will* come to ground. That I believe; that we must all believe.

'I beg you to ponder these things, however hard they seem, and to search for a way to discover the courage of love.'

He fell silent, and Privet, who had been successively astonished, dismayed, bewildered and filled with faith, noticed that his head and face and shoulders were streaked with sweat, and his body weak and limp from the effort of finding words to speak the thoughts he had won so hard.

None spoke. Fieldfare reached a paw to Chater's. Maple, more warrior and fighter than any of them, stared blankly at a future that seemed to have no place for him. And Drubbins sighed.

It was finally he who spoke.

'I feel old,' he said, 'and almost that this challenge and struggle is too great for me. Where are younger moles to take our place? Where is the leader who will go forth and speak of the things that Stour has spoken of?'

Since nomole was able to answer these questions it was Drubbins himself who continued talking.

'It would surely help us to know that there are others in moledom who feel as Stour does, and who, like myself, are persuaded by the quest for peace Master Sturne has extolled. Setting examples is all very well, but it would be easier knowing we might find support for what we do.'

'Well . . .' began Chater, frowning as if recalling something he had forgotten to mention, 'there was that business of rebellion against the Newborns that I mentioned to you before, Master . . .'

'Tell them, mole,' said Stour, 'it is a small comfort at least.'

'It was this,' said Chater. 'The vagrant mole I told you had helped me after I escaped from Garsington was one of those we journeymoles get used to coming across from time to time. Wanderers from system to system, of no fixed abode, who have no family and few friends and a disinclination to make either. They make interesting travelling companions, though a mole's inclined to wake up and find they've gone at the crack of dawn, never to be seen again. This one had come from Rollright a few days before he came across me, and told me that the Newborn moles there were abuzz with news of a revolt against them in the north.'

'You said –' began Stour.

'Aye, though the mole himself didn't know much about it he had heard mention that the leader of the revolt, Rooster by name, was being hunted for blasphemy, which fitted in with the kind of treatment that the Cuddesdon moles seemed to have received.'

'Did he say in which part of the north this revolt took place?' asked Privet. She seemed interested in this part of the news, and Fieldfare, who knew her so well, guessed that she felt special pride or interest in the fact that this first news of active resistance to the Newborns came from the north.

Chater shrugged and shook his head.

'The mole knew only what I have reported,' he said.

'No mention of Beechenhill?' persisted Privet.

'No,' said Chater.

'Well, at least it seems we are not entirely alone in our doubts about the Newborns,' said Stour, 'but then it would be surprising if we were.'

They all nodded, cheered a little by Chater's news, and then Drubbins said formally, 'Master Librarian, you have spoken to me before of plans and arrangements, and mentioned them at the beginning of what you said to our meeting. Can you speak of them now?'

'I shall,' said Stour. 'One way for moles to avoid fighting is for them to arrange affairs such that fighting becomes harder to begin. Those among you familiar with the Library – you, Privet, and you, Chater – will know that since my retreat certain important texts have disappeared. So they have. A mole in retreat does not sit on his rump all day. I have removed many texts, and all six of the Books of Moledom, deep into the Ancient System of our Wood where nomole will easily find them, especially those afraid of Dark Sound.'

There was a movement of surprise among the moles.

105

'You went in *there?*' said Chamfer.

'Aye,' said Stour, 'and nearly did not come out again. But it is done, and if the Newborns seek to censor our great Library they will find that many texts are no longer there to censor! Next, I must ask Privet to undertake a task. It concerns that outlying collection of Rolls, Rhymes and Tales, which she will know is uncatalogued and vulnerable. I ask her without delay to venture there and using her own discretion and knowledge and what help she may summon, bring those texts she values to my study cell, that they may be taken on into the ancient tunnels for protection.'

'But what of Husk?'

'Charm him, Privet,' said Stour with a smile. 'Lastly,' he continued, a little wearily, 'I now ask Maple and Chater to journey to Rollright, and to find out what they can of the Newborns' doings there and report them back to us. While you're there find more out about this mole Rooster and the revolt in the North. There may be lessons in that for us. Forgive me for suggesting this, Fieldfare, but needs must and Chater is the mole for such a task.'

Poor Fieldfare opened her mouth to object, but then closed it again without saying anything.

'It will be sensible if you take Whillan with you,' said Stour, 'for he needs a task and I have a feeling that he is one of those younger moles who, as Drubbins says, we have need of now. Such a venture will give him experience.

'For the rest, tasks will soon present themselves. I think we are not yet under pressure, but it is coming and we must be prepared in thought and ideas for it. Now, evening has come, and a Meeting was somewhat falsely summoned in Barrow Vale by Drubbins and myself. Let us go there, and speak of peace, and begin the task of preparing our moles for the struggle that will come.

'May the Stone guide us all in thought and in deed. May it protect us. May it lead us to the Silence.'

With that Stour had finished, and he did not wait for any comments or conversation. What he had said was a beginning, and it was one he wanted each of them to think about and discover for themselves.

Nor did the others speak, but went out on to the surface and paused briefly, and stared at the coming stars, thoughtful and concerned. Then they turned to each other to talk in low voices, and share something of their thoughts. All, that is, but Privet. For when Fieldfare turned to talk to her, Privet was already hurrying away, head down, not looking back, wishing to talk to nomole.

Fieldfare ran after her.

'Privet, my dear . . .'

Briefly, Privet turned back and faced her. But in her eyes was a strange lost look, and a look of terrible despair. But more than that, there was terrible hope as well.

'Privet . . .' said Fieldfare again, but Privet shook her head vacantly, turned, and was gone into the dark as surely as if the last light had suddenly fled from the western sky.

Chapter Ten

Privet did not waste time before beginning her task. After only a brief return to her tunnels to clear out some old nesting material and seal up a few entrances against the pre-winter trespasses of the shrews and voles, she crossed the Wood and entered into a small and inconspicuous grove of beech trees that lies adjacent to the High Wood and some way to the west of the Library.

It lay off any of the communal surface routes to the Stone, and she might easily have missed it had not Whillan some time previously pointed the place out to her, and told her who and what lay beneath its surface. The scene had an air of dereliction and decay caused, surely, by something more than the great tree that had fallen in some forgotten storm across the place and now lay rotted and broken upon the ground. Though the day was mild she shivered involuntarily before picking her way among the rotten wood and remnants of a patch of dog's mercury.

She peered about among the shadows for an entrance, wondering how Whillan had ever dared to make his way here, let alone venture down into the tunnels below and make contact with Keeper Husk. He must have more courage than she thought! And persistence too, for it took her a long time before she found a serviceable entrance, during which she was uncomfortably aware that if Husk was below he could hear her every move. But having found it she went on down into the tunnel beneath without further delay.

It was so dark after the bright light above that a short way in she stumbled over a pile of texts, which in falling brought down others across the tunnel floor. She did her best to pile them up again and noticed as she did so that they were a complete jumble of subjects, shapes and sizes and in no order at all. Then, with extreme caution, she ventured on down the tunnel which, she was not surprised to see, was shoulder-high in texts and folios all along its length.

Slowly her eyes adjusted to the light and she made out movement ahead, and then the shape of an ancient mole stanced poised and staring in a rheumy geriatric way in her direction. Keeper Husk.

'Go away, I'm busy!' he shouted. Indeed he did seem so, for he carried two texts against his scraggy furless chest with one paw, while he raised the other towards her, either to threaten her, or to shield his eyes from the light behind her so that he might see better.

'Keeper Husk?' she said, advancing in a friendly way upon him. 'The Master Librarian sent me.'

'Oh he did, did he? What for?' His voice was still loud, though she was so near him now.

'I'm one of his librarians. He would like me to help you.'

'Ha, ha, ha!' he cackled, genuinely amused and dropping the texts as he fell into a wheezing fit of such noise and duration that Privet thought that he might collapse on the spot. But eventually he caught his breath, wiped his eyes, put out a paw against the dusty wall to support himself, and said, 'Several decades too late I'd say, wouldn't you?' and grinned wickedly.

Privet peered around the place, and the more her eyes took in, the more untidy and chock-a-block it seemed.

'It does look as if you have needed some help for some time,' she said politely.

'What's your name?' he said.

'Privet.'

'I know that name!'

'I'm the mother of Whillan who used to come here.'

'You're the one from the Moors.'

She stared at him, astonished, and then remembered that Whillan had said that Husk had told him the same thing when he first came here.

'I wouldn't look quite so surprised if I were you,' said Husk; 'Whillan's a Peakish word and I assume you have some connection with the north to name him so.'

'I . . .' began Privet, but she drew back from further explanation. In any case, now she was near him she saw with a shock that he was staring not quite at her but to her left flank, and could not really see her at all. Husk was blind. He seemed suddenly very vulnerable.

'You were kind to Whillan,' she said quietly, 'and I'm glad to be able to thank you. He enjoyed his times with you.'

Husk's old face broke into a sudden and touching smile.

'Did he? Really? I used to tell him tales, you know. I miss him as a matter of fact, quite a lot. But I suppose he grew up and has gone off as young moles do, or something of the sort. When I heard you above I thought it might be him.'

He 'looked' at her again, his sightless eyes mottled and watery, and she saw his head had a continual tremor.

'I am quite interested in old and mediaeval texts, and in tales. I once studied them.'

'Yes,' he said, 'I studied them once, but I got over it. Studying's not the way with tales, is it?'

Privet smiled, appreciating his comment. Her tutor Cobbett in Beechenhill had sometimes said the same.

'I . . . I think perhaps it isn't really,' she said.

This unscholarly thought agreed, Husk turned from her, and reaching forward to guide himself along, led Privet on the strangest and most extraordinary textual tour she had ever ventured on.

Though before he really got started he stopped again, turned, and said in a testing kind of way, 'Any *particular* mediaeval scribe whose work you enjoy?'

It was a long time since Privet had been asked such a question, a very long time.

'Skelton,' she said without much hesitation.

'Ah, yes! Skelton. What a good choice. A pity his works are so rare.'

'I have only ever seen copies,' she said.

'Ah!' he said again, and turned once more and led her on.

She soon found herself in the first of a series of chambers of such utter chaos that it was hard to see which way to go. Texts and books, and folios, were everywhere. Piles of them, shelves bulging with them, stacks here and bundles there, dusty, torn, some half open, others standing on their ends, some stacked so high that she could not conceive how anymole could have got them there in the first place, let alone consult them later.

Husk seemed unable to move quickly, or to venture off what seemed his regular route through this chaos, and in any case he soon grew tired and suggested that she looked about for herself and come back to him. She picked her way through the clutter towards what seemed a tunnel to another chamber, but found herself in a dead-end of texts and had to retreat, discovering as she did so all sorts of textual delights, amongst which she browsed and dawdled with growing pleasure.

By the time she got back to where she had left Keeper Husk he had moved on and she had to follow him by sound, for in the confusion of stacks and shadows and muddle he was already out of sight. She went to the right, then forward, then to the left, and stooping down wriggled her way through into a low ill-lit chamber, which like the first was a chaos of stacks and shelves. There somewhere, heard but unseen, Husk moved about muttering, 'Where is it? Where's it gone?'

Perhaps he was a little deaf as well, which would account for the way he sometimes shouted when he talked, for he did not hear her now, and she saw him long before he became aware of her. A small, old mole, unable to move well, and surrounded by such piles and multitudes of texts that he seemed yet smaller than he was. She saw that the joints in his paws were furless and painfully swollen, and the talons of both front paws bent and skewed one way with the disease.

Pathetically he was snouting about, reaching his paws here and there, seeking something he could not find. Out of politeness and so she would not surprise him she called out his name, and then looked about a bit while he called that he was *just* coming, and wouldn't be long and couldn't she *occupy* herself, *please*. She began to feel that there was something peculiarly exciting about a place that was texts, and nothing but texts, all waiting to be looked at, browsed through, studied, and absorbed, and sorted. This *was* a worthy task.

Since Keeper Husk seemed in no hurry to emerge from among the stacks in which he searched, she began to browse as bookish moles like to do, and to her delight fround a fragment of a mediaeval verse whose script was of the Obverse Middle period and whose sentiments were all too familiar to her . . . 'My lefe is faren in a lond – Alas! Why is he so? And I am so sore bound I may nat com her to . . .'

Then, nearby and quite out of any sequence or order, was a much-worn text entitled 'The Cronycle of Feestes', though what festivities it referred to she did not have the inclination to find out because her eye was suddenly caught by a more ancient text whose title was at first hard to make out.

She ran her talons gently over it, snouted at it, looked askance at it to see the impressions better, and realized with a start that it was ancient scrivening. *That* she had not seen in all her time in Duncton. Indeed, she had not seen it since . . .

Then Husk was there at her flank, breathing in his wheezy way, though this time from the effort of a successful hunt rather than from mirth. His eyes seemed almost bright, his look nearly triumphant, and he held in his paw a text which he was careful as yet not to let her see, while he peered very closely at what she had been examining as if he could see it; but it was only when he touched it with his talons that he relaxed. He was suddenly in his element, and spoke quickly and with infectious enthusiasm.

111

'Ah! Yes! That's Berners' work. Quite a find, quite a chronicler. My father exchanged that text with a mole from Rollright for three worms and a burrow for the night. But Berners did better things and that's a rather tedious exposition of Whernish ways, in my view, and of course much more entertainingly done by Buke of Howlat. Now . . .' He silently gave her the text he carried. 'Have a snout at *this*.'

She examined the text carefully and with a growing interest that changed rapidly to awe.

'But . . .' she whispered, marvelling at the beauty of its script, and impressed by the good condition it was in.

'But . . .' she whispered again, turning back to the beginning to check again in utter disbelief what text it was, her talons tracing and retracing the mediaeval scribing there.

'Well?' he said at last, scarcely able to contain his impatience.

She ran her talons through its first folios, and then snouted carefully down its last. She stanced back from it, scented it, and weighed it quizzically from one paw to another.

'Impressive, eh?' he said, with a grin that revealed a few stubby yellow teeth. '*Well?*'

Then, with great reluctance, and glancing at him in some alarm, she said firmly, 'It's a forgery.'

There was deep silence. He looked about with what seemed outrage, and then cold anger, and then deep doubt, and yet throughout there was a half-hidden amusement about his face.

'In fact,' she dared venture, 'I would say it's a forgery by an Uffington scribe, and Early Modern.'

He thrust his withered snout at hers, narrowed his eyes, and said conspiratorially, 'So would I. Didn't get near to fooling you, did it? Didn't fool my father either. But he *liked* forgeries, you see, said the moles who did them loved their work.' He cackled again, and reached out for the script from her, which she put into his paws. He caressed it, and sniffed at it in a friendly kind of way, and with a final and affectionate pat put it down.

'Now, before you say anything, mole, let me show you some more of my little collection. That part you saw first I have really abandoned now, being old and my sight having failed so badly, and my work with them being over, but where we're going now I've kept my favourite texts and I can find *them* easily enough.'

With that Husk signalled Privet to follow him yet again and led her on a confusing voyage among the crumbling shelves and stacks of texts to chambers far beyond the first until they came to a drier, smaller, chamber which was a good deal tidier, though by the standards of the Main Library, it was still chaotic enough.

Cluttered it may have been but whenever Privet reached out to touch a text Keeper Husk followed her direction to it, touched it, and every time a gleam of recognition would come to his wrinkled eye and he would say things like, 'Ah yes! The oral tradition of the Welsh Marches, unsurpassed!' or 'Beatty? *There* was a rogue poet if ever I knew one, eh Privet?' or 'The "Lichfield Roll", eh! As scurrilous as they come! Challow who scribed it can always be relied on for some light relief . . . but of course he fought a hopeless struggle against his carnal desires. Yes, yes, some moles are like that.'

He clearly knew every text in his collection and loved them all and as they went he recounted their history – how they came to be discovered, and how they made their way to Duncton Wood.

'Ah, yes, my dear! There's a tale behind every one of these old texts, quite apart from what's scribed in them. Why, my father used to stance me down where you're stanced now, take up a Roll or Tale, and tell me all he knew about its provenance. Happy days! But of course young librarians aren't interested in this kind of thing these days; oh no, not they. Mediaeval texts were all the rage in my young days, but contemporary history's the thing now, as if there was ever really such a thing, since it's a contradiction in terms!

'But my dear, any one of these texts, whether Rolls recounting the doings of a system, or rhymes scribed for fun, or Tales told to scribemoles and scribed down, has more fascination to it than *modern* texts. Why? Because these days moles merely record the doings of others, which one way or another have to do with fighting and war, whereas in former times moles were concerned with the things they did themselves, like founding systems, or colonization, or delving, or love. Let me show you what I mean . . .'

This time he soon found what he wanted, and offered it to her almost diffidently, as one might introduce a mate to an old friend, secretly proud, yet uncertain that he or she will be appreciated.

'There,' he said, giving her a small and ancient text, '*there!*'

It looked modest enough, its covers faded, its scribing weak and hard to make out, its folios much worn and ragged at the edges. But for all that the text had a real sense of mystery and age about it, and the feel of something that had been scribed with love, and kept through the centuries since its creation by moles who had loved it too, the latest of whom stanced watching her, old and touchingly concerned to see how she reacted.

113

She did not need to examine it for long before she knew with utter certainty what it was, or rather, guessed what it could only be.

'But this is . . .' she began, unable to speak its name, so awestruck was she by what she held in her paws.

'Yes,' he said, taking it back from her, and holding it with love, '*this* is Skelton's "Adawe", the original.'

'But generations of scholars, knowing it once existed, have wondered where it was and searched for it,' she exclaimed. 'Most believed that it had long since been lost.'

'It *was* lost, my dear, but not destroyed. My father found it in a burrow at the deserted system of Ashbury Top, along with a number of Rolls of eastern systems.'

'May I . . . ?' she asked, reaching out her paws.

He gave it back to her and she laid it down and ran her talons over the title scribings.

'"Adawe", she repeated aloud, 'or "On the way to Silence, by Skelton of Blagrove Slide". I didn't know he came from Blagrove! How strange, I thought . . . but it's where Thripp comes from.'

'Thripp?' said Husk.

'No matter,' she said hastily, for mention of *him* here and in this context seemed almost blasphemous. She resumed reading aloud, turning the folio to the first full page of text: '"It was in the Autumn year of October, after the Scirpuscun schism had run its course, that I tired of my life in Uffington and, gaining a dispensation from the Holy Mole, set off into moledom . . ."'

'". . . with only the novice Butem to aid me on my way,"' continued Husk from memory, with his eyes half closed and a dreamy look on his face, '"and the sun by day, and the moon by night, to guide our faltering and uncertain steps. Of plan or purpose we had none, or if we had, we soon left it behind us like a shadowed time of past trouble that a mole has no more need to burden himself with. Thus set free, we turned our snouts north-westward, and before long Uffington, and all the cares of the world, seemed so far behind us that they might never have been. As for Silence, we sought to forget that that was what we desired, Butem singing a song when the shadows of that desire beset him, while I, for my part, resolved to seek the truth in the small things of each moment of the day and night and thus clear my mind of the dismay and restlessness a mole feels when he contemplates the fact that there is a Silence he has not yet reached. It was not long before we reached that great river which . . ."'

Husk stopped, smiled, opened his eyes and said, 'No text has ever given me greater comfort or greater food for thought than this. Skelton was a blessed mole indeed! His "Adawe" has greatly helped me in my work. Though now, alas . . .'

Privet saw that he peered round towards the far end of the burrow where, at a small raised and well-lit earthen dais which was, or had been, his scribing place, there was a clutter of torn and crumpled folios, and among them a pile of neat unused ones, intended no doubt for some future scribing that his blindness and infirmity meant he could no longer so easily do. Of finished work she could see nothing, and presumed that *that* was under the pile of rejected folios, or carefully hidden away somewhere else.

'Keeper Husk,' she said formally, 'I told you that the Master Librarian sent me here to help. He did so because he believes that these ancient texts you guard may be in danger of destruction by a sect of moles called the Newborns. But from what he has told me I believe that neither he nor any other Duncton librarians are fully aware of the importance of the texts you hold here, which makes the need to sort them, and get the most important to a place of safety soon, even greater. I hope therefore you will help me fulfil this task he has given me.'

'Yes, well, I wondered when you'd get round to saying something like that. Always was an organizer, Stour was. I've known that mole a long time – a long long time! Of course, he'll have found some way of making it all sound very important to come here and help me out but finally, when all's said and done, is anything so important as you know what? Eh? You *know*, Privet. Tales. That's important! But a few texts . . .' He waved his deformed paw about a bit and peered blindly here and there indifferently.

'And anyway,' he continued, 'the truth is that you may have some difficulty deciding which texts *are* important, even assuming that it is right to attribute relative importance to texts at all. The meanest, dullest-seeming scrap of text or folio may, for all you know, be seen as the *most* important by some future scholar. I have spent a lifetime learning that myself, and daring to assign to a lesser place in my work texts which once seemed the most important of all.'

'Yet the attempt must be made, Keeper Husk,' said Privet earnestly, 'for we cannot hope to protect *all* the texts in the Collections now in Duncton. The Master has made a selection in the Main Library, and he hopes I shall do the same here. He has of course started with the Books of Moledom . . .'

'Ah, yes, those,' said Husk rather more reverently than before. 'It

115

is a long time since I touched one of those . . . What precious things they are, what wisdom they contain. Would that the little book I'm working on contained a speck of those Books' wisdom, eh?'

'What is the book you're scribing?' she asked.

'Tales, or some of them. The best, or most interesting, or perhaps merely the most wise, since we're talking of wisdom. Yes, the most wise. But it is a mere compilation of final versions of the Tales that seem important, and even those . . . No, I don't know, my dear, about you working on the texts here . . . I'm not sure I want you poking about and disturbing things and more likely as not finding Tales and bits and pieces I should have included in my work . . .'

Husk looked again in the direction of his scribing place and Privet sensed that he was losing his interest in her task, and that soon he might grow tired and order her to leave. This was not a task she could ever do without his help. Perhaps if she talked to him of the work that seemed to matter to him most it would help. She wanted to tell him about the work she herself had brought, feeling that after so long lingering hidden in her burrow this was one mole who might enjoy it. But somehow it seemed so presumptuous to offer up her little text to a mole who was clearly such a master of tales.

'I wonder, Keeper Husk, if you are aware that there were other moles, or at least one other mole, who were working at something similar to yourself,' said Privet diffidently. She was hesitant, because no scholar likes to find another on his patch. But she need not have worried, for Husk's response was immediate interest and pleasure.

'Another mole worked on Tales? Tell me about him, mole, and what you know of his scribing, for no doubt I have much to learn, so much . . . What was his name and system, eh?'

'He was of Beechenhill, Keeper Husk, and his name was Cobbett.'

'Oh, *him*! You mean Stour's brother?'

'Brother?' repeated Privet, astonished.

'Oh yes, Cobbett's his brother all right. Fell out over a female seventy-odd years ago if a day they did and Cobbett wandered off on a pilgrimage to Beechenhill to recover himself and never came back. Funny tale that one, ha ha ha . . .' Husk fell into another fit of cackling at the memory of this ancient gossip.

'Why do you think Stour's got such a long face, my dear?' he continued when he had recovered. 'Unrequited love! Worse than worms in your guts that is! Eats you up, withers you, leaves you a mere shadow of your former self. I ought to know . . .' But he started laughing again until tears rolled down his scrawny face. For a mole so

116

infirm he seemed very much alive and to know how to enjoy himself.

'Dear me,' he said clutching his stomach, 'dear oh dearie me. Phew! Laughing'll be the death of me. You see, Privet, and you'll not believe this I know, being young and not believing old moles like Stour and myself, and Cobbett come to that, were once young too and had feelings, but – sorry, I've got to laugh, I must have been mad at the time – I loved the lass myself! Do you know what her name was? Mind you, you must promise never to mention it to Stour of course, as he'll have a fit at the mere mention of it. I expect I'm the only one who knows her name now, bar him and Cobbett. Her name was Pansy and she was fat.'

'Fat?' repeated Privet faintly.

'Stour called her comely, Cobbett called her magnificent if I remember right, but as I was the one to get closest to her first I think I have the right to tell the truth and call her fat. Fat Pansy, that's what others called her. Made a fool of all of us, as she took a Cumnor mole to mate and left Duncton Wood altogether. I ask you. Dear me! I haven't thought of Fat Pansy in decades and I don't suppose I ever will again! Can you imagine . . . ?' concluded Husk, laughing again, but more scurrilously than before.

But from the dubious and prudish expression on poor Privet's face it did not look as if she *could* imagine quite what he meant.

'Yes,' said Husk at last, 'I heard from a visitor forty years ago that Cobbett was scribing what he rather pompously called a Book of Tales.'

'Yes,' said Privet defensively, 'he did call it that. It's a long time since I was there . . .'

But Husk's mood seemed to have changed suddenly into almost depressive quiet. His head was low, and shook once more, his sightless eyes gazed at texts unseen.

'Though Stour was my brother,' he said at last, as if the fraternal state was one that could be sundered, and had been, 'Cobbett was my friend. It is a terrible thing to lose a friend. We don't have many chances of making friends, you see.' He reached out a paw and grasped hers with remarkable strength. 'Have you had true friends you've lost? Friends whose minds and hearts seemed to know your own? Eh mole, have you?'

'I . . . well . . . yes . . .' she began.

'Don't let them go,' he said urgently. 'And if they seem to have gone get them back. Do anything not to lose them. The Stone may never send you another and in losing them part of you has died! I

117

never found a friend like Cobbett, not ever again. Of course he's scribing a Book of Tales! It was what he and I shared, you see, and all this, and all my father taught us here. And that silly business with Pansy, and Stour being jealous and uppity, and suddenly Cobbett was gone, gone for ever. How strange you should have come here all the way from Beechenhill. Tell me of him, my dear, tell me all you remember.'

His old face was smiling, his eyes shone with tears, his paw held hers with trust and eagerness.

'I . . . I liked him so much,' said Privet. 'He was kind to me, and taught me much, and told me Tales I have never heard before.'

'Yes,' sighed Husk, 'my Cobbett was like that: now tell me . . .'

And so they talked, and night came, and Privet found herself inextricably caught up in the clutter and magic of Rolls, Rhymes and Tales. For when daybreak came, and she woke up, she found old Husk had wandered off and found her some food, and was already busying himself with sorting out some texts which he hoped she would agree ought to be saved.

'Later, you can help me with my work, that's the arrangement. I let you sort the texts, you help me with my work! Eh? Fair's fair. And seeing as you've been tutored by Cobbett it'll be like having part of him back here at my flank again, to share and advise, to sort and reject, to choose and decide, and then? Why then to scribe the chosen Tale, and after that to score bits out, and then to take still more away until—'

Privet laughed.

'I've got to eat first, Keeper Husk,' she said, looking around the cluttered chamber as it filled with morning light, feeling closer to her destiny than she ever had before. And thinking about so many things they had talked of the night before, so many memories, of friends, of loves, of tasks, of things undone that might, after all, still be done.

'I'll stay,' she agreed, not thinking it was paradoxical ending up agreeing to perform a task she had set out to do in the first place: nor realizing that perhaps the real task she was about to become involved in was really to do with Husk's own, and Cobbett's, which was not concerned to preserve texts but to explore them to find the inner truth of Tales.

'But I'll have to go back to my own tunnels for a short time, just to make sure they're safe for the winter, and to tell friend Fieldfare to keep an eye on them.' And too, though she said nothing of this, to collect her own small text and bring it here as an offering to this good old mole.

'Don't be long gone,' he said fretfully, 'for I'm beginning to get used to you being here!'

Chapter Eleven

Fieldfare responded very differently from Privet to Stour's appeal at the secret meeting, becoming restless and fretful, and suddenly concerned by issues that had never worried her before. However Stour had touched the others, with her he had disturbed her peace, and made her question the meaning of how she lived, and to wonder if perhaps the most living she had done was through Chater, and not through herself at all.

'Pups I've raised and sent them off!' she said to herself again, but it was not enough.

'I've made a clean and comfortable place for Chater to come back to!' But now that seemed rather less important than it once had.

'I've friends amongst all kinds of moles in the system!' But for what? What had she ever discussed with them? Nothing but trivia, it seemed. Not the great issues of peace, and serving the Stone, and suchlike matters as the Master had raised. It takes courage and honesty for a mole to confront 'suchlike matters' as these, and kindly Fieldfare had both, and was discovering the painful, uneasy consequences of it.

Perhaps it was best she was alone to wrestle with such things. But Chater's departure with Maple and Whillan for the dangerous mission to Rollright, soon after the meeting, left her without the companion she needed to debate these doubts and occasional excitements of thinking about what Stour had said. Nor did she have a task, as Privet did, to take her mind off her thoughts, or away from her worries that so soon after his escape from the Newborns in Cuddesdon, Chater was off again on what might be an even more dangerous mission, and for a period of time he had been quite unable to specify.

For long days she stayed in or near the tunnels she shared with Chater, her thoughts confused and her actions strangely slow and routine: waking, grooming, feeding, sleeping, waking . . . Then she took to wandering off to visit Drubbins, the only mole whom she felt it would be possible to talk to since she knew that Privet was now much occupied at Rolls and Rhymes and in what Fieldfare called her 'library mood', which meant preoccupied and uncommunicative. Somehow the time passed, and the last warm days of September gave way to a windy October and a reminder that she should clear out the deeper tunnels of her and Chater's place in preparation for winter. Since she knew that Drubbins needed help with his winter quarters, and what with discovering, or perhaps making, new things to do in her tunnels and his, Fieldfare continued to succeed for a time to suppress her excitement and dismay at all that Stour had said. Yet as the October days went by it became harder to do so, and she grew more restless still.

But then one day too many passed when she found herself discontentedly alone and without a companion, and she felt disinclined to go off yet again to talk to Drubbins. Oh, he was a nice mole, a likeable mole, but he was not suited to her need today; her need *now*.

For hours she dithered about her place, the great trees above her swaying in the October winds and shedding their leaves across the Wood's wide floor. Then suddenly her doubts were gone: it was a day for doing, a day for daring, a day for being dauntless.

Fieldfare patted her ample flanks, ran a paw over her chubby and wrinkled face, and thought that though being dauntless might not be her thing, dauntless today she must still be. And if friends were not for talking to when they were needed most they were NOT friends. And so . . .

'I'll visit Privet up in Rolls and Rhymes!' she said to herself. 'She's had time enough to get most of her task done, for there can't be *that* many texts for her to sort out. I dare say she'll be glad to see me now . . . and if she isn't, well . . . well then, I'll make her be!' Such, in Fieldfare's mind that day and thus far, was what being dauntless meant.

Yet as she neared the place, and peered among the dark trees there – for it was not an easy place to find – doubts set in. Perhaps after all . . . but dauntless was the word today! Perhaps she could make the excuse of having come to offer her services down in Rolls, Rhymes and Tales, for she knew that Privet might be working hard and imagined she might now be pleased to see her.

Alas, the reception she got at Rolls and Rhymes from Privet was even worse than she had feared in her darker moments of doubt. For Privet proved reluctant to take time off to listen to her, and when she did she was unwilling to discuss the issues Stour had raised, and could not conceal her desire to return to Keeper Husk, who seemed to have some kind of hold on her.

One of the things that Fieldfare had most wished to discuss was why it might be that Stour had chosen *her* to be part of the secret meeting. For surely she was no more than the mate of Chater and had no special gift or skill to give the system – the very notion which Stour had made her doubt, but which she wished to rehearse with a friend like Privet before rejecting it. Mind you, she had often said to herself in the troubled time just past, she was a mole who did not mind any challenge or any task. But then, until now such tasks as she had undertaken had been ordained by circumstance or custom.

'Now I've to find a route forward of my own through unfamiliar ways, you see' (she had wished to say to Privet), 'and, my dear, I'm not sure I know how to do it . . .'

But none of this was said, or could be said, to Privet, since Privet, after the briefest of conversations, said she had work to do and things to attend to and helter-skeltered off underground once more.

'Some friend!' said Fieldfare to herself, much hurt by this rejection. Then feeling most disconsolate, and unsure which way to turn to either confront the unexpressed thoughts which nagged at her, or escape them, she was on her way back to the Eastside in the vague hope that she might try to find Drubbins after all, when her brief outrage at Privet surfaced again in a more diffused sense of rebellion against everything in general, and her own acquiescence yet again in the idea that she needed another mole to give what she did any meaning.

''Tis not Privet's fault if I'm upset,' she told herself judiciously, 'it is my own! Fieldfare, my love, I despise you for being so pathetic! Today, here and now, you must be brave and dauntless like you said you would be earlier before you foolishly rushed over to Rolls and Rhymes!'

She stanced still a long time, staring among the trees, and breathing rather fast in an excited kind of way as unaccustomed thoughts of journeying crossed her mind in fleeting but alarming images of places to which she had never been, combined with thoughts she had never uttered. Not that either image or thought would have been very radical to moles like Chater, used as they were to travelling and thinking for themselves, or even Privet, despite her present flight into obscure seclusion with Husk and his texts.

No, plump Fieldfare's thoughts were parochial: 'There's nomole to stop me travelling this very day, if I so wish, to . . . to . . . why, to the Westside!' she declared daringly to herself. 'Or, *if* I wish, to the Pastures! Or to that mysterious stretch of the High Wood which lies *beyond* the Stone. I could, I could!'

As she thought of each of these places she turned and peered purposefully in their direction, debating the possibility of going there. But none of them quite suited the radical mood that was upon her, and that had to be satisfied.

Then Fieldfare furrowed her plump brow, and it was not long before a possibility more intimidating, and certainly more daunting, but infinitely more exciting, came to her.

'I couldn't!' she whispered.

'I mustn't!' she murmured.

'I shall!' she declared, and out loud too, to give her courage. 'I shall go to the Marsh End and see what these Newborn moles get up to on their home ground! They always did say moles were welcome at their meetings, and if they are as dubious in their intentions as Chater thinks and Stour says then I shall go and see what they're about for myself! Then, if I *do* have to confront them in the future I shall know all the better what I'm about!'

She could scarcely have guessed how original that thought and action would have seemed to many in the Duncton Wood of her day, nor could she have ever dreamed that it was his understanding that she might have such a quality of sensible enterprise and practical daring that had made Stour choose her as a member of his privy council. Perhaps it had not escaped him that a mole of Chater's calibre was unlikely to have a weak mole for a mate.

So Fieldfare set off directly downslope, with that sense of mounting and most pleasurable freedom a mole gets when she puts her normal daily cares behind, and goes off on a risky adventure from which there is no turning back.

'I've not talked to that mole Bantam in ten moleyears at least!' she said cheerfully to herself as she went. 'But she's something important and maybe that's done her some good. I'll seek her out for a start, and at the very least I can spend an hour or two in her company before returning to the Eastside. What fun it will be to have something to tell Chater for a change!'

It would have been hard for anymole, intent upon getting in among the Marshenders – who had become even closer since they veered the Newborn way – to have chosen a better day than Fieldfare had done. For arriving that same afternoon, tired and hungry, she found the Marshenders in a mood of excited expectation and open to visitors.

So much so, that strange though she was to most of them, they seemed not a bit surprised to see her, believing, as she quickly deduced, that she had come to witness for herself the visitation of some special moles whose imminent arrival was the cause of excitement all over the Marsh End. Indeed, other Duncton moles, mainly ones who lived on the edge of the Marsh End and who half accepted the Caradocian way, had come for that very reason, so Fieldfare's arrival seemed less remarkable than it might normally have done.

The cause of the excitement was that a group of Senior Brothers of the Order had been expected for some molemonths past and that very day news of their imminent arrival had come, and Chervil himself had set off upslope that very morning to the south-eastern Pastures to meet them. The Marsh End Newborns were now waiting excitedly for his return with the visitors, about whom they knew nothing but that they were Senior Brethren and were bringing joyful news that would end at last the Newborns' self-imposed isolation in the Marsh End away from the Duncton Stone.

Chervil! But that's Thripp's son! thought Fieldfare, her heart suddenly in her mouth to find herself so near so sinister a legend. For a moment she thought she should flee back upslope to the Eastside, but then, since the name of the day was dauntless she felt she should continue as she had begun and see things through. It would be quite a thing to be able to tell her Chater that his beloved had seen Senior Brother Chervil, Thripp's *son*, with her own eyes! And anyway, she felt hungry again, and fancied a nibble.

Worms aplenty were available and the Marsh End was in festive mood, and Fieldfare was at leisure, for the time being at least, to take in the scene. She had not been in those tunnels since she was a youngster, and the place seemed more modest, less dank, and less forbidding than it had then to her young eyes. Even so, the soil was darker and more moist than that upslope in the main part of the system, and the trees smaller, and the ground-cover thicker and muckier, making the surface ways winding and enclosed, and likely to confuse a mole who erred off the communal paths.

'Greetings, Sister!' moles said brightly when they saw her, approaching with smiling eyes and adding with irritating cheerfulness, 'This is a happy day, come celebrate with us!'

At first Fieldfare was uncertain whether these invitations were general to the day and season, or specific to a place and time within the Marsh End. Certainly the further she advanced along the Marsh End's main surface communal way, past entrances down into its tunnels, the more she came across the sight and sound of festivity of anything but a sombre religious sort. The Newborns, it seemed, could enjoy themselves.

Eventually she was stopped by the sheer force of numbers of one such group of brothers and sisters whose members had sprawled across the way, and through whose songs, prayers and eating it would have been hard to pass without seeming rude.

'Have a lobworm, Sister, and rejoice in the Stone's bounty!' a fellow-sister said to her, giggling as she presented Fieldfare with a broken lump of worm. 'It's a miracle, isn't it, the Senior Brothers coming this day and . . . this.'

Fieldfare looked in the direction indicated, which was a side turn off the main way, and she was astonished to see a massed tangle of shining healthy lobworms in a pile as big as a mole, and moving moistly. Fieldfare liked her food, but there was something over-generous about this mound of worms to which, in its juicy repulsiveness, the gluttony of the Newborns was a ghastly counterpoint. For the self-same paws that were soggy with the entrails of half-eaten worms were raised from time to time to the sky in supplication to the Stone, while those same stuffed and overflowing mouths were mumbling dribbling prayers of thanks.

Where the worms had come from Fieldfare had no idea, though she had heard it said that sometimes in the autumn, after especially hot summer years, there was a second breeding of such lobworms as these in the Marsh End, which resulted in their effusion from the worm-saturated soil on to the surface.

Perhaps this was the cause of the 'miracle' which Fieldfare's new friends were celebrating, but it was very soon a feast from whose nauseous sights and sounds she wished to escape. But out of the need to seem to be a part of things Fieldfare continued to nibble at what she was offered, whilst searching among the excited mass of moles to see if she might find Bantam or pick up a clue to her whereabouts.

Failing that, she talked a little to what moles were near and, between gorging and pious prayers, discovered that Sister Bantam was not far off below ground in a communal chamber, and that Chervil and the Senior Brothers were expected imminently. Mention of the fact, which came from two excited moles who had just appeared along the same route that Fieldfare had taken, had the effect of suddenly sobering up the joyful throng, as if they sensed that whilst celebration was in order, visiting Brothers, especially senior ones, might find fault with the present wormful excess. Having discovered where Bantam was, and sensing that the local festivity she had come across was not the best place to be, Fieldfare hurried on in the company of the two new arrivals, who led her underground to the communal chamber.

The place was crowded but orderly and since other moles came pressing in from behind her, Fieldfare soon found herself in the midst of what she suddenly realized was a congregation, whose prayerful actions and liturgy were being conducted by a mature male, dark-furred, whom she recognized as one of the Carodocians who had long since come to the system.

He was stanced at one end of the chamber, intoning prayers of praise to the Stone, which those all around her knew by heart, and cried out zealously after him. Fieldfare could only just see his head and snout, for the throng of moles in front obstructed her view.

She decided that just as she had nibbled at the worms on the surface to appear to be an enthusiastic part of things, she might as well nibble away at the service underground, to show willing and remain unnoticed by others there. But the liturgy being strange to her she had trouble keeping up with it and no sooner did she bob her snout low, in accord with the others, than they were raising theirs to the roof; and no sooner was she shouting out 'Stone I praise thee!' than they had fallen silent. Luckily other moles were scattered among the throng who seemed as ill-attuned to the service as she was, added to which there was all about her a certain undercurrent of spiritual chatter or noise, generated mainly by older and scraggy females, who seemed quite carried away by their own fervour. Ignoring the male leader entirely, they were conducting their own special form of worship, which consisted of half-prayers, half-songs, half-praisings, and half-gestures of abasement and joy, all to the apparent indifference of those nearest to them.

However, although they seemed utterly lost in a zealous world of their own, this proved not to be the case. For suddenly, the male stanced down and disappeared from Fieldfare's sight and in his place reared up a female, who cried out the single word 'Peace!' with such ear-splitting and harsh command that everymole in the room fell silent.

'Why, 'tis Bantam!' exclaimed Fieldfare to herself, instinctively retreating behind the mole in front of her, lest Bantam see her before she had a chance to decide if it was wise that Bantam knew she was there. Already grave reservations were coming into Fieldfare's mind about this whole venture, and she had decided that she had been dauntless enough, and when the right moment came to leave unnoticed she would take it. The silence did not however last for more than a moment or two before one of the oldest and wildest of the fervent females began singing out her joys once more in a cracked voice and disturbing the sudden peace.

Bantam nodded sharply to an attendant male who, Fieldfare saw for the first time, was one of several who were stanced guard-like at intervals around the edge of the great chamber. Although the other moles held their snouts low in expectation of some new turn in the liturgy for which Bantam's command of silence had prepared them, Fieldfare surreptitiously watched as the male, also dark, but younger than the seeming leader, pushed his way with a colleague through the congregation and unceremoniously grabbed the offending female and very rapidly and very roughly removed her, dragging her screaming towards an exit at the back of the chamber, and then up an unseen tunnel, whence her screams continued in a muffled way before suddenly, and most sickeningly, coming to a stop in mid-flight.

As all this happened Fieldfare noticed that the moles about her were uttering a humming, snoutish sound from the back of their half-open mouths in a rhythmic way, and seeming to say a word which sounded like 'oohhhnnnn oohhhnnnn oohhhnnnn!' Doing this, they seemed utterly indifferent to the fate of their aged friend and yet they must have had some consciousness of her because as soon as the males had silenced her – as Fieldfare assumed they had – they suddenly stopped. It seemed to her that the humming was their way of blocking out the fact that something unpleasant was happening which they wished to know nothing about.

For a moment there was dead silence again, but even as Fieldfare dared look up to observe everything the better, Bantam reared up and screamed out, 'Stohh oohhhnnnn!' and the humming chant began once more.

So that was it! Stone!

Half opening her mouth in semblance of joining the others, and half closing her eyes that her curiosity might not be noticed, Fieldfare watched and saw what she could.

Bantam was not much changed from when Fieldfare had seen her last; a little thinner perhaps, and her eyes, always forbidding, a little more so. It was plain that she held some sort of position of authority here in the Marsh End, and judging from the immediacy of the others' response, she was regarded either with great respect, or great fear. Having seen the speed and ruthlessness of the old female's removal Fieldfare had little doubt which.

Meanwhile there was some pushing and shoving at the entrance down which she herself had come, where it seemed that the same gluttonous moles she had met earlier were now being forced in by the 'guards'. Indeed, a wave of movement crossed the chamber, and brought the moles into even closer contact with each other, such that Fieldfare realized with sudden fear that she could barely move, and that she would find it quite impossible to get out of the chamber before others did.

Even as Fieldfare began to panic, and lose all idea of observing what was going on as she began to be desperate to get out before she was crushed further, Bantam cried out, 'Be still! Brother Worthing will speak a final prayer of thanks and then we will ascend to the surface to meet the Senior Brothers. For they have come at last among us, praise the Stone! Be still, or risk the dire crush of indiscipline.'

Just as movement had gone like a crushing wave across the throng a moment before, now a blessed stillness descended upon it, as each mole heeded Sister Bantam's word and one by one stanced still as death, so that Fieldfare could breathe again. Panic she still felt, and that grim phrase of Bantam's, 'the dire crush of indiscipline', seemed to throb in her mind as her blood throbbed in her ears until the panic subsided.

The good Brother Worthing's prayers she heard not, grateful only to be alive and know how relieved she would be to be outside again. Then, when the prayers were over, the guards stanced aside to reveal ways out through which they now unhurriedly directed those moles nearest to them.

As suddenly as the crush had come it eased away, and Fieldfare, beginning to shake with delayed shock, was herself at last able to stagger up a short tunnel, and out to the cool and infinitely pleasant surface of the Marsh End once again.

But she was mistaken if she thought that her tribulations were over and she could thankfully go home at last. They had only just begun. The same dark and silent young brothers who had been the guard-stewards below ground were now in place to herd the hapless moles into a clearing some way from the entrances down to the communal chamber.

The clearing, which appeared to be newly made, had recently delved ground about it which rose up on all sides but one, giving those in it the sense of being enclosed and vulnerable to anymole who took a stance up on the raised ground, which Sister Bantam almost immediately did.

Casting her imperious eyes across the throng she said, 'Brothers, Sisters, be still before the coming of the Senior Brothers . . .'

Then, from the far side of the raised ground, five males slowly appeared and with the sun-bright sky behind them they seemed like moles rising from the ground itself and bringing with them light. At this Fieldfare felt for the first time that sense, so alarming, so grim, that it might be much harder to find a way back out of the Marsh End and the ministrations of the Newborns, than it had been to get there.

No sooner had this thought crept uneasily into her mind than the one mole she recognized amongst the five, Brother Worthing, who had said prayers earlier, advanced and addressed the assembly.

'Brothers and Sisters in the Stone,' he began, 'we are gathered here to welcome three moles whose presence honours our small community in Duncton Wood, and whose coming this day marks a new and exciting era for true followers of the Stone. Brothers, Sisters . . . Senior Brother Inquisitors Fetter, Law and Barre.'

He waved a paw at each of these in turn and Fieldfare could not say she liked any of them, Barre looking decidedly brutal, Law having a cruel smirk on his face, and Fetter a calm and inexorable assurance. They nodded in that smug way new arrivals of importance often have when they are introduced to a company of moles. But it was not finally any of these three visitors that held Fieldfare's attention, but the remaining mole, who, she deduced from the fact that it was not necessary to introduce him to the throng, must be Senior Brother Chervil.

His eyes were black and intense, and his presence was strangely compelling in the way that a great rise of rock which seems about to fall because the heavy stormy sky behind it moves with cloud, is compelling. Though large enough, and strong, he was no larger than his companions.

Chervil neither looked at Worthing, nor anymole, nor smiled, but instead immediately hunched a little towards them in a slight movement that seemed massive and binding on them all, and said in a terse, commanding voice, 'Brothers and Sisters in the Stone, I have long looked forward to the day I should be able to welcome the Senior Brother Inquisitors to Duncton Wood. It is the last of the great systems of moledom which must be prepared towards the day when the main systems of moledom shall be ready to yield peacefully to the only true way to the Stone, and with your help and faith it will soon be so.'

'Aye! It shall be prepared by us!' cried out the moles enthusiastically all round Fieldfare.

'Join with me in a prayer of thanks to the Stone for their safe deliverance through the traps and dangers of moledom,' Chervil continued, 'so many of whose systems are not yet enlightened by the good news of the true way, and where the spirit of indulgence and indolence lingers to corrupt all moles.'

There followed some prayers that Fieldfare found interminable in their length, and irritating in their professions of joy, the more so because now and then, when she least expected it, the moles about her turned to each other and to her as well and embraced with cloying warmth with the words, 'Peace!' and 'Only the true way!' and 'Hail fellow Sister in the Stone!' to which Fieldfare replied with embarrassed smiles and mutterings of her own, which she trusted might be taken as suitable for the occasion.

'I mentioned,' continued Senior Brother Chervil suddenly, cutting across this spiritual bonhomie, 'that the spirit of indulgence is rife in moledom still. So too is the canker of dispute and faithlessness, at whose talons I myself have suffered these months past when I have borne witness of the Newborn truth. Aye . . .' and here he seemed to indicate a wound in his flank, though look as she might Fieldfare could see none, or nothing more than an indisposition of the fur where once there might have been a tiny scratch.

Nevertheless, this 'living' proof of the dangers to which Chervil had been subject and his witnessing of moles who dared to doubt the preaching of a Newborn mole, did not go down well with his listeners, who were incited to cry out in dismay and anger, especially the younger males.

Further mention of certain outrages against Newborn moles only fanned the flames of their anger, as a strong wind makes a fire grow across a wood, until suddenly Chervil raised a paw and said, 'Peace. Peace is the only way, an attitude of peace.'

'Peace,' hissed the Newborn rabble softly, and reluctantly.

'However, just punishment to make such moles suffer their own violence is also the Stone's way, for the Stone is jealous of the truth and will cast down into their own darkness moles who violate its Silence with their babbling doubt and discord,' ventured Chervil, his words rousing the Newborns to enthusiasm once more.

'Aye,' they cried, 'just punishment of wrongdoers!'

'Recently, it was Senior Brother Barre's duty to oversee such retribution in a system near here, a place of so-called learning, contemplation and scholarship. I refer to corrupt Cuddesdon. But we know

130

the dangers of such "learning", we have seen the blasphemy of much "textual scholarship". Aye . . .'

Fieldfare felt the cold shock of recognition as he mentioned Cuddesdon and heard no more as she realized with a start that she was now almost certainly looking at one of the moles who had so nearly killed her Chater.

'Elsewhere in moledom the blasphemous spirit of discord is being dealt with more formally,' continued Chervil, 'and so-called leaders such as the infamous Rooster of Bleaklow Moor have been, or are being, brought for judgement before the Stone . . .'

Rooster! The mole Chater mentioned hearing about. Caught, it seemed, and by now, perhaps, gone the way of those Cuddesdon moles. Fieldfare had heard enough, and though she could not get away, she listened to no more, sickened by a sense of pious righteousness which pervaded the meeting like the odour of a corpse.

Yet worse, far worse, was to come, and soon. For the moment Chervil had finished speaking, and as if at some signal, the moles dispersed in all directions, except that some who tried to follow, as Fieldfare did, were held back within a circle formed by the dark-furred guard-stewards.

Now Fieldfare's nightmare truly began. For she saw, with horror, that those detained included many of the moles she had first met gorging themselves. There was a short speech of accusation, by Senior Brother Inquisitor Fetter, not wasting any time it seemed, and a shorter speech by Brother Worthing who had officiated underground.

Then, as Fieldfare realized with mounting horror that she was one of the accused, they were forcefully herded down through a confusing thicket of brambles and sapling alder, all hurried and harried along the way, with some of them, who seemed already to know their fate, whimpering and crying out in fear.

Fearing the worst, and remembering what had so nearly happened to her Chater, she decided that it was now or never if she was to escape. She thought she chose her moment well, turned into a thicket, rushed through it, but before she knew where she was she was in the firm grasp of two of the guards, and worse, staring into the angry, powerful eyes of Bantam.

'But you *know* me, Bantam,' she said with relief. 'I'm Fieldfare, of the Eastside. I'm not one of these moles, I'm not even a Newborn . . .'

'I know sinners not,' said Bantam indifferently and then, turning to one of the guards she added, 'take her to the massing,' and was gone.

The massing? Cold fear began to overtake Fieldfare, terrible cold fear.

Round and about, over and under, through and by . . . Fieldfare, tired from her earlier journey, was shocked by what she had seen and heard, frightened by Bantam's non-recognition of her, and intimidated by the buffeting of the silent guards which seemed calculated to hurt and yet not quite draw blood or even make a mark.

Just as she felt she was about to faint with exhaustion Fieldfare was suddenly and violently pushed down a slipway into the ground ahead of her, the moles in front almost seeming to fall into the earth as she must have seemed to, to those behind her. A rough paw at her rump propelled her further down into darkness and confusion.

Down, down, stumbling, hurt, lost among screams and fear, the world turned turvy-topsy and most menacing.

In the murk she saw Bantam again, poised in a side tunnel's entrance and watching with a curious look of lustful hatred in her eyes. Fieldfare cried out for her to recognize her, saying she was only Fieldfare, an old friend, she was . . .

But she was nothing it seemed, and unrecognized. Bantam thrust her talons in Fieldfare's snout and tears of pain blinded her, and she tumbled headlong past into a great chamber, full, dangerously full, of others all frightened and confused like herself.

Then, from a raised and guarded area on two sides of the chamber, too high for moles below to gain access to it, and with exits behind which made coming and going by moles up there very easy, a dark brother appeared who began haranguing them for the error of their ways, shouting at them the horrors of the Stone's judgement, and informing them that mere apology was not enough. As he finished another began and so their arraignment began and went on, and on, and on . . .

And so did Fieldfare's nightmare truly begin. Desperately tired, she was not allowed to sleep; quite unknown, she was accused of every crime; a mole inclined to smile at life, she was now made to whimper out her fears. And she was not the only one. All of them, crushed together, half suffocating, agonizingly thirsty, desperate, and always, always, the dark-furred males, watching, pushing, dragging; and in the dark night that now fell, moles began to die about her. She could hear them, rasping and croaking and calling out for help; dying. She was sure of that.

'Moles dead . . .' she whispered, staring at the lifeless eyes of a mole who had died at her very flank. Seeing which Fieldfare knew that she too was on a terrible path now that led to death, or destruction or . . . acquiescence.

132

She turned then or later as a mole touched her and whispered most terribly, 'Help me, Fieldfare!' and she found herself staring into the eyes of the mole Avens, the one who worked in the library and whom Privet knew. His face was half crushed, his eyes bulged and staring, and the rigour of death began to destroy what life remained in his look of horror. Even as she tried to speak he died before her eyes.

Worse, worse, worse in that darkness. A crooked form came to him, snouted at him, and mounted him, a living mole covering a dead one. It did, they did, and Fieldfare closed her eyes on the nightmares that began.

A scream, of ecstasy, and then afterwards a nasally voice whispering, 'Take this one away . . .'

Fieldfare dared to open her eyes and she saw the dead, abused body of Avens being dragged away. The crush increased and moles about her were crying out their abject agreement to something or other they were being forced to do or say.

'Yes! Yes! Yes!' they chanted feebly or desperately, or screamed, or sang, 'Yes, we know the true way, yes we do! Brothers and Sisters . . .'

'Yes Sister?' a mole said fiercely to Fieldfare, looking up into her eyes. Up? Not down? His voice all nasal, his head low, his back contorting away into the obscure dark.

'I know you,' whispered Fieldfare.

The crook-backed mole's eyes widened.

'Snyde?' she said. It was Snyde here doing these things. Old fears surely, and old dislikes, surfacing as nightmare images . . . Was it the first light of dawn that made the chamber suddenly lurid and strange, and the motions of moles slow, and their voices drift away?

'Yes . . .' she whispered, that the livid nightmare moles might go away.

A mole came near and smiled a sneer, and Fieldfare knew it was Bantam who spoke to her. Then Bantam was gone, or her body was, for the voice lingered on, encircling Fieldfare's mind.

'She has admitted the Stone to her heart; what others are there now?' It was Bantam's voice, somewhere, drifting, far, far away, and near.

And Fieldfare, taken to the very depths of her pain, thought, most strangely, that Bantam was a pup once, she was, she must have been. And Fieldfare remembered then her first birthing, and the pain, like this pain, and how Chater had been there, right there.

'It'll end and you'll forget it,' he had said, in that way of his. Field-

133

fare smiled, for until now, until this terrible moment in a void she never before knew existed, she *had* forgotten it.

'It did end, my dear,' she whispered. 'Oh, it did. And this will, yes it will.'

'Sister, yes?'

It was Bantam back again.

'Yes,' whispered Fieldfare with a beatific smile, 'oh yes.'

'You know the true way to the Stone?'

'Yes,' screamed out Fieldfare, like the rest, 'oh yes!'

For she did, with utter certainty she did, and it was not these moles' way, not ever, ever, ever.

'Then sleep,' said a nasal voice, 'sleep and be still.'

'This will end and I shall live,' whispered Fieldfare to herself, and then tiredness came, and blissful sleep approached, and the dangerous beginning of forgetting.

'Sleep,' lured that voice one last time. But Fieldfare did not, must not, would not, not here.

'I want only to sleep,' she had told Chater that long-distant beloved day when she first gave birth to pups.

'Not yet, my dear, not yet . . .'

'Not yet,' she whispered now again . . . and watched unseen as others fell asleep, and the males went to and fro among the punished moles, and knew that if Chater were here he would have found a way to escape, and if he could she could, and *would*!

'Now . . .' sighed a voice, and in her nightmare images came that preceded any birth, painful or otherwise. Vile images of moles mating. Bantam? Snyde? The one mounted by the crook-backed other. And then more, the dark-furred moles, mounting, taking, punishing in this chamber of dawning acquiescence and just punishment.

'Yes!' screamed out Bantam, somewhere into Snyde's filthy extenuated sigh.

A talon on Fieldfare's flank, lingering and exploratory. A male face staring.

'Too old this one to bother with, too fat for me . . .' and the talons let her be, and the voices, sneering, drifted off.

Too old! Too fat! Could Fieldfare laugh madly to herself? It seemed she did. And she was glad of this rejection, for fearful though she was, and tired beyond words though she felt, it made her feel that never in her life had she ever felt more herself, never ever had she felt the value of life so much. Never had she felt so undaunted.

'Chater, my beloved,' she said to him she loved so much, addressing him as she sometimes did as if he were there at her flank, 'I'm coming home to you even if it kills me getting out of here!' And then a great black cloud of sleep mounted before her eyes, all dark, all forgetting; and whispering an ecstatic 'Yes!' in case any guards were listening and might doubt the nature of her faith, she slept.

Chapter Twelve

'Where is Fieldfare?' said Chater, as calmly as he could.

Then, 'Where is she?' he roared.

And then: 'If harm's come to her in my absence, if . . .' he threatened.

'We don't know,' said Drubbins, 'because only with your return have we discovered she's missing. *If* she's missing. She could have gone visiting friends or kin in your absence. She could—'

'Fieldfare is *always* here when I get back. She knows when I'm coming, as surely as a tree knows when it's leafing. As for friends and kin, she'd have left word for me.'

'Well, mole,' said Drubbins, who had gathered with several others at Chater's summons in his burrow on news of Fieldfare's disappearance, 'she'll not be far, for I saw her myself only three days ago.'

Chater, Maple and Whillan had returned from their expedition to Rollright only that morning, and in Stour's absence somewhere deep in the Library, delivered to Drubbins a brief account of their alarming discoveries, before Chater had gone to his tunnels and found that his beloved Fieldfare was absent. His search for her had soon developed into a hunt, and Stour had been sent for urgently at the library.

'Whillan here has been down to Rolls and Rhymes where his mother is,' said Chater, 'and reports her seeing Fieldfare the day before yesterday, so she can't be far. But I've just heard from a mole I packed off down to Barrow Vale that she's not been seen there for days past.

'All *he* could talk about was news of a Meeting being called by the Marshenders, of all moles. That's all I need at a time like this and bearing in mind what we heard about in Rollright! Where can she be? I'll not be answerable for what I do if she's been harmed, and bugger Stour's calls for peace and tranquillity.'

Chater's voice had risen, and he looked decidedly shaken for a mole who was normally well in control of himself and others, and who had just carried through a most dangerous mission with Maple and Whillan.

'Chater!' said Drubbins sharply, 'calm down and be quiet. Raising

136

your voice and threatening others will help nomole. You've just trekked back to Duncton from Rollright in only three days, barely stopping for sleep, and you're tired. Fieldfare's unlikely to have gone far and there'll be a simple explanation—'

'You don't understand,' said Chater more calmly. 'I *know* my Fieldfare. Something's wrong, very wrong, and she may need help. I was uneasy about going off to Rollright immediately like that, for she's a mole likes to natter and talk things through and I never gave her the chance. She was probably worried by things the Master said, and worrying herself sick about me, though time and again I've told her not to fret because I can look after myself. Now she's gone and done something she wouldn't normally and she's in trouble, and we've got to . . . we must . . .'

'We must think,' said a clear voice, 'and think carefully.'

It was Stour, come into the chamber where they had gathered with old Pumpkin, the mole who had tracked him down to some obscure part of the Library, and brought him as quickly as he could over the surface to Fieldfare's and Chater's tunnels.

'Now,' said Stour, quickly taking control of the gathering, 'if there's a simple explanation for what's happened to her then she'll reappear soon enough and nomole will be the worse off, except for you, Chater, and your frayed nerves. But if she's in trouble—'

'She *is* in trouble,' said Chater.

'Then if she's in trouble we will get nowhere by rushing about. There'll be an explanation, and it will be one we can find evidence for. *Then* we can act. Now, who was the last mole to see her?'

'It was Privet, but two days ago, at noon, and briefly,' said Whillan. 'I've just come from there and . . .' and Whillan reported the brief exchange that Fieldfare and Privet had had, concluding, 'the strange thing was that my mother wasn't in the mood for talking, either today, or two days ago to Fieldfare, by the sound of it. She's so involved with work in Rolls and Rhymes and with helping Keeper Husk it is almost as if she didn't want to know. But I don't think she can tell us more anyway.'

'Did she say if Fieldfare said anything special to her, about what she was doing, or . . . ?' began Chater.

'She said that Fieldfare wanted to talk about something the Master had said . . . but I don't know what. My mother said they had not talked for more than a few moments, which was about as long as she gave me!'

'Hmmph!' exclaimed Stour. 'We'll not get much more from her,

137

though I think it would be sensible if one of us went down and talked to her again. Perhaps you, Drubbins . . . Now I know of only one unusual thing in the past few days and that's what Drubbins here saw the same day as Fieldfare was last seen.'

'Aye,' said Drubbins. 'I saw a senior brother up on the south-eastern pastures, and saw three moles, all Newborns by the look of them, come upslope from the cross-under and then head off towards the Marsh End. They even greeted me, as a matter of fact.'

'And . . . ?' said Chater impatiently.

Drubbins shrugged.

'They were male, dark, humourless: Newborns to a mole. What more can I say? I was collecting husks of scentless mayweed at the time and had better things to do than interrogate Newborns. Not a task I'd be much good at anyway.'

'Anything else?' said Stour, looking round at them all. He was a mole who seemed almost to blossom and lose years off his known age in a crisis. These molemonths past he was proving himself as a leader of the system, as well as the Library.

'About Newborns?' said Drubbins. 'Well, there's a report that a Meeting has been called by the Marshenders down in Barrow Vale in a day or two.'

'It does seem that the Newborns have suddenly become active again,' said Stour, 'and it does seem too that Fieldfare disappeared at about the time they became active, doesn't it? Though that hardly constitutes evidence for anything.'

'It does suggest that the Marsh End might be worth a visit,' growled Maple, quietly. 'If Fieldfare is in trouble of some sort then that surely is the only place where mole might conceivably harm her. But of course if it's predator that's hurt her, owl perhaps or fox, or if she's been hassled by weasels, then surely other moles would have heard her cries?'

Stour nodded seriously. Duncton moles rarely had trouble with predators, for their tunnels were hard to get at, and their surface routes so organized that they were protected by overhangs of under-growth and fallen branches, and where they were exposed there were always escape routes nearby into tunnels below. But then . . . *that* thought did not bear thinking of.

'If there is to be a Meeting in Barrow Vale summoned by the Newborns,' said Drubbins, 'then it would be only right for us at least to go down to it, Stour. Also, we may more easily hear word there of Fieldfare, than wandering round the system asking moles.'

'Yes, and what is more,' added Stour himself, 'such a Meeting might be a very good time for others of us to visit the Marsh End, which will be less watched over by the Newborns than it normally might be.'

A thought which made Chater leap to his paws, proclaiming this the best idea yet, and he'd set off right away, and by the Stone he'd clobber anymole Newborn bastard who had so much as—

'Chater!' said Stour warningly. 'Chater! Rushing about will achieve nothing. If Fieldfare's disappearance *has* got something to do with the Newborns, and your expedition to Rollright produced some new information, then it might help us all to know what the three of you discovered. The more facts we have the better.'

'It won't have much to do with Fieldfare, will it?' said Chater impatiently. 'Since Rollright's there and Fieldfare's *here*.'

'But it might,' said Whillan suddenly and very firmly, stancing forward and staring around at each of them.

Stour looked at him with interest since he had not seen him since the expedition to Rollright. He saw immediately that there was a hint of new confidence about the young mole, which did not surprise him since ventures and expeditions beyond the system usually changed a mole.

'Perhaps you can tell us briefly what you discovered,' said Stour evenly.

'A good idea,' said Maple, 'since Chater's all topsy in his mind and Whillan here did well, *very* well.'

'Well, make it brief, mole,' said Chater indifferently, 'and perhaps then we can get on with finding my Fieldfare.'

'I will,' said Whillan with a smile, 'and the more I think about it, the more certain I am that the Newborns hold the secret of what's happened to Fieldfare . . .'

He paused, looked at them all, furrowed his brow seriously for a moment as he decided on the best way to tell his tale, and then, without more ado, began . . .

The three moles had set off for Rollright two days after the secret meeting with Stour. They had gone at dusk since the initial part of the journey, through the cross-under and thence along the edge of the roaring owl way, was best done in the obscurity of half-light when daytime predators were already gorged and somnolent, and night-time predators only just beginning to become alert.

Chater led the way, since the northward journey to Rollright was well known to him, and curbed the inclination of Maple and Whillan to go too fast in their eagerness to get to their destination.

'A journeymole learns early on that you start at the same pace you want to finish, for that's the quickest and safest way to get there. No good hurrying at the start, for you'll grow tired and slow down towards the end, and get dangerously careless too . . .'

They journeyed for four days before finding themselves beginning to ascend towards the higher, drier ground which leads up to that northward-facing stretch of sandstone on which the famous Rollright Circle of Stones stands.

Whillan had heard of it so many times, and of the moles who had passed this way before him on historic journeys to the north – and others who had returned and paused at Rollright before pressing on back to their beloved Duncton Wood – that he felt mounting excitement as they arrived at the first outlying tunnels of the system.

''Tis my habit to head straight for the Whispering Stoats,' said Chater, calm before Whillan's excitement, easy in the shadow of Maple's brooding strength and purpose.

'You'll both know that the Whispering Stoats are a group of Stones that rise a little to the south of the Circle itself, and a place where moles gather and gossip. A good place to get information about what's going on, seeing as it's a meeting place as Barrow Vale is in our own system.'

'But before we go a step further, come out on to the surface and mark well where we are, and the different ways we might get here, for if there's trouble and we get separated we'd best agree to have a meeting point. Now, 'tis not far off the moon's full wane – three nights at most – and if we're lost to each other that's the night we'll meet back here, and the following dawn is when whichever of us are here should leave to take our tidings back to the Master Librarian in Duncton Wood.'

This decided, and after each had had a good look about, and marked how a dead elm rose not far off the entrance to that part, they went below again, and continued on their way to the fabled Stoats.

The more the tunnels rose upslope, and the nearer they got to the system proper, the slower Chater went, snouting ahead, pausing to listen, staring down side tunnels.

'Danger?' whispered Maple.

Chater shook his head. 'Unease,' he said. 'Never did like Rollright overmuch – 'tis a second-rate sort of place compared to our own, but it's more than that makes me dubious. There's an untoward scent in the air which was not here in late August when I was last here. Stick close, stay watchful . . .' And on they went.

Certainly Whillan was watchful and proceeded as cautiously as his older and more experienced companions, but the truth was he could scent nothing but dry air, and hear little but the hiss of autumn wind across high open ground above, to displace the natural curiosity and youthful sense of adventure that had been with him for days past. As for Duncton, its cares and memory seemed a lifetime away.

It was not long before Chater, who knew the tunnels well, turned right and left and then left again – pausing each time to ensure the others observed the way he had gone – and surfaced suddenly into a small copse of mixed oak and ash. It was coming on to dusk, and he led them without a word through the undergrowth to some bramble cover where he stanced down.

'We'll pause here awhile to watch and listen; no good blundering about yet. But I like it not. There's a foul stench in Rollright and it reminds me somewhat of what I sensed at Cuddesdon . . .'

Whillan, who had always thought his snout was good, sniffled about but could not scent a thing, but since the other two were keeping quiet, and since he had the sense not to contradict Chater, he kept quiet himself. All, no doubt, would become plain enough.

Yet as dusk deepened, and nothing happened, his curiosity overcame his caution and he asked, 'Where's the Rollright Circle from here?'

Chater nodded north-westward and said, 'Takes no more than a few minutes. As for the Stoats . . . follow me, for there's nomole about at the moment and it's a chance to get nearer.'

Chater led them forward across a grassy way that held the sweet-sickly scent of two-foots, and thence over a small rise, until there, ahead of them, leaning hugely into each other, was a triptych of Stones beneath which was a shadowed secret place of bare earth.

'In the old days moles met there to seek a blessing before going on up to the Circle,' said Chater, 'and this was the spot where the Stone Mole himself once paused before he began his ministry, first at Rollright and thence to so many systems north of here until at last . . .'

But whether he stopped because they all knew the outcome of that holy ministry of moledom, or because he heard the approach of mole before the other two, Whillan did not know, but stop he did, and tense, and then signal them both to lie flat and watch.

Five moles came, a mixture of males and females, silent as the approaching night, close to each other as sibling young threatened by

141

a predator. They passed the hidden watchers without a word and went straight in among the Stoats, and there whispered nervous prayers whose implications were all too plain: help us, Stone, help us now . . .

The three moles listened for a time and then, after a hurried consultation, agreed that Maple would go forward and greet the moles in the hope of learning something of the state of things at Rollright. He would make a little noise so they heard his coming and would strive to seem as unintimidating as he could.

Out into the now starlit night he went, humming quietly in a cheerful way – a move which silenced the moles among the Stoats and had them turning to face him from the shadows there.

'Greetings,' he called out, his deep voice reverberating among the fissures and chasms between the Stoats, and then echoing into the whispers that gave the place its name.

The response was as sudden as it was startling, for there was a short cry of alarm from one of them and then they all scattered out of the shadows into the night, one of them almost running into where Whillan stanced, and then all back northward towards the Circle itself.

At which Chater looked around in alarm, started forward quickly, hauling Whillan with him, and joined Maple beneath the looming Stones.

'Scent the air!' said Chater urgently to Whillan.

'Aye,' growled Maple, ''tis sickening to be within . . .'

And Whillan scented, and looked about, and his eyes widened.

'It is the stench of fear,' he whispered, horror-struck. For there it was, palpable, thick, all about, heavy on the air where those poor moles had been. No sooner had Whillan said it than he heard, as the others did, cries and shouts of fear from the direction in which the five had run.

'They're in trouble,' said Maple, taking sudden and instinctive command. 'We've frightened those moles into trouble. Come, they may need our aid.'

At which Whillan, who though by now strong enough to wield a tough talon had never been near a serious fight in his life, found himself swept along upslope towards the Circle with Maple and Chater, to help the frightened moles they might unwittingly have driven into danger.

'Slow down!' rasped Chater from behind as they neared the Stones, but Maple did not need to be told. The great Stones of the Circle loomed ahead of them and he came to a smooth stop in their shadow, holding out a paw to make sure that Whillan did not go charging past in his haste. Then signalling them both to lay low and keep quiet, he went forward to investigate and disappeared from view.

Moments later he was back, even as they heard renewed cries of moles in fear somewhere within the Circle itself.

'The ones we saw are being arraigned by a whole group of moles,' he said urgently.

'Dark, male, cold-eyed, smiling?' said Chater.

'Not smiling,' said Maple, 'but all the rest. Newborns! There's ten or fifteen of them.'

'Too many for us to take on,' said Chater as a deep and terrible ritualistic shout came up from the Circle.

'I'm not so sure,' said Maple, stancing up as he heard more cries of 'No! We didn't mean . . .' and 'Please . . .' He continued, 'They look tough enough but I've a feeling they'd not stance up to us if we were bold enough. And we did get them into this trouble.' He looked dubiously at Whillan. 'We'll need you, lad, but for Stone's sake say nothing, and do nothing but look confident. Stay half a pace behind me at all times. Do you think you can do that?'

Whillan gulped, his heart beating violently in his chest, which was already heaving from their run to reach the Circle. Then he heard another pitiful cry, looked at strong Maple and confident Chater, and his fears left him and his courage came.

'I'll not let you down,' he said firmly.

'Right then,' said Maple powerfully, 'let's sort this little problem out . . .'

With that the three of them, with Chater to the right, Whillan to the left, and Maple huge and menacing between them, broke through the shadows at the edge of the Circle and into the moonlit sward in its centre.

The tallest Stone in Rollright, and the circle's natural focal point, rises on the northern edge of the circle, and round one side of it there was a cluster of dark male moles, their backs to where Maple had led the three out. The moles were chanting in a guttural rhythm, their paws keeping grim time with the chant as, almost imperceptibly, they moved steadily forward into an ever tighter mass, each more eager than the next to get at what lay in their centre.

But what they were intending, and what was in their midst, was not immediately clear to the three Duncton moles since their view was obstructed, nor could they see any sign of the five moles whose cries they had heard earlier; Maple looked round at Chater in puzzle-

143

ment. It was now probably but a matter of moments before they were spotted and the thought had occurred to him that they could still retreat back into the shadows, their coming and going never seen, and their presence in the system still unknown.

But then Whillan, staring intently at what seemed at first no more than a ritual by the Stone, suddenly hunched forward tensely, with a look of mounting horror on his face. Then he urgently touched Maple's flank, and when the great mole turned to him, he said, 'Listen!' in an angry voice.

They turned back to the massed and closing throng of Newborn moles whose chant grew suddenly louder and more urgent, their movements co-ordinated. The stamping feet were timed now with the sinister in and out and in again of talon thrusts, and the total effect was so evil that it made the fur on their backs rise sickeningly.

They listened as Whillan had bid them do, and slowly, from out of the darkness of that mass, from beyond its rhythmic vileness, each of them heard more and more clearly a sickening, gasping, rasping sound, muted yet mortal, a croaking, a choking, a dying of moles.

'They're being crushed!' said Whillan, even as Maple, also realizing that they were witnessing what seemed the ritual murder of harmless frightened moles – though so thickly massed were the Newborns that not one of their victims could actually be seen – rose up and rushed forward towards the frightening group.

For a moment Whillan and Chater were left behind, their horror replaced by alarm at the sight of Maple seeming to seek to attack so large a mass of moles all at once. Even so, after a moment's pause, and without concern for their own safety, they followed Maple across the clearing.

But as they caught him up at what seemed the very instant before his massive risen talons descended on the broad strong back of the nearest chanting mole – the chant was now a roar, the stamping now a rage, the in-out-in of the talons now a brutal act – he delivered not a death blow but a deafening, frightening, all-powerful roar.

'In the name of the Stone,' he cried, his voice even stronger than their chant, 'cease!'

For a few moments more the chant went on, moments in which Maple turned swiftly to right and left as if to make sure that Whillan and Chater were boldly at his flanks, and then the moles faltered, and the rhythm of the stamping and thrusting broke. Then the throng began to turn away and break up, some one way, some another, shouting, questioning, wondering, and Maple, maintaining his advantage of surprise, moved forward among the last rank of them, their backs still half to him as they struggled to sort themselves out and see from where the commanding shout had come.

Then even as the first of them managed to turn at last in the awkward space they themselves had created, and others at the side fell away in surprise and alarm, Maple reached forward to right and left and bodily pulled moles away and forced his way in amongst them.

At his flanks Whillan and Chater found themselves doing the same thing, the anger of the moment and the confidence engendered by Maple's leadership giving them not only courage but, it seemed, strength far beyond their normal measure. With grunts and muted roars they routed the Newborn moles aside to right and left without a single talon thrust, and so powerfully and impressively that the Newborns were too taken aback to strike a single blow in return, but fell away, and stared, and did not move.

As the last of them were thrust aside a terrible sight met the eyes of the three moles, made worse by the luridness of the moonlight that cast pale sepulchral shadows all about. The five moles they had seen earlier were there, turned, hunched down, huddled and terribly entwined one on another, the cause of the sounds they had made all too plain. The nearest was turned towards them, his mouth open in a ghastly cry of silent agony before his body spasmed and a gasping, throttled sound came from his throat. Beneath him another lay, the moonlight picking out the white froth that bubbled from his half-smashed snout. A third was crushed upright against the Stone, paws spread out above his head, which arced up towards the sky in mute appeal for help. Two more there must have been, buried somewhere in the paws and rumps and bent bodies of the first three. One of these, perhaps the least harmed of them all, was struggling to free himself and swearing in a youthful high-pitched voice.

'Hold *him*!' roared Maple, pushing Whillan towards one of the nearest of the silent Newborns. 'And *him*, Chater, I want to talk to *him*!' Without questioning Maple's order Whillan and Chater moved forward to grab the two moles he had pointed at. The others, staring at Maple in growing alarm and fear as if he was the very spirit of an angry Stone come alive amongst them, began to turn and flee. This Maple must have seen would happen and so wanted to hold one or two for questioning. His earlier guess had been right: the Newborns might look tough, but threatened as they now felt themselves to be, and utterly routed, their only thought was to turn and flee, leaving their companions behind without a further thought.

145

The two secure, Maple went closer to the half-dead moles and gently reached out to help the nearest of them. He had turned and slumped forward, his head low, as he struggled to catch his breath again. But when Maple touched him he managed to raise his head and whisper in a gasping, croaking way, 'The others, help them. I'm all right. I'm—' but more he could not say.

He eased himself forward and Maple went to the next, pulling them one by one free of each other, until four of the five were breathlessly struggling to recover themselves, the youthful one now helping the others as best he could. But the fifth, he who stanced against the Stone, moved not at all, until the one nearest him had stumbled away. Then, slowly, terribly, his eyes staring sightlessly in the night sky above to which he had appealed too late, he fell limply forward to where Maple caught him and lowered him to the ground.

The great mole turned silently to his two friends, a look of shock and grief on his face, and mutely shook his head. The mole was dead.

There was a curious mix of gratitude and awe on the faces of the recovering moles. One reached a paw forward as if for balance; Maple grasped it, and thus supported, the mole looked up at him, and then in turn at Chater and Whillan before turning back to Maple again.

But it was the youngest one, who was about Whillan's age but thin and hunted-looking, who spoke.

'You are Rooster of Bleaklow Moor!' he said, awe and gratitude in his voice.

Whatever any of them might have expected the mole to say, this was not it.

'Nay, mole, my name is—' began Maple before Chater suddenly interrupted him.

'We must leave here!' he said. 'If those others come back, cowards that they are, they'll bring many more with them, and we'll not be able to pull this same ruse twice.'

'Aye,' said Maple, turning to the mole Whillan held captive and subdued, though in truth the mole was as big if not bigger than himself.

'You!' said Maple, 'what's this all about, eh? What's this been *for*?'

The mole looked slowly up at him, his eyes curiously blank.

'Rooster is real?' he whispered. 'Rooster is here?'

Rooster again!

'Yes,' said Whillan suddenly, ''tis Rooster you face now, mole!'

At that the mole whom Chater held said, 'It is a lie, it was a lie.'

Is? Was? Before any of them had time to ask what he meant the

146

first to whom they had spoken said, 'This massing was a fitting punishment for what they did. Moles of the truth should not be disturbed at their night-time worship. They broke the curfew and had been warned.' He spoke with subdued outrage in his voice, but all the time stared at Maple with a look in his eyes that could only be described as reluctant belief.

'They'll not talk, Rooster,' said the recovered Rollright mole, 'they never talk but in rules and proscribings. You might as well talk to wormless ground as to them. Except—'

'We do not kill moles, it is against our creed,' said the Newborn, quite unrepentant, and not showing much sign of fear. 'We punish through the massing. It is your own foul-bodied crush that kills yourselves. We did not touch *him* with a single talon!' He was straining against Whillan's hold as he pointed to the dead mole. Then he added, with contempt in his voice, 'He killed himself with your help!'

'We must get out of here,' said Chater urgently. 'Let's lose these bastards now.'

'Aye,' said Maple, coldly. Then he grabbed the one Whillan held and lifted him off the ground. 'Tell them Rooster's come if you like, and tell them there's more where he came from, many more. Now get out of here . . .' With that he hurled him bodily away.

'And you!' said Chater in disgust, pushing the one he held after the first. Both scrambled up, stared one last time, and were gone.

'That was well said, Whillan!' said Chater with a wink and a quick grin at them both. 'Rooster indeed! You're quicker-thinking than me! Now, what's the way out of here?'

'I'll show you,' said the bright youngster with the thin face.

'Right,' said Chater, taking overall command once more, 'lead off sharpish. This kind of work is not just a matter of knowing where and when to turn up, you need to know when to scarper too. What's your name, mole?'

'Fiddler,' was the reply, and off he set.

This extraordinary and frightening incident, early though it was in Whillan's account of the venture to Rollright, was the most dramatic and telling of all the events and discoveries of their three-day stay in that subdued system.

But before Whillan's account concluded with the rest of what they discovered of the mysterious Rooster, Stour interrupted him; 'This "massing", as they call it, was something they had done before?'

'Yes,' said Whillan, 'mole after mole told us about it. The rules of

147

their belief in the Stone, if it can be truly called that, say they cannot themselves kill a mole *with their own paws*. But moles who are deemed to blaspheme may be *punished even unto death*. By performing the kind of massing we witnessed they can claim that the victims effectively killed themselves . . . It needed only a few massings, always of three or more moles, to subdue the Rollright moles. As for Rooster—'

'Aye, mole, but more of him later,' said Stour. 'You have told us enough now for me to think it a matter of urgency that we satisfy ourselves what has happened to Fieldfare, and confirm at least that she is not in the Marsh End. For if she is . . .'

'And if she has been "massed", Stour?' said Chater bitterly. 'Where does that put your ideas of peaceful resistance then?'

'It changes them not a bit, Chater,' said Stour sternly. 'There will never be peace, never be Silence, for moles who match talon thrust with talon thrust, and killing with killing. Now, Drubbins and myself will hurry down to Barrow Vale in response to the report that there is to be a Meeting. If so, and if it has been invoked by this Chervil and the Newborn moles then we shall ensure that as many of *them* attend as can before the Meeting starts. That will be your opportunity to see what you may find in the Marsh End.'

'I would prefer to go in there now,' said Chater, 'for if Fieldfare's there she'll be in danger – she's sure to say or do something that's seen as blasphemy. She's a mole who always speaks her mind.'

'No, Chater, give the Master and Drubbins a start before we leave,' said Maple, 'what he says makes sense.'

'Well . . .' growled Chater miserably.

'And you come with us, Whillan,' said Stour. 'We may have need of a younger mole.'

At which the two older moles and Whillan turned off downslope to the north-west for Barrow Vale, and the other two slowly made their way northward, to reach the edge of the Marsh End and wait until a little time had passed, and they judged it right to go further on, and try to find out what had happened to Fieldfare if they could.

Chapter Thirteen

Privet's work with Keeper Husk had soon settled into the companionable routine of two moles who shared a passion for mediaeval texts and molish tales, and for whom 'working' at such things was a continual round of enjoyable study and enriching conversation.

Husk had accepted with glad grace the text of tales Privet had brought with her, the more so when he learned that many of them were gleanings from tales that Cobbett himself had told her.

Some of the old rivalry between himself and Cobbett, as well as Stour, might still survive, but he was obviously pleased, even so late in life, to have this addition from the North to his Collection, and one touched by the knowledge of so old a friend.

Had the ages of Privet and Husk not been so disparate, and their inclinations so clearly celibate, others might almost have thought them mates, so much together were they, and so lacking in interest in the world beyond Rolls, Rhymes and Tales. Indeed, so suddenly and completely absorbed was Privet with her new-found task that a mole might almost have thought that she was escaping from something.

As it was, Husk continued his disconcerting habit of sleeping when and where he felt like it – usually for only short stretches of time and with a text or folio clutched in his paws – while Privet delved a small uncluttered burrow near the only serviceable entrance into the tunnels, and retired there at night, usually after a lengthy conversation with the old mole which often ended with him telling a tale or two.

As for their respective tasks, each kept to their agreement in meeting the other's needs. Privet was allowed to work her way through the texts as best she could, separating out those she felt should be preserved in the Main Library. Initially she approached Husk formally over each one she wished to remove, but this so upset him, and provoked such lengthy and indecisive discussion of the relative merits of one text against another (which he could not quickly find) that both agreed it best she consulted him no more.

The only time she left Husk and ventured over to the Main Library was soon after she started, when she told the Master what she was about, and asked that Pumpkin or some other aide might come routinely and take the rescued texts across-slope to safer sanctuary in the Library.

'Pumpkin it shall be,' said Stour immediately. 'As for the relationship of Husk to me . . .' (for Privet had mentioned Husk's claim, though without reference to Fat Pansy) '. . . it was all a long time ago. He has his task and I have mine.'

At first Pumpkin had come only sporadically, but it was not long before Privet had got herself into an efficient routine, and he came daily to see her to remove texts, and found another aide to help as well. But as time went on they rarely saw her, for it seemed she wished to get on with her task uninterrupted and chose to leave what texts were ready for collection set apart for them near the tunnel entrance.

As for Husk's work with scribing tales, Privet kept her side of the bargain she had made, and for a time each morning and afternoon joined Husk in his inner chamber, and helped him as best she could. It soon became obvious to her that the 'task' that he wished her to do regarding his work was very different from the task she felt sure she should be doing, whose nature put her into something of a quandary. For it seemed that so far as his Book of Tales was concerned Husk had been too close to it for too long and had lost his judgement of what should be included, or more particularly, of what should be taken out.

The mystery of the discarded and scored-out folios about his scribing place, and the seeming absence of completed and corrected work was soon sadly resolved. From what he told her and what she observed it seemed that he had long since completed his great work, in which, successively, he had retold the great tales of moledom, extracting them in much the way that Privet had observed Cobbett do in Beechenhill, from the hundreds of tales in his great Collection, made originally by his father, his own work being based on the collecting rather than scholarly zeal of *his* father.

The reason why this great Collection was not in the Main Library was one of inertia – arising from the difficulty of moving it – combined, Privet suspected, with stubbornness on all sides arising from the argument originating over Fat Pansy.

Quite when Husk had completed his 'book' – it was less a book than a portfolio of tales – Privet could not find out, but certainly a long time before. However, he himself had not judged it complete, feeling there was too much in and that before he declared it satisfactorily done, and showed it to other moles, he must excise parts to make it ever more simple, more direct, more 'true', whatever that might mean.

Privet had arrived at the end of this second stage of his self-appointed task in time only to see the ruins of the great work that had once been – literal ruins, in the sense that the discarded material was all about in the tunnels, or if it was retained in the book itself, was now in the form of scored and broken folios.

It was this hotchpotch of a thing, hardly book at all, over which the now blind Husk huddled painfully every day, and had never shown to anymole, and would not show to her. She saw its battered birch-bark covers, white and peeling, and its crumbling crazy contents, from a distance, but never more than that; and even when he left it on his dais and went up to the surface to groom, and she might have looked at it if she had cared to, it was understood that she would not, and this was a trust she would have preferred to die before betraying.

Husk's obsessive work now seemed to be but a process of dimin-ution whose inevitable end was that sooner than later there would be no text left at all of what might once have been moledom's greatest book of tales.

The discards, as Husk himself called them, were another matter, and scholar and librarian that she was, once she realized their possible importance she felt that by rejecting them Husk had no further claim on them. At first she had barely looked at them, for it was Husk's grubby habit, particularly on colder nights, and at even colder dawns, to use these crumpled and broken discards as nesting material into which he snuggled down to keep his scraggy old body warm.

The day when she realized these were rather more than mere scraps was when she discovered that he had been sleeping for several days on what, when she looked more closely at it, turned out to have been (at one time at least) the very first folios of his great work. What caught her eye and talon as she followed his scribing down the folios, was a tale whose title was, 'The First Tale of Balagan, and how all moles began'. It was scribed more neatly and boldly than other things of Husk's she had seen, and she concluded he had scribed it many, many years before.

The tale began, 'There was a mighty Stone that stood in the eternal silence that was before mole began. This was the primal Stone, in which all life and all things were. This was the Stone out of which Balagan sought to find a way.

'One day the silence of eternity was broken by the sound of the Stone cracking, and at first the tip of a talon, then more talons, then a paw, and then a mole's arm, struggled out of the Stone, and there was a panting, and a heaving, and groaning and roaring and thunder was born, which was Balagan's voice; and lightning was born, which was Balagan's eyes; and the wind was born, which was Balagan's breath.'

At this point the first folio ended, and she had to scrabble round in the muck and filth of Husk's chamber to find the next. It continued, 'Then was a storm where the primal Stone had stood and Silence was no more . . .' and then was Privet carried away into the oldest Tale of them all, which is of the coming of Balagan the First Mole, and how moledom was made, and how its stones came to be, each of them fragments of the Primal Stone he cracked and broke in his desire to be free.

It was a long telling of a story she had heard, though in Peakish, when she was young. Yet skilled though her mother had been at such a story-telling, she recognized in Husk's account something more. The language he had used was not one of the local dialects in which most tales are recorded, but ordinary mole. There was something strong and simple in the way he told it that made her see that the tale was no mere fantasy, or way to occupy an idle hour, but a reminder, deep and true, of something of where all moles began, as fundamental to all their lives as the Primal Stone itself.

Why then had he discarded so much of the book he had made, including even this most fundamental of the tales of moledom? When she asked him, which she soon did, for Privet was not a mole to be surreptitious or indirect on matters involving library work, his explanations were reluctant and vague.

Balagan's story was too well known, he said, and anyway, he was dissatisfied with his telling of it. Then again, he said, when a mole tells a tale it is finally the gaps and silences between the words that mean most of all, for words themselves are but paltry unsatisfying things, which taken together rarely say what is in a mole's heart when he makes a telling to another.

'So I work at my Book of Tales to simplify them, and you can help me, my dear, by listening . . . This is not work to do alone.'

'But do you mind if I collect what you call the discards?' she asked him one day. 'It will make this place tidier for a start . . .'

'Collect them, if you must,' he said indifferently, 'but leave fresh folios out for me, for old and tired as I am, I scribe new things, or rather new versions of very old things! My scribing however becomes more arcane, meaningful perhaps only to me; but there we are, a mole must scribe what he can. As for whether another can make sense of it, well that I rather doubt. And there you can help me too, by going over what I scribe until I feel it is ready to put into what remains of my little book.'

In this way Privet's historic collaboration with Keeper Husk evolved into several tasks at once – rescuing his discards, which she kept separately in one of the chambers she had begun to clear of texts, re-scribing what he had scribed in a firmer hand, and listening when he felt it incumbent on her to scribe down what he said, just as he said it, and these tales too she carefully kept in folios, somewhere where he could not find them until she had gathered them together and created once more a text that might truly be called a Book of Tales. Some of her own work was in it, and all this she one day commanded Pumpkin to take to safety up in the main library.

So developed a relationship between two moles who spoke each other's language, and shared the same love of words and old texts. Two moles who seemed never to stop talking, one of all he knew, and the other of all she could learn. Was it some time then that he first told her of a long lost tale entitled 'The Sound of Silence'?

'It's here somewhere,' he would say vaguely. 'I'm sure it is . . .'

Above them, almost unseen – for now they rarely ventured forth from Husk's tunnels, and Pumpkin had learnt not to venture down into them except to collect the texts left by Privet at the entrance – September ended and blustery October began, and the days drew in. The tunnels grew gloomier, the air more dank, but as the rest of Duncton Wood prepared itself for winter Privet and Husk barely noticed it, working now together in that world of tales that had been Husk's alone for so long, and into whose endless tunnels, and eternal time, he had now welcomed Privet.

Yet removed though they seemed, and abstracted as Husk increasingly became in the throes of his solitary re-working and steady reduction of his text, Privet herself never quite lost sight of reality. As the days continued and the weather worsened, she could see that the old mole was visibly slowing. Sometimes he seemed unable to work at all; or, he was lost in some tale he had scribed before, weeping and laughing for moles whose lives he had made permanent between the folios of his Book, but whose record he now felt obliged to finally discard, muttering, 'To Silence, aye, to Silence it must go! No good, Privet, not this tale, not near the truth of it at all. Better that moles make their own tales you see, live their own tales, that's the thing; but I don't know . . . I just don't know any more!' And he stared at his ruined portfolio, closed the birch-bark covers on it and rested his weary paws for a long time, thinking.

'Perhaps tomorrow, my dear, we can delve at this some more, and make some sense of it, so that something useful's left,' he said at last. Then, more cheerfully, he added, 'Mind, I have something to scribe down, not a tale you know, but just a thought, a *thing*. So give me a clean folio and leave me be, and I'll do with it what I can. Dear me, what a to-do life seems when a mole gets to the end of it. All a big to-do about nothing much at all. Now, let me see . . . ha! That's a laugh! I'll never *see* again, and you know what, old Husk doesn't care a jot because he's got imagination to see with, and voice to speak with. That's all you need for tales, my dear, for a mole to listen, and time to make a telling. Such a to-do, and it's all so simple in the end. Now! Leave me, mole! Take away all these discards of mine before I sit on them or sleep on them or otherwise do something you'll disapprove of with them. I know, I know, you're a hoarder like my brother. A true librarian. But what would librarians say if the grubby moles who made the texts they love to hoard came ambling along their way? Eh? Ha ha ha!'

Then in mid-October Husk was taken ill, and grew incapable of any work at all, even the discarding of what little remained in his portfolio. Privet hardly left his flank, for she knew he was ailing and had come now to rely on her, and grew distressed if she was gone to the surface too long.

She managed to continue her sorting work – indeed she did more than formerly, because there was no work of his to do except some-times to scribe down tales he told in his delirium, strange tales of endings and beginnings, of beginnings and endings.

'Stone,' she prayed quietly as he slept, 'help him find peace and an end to his great task. Give him strength to take it to its conclusion . . .' For she sensed that near though he was to death he still did not himself feel his task was complete, and wanted to stay alive until it was.

'Shall I get Stour?' she said one day.

'No!' he said loudly. 'He'll only blather on about Fat Pansy like he did last time.'

She could not help smiling. 'Last time' was more than seventy years before. So many decades, such a waste . . .

'Did I tell you the story of Fat Pansy?' he whispered, turning pain-fully to her, his paw out to hers, his unseeing eyes upon her.

154

'Some of it,' she said.

'I'll tell you the rest then . . .'

But he never did, for it was that same day, that same time, that Privet heard mole sounds at the entrance to the tunnels and went out to investigate. It was Fieldfare, and for the first time since Privet had been in Duncton Wood she was not glad to see her friend or eager to talk. Even less so was she when Fieldfare went on about her worries about the things the Master had said at the secret meeting. Why, all *that* had long since fled Privet's mind, and now Husk was dying, and in his last days he had to be helped to find strength to complete his work. She could not have stopped, her mind was only on Husk and there seemed so little time.

But within three days of Fieldfare's visit, Husk had recovered somewhat and was even grumbling about wanting to get back to his scribing, and Privet was suddenly filled with a sense of guilt at having given her friend so little time. So much so that she could not bear the oppression of the tunnels any more and went up to the surface. It was morning, and misty, and the ground was wet with a heavy dew. But looking up Privet could see the mist adrift among the nearly leafless branches of the trees, and it held that pink warm light that suggested that the late autumn sun was trying to break through.

She watched the mist lighten all about, and autumn colours come to the branches and leaves above, and then to the surface of the Wood on the slopes above, where sun began to shine through hazily at last.

But downslope of her the mist was still thick, and resisting the warmth of the sun. Fieldfare had told her that at this time of year such mists as these lingered in the lower parts of the Wood and particularly about the Marsh End.

The day could be warm and bright in the High Wood whilst down there the chill mists lingered to catch at a mole's throat, while the day stayed gloomy, and dank. Privet stared that way, shivered with unease, and turned back down to the realities of tunnels she knew rather than a contemplation of tunnels she did not.

That same dawn Fieldfare awoke and knew that her resistance to the Newborns, which had been waning for days and nights past, was near its end. How hard she had fought the pressures of the Brothers' ministering in that chamber of subjugation, acquiescence, and death.

Her strategy of pretending that she agreed with what they said had finally failed, because *what* they said, to which she and others said, 'yes, oh yes' changed, oh it changed. What was right one hour was wrong the next; where cries of 'yes!' in response to a question were greeted by food and caresses one moment, they were ridiculed and punished the next, though the question was the same.

The tiredness grew, for though they were allowed to sleep they were woken at sleep's deepest point, and dragged with blows and smiles, shouts and caresses, back into this world of contradiction, where there was no right or wrong but what the Brothers said was right and wrong, however much it changed from one moment to the next.

'The Brothers are always right!' Fieldfare declared – still stubborn and clever enough to think that this nonsense might be the way to survive. But no! More blows.

'The true way to the Stone is right!' they said. Ah! Yes! The true way. Sleep, that would seem true enough. Escape from the images of Bantam, and the nightmare of snurtish Snyde, and Fieldfare unable to feel anything at all in the long days that shifted into nights, and nights that changed back to days in which the light was so bright, and hurt her heavy painful eyes and felt like talons thrust deep into them. Yes, no, yes, no, she would do anything and say anything if the Brothers would let her sleep. But doing, and saying, was not enough. She must *become*. Day, night, day – it was enough to break a mole, or drive her mad.

And that morning, when she woke, the light was dim and she thought that she was going blind. She peered, moved, expected a blow and none came; said yes, said no – no response. She peered, and saw the Brothers across the prone unconscious bodies of those others being punished with her.

The 'oohhnnn' hum was starting; Bantam was there, no sign of Snyde. Perhaps he had never been. The Brothers were beginning a chant to the Stone. She scented the air. Darkish, dankish, moistish, the scent of a Marsh End mist. Memories of puphood. Memories of a mole she had been before . . . *this*.

'I'm Fieldfare,' she said. 'I'm still *her* . . .'

'Oohhnn . . . oohhnnn . . . oohhnnn . . .' they went on, and Fieldfare remembered she had heard this ritual before. Up on the surface . . . no, in that other chamber. Yes. It went on a bit yet . . . on for long enough . . . yes! Oh yes!

'It goes on long enough for me to escape,' she said, whispering that heretical word 'escape' and feeling mortal fear for doing so. They would kill her if they knew she even thought it . . . would kill her if she tried . . . But dear Stone, they *were* killing her.

Then . . .

'Come on, my dear,' she said wearily to herself, 'it's really time you went home at last. Come on . . .'

Then Fieldfare did the bravest thing she ever did in all her life. She began, bit by slow bit, to the rhythm of that ritual chant from the far end of the chamber, to crawl unseen towards the nearest slipway up to the surface she had not seen for days. She knew that if she were once seen she would be dead, yet on she went.

As she reached the slipway, the air grew suddenly cooler, the light brighter yet grey, and she looked back in fear at where the Brothers were gathered in their chant. She could see Bantam facing her way, but her eyes were closed in prayer.

'Now!' said Fieldfare to herself. 'Now I *must* try!'

Then she stanced up on her shaky paws, pushed herself forward among the sleeping bodies of her fellow-victims of the massing, and reached the portal of the slipway.

But, too soon, she let panic overtake her and abandoning caution she noisily ran and scrabbled and pulled her way up the steep ungiving slipway, panicking the more when soil rolled back under her paws, and stones went down and her scrambling made more and more noise. Even as she reached the misty portal out into the real world the chanting stopped below, there was a cry, and she knew, dreadfully she knew, that she had been seen and pursuit of her had begun.

Out into thick white nothingness she went, utterly confused. Three steps and she could not even see the portal she had just left. Another and she was back at it, with the Brothers coming up . . .

She cried out in fear, turned, and ran towards the dark murky bole of a tree nearby, the only shape she could see. The dew was sopping at her paws, and with the cold air her mind began to clear, though she felt almost paralysed with fear.

'Find another tree ahead,' she told herself, desperate not to run back again towards her captors as she had momentarily before. She took a line on the next tree she could see and ran wildly to that.

'Follow his trail in the dew!' she heard them cry. '"*His* trail!"' Of course! This much she had discovered of the Newborns: they thought little of females – except Bantam, who might almost not be one at all – so little that an escape could only be a male.

'Well,' thought Fieldfare as she ran, 'first I was old, then I was fat, and now I'm male! What would Chater say? Oh Chater . . . I'm coming home!' This last was spoken aloud, as a gasp that ended as a sob.

'"Follow his trail in the dew,"' they had cried. She looked round and saw her trail could be easily seen. Behind she heard their angry pursuit and their hypocritical cries: 'Brother, be not afraid of us!'

She was a Brother too it seemed! But, oh, she was very much afraid. She veered into some undergrowth, knowing that it might obscure her trail better than plain leaves, and then when she saw the bole of another tree she ran up on to it and did her best to scramble round it and then off into a mess of brambles – all the better to break her trail. Again and again she did it, growing tired, trying to get a line upslope in the thickening mist, for upslope was safety.

Thickening mist! Colder air! But this must be downslope and away from safety; she dared to stop and listen, so far as she was able to for the sound of her own gasping breath. She could hear the Brothers chasing and crashing through the undergrowth. But though they got no nearer yet they veered no further off. It seemed a matter of time before they found her trail again. But which way? The mist billowed about her, now thick, now thin, so that the trees appeared and disappeared around her, and all was muted and strange. Then for a brief moment, the grey light above brightened and panic overcame her once more as she realized that she was only still free *because* of the mist. Once it lifted she would not stand a chance against her young male pursuers.

She controlled her panic, waited for the mist to thin again, stared along the ground to gauge the slope, and saw that it went upward more to her right paw than her left. She listened, heard nothing to the right, and more slowly now began to progress as silently as she could upslope.

Once she was moving again, and realized the mist was her ally and that the Brothers were not too close behind, she felt more calm. Slow and steady was the way, and not to think of getting caught. Creep away and hope the mist would not thin too fast; and hope that the Stone was with her now.

The Stone! How blessed did it seem, how precious to her now. She whispered for its help, went from the safety of one tree to the next, or from one bramble patch to another, looking behind to be sure that her trail, still clear enough in places, was broken here and there. Her breathing recovered something of itself, but with that came growing tiredness once again.

'Oh, oh, oh, I want to sleep,' she whispered to herself, turning right and then right again and realizing that for a moment she *had* slept and veered back the way she had come. The trees circled her about; she paused again; her pursuers cried out through the mist that they had her trail, and sounded suddenly near, so near.

'Here's his trail again! This way!'

It was a female voice: Sister Bantam's. Nothing could have put more fear or energy back into Fieldfare's failing paws. She stirred herself forward, desperately watching the ground ahead to be sure that it still was the upslope way, but she was tiring, and the roots across her path seemed now like great and awkward obstacles which caught at her and slowed her progress. The mist thickened once again, cooler, and she plunged on into it, on and on, the cries closer behind, her paws bloodied by thorns and brambles and rough roots, another tree ahead, help me Stone and—

Her heart seemed suddenly to stop.

The 'tree' turned into a Brother. Staring, waiting, and most terrible of all, smiling from out of the shining gloom.

'Sister!' he said, welcoming her back to his vile world.

She cried out in fear, turned, sought out the thickest of the mist in whatever direction it lay, and ran back into it, the wrong way she knew, and him chasing and others near all chasing, all nearer, coming from her right and left and from behind and she caught now with only the wrong direction in which to go.

Her breathing came in desperate gasps, her paws fell almost out of control ahead of her, her whole body ached, and when she heard them cry, 'She's just ahead,' she knew that not many moments of her liberty remained.

Not just physical liberty, but freedom of the mind as well. The freedom of which old Stour had spoken and which had troubled her so much. With their cries, with the sound of them just behind, with her final sliding, turning, hopeless steps she knew that nothing more was left. Fieldfare would be no more.

The mist loomed white and lighter above, a tree ahead seemed to fall towards her, and she cried out at last, cried out hopelessly. A mole, another Brother, another . . . Chater.

'Help me,' she gasped with her final breath before they came. 'Help me!'

Oh yes, oh . . .

'Oh Chater . . .' she whispered as she fell.

For the briefest of moments his paw touched her flank and then her face, gentle, warm, real, beloved. Then he looked past her with an expression on his face so frightening, so terrible, that it seemed a nightmare in itself.

She fell, and turned, and looked back where he stanced, his paws spread out to stop them coming on. She saw them stop, three and four, then five of them. Brothers, dark-furred, panting, a dark and angry mass. Then Bantam joined them, eyes staring out with hate.

'You!' she hissed, more than hatred in her eyes. Female to female, as if in seeking to escape she, Fieldfare, a female too, had affronted something especially deep in Bantam's corrupt imperious soul.

Yet they, and even Bantam, were all stopped as one by Chater's roar.

'You cannot . . .' Fieldfare tried to say to him, her brief moment of hope quite overcome by the sadness that he too would now be caught, and that it was she who had brought him here to this.

The mist thinned, the trees above caught sun, all poised in a long and silent moment of confrontation in the Wood. And then, the final horror, as a huge paw descended on her shoulder from behind, and she screamed and swung round and the mist began to turn to darkness before she saw looming as high above her as the trees it seemed, great Maple.

Huge Maple.

Towering, solid, oh bigger than a tree, darker than *their* dark, more terrible than their terror. Maple and Chater.

'Stance where you are, Fieldfare, and leave them to us,' he said.

'Fieldfare,' he had said. And then, 'Leave them to us . . .' and Fieldfare knew the rebirth of herself and all the possibility of life once more.

Maple passed her, stanced huge alongside Chater, and then together they charged, but slowly, powerfully, like storm clouds mounting in the sky. Beyond them Fieldfare watched the mass of Newborns break. She saw their shock and fear. The Stone had failed, was failing them, and they were afraid.

The mist thinned more, the nearly leafless trees found colour, the sky was pale and misty blue, and then downslope, through the wood, back into their rank mist the five Newborns fled. The last was Bantam, who turned with eyes narrowed and red, and hissed the single word as a threat to wither a mole's soul, 'You!' Then into the mists she too was gone.

Then Chater turned, reached out his paws to her as she reached out to him. Tears she did not shed. Fear she did not feel. Anger she did not speak. She felt only a mortal certainty.

'They must not be allowed to be,' she said. 'They are a sickness in our Wood. We must not . . .'

Then, wondering, Chater and Maple led her from that place.

Chapter Fourteen

The misty weather that had helped make Fieldfare's escape possible clung on mysteriously to Duncton Wood for three more days. Nights when the mists deepened – days when the sun broke through once more to glisten in the heavy dew among the old trees of the High Wood, whilst down in the Marsh End the mist stayed thick and the air cold and the Newborns, who knew some upset had occurred, dared not speak of it, but looked round sharply at the dark vague forms that shifted through the wood, and wondered what they were.

Long and ominous days of waiting, when leaves in the highest branches broke free and fell solitarily down, their sound clear in the hushed Wood, and blackbirds rustled wetly unseen and flew off no-mole knew where.

Evenings when the Newborns mustered through the chill mists to listen to the zealous prayers and plans of the Senior Brothers to bring a reformation to a system they saw as wayward; evenings when the apprehensive few in the Eastside and the High Wood wondered when, and how, the change they sensed would come.

It was during the morning of the fourth day after Fieldfare's safe return that the weather began to break. The trees of the High Wood stirred with a decisive wind, the mist shifted and was gone, and moles saw that autumn's colours had fled with it and left behind a dank, dull, pre-winter Wood that shook before the wind. At noon the wind veered and began to blow steadily from the north and those eerie, fearsome, unsettling sounds that come to the tunnels of Duncton Wood when such winds blow, began to come again. Throughout the Wood, moles of the old ways of the Stone and Newborns alike felt fretful and uneasy, and wondered whatmole it was who seemed to be trespassing malevolently at the portals of their tunnels.

''Tis only the wind.'

And so it was: the wind of destiny. For already a mole had hurried up to the High Wood from the Marsh End, male, dark-furred, a nameless messenger from Senior Brother Chervil to Master Librarian

Stour. Now, the message delivered, he was on the point of leaving.

'Tomorrow then, at noon,' he said. 'The Senior Brother will wish to know then whatmoles will be in the delegation you send.'

Stour, with Snyde expressionless at his side, nodded his understanding and acknowledgement, and confirmed that on the morrow he would come to Barrow Vale again.

'It is certain then?' persisted the Newborn messenger.

'As certain as this northern wind,' said the Master coldly.

Snyde watched the Newborn leave and frowned. 'He is insolent, Master Librarian, and yet you treat him with courtesy.'

Stour shrugged, his eyes alert, but said nothing.

'And you will do as this Newborn Chervil bids?' persisted Snyde, the ugly bones of his crooked back tight and sharp beneath his fur.

Stour shrugged again. 'Courtesy costs me nothing,' he said softly. 'Eh, Snyde? You are too quick to feel resentment, and always have been. A fault of yours, you know.'

'Yes, Master Librarian,' said Snyde bleakly.

Stour turned to him and Snyde did his best to hold his gaze, but eventually it slipped away to somewhere shadowy.

'Tell me, Deputy Master, what do you know of the Newborns? What do you feel for them?'

Snyde's eyes did not blink as they came back to the Master's and feigned honesty. 'Nothing, Master Librarian. Nothing at all. Nothing more than others who follow the old way. They are, perhaps, too . . . persistent.'

'Are you Newborn?' said Stour, his voice very, very quiet, and his gaze strong. To a worthy mole, who might have erred, the question offered a way of escape and restitution. But Snyde was not worthy, and nor was he honest, and nor could he tell that in that direct and open question the Master Librarian was giving him a chance.

He did not take it. Instead he affected a swift dismissive smile, his tongue flicked briefly at his mouth, he shifted his body uneasily, and said, 'No, Master, I am not.'

Stour stared at him a moment longer, smiled, and said, 'It is well then. Now, I wish to be alone.'

'And the delegation, Master Librarian?'

'What of it, Snyde?'

'What moles will form it? We must decide.'

'Only worthy moles, Deputy Master, only worthy ones.' As he climbed slowly up the slipway to the privacy of his study cell and gallery he added, 'But you of course must go.'

162

Unseen behind him Snyde watched him go, his face showing signs of concern and doubt. 'Me, Master Librarian? But we cannot both go and I thought—'

'You're right,' said Stour wearily, 'we cannot both go. Quite right.' Snyde's face relaxed into his habitual look of smug satisfaction. He stared at the shadows into which Stour had retreated.

'Yes, Master Librarian,' he whispered with the mock obedience of an arrogant mole. Then he told himself, 'One day I shall come and take back the texts you have filched and stored away up there, Dark Sound or no, and restore the holy rightful ones to a place where moles of the true way can study them. And it shall be me who cleanses moledom's greatest Library by directing the excision and destruction of the texts that blaspheme the holy Stone, and bring shame and ignominy in the Senior Brothers' eyes to this system of ours.'

So Snyde declared himself only to himself, before he slid away, his going watched from the gallery above by the Master, who shook his head sadly.

'Stone,' he said, 'pity him, be merciful to him, but spare us from him and guide me through the traps he and his like will set.'

After a long time, when he was sure Snyde was not coming back, Stour went back to the slipway, came quietly down, and found Sturne, his most trusted Keeper.

'Keeper Sturne, be kind enough to arrange for the aide Pumpkin to be found and sent to me.'

'He's off at Rolls and Rhymes, Master, though there's been little enough from there these few days past.'

'When he comes back then . . .'

'Aye, Master Librarian, I'll send a mole for him.' He turned and did it, and was back a few moments later.

'And Sturne, nothing more of this to . . . anymole.'

Sturne nodded, his face expressionless. 'The Deputy Master was here,' he said, with reference to nothing in particular. But then he added, 'I never do say anything about your business or your work to . . . anymole. Never did, never shall.'

'I know, Sturne. I know it well.' He came closer to Sturne, and most uncharacteristically reached out a paw and touched him. 'Mole, you know why I made him Deputy Master, and not yourself?'

'I can only guess, Master, I have only the comfort of guessing.'

Sturne, a thickset mole with a craggy face flecked with white fur, lowered his head a little.

'Guess,' said Stour.

163

'He is a greater scholar than I, Master, that's for sure. A brilliant scholar perhaps.'

'Guess,' said Stour again.

'He is younger than I and energetic. Such a mole may be needed for succession.'

Stour stared at him. 'Guess again, mole. Speak what is in your heart.'

'The better to watch him,' growled Sturne.

The faintest of smiles lit Stour's eyes. 'And why did you stay on and suffer his taunts and plaints? Eh, mole? You who—'

Sturne whispered, 'Guess, Master. Forgive me, but *you* guess now.'

Stour looked at where Sturne's great paw rested on the text at which he had been working, and then at the great Collection of texts of which he had been Keeper so long.

'You did it for love of these texts,' said Stour softly. 'Only for that.'

'They have been a comfort, Master,' said Sturne, much moved. He was quite unable to look at the Master.

'Mole,' said Stour gently, 'follow me now for I have something to show thee. Bring that text and talk loudly of it that others think it is for that we go up to my study cell.'

Sturne looked up at him in surprise and some bewilderment, but when he saw that Stour was already heading back up to his study cell he quickly followed.

They did not pause at the portal at the top of the slipway, but passed straight through it into the modest chamber, and went immediately across it towards the further portal that led as Sturne guessed, for he had never ventured there, into the deep recesses of the Master's private library. It was there the originals of moledom's oldest texts were kept. From there now came that dire wind-sound so many in the Library feared, a rush and a hiss, a dark whisper and a distant crying.

Stour stopped at this second portal and said, 'Say nothing to any-mole of what you shall see now, and what I shall tell thee. Remember that though certain others in the system will shortly know something of what I shall show thee, only one will understand it as well as yourself.'

'Privet?' said Sturne.

'Aye,' said the Master, 'Privet. She is a worthy mole. But none of these moles shall know that you know. Remember that, Sturne, and tell nomole. All must think that you are but subordinate to Deputy Keeper Snyde. But here, and now, I tell thee that you are my

164

appointed successor. You who have been loyal so long, must one day succeed me, and continue that work I have tried to do as best I might. This shall be your task, Keeper Sturne, and worthily will you do it.'

'But Master, you are . . .' faltered Sturne.

'. . . I am near my end. Or near a retreat from which I may not wish to return as Master Librarian. Today is an ending and a beginning, and our whole destiny is in doubt; a few must be entrusted with our future. For many moleyears I have foreseen and planned for what must begin with tomorrow's dawn, before the Newborns begin what I fear will be a destructive takeover of our Library and heritage.'

Sturne made to speak, or protest, or express alarm, but with a gesture Stour silenced him.

'Listen, Keeper Sturne. One apart from all of them must know what I shall tell thee. None must suspect, and for this did I deny you the Deputy Mastership, to prepare you for the difficult times ahead when your patience, your knowledge and love of our texts, and most important of all your knowledge of the vices and the virtues of our Deputy Master Snyde may be needed.

'Now, we have little time, for your presence up here will have been observed, so come, and be not afraid of the Dark Sound, for it was made to defend good against evil, and now for a time it may defend our greatest texts against the depredations of the Newborns. Follow me and see what I have done.'

Stolid, calm, determined, purposeful, good Sturne followed Master Librarian Stour through the dark portal and into those lost tunnels so many feared, which in those days had only ever been visited by Masters alone. Then, at last, Sturne learnt those things that helped him understand so much that had puzzled, hurt and sorely tried him for so long.

Later, as the day began to wane and the sky to grow dark grey with cloud, and Sturne was back down at his post again, Pumpkin returned from Rolls and Rhymes, empty-pawed.

'Somemole said you were looking for me,' he said.

'The Master is,' said Keeper Sturne.

'Trouble?'

'Were you ever in trouble, Pumpkin? I thought your life was devoted to avoiding it.'

Pumpkin grinned, and turned for the slipway.

He was back down again but a short time later.

'Trouble?' said Sturne ironically.

'Change,' said Pumpkin, hurrying on his way.

'Aye,' said Sturne to himself, 'change indeed! Now, what have we here . . .' and he took up a text that an aide had brought some days earlier, and in his strong and gentle way, turned its folios, and snouted at it, and examined it with love.

'Trouble?' said Snyde, creeping up as he always did.

'Mediaeval beauty,' said Sturne, looking up obediently.

'Ah, yes,' said Snyde, giving the text an indifferent glance. 'You stay with that, Keeper Sturne, and just with that, and we shall be well pleased.'

'I shall, Deputy Master; texts are all that has ever interested me.'

'Good,' said Snyde, satisfied, going on his bent and crooked way.

Sturne closed the text, his face expressionless. 'May the Stone give me patience,' he muttered to himself, 'or rather, continue to!' His face cracked into a smile. Then he took up another text, began to browse through it, and soon his sense of calm and peace returned, mixed with a sense of purpose and determination of a quality he had never felt before.

'She'll not come, Master Librarian, not yet at any rate,' said Whillan sombrely. 'She said she regretted being unable to come here this evening but that though her sorting of the texts is more or less complete, and Pumpkin and other library aides have brought them into your custody in the Main Library, she feels her task is not yet done. The Keeper Husk is near the end of his own great task and wishes her to help see him through it.'

'But you judge *him* well enough?'

'Yes, well enough. Weak, but not near death, if that's what you mean.'

Stour was silent for a moment. 'May the Stone give me time to go to Husk myself tomorrow before . . . before everything! I shall strive to see him then.' He seemed relieved to have made this decision and turned his mind back to the urgent task on paw.

As late afternoon and all the moles of the secret meeting but Privet were gathered in the half-light of Fieldfare's and Chater's tunnels once more. Fieldfare looked much recovered from her ordeal in the Marsh End though she had not yet talked about it to anymole but Chater, who was watchful and subdued, much chastened it seemed by what little she had told him.

Drubbins had been with them some time, and Maple too, for as chance would have it Pumpkin, whose task it had been to discreetly gather the moles together after seeing Stour in his study cell earlier that day, had come upon these two first.

Whillan was windswept and his fur was damp, for he had been caught by one of the driving showers that had accompanied the day's changing, cooling weather.

Then, his face stern, Stour had arrived from the Library, and immediately asked after Privet. When he had earlier been warned by Pumpkin that she was unwilling to come he had asked Whillan to go and find out what the matter was.

'We shall have to begin without her,' said Stour, 'and that being the case and the weather being as unpleasant as it is, we may as well talk here as in my study cell, as I had originally planned.'

There was a stir of surprise among the moles, for none of them but Drubbins had ever had that privilege before.

'We shall go there later, or perhaps at tomorrow's dawn, and then on into the Ancient System itself so that you may all know what preparations I have made to defend our ancient texts.'

All of them but Drubbins perhaps were astonished at his casual mention of their imminent entry to the Ancient System. Strange and troubled times indeed!

'Today,' Stour continued, 'I received a visit from a Newborn messenger informing me that Senior Brother Chervil, of whom I suppose all of you by now know, is summoning a second Meeting in Barrow Vale tomorrow. Its supposed purpose is to allow me to declare the names of a delegation we have been invited to send to Caer Caradoc, to attend a Convocation of moles summoned by none other than the Elder Senior Brother Thripp himself. His intention it seems is to discuss proposals to reform moledom's libraries, whatever that may mean. I think I know!'

He looked around at them, allowing time for this to sink in and the natural questions to rise in their minds.

'The delegation will be of all important moles, and I must tell you now that for reasons of my own I believe that Deputy Master Snyde should be one of them. But who else?'

'Take Chater or myself to give you protection, I beg you,' said Maple.

'Protection we may need, Maple, though not in the way you mean, but I am grateful for your offer. I doubt that Fieldfare will wish Chater to be counted among those who will leave Duncton Wood!'

To everymole's surprise Fieldfare said passionately, 'I will disagree

167

with nothing that serves the purpose of obstructing and defeating the Newborns!'

'Good! But we jump ahead. I have no intention of attending tomorrow's Meeting in Barrow Vale, but intend instead to retreat once more into the Ancient System, to a place I have already set aside for the defence of our textual heritage. I shall need nomole with me in person, but I *shall* need your moral support and understanding.'

'In the Ancient System, Master?' said Maple. 'But the tunnels there are not fit for mole to live in.'

'Quite so, they are not. Yet a mole may survive, if he sets his mind to it. And Dark Sound is a great protector of old texts, especially from moles filled with noisy desire to get their paws on them. Believe me, nomole will easily get to where I intend to go, and have indeed already been many times carrying texts. I confess however that I have never been in that great Chamber of Dark Sound, as our predecessors accurately called it, for very long. Meanwhile, I have summoned you here for the second and perhaps the last time, that we may understand each other's views on a number of matters – some of which I raised when we last met, when, if I am correct, Drubbins and myself were in a minority of two in supporting peaceful resistance as opposed to violent resistance.

'I welcome to Whillan, whose courage and purpose, of which we may shortly hear more, makes him a mole worthy to join our number in the coming struggle against the Newborns.

'I do not want to seek your views on that until we have heard each other out, and considered those matters that have occurred since then and for which this is the first opportunity to report . . .' He paused to look up at the chamber's roof as a stronger gust of wind than most shook it, and stirred and flurried at the tunnels' entrances leaving behind the stress and strain of shifting roots and wind-sound.

'We all want to hear what happened to Fieldfare, and I hope she will be willing to tell us.'

Fieldfare nodded grimly, and shot a glance at Chater, who looked grimmer still.

'I hope too that we may prevail on Privet to come and join us before the evening's out—'

'I swear she'll not come, Master Librarian!' said Whillan.

Stour smiled and said, 'She *should* be here, Whillan, and I have noticed that the Stone has a way, always mysterious to me, of arranging matters as they should be, and not as moles wish them to be. I may incidentally observe that your presence here, Whillan, makes us six, and if, as I believe she will, Privet joins us then that will be seven. Which means we shall form what in more superstitious or possibly more reverent times, was called a Seven Stancing, which is to say seven moles taking council amongst themselves to try, with the Stone's help, to right some wrong, or prosecute some great and holy purpose. Let us therefore be patient and, meanwhile, hear the rest of your account of your expedition with Chater and Maple to Rollright.'

'That's easily told . . .' began Whillan; and so it was.

Once the Duncton moles had got the four they had rescued from the massing by the Stone in the Circle to safety, it was decided that Chater and Maple would go back briefly into the system and talk with one or two moles Chater knew of old.

'I know the way there,' he said, 'and they'll know as much as anymole. Meanwhile, you can talk to this lot, Whillan, and establish what you can about the intentions of the Newborns. We'll meet by or before the new moon at the spot I showed you on our way here, and if we're not back by then, don't dawdle – set off to Duncton and tell them what you can.'

So Chater and Maple bravely went back into Rollright's tunnels, and were successful in making the contact they sought. They learnt much that confirmed not only Stour's fears about censorship and destruction of texts, but also accounted for the attack on Cuddesdon which Chater had reported on. It seemed that the Cuddesdon moles had heard of the censorship in Rollright and, foolishly as it turned out, sent a delegation to the Newborn Brothers there to attempt to reason with them. This was interpreted as blasphemy, and in the face of the Cuddesdon moles' 'intransigence' the attack and killings that Chater had seen the evidence of were perpetrated.

This information gathered, and certain additional facts about Chervil ascertained – namely that he was not himself one of the Brother Inquisitors and had been sent by Thripp to Duncton Wood to keep him out of harm's way as strife within the Caradocian Order reached a climax – the two moles returned to where they had left Whillan, content that they had gathered sufficient information to make the expedition worthwhile.

But when they got there Whillan was gone, along with the four rescued moles. It was for Chater and Maple a grim and terrible moment, and their earlier elation gave way to grave doubts and fears. The only consolation, and that but a small one, was that there were no signs of struggle, blood or bodies.

'We'll search the tunnels and surface nearby, and if that fails we'll fall back on our arrangement to meet at that place we stopped at on the way here, and hope that Whillan leads the others there,' said Chater.

'He's not a fool,' said Maple, 'and he kept his head earlier. The chances are they got disturbed by Newborns searching for them and scarpered.'

So they made their search, and finding no clues at all, and not wishing to risk more, went to the place where they had agreed to meet and since Whillan was not already there, stanced down in the hope that he would come.

Of their long wait and increasing concern moles can imagine for themselves. But the days passed, the moon waxed, and the night came in when it was full and they must leave. With heavy hearts they watched its inexorable rise above the horizon, scanning the tunnels and the silvery surface that led towards Rollright, and listening out for mole. The more they waited the more Chater and Maple needed their resolve and confidence to stay just where they were.

'He'll come!' said Chater, time after time.

'Aye!' said Maple heavily, shaking his head and in great distress, 'but we should never have left him.'

'He'll come, mole. That one was a survivor from the moment he was born. He'll come.'

But the moon was already waning, and the dawn coming through before which they should have long since left, when they heard moles at last.

''Tis trouble apaw,' said Maple, stancing up fiercely. He was in the mood for a fight.

And trouble it was. For out across the surface, running helter-skelter along, came the mole young Fiddler, fur flying, and behind him, wounded in the flank and hobbling along, was Whillan.

Fiddler did not waste words.

'Patrol's behind, safety's in front, the scribemole's wounded, the big'un take up rear and clobber them if you have to, the old'un shove the scribemole up the rear to hurry him and the whole lot of you follow me! On to liberty and fraternity! Out, up, over, down! Away!'

With this third-explanation, third-command, and third-rousing-speech, Fiddler, looking excited and pleased with himself, led the escape from the Newborn Brothers who chased behind.

It was clear to Chater who the 'big'un' and the 'scribemole' were, which left him as the 'old'un', and this pleased him not one bit. But needs must, and off he went, taloning Whillan in the rump as much to express his annoyance as to hurry his young friend up.

The route Fiddler led them on was a windy one to the west and far from that along which Chater himself would normally have taken them. It eventually left the ups and downs of the high ground and dropped into the moist coppices that lie above the River Evenlode, and there Fiddler suddenly stopped.

'The Newborns don't like low, wet ground that's wooded,' he said, cocking his head on one side to listen. 'Yes, listen . . .'

The four moles heard much crashing about in the dry grass and undergrowth on the slopes above them. Then mutterings of deep angry voices until the noises faded and they were gone.

'Don't want to come down here, you see,' grinned Fiddler wickedly. 'Newborns don't like alders. Strange lot. But good fun, eh? We're safe now.'

'You better go back, Fiddler, you'll be safe enough by yourself,' said Whillan. He spoke affectionately, and it was obvious real trust had built up between the two moles.

'Don't want to go, shan't, and will not,' said Fiddler. 'Been thinking as we ran. Glad we got chased. Good fun. *You* are where the action is, scribemole, and I'd like to stay with you and help you out.'

'You can't,' said Whillan. 'We're going back to Duncton.'

Fiddler grinned and said, 'Duncton? Good! The Newborns fear it. I'll be *useful*.'

'You can't,' said Whillan uneasily, not wishing to send him back at all, 'and you probably won't.'

'But I can! I can!' declared Fiddler. Life, it seemed, was a game to him.

'Come on, Whillan, thank your new-found friend and send him packing,' interrupted Chater impatiently. 'If I'd allowed all the moles who asked to come with me to Duncton Wood the place would be overcrowded. They all want to come. No offence of course, Fiddle or whatever your name is, but if I may sum up the situation: we rescued you, you helped us, we're quits and we're off, leaving you behind. What's more, your friends in Rollright need a mole like you, so stay and help them.'

Fiddler raised his paws in a look of abject agreement.

'Yes! Quite understand. Very well put. Makes sense and sounds reasonable, except for one thing: if I can't come with you now I shall come one day. Since Duncton is the home of liberty it will no doubt welcome me. See you later, Chater!' He giggled madly to himself, and was gone.

'Chater, that wasn't necessary,' said Whillan angrily. 'He saved my life.'

Maple frowned and nodded in agreement.

'I know a good mole when I see one,' said Chater, 'and that's a very good mole, and very useful. But we can't be too careful. If he's as good as I think he is we'll see him again one of these days. It never hurts to try a mole.'

Whillan and Maple laughed.

'You're a rascal, Chater,' said Maple, 'and Fieldfare's got my sympathy! Now, Whillan, where are the others?'

'Safe enough. We nearly got caught by a patrol, which is why we weren't there when you got back. But Fiddler led us back through to where a lot of the Rollright moles live and we were safe enough there. The Newborns get worried when moles wander.'

'Well, I'm glad you're safe,' said Chater.

'Got a lot of information,' said Whillan.

'Us too,' said Maple.

'Let's keep it until we're well out of here,' said Chater.

That evening, tired but safe, and on course once more for Duncton Wood, Chater led them to an old run of tunnels and burrows that overlooked the River Evenlode, and had been used in the old days by wandering scribemoles. They settled down to eat of the thin worms that they found in the gravelly soil and to listen to what Whillan had to tell them about his discoveries.

He recounted what he had been told of the slow and steady takeover of Rollright by the Newborns, who had sent what they called a cell of moles to settle in the most lowly part of the system a Longest Night before, just as they had at Duncton Wood.

The Newborns had kept themselves to themselves, causing no trouble at all and it was not long before two of them had gained positions as aides in the Library and another who could scribe got a task as a librarian and won the Rollright moles' confidence.

'They were visited by some Senior Brothers last autumn and from what they told me it sounds as if Thripp was one of them,' said Whillan.

'Also, the Rollright moles believe that a Duncton Newborn, probably Wesley, came over and saw this Thripp.'

'To make a report no doubt,' said Maple.

172

'No doubt at all,' declared Fiddler.

It seemed that from the time of Thripp's visit the numbers of Newborns were increased in Rollright, and the pressure they put on the system began. Moles who resisted them disappeared and it was not long before the system was subjugated to them, and with barely a show of force at all.

'You mean they didn't fight?' said Maple.

'They were persuaded that the Caradocian way was the true way,' said Whillan, 'or most of them were. Anyway, the Caradocians don't fight, they punish. They use what they call a ritual cleansing of moles needing punishment which is called a massing. On a small scale that's what we saw them doing to the five moles by the Stone.'

'A *massing*,' whispered Chater in horror and disgust.

'Normally they do it underground,' continued Whillan as the others fell silent and listened. 'They shove a lot of moles into a high-roofed chamber, panic 'em, deprive them of sleep, harry them with questions and doubts and kindness followed by blows, guard the entrance with Brothers who believe in what they're doing, and slowly break them. Put simply, that's a massing. The moles "punish" themselves and die of crushing, heat, suffocation and Stone knows what else. The one we witnessed was pup's play by comparison.'

'And they do this often?' asked Maple.

'Enough to subdue a system. Always by surprise. And most moles survive, they make sure of that. But few are the same again and all become tractable.'

'Don't moles fight back, or something?' said Maple.

'Not in Rollright they didn't. Nor in any system I was told about. In fact there's only ever been one successful break-out from a massing that I've heard of.'

'Yes, I was coming to that,' said Whillan. 'It was to learn more about that I stayed on in the system for a time.'

'And?' said Chater.

'You remember when we came into the Rollright Circle and Maple broke up the massing?'

'Yes?'

'Then whatmole was it they thought Maple was?'

'Rooster,' said Chater immediately. 'Though Stone knows why. And you played up to it.'

'Aye,' said Whillan, 'they thought he was a mole called Rooster, the same mole you heard mention of before.'

Chater stared and blinked, making the connection. At the mention

173

of Rooster's name they were all suddenly still. Stour had wanted to know something more of him and such information would make their expedition doubly successful.

Then Whillan said, 'He's the mole said to have led the only known escape from a Newborn massing?'

'He's certainly the one Stour wanted to know more about. Well, I *did* learn more about him. He's from an area they call the Moors . . .'

'I've heard of it,' said Chater without enthusiasm. 'It's somewhere up beyond fabled Arbor Low, the Stone circle beyond which most journeymoles agree civilized moledom ends. But it's grike country, not safe for ordinary mole . . .'

'It may be,' continued Whillan, 'but that's where Rooster is said to be from. The story goes that he came south into moledom with some of his followers *in pursuit* of the Newborns, and they didn't take kindly to it and tried to get rid of him. Rooster put up some resistance and since then he's been something of a hero to all who choose to resist the Newborns. What's more it's said he was caught and subjected to a massing, but he escaped. Now there are dark rumours that he or some of his followers have been caught and killed.'

'When was all this? Recently?'

Whillan shook his head.

'It was during spring, about when I was born.'

'And he's not been heard of since?'

'That's it. He has. Recently. Word came to the Rollright Newborns that he was caught again, arraigned, and punished, successfully this time. Others say it's rumours put about by Newborns. Nomole wants to believe Rooster's dead or even in trouble because he's the only hope most have now. When you came, Maple, moles like Fiddler believed what they wanted to believe, that Rooster is alive after all, and able to come to their aid. Even when I said you weren't him they said that you must be part of his group and wouldn't take no for an answer.'

'He seems to inspire a following, that one,' said Maple.

'I should think every dissenting group from the Caradocian way is hoping he'll visit them, just as the Rollright moles did,' said Whillan soberly.

Chater nodded. 'He sounds like the leader Stour was hoping for. But if he's been caught then a fat lot of good he'll be to us.' The moles stared at the ground in silence, reflecting on what Whillan had reported. 'We'd better get some sleep. These are things the Master will want to hear of as soon as maybe. We'll get going before dawn.'

'There's one other thing,' said Whillan, before they stanced down for the night, 'though I can't make sense of it. Moles who've had contact with others from the north say he's earned a title of his own. He's called Rooster, Master of the Delve.'

'"Master of the Delve?"' said Chater. 'That's as strange a title as I've ever heard in my life.'

'I wonder what it means?' said Whillan sleepily.

Chapter Fifteen

'I can tell you what it means,' said Stour with great excitement in his eyes, when the last part of Whillan's account, describing the three moles' safe journey home was complete.

Fieldfare too was excited and at the mention of the mole Rooster she had looked almost as if she were about to speak, certainly as if she had something important to say. But she finally did not, but only repeated at the end, 'Master of the Delve . . .' like some incantation of past times.

'I've a feeling you've heard the expression before, Fieldfare,' said Stour, perhaps to draw her out.

'Only in tales and legends, Master Librarian, as told me by my mother. But, as you know, she was a northern mole originally and the Masters were last heard of up there. Yet it was not of that I was thinking. It was . . . no, it's all right, Master, I'll think more before I speak. You tell them,' said Fieldfare. Yet as he began she seemed to drift away into her thoughts, and mutter to herself what sounded like, 'Rooster?' in a tone of surprise.

'Master, what *does* "Master of the Delve" signify?' asked Whillan impatiently. 'I'm sure I've heard my mother Privet mention such a thing in tales she told me when I was young, but I can't quite remember. What *does* it mean?'

'Well then,' said the Master Librarian, his eyes shining and eager, 'if this mole Rooster is what the title given him by other moles implies him to be, then much of what has happened in recent times begins to make sense to me. And what's more, this would indeed have been something Privet told you about, Whillan, and she should be told about this Rooster now, for it will mean much to her.

'In mediaeval times and before there was a fraternity of moles who were known as the Masters of the Delve. Many are the legends associated with them, and with their coming, and some say that the first such Master was a half-brother of great Balagan himself, the First Mole.

'Be that as it may, the Masters of the Delve were moles whose skill

176

at delving was so great that it came to be regarded as a holy gift. They worked in small groups of five or so, and were itinerant, travelling moledom with their mates and offspring, to whom they passed on their secret skills.

'You see, these were the moles who delved the great chambers and tunnels of the Ancient Systems of moledom – Uffington, Avebury, Fyfield and all the others. And, of course, the Ancient System beneath the High Wood of Duncton Wood itself.

'When systems felt they were ready, or when these strange awesome moles felt a place was right to delve, they went there, guided by the Stones, and made the great works that survive in so many places to this day. Many scholars have said that moledom was at its most harmonious and reverent when these moles lived and worked. Sadly there are few records of how they delved, or what methods they used to achieve the extraordinary chambers and tunnels with such purity of wind-sound as they created.

'Nomole in modern times has ever been able to emulate the delvings they made, nor replicate the clarity of sound which their tunnels, even after so long, retain. They were never moles for scribing, and each took a vow never to talk of the work they did. Indeed, such accounts as there are of the coming of the Masters of the Delve consistently record that they were a silent, taciturn lot, disinclined to talk, even amongst themselves.

'Yes, their "speech" was of a different kind than ours. It lay in the beauty and the purity of what they made, and all their passions went into what they delved. Their desire to defend their work against the attacks and depredations of the corrupt, irreverent or evil was achieved in the carvings of Dark Sound. These are much misunderstood, and have been subverted to evil usage by moles in the past like Scirpus and Rune. But in the paws and talons of the Masters, Dark Sound carving was a device to protect what they had made, to warn moles off, and to test moles' faith and purity of heart. A mole approaching a place of such carvings hears reflected back upon himself his own darkness, his own fear, and so only pure moles, or moles of great courage and stamina, can go into such places.

'Few dare to do so, and so through time many places that the Masters of the Delve made have become feared, and have survived.

'I believe that we in Duncton have some of the greatest of such Dark Sound carving, deep in the Ancient System, and that the reason why even today moles fear such tunnels, is that we have lost something of our faith and have not the spiritual courage to face Dark Sound.'

177

He paused and looked about the group.

'What happened to the Masters of the Delve?' asked Whillan.

'With the Scirpuscun schism in late mediaeval times following the split between Scirpus, who scribed on Dark Sound, and Dunbar, one of the greatest leaders of Uffington who ever lived, the art of delving in the old way began to die. Perhaps the spirit left it. Their work in the Ancient Systems of the south seemed done, and the groups began to die and disappear. Some believe that they travelled north to delve in the wake of the evil Scirpus, an early attempt to combat the fatal Word. It is thought that his grikes put most of the Masters of the Delve to death. Others believe too that Scirpus learnt how to turn Dark Sound carving to an evil end, and rather than teach him more the Masters submitted to death by snouting.

'Yet a few lingered on secretly, or protected by communities that dared resist Scirpus, passing on the mysteries of their ancient skills how and where they could – to their sons perhaps, or to moles whom they judged to be of sufficient faith. The last Master of the Delve was said to live in Wensleydale, a place of pale and shining stone, and it is thought he bravely chose that place because of its proximity to Whern. He wished in some way to combat Whern's evil with what delvings he could make, which would reflect back upon Whern the darkness that emanated from it.

'We do not really know the truth. Many are the legends of that last mole who knew the delving art, but most say he did not die. They tell of a mole who went into retreat in a perfect place he had delved, there to sleep and await the coming of one who would know how to find a way to waken him. The stories say that in every generation a Master of the Delve is born, ignorant of who and what he is, a reincarnation of that last Master of the Delve, changed and transmuted in some way through time and place from the last great, but secret, delving that was made near Whern.

'Many are the moles who have sought that delved place, but perhaps it exists only in moles' minds! Meanwhile, these unknown and unknowing Masters of the Delve are born successively so that when at last the time is come when those lost arts are needed once again, a mole will be there with them in his graced talons. But the legends tell that such Masters can only fulfil themselves, and reveal their art, if they have never harmed or killed another mole. You see, a Master cannot delve who is not at peace with himself, and peace does not lie the way of killing. How few are such moles as these! How many the Masters who in a fit of anger, or from ignorance of their true natures, have destroyed for ever what they are and all unknowing left it to another to take their place.'

'But when would such a great mole be needed?' asked Whillan.

'Why, mole,' said Fieldfare quietly, 'your mother surely told you that. Or if she did not . . .' Fieldfare paused, a strange mixed look of puzzlement and understanding on her face. 'Surely,' she continued, 'Stour will tell us what the old tales say of the coming of the Master of the Delve.'

'Aye,' said Stour, 'and so I shall. He'll be needed when that holy day comes that the lost and the last book, the Book of Silence, comes to ground. Though he himself may not know what he is, or what his art may do, only then will he come, brought to us by the Stone. So shall that last Master be reborn again – aye even newborn! – but by then unknown even to himself, awaiting his own awakening. How *that* will be achieved I am not wise enough to know!'

'Yet what would he do with the Book?' persisted Whillan, his imagination carried away by Stour's tales.

'Maybe make a delving to *hold* the Book?' offered Chater, who though a journeymole who prided himself on his direct speaking and common sense seemed as much affected by the legends as Whillan.

Stour shrugged.

'To hold the Book. To find the Book. To inspire the Book. I know not. It is a strange and half forgotten legend that I have told you. Yet such memories have often the strength of prophecy. Was not the Stone Mole a mere prophetic legend before he came alive, right here in Duncton Wood? Now, most strangely, we have this mole Rooster, given the title Master of the Delve, and not I suspect by himself. A true Master would give himself no title at all. He would not *know* what he was. Yet out of nothing he comes, out of the north, out of Bleaklow Moor where only outcasts live. And alone of all moles of our generation it seems he has the power to put fear in the hearts of the Newborn moles.

'This is strange indeed. I would give much to know more of him, for if he is what his title suggests then we may proceed more boldly and with more certainty with the strategy that I have planned. And, too, since such Masters were moles of peace, and were renowned for their unwillingness to defend themselves against anymole, preferring to die than harm another lest the blood of mole should taint their delving, I believe that this is a sign that the peaceful way is the only way forward. If we but knew more of this Rooster!'

There was silence again, broken only by Fieldfare, restless, uneasy, concerned.

'Master,' she said hesitantly and not like herself at all, 'I think there may be a way to know more.'

'If it were only so, Fieldfare! For this mole is in danger and may need others' help. If you know a way . . . ?'

'In my time in the Marsh End, of which Chater has told you something already, I too heard mention of Rooster,' said Fieldfare. 'I felt strange at the mention of his name. I felt I had heard it before, as if in a dream, or when I was a pup. As if somemole spoke it once to me. So strange was it, so powerful that I have thought of little else since. It makes a mole restless not being able to quite remember something she knows she's forgotten. But just now, when Whillan mentioned about this mole being a Delver in the old way, and when you told of it, I realized that I knew of him, Master, I knew of him very well.'

She had stanced up and her eyes were determined and rather fierce. Above them, in the darkening evening, the north wind blew hard and made the trees fret. Somewhere roots shifted and stressed, and even Fieldfare and Chater's comfortable and well-made tunnels seemed beset.

'Master, let me go from this Stancing for a time, and I think I can return with the answers you seek.'

'I'll not allow her to go anywhere alone, Master, not without me,' said Chater. 'It's not a night for going out in. And she'll be afraid and get herself lost again.'

Fieldfare turned to Chater with the most tender and loving look on her face. She reached out a paw to him and drew him near, and spoke to him so personally that the others there looked away.

'Beloved,' she said, 'I lost my fear in the Marsh End. This is now more than all of us, and I think that this mole Rooster has been coming towards us for a long time. His name awakens something in me. I'll not be gone long.'

'I'll not allow it, Master,' said Chater fiercely.

'But this is *my* task,' said Fieldfare, as strong as him, but more gentle. 'Master, let me go, and if I must have a mole with me let it be Pumpkin, if he can be found.'

'He's nearby these tunnels on my instruction,' said Stour. 'Chater, take her to the surface, call out for Pumpkin, and then let them be. The Stone's Light is on this, she shall be safe.'

Out into the chill and windy night they went, and Pumpkin came when he was called, seeming almost to expect them.

'Where are you going to go?' asked Chater, wretched to let her go from him, even for a short time.

'It's best you don't know. It's best nomole knows, for I may be wrong and if so then the matter can rest. But if I'm right, Chater, my dear, then it is all of a piece. Pray for me!'

He embraced her, told Pumpkin not to let her out of his sight, and then was gone back underground.

'Where did she go?' asked Maple.

'She would not say,' said Chater grimly. 'All she said was to ask me to pray for her. In all our lives together she's never asked that.'

'Then 'tis best to do it, mole,' said Drubbins.

'I'm not one for making prayers,' growled Chater.

'Nomole is until they try,' said Stour. 'So try!'

Chater nodded his head, stared at the chamber's floor, and slowly, and falteringly, and not like himself at all, began a prayer for his beloved Fieldfare, and ended with a prayer that was for them all.

'Where *are* we going?' shouted Pumpkin against the wind, as soon as Chater had gone in.

'To Rolls, Rhymes and Tales,' said Fieldfare, setting her snout determinedly westward across the slopes, 'for I've a question to ask of Privet.'

'She'll not come *here* tonight,' said Pumpkin. 'I tried and Whillan tried. It is with Husk she'll stay.'

'We'll see,' said Fieldfare, setting a pace through the gloom which poor Pumpkin had to struggle to keep up with. 'Yes, we'll see about that!'

'You don't seem in a very good mood, Fieldfare, if I may say so,' said Pumpkin breathlessly.

'Don't I? Well, I might soon seem in a much worse one, I'll warn you of that now. As for Newborns I wouldn't worry about them tonight if I were you, Pumpkin. The mood I'm in I could *eat* Newborns. Now, hurry up and let's get on!'

Yet, for all Fieldfare's angry energy it was as well Pumpkin was there, for in the gloom of the night, with only the moon's light shining out between high, racing clouds, it needed his guidance to get them to the obscure clearing beneath which Rolls and Rhymes lay.

But having got there Fieldfare did not waste time, or approach her errand with much tact.

'Privet!' she called down sternly into the tunnel. 'I know you and Keeper Husk will have heard us so if you're hiding thinking it's *them*, don't. It's me, Fieldfare. And Pumpkin, your long suffering aide. Now

181

come on up to the surface because I don't have time or inclination to flounder about in the murk finding you.'

Then she added softly for Pumpkin's benefit. 'That'll get her to hurry up!'

It did, and to their mutual surprise it brought not only Privet hurrying along, but old Keeper Husk as well, slower, breathless, staring, but there all the same.

'Yes?' he said.

'It's Privet I've come to see.'

'Well?' said Privet, behind Husk, evidently annoyed. 'I was asleep!'

'Well wake up, I've got a question to ask.'

'She's in a bad mood,' said Pumpkin helpfully.

'I can hear that,' said Husk. 'An irritated kind of mood. There's a tale in this, that's for sure.'

'Well?' said Privet coldly again, trying to keep calm and seeming to have no idea at all what Fieldfare wanted.

'Have you heard of a place called Bleaklow Moor?' asked Fieldfare.

'I have heard of it,' said Privet cautiously, and after a moment's hesitation.

'It is part of the Moors, is it not, from which you originally came?'

'That was a long time ago, Fieldfare. You know I prefer not to . . .'

'I no longer mind what you prefer not to talk about, Privet. I am concerned with what you must talk about, if not for your own sake then for the sake of others.'

'What good will it do anymole for me to talk of my past? I came to Duncton to escape from it, to start a new life, and here with Keeper Husk I have found a task to absorb me. He needs help with his Book of Tales and the Stone has given me the skills to help him . . . Is that not so?' Privet turned to Husk for support.

'It is so, so far as it goes,' said Husk. 'But if there are things you could tell us that would help others, then you should do so . . .'

'What others can I help?' cried out Privet in a voice of growing despair, as if she sensed that even here her past was catching up with her, and she could run no more.

'There is a mole you can help,' said Fieldfare.

'What mole?'

'A mole you loved once long ago.'

'I do not think I truly loved anymole . . .'

'A delver, he was a delver. You told me that yourself.'

'No!' cried out poor Privet.

'Was his name Rooster?'

182

'I cannot help him, I cannot! He went beyond my help. Don't make me speak of him!' Her voice had become a wail, a whine, a cry as of a pup who does not want to do what it knows it must.

'He needs your help, Privet.'

'No, no! I am not worthy to give him any help. He is, he was . . . before he knew me he was . . . he would have been . . .'

'A Master of the Delve?'

Privet cried out in utter despair as Fieldfare said this, and would have collapsed had not Pumpkin and Fieldfare between them, and even old Husk as well, clung on to her.

'I know nothing of him!' Privet whispered. 'I cannot help, I cannot help him . . .'

'Mole,' said Fieldfare quietly, 'I'll ask you one last time. After that, if you deny it, I'll not speak his name ever again, and nor will any but these two you trust know I ever asked you this. It will be like it never was. But you see, Rooster is in trouble now, my dear, and he may need your help. He's a mole sent by the Stone, oh I *know* he is. But the Master thinks that if we are to know best what to do, we need to know more of him and so I've come here to ask your help. I know you've never spoken his name since whatever happened all those years ago. But, mole, you can't run for ever from the past, and we may all need you now and what you know.

'So Privet, my dear, for the final time, and perhaps for all our sakes and his as well, *if* Rooster was the mole you loved will you speak of it at last?'

For a moment Privet held back the tears that she had kept at bay so long. But then her hold on Husk's thin paw tightened, she opened her mouth to speak, and *then* her tears came, and her weeping started. The tears of a mole who has lost years of a deep love; the tears of a mole wanting to talk at last of what she had run from for so long, the tears of a mole who knows too well what she has lost, perhaps for ever. Tears to cry in Fieldfare's warm embrace. Tears to share with moles as good and honest as Pumpkin, and Keeper Husk. Tears which must be shed before true feeling can begin again.

Then, finally, Privet dared to ask what Fieldfare knew of Rooster, and what had happened, and and . . .

Quickly Fieldfare told them all she had heard that evening: of the rumours Chater had heard in Cuddesdon, of all that Whillan had learnt in Rollright, and of her own experience of a massing in the Marsh End and so of what Rooster himself might have suffered.

183

'One more thing,' said Fieldfare. 'In the north they call him a Master of the Delve and that means—'

'*I* know what it means,' said Husk urgently and with that same excitement Stour had shown. 'If *that* be true, mole, go now and tell Stour what you know. Moledom's future may depend on it, and the finding of the Book of Silence.'

Privet said not a word.

'You knew that, mole,' said Husk. 'You knew it all.'

She reached out a paw to him and then stared wildly all about the night.

'He *is* a Master of the Delve, I know it for I have seen what he can make. He delved once for me. But . . . but Husk . . . Fieldfare . . .'

'What is it, my dear?' said Fieldfare holding her.

'Such a mole may never hurt another, never talon another, never kill another . . .'

'Mole,' said Keeper Husk sternly, 'go to Stour. Tell him what you know. I *order* it. Go now, and don't worry about me, for Pumpkin will see to all my needs while you are gone. I have one more thing to scribe, one more thing and my own task is done. But yours, my dear, begins anew. Turn and face it, be not afraid before it, for the Stone will always give you strength. Now let me hear you go.'

Then, with a last wild look at him, and a quick embrace, and a whispered farewell, Privet turned with Fieldfare, before her courage fled her, to tell of her tale of Rooster, and her love for him, and all the burden she had borne alone so long.

Duncton's eternal enemy, the cruel north wind, which had gathered such force as that fateful day of change in Duncton Wood progressed, grew ever more wrathful and violent as Fieldfare led Privet back across the night-struck slopes.

It seemed it sensed that in the tale that Privet had now agreed to tell there was a light it did not like, a hope it sought to kill, and a way forward it wished to block.

'We must hurry, my dear,' shouted Fieldfare against its noise, 'for we've been longer than I thought and the worse this weather gets the more likely it is that my Chater will fret too much and come out in search of us.'

So hurry on she did, with Privet at her flank, fur flying in the wind, fighting the hurled wet leaves, scurrying from falling and crashing branches, seeking to avoid the rain and litter that was blown up into their eyes.

Sometimes the violence in the air was so great, so confusing, that they were brought to a stop by it, and were forced to shelter among the enshadowed surface roots of trees, and clutch on to what support they could find, lest they be blown off their paws and separated. At other times it seemed that the wood ahead all changed, its surface sloping to the right instead of to the left even as they peered out into it, and they were thrown into confusion and uncertain which way to go.

Then once, the worst moment of all in that grim trek back to Fieldfare's tunnels where the other members of the Stancing waited, it seemed they saw the hurrying spectres of moles pausing to peer out of the confusion at them, poised for a moment to come out and attack them, but then hurrying on. Male moles, dark-furred, half shadows, half substantial in the night.

'There was *something*, Fieldfare,' cried Privet in alarm, half turning to look back the way they had come and they had gone, 'and I do not like to leave Husk alone on a night like this with only Pumpkin for protection. Let me go back . . . tomorrow will do as well as tonight to tell what I know of Rooster.'

'No, Privet!' replied Fieldfare with determination, grabbing her unwilling friend by the paw. 'Tonight's the night. Nomole but us would be fool enough to be out and about. 'Twas the spectres of your own memories and fears you saw! You cannot run from them for ever.'

So the storm tried to defeat them, but so they conquered it and arrived, staggering, wet, bedraggled, heaving and puffing with the effort of it all, back at Fieldfare's place where Chater waited at the surface entrance, Maple at his flank.

'Thank the Stone you're here!' declared Maple, seeing Fieldfare come out of the night. 'I had to stop your mate coming out after you and losing himself in this storm!'

'Where have you been?' demanded Chater, his sudden anger but his way of being concerned for her.

'Fetching Privet,' said Fieldfare turning to her friend as she came out of the dark, 'for she's the one to tell us of Rooster.'

'*You?*' said Chater in doubtful surprise on seeing Privet, who was quite unable to say a word in reply.

'Stop worrying, beloved, and let us in out of this wind. And fetch poor Privet food, for it's thin fare she's had with Husk these mole-months past.'

Then turning to Privet Fieldfare said more gently, 'Now, my dear, come down into the warmth and be with friends, and tell them what you must . . .'

It was only later in the night, when the wind had abated a little and the rain settled into a steady roar that sent its drips and runs of water down the entrances above, that Privet recovered enough to break her silence.

'You're welcome here,' Stour had said, 'and welcome back! Fieldfare has told us only that she thinks you may know of the mole Rooster of Bleaklow Moor, also known as Master of the Delve.'

'She said he was in trouble . . .' Privet said, worry on her face as Whillan came nearer to comfort her.

'Aye, it may be so,' Stour had replied. 'Let each of us here tell you what little we know and then you tell us what you know, and between us all we may find a way forward from this mystery, or opportunity, or whatever it may be.'

This they had done, and Privet had listened in silence, distressed and saddened by it all and all the emotions the memories of love, of trial, of loss and of loneliness may bring crossing her thin and sensitive face.

At last she had heard all they knew, and Stour glanced up at where the muted roar of rainfall came, and round at the largest tunnel out of the chamber, down which the steady sound of dripping came. Sometimes it was lit up with flashes of lightning, and at other times with the slower paler light of the moon as it came out from behind the huge, racing storm clouds of the night.

'It is a night for staying aburrow and telling tales,' he said. 'A night when only moles with urgent business or mal-intent go forth. You, Privet, came to this system a full cycle of seasons ago and know that you have our trust. We have all seen how deep your feeling and experience runs concerning matters we so far know too little about. We ask you now to tell us what you know. I think perhaps we seven may never be as one again, and that after this night, and with the coming of the dawn, a trial will begin for each one of us whose outcome nomole can know. Much comfort and good may come from sharing what you know, which knowledge will provide us all with light to guide us on our separate ways in the days so soon to come. Therefore we wait in silence, Privet, to hear what you may say.'

Privet glanced nervously at them, reached out a paw to Whillan, and said in that quiet way she had, 'The place and time to which I must take you is far, far from here. Of you all, perhaps only Chater, being a journeymole, can begin to imagine what the Moors of the north are like. Whilst only the Master Librarian, and perhaps you, good Drubbins, whose memories are long and experience of mole so wide, can truly guess the nature of the times of which I must first speak.

'So though I will do my best to tell my tale that all may make the most they can of it, if there are parts one or other of you do not understand, then tell me, and perhaps with others' help I can make it plainer still . . .'

Then began Privet's telling of Rooster's tale, which was scribed down at the time by Whillan on Stour's instruction and with Privet's agreement. Scholars in later times have expanded parts of it, corrected details in others, but no subsequent research or recounting has ever bettered the extraordinary tale as she first told it. Nor has any ever doubted that the emergence of Rooster, Master of the Delve, out of the dark Moors whence he came, and into the ken of moledom as a whole, marked one of the great turning points in moledom's modern history.

Privet had believed, sincerely too, that her concern was with a Book of Tales, but now she herself told a tale that might make moles see that Book as being a way towards another, greater one, the long lost Book of Silence whose coming allmole sought.

PART III

Rooster

Chapter Sixteen

The Bleaklow and Saddleworth Moors form the northern flank of the High Peak, though moles who live in systems about its fringes and know it best give it the more ominous name of the *Dark* Peak. To its north, through those fastnesses which moles traditionally believed impassable, lies the dreaded Whern, harbinger of the moles of the Word, for so long a source of vile imposition upon moles of the Stone.

To the south are Beechenhill and Ashbourne, and famed Arbor Low, that circle of Stones which most accept as marking out the end of wormful moledom, and the true beginning of the north.

Whichever way a mole approaches the Moors, whether from the sunnier south or glowering north, they rise up formidably into rank peat bogs, and gullies, in which brown-stained rivers race, and slurp, and suck to death all living things that fall, or slide, or are pushed into them.

Dark are the Moors, high, worm-poor, desolate, nearly unvisited, forsaken, terrible, corrupting of a mole's spirit, a place of desertion and death. It is the last place in moledom where mole would choose to live. A place indeed to which even a guilty mole fleeing from his righteous persecutors, might, if he knew its full terrors, and realized its final desolations, choose to balk at entering.

For make no mistake, a mole *enters* the Moors, climbing in among the peat hags, searching among the dried-up heath and noisome pools, seeking whatever scraps of food and distort worm he can find. Or she, perhaps.

Once into them, a mole soon feels he may never get out again. This is truly a place of death and ending, for if a stranger ventures here, and loses his way among the high hags that hem him in, he's as like to starve as to be picked off by the ragged rooks that are the only form of life that seems to thrive. Though even these are skinny, errant, aged things driven from the easier and more desirable pickings in the valleys below by their plumper and more powerful peers. Has-been rooks clinging meanly on to life, feeding off other vagrant creatures that crawl, and limp, and snivel their way about.

What moles then could ever wish to live there?

Until the wars of Word and Stone ended with the Stone's victory, nomole lived there that was not mad, or bad, or both. But afterwards . . . afterwards one group of moles was glad of any sanctuary it could find, even Saddleworth or Bleaklow Moors.

These moles were the filthy relics of the Word, those who through murder or guile, dark chance or strange destiny had survived pursuit by followers of the worthy Stone and then, sneaking, slinking, skulking, like noxious fumes absconding in the night, had made their way to the one place in moledom where not even righteousness and justice followed them: the Moors.

Most, in their unpleasant way, were strong and competent. Well able, that is, to betray another to make their way, or lie and cheat to escape, or to kill a friend to survive.

They came from two directions. The earlier incursion on to the Moors was from the south and west, of moles of the Word and their creatures and minions, mainly corrupted Stone believers, fleeing the justice of followers of the Stone. These moles made their home in the marginally less desolate Bleaklow Moor.

The second and larger group came from the north, and these were grike moles, that darker, dimmer, nearly prehistoric form whose vile genesis and talent for obedience to the Word is described by Woodruff in the Duncton Chronicles.

These grikes escaped in powerful gangs when their bases near Whern were taken by Stone followers, and fleeing southward they settled initially in forsaken Saddleworth, which lies but a few days' journey north of Bleaklow.

Soon these gruesome murdering grikes, driven by a wormless period following drought, crossed the vale of Crowden and went up into Bleaklow. We dare not even think of the chaos their coming caused as, in the darkened secret places of the Moors, grike marauders met the already established relics of the Word. A decade of anarchy followed all across that wretched place, until under a grike leader called Black Ashop, peace of a kind prevailed. There was law, there was justice: the one simple and clear and created by Black Ashop, the other swift and brutal and meted out by Ashop's aides. It was the last place in moledom where snoutings continued, but at least the initial anarchy, rape and mayhem ceased as grike learned to live with Whernish mole and a kind of civilizing began.

Such was Bleaklow Moor twenty moleyears after the end of the war of Word and Stone. A place unto itself, a place where nomole went, a place where moles, guilty of past crimes, hid and eked out a life that some might say was a punishment for what once they had done to innocent moles. While northward, across the Crowden Vale, a few families of brutal and secretive grikes vied for power in their ruthless way.

As for the rest of moledom, it knew of the Moors only as the name of a vile and lawless place to which grikes and others had fled, and in which they were welcome to stay for eternity. Out of sight was out of mind, and apart from the occasional incursion of Bleaklow mole down to the richer valleys below, the one was not disturbed by the other, and each might have regarded the other as a race apart.

Yet, for all the dark history of the moles who had made their way to Bleaklow, they were not entirely forsaken by the Stone, and for those few moles there who might somewhere in their dark hearts find a place for Silence and Light, there was the possibility of redemption.

For one thing, there existed then a small and sturdy community of Stone followers in Crowden, the system that lies in the flooded vale that divides Bleaklow from Saddleworth. This community prided itself on its independence, on its successful defence of itself against successive waves of grike fugitives through the years, but most of all on the fact that to any moles but grikes who would accept the guidance of the Stone, it would give sanctuary. Those who merely professed such acceptance but lived otherwise were soon ejected, whilst more grimly, those who betrayed the Stone, perhaps by treachery towards the Crowden moles after gaining their trust, were killed. In this community the Stone's justice was rough, and the moles its willing practitioners. But at least new blood was admitted from time to time and this kept the isolated Crowden moles healthier than those who subsisted on the Moors that lowered over them, and in touch, if at a distance of space and time, with moledom as a whole.

Sometimes grike moles came to its portals and asked to be instructed in the ways of the Stone, but having been betrayed by such a mole in the past, and nearly wiped out, the Crowden moles continued to reject all grikes. But for those other moles who glimpsed the possibility of a better life, and were willing to live with the suspicions of their peers for a time, Crowden was a light to turn to in their time of darkness.

But there was another light on the Moors to lead moles towards the Stone. For there rises, in the very heart of Bleaklow and almost at its highest point, the Weign Stones, a place of sanctuary for moles lost in that heart of darkness. Unvisited for decades, perhaps centuries, before those fleeing moles came after the wars, the Weign Stones were known only in myth and legend to moles who lived in the small and humble lowland communities that lie adjacent to Bleaklow itself. By the time of which we speak, most moles might justifiably have doubted that these fabled Stones existed at all.

Yet there they were, unvisited but waiting, a last chance for moles whose lives seemed otherwise irredeemably lost to discover the Silence and Light that all moles may find if they but seek for it. These great Stones, stolid and massive as they are, do not rise as tall as the great Duncton Stone, or those of Avebury. They are, relative to those, squat and strange, and some might think are not of the Stone at all. Yet in its wisdom the Stone takes many forms, and there on Bleaklow its form seems fitting enough, for strange though they are, more lowering than light, more inelegant than beautiful, their circle offers peace from the endless bitter winds that blow, and kindness to the spirit of a mole who visits them in openness and humility.

In the years after Black Ashop had imposed his tyrannical peace across Bleaklow and Saddleworth and as he and his henchmoles began to grow weary and old, the moods of anger and fear that had beset the Moors so long were replaced by strange despair and lethargy. Moles who despite all had still taken pride in grooming themselves and keeping their barren tunnels clean, now began to let them and themselves go. Moles who had once survived only because they were cruel and aggressive to anything that moved, now turned away from violence, snouts humble and low. Eyes that had been bright grew dim, eyes that once had a glimmer of hope were wan, eyes that had once looked boldly, now looked away.

The seasons drifted by in rains and grey skies, winds blew through tunnels that were unrepaired, males turned from females and did not mate. It seemed that a plague of spirit came upon the Moors then, as if the crimes and sins of moles to which it had given refuge could be borne no more, nor moles escape the truth, which was the darkness of themselves.

A terrible change then, and one made worse by the arrival still in Saddleworth and Bleaklow, from north and south and east and west, of dribs and drabs of moles, of outsiders, or sad moles, upon whom the shadow of life had fallen hard. Like moles who are dying slowly, and desire no company, nor know where to seek solace, they came to the one place in moledom where their scant bleak needs might best be met.

These were the shades and troubles of the past, moles or the kin of moles now dead, whose malfeasance during the war of Word and Stone had stayed secret to all but themselves or the pups they had borne. Now, dreadfully, unable to bear their secrets any longer, they came to pay the penance of their lives. Despair was in the very wind of the Moors, and melancholic resignation.

It was then that a mole came to Bleaklow, unseen and unknown, and chose to live at first on Saddleworth Moor. She was thin of fur and gaunt of face, and her body bore the marks of punishment and suffering. Scarred and maimed of paw, if she travelled it was only by night and by shadows, and many were the names she gave, and none.

Of her past nomole knew, nor could any have easily guessed. At first sight of her it was a wonder she was alive at all, for how could so slight and weak-seeming a mole have survived so long? Yet, vulnerable though she seemed, there was a clue in this: nomole, not even the vilest and fiercest of those who first saw her in Saddleworth, touched her.

Indeed, even when her wanderings took her into the infamous Charnel Clough, the stronghold of that Ratcher clan of grikes who had won the struggle for dominance on grim Saddleworth, she survived. She wandered on to Bleaklow and yet again, among moles themselves tainted by sin and despair she seemed more tainted, and exuded such misery of spirit, such desperate desire to escape herself, that to touch her would have been tantamount to becoming something *of* her. Far though those moles had gone down the way into darkness, none felt they had gone *that* far.

This anonymous mole was an outcast among outcasts, who seemed to have journeyed all moledom in search of inner peace until she reached a place from which she could journey no more. Moles knew only that after leaving Saddleworth she had tried to gain acceptance among the community of Stone followers at Crowden, but though she had been willing to accept fully the Stone, they had rejected her for reasons unknown and she had drifted on up into Bleaklow Moor.

After that she chose to live alone, scraping her food from among the peat hags, and never raising her snout from the dirty sods in which she rooted out her life. If mole approached she hissed and squawked, and cried out her curses on them, and they backed away.

'What is your name?' moles would call out in jest, for taunting the likes of her was one of the few pleasures they could find.

195

A hundred names she gave, a thousand perhaps. Until a day came when that scrawny thing was mocked once too often and looked up into the eyes of her tormentors at last. So strange and wild was her look, so red her eye with tortured grief, so great the sense of bereft vagrancy she evoked, that they backed away and stared. It was then she whispered out a name she had never given for herself before.

'Call me "Shame",' she said. 'I am the guilt of mole. Where is an end to the shadows that follow me?'

These were her words, and in them was a truth for all the moles who heard her. For guilt at what they and theirs had done was truly theirs as well, and endless seemed the shadows that followed each of them.

'Why "Shame"?' one cried out.

'Guilty am I of the greatest crime of all. I it was who killed the Love that came.'

So spoke the female, and from that day she rose from the filthy spot in which most had expected her to end her days and began to wander Bleaklow fearlessly, speaking not of others but of herself and guilt and shame and sadness at what she was, and in that speaking for them all.

'But what *is* your name?' asked mole after mole, for there was a fearful spirit in her that made moles curious indeed. Her true name, perhaps, might serve to assuage the guilt they felt by permitting them the indulgence of saying 'Her name is not "Shame" but . . .'

But what? For sure, 'Shame' is no name for mole.

So, 'What is your true name?' they persisted uneasily, for in the name she had given herself was a name too near their own.

'I dare not speak the name that once I had,' she would reply, turning to wend her away out among the dark peat hags and be gone. But in speaking as she had the female touched something at the very heart of the malaise that had affected so many on the Moors: shame at the past and present, despair and hopelessness of the future.

At last Black Ashop, aged now but no less cruel, heard of this mole and sent out his aides to find her. They brought her to him finally, much chastened by her fearlessness, and he listened as others had to what she said. Pig-eyed, he stared, wondering why his talons did not itch to crush a mole who out-stared even him. 'Shame' was not a name *he* knew. The fugitive in her he recognized, but from what she fled he could not tell.

He asked, 'Must a mole be for ever what you say you are, ashamed of what they've done?'

A perspicacious question, but then often moles that rise to power as he had done have insight and intelligence of a sort, distorted and misapplied though it may be. The best torturers see deep into their victims' hearts. But to his question she did not reply.

'Is there nothing you're afraid of if you're not afraid of me?' he said, trying to find her secret once again. From the widening of her eyes he saw there was. Strange and distasteful though it is to tell, Black Ashop found something appealing in her stubbornness. Tyrants are intrigued by those who fear them not, and if they sense a mole fears something more they'll not sleep until they find it out. So Ashop studied her, and he reached out his brutal talons to her ragged flanks and thought that what he could not know he could at least dominate. Aye, Ashop, in his need to understand, took the thin, unkempt old thing. Yet he knew her no better after it, and so did what all moles do whose lusts are satisfied but whose questions remain unsatisfied: he grew bored with her.

'Take her to the Weign Stones,' he said with wicked insight, 'she'll fear them more than me. Take her now, and let any of my aides that wish to do so, despoil her there.'

His aides saw that day that there was about Ashop a touch of the clever tyrant he once had been, and as they turned on the filthy, scraggy female they felt anew the power they once had in his black shadow. Their victim screamed, and struggled, and begged, and asked for anything but that.

What? Despoiling by the mob?

She wept, and shook her head, and said, 'The Stones!'

Ashop's aides dragged her there despite her screams, there where light was, and where a mole might hear the Silence and know that love was not quite dead. If they but knew.

'What now?' they laughed, throwing her at the base of the biggest of the Stones. Then poking their talons into her they said, 'And? Eh? What now?'

What now? It is what all moles must ask when their fugitive days are done and finally and at last they must turn upon themselves and raise their snouts and seeing what they are must say, 'I am nothing.' In saying which a mole begins to be. To this great mystery of life renewed at the moment of the death of self had that suffering female finally come. All ways, all routes, all paths lead finally to this: the Stone, a mole, and nowhere else to flee.

So then: *what* now? Slowly she raised her head, looked up at the Stone which rose above, and wept for all she had known and yet

197

denied, all she had done, all she had undone, all of everything that had led her there.

Watching her pain the aides of Ashop laughed some more, knowing nothing of the new journey that the mole they tortured was about to start.

'What's your name, mole? Tell us the real one and we'll kill you quick instead of slow. Come on, what's your name?'

It was then, subjugated and humiliated that she spoke her name at last, not to her tormentors, but to the Stone itself.

'I am the Eldrene Wort,' she said. And as she did black clouds mounted in the sky, and the very Stones about them darkened and shuddered at her name.

'Wort!' hissed the aides among themselves, backing off and looking at their talons as if to say, 'These have struck a leprous mole, how can they be made clean?'

' 'Tis Wort!'

So there she stanced, the mole who in the days of Word and Stone had held great power for a time and had been the one to kill a mole whose name was love and whom all moledom might have loved; a mole whose life was dedicated to leading us to Silence.*

'I am that same Wort,' she whispered to the Stone, unaware of the consternation and fear she created among Ashop's aides, who until that moment had thought only of tormenting her. Then, harder even than her name to speak, she spoke these words: 'Forgive me for what I did to thee. Forgive me that I may die at peace.'

The Stones around her were silent and impassive, the aides staring and impassive too. A fretful breeze troubled the withered heather there.

'Wort!' the aides said again, as if to spit a taste that would not leave from out of their mouths.

Wort! Then anger came to the aides because of the deep self-disgust she made them feel. To a mole they turned back from that dangerous path of self-examination to the safer tunnel of their lord's instruction: despoil her by the Stones.

Anger and disgust gave way to insane lust and urging each other on they savagely despoiled the Eldrene Wort, hurting her, taking her, destroying what ragged remnants of self she still had left and besmirching her with their sweaty, loathsome need to forget for their

* The full story of the Eldrene Wort, former inquisitor for the Word, and murderess, is told in *Duncton Found*, Part III of the *Duncton Chronicles*.

brief panting moment the frightening way towards self-feeling she had exposed them to.

Then, when each had had their turn at her and she lay unmoving by the Stones, they stole away, wondering why they felt so cursed by what they had done, or been made to do. Guilty. Despairing. *Shame.* The name which was theirs now.

But enough of them, for now. If they must journey back into our consciousness let them do it by themselves.

When they were gone, and night was come, and the Stones were silent, Wort roused herself and pulled her besmirched body to the largest of them and said, 'Now I am nothing but what you make of me. My name is Wort and from it I'll flee no more. Only forgive me and put peace into me and guide me.'

Did the Stone speak then? To this day many on Bleaklow say it did, believing the hour of Wort's redemption marked not only the turning point of the Moors away from their dark decades, but of all moledom too. Aye, mightily, with thunder and with lightning, across the benighted sky, in the full majesty of a great storm, the Stone spoke that night to Wort.

'You are forgiven, mole! You saw Light once long ago and lost it. Now you have found the courage and humility to see Light once more. From you much came, and much is still to come. Be fugitive from our Silence no more and let all who one day hear your story know thereby that all moles may find forgiveness in our Silence. Even she who killed us, even from *her* may good come out once more.

'Therefore discover how to help the mole that becomes closest to you, and teach that mole to know the Light. Teach that mole what you have learnt. Bequeath that mole a way to leave this place of darkness, that all moles, wherever they may live, may know that they can turn from the Bleaklow of their hearts and be reborn. Do it for the love you saw and which in me you see again.

'Now, Wort, give up the last of thyself to me and be reborn! From the sin and dust of thy poor past life let new life come! Come, mole, speak thy name to me in joy!'

So did the Stone speak, and the black clouds mounted and broke with thunder and lightning, and rain poured down and cleansed the stricken body of old Wort, cleansed it of all its filth from Ashop's aides and of all its darkness from the decades past.

Until at last when dawn came Wort found strength to rise from the shadows into which she had fallen and gazed upon the Stone with love, and raised her paws in adoration as the great light of the eastern sun shone forth and dried the ground and all her tears. As it caught the Eldrene Wort in its brightness, she was reborn and whispered without shame, 'Yes, I am Wort as Wort was born. My past is done. My future begins now and is with the Stone. I . . . am . . . Wort.' It is given to few moles to speak their name so true.

Indeed, in truth, sterile Wort (as she had once been known), arid Wort (as in appearance she seemed still) was no more either of those things. Life, so vilely made in her by the aides of Ashop was transformed thereby from hate to love within her, and it stirred, and was safe, and was good.

'Go now, Wort, and bring that life made new in thee to birth, bring it to safety, find a way to nurture and to guide it,' whispered the Stone, whose voice was a spring breeze among the Stones.

Then the Eldrene Wort turned at last from the Weign Stones, and she made her way through the molemonths that followed among the hidden places of the Moors. Life grew in her and the Stone watched over her and led her to that high wet place on the Moors above Crowden, which moles call Shining Clough. She grew near her time, and crept into a gully there, though few can find it now, so turned and out of the way it is. But there the sun shines warm even on a chilly day, and there did Wort give birth to three pups. But such was her weakness of body, such had been the hardship of survival these molemonths past, that only one survived. A female pup.

To it she tried to give love. Tried to teach of suffering; tried to bring joy; until finally, when she grew too weak to take care of it, she took it to a place of safety . . .

'That pup . . .' whispered Privet, whose tale of Wort had so stilled the moles listening to her that they seemed made of stone, 'that pup the Eldrene Wort named "Shire".'

For the first time in all the telling of her tale, a hard glitter came to Privet's eyes, a coldness born of bitter memory. All stared at her. Not one mole moved.

'Shire was my mother and the loveless life that I have had as penance for Wort's shame is my only heritage.'

'But mole—' began Stour gently, who wished to say for all of them that such a heritage could not be Privet's personal fault, as she seemed almost to think.

'Hear me more!' she said, cutting savagely across him, her eyes staring blankly towards the chamber's entrance as if at memories which were no longer the history of another time, but lurked now, waiting to enter in as part of what had brought her *here*, and might yet shape them all.

'Hear a mole whose life is penance for what Wort once did; a mole who came to Duncton Wood in search of that same peace and Silence the Eldrene Wort once sought; a mole who brings trouble and pain to others wherever she goes, whatever she does . . .'

Privet's snout was low, her eyes downcast as each of her listeners understood in their own way the depth into which she felt she had been brought, and the courage she needed to speak of it.

None more so than Whillan, her adopted son, who came closer still as if to support her through the time of trial this telling might yet prove to be.

'You have not caused us trouble, or pain, Mother,' he said quietly.

'I may yet do so, my dear,' she whispered miserably, 'as I did once to moles I dearly loved.'

'Tell us this history, mole,' said Stour gently, 'and be reminded that you are among friends, and within the orbit of one of moledom's greatest Stones.'

Privet nodded silently, and began her tale once more as around them in the chamber the night grew darker, and the winds above more troubled.

Chapter Seventeen

It was on the eve of Midsummer that the Eldrene Wort, with heavy heart, brought the young Shire to the portal of Crowden and sought to enter in. Rumours of her survival and the birth of Shire had reached the ears of Ashop's aides and they were in search of her.

'What would you with us, mole?' the Crowden moles asked, staring suspiciously at the weak old female and the innocent youngster at her flank.

'Sanctuary in the name of the Stone, for my daughter and myself.'

'What is your name?' they asked, though they knew it already, and whisper of her coming had long since reached them.

'It is Wort,' she said. 'But it is for my daughter that I come. I wish her to know the Midsummer ritual. I wish her to be reared to the Stone. I wish—'

So there they waited, the dark Moors rising behind them, the safe tunnels of Crowden before them, and Wort trembling with illness, her flanks wasted with the effort of raising her pup, her snout low with memories of shame she had felt when Crowden had rejected her before. But now perhaps . . .

Returning, the spokesmole for Crowden, the forbidding Librarian Sans, a bitter unpupped female, said, 'You are not welcome here, for you are Wort, whose crime all Stone followers know. The Stone shall punish you as it sees fit. We shall not succour you in our tunnels.'

'I am forgiven,' said Wort, 'but if only for my daughter's sake take us in. I am near my end, Ashop's guardmoles hunt us, and my daughter will not survive on the Moors alone.'

Cold eyes appraised young Shire, who sank back into her mother's flank in fear. Cold whispers. Sans' snout, long and thin, came out and poked at Shire's flank and scented her.

'She is willing to be reared of the Stone?'

Shire nodded, eyes wide in fear.

'She is not tainted by Word or Whernish blasphemies?'

'She is not!' said Wort fiercely.

'She is obedient?'

'And clever,' said Wort, 'for already she can scribe a little. I have been able to teach her that. I beg you, take us in. I have not long to live and would see her through the Midsummer ritual and know that she shall be reared towards the Stone's Silence.'

'What can you scribe, mole?' the cold female asked of Shire.

Shire stared, paralysed with fear.

'Scribe them a word, my dear,' said Wort. 'Scribe them what I taught you.'

Then did Shire scribe down her name in the ground, her scribing puppish and ill-formed. The female stared and ran her talons over it.

'All moles in Crowden can scribe their name,' said Sans dismissively; 'what else can you scribe?'

'I can scribe the names of the seven Ancient Systems of moledom,' she whispered.

'Do so.'

Slowly Shire did, scribing them out one by one, and repeating their names as she did so: Uffington, Caer Caradoc, Avebury, Siabod, Fyfield, Rollright . . .

'. . . and Duncton Wood,' she concluded, gaining confidence. Her eyes lost their fear and she said excitedly, 'My mother was there once, my mother—'

'Your mother was in Beechenhill as well,' said cold Sans, hatred in her eyes as she glanced at Wort and made this reference to the place of Wort's greatest crime and shame.

'I can scribe that too,' said Shire, not knowing what she said.

The Crowden moles stared, huddled, and whispered long and hard until at last Sans turned back and said, 'We feel it our duty before the Stone to raise the pup, but you, Wort, are a cursed mole. You shall not enter in.'

'But she is all I have and I—'

'Decide now or we shall take neither of you in. Decide.'

'Whatmole will raise her?' whispered the ailing Wort.

'I shall raise her,' said bitter Sans, vile possessiveness in her grey eyes.

'I won't go with her!' cried poor Shire, backing away to her mother's flank.

'Decide. There will be no second chance. She shall be reared to the Stone, rest assured of that.'

What greater agony is there for a parent than that they must part from their only pup for that pup's good, knowing that in the parting something of the pup may die? How much more is such an agony

203

increased when the pup must be raised by such a mole as Sans!

'Don't let them take me,' screamed Shire at the portal of Crowden. Cold eyes on Wort's eyes of agony, whose light was the bleak despairing love that had brought her there.

'Take her,' she whispered at last, 'but teach her that I loved her.'

'No!' cried poor Shire.

'My dear, it is the only way for thee. Soon I shall die alone on the Moors, and then you too would die. One day you will understand. And when you do, leave this place and all these Moors behind. Go to Beechenhill and seek forgiveness for what your mother in her ignorance once did.'

'No!' cried Shire, her screams a torture in Wort's ears.

'Take her,' she said, and stumblingly, her old paws scrabbling across the little scribing Shire had made, she began to turn away. But then she paused, and as she looked around again at all the moles who were gathered watching this scene something returned of her old authority to her, mixed with the new-found sense that the Stone was with her in all things, even in this.

'Moles,' she said, addressing all of them gently as a mother might her pups, 'I am old and near death, and have done much wrong. This pup is all I have to leave behind, and the best I have, and she is innocent. She needs only love to grow and blossom. I would not leave her to any other mole to raise from choice, least of all to moles whose minds I do not know, whose natures may be cruel, as mine once was, and whose hearts may be barren, as mine has been. Therefore, if there is one among you who believes the Stone has forgiven me, as I feel it has, watch over my pup with all your love, and one day tell her that her mother gave her up that she might live.'

'No!' wept Shire.

But cold paws pulled her into Crowden's tunnels, and speaking no more words, Wort turned away, and began her final trek up into the Moors.

But two moles stayed at the portal of Crowden, both males, both young then, who seemed of no consequence at all. The older of the two wept openly for Wort, and stared at the scribing her pup had made. All was broken and scored by Wort's frantic paws as she had turned to go.

'Shire': scored out.

'Uffington': scored out.

Avebury, Rollright and all the others but one scored out.

204

That last was untouched and clear, and as the two moles looked down at it a special light caught it and held their gaze,

'Duncton Wood,' whispered the mole to his younger companion, and as he did so they both saw that its scribing seemed to shine and shimmer even more. 'We shall remember. And, too, what she could scribe but was not allowed to: Beechenhill.'

'We shall remember what her mother said,' whispered the other, a thin mole with wild fur and a roving intelligent look in his eyes that ever gazed up and away from the confined tunnels of Crowden towards the Moors above.

Then he went a little way after Wort and watched her slow and terrible trek away from the only life she had ever made, and he said, 'Stone, guide her, protect her, and bring her to thy Silence, for surely you have forgiven her. As best I may, I shall heed her final words and watch over her daughter, and one day tell her that her mother loved so much that she gave up what she most loved.'

'That was well said, mole,' said the older of the two, 'very well said.'

'The older mole's name was Tarn,' said Privet through tears that the others shared with her at this memory, 'a junior in the Library who never gained much rank or respect. Yet what little love there was in my mother's upbringing in Crowden, what little light, Tarn gave it. And later, when he felt that what he gave Shire was too little, and too late, he gave her something more, for he summoned a vagrant mole from off the Moors and guided him towards a task and a fulfilment.'

Then a soft smile broke like sunshine across Privet's face and she nodded to herself with pleasure at Tarn's memory and what he had once done.

'Was that the second mole, the younger of the two?' asked Whillan softly.

Slowly, Privet nodded. Then she smiled again and said in a firmer voice, 'Yes, indeed it was. His name was Sward, and he was known as Sward the Scholar. After decades of wandering about the Moors, making a great collection of texts, and recording much that moles told him of those strange dark years, old Tarn got Sward to come back and settle down in Crowden. As I said, Shire was my mother.'

'And Sward?' said Whillan intensely, as if he already knew.

'Yes, my dear, Sward was my father, and what love, what patience, what good humour I may have had in raising thee I owe to him. But before I tell of that I must tell of Wort's final act and affirmation before she died, and of how the Stone came to answer Sward's prayer on her behalf; and I will speak too of Shire's bitter life, and say more of how I was born.'

She turned to Stour then and said, 'Master Librarian, you have asked me to tell you what I know of Rooster, but I must ask you to be patient whilst I tell of these things that came before. For I believe that in some strange way, the events of which I was both product and witness all those years ago, were guided by the Stone. What seemed to me then malchance and fell circumstance, and caused suffering to many moles, myself included, was the Stone's will and of its mysterious pattern for ill and good, for darkness and for grace, of which we are a part.

'As it was my destiny to be raised in the shadow of the Moors, so was it Rooster's. Our paths crossed for a time; that gave meaning to my life which until the mention of his name earlier this day I thought I had lost for ever. But now . . . I begin to see that what seemed finished continues still, and a pattern of grace is still there waiting for moles to find and help fulfil. So, I must tell of these things preceding my meeting Rooster just as the Stone guides me, and then of how the delving arts were preserved against the vicissitudes of time and faithless moles. Moledom will, I believe, one day find its recovery through him, though the last mole in moledom to even guess such a thing would be Rooster himself.'

'Tell it as you will, good Privet,' said Stour, 'for the night is deep and will be long, and its wild winds too strange and unsettling for mole to sleep.'

'I will,' replied Privet with the smile of one who has found courage to trek a hard journey, and will see it through right to the end.

Sward the Scholar! What legends came to be attached to his name in the decades following the pup Shire's sad deliverance to Crowden, and Sans' guardianship. Sward the Vagrant! Sward the Eccentric!

Perhaps, most truthfully, Sward the Obsessive, for once he had served his apprenticeship in Crowden's Library, the confines of that worthy but parochial system became too much for him to bear and the discovery and recovery of texts was his only passion. How often he tried to persuade his good friend Tarn to accompany him on his journeys over the Moors! But how he failed! For kindly Tarn was not a venturesome mole, but liked the dull safety of routine library work, the pleasures in his life being of the quiet and loving kind that come with loyalty and love not to work but to a partner who loved him equally, whose name was Fey.

These two were Sward's only family, and the true starting point for all his journeying, and the true end as well. While he, living a vagrant's life out on the dangerous Moors, chased by the grikes who had hegemony there, sometimes in danger for his life, always with adventures to report, and texts to hoard in his secret place up near the Weign Stones, was *their* journeying, their portal on the world beyond.

In time Sward gained such respect for his scholarship and harmlessness that even the grikes let him be, even the dreaded Ratcher moles who lived over on eastern Saddleworth at infamous Charnel Clough.

Strange decades those, when the moles of the Moors turned in upon themselves and none, not even those like Sward, thought to venture beyond their edge. How could they know that all moledom was the same through those long decades of recovery from the wars of Word and Stone? It was not a time of travelling.

One dream, and a strange one, kept Sward a wanderer. It was to find a certain text, one that moles up on the Moors told rumours of, a text written in the last days of her life by Wort *after* she had left Shire in Crowden's cold care. It had a name: 'Wort's Testimony'. And Sward, who as a youngster had witnessed Wort's last coming to Crowden with Shire, believed that no text he could ever find would be as important as that.

So he wandered on through the years, growing older, his fur going grizzled and grey, and his friends Tarn and Fey despairing that he would ever stop. Until, one winter, he came back, tired and beset, the spark of vagrancy gone from him, and desire to rest and sleep dominant at last.

'He's ill,' said kindly Fey.

But Tarn shook his head and said, ' 'Tis more than illness ails our friend, for he mopes like one who has seen a ghost.'

Winter set in, Longest Night came, the time of tales and the seasons' turn, time to cast off the past and turn towards new life once more. On that Night of Nights Sward told his friends why he had come back to stay and why he might never venture forth again.

'I found the text it was my life's work to seek. I found Wort's Testimony.'

'Where?' asked Tarn.

'Off across Saddleworth, through the mists and drizzle of the Tops and beyond to Chieveley Dale. Then to a high place called Hilbert's Top.'

'Hilbert's a northern name,' said Fey.

'Hilbert was the last Master of the Delve,' said Sward, scholar-like. 'He made a place of great grand delvings which nomole but I have visited – except that mole who took Wort's Testimony and placed it in safety until the years of my life of journeying passed by and led me there.'

'This Testimony . . .' began Tarn.

'I kenned but its beginning,' said Sward in a voice filled with awe and with shadows in his eyes, 'before I saw . . . I heard . . . I knew it was of the Silence and that her work, scribed I think near the Weign Stones even as she lay dying there, was meant for the eyes of but one mole alone. Certainly not mine.'

'What did you do with it?' asked Tarn.

'I left it where it was, secret and safe. It was not for me to know more than its beginning; more I could not know and live. But one day that Testimony will be kenned right through by the single mole for whom it was meant. That mole . . .' His voice grew more hushed as he continued; 'Tarn, I heard the Silence, I saw the Stone's Light, and I was afraid. So I came back here, to you, who are my friends, and I have no heart for texts now, nor desire ever to venture forth again. I feel I am on the way to death.'

'And you have nothing left undone?' said wise and humble Tarn. 'No more task that the Stone might have set you?'

Sward shook his head.

'And when we were young, Sward? Was there not a vow we made together?'

How silent Sward was then, and how he wrinkled his thin grizzled face, and narrowed his eyes and tried to think of that distant day when Wort had come to Crowden Dale.

'The pup Shire?' he said reluctantly.

'You know well she is a pup no more, but old now, as ourselves, but unhappy. I have done what I could to give her love, but against Sans' cold and dreadful power it was not much. But now I am old and you have come back and this Longest Night you have told us a tale of fear and awe and something you have seen. But my friend, forgive me, but you think most of yourself. Well, Sward, think this night of Shire . . .'

'She has no friends,' said Sward, 'nor, from all I hear, does she want any. She's a bitter mole, and has taken over Sans' librarianship as if she was born to it. What would she want with me? She calls my texts all nonsense, and casts doubts upon my scholarship. She has no need of mole on Longest Night, least of all me!'

'Allmole has need of mole, my friend, especially on Longest Night. No doubt of it, she is alone, and by her own choosing too. Unpupped like Sans, almost incapable of love. And you, Sward? Are you capable? What have you got when all is said and done? Some hoarded texts and a wish to die! No real wish for anything. At the very least you could bring your texts to Crowden, and at the most—' But Fey glanced sharply at him, and touched his paw, and he did not elaborate further.

It was Fey who spoke next: 'What Tarn says is true. Is that all your life has been? You saw a young and frightened mole once, and her name was Shire. That Shire still lives. Go to her, mole, tell her about the text her mother made, tell her what you believe this Testimony to be. Mole—'

'I will!' declared Sward, half laughing, half shouting to stop his best friends' demands. 'I will. At least, I'll seek her out and wish her well of Longest Night and if she bids me leave I'll . . . I'll stay my temper for thee and Fey, who I love more than anymole!'

'Go and do it then!' said Fey with a friendly buffet, 'and for goodness' sake, Sward, eat more, sleep more, care for yourself this winter, for if you go on as you have you'll not last it out and we two need you! Now, get along with you!'

Thus scolded, and grinning for the first time since his return, Sward set off on what anymole in Crowden would have told him was a hopeless, thankless task.

Enough has been said already of poor Shire and the circumstances of her parting from Wort and adoption by Sans, for anymole with half a brain to guess that she had little chance of being reared as a loving mole. But it was worse than that. Whatever Sans had been, Shire was doubly so. Doubly forbidding, doubly dogmatic, doubly cruel to those she had power over, doubly dour and bitter and withered, and shrunken in her soul. Her only attributes were her skill in matters textual and a gift for teaching scribing and scrivening to those who could stomach her chill manner.

Never, in all her life, until that Longest Night when Sward the Scholar came, had male dared go to her in friendliness. Or if they had, their smile had lasted no more than moments before it withered and died away before Shire's icy gaze.

Yet Sward went, leaving the festive moles behind in Crowden's communal chambers, and heading off to the austere place near the Library where Shire chose to live. There he found her, a look of displeasure on her bitter face because the distant festive sounds disturbed her work.

Work? Aye, Librarian Shire made a point of working on Longest Night.

'Heathen, their dancing and their singing is,' she hissed, when, with ill grace – and ill-concealed surprise – she had heard out his seasonal best wishes. 'Longest Night is a night of contemplation and self-assessment,' she observed, for want of anything better to say. 'Now, if you don't mind—'

'But I do!' said Sward as jovially as he could. 'This is a night of joy . . .'

'. . . of penances.'

'Penances, for what?'

'Past sins!'

'No, mole, 'tis a night of hope and thankfulness. A night of future dreams.'

'No, no!' she cried bitterly, 'it is . . .'

And so they argued, and Sward saw the depth of her joylessness, and the cheerlessness of her narrow faith. He saw and began to quail, he saw and began to lose words to argue back, he saw and understood the dark void in which she lived.

'You shall leave now, Sward,' she said.

He stared and found no words to reply. He stared, his eyes on hers.

'You shall go. I . . . am grateful to you for coming. But you, I do not need your wishes, I . . .'

He stared.

'Shire,' he said at last, and so gently did he speak, and with such love for the young mole he remembered Shire had been once, that she fell silent at this single speaking of her name.

'Shire, it is I who need you,' said Sward.

'You?' she said faintly.

Bleakly he nodded. 'Did you know I was there when your mother Wort brought you here?'

'I know only that she abandoned me here,' she said. 'Gave me to her.'

'Oh no,' said Sward, shaking his head and half turning towards where the sounds of Longest Night, laughter and companionship and seasonal cheer, came to join their strange communion; 'no, Shire, Wort never gave you away.'

'She . . .' began Shire, then fell silent again before his presence and memory, and the understanding, new to her and disturbing, that she should say no more, no more at all: it was he who needed to speak, he who *needed*, and she who after all those bitter years had

210

found at last that she had something to give. So Shire was silent, and Sward the Scholar, Sward the Eccentric, Sward the Courageous, Sward the Obsessive, and now, Sward the Needful, talked of a Testimony he had found that was her mother's, addressed to a mole who was neither of them, but another, and one they must find.

So began the strange late love – strange awkward love though it was – of Shire and Sward, which led to their discovering they had things to share through those winter years whose theme was a love of texts born of a fear of life and giving.

Until, come early spring, and with news that the Ratcher moles were becoming active and violent across Saddleworth, they set off over the Moors to the Weign Stones, to recover the great collection of texts Sward had hidden away.

'At least, that's what they *say* they're going for,' chuckled Fey to Tarn, as she watched them leave, for though Tarn was too old now for such things himself, his Fey was still spirited enough to remind him of why it might be, when the winds grew warm and the sun melted the snows across the Moors, a male and a female should, for a time, wish to find a place to be alone together.

'No!' said Tarn.

'Oh yes,' said Fey, thinking that perhaps, after all, if the sun made the heather seem so sprightly, and the streams continued to run through Crowden as purposefully as they did, her Tarn might not be too old after all . . .

'No,' said Tarn again.

But Fey, who knew him well and loved him so, came closer still, all flank to flank and fur to fur, and spoke to him of love, and said that spring makes all moles young again.

Neither Shire nor Sward ever spoke of what occurred when they reached the Weign Stones up on the Moor, though much later, Shire, near her end by then, could not quite resist scribing something of it down.

How *could* she resist? For that trek up into the Moors that spring morning, that afternoon of discovery, that evening of touching the texts he showed her and that night by the awesome Weign Stones, all of it was the spring and the summer of Shire's sparse life. Like a butterfly that opens its wings to the warmth of a dawn sun, and flies for a solitary day, Shire awoke to another mole for a few brief, unaccountable, frightening hours of her life.

Through that strange afternoon and evening she awoke to Sward's

211

instinctive sense of what she needed, until there, by the Stones, deep in the night, she was not Shire any more, but somemole other than any she knew. Then she was free to come to him at last.

Whilst he, at first puzzled by her ardour, astonished at what she seemed to know of the loving art, understood at last that here and now in that springtime night was when it was and all it would ever be for her. A solitary night in a whole lifetime when a mole was made to forget what life and circumstance had made her, and could be herself as she might have been.

'Why?' he might have asked, but didn't.

'Because you never criticized my mother Wort, nor looked as if you thought of her with anything but love, and made me believe she was forgiven, and through her Testimony will one day be redeemed,' she might have replied, but had no need to. In that too short time she could reach out to him, she enjoyed it all without the need for words.

But when their sighing was done and in that afterlude when Sward felt the pain of Shire reverting to her bitter dismissive self once again, but then . . .

'What did we do tonight?' whispered Shire, for one last moment letting herself be her better self, and wonder at the stars as well. A star went right across the sky.

'What did we do?' she asked.

Then Sward reached out to her and touched her flank. Suddenly he knew, he knew so much. In the starlight he smiled and said, softly, 'I think I know.'

'Know what?' she asked.

What they had done, and whatmole the Testimony was for. He held her close as long as her drifting back to coldness would allow, and prayed that if he was right one of the pups born of their brief union might one day be the one for whom Wort scribed her Testimony; and if that was so then perhaps the Stone would bless that pup with the love and companionship its parents never fully had.

Silence came again to the chamber where Privet told her tale. Not so much as a breath was heard, and above the wind roared on, and the rain came in swathes across the wood. They waited for Privet to resume, and then she did.

'It was I who was conceived that night,' she said. 'I and my sister Lime. There came a day when my father Sward told me that he thought Wort's Testimony was scribed for *me*!' She laughed dismissively and shrugged.

'For me? Who as you shall find, harmed so many and brought happiness to so few. For me? Who in my arrogance tried to find Wort's text but lost courage. Such a thing for me? No, no, dear Sward was not always right, you know! But I am sure he was right to think that one day a mole will be worthy to ken the whole of Wort's lost Testimony, and then it will be recovered and moledom's understanding of Silence much increased. For my grandmother Wort journeyed into the void, and came back again. Few moles have courage to do that. Well . . . what will be will be, and we must strive meanwhile as best we may. But now, back to the Moors! Back to my bitter puphood and how I broke free of it!'

Chapter Eighteen

Shire did not enjoy being with pup and from the first she longed for the day she would be rid of them. Throughout the long molemonth of April she was sick and uncomfortable, and afraid, and at the end she felt imposed upon, and what little care she had felt for Sward was all used up because of what 'he has done to me'.

Not for Shire any pride in what she would soon make, or the joys of reverie about her pups-to-be, nor even the natural wish to make a place to nest, a secret place where she and her pups might for a time be one and all unseen. Poor Shire, so coldly reared by Sans, did not know feelings such as those.

At least when her pups started, the first, Lime, came with sudden and consummate ease, and for that Shire felt only eternal gratitude. But the second, Privet, came only after hours of pain and difficulty, and for that Shire never forgave her. Lime was large and healthy; Privet, puny and weak. Shire eyed her when she came out and wished her dead, and only Tarn's ministrations kept the pup alive until it found strength to take suck.

So Shire loved and favoured Lime from the first, the more that she behaved as Shire felt a pup should, which is obediently and to its parents' greatest convenience.

'But this Privet never sleeps or sucks when she should, and mews and bleats until she drives me half mad with tiredness,' Shire complained to Tarn.

She might have spoken more to Fey, but her only female friend had, by some miracle, got with pup as well and was joyously raising a brood of four in her own burrows and would not venture forth, not even to see Shire's two.

'Aye,' said Tarn, 'we've a couple like your Privet. But our first-born, Hamble, why, he's like your Lime – big and strong and never a moment's trouble. But Privet will come right, you'll see; be patient and nurture her. The weakest are often the best.'

But it seemed not in Shire's heart to want to feel so, and from the

214

first Tarn felt an instinctive need to watch over that one especially, and to seek to persuade the reluctant father to do the same.

But Sward, having to the astonishment of all of Crowden succeeded in getting the dreadful Shire with pup, soon found she did not want him more, and blamed him for her continuing trials in raising pups. He tried to take an active role but failed, and devoted his attentions to the easier task of retrieving his hoard of texts from the Moors. At the same time he began to enjoy acceptance in the system, and for the first time in his life felt he had a home better than a temporary burrow in a stinking hag of peat, and one worth getting to know better.

The system he had finally found acceptance in was well established, had learned to live in the shadows of the Moors and had a long history of successful defence against grikes and anarchy. In earlier decades, when Ashop was alive, it had had a fiercely pioneering spirit about it, and its worship of the Stone was obsessive, and its prejudice against all things grike and Moorish was complete.

Things had become easier in recent years, and moles like Sans, who had reared Shire with such discipline, were rarer now, whilst half-grike moles like Sward, provided they showed they were loyal and useful to the place, were accepted well enough.

The main system was located to the south of the Crowden Tarn and river, which formed its northern defence. At the East End, as moles called it, was a series of interlocking tunnels which confused moles who did not know them and provided many traps for the unwary. It was the task of young moles to maintain these tunnels, a process by which they got to know them well.

The southern flank of Crowden was marshy and except in dry weather difficult for mole to cross who did not know the way, whilst to the west few dangers lay, for anymole coming that way would have had to outflank all three other sides and have long since been seen and attacked.

It was a system in which aggression and fighting were appreciated, the delving art as well, for delvers were always needed to maintain the tunnels and improve them where they could. Crowden moles were rugged and proud of their system's independence, but they were dull moles with little originality or willingness to do anything that might draw attention to themselves, whilst their faith was of a simple dogmatic kind in which right was right and wrong was very wrong indeed. Unfortunately, in such matters Shire had a certain sway and status, for moles were in awe of her great learning.

The Crowden moles had no Stone about which to enact their rituals, but there was a spot, a little raised, in the centre of the system, at which moles collected to worship the Stone, whilst most families had a prayer or two they said each day – prayers which spoke grimly of protecting Crowden against the dark forces that surrounded it.

Through the years the tradition of scribing, started by one of the moles who had first come to the system at the end of the wars of Word and Stone a century before, had become firmly established in Crowden. The Library Shire inherited from Sand had been created partly by the same acquisitive process that Sward had long practised, but also, and more interestingly for later scholars of that time, by the Crowden scribes who had maintained their own chronicles, concerned mainly with recording the vicissitudes of defence and attack that future generations might know what former generations had done to defend the place. Sward soon noticed that though the Library, which lay centrally beneath the place of worship, was the place moles liked to say they most wished to defend, the fact was that few moles ever visited it, or could even scribe very well. In that regard things had declined at Crowden, and Sward noticed that some of the defences were unrepaired for lack of moles as skilled as the older generation in such delving work.

Meanwhile it mattered not that librarians like Shire were disliked for it was not them, but the idea their work maintained that ordinary Crowden moles were dedicated to defending, and despite their ignorance of scribing, would have defended to the death. Which being so, Sward did not find it difficult to persuade some of the younger males, together with Tarn who came along out of interest, to venture up into the Moors to the Weign Stones and recover his collection and bring it into Crowden.

With this lengthy project completed, and Shire's continuing rejection of his attempts at helping to rear their pups, Sward felt he had done enough to earn the right to spend his days contemplating life and chatting to older moles like Tarn. The time soon came when he and Shire barely talked at all. They were bound only by their pups, and for the time being that was Shire's province and if Sward was allowed to venture near them, as at communal ritual times, it was as a token gesture which he was encouraged to keep as brief as decency allowed.

He enjoyed much more his status in Crowden as 'conqueror' of Shire, and took to wandering the edges of the system when he was not working in an increasingly desultory way among his own texts in the Library, staring out at the Moors to which it seemed unlikely he would ever return. As for his attendance at Stone worship, it was erratic and disconcerting, for he was inclined to mutter provoking comments about life, atheism and the void during the solemn liturgies. It was a testimony to how far the defensive Crowden system had come that Sward was tolerated at all. He spoke like a Moorish mole, and some said it was obvious from his dark thick coat, now flecked with grizzled grey, and the way he talked of heathen things, that he had grike blood in him.

But raggety and wild though he seemed, Sward soon established a niche for himself with his gift of the gab and a demonstrable knowledge of the Moors which surpassed that of anymole in Crowden. Older males riposted the plaints of the religious females about him by saying that if ever Ratcher out on Saddleworth became serious in his attacks on Crowden moles, then Sward's knowledge of the Moors might be invaluable.

Meanwhile Shire brought up her two daughters in a way as partial as her response had been at their birth. Lime was favoured, Privet unfavoured. The one was always right and spoilt, the other always wrong and rejected. The one was pretty, the other plain. The first was first in every thing, the second last in all.

Privet might have helped herself more had she not done so much to exemplify Shire's unpleasant view of her. She *did* whine, and she *did* do wrong, she *was* clumsy and timid where she might so easily have been elegant and bold. But there it was, and there *she* was, miserable, isolated, beset, unattractive, and everything her mother said she was.

Yet there they were, trying to live as a family. Midsummer passed, and Privet survived, smaller than Lime and plain as a puddle, the weakest not only of her little family, but also of the gaggle of youngsters that formed around the tunnels in that part of the system. Like all such smaller ones she learned how to avoid trouble and keep a low snout, and to say nothing when Lime put on her airs and graces and was unkind and unfair.

Yet such hurts run deep, and for Privet they ran deeper when their mother continued to take Lime's side as the two grew up. Shire always had time for Lime, time to talk waspishly of other moles, time to chatter as they re-arranged their respective burrows, time most hurtfully of all to laugh in a way that excluded others; Sward, for example, when he came visiting, but most especially Privet.

How Lime posed and preened when Sward was there, and shared

217

those secret offensive laughs with Shire, throwing glances at poor Privet, to be sure she knew she was not part of things.

'Privet, fetch some food! Privet, clear out that nesting material by your burrow . . .'

'It's Lime's and it's not fair I should do it.'

'Do it, Privet,' hissed Shire, cold and threatening. She said the name 'Privet' as if it needed spitting out. She never said it with love at all.

'But—'

'Better do it, mole,' said Tarn, 'look, I'll get you started . . .'

Then Lime's smirking glance, and tears in the dust as Privet worked and ached with that most unanswerable of the questions of beset youth: why are things unfair?

Yet Tarn was always a comfort and so too was Sward on those rare occasions when he could see her while Shire was absent and so unable to spoil their meeting. She would listen as her father told his tales of the wild Moors and of days when he was young and danger lurked between and behind every peat hag, and moles were known to set forth to drink in a nearby clough and never be seen again.

'Where did they go?' wondered Privet, wide-eyed.

'Eaten by the ghost of Black Ashop!' said Sward with a manic grin. For Ashop had already become a nightmare legend across the Moors.

Lime sneered at such tales and superstitions, affecting a boredom with it all and yawning in a preeny way, and licking her glossy coat and let Shire groom her head with quiet complicity.

In one thing at least Privet was better than Lime, though a mole would not have guessed it from the criticism Shire directed at her: scribing. Privet had a snout for it, and inelegant (compared to Lime's) though her talons were, poor crabbed things and weak, yet she learned scribing well – the love for it coming from her father, and the discipline from harsh Shire.

Lime would not and could not scribe, and in this she was a disappointment to her mother, who soon gave up making the spoilt mole even try.

'*She* can do it well enough for both of us!' said Lime, pointing spitefully at Privet. 'And if she wants to spend her life with her snout in boring texts, bad luck to her! I don't!'

'I do,' said Shire reasonably, for once not altogether pleased with Lime.

'You're Shire,' said Lime fawningly, all fluttering and warm, 'and you're respected in Crowden so it's different. She's not and won't be, and anyway . . . she can't delve for anything, not even love!'

'Don't be unkind, Lime,' said Shire, smiling despite herself and looking at Privet coldly and thinking it was true. So weak, so graceless, unable to delve even for love! Thin, gaunt, hunted, but with eyes that were clear and from somewhere deep inside accusing.

'Moles say she's like the Eldrene Wort,' crowed Lime, pointing a talon at her weaker sister and gloating over the anger this caused her mother to feel. For at mention of that dread name Shire grew yet colder, and hit out powerfully at Lime for mentioning it (who dodged the strike and ran) and viciously at Privet, on whom it landed and drew blood.

Yet it was true. Moles with memories long enough said that there was about Privet the look and stance of Wort, a likeness that increased as she grew up. A likeness too that made old Tarn come to believe that his first instinctive wish to protect Privet was well-founded – there was something about the youngster and her suffering that stirred in him a sense that in Privet there lay a destiny, terrible perhaps, great perhaps, but one which had started long before with Wort, whose rejection from Crowden and last trek back into the Moors he and Sward had watched with such tears.

Meanwhile Privet could at least scribe, and Lime could not, and there was a kind of comfort for the bullied youngster in that. At least when she was in the Library helping, her mother was less hurtful to her, and so it was to there she went more and more as the summer years passed by. Until the day came when Lime said yet again, '*Please*, I don't want to scribe, I never want to scribe, ever.'

'Well then,' said Shire softly in a voice Privet never ever heard her use to her, 'there are things other than that, I suppose, many other things. Come, my dear . . . and you, Privet, stop staring, and find something useful to do in the Library.' And Privet knew that she had found a place at last in her mother's heart, however small, and that now at least in scribing she would never be surpassed by Lime.

Such were Privet's memories of her puphood with Shire and they were hard and bitter and ungiving, and as she spoke of them on that long night of change so many moleyears later in Duncton Wood she felt again the unassuaged hurt and anger she had felt then, and remembered dark nights when she was young, and heard her mother go to Lime and talk and laugh, and wished it was to her she came.

Yet it was not in Privet's nature to let bitterness override her better

219

memories and her eyes lightened again as she said, 'But I did have friends, oh I did . . .' And she smiled with eyes that filled with tears for a mole remembered with affection.

'You mean Tarn, my love?' said Fieldfare, to encourage her. 'And your father Sward, he seems to have been nice to you.'

'Oh yes, them, them . . . but mole wants a friend of her own generation too and there was one, just one . . .'

The mole she was thinking of was Hamble, the strongest of the males pupped by Fey in the tunnels adjacent to Shire's place, who was soon the natural leader of the gaggle of youngsters from that end of Crowden's system. Although not the largest of the males he was powerfully built and had a decisiveness and sense of justice that others liked. He was a good-natured mole whose face though not handsome was pleasing to look at, but when he was crossed, or otherwise felt he must assert himself, he came forward without fear, frowning and formidable.

As such natural-born leaders often will, he protected the weakest even while asserting his rights as the strongest, and since Privet was the weakest he took her part from time to time, his stolid shadow falling over whatever mole was picking on her, even Lime, and with a glance and a buffet if need be, he made them clear off and leave her alone.

Not that he ever said much then, for Hamble was a doer, not a talker, and his pre-eminence he gained as much from strength as cleverness, though tunnel-wise cunning he certainly had.

'Stop provoking them, mole, and they'll leave you alone,' he would say to her. But her very weakness and vulnerability provoked.

'Stance up to them and they'll clear off,' he would suggest, but Privet barely knew the meaning of 'stancing up' to anything. Aggression was not her way and those few and feeble attempts at assertion she had made earlier on, Shire had crushed and destroyed.

'Well then,' said Hamble, despairing, 'keep out of their bloody way.'

He little knew how grateful she was to him, and would not have guessed that for a time she thought she loved him with a passion that felt stronger than the fiercest storm, and brighter than the brightest sun. But shy Privet never spoke of such things, never once, not even to Sward. She only dreamed them, and hid herself away miserably, and lost herself in texts.

The summer years passed and bit by bit that generation changed and grew apart, the tensions growing subtler, as did the likes and dislikes of one for another, shifting and changing as old passions faded and new passions dawned.

'Did I love Hamble?' Privet asked herself one November day, when she saw him across the sun-filled surface, the moorland rising far beyond. The bullying by others was long since over and the old wounds had healed but left their scars, and she had become what she would always surely be, physically the least significant of her generation, already bound to Library work and scribing, under the influence and control of her disliked mother Shire.

Lime had fallen out with Shire over a male from the East End of Crowden, whom Shire thought beneath her precious elder daughter. But Lime tossed her head and said she would see him anyway and with not a jot of gratitude, left their home burrow never to return.

So Privet was left alone with her mother, having nowhere else to go and no other mole to turn to; nor did she have the nerve to break away as Lime had done. They maintained an uneasy truce helped by living at far ends of the same tunnels, talking mainly in the Library, and seldom in their home. It was a comfort of a sort. Yet a creeping loneliness, whose name she knew not, had come to Privet. An ache to be alone, a restlessness, a failure to be absorbed in the scribing that had, thus far, been her only solace. A longing, an understanding of which she only came near when she saw others of her generation with companions, or her sister Lime, flaunting her male friends. Poor Privet, shy timid Privet, did not know how to talk to other moles, and if they tried to talk to her she shied away, snout low and blushing pink. What a dull mole she seemed, how worthless, and how uninteresting.

'She'll be like her mother before long!' she heard one mole say to another, and though it hurt she did not know what more to do than grieve. She hated Shire sometimes, *hated* her, and yet knew that sometimes now she herself looked as severe as Shire did, or turned her snout as Shire did, or felt arrogant about her learning, as Shire did. Such experiences felt like a clinging plague upon her, and one she could not get rid of, ever. She felt doomed to loneliness, and yet, each day, turned to the tunnels of the Library once more and felt the comfort of familiar greetings of moles who knew her rounds.

'Nice day, Miss Privet!'

'Yes, it is.'

'Busy are you then?'

'I am.'

'Well, then, see you around.'

'Yes, yes.'

But that November day when she saw Hamble on the surface, she had felt a little wild. The sun was shining, the Library did not appeal, her mother was not around to make her feel guilty if she did not work all day, and so, deviating from her normal route she had surfaced to scent the fresh air. And there was Hamble, looking . . . well, not quite like himself.

She had not talked to Hamble for molemonths past, and never, as far as she could remember, in any personal way at all. He had simply been there, and her gratitude to him had never been expressed. Seeing him now, stanced by himself in the sun, she felt a surge of affection that took her by surprise. She was diffident about going up to him, and so began to turn away towards the tunnels and the safety of the Library, where in any case she *ought* to be, but fortunately he saw her and called out a greeting.

And then again, 'Hello, Privet,' when she drew near.

Yes, she thought, I feel *affection*. She analysed it like a text. Affection, not love. In that was freedom! She dared to look into his eyes and was not afraid. She saw friendliness and disquiet.

'You—'

'Yes, mole?' he said. He was so strong, his fur so good, his presence as good to her as it had always been. She might not feel love, for how can a mole love one who has been almost a brother, but shyness she felt, and curious pride to be talking to him at all. And comfort that she had known him, in a way, so long. And yet . . .

'Well?' he said persistently. 'You always were the quiet one, Privet. You can say what you were thinking, I won't bite.'

'You . . . looked sad,' she said. 'I was thinking it isn't like you.'

'No?' he said, a little mournfully.

'No,' she said very firmly, much surprised at her own daring and hoping that her snout was not going pink.

'Have you ever been in love?'

The question was so unexpected, and so apposite, that Privet giggled, which is not something she ever did.

'It's not funny,' growled Hamble, settling down comfortably. He seemed so open and trusting that she felt her diffidence leave her and an almost daring relaxation overtake her body. She stanced down near him.

'It is funny really,' she said, 'because I did once love a mole.'

'Who?' he said.

It was precisely the question she had hoped he would ask, but now he had, her heart beat faster and she was unsure what to say. But the sun was warm, and his presence good, and thinking it was him she had loved she could not but smile. It was a day for smiling, and for being *here*. She felt suddenly so tired.

'You,' she said archly.

He stared at her astonished. 'Me? But you never said! And anyway . . .'

Yes, anyway; she was merely Privet. It felt a long time ago.

'It's over now,' she said.

He looked relieved and grinned at her and said, 'Just as well, really.'

She stayed silent, staring, and suddenly knew whatmole it was he loved.

'It's Lime!' she said. 'Oh dear!'

He nodded sadly and since she was silent he began to talk. Oh, how she knew the passion he described, how fierce such passions are, how very bright they seem.

'Will I get over it?' he said at last, for he had told how Lime had laughed at him when he declared himself and called him 'clodhopping', a term she had learnt from Shire.

'I did, eventually,' said Privet a little unhelpfully. They were silent for a time.

'Hamble . . .' she began at last. He had the sense to stay silent. 'I never dared say before, and I might never be so bold again. Thank you for what you used to do for me. I . . .'

Her eyes filled with tears and suddenly she felt a fool. She stanced up to escape from him and *this*. Then he did that which once she had so wished that he might do. He reached a paw to hers and said gruffly, 'Never did like seeing a mole hurt who couldn't defend themselves and especially not you, Privet. You're cleverer than all the rest of us put together and fighting isn't your way.'

Me? Cleverer? she thought. He had thought *that*? But then clever moles are not loved moles, not by males at least, *that* she knew.

'Never liked the way your sister treated you,' he said.

'But you love her, Hamble.'

'Do I? *Do* I?' He frowned, his paw still on hers while he thought. 'I do, I suppose, but that's because I can't help myself. It's different moles than me she wants . . .' He named two males who lived at the other end of Crowden, whom Lime seemed to think were more worthy of her. Privet listened patiently and sympathetically, nodding her head now and then but rarely commenting, and never once criticizing Lime.

'I like your father Sward,' said Hamble suddenly, changing the subject. 'He's told me all about the Moors and said if he was younger he'd take me up there and show me the routes. You're lucky having a father like him. I envied you that.'

'But I envied you your parents. I used to wish I could wake up and find Tarn was my father, and Fey my mother, and you . . .'

'Me?' grinned Hamble.

'Well, not my brother,' said Privet coyly. She marvelled at how easy it was to talk like this. 'And my mother?' she said. 'What did you think of her?'

He shrugged. 'Shire's Shire, everymole knows that. At least she taught you scribing and that's a gift to have. You could travel away from here with that. They say there's other libraries all over moledom.'

'They wouldn't want a scribe from Bleaklow, or be interested in Whernish, I would think,' she said. She meant it, and looked down modestly at her talons. 'I *would* like to go and see some of the places I've heard about but I suppose I never will.'

'You should!' he said. Her eyes had the far-away look of a mole who had courage only to dream of such things.

'I'm needed here,' she said. 'By my mother and others in the Library. There aren't so many scribes in this new generation.'

'What do you *do* in the Library? I'm not good at that sort of thing. I mean what are texts *for*?' He looked suddenly vulnerable, as if revealing an ignorance he would prefer nomole to know of, but it was something she had seen in other moles, and she understood.

Then, slowly, she told him about texts and scribing and how a mole could get quite lost in it.

'Like thoughts of love?'

'Better than love,' she smiled, 'and more dependable.'

So they talked as the day went by, and discovered the surprise of mutual trust and dawning friendship. Both found solace in sharing their disappointments; Hamble for a mole who did not want him, and Privet for the love of a mole who was so far no more substantial than a dream, yet for whose presence she felt a growing ache and longing.

The hours passed by unnoticed as they talked, until the shadows lengthened and Hamble declared with a start that he had to go to a meeting summoned by the elders about renewed threats from the Saddleworth moles; Privet had work to finish in the Library before dark. They went their different ways feeling much the better for having talked, and each looked forward to the next time, for there seemed so much to share.

Chapter Nineteen

A pup's life begins in darkness at his mother's teat, and only after moleweeks have gone by does he emerge into light and out into the safe confines of a nesting chamber.

Then he begins to understand that there are pups other than him, and he becomes aware of an entrance to a tunnel, dark and dangerous, of which he is afraid. The moleweeks turn into months, strength comes to his paws, he dares to venture down the tunnel, and the darkness and danger recede to the tunnels and surface beyond.

The pup grows and explores the further tunnels and the surface too, and bit by hard-won bit the darkness and the danger recede still more, and become less palpable. Yet the fear remains, deep, lurking, a profound constraint.

The pup matures, learns to defend himself, comes to realize that the darkness and the dangers, though not imaginary, are controllable. According to his strength and intelligence, and his natural boldness or timidity he ventures far, or only near. He turns in sleep, he learns of other moles, he sees suffering and joy, and new darkness comes, new dangers appear, of mind and spirit now, much less of place. He discovers that others, weaker than him in body, are stronger now in spirit and begin to catch him up in life's endless journey.

Thus, Hamble, elder son of Tarn, learning of the sufferings of love, grasping something of the joys of friendship, feeling his strengths, yet discovering his weakness. And finding strength and support from Privet, a mole who had only ever seemed weak to him.

Thus Privet: full of fears and self-doubts, born of a mother who made her feel worthless, living with a low snout and no thoughts of venturing far at all until she made a friend of Hamble one September, and began to dare look up.

Yet both were still parochial, both reared to a view that Crowden was the only place there was, the safest place, the best. The place they owed their loyalty to, the place they might, as others did, complain of and yet would never leave. Even warrior moles like Hamble were discouraged from crossing the boundaries of the system until they had lived a full cycle of seasons and were adult. By then their first mating was of greater allure than exploration of a dangerous unknown world, and in this way Crowden secured for itself its succession before its brighter and more enterprising males set forth from their home system to explore, as explore they must.

Not that many went far – just far enough indeed to realize that the Moors were uninviting, the grikes unpleasant, and the only direction worth going in was west. Except that Crowden needed them, and other systems did not. Most came back soon enough, sadder and wiser for their discoveries, and settled to the life they had been reared to, which was to defend Crowden against the Moorish grikes, the infidels.

As for Crowden's females, most were got with pup that first adult spring and so did not have any desire to journey away at all. In fact, Crowden was the place to which moles *came* to seek sanctuary and, all in all, there could hardly be a better place for a mole to be born, reared, live and to die than there.

Such was the narrow view shared by Privet and Hamble that September when she turned Hamble into a friend, and by October, when they had learnt to trust each other and share what secrets they had, neither had changed it much, though Hamble was beginning to feel a restlessness. Privet meanwhile was all dreams, all wishes, all half-formed desires, all timidity – and restlessness as well. But hers was of a kind different to Hamble's – it was the aching need of a mole who had no mother-love, nor real father's care, who longed to be safe and valued, but most of all to be needed, and was beginning to realize that she would never find such satisfactions in her home system.

'*I* need you!' declared Hamble one day when she admitted these things to him.

She smiled her wan smile, and touched him in friendliness, and looked past him to the Moors.

'The trouble is you're like a brother, Hamble, and that's not what I meant.'

'I know,' he said, 'because sometimes I feel the same.'

'Will we ever find moles to love, whatever love really is?' she asked.

'We better!' declared Hamble stoutly.

'We might,' replied Privet doubtfully.

In mid-October the closed world of Privet and Hamble and many of their peers was opened up for ever by the renewal of interference from Ratcher's grikes on Saddleworth. There had already been some slight disturbances in September – Crowden moles venturing beyond

226

the system's edge had been half-heartedly attacked, and grikes had been seen lurking at dusk across the waters of the Crowden Tarn at the system's north-eastern boundary. A grike's body was found, wasted and diseased near one of the defences.

'Left there to intimidate us!' declared the older males. 'Let the rooks take it!' Young males like Hamble had watched silently as all day rooks wheeled and dived upon the corpse. There was growing up in that.

But not since then had there been anything serious, for Ratcher and his moles had gone quiet, a quiet that had seemed ominous until Crowden heard rumours that the plague of murrain had come to north Saddleworth the previous spring and blighted the mating period, forcing Ratcher to retreat to his home ground and stay there.

Since spring nothing more had been heard of the grikes until the September incidents, when moles like Hamble had found their duties as watchers and delvers along the boundaries of the system had been increased. Now the grikes were active once more and Crowden was confronted with a crisis from the Moors that would change all their lives.

Grey weather had come, and the first cold damp winds of winter which affect the Moors sooner than the lowlands to the east and west, and a molemonth or two before more southern parts. As one of the strongest and most dependable of his generation, Hamble had been given the task of night-watching over on the north-western defences.

One night he saw ominous shifting shadows, moles beyond the perimeter, talons glinting in the stars, eyes staring from afar. Then calls, strange and haunting and carried on the wind. Hamble reported it, and others came and watched. Nomole appeared from out of the dark, but shadows were seen, now here, now there, and an alert was sent out and moles were deployed to the defences. As yet it was nothing too unusual, and the system went through these precautions smoothly, with most moles asleep and not even knowing anything might be apaw.

'No point in going forth after the bastards,' said the commander of the night, 'we'll wait. If they attack, the defences will slow them down and we all know what to do. You, Hamble, and those with you now stay alert.'

All night Hamble watched on, but heard only those plaintive calls and saw only grey shadows like frightened moles too timid to approach, not grike warriors at all. Vagrants wanting to get in perhaps, or . . .

Then screams out of the darkness, and the sound of moles chased, and then bigger, darker shadows and gruff voices. Screams then, and lingering cries, the sound of moles being killed.

'They might be some of our own returning,' said Hamble urgently, 'or moles seeking asylum, caught by grikes. Couldn't we go to them?'

'Ours would not come that way, nor be afraid to enter in. If it's bloody asylum seekers they can wait until the light of day when 'tis safe for us to go to them. Most likely 'tis grikes' trouble with their own. Leave them to it!'

Dawn, which came with the slow rise of light into the wintry sky, was accompanied by the moans and weak cries of a single mole out beyond the system's edge.

'Can't we go to him?' said Hamble, unable to bear the sound.

'Listen to that sound, youngster, and get used to it. Listen and be strong. That might be you one day if you're ever weak. Aye, it's a mole dying, a grike mole no doubt caught trying to get here.'

'But –'

'We'll have a look when the light's better, and when we've made sure there are no grikes about. They have been known to maim one of their own to decoy us out. Or the mole may be putting on his agony. Eh?'

It could be so, thought Hamble, if the moans had not been so deep, and the sense of despair spreading across the Moors not so strong with the risen dawn. In the time of waiting he went to his burrow and slept, for his watch was done, and when he woke Privet was nearby, waiting for him to tell her what had happened in the night, news of which had travelled quickly round the system.

He told her, and together they went to the East End, to find that a reconnaissance had been made and moles were just going out to investigate more thoroughly the dead bodies which had been seen.

'You stay here,' the commander said grimly to Privet, 'this isn't for the likes of librarians. But you, Hamble, follow me. Since you saw the beginning of it, you may as well see the end.'

But some small spirit of rebellion came to Privet then, and despite Hamble's protestations, she followed him through the twists and turns of the defences, down one level and then up two and finally out on to the wild Moor beyond. It was the first time she had ever in her life been beyond the system's bounds, and as she emerged into the grey light of early morning and felt the cold winds across her snout, she felt fear and a surge of freedom all at once.

'Well, if you must come, keep close by me, Privet,' said Hamble

228

protectively, going on. And so she tried, nervous of doing anything else. Slowly they went among the hags, turning here and there, the watchers calling to each other to keep in touch.

'Over here, mole! Here!'

'Aye!' cried out Hamble, 'I'm to your left.'

Then, 'Here! A body here!' A call from a mole to the right.

Privet's heart seemed to stop inside. Death was not a thing she yet knew.

'Here, Hamble, look at this!' The voice was horror-struck.

Privet followed behind Hamble, they turned a corner, saw the mole who had shouted, and there, her view half obscured by Hamble in front of her, Privet caught a glimpse of death. She saw the bloodied open eye, the paws arced back defensively, the brutally-taloned stomach wounds; and the flies already at the flesh.

'Go back, Privet, go back!' said Hamble urgently. 'Go back, this is not for you!' She saw his eyes were shocked, and without argument she turned back the way she had come. Or thought she had come. For one hag rises brown and dank much like another, a black puddle has many replicas; the Moors delude a mole.

'Go back!' Hamble had ordered her, but it was to the left she veered, uncertain, running to get away from death. She paused, decided on a different way, turned round another hag and into worse than death.

Three moles lay slaughtered, their blood thick at a puddle's edge. One's head was half submerged; another smaller mole, a youngster, was curled up as if asleep. The blue-white sheening bones of his spine showed bright through his flesh and fur where grikes had broken him. The third was a little beyond these two and Privet would have turned and run away had not the slight movement of that mole's front paw stopped her.

She stared, her horror mounting, and saw the mole was still alive. Privet stanced quite still, her heart like thunder in her breast. The mole moved the other paw and tried to turn. A female, and young too. But her fur seemed old, all patched and thin, and from her haunch, blood had flowed and dried and was thick down to her paw.

Her head shook with effort or with pain, and on the hag above short grass trembled in a breeze that wafted over it. A sound, the moan of pain, and fear was all gone from Privet, and all sense of anything but the need to help the mole who tried so desperately to crawl away.

'Mole,' whispered Privet, moving at last, past the two bodies to the injured mole's flank. 'Mole . . .'

For a moment more the mole tried pathetically to flee, but her frantic front paws soon stilled. She turned her head and stared into Privet's eyes. Her face was caked with the sweat and blood of death, and vomit was on the hag's edge nearby. There was a stench.

Yet though Privet saw and scented all of it, all she knew was that mole's suffering. The mole opened her mouth and Privet reached a paw to hers.

'Help us in Chieveley Dale,' said the mole.

Privet had not even time to think she had never heard of Chieveley Dale when the mole's head turned and seemed to snout up towards the breeze that blew beyond her reach. She tried to turn to look at Privet once again, but stiffened, moaned once more, and even as Privet touched her, she died.

Long moments later Hamble came, and saw the scene, and poor Privet stanced near a dead mole. He went to her and she turned to him and sobbed, 'They wanted help, they wanted help from us.'

So it was that the first of the refugees from Chieveley Dale across Saddleworth came to Crowden. Eight were found, all showing the swellings and fur loss of virulent murrain and all killed by Ratcher's grikes for fleeing during the night.

Three days later there were more screams in the dark, and this time one was found alive, though barely so. At least he survived longer than the one Privet had seen die, and was able to tell them something of Chieveley Dale, and of recent happenings on Saddleworth. Though weak from the taloning he had received, he lived a few hours more and in that time repeatedly asked to be admitted into Crowden, as if he were certain that he would find healing there.

But the elders decreed against it and several of the younger moles made him comfortable where he lay, while others watched out for grikes returning. It was then he told what he could of his system's circumstances, and Shire, being unwilling to come beyond the system's bounds, sent Privet to scribe down what he said, or tried to say, for his speech was wandering, and he mentioned moles and places that meant little to those who heard him.

Since the first incident Sward had explained where Chieveley Dale was, and something of the mystery of the delvings on Hilbert's Top, the high part of the Moors that formed the Dale's eastern flank. Privet had heard from him too of the Charnel Clough, the den of the Ratcher mob, which no outside mole had ever visited voluntarily, and from which none ever returned; the Charnel was an ancient source of fear, and of rumours of gorges and raging rivers, and ogreish moles who ate their young. This place was Red Ratcher's home.

That much she had heard and was able to understand when the Chieveley mole referred to it, and she knew that the system of which he was a part consisted of moles who in very recent years had made an exodus from the Charnel and occupied Chieveley's long-deserted Dale.

The mole talked of disease and death, and siege as well, and of Ratcher's desire 'to kill us all'. And, of other moles, 'their delvings will not hold out much more'.

'What delvings?' asked Privet, for the matter seemed pertinent and worried the dying mole.

'Rooster,' replied the mole, his eyes gentling at the mention of this odd word.

Rooster? He did not say more.

Except that when she asked him to explain he said, as if it meant much, that 'she is dead, like others, like our best delvers. Rooster's in retreat.'

Such fragments as these did Privet scribe down, urging the mole, as much as she dared, to say more.

Hilbert, he mentioned him. And Rooster, that again. But most memorable of all, because he said it as clearly as a lark's song in the spring, and it was the last thing that he said; 'Thank the Stone, we have a Master of the Delve at last, Rooster . . .'

It was not much, and yet it was enough for Sward to say, 'A Master of the Delve, he said? That will be the day!'

'What is that?' she asked.

He gave an answer steeped in legend and history, and as he did she remembered kenning of such a thing somewhere, not in mole but Whernish. She had thought that such Masters were evil things who practised Dark Sound.

'No, no, my dear,' said Sward, 'the Scirpuscuns corrupted them and wiped them out in mediaeval times. The mole was babbling of the past, for there'll never be more Masters of the Delve.'

'And Rooster? What did that mean?'

Sward shrugged. ''Tis not a thing I've heard of before.'

'Perhaps it is a mole,' said Hamble simply.

Yes, thought Privet, strangely thrilled, it *is* a mole. That explanation makes most sense. 'Rooster's in retreat', the mole had said. On Hilbert's Top, perhaps. And so began a dream.

Such was all that last survivor said, and it did not amount to much. Yet his coming, and more particularly the decision of the Crowden elders to deny him access to the system, began a fierce debate about what to do if others came.

'If we are of the Stone then we must admit moles to our sanctuary,' argued the younger moles, and with them, for the first time in her life, Privet found her voice. She was angry, and upset, and at night could not close her eyes without remembering those other eyes that stared into hers before they died, and a voice that called out, 'Help us in Chieveley Dale!' So with Hamble she persuaded others of like mind to complain and argue with the elders.

But most were against them, including many like Lime who were of their own generation, who sided with the majority of older moles and began to call them grike-lovers, and sneered at them. Whilst Shire, who as Librarian had elder status, mocked Privet and turned the elders against her and Hamble and others like them, saying they had too little experience to judge such things and that Crowden had not survived this long by giving space to grikes.

Then two moleweeks later, four more refugees from the Dale arrived at the western boundary, attempted to enter Crowden, and after a near-violent argument led by Hamble and Privet in favour of allowing them in, against the majority who refused them entry, the refugees were denied admission. Nor was Hamble or any other mole allowed out to talk to them, though over that there was more dispute.

That night the grikes came, and the Crowden moles heard the refugees tortured and murdered but a short way beyond the defences. It was a shameful night in Crowden's history and as red sun bloodied the dawn sky, the refugees' corpses were found taloned to the ground.

Had Privet been a bolder mole, had Hamble had less common sense, either one or both would have left the system that day. As it was they watched the rooks wheeling and swooping over the fodder the grikes had left, and for days after watched the Moors. If refugees had arrived then, violence would have come to Crowden over their admission and perhaps, after all, the system's elders would have relented and let them in.

But none did, and Hamble and Privet and their few friends were left with bleak looks in their eyes, and faces that had aged more in a few days than in all the moleweeks past; and would age still more in the moleweeks to come. Whilst into their hearts had come a restlessness and impatience whose satisfaction could no more be found within the confines of the system in which they had been born.

But now to the system and to both these moles came a new worry. Sickness began to go through Crowden like rank mist across a heath which, when it has gone, leaves the heather wan and fading. Once again the mood of the system swung, for none doubted that the sickness was the beginning of a form of plague, and contact with the sick refugees had brought it into the system.

It affected the older moles most, as sickness always does at autumn's end, and suddenly both Hamble and Privet had new and more immediate concerns than refugees, for Tarn and Shire were both struck down. While Sward, if not sick, became distracted, his eyes rheumy; he wandered away towards the Moors, saying he was off on a journey to find a text. At first Privet got Hamble to stop him – he would not listen to her – but soon they realized it was all talk, and after a short time he always came back again, muttering that he had not found 'it', but he knew where it was, he did.

Of more concern was Shire, whose sickness filled her with lassitude, and whose voice, always so disciplined and clear, took on a querulous tone. She began to stay in her burrow and had reluctantly to accept Privet's help with food and grooming, which she did with venomous and unpardonable criticism, while calling all the time for Lime. But Lime did not want to come, seeming to take her mother's illness as a personal affront, worried, too, that *she* would catch the sickness herself.

In their different ways Privet and Lime discovered how shocking it was to find that a parent who has always been there and seemed so strong may in a matter of weeks or even days become weak and changed. It was as if the wall of a great strong chamber where a mole has felt so safe had suddenly collapsed, and the bitter winds and rain of the world driven in. This Privet saw more clearly than her selfish sister, and for all the anger and hatred she felt for Shire, she felt her world was on the edge of ruin now, and a change was coming of which she was afraid; yet she did not want to prevent it.

Meanwhile, in the Library, moles began to consult Privet directly, and she realized that despite her youth the training her mother had so ruthlessly given her, and her natural ability with texts, had made her indispensable. Caught as she now was between these growing duties, and caring for her ungrateful mother, Privet retreated into days and weeks of nothing but work, and hurrying along winter-bound tunnels to one onerous task or another.

Her only relief from Shire came not from Lime, who stayed as clear as she could from her former home burrow and avoided caring for her mother, but from Sward, who once he recovered himself, began for the first time in years coming by the burrows to help out with food

233

and nesting material. At least with him Shire did not shout and criticize, and when he was there poor Privet was able to get some sleep. It was the first time she had ever seen a show of concern between her parents, or any sign that once, however briefly, they had cared for each other.

But meanwhile the sickness – moles now openly called it murrain – afflicted others in the system, including Hamble's parents Fey and Tarn. For days they lingered near to death, suffering much, yet each striving even then to help the other.

One day at the end of October Hamble came to Privet in the Library, and seeing how he looked she went straight to him.

'My mother died this morning,' he whispered, 'she just turned away and died. My father . . . he would speak with you, Privet. He too is weak and I do not think will last the day. Others have died these few days past, and more will die. Privet, it is murrain, isn't it?'

'I will come to him now,' said Privet; 'he was like a father to me when I was young.' As for the murrain, she did not know. She supposed it was.

She found Tarn weak but clear-headed, his benign and gentle face warming to see her, his paws squeezing at hers. Her father, his oldest friend, was nearby, and he grinned manically when Privet appeared.

Then, winking, he said, 'The old fool thinks he's sick. Eh, Tarn? He's not so ill he couldn't think to call us here.'

'My dear,' said Tarn, his voice barely more than a whisper, 'I want to tell you about your mother's coming here. Your father prefers not to talk of such things, never would, but he can listen and you'll make him talk when the time's right. Ask him about the Testimony your grandmother Wort scribed, and which he found at Hilbert's Top. Aye! That's pertinent!'

'Pertinent my arse!' said Sward.

'Well then,' continued Tarn as best he could, 'tell her how we failed to keep our promise to look after Shire. We did, you know. Yet maybe . . . we fulfilled our task through Privet here. Aye, Sward! *That's* pertinent and damn your arse.'

So Tarn talked, rambling, worried, feeling he had failed to keep some secret promise he had made to the Stone long, long ago. He dared talk more of Wort and told Privet how she had been concerned for Shire, of the sacrifice she had made, of what she must have given up. Of all that long-distant past he told, when Shire was but a pup and he but one Longest Night old.

Until at last he told how she had scribed in the earth at Crowden's southern portal, her name, and the names of the seven ancient systems: Uffington, Avebury, Rollright, Fyfield, Siabod, Caer Caradoc and . . .

'. . . and Duncton Wood. 'That was the one, my dear, the one that there was a strange light about, and which stayed clear as day in the earth: Duncton Wood. Remember it, Sward?'

'I do,' said Sward, 'old friend, I do.'

Then Tarn told of how Shire wanted to scribe down 'Beechenhill', but *that* Librarian Sans would not allow.

'I stanced there and made a prayer, as did your father too, and knew one day I must tell a mole those two names and how they seemed to speak out to me. Well, I never did tell Shire, nor can I now, but you, my dear . . . you I can tell. Those names were scribed for you . . .' he began to cough, as a mole near death coughs, deep, and long and terrible.

Yet when he had calmed again he grasped Privet's paw and said, 'You remember when you were a pup they said you looked like Wort?'

Privet nodded, tears in her eyes, as much for love of Tarn and to see him fade, as for memory of how she was hurt when young.

'I came to you and asked if it was true, and you said it was not.'

Tarn nodded feebly. ' 'Twas the only lie I ever told in my whole life, and I'll unsay it now. I saw Wort with my own eyes. These months past as I have seen you become adult, and your face begin to show the cares and passions of the world, I have seen that you look more and more as your grandmother did. But mole, the Wort I saw was not the Eldrene all moles love to hate, but a mole who had learned of life, who had had courage, who had turned finally towards the Stone. A mole who gave up what she thought was the best thing she ever made, which was Shire. But you, my dear, might have been much closer to her. Why, had she been younger when you were born and if circumstances had allowed her to live here as Sward was allowed, you might have been closest to her of all. 'Tis often the way with grandparents and grandpups. Aye, you would have been closest of all. It is an honourable heritage you have and no bad thing to look like such a mole.'

'Yes,' whispered Sward, who saw that his friend was near death, 'you were always the one like Wort, my dear, same eyes, same pointy snout, same *quality*.'

'Now he's talking!' declared Tarn. 'Said he would!'

His voice faded and he drifted towards sleep, but his paw kept its tight hold on Privet's.

He started back into consciousness quite suddenly.

'Promise me something, my dear.'

'I'll try,' whispered Privet.

'When you can, when it's safe, leave Crowden. Don't get stuck here as Shire was, down in the Library. There's places in moledom you've never dreamed of, and tasks you never knew you could do. Find a dream to give you courage to leave Crowden and the Moors. Go to Duncton Wood, my dear, that's dream enough for anymole, and when we saw your mother scribe it there was a light a-shimmering over it, like the Stone's blessed Light. Promise me you'll make it your dream.'

''Tis so far,' said Privet, 'too far for a mole like me.'

'Then go to Beechenhill, for they say that's not so far away. Go and scribe a prayer for your grandmother, whose greatest shame was there, yet whose life began there as well. But one way or another, promise me you'll make a dream to carry you off from here.'

With tears in her eyes Privet looked wildly about the hushed burrow, first at Sward and then at Hamble, who smiled for a moment at her, and nodded his head in assent.

'I'll find a dream,' said Privet. 'I'll try to find courage to leave.'

'Yesss . . .' sighed Tarn, closing his eyes and seeming satisfied, 'yes. Now, I would talk with good Sward, and then with my son. Goodbye, my dear, I did my best for you, and Sward still has time to do his!'

If there was a twinkle in the old mole's eyes as he said this, Privet did not see it, for she was sobbing, and could not but embrace Tarn with gentle passion, for she knew he was near the Silence now and he had spoken to her his last.

'I will leave you with your father now, Hamble,' she said at last, pulling away. She knew in that moment that all her life Hamble would be her friend, for what they had shared in the moleweeks past, with the grike refugees, and now with their dying parents, was bringing them out into a world that was alien and strange, and was bonding them for ever in ways that could never be sundered, whatever happened to their lives.

Before she left the chamber she went to Hamble and briefly he held her close, and she knew he was thinking the same thoughts. When she turned away from him to leave, there were tears on her fur where his face had been.

Chapter Twenty

Two days later, with Hamble at his side in the hushed burrow, Tarn quietly died, his kindly spirit drifting to the Silence as the seed of rose-bay willow-herb drifts past a watching mole and out of sight. No sooner had the news of his death reached the system as a whole than Shire, too, went into a final decline, her mind wandering and much distressed as Privet and Sward both tried to comfort her and relieve her misery.

She called continually for Lime, who after one more reluctant appearance did not come, declaring that everymole knew now that the sickness was virulent murrain and therefore infectious, and moles must let those affected by it die alone.

'It's your *mother*, Lime, and she calls for you,' said Privet.

'I owe nothing to her or to you either, come to that,' replied Lime. 'Do you think *she* would have gone to her mother, our grandmother, Wort, if to do so meant risking death? I don't think she would and for the same reason I'll not go to her. Anyway, parents must expect their offspring to fend for themselves and I'm staying over at the East End. Also . . .'

'Yes, Lime?'

These days Privet had the measure of her sister and was not so intimidated by her as she once was.

'I think I may be with pup. A late-autumn litter. I must think of them.'

Faced by what was most likely a lie or half-truth Privet could think of no more to say. And so it was that when, as November started, Shire's last hours came, Lime was nowhere to be seen despite the pathetic call from her mother: 'Lime, Lime, where are you, my love? You're the only one I want.'

Privet watched over her as Sward attended to her final needs with surprising gentleness. She heard the wandering voice, and saw the bleak puzzlement because Lime had not come. Then Shire seemed to slip back slowly through her life, shouting pathetically at Privet as if she were still a pup, crooning over a Lime she seemed to think present again, but now no more than a few days old.

Shire's gaunt face grew gaunter by the hour, and since she had not eaten for days it seemed that her body withered and grew thin before their eyes. As for her eyes and face, they expressed more and more that worry and fear they had held all her life, as if whatever it was she had feared had come now to visit her.

Yet suddenly all changed and her face relaxed, and her eyes gained a lightness, even a joy, Privet could never have guessed could be there.

'Are you taking me back to the Moors?' she said, her voice soft and trusting like a pup's. The question was asked of Privet, to whom throughout her illness as throughout her life she had always been unpleasant, showing not the slightest gratitude for anything she had done.

But now all was changed. She reached out for Privet's paw for the first time Privet could remember, and when she found it her touch, so unfamiliar to her daughter, was as light as the look in her eyes.

'Are you?' she said.

Privet hesitated, looked at Sward who nodded, and she said, 'Yes . . .'

Shire spoke in whispers, of places, it seemed, she remembered as a pup; some of them she liked and others she feared, but in all of them she felt safe in the company of the mole to whom she thought she spoke.

'It's the Eldrene Wort,' whispered Sward, during a time when Shire slept fretfully, 'she thinks you're Wort. So speak to her as if you are. She cannot have long now and it cannot hurt. If you are willing, that is . . . Stone knows she has done little enough for thee.'

A look of resignation came over Privet's face and she said, 'I'll try, but I don't know how Wort spoke, or what of. I never knew her, Father.'

'Didn't you?' he said vaguely.

Shire stirred and smiled and closed her eyes again, her paw in Privet's.

'You didn't either,' said Privet.

'Oh, but I did in a way,' he said suddenly, 'yes, I did. I . . .' and he grinned and said, 'I won't be long. I have something for you now. Yes, I have. For you, now, this is the right time. It has long troubled me.'

He left her and seemed gone for hours, so long indeed that when

238

Shire next woke, her mind wandering across the Moors, crying sometimes for some long-forgotten hurt, giggling too, Privet felt she might slip away from her at any moment. But then, as well, when Shire asked her some puppish question Privet felt curiously like a mother, like Wort herself might have felt at such a moment perhaps.

Privet felt the cycle of life turning, and the growing up that had been upon her since the autumn came seemed now near its end. She felt guilty to be at once so involved with her mother's sickness and yet so removed from it. When Shire slipped away into sleep again, she thought calmly to herself that with her mother's death her life could then begin.

Sward returned, bringing with him a text which she saw was scribed in his own untidy paw.

'For you, mole,' he said, giving it her quickly as if that were the only way he could part with it.

'For you.' She was conscious of him watching her as she took her paw gently from her mother's so she could look at the text.

'I'm afraid,' said Shire, suddenly starting out of sleep again, and in acute distress at some imagined danger. 'I'm scared.'

'It's all right,' said Privet instinctively like a mother, 'I'm here and I won't go away.'

'You will,' said Shire. Then opening her eyes she stared at Privet almost wildly and trying to rise shouted out, 'You *are!*'

She fell back immediately and closed her eyes, her rapid breathing slowing towards sleep once more.

Privet opened the text at last and ran her paws over its first words; '"I have found the sanctuary of the Stones again and I am thinking what it is I must say to you. You whose name I do not know, you whose life was all my purpose, you for whom my little love was meant . . ." What text is this, Father?' she said, interrupting herself and flicking expertly through its remaining folios for some general clues to what it was about.

'Why have you brought this here to me now, when –' But she stopped, for she had turned to the last folio and seen that he had written there, 'ALL I REMEMBER OF WORT'S TESTIMONY'. Privet stared at it, and then at Sward, in silence.

'What is this?' she whispered in an awed voice.

'It is that first part of Wort's Testimony I discovered on Hilbert's Top and which I kenned and later scribed down as best I could remember it. I believe, my dear, that it was addressed to some such single mole as thee, or . . .' and here he looked at Shire, 'perhaps Wort scribed it for Shire, the Shire she knew as a pup before she was forced to part with her, a pup that was lost, but to whom Wort speaks still and for ever more through those words she scribed.'

As Privet stared down at the copied text once more, her right paw running steadily over the scribing, Shire opened her eyes again, and seemed to see and understand what it was she did, though not of course the nature of the text.

'Mother,' she whispered like a pup, 'what are you doing?'

'I'm kenning a text,' replied Privet, 'a very special text.'

'Ken it to me. I want you to ken it to me. To me!'

Her frail old paw reached out and took Privet's and her look and voice were as near to being a pup's as an adult's can be.

Privet did not look up, but instead nodded and smiled such as a mother might, and whispering at first and then with growing confidence, she said, 'My dear, this text is for you, especially for you.'

Then she began to speak out Wort's words, scribed down by Sward. For a moment Shire's eyes opened wide again, a look of pleasure came to her face, and her breathing calmed. Then Privet spoke on, folio after folio, and more and more she spoke the words with gentle confidence, and knew as she did that for a time at least she was becoming Wort, she *was* Wort, and she was as caring as Wort would have been with Shire, had circumstances allowed, or if by some miracle she were resurrected here and now at her dying daughter's flank.

While from the text, through the miracle of words scribed long since, Wort *was* present again, and poor Shire, abandoned as it had seemed, never discovering true comfort and security since, found at last a comfort in the words Privet spoke out, a comfort only a mother can give, to ease a troubled passage through the final sickness of murrain to the Silence of the Stone.

While Privet herself found comfort too, in knowing that her grandmother had cared enough to scribe down testimony, and though it was only the first part that Sward had copied, never having kenned more, it was enough, for before its end Shire had slipped away, not to peace, but in peace, and with a smile and a touch that bespoke a faith that her mother truly loved her, and abandonment, and Sans, and all that later life of unhappiness, had never been.

Something in Privet, too, was healed. There, in that death-burrow Privet herself was reborn, where, as night came, and darkness, Shire died as the text's last words were spoken. One moment that grip on Privet's left paw was living, the next she felt the life pause, turn, and leave for somewhere else. And two moles who had not known a mother's love, knew at last a mother's touch.

A long time later, Sward came near. He touched Shire on the face. She who in life had looked so bitter and disagreeable, in death looked serene.

'It was meant to be so, my dear. Now listen to what I say. You must leave this place. I mean not this burrow but this system. Remember what Tarn said about Duncton Wood and Beechenhill. Those are the kind of places you must try to go to. Saddleworth, Bleaklow, Crowden, they're not for you, my love, and were never meant to be so. Take this fragment of a text, for perhaps it will give you credence in one of the great libraries of moledom. It will teach moles to know they can be forgiven, as it taught your mother she was loved. The two are the same you see, forgiveness and love. Just the same. You must leave before the murrain takes you, and before the grikes return. Take Hamble with you, for you were meant to be together . . .'

Privet shook her head. 'He's like a brother to me, nothing more.'

'Well then, as a brother he'll protect you.'

'And you, Father? What of you, and of the Library? What protection for it will there be if the grikes come as you say they will? Our system is weaker than it was; Hamble is one of the few strong males left and is needed here, as I am.'

Sward shook his head, unable to argue but sure that he was right. 'You must leave, you *will* leave, for I sense that in you is a destiny which is for all of us. Your grandmother knew it, you see. I have known it since the night you were conceived.'

'Known?' repeated Privet, wide-eyed.

Then there, as they paid their last respects to Shire through the night, he told her in his wild and rambly way all that he had not told and if, towards the end, Hamble quietly joined them he did not mind for surely Hamble was part of it as well. A pattern, a destiny, a purpose, a fulfilment.

'You're *definitely* part of it too, Hamble my lad,' he said with a smile, 'and you'll look after Privet, won't you?'

Hamble grinned.

'I always have, Sward, it's what my father told me to do, look after Privet.'

'You never said that!' said Privet.

Hamble shrugged.

'It's true all the same. He said it was a promise he had made, the same as he watched over Shire I was to watch over you. I thought I told you that.'

'You males are always telling me things unexpectedly which you say you told me before! You . . .' But she was suddenly tired, so tired.

'Come,' said Hamble, 'come to my burrow now and I'll see to your mother. Come, 'tis best.' So, taking up the text that now meant so much, Privet and Sward followed Hamble, to find another place to sleep.

Even if Privet had felt inclined to take Sward's advice to escape from the Dark Peak and seek out a system like Beechenhill to make a new life for herself, the circumstances were against it. With November the weather darkened and the clouds lowered down across the Moors, and the murrain hit hard and plunged the system in crisis and gloom and all healthy moles were needed as helpers or watchers over the Moors.

The safety of the Library now began to seriously concern Privet, whose position had grown in importance since her mother's illness and the death of other senior librarians. For all her youth, she seemed now to be the one to whom the others turned, or the only one not so shocked and beset by all that was happening as to be unable to think about risks now the system was so vulnerable. To her concern was added Sward's, who since Shire's death and his giving of Wort's text to Privet, had aged and retreated into himself. The world of the Moors was lost to him now, and of the surface too, for again and again Privet found him sequestered in that cramped corner of the Library to which Shire had consigned his texts, and there he browsed and muttered and grinned to himself, or with furrowed brow warned of the dangers of the grikes, and spoke of how he had brought his texts here for safety, saying they were safe no longer unless something was done.

'What can be done?' asked Privet, trying to reason with him.

'Delve!' said Sward grandly. 'Delve them so deep that if the grikes come the buggers'll give up before they reach the texts.'

'We have few moles strong enough to delve the defences into proper shape,' said Privet, 'let alone begin such a work, and none skilled enough.'

How desperate Sward looked then. 'The grikes will destroy all they don't understand, which means all the texts we have. Only the murrain has saved us from invasion so far but they got it before us and they'll recover before us. Then's the danger! Old Sward knows!'

As if his words were heard somewhere, that very night there was an alarm from the watchers at the East End: 'Grikes! Lurking grikes!'

'Lurking fears more like,' said Hamble when he was summoned. By now he had gained rank and respect, as Privet had, and along with other warrior moles stared out into the gloom.

'Listen to them calling us. 'Tis refugees from Ratcher once again, come for sanctuary. And this time . . .'

But there was argument once more, and the night deepened, and the calls came weaker through the dark as Hamble sought to persuade his peers to do their duty by the Stone and give sanctuary when asked.

'Anyway,' he said, 'there may be moles amongst them who can help us, for the grikes may use the coming of the winter to seek better shelter than the Moors, as they did before.' He was referring to a grike campaign generations past, whose heroic memory was kept alive in records in the Library and retold on winter nights.

There is a time when a warrior mole must stance up to his peers and fight for what he thinks is right, and with that dawn such a moment came to Hamble. He was a stolid mole, and strong, and though not the largest there, by the time dawn came he was easily the most angry. But Hamble was a mole who knew how to curb his talons and his tongue, and that the right stance and the right action at the right time were more powerful than a thousand words or talon thrusts.

At dawn he suddenly rose powerfully from among the group of moles who had listened to the refugees and without a further word resolutely set off through the defences. None followed him, except with shouted warnings he ignored; all watched and waited. They saw him emerge on to the surface in the gloom and then, with a shout, call to the moles that he was of Crowden and coming among them.

News of what he had done spread back into the system and moles came hurrying, Lime among the first, to support those who said that no strangers should be allowed in. But then, a little later, others came, including Privet, and all stared apprehensively into the Moors to see if Hamble would come back.

Minutes seemed hours to Privet when nomole came, nor any sound was heard. But then, as dawn lightened across the sky, they saw Hamble lead back a group of bedraggled-looking moles from among the peat hags, before they dropped down into the defence tunnels out of sight.

'He's not bringing them into Crowden!' roared one of the more belligerent moles.

But he was and he did. Boldly he led them through, and when he emerged on the safe side and his fellow-watchers ranged before him to prevent them coming on, Hamble thrust through the grike refugees and said fiercely, 'If there's any here who wishes to strike them they'll have to strike me first. These moles are not diseased at all. These are survivors of the murrain, but they have been besieged and starved by Ratcher's moles. Ten of them left Chieveley Dale to come here and five have got through and now come to ask for help, as those others did before them.

'As the Stone is my witness, ours is not the right to deny, but the duty to give them help and sanctuary. The Stone will be good to those who protect its own.'

But one of the belligerent ones came forward and with a great shout to the others to attack, talon-thrust at Hamble. But so quick was Hamble in moving to one side, and so resolute in talon-thrusting back, that the mole was off-balance and at Hamble's mercy before any could blink; and not another mole there had time to do a thing.

'You'd leave these moles to the mercy of Ratcher's crowd?' said Hamble, staring them all out. 'Look at them and see what you yourselves might be!'

There were five refugees: two adult males, a female, and two frightened and shivering youngsters. All gaunt and thin, and with near-defeat about the way they stanced, as if they expected that life which had dealt with them so hard would not forgive them now. Clustered about Hamble as if he were the only thing between life and death, they stared pathetically at the Crowden moles.

Then with a look that combined impatience with contempt Hamble signalled to the leading male among the refugees to go forward.

'Hold your head high, mole, for what you've done was brave. There's not a mole here will harm you now. May you and your friends and kin teach us all you know that we may the better resist Ratcher when he comes.'

Then a light of hope and courage came to that mole's eyes, and turning to one of the youngsters he put his paw on his shoulder encouragingly.

'Come,' he said gently, in that deep and guttural voice of the Saddleworth moles, 'we're safe now, as Rooster said we would be. Come!'

With nervous smiles and muttered thanks they advanced among the Crowden moles, none smiling back until Privet dared come forward and with a glance at Hamble said, 'Follow me, there's moles will take care of you and your young and find you a place to eat and rest. Come!'

Many including Lime muttered and stared venomously at Privet and the strangers, but with Privet bold in front, and Hamble bold behind, none dared question it.

When they had gone Hamble said quietly, 'For Stone's sake, moles, let this be an end to our rejection of moles who seek our help. Our strength now will be more in the care and mercy we show others than in what we give only to ourselves. Crowden must look beyond itself at last.'

Hamble was never a mole for speeches, but such words as these he had heard his father say and they seemed to serve the purpose now.

'Aye! The lad's right! Moles like this could be our strength!' muttered the others amongst themselves. 'These moles have shown courage coming here. Stone knows we would not show as much out upon the Moors, and this place must be as alien to them as the Moors would be to us!'

It did not escape Privet's notice that the name of Rooster had been invoked once more and, after all that had happened, how much more she wanted to learn about him! Once again she scribed down all that the strangers told her of him which only confirmed what she had heard before.

'He is a mole of peace,' they said, 'and refuses to fight or hurt another. He came to us from Hilbert's Top where he has retreated since Samphire's death. He told us not to hurt another mole, but to turn from Ratcher's moles and flee and find a place where we could learn of the Stone in peace. He told us to come here, and warn you that the murrain has been and gone in Ratcher's place. These moleyears of summer past Red Ratcher has travelled north and gathered a great army of grike moles. Come the spring they will descend on Crowden. We cannot stay here after that. This much he believes.'

'We'll fight such moles!' declared Hamble. 'Crowden always has, and it will do again.'

'But did you meet this mole Rooster?' asked Privet of one of the refugees one day. The fact was that they were curiously reluctant to talk too much of Rooster, or to say anything of their previous history in the Dale.

But this one said, 'Me? I saw him delve. I lived among his delvings. What need to see a mole when you've lived so, for there we knew him better than he did himself.'

'What is this delving that he does?' asked Sward excitedly.

But it was a question none of the refugees could easily answer. They looked vague, and shrugged, and searched for words they could not find.

'He is a Master of the Delve,' said one eventually.

'What's that?' asked Sward.

'I don't know,' whispered the mole, 'it's something that he is. He hurts nomole nor ever will. They say that if he does so he will die. A Master cannot fight or kill except himself, he delves.'

'Rooster, Master of the Delve . . .' whispered Privet in the darkness of the burrow where she told her tale, where now, though it was black as night, the first dawn birds could be heard up on the surface of Duncton Wood. 'Each time I scribed his name, or that word "delve", I felt a tremor of destiny upon me. The idea of meeting him, a Master of the Delve, stirred me in a way that I had never known . . .'

She stared at each of them in turn, and they moved not, like shadows that were divorced from everything but the distant time and place to which she had taken them, and with which she was the only link.

'It seemed that all my life had been moving towards the decision I made one night then, at such a pre-dawn time as this. In my innocence of such things I decided that Rooster might be the mole to delve a place of protection for our Library. Therefore, I, Privet, weakest of moles, would set forth alone across the Moors, and using the infor-mation those refugees had given me, I would find him, and ask him to come to Crowden. He would delve for us, and teach us if he would. He might even lead us. Yes, that's what I decided to do! Of course, I told myself it was only for the Library that I was going: how could a mole like me have guessed that deeper passions than libraries stir young females to set off on perilous missions across the Moors?'

'I don't understand what you mean,' said Whillan, as innocent now as his mother had been then.

'She means love, dear,' said Fieldfare cheerfully. 'For Rooster!'

'Ah!' said Whillan in a bemused and academic way. 'Of course!'

There were smiles and then more silence, until Chater stirred and said what all were thinking, and speaking as if it was *now* Privet was making such a decision, not long before: 'But mole, you're not a warrior or fighter, but a female and a scribe. You'll not survive on the Moors in winter, or among the grikes, not all alone. This part of your tale I'll not believe!'

There was a murmur of assent at this from all but Stour, until Privet nodded, and smiled and said, 'Yet that is what I had decided to do.

246

Then and there! With no word to anymole, for they would only stop me! Well, it was time I was impulsive, and I had not forgotten that sense of freedom I had felt when I had first set paw upon the Moors, nor my father's plea for me to leave Crowden. It all seemed to make sense then in that dark hour.'

'Things often do,' said Drubbins wryly, 'at that hour! The true light of dawn returns a mole his common sense.'

'Well, be that as it may, I rose from my burrow and set off for the East End there and then. My only fear was not the Moors but getting through the defences, but by then I had seen enough to remember them. My training as a scribe had given me a good memory. It took time, and I had to hide from the watchers more than once, but eventually I got out at last to the Moors and –'

'And?' said Fieldfare impatiently.

'Hamble was there waiting for me! "You!" he said, laughing. He had long since been warned that a mole was skulking among the defences and had guessed it was one of the refugees wanting to escape the confines of Crowden. I explained as resolutely as I could what I was doing. He told me I couldn't. We had an argument . . . I wonder if all ventures begin in such a way?'

'Some do,' said Chater, glancing at Fieldfare with a grin. Above them a blackbird scurried near and called. Dawn was coming fast.

'We argued until at last I told him it was for me as it had been for him when he had gone out to bring the refugees into Crowden. "I will do it, my dear," I said, "whatever you do."

'"Well then," he said at last, resigned, "you'll not do it without me. I'll go with you, or you'll not go at all."'

'For an innocent female, as you called yourself, you didn't do badly!' declared Fieldfare approvingly.

'It gets worse, I'm afraid,' said Privet contritely. 'For then Hamble said, "But we'll need a guide, and there's only one mole can give that service – your father Sward, and don't tell me he's too old. He's hankered after travelling the Moors again for years and a mole like him will find his strength again when he needs to!"'

'Well!' declared Fieldfare. 'Hamble's certainly a mole who knows how to get things moving.'

Privet laughed. 'He always was.'

'And he helped you go to find Rooster?' asked Drubbins.

'Of course,' said Privet, but the calm way she tried to speak was belied by the shadows of new memories that now crossed her face.

247

Chapter Twenty-One

Although alarm and horror spread through Crowden when the news broke of Privet's and Hamble's foolhardy venture with Sward on to the Moors to contact Rooster, it was too late to send a party off to bring them back.

All moles could do was stare up from the safety of Crowden's ramparts to the Moors and the drizzly cloud that rode on the wind there, and ponder on the stupidity of youth, and reflect what a loss the system had sustained: its most promising young campaigner, and its best young scribe. As for Sward, he always was a daft mole anyway, and had not been the same since Shire and Tarn had died. Perhaps it was best that he was away; but then, if any mole could guide Hamble and Privet back to safety, it was he.

The fears for the trio's safety were well justified, as they themselves might soon have agreed had they known what they would find if fate and fell circumstance combined to deliver them to Ratcher's moles. But they did not, and proceeding on to the Moors oblivious of what lay ahead, they were concerned only to make their way towards the secret system of Chieveley Dale as quickly as they could, and then find clues to Rooster's whereabouts.

They journeyed in single file, with Sward taking the lead, Privet in the middle and Hamble at the rear. Sward knew the first part of the route quite well, and went south-east across the Moors to keep well clear of the great stretch of water that floods the vale eastward and might have hemmed them in if grikes were about.

They travelled in silence, partly because of the need to go unobserved, but also because each in different ways was greatly affected by the emergence from the limitations of Crowden and its Vale on to the wider expanse of the Moors.

Sward was simply happy, for the Moors had been his life, and only as he set paw on them again, and scented once more the dank clean smell of peat, and heard the curlew's cry, did he realize how much he had missed such a sense of freedom for so long. He felt liberated from what he had come to regard as his responsibility to Shire and through her to his texts, and now it seemed he had only this final task of bringing Rooster to Crowden to delve a safe place for the texts, before his life's work was done and he was free to live only for himself once more.

Hamble, for his part, felt not liberty but responsibility, though it was a feeling he welcomed. He knew he was the warrior in the group, and that on him would fall the task of protecting the other two should danger threaten. Not for the first time he looked at Privet's slight form as she picked her way through the heather and peat hags ahead, and felt affection and liking for her, as well as a wish that he might have loved her as a mate would. But that had never been and he was content to travel out on this first great venture from Crowden with the mole he now regarded as his greatest friend.

For her part, Privet felt nervous of where she was, but safe: for she trusted her father Sward's knowledge of the Moors, and knew that she could have no better fighter at her flank than Hamble, if fighting were needed. But that much known, her thoughts moved on swiftly to other things: the sense of escape from her home system was one of them, the realization which grew as the day went by that moledom was vast indeed, and thus far she knew so little of it. With each step she took, Crowden seemed to grow less important, and less like the place in which she wished to spend the rest of her life. Had not Sward often mentioned Beechenhill as a place to which a scribemole might go, and fabled Duncton Wood? Of course he had, and now with beating heart she began to see that if she could come out on to the Moors, why, she could go almost anywhere!

But more powerful than such ideas by far was her growing sense that this journey to find Rooster had something of destiny about it. All that she had heard of him, and all the circumstances that had given her the impulse to come on to the Moors, made her think that in some way her life and his were bound together. So it was that in those first hours of their journey, until nightfall brought them to a halt, it was dreams of love fulfilled that Privet had, the natural but naïve dreams of one who has never loved or been fully loved, but who has ached and hoped for it, and secretly prayed that one day it might be.

That love was not so easy, that the chances of finding love in such a way and such a place were slim, that Rooster was not by all accounts a mole a female would especially love in *that* way, did not concern Privet. She was young and inexperienced, she was abroad on a dangerous venture, she was with two moles she trusted, and she was seeking to find a third whom she believed it was her destiny to meet. Thus far doubts did not, could not, play a part in the dreams that drove her on.

It was in the middle of the next day, after crossing rougher and more wormless ground, that Sward judged it right to veer north-east to drop down and cross the stream that flows down that part of the Vale.

'We've passed by the lake now, and the harder part of the journey's to come,' he said, pointing a talon north across the Vale below them towards a bleak black rise of ground that stretched interminably out of sight and higher than where they stanced.

'That's Pikenaze Moor,' he explained, 'which I have traversed only once before. Beyond it lies the greatest challenge on our journey to Chieveley Dale, the rising fastness of the Withens Moor where many of the grimmest battles among the grikes and others were fought in decades gone by. Stone knows what dark deeds were committed there – it was a place I swore I would never cross again and certainly not alone. But with a strong young mole with us like you, Hamble, and with your common sense, Privet, I suppose an old mole like me should not be nervous.' He shrugged and smiled wryly.

They had crossed the stream and trekked halfway up Pikenaze Moor before dusk came and Hamble suggested they should delve a temporary burrow. All were tired, and a little concerned by the prospect of travelling on to Withens Moor on the morrow.

So far there had been no sign of recent mole, though here and there they had come upon traces of temporary burrows such as the one they themselves delved now. These were not parts that moles dallied in, the less so that the wind was never-ending on the higher parts, and the heather among which they hid hissed about their heads, and creaked, and made a mole feel there were others lurking about when there were none.

They all woke with the dawn, feeling they had not slept at all, and after the briefest of groomings and a quick bite at the sour-tasting worms they found, they were on their way up to the top of Pikenaze to view the next part of their journey.

It was a grey and drizzly day, and they found themselves looking up a long steep clough with dark looming sides, which led up in the far distance, and more than a day away, to a steep rise on to the highest part of the Moors in that area.

'Twizle Head Moss,' said Sward grimly. 'Beyond it according to the moles we've spoken to is Ramsden Clough which we must find a way into if we are to descend to the vale that leads to Chieveley Dale.

Now the part I came down when I was here lies to the right where that mist hangs. That's Withens Edge and not a place for mole. Wormless and vulnerable to rook and buzzard. *That* way, and on to the east, takes a mole to the notorious Charnel Clough where Red Catcher's clan resides. We'll stay well away from that . . .'

Privet heard what he said, but her eyes were drawn to the lower part of Withens Moor which lay beneath them in the mist and rain. The white-brown run of a stream was visible, and the fearsome and inexorable climb up towards the distant Twizle Head Moss. It was the widest expanse of ground she had ever seen in her life, and its slow rise to darkness and shifting mists filled her with a sense of desolation. Surely nomole could ever have fought others and lost their lives over possession of such a place? Surely none could live there? Yet no sooner had they trekked downslope to the bank of the grubby brook that drained this vast rising moor than they saw evidence of mole in the form of ruined mounds of stony earth and collapsed tunnels of a mean and meagre kind.

'The moles hereabouts stick to the brook's edge as being the most wormful, or least wormless,' said Sward, 'and for the same reason we'll take that route up. Hamble, your eyes are better than mine so you take the lead, but we must be watchful behind, Privet, for the peat hags give plenty of hiding-places here for malevolent moles. But we're far enough from the Ratcher clan's place not to run into any grikes that would wish to harm us. The moles who are here will be more curious than anything else, but of course once they see us word of our coming will get about and we may be pursued. So once we start there's no hope of stopping for long until we find somewhere safe, or moles we can trust to give us sanctuary. It's many a year since I was here, so much may have changed. But I picked up some useful texts on Withens when I was here in a community some way up this vale whose location I may with luck recognize when we get there.'

With a brief sad smile for times past, Sward gave way to the younger Hamble, and with Privet taking up her place between them once more they set off upslope among the mass of hags and pools, wet moss and ferns, through which the Withens Brook rushed down its miserable way.

Times had changed and so had the place. Nowhere did Sward remember, and feeling increasingly despondent on his behalf, Privet steadily plodded on, marvelling for the first time in her life at the adventures her father must once have had, and the courage too to have travelled in such places alone.

251

'I'm sure it was here . . .' said old Sward at every new turn in the stream on whose higher banks they travelled, 'or was it . . . yes, it was just ahead.'

But it was not, though several times more they found signs of itinerant mole and each felt that life was not far away. Until the rain that had spotted down upon them through the day thickened into drizzle, the winds grew gusty, the temperature began to drop, and Hamble decreed that the time had come to find shelter for the night.

It was while they were exploring the hags surrounding a little terrace of drier ground above the brook that Privet saw movement and Hamble went ahead alone to investigate, his two friends huddling together among the peat to shelter from the now driving rain as best they could. Then suddenly Hamble reappeared, his face set grimly.

'Follow me,' he said, without further explanation.

They did so, wondering, turning away from the stream to a half-hidden and tortuous path that they would never have easily found except by chance, or prior knowledge. It was running with water, and the rain dripped from the heather that overhung the hags through which it went. They turned a corner and the path widened into a shallow black pool on one side of which, blanched by water and picked clean by rooks, a dead sheep lay, its grey wool spread grotesquely over the hag on which it had stumbled its last, all sodden with rain and filthy with peat.

Hamble hurried them past this and they climbed a short grassy way on to a higher terrace carved in former times by the stream which now rushed noisily below. The terrace had all the bumps and pits of an ancient system, and a fresher scent of life than any they had so far found.

'It was here!' cried out Sward suddenly. 'The community I knew was *here!*'

Even as he said it, Hamble pointed ahead of them to one edge of the terrace where the ground rose steeply into heathery moor once again, and there among the shadows they saw the bedraggled forms of a few wretched moles.

Privet gasped in astonishment and sudden fear, for it was plain from their size and dark fur, as well as their short snouts and lumpy paws, that the moles were grikes. But these were no rapacious monsters, nor fearsome warriors, just moles brought by starvation and disease to the very edge of their lives.

Instinctively Privet held back with Hamble, for both had spent a lifetime that spoke of grikes as dangerous killers, but just as instinctively old Sward went forward, with a gesture of greeting, and a quaint nod of respect.

A single mole, older than the others and with grizzled grey fur, broke clear of the pathetic group and came towards Sward with a grimace that Privet took to be a smile.

'You're welcome, mole, as any living mole would be. But we've little to offer.'

The grike spoke mole, but in a thick accent which Privet found hard to follow. To her surprise her father replied in Whernish, raising a paw and then going forward and smiting the other mole's outstretched paw. They spoke quietly for a moment or two but with increasing intensity until suddenly the grike reared up with what Privet took this time to be a laugh, though it sounded deep and threatening to her, before he said, 'Bugger me but it's Sward! Well!'

He turned back to the group, went to an old female there, and said in a loud voice that suggested she was somewhat hard of hearing, 'Myrtle, it's Sward the Scholar. Aye, Sward! And he's not come to harm us, not him. Why, you remember he came before?'

Remember? The two old moles forgot everything in remembering their dim and distant former meeting – the rain, the Moors, their companions, the gathering night. Never would Privet have believed her father could grow young again, but young he suddenly became. As she watched him talk to the old grike, and heard his laughter, and saw the interest and sympathy he showed for the sorry story they soon told him, she felt again that sense she had had earlier that for the first time she was understanding what Sward had once been.

Then, when she was brought forward at last and introduced to this 'old friend' as 'my daughter Privet' she felt proud of that introduction. Proud too of the affectionate way Sward introduced Hamble, and humbled by the deep respect Sward showed these poor, half-starved grikes, stranded by life and circumstance in this forgotten and desolate part of moledom.

The old grike's name was Turrell, and if first impressions last longest, and the Stone's Light shines on all moles, then to Privet and Hamble these were worthy representatives indeed of the grikes.

What little food they had they offered to share with a mole and his kin (for they included Hamble in Sward's family) for memory's sake, and such dank and cramped quarters as they had they made over to their visitors, with gruff apologies and humble pleas that times were hard, worms scarce, and their strength low.

'But it'll get better, Sward, it will,' said Turrell hopefully, looking round with concern at the four young moles with him. They were not his kin, but the surviving young from two families the rest of whom had died of plague in the bitter molemonths just past.

'That, and the Ratcher clan's predations on us – they took the only young female who had her full health back to Charnel Clough – have brought us close to ruin and extinction in these parts,' Turrell went on. 'You go higher up the Withens and you'll see moles worse off than us.'

Once they were rested, and before night came, Hamble and Privet set off back downstream to a wormful spot they had noticed and soon brought back some food for the others. Three trips they made, while Sward helped Turrell delve a drier chamber, and the youngsters, too shy to speak, visibly perked up.

The rain got heavier and all the moles settled down for a night of talking and exchange, in which Turrell and Myrtle told of the troubled years they had had. When the grikes heard that the trio had come direct from Crowden they were interested indeed, and grew positively voluble when they discovered that it was for Rooster they had come.

'You know of him then?' asked Privet.

'Know of him lass?' said Turrell in his rough, accented voice. 'You'll not find a mole on the Moors who doesn't these days. Know him and admire him, for so far at least he's got the better of Red Ratcher, and he's the first mole in generations who's brought hope to this forsaken place. There have been others no doubt, but they've gone or have died and we've been put back to what we've always been. But Rooster, by these old talons of mine, he's a mole like nomole I've ever heard of before.'

'Do you know where we'll find him?' asked Hamble.

'I've an idea where he lives, but you'll not find him easily, that's for sure. If *you* could, a stranger to these parts, then Ratcher's mob could too. Mind, you've rascally old Sward here and he's a legend too in his own way.'

'Tell us what you know of this Rooster then,' suggested Sward, shoving the fattest worm he could see towards Turrell, adding as he did so, 'though I should warn you that my daughter Privet is a scribe and scholar like me and will scribe down all you say one of these days!'

Turrell laughed and looked round at his mate, and the youngsters.

'It does my heart good to see moles gathered like this again and yarning. Aye, it does me good!' He munched the worm for a while, settled close to the scraggy form of Myrtle, and finally said, 'So, it's Rooster you want to know about. Well, I'll tell you what I've heard –

it's a tale will do anymole good on a night like this! But I'd best begin with Red Ratcher, for he's the start of it and will be the ending of it one way or t'other.'

'Red' Ratcher was so called from the fact that when the sun struck his coarse fur it took on an unsavoury russet or reddish tinge, particularly about his short thick neck and massive shoulders, an effect increased by the untoward redness of his eyes.

He and his clan had as their base the obscure but wormful valley called Charnel Clough, discovered and used as a hiding-place by their ancestors in the decades after Whern's fall to the Stone. This narrow and forbidding gorge, some three days' journey north-east of Crowden Vale, could only be reached by a narrow valley between cruel juts and overhangs of rock which seemed always to threaten anymole who hurried by underneath. A place impregnable and easily over-watched by guards, though few would be so foolhardy as to risk venturing there. A peat-stained torrent of a river, the Reap, plunged down a succession of straits and waterfalls through the Clough, from whose obscure and dangerous depths spray blew up dank and cold and assaulted a mole whichever way he turned.

This perpetual wet combined with a trick of geology to produce a lush vegetation of ferns and other shade-loving plants, as well as many places of worm-rich soil. The only other creatures which inhabited the place were rabbits in the grassy lower slopes, and the ravens that fed on them from the cliffs above.

The system itself was in one of the higher, more secret parts of the Clough, where after steep falls down from the Moors it opened out into a strange flat area hemmed in by cliffs. At its upper end the Reap stream tumbled down until it entered into a narrow cleft that dissected the plateau in which the system was delved.

The northern of the two resulting halves was called the Charnel, the southern was the Reapside, and they were connected only by a treacherous arch of rock, the Span, which was perpetually wet and slippery and at whose steep sides, in clefts, wet ferns and mosses hung. Since the way out of the system and down the Clough was on the Reapside, anymole that had crossed the Span into the Charnel must come back that way, unless he cared to risk climbing the heights of the Creeds, the raven-infested cliffs, to the Moors above. Some had tried; none succeeded, few survived.

Through the years the Ratcher clan had grown infertile and in-bred, so that it had an unusually high number of deformed and idiot moles, and a line of females who had goitres disfiguring their necks, and the short and running snortle snout to which such moles are prone.

These unfortunates were banished to the Charnel side of the system to join the small and desolate community of moles already there – all disfigured, mostly diseased – who were said to be the original occupants of Charnel Clough. These miserable moles kept themselves to themselves – but for the occasional sacrifice of their offspring into the Reap – and the Ratcher moles stayed well clear of them, fearful of the diseases they suffered, and the vile and ugly primitiveness of their lives in so enshadowed a place.

Meanwhile, from the grim facts of Ratcher interbreeding and consequent sterility had come an awareness of the need for fresh blood from moles outside. It was the habit of the fitter males to raid neighbouring systems in late summer and early spring and find moles for breeding purposes.

Red Ratcher was pure grike, and won his place as head of the clan by fighting his father to the death, and unceremoniously hurling his two brothers down into the foaming Reap. He was formidable, though no more so than any petty tyrant who rules a system and a region for a time before his own advancing age and the youth of others displaces him. He had no subtlety of intellect and his intelligence was of the crude and cunning kind that knows most moles are biddable under intimidation and fear.

So Red Ratcher – or Ratcher as he became universally known – gained the ascendancy, though still unknown to anymole outside that dreadful area. The only real insight he ever had came during his first raid to get a mate, when his group were stranded for some weeks to the south of Saddleworth on Bleaklow Moor, during which time they made merry with the few poor local moles they found, and much enjoyed themselves.

From this brief encounter with the world outside it occurred to Red Ratcher that the system might expand a little and put out some of its members to breed in other places, and so spread the Ratcher blood about.

This he did, though not with any real strategic forethought. But since this small expansion coincided with Ashop's demise and nomole held sway across the Moors, Ratcher's moles found it easy to establish themselves here and there. From small beginnings do larger evils grow.

At that same time a grim doubt came to Red Ratcher about his own possible sterility. It was not easy to tell for certain since it was the clan's brutish way to share their females out like food. The head or master at the time had first choice, but when he had had his way with those females he desired he passed them on and others had them too, according to rank and strength. In that way the true father was never known for certain. However, communities have a snout for such things and the word got out two springs running that not a single pup born was of Ratcher's spawn – a possibility he liked not one little bit. It dinted his pride. It made him doubt himself. It made for insubordinate laughter. It irked him sorely.

Therefore he decided to take a female all his own when next he raided forth, and since the eastern population of moles was thin, and Crowden was still too strong a system to risk attacking, it was to the north he went, to a quiet Stone-fearing vale called Chieveley Dale. Little more is known of that raid but that Red Ratcher and his mob found a small and peaceable community of moles, half-grikes, doing their best to keep a low snout and worship the Stone and so escape the thralldom of their past. Ratcher killed them all, except for a solitary female, dark, molish, civilized, and one he intended to call his own.

Her name was Samphire, and she was a mole of exceptional grace and beauty, who was of the Stone and in intelligence and common sense far more than Ratcher's equal. But without friends or kin she had no chance, and it is easy to imagine her terror after her abduction by such moles, as the sheer cliffs of the Charnel Clough closed in on her and she began to realize escape would be nigh impossible. More than that, that her role was consort to the infamous and loathsome Ratcher, whose rude attentions spring and autumn would surely make the prospect of never escaping from the Charnel Clough more like a living death.

Added to this was an experience she had soon after she arrived on the Reapside, so horrible, so searing that she shivered at the thought of it for days after. Even had she been able to make sense of it – which later she did – it was not something a mole easily forgets.

It was this: on a certain day, known to the Reapside moles, they gathered along the Reap in festive mood and chattering and pointing in their rough brutish way, peering through the spray and mist to the other side until, as if on cue, the deformed moles of the Charnel appeared, pushing, carrying, driving some of their young before them to the wet and slippery edge of the Reap itself.

The adults were bad enough, though the spray made it hard to make out the extent of their deformities. But Samphire saw enough to know that these were almost mutant moles, with split paws, and spaddled snouts, all ulcerous and huge, and swollen eyes that stared as if in fear. Whilst many had goitres at their necks, all round and shining and furless, big as their heads, most horrible.

Their pups were worst. Did one have two living heads? Samphire thought it was so. Was one without limbs at all, yet alert of eye? It seemed to be. Were several huge of limb, bodies without brains? And some thin and furless and ulcerated? They were.

Then, to Samphire's undying horror, these pups were one by one pushed into the treacherous Reap, with gesticulations of joy, and strange savage shouts whose muted sound was echoed by the Ratcher moles, who, as the helpless pups fell and bobbed and drowned, laughed at their plight, wagered on how long they would float, and jeered at the monstrous parents of these doomed young.

All this Red Ratcher much enjoyed, and he grew angry with Samphire when she tried to turn away and angrier still when she dared cry. Ratcher moles should not show such weakness; Ratcher moles had little enough to entertain them and this routine ritual (for so it was) should not be spoilt by the bleating of a consort.

Somehow Samphire survived these ordeals and got with pup, and as her pregnancy advanced she began to come to terms with the life she must lead and decided on the secret strategy she must adopt. It was based on the astonishing discovery that Ratcher 'loved' her, if love it be that is ever-possessive, and seeks to hold for ever the body and the spirit of a mole to one's use.

This hold on him grew stronger when she bore him a five-pup litter, not one deformed, all large, all strong, thus proving to all the clan that he was a fertile mole. What pride did he feel then! What love for her! What wish of hers would he tumble over himself to satisfy – any but two: her desire to worship the Stone out loud in prayer and ritual as she had been taught, and her wish to leave him and his wretched system for ever and forthwith. Ah, no, those two he could not grant.

Therefore, to punish him (though it must have hurt her as much) she suckled his young without love, and with coldness watched them grow; with indifference she let them roam from the home burrow, and when two tumbled over the void and into the stream, then let Ratcher grieve for both of them; and if another was blinded in a fight, let Ratcher decide how best to put him out of his misery, for she would not, and did not care.

She could not, for she grieved still for the kin she had lost so violently in Chieveley Dale to the mole who now held her as captive in body as she increasingly held him in spirit. But she was clever enough not to be too cold and so, at least, Ratcher permitted her to stay on the sunnier Reapside and abide with him.

A cycle of seasons turned and she must let him come to her again and make love, so that for the second time she was with pup. Again a five-strong litter, again all healthy, again all fit for a father's pride. Again and again and again she reared them lovelessly, biding her time until the day might come when the never-mentioned Stone, to whom she whispered her secret prayers of hope, would send her a sign of what to do. The Stone sent her no sign, but subtly it put into her mind this thought: that the third litter she had by Ratcher she would at least try to love. She might have lost her liberty, but could she not inculcate into her future pups thoughts and ambitions that might undermine their father? Aye, she surely could, and surely would try.

It was in the ensuing moleyears of that following summer that Red Ratcher began to expand his realm, and it was Samphire's sons who were sent forth to colonize Saddleworth and Bleaklow Moor. These were Ratcher's mob and they took time to learn their task for they were full of fear and superstition, thinking the Weign Stones a most dangerous place, and Crowden much stronger than it was. Had they but known the truth, how different might moledom's history be!

The moleyears of winter wore on and internecine feuds stopped Ratcher's mob expanding more. Meanwhile, Samphire's third spring in Charnel Clough began and this time she allowed Red Ratcher to her burrow with a certain joy, thinking she would make a brood to destroy the clan without the rapacious Ratcher ever knowing what she intended. There was a certain cruel ecstasy in feeling him touch as gently as he could the body he now worshipped, aged a little, lined as well, but more beautiful and holy to him than it had ever been and him *not knowing* what the mind that lived in that body thought.

'Forgive me, Stone,' she whispered when he had done, 'forgive me for such hateful thoughts, but without your guidance I can see no other way to fulfil my purpose here.'

In truth, with that third mating Samphire first felt the fullness of the love Ratcher had for her, and in that she felt a dreadful pity for all he was, and for the confusion such lost moles suffer in their lives.

'Why make me pity him, Stone? Why do you make it so hard for me?'

The Reap's grim roar was the only reply she heard.

But her pregnancy was not good. Sickness came, and fevers, and loss of blood, and her worry for her pups grew even worse when over on the Charnel side others made pregnant that same spring began to abort, or worse, give birth to premature deformities that lived until they had to be put down.

'It is the plague murrain!' moles cried.

Murrain had come upon the Ratcher clan and history would show that theirs was the first area it reached after beginning a cycle of seasons before in Whern.

Yet Samphire's hopes rose as the weeks progressed and she did not abort, while some others gave birth to healthy litters. Fear of the murrain declined, Charnel was safe, all was well, forget what happened earlier.

But near the end, Samphire knew in her heart that all was not well and when her litter came, though it was five-strong once more, every one was deformed. The first was pawless. The second without snout or eyes. The third had an open back like one great wound. The fourth was shrivelled-up and old. The fifth was dark, ugly, odd of face, deformed of paw, and still, quite still except for the shallowest breathing she had ever known. He could not last the day.

'All must die, Samphire,' said Red Ratcher, peering at these deformities. 'You know it must be so.' He spoke gently, as even such a mole will do when he has found it in his rough, closed heart to love.

She stared at him, weak with the pupping she had made, but knowing what he said seemed true. And yet, as she stared down at the pathetic things, she still felt that love for them she had from the very first, and which she had never felt for those perfect ones she had borne before.

'My dear,' she said . . .

'It must be so.'

'Great Ratcher,' she said, determined not to give up while there was still life within her pups, 'grant me only this. Give me one day and night with them, that I may give them all my love before you take them out to die. Grant me only that as a reward for all I have given you, and all the good pups I have made.'

He stared at the wretched things and nodded his slow head.

'At dawn I'll come. Then I must take them from here. The system will expect it. There will be other broods. Remember, there will be more for you to love.'

Did he understand then that these ones she loved more than the ones before? Perhaps.

But what she knew he could not know was that there would be no more broods from her, never. The murrain had taken that ability away. She *knew* it to be so. These poor things, then, were the first and last she could ever call her own, they were the Stone's gift to her made in love, and in them she must find love by giving it.

'Teach me,' she whispered up in prayer when he was gone, 'teach me to love them through this day and night with all my heart and body. Teach me what I must do.'

There, to the thunder of the River Reap, in air all dank with its endless spray, with great Ratcher brooding out on the Span, the Stone found an answer to her prayer. Good Samphire rediscovered all the love she had lost, and much more as well. In those few hours that she had, she gave her love to her poor litter, each one encircled in her paws, each one that could suckled at her teats, each one living in the endless moment which is a pup's consciousness. Each striving to live that soon must die.

Except the fifth, which lay inert, silent, beyond even her dear love; yet breathing still and only just alive.

What words of love she whispered to each one of them, what tears she shed, what agony she felt to feel them weaken with the chill advance of dawn, what stabbing pain of loss she began to feel when Ratcher's shadow crossed her portal once again.

'One here,' she said immediately, 'has not yet known my love. This fifth and last has not stirred for me. Let him stay by me to the very end for perhaps even yet he will know a moment's consciousness and sense how much he is loved by me.

'But these others, all nameless, have known my love. Each one is weakening even as we speak, and suffering more, but each has acknowledged its mother's touch. Take them now, my dear, and give them peace.'

Then, gently for such a mole, Red Ratcher took each one out into the dawn, carrying it in his great maw before the gaze of other moles. Even as he trod out upon the treacherous Span to throw them off he felt them fade away and die. Not one but died before it was dropped down, and whatmole can say they had not had the happiest of lives, encircled by a mother's love, carried by a father to their end? Returned to the Silence of the Stone before they were dropped into the oblivion of the Reap below. Who dares say that?

But when Red Ratcher went down into Samphire's tunnels for the fifth, she would not let him go.

'I felt him begin to stir, my dear. I felt him begin to know my love. Let him be with me a little more for he may yet live and be your pride.'

Red Ratcher stared at her whom he held more beautiful than any

261

mole he ever knew, whose life he had stolen, whose family he had destroyed, then down at the inert pup.

'He is deformed and must die even if he lives,' he said, 'look at his paws! Look at his great strange head! We have made better pups than this before and will again. Let me take this one now.'

She licked at the pup's paws, which were large and strange; she nuzzled at his head, which was huge, swollen and wrinkled at once. Yet she felt love for him, and felt deep within his tiny body the first stirrings of real life.

Watching, Ratcher said, 'Tend him a few moments more before I take him then.'

Desperately she licked her pup, and caressed him, and tried to whisper movement into him enough that Ratcher might relent. But he seemed barely alive at all.

'I must take him now,' said Ratcher.

'Yes,' said Samphire blankly, giving up, 'yes, take him and may the Stone take him for ever to its care.'

'The Stone?' said Ratcher uneasily.

'The Stone.'

'It is not of this system,' growled Ratcher, suddenly angry.

'It is of everything,' Samphire dared to reply.

His love was great, but mention of the Stone was too much. Frowning and without another word, Ratcher took up the pup and went out with it to the Span, while Samphire, her moment of defiance gone, lay thinking that with the last pup's death her life would end. She began to weep for the nameless pup and all the love she had known and lost that day and night just past. As ever, the thunder of the River Reap was sole companion to her despair.

Meanwhile, as Ratcher crossed the Reapside and set paw upon the Span once more, moles watched him, and stared without compassion at the still form of the ugly pup dangling from his mouth. The Reap was heavy with recent rain, and spray drifted all about. Before and behind the cliffs loomed dark, and juts of rock were stark against the sky.

As Ratcher went to drop the pup into the void a raven mother's desperate cry came forth across the Charnel as one of its fledgling young pushed off too soon from its ledge and the downdraughts carried it helpless, straight into the depths below the Span. Several ravens flew up, the mother called out again, but none could help the hapless bird, as spumes of dark-stained spray came up like talons to engulf its feeble wings.

Ratcher, pup in mouth, stanced still, watching the bird's last flight, when suddenly a shaft of light which seemed almost too bright for sun came from between the grey, breaking clouds and lit the depths where the bird, its wings still beating frantically, tried to rise. Light shining on the wet gorge sides, surging light in all the spray, greens, blues, yellows, shining greys and blacks, all alive in the gorge right then, as if declaring that life *was*.

The fledgling paused in flight, turned on its back as it had seen its parents do, then righting itself, stooped straight towards the raging water just below, opened its wings as wide as it could and with a mighty, flapping, desperate pull, succeeded in halting its fall just above the water's surface. Then heaving, struggling, fighting, it rose through the spray that tried to drag it down, up and up to the level of the ground once more, and then beyond and up into the fullness of the light, up to safety once again.

Even as its frantic mother stooped through the air to guide it back to the ledge the watching Ratcher felt the pup he held suddenly stir with life, in the light that seemed brighter than the sun, stir strong, and then he heard it bleat and mew and bleat again.

Awed by this sudden surge of life Ratcher pulled back from the void and placed the pup down on the slippery Span. In some alarm he stared at it, thinking he must hurl it from him now to death but knowing even as he thought it he could not. And all he could think of was Samphire's mention of the Stone, the very thought of whose name froze his mind. Caught between desire and incapacity he raised his head and roared out his frustrated rage. The roar seemed only to stir the pup still more, for it rolled on to its paws, stanced up shakily, and blindly crawled forward all unknowing towards the void once more. Its head dropped, the rocky surface gave no grip, its weak paws lost their hold and it began to slide down towards its death.

Ratcher rushed forward, stooped, and snatched it up again. The watching moles blinked their puzzlement and displeasure at this first show of weakness they had ever seen in their leader. Yet caring not a mite for that but only for the fear and awe he felt, and the sense that the dreaded Stone had sent its Light into this place, Red Ratcher turned back the way he had come, back to where Samphire lay defeated in her birthing nest. From the portal he stared at her, the struggling pup hanging from his mouth.

She heard him come, but dared not look up for grief, and for fear of what he would do to her because of her earlier mention of the Stone. But then his shadow fell across her face and she scented mole apart from him. Soft scent, sweet scent, fresh as grass in spring. A pup's scent. Not believing what she knew, she felt a surge of love and joy as she realized it was her own pup's scent, the last one of all, alive; and then she heard it mewing for her love.

She turned, looked up, and instinctively reached out her paws to take back what she had trusted to the Stone and what the Stone had given back to her. She began to cry.

'Why?' she sobbed in relief and gratitude. 'Why?'

'He stirred,' said Ratcher, helplessly, frowning in puzzlement at himself as he stared down at the scrabbling pup.

Samphire rose and embraced the rough cruel mole who had robbed her of all joys of life and love and yet, now, granted her this charge. She felt that finally the Stone had heard her cry and answered it.

'He has no name,' she whispered as she cuddled the pup and Ratcher pulled away from her as if he might be made contaminate. She stanced down again, encircling her last and only pup within her paws, and brought her teats where he could more easily reach them. Already he was seeking one of them out with his strange grotesque head and misshapen paws; oh no, to her his beautiful head, his beautiful paws.

'My love, my beauty, my only one,' sighed Samphire.

Perhaps remembering then the roosting ravens that had watched that fledgling fall into the Reap and then emerge again, Ratcher said, 'Let him be named Rooster, and whatever he may be he shall not for now be harmed by others here. He is my son.'

'Ratcher . . .' she began, wanting to share her joy with him, to show him what pleasures a pup can give.

'No,' said Ratcher retreating, his eyes hard, 'it is enough I brought him back to you, mole. Be glad of that. No more weakness can I show.'

'It is not weakness,' she said.

'It is so!' said Ratcher turning to leave. 'It is more than I should have done. But take him this day and raise him on the Charnel side, for you and yours are tainted by something worse than plague now – you are infected by the Stone.'

'He'll not be harmed then?' said Samphire, sensing a retreat in Ratcher's heart and already fighting for her pup's future.

'Not by me, that much I promise. But from his siblings I cannot long protect him, for they will not tolerate his deformity or your Stone beliefs. Therefore for my sake and your pup's leave the Reapside. I cannot be seen to love you more.'

With that Red Ratcher left, his heart hardening against them both even as he went, and where for so long there had been the warmth of love now came the chill gloaming of no love at all.

That same day moles saw Samphire, weak and gaunt from the fateful pupping she had made, carry the dark pup over the Span into gloomy Charnel, and thence plod steadily up past the dreary entrances into the tunnels there and climb the slopes beyond to make a place higher than any others dared among the moist scree beneath the cliffs.

The torrent's roar was muted up there, and not far above the ravens chuntered to themselves, or croaked loudly as they flew out and turned on the updraughts of the cliffs. Nearby a sudden cracking of rockfall came, loud and clear, but Samphire disregarded it and all else and trekked on upwards until she found a place that suited her.

There, where no sun shone, nor mole came in kindness, nor mate came to relieve a sleepless midnight hour, Samphire made a home to raise her pup, all deep and dark and secret.

The night out on Withens Moor had grown wild and rough, and all the youngsters had fallen asleep with Turrell's tale.

'They've heard it before,' said Myrtle, 'and will hear it again before they're done. Now, you can see our visitors are tired, Turrell, so you can stop talking now and tell the rest another day.'

It was true enough – Hamble was almost asleep where he stanced, while Sward, whose snout was extended along his grey-furred paws, had in the last short while begun to feel more tired than he had ever felt. Only Privet was bright-eyed and listening attentively, excited by all they had heard and feeling again that sense of destiny that almost from the first the mere mention of Rooster's name had stirred in her.

'You *will* continue tomorrow?' she said quietly.

Turrell, nodded his head and fixed her with a stare.

'I can see you're a mole who knows how to listen,' he said. 'But venturing out on the Moors? A scribemole from Crowden? Seems strange to me.'

She grinned and looked at her two companions. Hamble was already asleep while Sward was humming to himself with his eyes half closed, some old and tuneless song he remembered from his youth.

'I'm in good paws,' she said, 'and I'm not really scared. I'm glad . . . I mean . . .'

'Glad we're the first grikes you've met?' said Turrell. 'Eh, lass? We're not all bad you know. 'Tis circumstances and missed opportunity degrades a mole, not original malevolence. We grikes were never taught anything but violent ways.'

265

'No,' said Privet quietly, humbled that he should see into her thoughts so well.

'You sleep now, and one way or another I'll finish off this tale when next we've a moment to stance still. Sleep, mole.'

The last Privet remembered of that night was the racing of wind among the heather, and a mole coming towards her through it, who was no more than a pup and yet had huge paws and a monstrous head, and eyes she could not see.

Chapter Twenty-Two

When Privet awoke next day she lay dozing for a time, knowing it was late, yet unwilling to stir, for the images of the places in the dreams she had had in the night lingered with her still and dark though they were, and troubled though the moles who inhabited them seemed, she was reluctant to leave them for the realities of the journey she must resume.

When she finally went out on to the surface to groom, she found that the others had been long up and about, and were talking in low voices in the same safe overhang of peat where they had first found Turrell and his group.

'We're not going to move until late in the morning,' said Hamble, 'because Sward thinks we need to rest a bit before the climb up Withens Moor to Twizle Head. But Turrell's told us how best to reach Chieveley Dale without being seen by grike patrols.'

'But we won't delay too long?' said Privet, who was filled with a desire to track Rooster down.

'Always take the third day of any journey easy, my dear,' said her father, 'for it's when travelling moles are at their most weary and vulnerable. I'm going to show these youngsters how to make a burrow in the *molish* way . . . We'll set off again at noon.'

He grinned happily as the four youngsters tugged at his old paws and took him off upslope; Privet watched him go, thinking she had never seen him so relaxed and wishing wanly she had been allowed by her mother to get to know him as these youngsters seemed to be doing.

'Perhaps one day I'll have young of my own,' she thought, 'and if I do I'll tell them stories and teach them things and give them what I never had.' She stared at the grim Moors about her, which if anything seemed duller and more desolate even than they had the day before, and was adding to her thoughts the resolution that she would never raise young in such a place and so must leave, when Hamble put a paw to hers.

'You look sad, Privet. Things will get better now. We'll find Rooster and bring him back to Crowden and things will improve.'

Privet nodded vacantly and took up some food and pecked at it in silence.

'Come on, Turrell,' said Hamble, perhaps guessing at the cause of his friend's gloom and determined to find a way to cheer her up, 'tell us the rest of the tale you started last night. I fell asleep just when –'

'Just when Rooster was born,' growled Turrell. 'A fat lot of good it is telling tales to moles who fall asleep, but at least Privet here heard me out, which fortunately for you, Hamble, was not long after you started snoring. Now . . .'

That morning, the unforgettable morning when Privet first heard of the raising of Rooster in the infamous Charnel and the circumstances of his escape from it, went swiftly by. But before she could take stock of what she had been told and begin to ask the questions that occurred to her, Sward came back and the time had come to leave their friends and set off once more into the Moors.

'Come back this way!' said Turrell. 'It's done us good to see you, and 'tis good for these youngsters to talk to other moles than me.'

'I've given them their instructions, old friend!' said Sward, touching his paw to Turrell's great shoulder, 'and sworn them to secrecy too.'

Turrell laughed and told his wards to accompany 'the Scholar and his kin some part of the way upslope, as courteous moles should', and then they were off. Only much later, when Sward had sent the youngsters back to their patch again, did Privet ask what instructions he had given them.

'Told them that in return for all Turrell's done for them it would be their task one day to get him off the Moors to a place more amenable to mole. He'll never go of his own will, but he might if they make him.'

'Perhaps he's happy here,' said Hamble, amused.

Sward did not smile, but looking serious paused in the climb upslope and said to both of them, '*He*'s happy enough, as moles are when they know no better. But it's *them* I'm thinking of. Without a task like that they'd never leave themselves, and it's time my generation saw that whatever sins first brought moles to the Moors have been expiated, and it's time moles stopped punishing themselves by living here.

'Same goes for Privet, as she knows. It's my great wish she leaves the Moors and goes somewhere where her scribing skills will be appreciated. As for you, Hamble, there's better things for those talons of yours to see to than matters on the Moors, and better things for your mind to think about.'

'I'm surprised you agreed to lead us on to the Moors then!' said Privet.

'Want you to see it while you can, and to meet some of its suffering moles. A mole should know his own place, and learn what there is to love in it, before he ever leaves it. I think there'll be things you'll learn on this journey. And anyway, I didn't want to end my days in Crowden – too safe, too limited for me!'

'You'll not be ending your days for a long time yet,' said Hamble.

To which the only reply Sward gave was a look, long and deep, at each of them, and a slight shake of the head. Then he turned and headed slowly upslope once more, with Hamble close behind, while Privet paused some brief moments longer and watched her father become but a vague distorted shape in the mists above and felt a curious sense of loss, as if he were leaving her for good. Then she sighed and hurried after them to take up once more her place of safety between them.

All that day and the next they trekked on into heights more worm-less and desolate than any Privet could ever have imagined. The mist never cleared, but swirled in the chilly air to catch at the back of their throats and sting at their eyes as if it were malign and wished them to turn back.

To Privet it was a wonder that Sward pressed forward with such confidence, for she had long since grown confused as to where they were, or in what direction they trekked. Whichever way she looked there was only the white light of mist; no sign of sun or even a lighter sky to indicate where it might be. All colour was drained out of the heather and peat hags through which they passed, for their shadow-less, dark brown hue seemed no colour at all but the negation of all life.

'You wait till the mists clear and the sun comes out and you'll see colours you'd never guess were here,' said Sward. 'You just wait and see!'

'How do you know which way to go?' she asked him.

'By the lie of the heather and the run of the ginnels in between. The prevailing wind hereabout is westerly and you judge your direction by that. As for place, well, that's a matter of experience. We'll find a drainage valley and trust to the Stone we get the right one for Chieveley Dale.'

He scratched his grizzled fur and screwed up his eyes against the mist in the general direction in which they seemed to be going. Around them the breeze hissed in the heather, and the hags loomed; now near, now far, according to the thickening and weakening of the mist. Their face-fur was wet with condensation. Each of them was hungry, though nomole mentioned the fact, for the brackish black water in the puddles and small tarns they passed was their only sustenance. They knew that this was as wormless as a place could be and that if Sward could not get them off the Tops to lower and more wormful ground to the north they would surely starve before ever they could make their way back the way they had come.

Despite the desolation there was the sense, peculiar and frightening, that grikes might be about, a possibility confirmed by the sudden discovery of pawprints by a place where they stopped to drink, which though blurred by rain and wind were recent enough to warn them against complacency.

Yet they saw no other sign of mole and as dusk gathered on the second evening after leaving Turrell, and they might normally have considered establishing a temporary burrow, the ground began to slope northward and they came into the beginning of the upper end of a drainage gully that Sward thought might help lead them off the Tops.

By now Privet's paws were as weary as they had ever been and the sudden drop through rocky outcrops and among sharp shards of scree taxed all her strength and endurance. She stumbled more than once, and cut her paws on the sharp stones, while the wind drove sharply up at her and brought tears to her eyes to impede her downward progress still more.

'Not far now, my dear, and we'll be at the stream's edge and the going will be easier,' Sward called over his shoulder from below.

'What stream?' she said dubiously, for the mist was as persistent as ever and all the wind did was blow it about some more.

'You can hear it,' growled Hamble behind her.

And so she could, a racing sound somewhere below which grew louder and louder until the mist cleared for a moment and she saw the blessed sight of swards of green grass along a small stream's edge.

Easier going! Food! Clear water! Rest! Sleep!

Not quite! For Sward and Hamble were for pressing on to find a place less exposed than what seemed too obvious a route off the Tops for them to risk stopping near. The light had long since gathered into gloom, but after the most perfunctory of rests Privet was prodded awake again by her father; with her paws only half responding to the way she wished them to go, she tottered and dragged herself on downslope for what seemed to her half the night. Then she became aware of the sound of wind in trees, looming shapes on either side, the stream growing ever bigger, the scent of wormful soil and with a turn off their route and a shove from behind by Hamble, she followed Sward to a den of a place at the edge of a copse.

Perhaps she ate, perhaps she burrowed, or perhaps she simply laid down her head upon her paws and without more ado fell into the dead and heavy sleep of the very tired. She did not know. But when she woke it was still pitch-dark, and there was the sound of rain on trees, and Hamble's great strong flank was warm against her own, and gently moving with his breathing. They were in a burrow of some kind which scented fresh and newly delved. The stream's racing roar was nearby, and somewhere across from where she lay she heard her father's laboured breathing, and the occasional snuffle of his snout. But nothing could she see, no light at all.

Tired though her body felt, and sore though her paws and talons were, her mind was active, even excited. They had crossed Twizle Head, they were on wormful ground once more, and soon, perhaps very soon, they would reach Chieveley Dale and begin at last the final part of their journey to find Rooster.

At the very thought of him, and the silent repetition of his name, she felt again the stirring of curiosity and a determination to meet him. But when she thought of the second part of the tale Turrell had told, that stirring turned to the breathless excitement and nervous awe moles feel when they sense they have caught a glimpse of their destiny, and know that whatever the future may bring, and the dangers they may face, their paws are set on a journey from which there is no turning back.

Until the day of Rooster's birth and her banishment over the Span, Samphire had little knowledge of and no contact with the moles of the Charnel, and that nightmarish first sighting of them at the Midsummer sacrifice so many years before was mercifully now almost forgotten.

So it was not until she was across the Span and halfway towards the slopes that rise to the cliffs on the Charnel's dark north side that her distress and anger with Red Ratcher, and maternal need to save at least one of her pups, gave way to those fears that distant memory, and all she had heard since, had nurtured, if only unconsciously.

But so enshadowed was the place she found herself in, so alien its rough grassy surface with huge rocks and boulders that seemed freshly tumbled from the great black cliffs ahead, that fear suddenly beset her, and a moment of paralysis. Her pup hung from her mouth as she stared nervously about her, fearful of the shadows and the slight movements, of watching moles perhaps, or something worse she seemed to see there, and only the pup's bleats brought her back to the reality that another now depended on her, and she must do her best for it.

She had no doubt at all she was being watched – indeed, soon after her numb pause and recovery from it, she saw in the dark lee of a huge boulder an ogreish female all swollen and vile staring malevolently at her – and resolutely decided that the best thing to do was to force herself to keep moving, and seek out a place up on the slopes above beneath the cliffs. She believed that such a spot would be unoccupied because of the danger of raven and rockfall, and that and its height would give her some vantage if Charnel moles came after her.

Tired though she was she went steadily on, keeping to the surface and as clear as she could of rocks and boulders where moles might be lying in wait for her. On and on she went, with only one more mole seen – again a female, this one bald and so ulcerous her appearance was a blotchy red – until she gained the slopes and was able to relax a little, for she found no more evidence of mole.

The place was dark and damp, and so steep that the soil was scattered in pockets among the boulders and rock fragments that had fallen from the cliffs above, whilst in one cranny directly beneath the cliff a pocket of snow remained in a spot where the sun never shone.

The tunnels she made over the next few days were convoluted and most strange, running at odd angles among the jags of buried rocks before petering out on to the surface for the lack of an underground route to other soil. She did her best to give these overground runs protection by taking them under the lee of fallen rocks, but with the ravens watching above, and the continual threat of further rockfall – the sudden sounds of which she heard sporadically both day and night – it was in truth no place to rear a pup; but it was all she had.

It seemed that others must have thought so too, for apart from occasional sightings of those same terrible hulking females she had seen on her way across the Charnel, who came snouting the slopes

272

below her sometimes – though at dusk when she could barely see them – she was left alone.

Gradually, as Samphire became absorbed in the hard work of raising her pup and she remained undisturbed, she put worries about these other moles behind her and concentrated on the task in paw. The weather was inclement, the tunnels liable to slippage and damage from the frequent rockfalls, the wind continual and often ferocious.

All these factors meant that the first moleyears of Rooster's puphood, right up to the end of April indeed, were spent solely in the company of his mother. She was not at first much encouraged by his appearance and seeming stupidity. She had hoped that the growth of fur might mask somewhat the grotesqueness of his paws and wrinkled massive head, but it did not. He was certainly large, certainly powerful, and in that he took after his father. But his head seemed over-size for his body, and his paws were deformed in the sense that one – the right – was larger, much larger than the other, though neither was small. His fur was hopelessly awry, and however much she strove to groom it, it remained so, becoming thicker, more wiry, less manageable with each day that passed. His tail was askew, twisting awkwardly to the left and to this she attributed his clumsiness, for tails help moles know where they are. Poor Rooster was for ever tumbling this way or that, or veering off from the direction in which his awkward paws sought to take him.

All this she might have borne with equanimity if he had shown an alertness of mind, or ability to learn, or even speak, but he did not. Nor was there much sign that he would do so from his expression, which once his eyes opened remained deep and dark beneath his heavy furrowed brow. Yet love him she could not fail to do, for in his ungainly silent way he would run to the safety of her flanks when danger seemed to threaten, such as the rumble of a rockfall, or the scuttering of raven on the surface above.

Then, too, he would stare up at her with his black eyes, and if the light caught them she fancied she saw trust in her there, and perhaps even love. From that deep instinct mothers have, which seeks no reward from a task that seems fruitless, she talked to him, telling him stories of moledom and the Stone, and as time went by and his attention on what she said seemed more sustained, about her own upbringing in Chieveley Dale. Indeed, the very fact that he did not, or could not, respond, seemed to give her courage and space to speak out her heart's old longings for her home system and lost family, the memories of which for so long she had found it easier to suppress.

That same maternal instinct began, too, to tell her that slow though he was to speak, and ungainly and awkward though he was in all he did, he had positive qualities which she did not remember any pup in her earlier broods displaying so young, or at all. For one thing he grew so fast that he weaned himself on to the solid food of worms and other scraps she found very early for a pup, and developed an encouraging ability to find the living worm – a talent most pups develop late.

Not Rooster. He seemed to know when and where to find the poor thin things that the Charnel soil supported, and in this they found their first real communion, for when she praised him for what he did he chucked and purred and made those sounds she had thought he might never make, sounds that are the precursors of speech.

Soon after this he developed a second, perhaps related ability, though one so strange to her that for a long time she thought it mere coincidence. It seemed that Rooster knew when and where rockfalls from the cliffs above would occur, long before they happened. More than that, this knowledge gave him the confidence to judge when to flee or not – and, finally, to her alarm, when to go out on to the surface and watch! It seemed then that for all his clumsiness he had his own sensitivities, and in that she found strange and wondering comfort.

With the warmer weather of mid-April she began to allow him out on to the surface, and there the rocks, the emergent green-white flowers of lady's-mantle and saxifrage, became his friends. While the ravens above, stooping, turning, croaking, became . . . well, not his enemies. As with the worms, and the rockfalls, he seemed to sense their movements before they ever made them, and learnt that a mole who turns to face a stooping raven, raising his talons before it comes too near, will cause it to swerve aside. Ravens prey on carrion, or on injured things, and fear life that confronts their beaks and claws.

This much Samphire knew herself, though like most moles she avoided exposure to ravens and any bird too big, but she knew as well that moles like Red Ratcher disdained to cower from ravens, and went about their business unafraid of them, heaping invective on them when they came near, and raising their talons at them as Rooster, so young, had taught himself to do.

With these excursions on the surface, in which Samphire was forced to learn to trust that Rooster could defend himself, the youngster's speech began to develop. His voice was rough and husky, his speech slow, qualities that he never lost. He talked more to himself or to the rocks and tunnels among which he played than to her, prattling and speaking to them as if they were alive, as solitary youngsters sometimes will. And, too, early again, he began to delve little tunnels and half-chambers of his own, slowly and deliberately, and she was glad to see that his large ungainly paws were, if anything, an advantage in doing this.

Throughout this time they saw no other moles, and nor did Samphire hear any, though sometimes it seemed as if Rooster did – a fact which, in view of his percipience with worms and rockfalls, would not have surprised her. It was always at dusk, and always in the direction of the slopes below, and Rooster's squat and wrinkled snout would whiffle at the air, and his dark eyes narrow, and he would mount up in mock aggression as if to defend their territory against all comers. The all comers never came, and always such occasions ended with Rooster looking curious, and taking a few steps out of their family chamber in a friendly way as if he half hoped other moles would come.

That they *were* moles Samphire had no doubt, and to confirm it Rooster asked what moles they were and when they would come. His defensive stance was one instinct, his fearlessness was another deeper one, and Samphire was wise enough not to seek to damage it.

She had told him in various ways of the Reapside, and the Charnel, and that the moles in each were different. He knew that his father lived in the Reapside, but having no other experience Rooster had no expectation, nor much curiosity, to see him. Since the Charnel moles had not molested her, and seemed, if anything, somewhat afraid, she did not yet warn Rooster against them, or even say what she already knew, that they were sometimes deformed, and perhaps diseased. He would find out in his own way, and if need be she would be there to help and defend him; though, as the days of April went by and he grew bolder and stronger, she began to think that if the Stone continue to bless them both with this solitude and lack of interference, then by the time that contact with other moles was made he would be very near to being able to defend himself.

But this was not to be. Towards the end of April the weather suddenly warmed and for a time their tunnels were wet as the great patch of snow above them and beneath the cliff finally thawed, sending rivulets of water down the slopes. There were, too, a number of rockfalls uncomfortably close to their tunnels, and one which destroyed part of them, though such was Rooster's ability to sense their coming that he had long since warned her and removed her to safety, muttering in his laconic way, 'Coming, rocks. Get downslope.'

The rocks did come, and the cliffs echoed with the fall, and that same evening came one of Rooster's observations of the silent, unseen moles downslope from them. For the first time, and with only a brief, 'Will see,' to his mother, he ventured out into the tunnel, and then on to the surface.

Samphire called after him to stay near, and followed, watching his progress downslope to the shadows of the boulders there. She watched as any mother might, resolving that if there were a sudden movement, or a call, or anything untoward at all, she would rush down there to his defence; until then, she must let him begin to discover something of the world beyond the little one she had reared him to.

But there seemed no cause for alarm, and nor did he even disappear from view, though it was plain he met and talked to a mole or moles in the shadows, for she heard his young husky voice, and some kind of a reply. But whatmole it was he saw she knew not, and nor, being a youngster, did he say when he returned, except that the mole was a 'they'. He said no more than that, and seemed to accept what he had done, and the moles he had met, with that same calm boldness with which he had met all else in his so-far restricted life.

It was only two days later, in the fading light of late afternoon, that Samphire saw the moles her son had met. Or rather, turned a corner, surfaced, and to her astonishment and alarm, found herself face to face with them.

'Rooster!' she called urgently, as much for support as from any certain knowledge that these were moles he already knew. 'Rooster, come here!'

For the first time in her life Samphire experienced a new and very different quality in her strange and slowly-revealing son, and one that in time would endear him not only to herself but to many other moles, and in a way to all moledom. For Rooster came running, ungainly, awkward, but massively protective in the gentlest of ways. Indeed, her second calling of his name was barely made before he was there, a little in front of her, his great paws before him, his huge head making his young body seem bigger than it was. It was as if one of the great dark boulders that lay about that surface had come alive and taken the comforting form of a huge benign mole.

Rooster saw the moles she had come across, and Rooster laughed.

'Friends!' he said. Even as he said it, he went forward and touched one of the moles with his big right paw, and nodded at the other, and the three of them moved off among the scree as youngsters will who wish to be free of the adult world to explore and journey into those discoveries of place and community which are such moles' challenge and delight.

Yet moved as she was, Samphire watched with a grave concern tinged with horror. For though the two moles that Rooster had made companions of were youngsters like himself, born no doubt at much the same time, they were anything but normal moles and by going with them as he now did it was as if she were watching him take a turning into alienation and abnormality for life; as if, in fact, her son Rooster had declared that he too was abnormal and deformed, he too would always be an outcast.

What was it that Samphire saw first? First, and only slightly the less strange, was the bigger of the two, a mole already larger than Rooster, a hulking thing, its reddish fur patchy and in places so thin that pink-grey bald areas mottled its body. Its protuberant eyes were milky-white and blind, and its great head hung down beneath hunched shoulders. Its reactions seemed so slow and strange that Samphire rightly guessed the mole was stone-deaf; she could not know that it was dumb as well.

'It'. Such might well have been its name, so alien did it seem to her. But the mole was male. Even as she watched, Rooster put his left paw to this seemingly helpless mole's flank and spoke. The lumbering male raised its slow head, stared out of its blind eyes, and reached out to touch Rooster's face and snout with surprising gentleness. Its paws at least were good strong things, their talons shining black, all well-formed. So the two moles greeted one another, and life, of a kind, came to the blind mole.

This brief, touching, and to Samphire, tragic proceeding was watched by the second of the moles, a female. That much at least could be said for her. For the rest . . . Samphire stared in horror despite herself, for she had never seen such a thing, such a mole, in all her life, or imagined it, though from time to time she had heard that such things had been born and quickly destroyed, for they have little hope of survival into adulthood.

She was thin and small, and most strangely shaped, more like rat or mouse than mole, her snout barely formed, her paws extenuated and weak. And she was pink-white.

'Albino,' whispered Samphire to herself.

Indeed she was, and with it went pale white talons, and such snout as she had was pink-white. But her fur was more yellow than white.

'But her eyes . . .' whispered Samphire again, for she knew enough to know that albinos' eyes are pale and the fur about them white. Yet

277

her eyes were shining black, alert, amused, sharp, intelligent. But that was not all, nor what made the two of them so compelling to watch. No, it was that those intelligent black eyes, so alive, so aware, seemed all the time upon the hulking male, and filled with care, concern and . . . adoration. An alien pair, perhaps, but the more Samphire stared and got used to them in those moments, the more she thought they were a striking pair as well.

Now, as Rooster made his easy hello to the big male, the albino's eyes filled with pleasure too. Clearly she liked mole who liked her companion and made contact with him. Then, after reaching out and touching the male briefly, she darted away from him, moved around Rooster's flank and fixed a stare on Samphire.

'Your mother?' she said.

Rooster looked round with some embarrassment and grunted a reluctant acknowledgement, as if he wished his mother were not there.

Youth! That much, at least, was normal here, thought Samphire.

'Ha!' said the strange female in a disconcerting way, and then, 'Ha!' again. Her voice was softer than her look, and the sound she made seemed to express the sense of 'Ah, now I know, now I see, so *that's* the mole who came from the Reapside; I see!'

With that the three moles turned their attention to each other and moved off among the boulders in a tight, exclusive group, affirming Samphire's sense of a day or two before that freedom of a kind was coming back to her as Rooster began to make his own life.

But, when the youngsters were gone, and she looked across the grim undulations of the Charnel towards the rising spray of the Reap, and beyond to the Reapside, which that day was bathed in soft spring sunshine, and then back up at the cliffs that towered above her, she had pause to ask herself, 'Freedom for what?'

Rooster's venture that day with the two Charnel youngsters began a pattern that was to recur day after day, as April grew warmer and May approached. In time the two youngsters grew used to Samphire, and she to them, and though they were lost in their own strange world of silence and whispers, touches and disappearances among the rocks and tunnels, they became part of her new world, and expanded it.

Since Rooster had become morose and unforthcoming in his mother's presence, Samphire only found out their names when she asked the albino directly, having found her alone one day.

'Me, I'm Glee,' said the albino.

278

'And your friend?' said Samphire.

Glee's eyes grew both serious and warm. 'He's Humlock,' she said, unwonted shyness creeping into her look.

Samphire wished suddenly, and irrelevantly, that she had given birth to a daughter just once. Now she knew she never would. She stayed silent. Glee's bright-dark eyes studied her, and seemed finally to trust her.

'Humlock and Glee,' she said with a lilt to her voice, almost as if it were a snatch of a familiar song: 'Humlock and Glee! I protect him and he protects me!'

Samphire smiled and Glee grinned back and giggled, and suddenly all her abnormality seemed gone, and it seemed to Samphire that she had touched for a moment those past days so long ago in Chieveley Dale, before Ratcher came, when she had siblings and parents and friends, and the sun shone, and the little river through their vale was gentle, and all was good.

Then a cloud went across the sun that seemed to shine from Glee's black eyes and she said, 'He can't hear, or speak, or see, but I know he thinks. He thinks a lot. My mother and his mother don't believe he does, but I know he does. Rooster knows it too. One day me and Rooster will find something useful that Humlock can do better than any other mole. We will!'

Little Glee's pale pink face had aged, there was a defiant frown between her eyes, and she stared at Samphire as if daring her to say different.

Samphire said judiciously, 'I'd like to meet your mother. Is she the one who comes sometimes to the shadows in the lower slopes?'

Glee nodded. 'She's afraid of you, and doesn't want a mole like you to see her. She's a goitre.'

Samphire's gaze remained steady, though she knew well enough the horror of what a goitre was. Those had been goitres she had seen in the shadows when she had first crossed the Charnel to make her tunnels up here on the slopes. Goitres died a terrible death – breathless, bloated though starving, ulcerated.

'But she wasn't always a goitre. She told me to come and look at you because that's what she was like once. Will you become a goitre?'

'Tell her I would like to meet her. Will you tell her that?'

'She won't come.'

'I let Rooster go with you,' said Samphire with sudden purpose in her voice, 'so you bring your mother to see me!'

'That's fair,' said Glee after a moment's thought. 'She might come if Humlock's mother Sedum comes. She's dying to see you. She's probably the one you saw downslope.'

'Bring them both then,' said Samphire firmly. Glee was a mole who seemed to appreciate strong moles.

'Will do,' said Glee, 'but you'll regret it. My mother's all right but Humlock's, well . . . she can only talk of one thing: Midsummer.'

Suddenly Glee's eyes were cold, clear, and purposeful.

'Midsummer, my dear?' said Samphire, fearful that she knew what Glee meant.

'"When Humlock's got to go to peace",' said Glee as if repeating an oft-heard turn of phrase she did not like. 'In other words, die in the Reap with the other youngsters judged to be too . . . abnormal. Get it?'

'Umm . . .' began Samphire, unable to think what to say.

'Well, I won't let them. Not then, not ever. There's nothing really wrong with Humlock, not where it matters, not in his head. And he's very brave, because he's clever enough to *know* what his mother thinks must be and he's not giving up like some do. We're all working on it.'

'All?'

Glee grinned. 'Humlock and Glee and Rooster, though I don't think Rooster knows yet.' She giggled again, looked sharply at Samphire, and said, 'Course, *he's* odder than either of us two. By comparison with *him* we're positively normal.'

'Really?' said Samphire.

'Without a shadow of a doubt,' said Glee very firmly indeed.

Privet might have continued rehearsing Rooster's story as she then knew it in her mind but the sudden unmistakable sound of approaching mole broke through her reverie, and brought her back to the present with a jolt.

Night had gone, cold dawn had come, the mist was clear, and somewhere nearby were moles, galumphing heavy moles, alien moles. She quickly reached out to touch Hamble awake, and then went over to her father, whose restless heavy breathing seemed suddenly dangerously loud.

'Wh . . . what?' he began, before Privet and Hamble shushed him.

All three started silently forward to the edge of the little place that Sward had insisted they made their night's temporary burrow, and Privet was grateful for his prudence. In the dawn light on the dewy path beneath them, along the bank of the stream, there passed by four great dark moles, ugly of snout, cruel of talon, unpleasant of mien. One of them, the second in line, was considerably older than the rest, his fur partly grizzled grey. But where the pale dawn sun caught it, it had a reddish tinge.

Privet stared in horror and alarm, even as Hamble's paw tightened on her shoulder and pressed her lower to the ground. Yet even with the soil and grass pressed into her mouth and snout she still managed to see the moles pass by and out of sight, set it seemed on a murderous and malevolent mission.

But it was that reddish fur, that most cruel and brutal of profiles, that aura of ruthless power about the older mole that had her heart thumping in her chest, and beads of sweat pricking at her neck.

'Was that . . . ?' she began, when they had gone.

'It looked like the mole they described as . . .' continued Hamble.

'Red Ratcher,' said Sward grimly, 'and heading for Chieveley Dale.'

'What are we going to do?' said Privet.

'Follow them,' said Sward, 'it's the best way not to get caught!'

'Follow them!' gasped poor Privet.

Hamble chuckled and buffeted her rump towards the path below. 'If it's Rooster you want to meet this is likely to be the quickest way!' he said, taking the lead for the first time in their long journey, as the three of them set off in discreet pursuit.

Chapter Twenty-Three

'At least the mist has cleared!' said Privet, as much to take her mind off the frightening notion of tracking the four huge grikes who had just passed by, as to express her relief that the day was a little brighter than the previous ones.

'It hasn't cleared, my love, it's just that we're not so high up now,' said Sward, pointing a talon back up to the Tops from which they had come the evening before, where the mists still swirled. Privet shivered, for the dawn was cold, and she felt stiff and aching from the dark hours of the night and she wished she might rest some more . . . Then there was a prod in her rump from her father behind, to tell her to follow on after Hamble, who had already cautiously set off after Red Ratcher and his moles.

Although such tracking of other moles was not within Privet's previous bookish experience, even she could follow the fresh and heavy pawprints that the four moles had made before them in the soft ground along the stream's bank.

Even more ominously, she could scent their rank smell hanging in the air, especially where the pine trees of the forest came down to the rushing water's edge, and the air was trapped and still. It somehow made more real, and almost too close for comfort, the nature of the dangers that had confronted Rooster and Samphire when they left the Charnel, as Turrell had told the story.

But she could not think of that now, as they trekked on downslope, the pines growing ever thicker, and the vegetation along the stream's banks ever more lush the further they went down. The tracks, and the evidence of freshly-broken ferns and bracken, suggested that the grikes were either in a hurry, or did not care if others saw where they went – or both.

'If you ask me they're hurrying like this because they're meeting other moles,' whispered Sward during an enforced halt, when Hamble had thought he heard voices ahead and had gone on to check. The path had veered a little from the stream, whose muted babble was off to their right, and they had stanced down in the russet shadows of pine-tree roots.

Hamble reappeared, his fur untidy with dry pine-needles, his eyes excited and resolute.

'I think we're near to Chieveley Dale,' he said, 'for the forest stops ahead and opens out on to a secluded vale just like the descriptions we've been given. The Ratcher moles, if that's who they are, have gone ahead into the open, but not very far. If you follow me we can observe them and decide what to do next. But the going's rough, because there's no way we're staying on this path. Others might be coming down it . . .'

He had barely spoken these words before the unmistakable sound of more large and lumbering grikes came to them from the way they had come, and with a calm gesture to remain as silent as they could, Hamble led the other two off the path and out of sight.

The way took them through musty mounds of pine-needles, which pricked at Privet's snout, and past whipping branches which flew at them from all directions, until the sky lightened ahead and they found themselves on the forest edge, looking down at hummocky Chieveley Dale, which had been their objective for so long.

Not far downslope, their voices but not their words audible, were now not only the four moles they had been following, but several more who must have been there already. Then, with a crash through the undergrowth along the path to their right flank, five more Ratcher moles appeared out of the forest, and went forward to join the others. They were greeted with rough salutes and boisterous buffetings at each other before the older one Privet and the others had seen earlier raised a massive gnarled paw and called them to silence. A hush fell on the grikes and they turned to face the older mole, as Sward whispered, 'That's Red Ratcher himself all right. No other mole could hold such sway over such a mob of moles as those.'

Ratcher's words remained frustratingly indistinct, and the ground beyond the forest was too open for them to risk trying to cross it to find a better vantage point; but such was the nature of the meeting, and so frequently did Red Ratcher point downslope towards the centre of Chieveley Dale as he spoke, that the grikes' intention became all too clear.

'They're planning an assault,' said Hamble, 'and there's nothing we can do about it, nor any warning we can give. We can only watch.'

'But if the Chieveley Dale moles are below ground perhaps we could find a way of reaching them,' said Privet, her natural fear giving way to concern for the moles who could not see this mounting threat, and a desire to help them.

Hamble turned to her and said, 'None of us knows this ground and if we started wandering round now looking for the way into the Chieveley Dale system, the Ratcher moles would pick us up in no time at all. And the grikes don't take prisoners.'

'I'll warrant that if the Chieveley Dale tunnels are as well constructed as we've been told,' said Sward, 'then the moles inside them will already know that the Ratcher moles are here. The best we can do is wait and see if we might be of help to any survivors or refugees later. The only advantage we have is that our presence is not known, and that fact may yet prove useful.'

They watched for some time more, until at last Red Ratcher led most of the moles off downslope to begin whatever operation the three Crowden moles were so reluctantly witnessing. But he left several behind, who quickly dispersed themselves across the slopes of the Dale.

'They must be posted to watch for survivors, like us,' whispered Hamble, 'so we may be doing the right thing staying here.'

'We could disperse a little as they have,' said Privet, surprised at her own calmness.

There was a respectful twinkle in Hamble's eyes towards his friend. 'Just what I was thinking,' he said, 'so if you're both willing we'll spread out a bit. You stay here, Privet, I'll go down nearer the stream and main path into the Dale, and you, Sward, go further along the edge of the wood – and don't wander off too far!'

He pointed to a dead pine that leaned out from living trees a little behind them and said, 'Let that be the point where we all meet again, whatever happens. All right?'

Sward grinned, his eyes excited. 'It's like old times, when I was young and wandering and dodging grike patrols. They never caught me then, and they won't now. Just remember, you two youngsters, surprise is on our side so they'll take time to work out how to respond to us. But if they see you and give chase, keep your heads and keep changing direction until you get back to base, which is here with you, Privet. In this situation a few always have an advantage over many.'

With a final grin at Privet he went off along the edge of the wood and out of sight, and shortly afterwards Hamble went off downslope to the stream, and Privet found herself utterly alone, but for the two or three grikes in the Dale below, whose skulking rough backs she could just see.

She looked behind into the shadows of the wood, and resolved that if mole saw *her* she would burrow under the cover of the pine-needles and stay very still indeed. But with all in view before her, and the safety of the trees behind, she felt surprisingly secure.

She ran her snout along her paws, felt a shiver of excitement and apprehension tingle along her flanks, and began the long watch. The sky lightened a little, but remained overcast with low cloud and the wood behind was silent; she saw occasional surreptitious movements by one or other of the grikes, getting into a better position for whatever they expected to come upslope, and time began to meld into a limbo nothingness.

There was distant movement to her right, and she looked round and saw nothing, except that something was different, something . . . unfamiliar. A breeze touched her face-fur, she looked higher, and saw with a start that the mist that had dogged them so long had all but gone from the Tops. Even as she watched, the last of it lingered on the very peak of what she knew must be Hilbert's Top. Lingered and did not leave, for the mist swirled here and there so that the Top's form did not quite make itself fully plain.

'Strange,' she whispered to herself, 'and I wonder if he's there.' Then, in a spirit made urgent by the fact that story and reality seemed now to be catching up with each other, she permitted herself to ponder the final part of the tale that brought Rooster in safety to the very Dale over which she now watched, and thence to Hilbert's Top itself.

It was not long before the youthful Glee fulfilled her undertaking to bring her shy mother, Drumlin, in the company of Humlock's more sociable parent, Sedum, to meet Samphire.

They came with the dawn of a May-day morn, and even in the Charnel the air, though chill, felt light and good and across on the Reapside the sun was soft among the grass and rocks. The Reap itself was subdued, with barely any misty spray rising from the gorge through which it ran, while up at the top end of the Charnel, beyond the great rockfall, the gullies between the three Creeds rose stark and black, the Creeds themselves bold, buttress-like and clear, not yet touched with sun.

Drumlin and Sedum came up by a surface route, breathing heavily from the effort of the climb, and keeping to the shadows among the rocks. Glee made her chirpy introductions and quickly left, saying she wanted to find Rooster and Humlock who were already off higher up the slopes to be by themselves and clear of the adults. It was only when the three had exchanged pleasantries that the two visitors emerged out of the shadows to which they clung and Samphire saw what it was they were so eager to hide.

Each had a goitre half the size of her head protruding from her neck, all blue-veined and bald, and accompanying the symptom of breathlessness she had already noticed were further signs of disease – scurvied patches of fur riddled with unpleasant sores and ulcers, and in Sedum's case, protuberant staring eyes.

Glee's prediction proved right; Sedum was the more voluble of the two, and she began almost immediately to talk in a resigned and fretful manner of the 'pity' of what Midsummer would mean for 'poor Humlock, bless 'im when 'e'll be the better for being gone from this bitter world'.

As she spoke thus, seeming almost to relish the inevitability of Humlock's death (or 'sacrifice to the Creeds' as she strangely put it) there grew in Samphire the grim realization that however a mole might object to the tone and assumptions behind what Sedum said, something terrible *was* going to happen soon: moles *would* die when the Midsummer ritual took place. On this side of the Reap, what to the Ratcher moles was merely one of the seasonal cycle's great spectacles seemed suddenly tragic, and real. Until that moment Samphire had thought only of the fit and able who crossed the Span, moles she had pitied for the brutal training they would receive; now she was able to put faces to the ones who were left behind – moles like poor Glee and tragic Humlock, moles who would die in a warped ceremony which was meant to prevent them suffering further, but which, from what Sedum was saying, had much also to do with propitiating the Creeds, which seemed to be some kind of Charnel deities.

All the while Glee's mother Drumlin, whose eyes had the same dark, alert quality as her daughter's and belied the ravages of goitrous disease her body was suffering, stared silently but intelligently at Samphire, who began to think that she was being summed up. She, in her turn, said little, at first because it was hard to interrupt Sedum's litany of gloom and doom, but eventually because she was simply too shocked by the implications of what was being said. Whether or not a mole was 'vacant' (as Sedum further described her son), if he had survived this long and grown so strong, should he not be given the chance to live and die as the Stone, not other moles, willed?

It was as Samphire was silently worrying about such things that Sedum suddenly let slip something very odd indeed. She said, 'And anyway, 'tis not just him being mindless as I believe, so the lad won't suffer when Midsummer comes, nor even see what's coming to him so it'll be merciful, but he's not delved a single pawful of soil in his life, so *that* chance can't come his way either. No, moles say as he will be one of the Chosen, and I must say I . . .' Sedum puffed herself a little with pride as Samphire realized that 'Chosen' was a mere glorification of 'chosen to die'.

But *what* chance? Did the way Sedum had said 'delve', with a slight lowering of her voice, almost as if delving awed her, give a clue to what she meant, and that quick look she glanced at Drumlin as if to say it surely didn't *matter* her mentioning delving? The fact that she hastily went on to other things suggested she had let slip something she should not have.

Even as Samphire puzzled about this Drumlin shifted her paws uneasily, and stared in a sharp and almost impatient way at her friend. But then that look gave way to something kinder and more tolerant which Samphire instinctively understood to be the way one mother responds to another whose pup is so damaged and helpless as Humlock seemed to be.

'How could delving help?' Samphire asked, cutting across what Sedum was saying, for she did not want their conversation to be all politeness and nothing of substance. Midsummer with its sacrifices would be upon them soon, and Samphire wanted to understand what the mystery was about the ritual.

Sedum seemed about to reply when Drumlin cast her another glance, a 'please be quiet' kind of look, and speaking for the first time, responded to Samphire's question with one of her own.

'What do you make of Humlock?' she asked. Her voice was gentle yet firm, and the gaze that accompanied it was penetrating.

'I don't know him well enough,' said Samphire carefully, 'but . . . well, my Rooster seems to like him, and Rooster's not a fool. Is he really deaf and dumb as well as blind?' She hoped the answer would be 'no'.

Sedum stared, seeming a little shocked by the directness of the question, as if it was a reminder of a reality she had long since turned her back on.

Drumlin said slowly, 'He is all those things, which a mother cannot tell at birth, and so he survived. We have often had moles such as him in the past, and they are gently dealt with and cannot have known much before . . . going to the Silence. But with Humlock, well, you see my daughter Glee *likes* him and seems to think he has intelligence. Perhaps it's more the pity if he has and I was beginning to think as

Sedum does that come Midsummer it might be kinder if Humlock was Chosen. But then your Rooster took to him as well, and seemed able to talk to him in some way, or at least to make him understand . . .'

Her sudden gaze upslope was followed by the other two and they saw the three youngsters huddled together, Glee's whole fur bright and dangerously noticeable, the more so for Rooster's dark brooding presence next to her, huge and powerful; while Humlock, larger still, made up the trio, snout to snout, Rooster and Glee periodically touching him and he reaching out to them.

'He never smiles,' said Sedum suddenly. 'Not ever.' As she said it she smiled wanly.

Nor was he smiling now, so far as they could see. Just there, accepted by the other two, hulking and slow, his snout low, and just his great paws moving occasionally to touch the ground at his sides, or a rock nearby, or his two friends, the only friends in his dark and silent world.

As they watched Rooster gently pushed Humlock to one side and signalled to Glee to move away on the other, and began suddenly and rhythmically to delve.

'So he does delve,' said Drumlin, half to herself.

'He likes to do so,' replied a puzzled Samphire.

'He's well formed too,' said Sedum, a little enviously, 'so he'll have no trouble crossing the Span. It's always the ones who don't need it can delve.'

Drumlin nodded and added mysteriously, 'Yes, he looks well-made enough to be passed to cross the Span at Midsummer, but if not, with a liking like that for delving, he'll be all right.'

How delving would make things 'all right' for Rooster Samphire could not imagine. Surely moles that didn't 'pass', in other words moles that were 'Chosen', had little to look forward to but that last, brief plunge into Silence in the Reap?

Yet, despite that, Samphire did not welcome the sudden image she had of him crossing the Span back to the Reapside to . . . to what? A training in brutality at his father Red Ratcher's paws; a life she did not want for him, which would be for ever beyond her reach; a spiritual death.

'I do not want Rooster to cross the Span,' she said impulsively, 'but I don't want him to die.'

'But you're from the Reapside, mole,' exclaimed Drumlin in evident surprise.

'I don't want him to go back to all that I have had to suffer these years past, with Ratcher and all of that!' She waved a paw somewhat wildly up towards the surface and in the direction of the Reapside. 'You see, Drumlin, I was never happy there, I mean I didn't want to be there at all. Perhaps you don't realize but –'

'We know nothing about you,' said Drumlin, 'though a few of us think . . . but no matter. Tell us about how you came to be a Ratcher mole.'

The request was put politely, almost indifferently, and Samphire was tempted to ignore it and press on with her own questions. But there seemed no harm in saying a little of how she came to be there, even if for the first few moments of her account of her life Drumlin's attention was as much engaged in watching the three youngsters upslope as with what her new friend had to say. But the moment Samphire mentioned that she came from Chieveley Dale all changed.

'Chieveley!' whispered Drumlin, looking round at Sedum and then hunching forward into an attitude of intense concentration, while Sedum's breathing grew more rapid, and she blinked her protuberant eyes several times as if not quite believing what she heard.

'Yes, Chieveley. You know of it?' said Samphire, and if she sounded surprised it was because she thought that the Charnel moles could know nothing much of moledom beyond the Span, and certainly nothing of an obscure Dale which probably few moles now remembered.

'So you will have seen the mountain called Hilbert's Top?' said Drumlin.

'It's not quite a mountain,' laughed Samphire, pleased to hear that name again, 'but more just a high fell to the east side of the Dale. My father took me there a day or two before Red Ratcher came. It was, it remains, the happiest day of my life.'

'You have *been* to Hilbert's Top?'

'Yes. Is that strange?'

Drumlin waved a paw for her to continue, saying, 'Of *that* we'll talk later, and its strangeness.'

'You don't know who Hilbert was, then?' said Sedum.

Samphire shook her head, her puzzlement increasing, but neither mole said more and she continued to tell of how the moles of Chieveley Dale were slaughtered, and she was the sole survivor, brought into the Charnel for the personal gratification of Red Ratcher himself; of how she learnt to tolerate Ratcher and his love for her, and finally of his rejection of her and her sole surviving pup, and her banishment across the Span.

It was a sombre telling, and one which more than once brought tears to the eyes of her listeners – tears which were more eloquent of their sympathy and trustworthiness than words could have been; tears, indeed, that eventually brought out many sweet memories of a lost past she had kept hidden too long, and bitterness at a wasted life that she had not expressed before.

Yet, along with the tears in her listeners' eyes was excitement too. This was especially true of Drumlin, who by the end looked more amazed than anything else, as if some kind of prayer she had offered up in times past but long since given up hope of receiving an answer to, was being answered now.

'. . . Of course,' Samphire concluded, 'I was very nervous when I crossed over to the Charnel. You see, I saw the sacrifices when I first came and I was told that pups who are not deemed fit to cross the Span are thrown into the Reap – "wasted" is the crude word Ratcher uses.'

Drumlin winced, and nodded. 'Yes, we know that they see it as a kind of summer entertainment,' she said quietly, 'and us Charnel moles as deformed cruel moles who wield dark powers in our talons of which they are afraid. No doubt too they fear that they will catch disease from us, or bring down upon their snouts evils they cannot combat with the strength and ruthlessness that they regard as such virtues. But Samphire, the truth is very different: we are the moles who are cursed by their presence, and the diseases that beset us and now threaten us with extinction, come from *them*.'

'Are you going to tell her?' said Sedum suddenly, breathless, tired, frowning. 'She doesn't know a thing, Drumlin, can't you see that?'

'Tell me what?' said Samphire, wishing suddenly that Rooster was near, and feeling impatient and suspicious of these two moles who seemed nice enough, but gave nothing away and said such strange things about delving and Hilbert's Top.

Why, despite what Drumlin said, she had *seen* the sacrifices at Midsummer, and through the years she had seen the bodies of deformed and wasted moles in the Reap, and washed up sometimes on the Reapside; and since she had lived here in the Charnel, had she not seen moles being forced upslope towards the Creeds, to take part in some primitive rites that ended in their death and disappearance?

'I don't believe there can be any truth about this place, and the moles who live in it, but a horrible one; and even if you carry out your rituals and sacrifices in the name of a faith of your own, I don't like it. Your assumption that moles must die if *you* decide they can't live is not one I would make. 'Tis not of the way of the Stone by which I was brought up in Chieveley Dale.'

'"The Stone",' whispered Drumlin dreamily, as if that were a thing far, far from the Charnel. Then she whispered 'Chieveley Dale,' as if that place were further still.

Samphire decided to say no more, but stared in what she hoped was an unyielding way at Drumlin, and waited for her to do something other than not answer questions and ask ones of her own all the time. Then Drumlin smiled in the most disarming way, drew a little nearer as if in conspiracy, and asked what proved to be her last question of Samphire for a long time.

'You mean us no harm, do you, Samphire? You really were banished here, and not sent to spy on us? You –'

'Is that what you thought, all of you,' cut in Samphire wildly, 'that I was hostile to you, and a minion of Red Ratcher? Is that why I've seen nomole at all in the time I've been here but those you are taking to sacrifice up by the Creeds? Is that . . .'

But she could not go on, for she felt suddenly very alone, rejected not only by the Reapside moles, but by those of the Charnel as well. Whilst, silly though it seemed, the sight of Rooster upslope and absorbed in his games with Humlock and Glee reminded her that whatever happened, very soon he would have grown up and away from her and she would be left alone for ever in a place that was as alien as any place could be. The thoughts flooded into her as the tears flooded out. All this time raising Rooster, afraid for him, afraid for him *still*, and not another adult mole to talk to and now these two thinking she was a spy when it seemed to her they had come to talk to her for no other reason than to spy on *her*.

So she wept, then stopped, only to start again even more deeply when she felt come around her the motherly paws of Drumlin, and heard her whisper soft words of comfort and explanation.

'My dear, in the circumstances it was natural for some of us to be suspicious of you, and to fear you.'

'But n . . . n . . . not *all* of y . . . you?' said Samphire through her tears, seeking some comfort where she could find it.

'Some of us felt your coming meant something very special, and that *you* were sent to us by the Creeds to help us,' said Drumlin, still embracing Samphire, who in her turn clung on to Drumlin, goitre and all, as if to let her go was to be abandoned for ever.

'I'm just an ordinary mole,' mumbled Samphire.

'An ordinary mole from Chieveley Dale,' said Drumlin, a little ironically. Then pulling back a little and looking up at their three youngsters, Drumlin added with strange wonder in her voice, 'But perhaps it is not *you* who were sent but *him*.'

'Rooster?' said Samphire, her face all wet with tears as she too looked upslope.

Rooster was delving once more, but this time with Humlock at his flank as he tried to guide the silent mole's paws in the act of delving. Meanwhile Glee stanced before them both, urging Humlock on with words he could not hear and actions he could not see, hoping that somehow or other he would understand what his friends were trying to make him do.

But it was no good, for the moment Rooster took his paw away Humlock fell still once more, and his snout lowered as he hunched back into the position that seemed to exclude the world from himself, and himself from the world.

'But he must learn how to do it!' Glee said, loud enough for the adults to hear. There was desperate sadness in her voice, and mute appeal in the way she looked at Rooster.

Rooster stayed still a moment more, and then he separated from his two new friends and went upslope a little and stared up at the cliffs, and then round and up the valley towards the three dark scars of the three Creeds. Perhaps he was praying, perhaps just thinking, but whatever it was it seemed plain that in his own dark ungainly way he was trying to find a way forward for Humlock.

Then, in a resigned yet thoughtful manner, he turned back to the two moles, and reaching them he raised his two great paws to touch them both in a way that was so gentle, so expressive of concern and determination, that he looked not like the clumsy youngster he often seemed to be, but a much older mole whose power of spirit and purpose made watching moles forget entirely that his head was mis-shapen, and his paws grotesque.

So striking was this sense at that moment that Drumlin and Sedum drew instinctively closer to Samphire, and, indeed, their paws reached out to each other in such a way that they echoed that same triumvirate of shared concern they saw in their youngsters above them.

'It *is* your Rooster who's been sent,' whispered Drumlin, 'and the power of the Creeds is with him . . .'

'. . . and the Stone is with them all,' added Samphire, thinking perhaps that she must offer hope of the Stone's trust in the other two, and not yet understanding Drumlin's meaning.

The Reap roared, ravens turned and scuttered high above, the clouds moved in the sky beyond, as Drumlin said, 'My dear, there comes a time when a mole must trust another unreservedly, as I now, having heard what you have said, and seeing the love of mole and gentleness that abides in the son you have reared here in the Charnel, will trust you.

'Let our youngsters play on, and seek out for themselves a way forward that may be perhaps for us all, as I try now to answer the questions you have raised about delving, and about the moles of the Charnel.'

When Turrell had reached this moment in his account of Rooster's life a tear had coursed down his face at the thought and memory of it; and a solitary tear coursed down Privet's now.

Blankly, she stared out beyond her outstretched paws, seeing not Chieveley Dale, but that former time in that place unvisited by her, where Rooster was born and raised, and where now a secret must be revealed . . . Yet even as she thought of it and its consequences there came a rough brutal shout from the Dale below and Privet was jolted back to reality by the renewed perils of the present moment.

The shout she heard was from one of the grikes below her as he reared menacingly up from his cover to confront two moles, both young males, who had broken out of a hidden tunnel upslope of him and were now trying to make a run for it towards the forest, and the very place where Privet now stanced.

Chapter Twenty-Four

Privet stared in mounting horror as the two fleeing Chieveley moles struggled across the rough ground towards her, the huge grikes in close pursuit. Her heart beat painfully in her chest and she could not even catch her breath as she tried desperately to think what she should do.

From where she stanced it was plain that the two moles were no match for their pursuers, either in speed or size, and to make matters worse other grikes were already running up from the lower slopes in response to the shout.

It seemed to Privet that pursuers and pursued, racing upslope as they were, would all shortly converge on the very spot where she had until now laid watching and unseen. If the grikes had come alone she would simply have hidden until they were gone; and if the two Chieveley moles had not been seen, she would have attracted their attention in some quiet way and led them off unnoticed.

But with them all coming together in the open, what was she to do? What *could* she do? Hide, and abandon the moles she and the others were committed to help? Or show herself, and risk capture and perhaps the lives of the very moles she wanted to save?

Even had Privet been able to find a clear answer to these questions in so short a time, the situation suddenly changed again and she was faced by new dilemmas. For more Chieveley moles emerged from secret exits off to her left flank somewhere up near where her father had deployed himself, and were making a dash for the forest with grikes in pursuit of them as well.

Privet glanced downslope to her right in the hope of seeing Hamble, and getting some guidance from him about what to do, but he was out of sight. Meanwhile, though the two Chieveley moles were much nearer now, their pace had slowed as they struggled to cross the rough ground adjacent to the forest, and she could see that their bodies were thin and wasted as if they had had too little food, and their eyes were wide with fear. Then one of them made the mistake of turning to look back and see how near the grikes were, and stumbled sideways with a hopeless cry as he did so. His companion paused, turned, saw how near the grikes were, and then rushed on desperately.

It was then, wishing to give him encouragement and with no thought of her own safety or of the consequences of what she did, that Privet involuntarily stanced up to cry to the moles to try to press on to the cover of the trees. But the moment she rose out of the undergrowth she knew it was a mistake, and perhaps a fatal one. The approaching mole paused in alarm at what seemed the new threat ahead of him, the grikes pressed on ever faster behind, barely pausing in their stride as they looked up, decided that Privet was the enemy as well, and charged resolutely on.

They caught up the mole who had stumbled and dealt him a disabling sideways talon thrust before they came on, the one in front pointing ahead first at her, and then at the fleeing mole as he grunted, 'I'll get 'er, you get 'im.'

To her credit Privet stayed still and upright on the spot from which she had risen from the undergrowth, not from the utter panic she might well have felt – in fact a deathly calm had overtaken her – but from a wise appreciation of the fact that if she was going to dodge the grike and have some chance of escape, she had best do it at the last possible moment, when, she hoped, he might have such momentum that he would carry on by her and straight into the bole of the dead tree near where she had stanced and towards which – surprised at her own coolness – she now backed.

She saw the slower of the two moles tumble and lie still from the taloning he had suffered, she saw the second grike come on as the first passed by the faster of the moles and headed straight for her. Then, quite unexpectedly, she heard her father's voice cry out from far upslope: 'This way! Now!'

Was it intended to distract the grike about to charge her down, or was it to help the fleeing moles who were striving to reach the forest where her father had been? She did not know, but in some wonder she found that events which until that moment before had been overtaking her with their speed, now seemed suddenly to slow so much that she had time to think about such things, and others too. In this new slowed-down world, in which the great grike looming over her appeared to have paws and talons that were merely floating lazily through the air, she had time to glance to her left flank once more in the hope that Hamble had made an appearance at last, but still he was not there.

Then, too, she was able to turn in time to see her father Sward rush out into the open on the slopes above and signal to more Chieveley moles which way to go. She watched the grikes pursuing them falter for a moment, even as she turned back once more to see the grike who was intent upon harming *her* slow fractionally in such a way that she knew how and where to place her paws and then how to move, such that his talon lunge missed her and he crashed on by, hitting the tree with a roar of rage.

These things happened like a living dream, as did her father's move out from the forest edge into a greater danger even than the one she faced, as the moles he was trying to help passed him by and took cover in the forest, and he was left alone to face the grikes.

'It's what he *intends!*' she whispered to herself in this strange, sluggish, muted and unemotional world in which she found herself. 'It's what he wants.'

But then the likely consequence of her father's appearance in the open jolted her back to reality, and the world speeded up again, and danger and panic were upon her. The second grike approached and his paws began to crash down towards her; there was an ugly roar of shouting; the stricken mole on the slope before her cried out in pain; the other, so near her now, had stopped still in terror.

All this, and her paws and body continued to obey that guidance they had received from her calm self a moment before. She instinctively moved to one side even as the grikes before and behind tried to strike her. For a terrifying moment she saw them both, ugly and threatening, before the second pulled back his talons with a contemptuous sneer and nodded towards the first, as if to say that Privet was *his* victim.

Then as he turned back to attend to the two Chieveley moles, Privet turned from him to face the larger of the two grikes alone. He had recovered from his crash into the tree and now stanced staring down at her, frightening in his power and the ruthlessness of his purpose. With a cruel smile he raised his talons in a slow deliberate way and Privet saw death coming upon her, and it was ugly, and frightening, and terrible, and it gripped her whole body as if a cruel paw had come out of the sky and taken hold of her and was squeezing whatever calm she had felt right out of her, and leaving her in death's sickening company.

Again the world receded to mute slowness, but now she was the victim and this time it was her limbs, her talons, her mind that could not seem to respond with speed or purpose, or do anything at all. As she saw the sharp talons begin to fall she knew it was the last thing she would ever see.

Yet even as they began to drive down towards her snout they too slowed and stilled, and as she dared look from them to the grike's face, she saw his expression change from murderous anger to one of puzzled surprise. The look of surprise changed as quickly to one of mortal pain, dark and deep, and his eyes bulged, then rolled as she saw loom over him a mole she knew, though never in this way before: angry, ruthless, strong. Before she could even speak his name he pulled back the talons of his right paw from the grike's back into which they had lunged with such effect, and brought down his left paw sideways in a thrust that not only ripped open the grike's flanks and exposed the white bones of his ribs, but served to throw him to one side too.

Hamble had come, and he was a youngster no more. The blood of killing was on his paws and a terrible look of controlled and deadly intent was in his eyes – more formidable by far than the grike's cruel smile, for it was intelligent, and thinking, and purposeful. Hamble the warrior had been born.

Without pausing to speak or acknowledge her or what he did, his fur red and wet with the grike's blood, Hamble trampled over his victim's flanks and snout and surged past Privet to charge down upon the second grike. As Privet turned to follow all of this she felt a strange shudder at her side and saw the grike's talons at her flank, stretched out and shaking as he gasped his last and died.

But now her attention was taken by the brutal sight of two great moles, Hamble and the second grike, beginning what was evidently a fight to the death. They were locked in a straining, grunting brawl of talons and snouts, bared teeth and sweating fur, falling now this way towards Privet, now that way away from her.

Nearby the uninjured Chieveley mole had recovered his senses enough to turn back to his hurt friend, and was huddled over him, watching the fight one moment, and the next the other grikes across the open space who had earlier been coming after him as well, but now had veered off upslope where Sward had been, and where a greater number of the Chieveley moles were escaping still.

The scene was like a rough sea of death, with wave on wave of moles, rushing one way and another, fighting, screaming, fleeing. Then, as Hamble fought on bloodily, the sea shifted once again and with a pounding of paws from above where her father had been, several grikes, having killed or lost the moles they had been pursuing, were now charging down to rescue the one that Hamble fought.

Panic had already rooted Privet to the spot when, from some place beyond them, among a mêlée of other grikes, her father rose into view and cried out, 'Run, my dear! Run *now*!'

Even as he did so he disappeared once more under the murderous paws of the grikes who had surrounded him and she stared, numb with horror and unable to move at all. But then behind her Hamble cried out, 'Do it, Privet, do as he says. Run!'

She turned back to him and saw him make a death thrust into the second grike's snout and eyes and, with blood all over his flanks and paws, though whether his own or that of the grike he had defeated she could not tell, he rushed towards her and beyond to head off the new threat of the oncoming grikes.

Pointing to the two moles whose emergence had first started this time of terror, Hamble cried out, 'For Stone's sake, Privet, run! Run to the stream with *them*! Runnnnnn . . . !'

Then he was lost in battle once again as she, freed by his voice from the spot to which she had seemed for ever rooted in her fear, ran stumbling downslope in the wake of the two moles, towards the stream, away from all of it. She did not look back as the sounds of renewed fighting, cries and grunts, bloody thuds and gasps, came after her as if the noises themselves were enemies which sought to blot her out. On, on and on again she ran, the rough ground rushing up towards her, the two Chieveley moles struggling on ahead, her gasping breath an agony and a fainting darkness overtaking her and blotting out all the madness and the terror until all was gone from her but the struggle to escape.

Of the rest of that day, or the night that followed, or even of the days and nights that followed them, Privet afterwards remembered little more than brief and terrible glimpses of horror and feelings of loss.

She lost track of the two moles she had fled with, and hid somewhere by the stream to which Hamble had ordered her to run. She remembered emerging from a dark place to a deserted vale, and searching in vain for Hamble, for her father, for anymole at all. She came to believe she had found her father with some of the Chieveley moles, and a few grikes, all dead and half eaten by the rooks.

But Hamble, he had gone; and the tunnels of the Dale had been ruined. She woke from her nightmare slowly to the aching reality that she was alone and all but lost, with nomole to help her but herself, and the wide Moors to cross if ever she was to reach Crowden again.

Days of wandering and aching, days and nights of sleepless wondering, of shock, of being too numb to be afraid that the grikes might come; or so lost that if they came it might be preferable to being so alone. Days when the mists on the surrounding Moors lowered ever more, and the air gained the chill of approaching winter.

Until a day came when she awoke refreshed, free of her nightmare at last, and knowing that all that past was in retreat – not conquered but repressed to a place deep within where she could control it, and for a time forget. A day when a wintry sun shone down in the Dale where she wandered, and up on the Tops above, and Privet saw that the mists were gone.

It was then that she saw Hilbert's Top for the first time, its sides steep and dark with exposed millstone grit, and she felt the weight of the past, and of the past days, drop off her, as if it was all long ago, and she free of it. Her father . . . was no more. Hamble . . . was beyond her reach now, but the Stone would protect him, and all of this and these events were part of a pattern greater than she could comprehend or seek to control.

For now the fresh autumn wind was in her fur, and the sun warm on her face, and before her rose Hilbert's Top, the place to which she knew from all she had been told was where the mole they had set out to find had gone into retreat.

'Rooster must be up there!' she declared to herself, feeling that he was all that mattered now, and her whole life had been leading towards finding him. Thereafter . . . She could not guess and did not even care to try, as she set off to climb up the slopes towards the Top, and leave her past behind.

'Rooster,' she whispered to herself as she went, as if speaking his name, and thinking again of the remarkable story that lay behind his coming to Chieveley Dale and his later retreat to the heights above, might make it the more likely that he would be waiting for her up there when she reached Hilbert's Top herself.

Rooster's mother Samphire could scarcely have imagined what story it was that Drumlin and Sedum were to tell her, that day in May when the three moles had shared their confidences. Nor that its outcome would be a visit to see a place, and meet moles, unlike any other in all of moledom.

'But first, my dear,' Drumlin began, 'I must tell you of the great task whose challenge and hoped-for outcome has given meaning to the lives of so many generations of the moles of the Charnel over the centuries since our forebears were first outcast here. You already know of Hilbert . . .'

'Little beyond the fact that it is the name of that part of the Moors which rises to form the eastern boundary of the Dale where I was raised,' said Samphire. 'There were rumours that there were ancient delvings up on the Top, and that a mole called Hilbert had lived there, but of the delving arts or that he was the last Master of the Delve, we knew nothing.'

'So!' declared Drumlin after a pause in which her face expressed surprise followed by sudden understanding. 'So, the Stone must have intended that his history was forgotten in these parts, all the better to preserve the secrets that he left behind. I had better begin at the beginning then, though what I shall tell you is known to every adult Charnel mole, for it is our earliest heritage, and provides us with such pride as we may have, and such purpose as we may follow – a purpose far nobler, far greater, than the narrow confines of this dark, beset place might suggest to you. The youngsters ought to hear it too!'

'Even Rooster?' questioned Sedum suddenly.

'Especially him,' said Drumlin shortly, 'for isn't he as much a Charnel mole as any other, seeing as he was brought here at birth, and lives as near to the Creeds as it's safe for mole to get? And have I not the sense that he is the one for whom our generations of ancestors and ourselves have waited for so long?'

Drumlin called to Glee to stop what she and the others were at and all come on down, since she was about to tell a tale they ought to hear.

So down they came, though not without some delay, for Humlock did not understand, and seemed determined to stay where he was, hunched in that drear way of his over the delving Rooster had made but could not communicate. But at last he turned and came down between his two friends, and all three stanced down near Samphire to hear of the great events of which Drumlin wished to speak.

Then she began to talk at last of the history of the Charnel moles, a community of moles whose past and present lives were surely as secret, strange and awesome as any in all the annals of mole history; a community to whom Samphire's and Rooster's coming brought to an end long centuries of isolation, and ways onward which might in time touch all moles, and bring back to moledom the lost secrets of the delving art, and finally a way towards the Silence for allmole.

*

It seemed that the settlement that the Ratcher clan disturbed when first they came to the Charnel decades before was far older than they knew or could have guessed, had they been interested in such things. Indeed, its antecedents went back centuries, to the time, well-recorded in ancient texts, when there was a schism in Uffington, and dread Scirpus, creator of the Word, came north to Whern and began that inexorable train of dark events that had so nearly led to the extinction of the Stone in more recent times.

Drumlin told how the Scirpuscun movement began the dissolution of the holiest places of moledom, whose importance had been enhanced by various Masters of the Delve who had created there mysterious and awesome tunnels and chambers, marked out with delved carvings that carried the sounds of Silence.

'Such places gave all who visited more than merely a sense of peace: they put into their very souls the sense of a way of living, and a way of dying, that was of the essence of the Stone. It was the Masters' art to be able to delve such places, and their mystery that they themselves were not always holy moles, nor even personally awesome, or even close to the Stone.

'No, their gift was of a deep unspoken kind, a gift of touch and feeling, a gift of expression through their paws and talons such that they themselves were often taciturn, ill at ease with words, poor at talking to others or speaking of the Stone whose Silence and whose Light it was the task and the glory of their lives to honour.

'I speak of a "gift", but in truth such art is not easily acquired, but comes only from long years in the service of a Master who teaches what he knows by example, and whose art is learned by experience alone. Some delvers learn more easily than others, but most are able only to learn so much and fall far short of being true Masters of the Delve.

'But such moles are much needed and much loved by the few Masters who emerge and whom they serve, for no single mole could ever have delved all that was needed in the holy places of the Stone without the help of many other trained and expert paws. So each Master must have his Disciples of the Delve, to perform the simpler or more routine tasks and so help construct, carve and delve the basic tunnels and chambers, portals and retreats, which the Masters complete with their own delving.

'Be that as it may – with the coming of Scirpus began the demise of the Masters of the Delve, for he learnt their art and corrupted it, turning all its effort towards the creation of Dark Sound, whose origins

301

had been wholly good and intended only to protect the holy places from those who might destroy them, the enemies of the Stone. It was Scirpus' evil genius to turn Dark Sound upon itself and, as a consequence, signal the end of the delving arts.

'When he and his followers judged that they had acquired all the skills they needed the order went out that the Masters of the Delve be hunted down and killed by the Scirpuscun moles, and their Disciples dispersed. Many tried to flee and hide, and some succeeded for a time, passing on their knowledge in secret down the generations of their family. But inexorably their numbers dwindled and their art declined until at last only one true Master remained, of a line that had hidden itself in the very shadow of Whern. This Master was finally betrayed and forced to flee, taking with him but a few aged Disciples to help him in his work.

'His colleagues gone, his assistants taken or killed, he fled southward from Whern warning that with his death the delving art would be lost to moledom for all time, and with it the true way to Silence.'

As Drumlin spoke, the day around them grew quiet and the roar of the Reap more muted; but the ground beneath their paws seemed to tremble, and Samphire felt troubled and uncertain in herself.

'This last Master was Hilbert of Wharfedale, known as Master Hilbert to ourselves. Harried and chased, his friends dying or killed, he came at last into the Moors and lived for a time within the sanctuary of the blessed Weign Stones over on Bleaklow. But even there he was traced, and was forced back into darkest Saddleworth, and thence to Chieveley Dale. Aye, Samphire, to the very place where you were raised.

'There he found a time of retreat and peace, beloved in that little community of moles, nurturing those few Disciples who remained while he fell into communion with the Stone, having the belief that it would ask of him a final task. Until at last, when he had but two Disciples left, both old and near their time, Hilbert understood that he must, with their help, make a final delving – perhaps the most important that any Master would ever make.

'That much he knew, but what the delving would be, or what its intent, he did not know. Yet having faith, he led his two followers out of Chieveley to the highest place thereabouts, whose name we now know as Hilbert's Top. And there he began his delving once again.

'Long moleyears he worked, nomole in Chieveley telling others he was there, even when the Scirpuscun moles sent their inquisitors out upon the Moors to track him down.

302

'"An old vagrant died here years ago," the Chieveley moles lied, "perhaps that was the mole you seek. Had we known . . ." It is said that the inquisitors, suspicious, tortured Chieveley moles, but none ever confessed.

'Then something worse befell the Dale: virulent murrain, which left the Chieveley numbers low, and the survivors diseased and maimed, their offspring all deformed. Of course, moles of dogmatic faith such as Scirpuscun moles perceive disease and deformity as judgement of the Word, and stricken moles as guilty, fit only to be killed.'

Here Drumlin paused and glanced at Sedum and half raised a paw as if to touch the goitre that so disfigured her, and then pointed at her patched and raddled fur before smiling wryly at Samphire once again.

'It is the lot of moles like us to be rejected by moledom, and to be treated as if we had done something wrong. Dogma makes mole heartless and punitive; but to us, dogma is a worse disfigurement, for it spoils the heart. Such is one of the wisdoms Hilbert taught us.

'That being so, it is not surprising that the Scirpuscuns were reluctant to touch the Chieveley moles with their own paws, lest they become tainted themselves. So they were driven over the Moors, and up into the Charnel – a place where other plagued and deformed moles were already confined until they died forgotten and unloved.

'So it was that Hilbert saw from afar disease afflict the community that had protected him, and then that community herded from the Dale to be condemned to live out their suffering until death in the shadows of the Charnel, and he was powerless to do anything about it. He worked on in the company of his two friends, striving to perform the task he felt he had been set; striving but failing, for despite all his art his delving would not come right. Until at last his friends grew old and died, and he was alone once more.

'We know that it was then he made great dark delvings, delvings that explored his grief and last anger, delvings that delved into the last shadows of his soul; delvings that took him on a journey into darkness that only a Master could have endured. With these he surely made Hilbert's Top a place to fear, for nomole could approach that place without suffering the Dark Sound that Hilbert created in the tunnels there.'

'It *was* a place we were taught to fear as youngsters,' said Samphire, 'and there were many stories of moles venturing there and never coming back, or if they did, they came back mute and mad.'

'Aye,' said Drumlin grimly, 'it would be so, it would be so. But

Hilbert, his dark journey done, came through that final time of trial, redeemed and made pure, and understanding at last what he must do. Where his friends the Chieveley moles had gone, he must go too, and he who had conquered darkness of the mind, must journey now into darkness of the body.

'We know little of his journey from the Top out on to the Moors again, or how it was he reached the Charnel. We do not even know if he already knew that the Chieveley moles were there with other outcast moles. We think he was chased and harried there, yet one thing we do know, one strange important thing . . .'

Here Drumlin turned and pointed a talon towards the dark fissures of the Creeds at the head of the valley.

'He came among us by that route. Aye, down one of the three Creeds he came.'

'But that's impossible!' declared Samphire.

Drumlin shrugged, and said quietly, 'We are certain it was so. He was chased to the cliffs above, harried along the Tops, and then somehow tumbled into the void of the Creeds and was presumed dead and gone. Perhaps it was the Stone's way of giving him the protection from the Scirpuscun moles he needed to complete his final task. Certainly it was not across the Span but down from the valley head, from the direction of the Creeds, that one day he came to our forebears, like a light shining from the Stone itself.

'In his reunion with moles he loved, and his meeting with the strangers here, all deformed or diseased, Hilbert understood at last that his time on Hilbert's Top was but a trial, and that his final and his truest task was *here* in this place of outcasting and hopelessness.'

'Here?' repeated Samphire, while Rooster and Glee stared with wide-open eyes, with Humlock between them, hunched, unseeing and unhearing, in his eternal silent darkness.

A look of great pride came over Drumlin's face as she resumed her tale.

'Master Hilbert understood that in all of moledom this was the only place where the delving arts could be preserved until that day when moledom would have need of them again, and that these outcast moles, diseased and forgotten, deformed and reviled, must be his last Disciples, and must be taught all the arts he knew. Aye, to them he brought a great task, and gave them and their pups, and *their* pups after that, down to this very day, a most holy and a most secret trust. For it was then, not far from where we are stanced now, that the Master made his greatest delving, using it to teach our forebears all he knew, and giving them a place and the means to teach others, that the delving arts would not be lost.'

'But I see no delvings, nor any delving moles,' said Samphire incredulously. 'I see no portals, nor tunnels, and I see no great chambers.'

'Yet they are near here, my dear, and much more than that, and soon I shall show his great work to you. But I must prepare you a little, for what you shall see nomole from outside the Charnel has ever seen, nor anymole that was not born deformed, or mutated, or in some way imperfect, and so knowing that they are but part of what they might be. But together . . . we are whole. This is the understanding our condition gives us.'

'But you sacrifice your deformed young, you . . .' began Samphire, more angry than she should have been because she felt herself on the brink of a revelation of which she was much afraid, and because it was plain that Drumlin saw Rooster as such a mole, as part of a whole, whereas to her he was quite whole enough.

'My dear, we do not sacrifice our young. We nurture them as best we may, even the blind ones, even the snoutless ones, even those with no limbs, or with gaping backs, or with no hope of independent life. We bear them and we nurture them, as the Master Hilbert bade us do. But when Midsummer comes we seek the Stone's guidance over their future, knowing that some cannot pass into adulthood and hope to live. These we give up into the Reap. But the others, the ones the Ratcher moles never see when they gape and jeer at our ritual farewell to those we love but cannot help, these are given the task that Hilbert set them so many centuries ago – to learn what delving arts they can, and so maintain that great delving he made to preserve all that the Masters once knew until that day when a new Master will come among us, and moledom has need of him. For you see, Samphire, Hilbert believed that one day a great Master would rise up once more, and that moledom, no longer beset by the Word, would welcome him, and be ready again to learn what a Master of the Delve may teach.'

'But what of the moles I have sometimes seen going up towards the Creeds? And the ones whose bodies have been cast up along the Reap?'

Drumlin nodded gravely. 'I told you how the Master came among us from one of the Creeds. We know not which of the three. But he told us that the new Master who comes to moledom will be saved by a journey back up through the Creeds, back to the Tops above, back to moledom. So it is that when our moles feel their task is done, or that their disease and deformity worsens and the Silence draws near, they, in a time of their own choosing, have the right to leave us and try to ascend one or other of the Creeds. In their hearts is the hope that they, after all, might be the Master we await, *they* might have a task far beyond all they have done here.

'So it was that the Master gave us our pride and our purposes, and our rituals too – unknown though they mostly are, strange though they must seem. But now I must show you of what it is I speak, for delving is not a thing of words but deeds, and the Master intended that it should be seen and experienced, not merely talked about.'

'Now?' said Samphire faintly. 'All of us?'

Drumlin nodded.

'Can Humlock come?' said Glee suddenly.

'It's not for the likes of him,' said Sedum, ''tis best he doesn't come.'

'But –' began Glee.

'Aye, 'tis best, my dear,' sighed Drumlin. 'Where we must go is not always easy, not always safe: Humlock might be endangered there. Then too, how could he know what it is he cannot see, or what it is he cannot hear?'

'He . . .' said Rooster suddenly, all gruff and close to tears, 'he *might* know.'

A sad smile came to Drumlin's face, and Sedum went to Rooster in her direct and kindly way and touched his paw.

'Would his own mother deny him any right if she thought it was for the best?' she said with tears in her eyes. 'I've done my best to love my Humlock from the first, from the first suckling, but never once has he responded to anything I've done, not because he won't but because he can't. To this day I must find his food for him, I must feed him, I must clean after him. 'Tis not his fault, but he was born not only without sight and speech and hearing, but without much of a mind as well.

'Bless you both, and I'm sure he gets something from your company, though nomole can know what. But you see he'll never be able to be independent, he'll always need the support of others to survive, he'll never be able to give a thing in return. It might be easier if there were more outward signs of what he is but there aren't. And he can't even delve, you've seen that yourself, Rooster – he can't learn it at all. Don't you think I've tried day after day before now, like you did today? Don't you think I know what must happen when Midsummer comes? I've suffered so much on his account, and the only thing that keeps me going is having faith that the Stone knows best and there's a purpose to his life beyond my simple understanding.'

'Why would his being able to delve make things different?' asked Samphire gently.

'Because Master Hilbert said that a mole who can delve can learn, for each time he puts his talons to the soil he joins himself back to moledom and allmole, each time he makes a delving stroke and takes away what was there he comes nearer to something of himself. But poor Humlock here . . . how can he ever live like this?'

At this she broke down utterly, and putting her paws about her great hunched son, hugged him, and petted him, until her tears wet his fur, and her sobs grew quiet. But all the while Humlock hunched still, unmoved, and all uncomprehending as it seemed.

'Well,' said Glee in a tight voice, 'whatever anymole says I know he knows. I can feel it. Humlock's . . . *Humlock*, just as I'm *Glee.*'

As Sedum pulled away from Humlock, Rooster said, 'Well, we could try just once more, just once . . .' And so he did, delving the ground in the midst of where they stanced, guiding Humlock's great paw, raising the rough Charnel soil, and then casting it to one side. But it was no good, Humlock would not, could not do it for himself, and when Rooster let his paw go, it went back to the ground and did not move.

'Well,' said Rooster at last, 'it doesn't feel right not to take him with us, and I agree with Glee, there's something there. But – I'm sorry, Glee. We must . . .'

She nodded in a sad resigned way and tried to get Humlock to go below ground, pushing and shoving him with all her might. But like some great rock he stayed where he was.

'It's all right,' she said with a grin, 'he likes to stay on the surface sometimes. I'll take him to the protection of those boulders on the slope above, and don't tell me he hasn't got brains, for he'll come with me now as if he heard the words I said.'

Which was true, for the moment she put her paw to his flank and pushed him in the direction of the boulders, he padded meekly upslope, and when she ran ahead to one side of him, his head touched her flank as they went, moving together like one mole, her white-pink body dwarfed by his dark flank and limbs. Once she had settled him among the boulders she scampered happily back, and the mood of the party changed to one of expectant excitement.

'We won't be gone too long?' she asked, looking back up at Humlock.

307

Drumlin shook her head and said, 'Not this first time, no. Later there's no knowing. Now, follow me, and do as I say, and when we go down-tunnel Sedum will take up the rear lest any of you go astray. It's this way.' And they began to traverse gently down-valley towards a group of large rocks that lay ahead and a little below them.

It was as they were dropping down a steeper part of the slope just before them, with the cliff seeming to loom higher and darker above them to the left and the ravens wheeled restlessly in the sky that they heard, suddenly, like a gust of stormy wind out of air that has been still too long, a strange and desolate cry. That it was of loss there was no doubt, but that it was mole was more questionable, for it had a sub-mole quality about it, which struck alarm into all who heard it, and awe as well. It was Sedum who responded first, starting up with a mother's instinct.

'Humlock?' she said, or gasped, even before she turned to look back along the distant way to where they had left him.

'*Humlock?*' she cried, disbelieving what she saw.

He was no longer by the rocks where Glee had left him, but seemed to have managed to find his way back downslope to where they had been when Drumlin had told them Hilbert's tale, where Rooster had tried yet again to teach him to delve.

There he was, staring blindly at the ground, and seeming to reach towards it, though if it had been he who cried out there was no sign of it now. As they watched they saw his right paw touch the ground, and he seemed to hesitate. Then he shifted forward a little even as Rooster, watching as the others did, whispered softly, 'Yes, mole; *yes!*'

Then, his stance firmer, he pulled back his right paw for himself as Rooster had showed him, and without more ado lunged it powerfully into the ground. For a moment he held it there before, with a mighty delve, he raised it out again, soil and all, high. Then he slowly raised that great hunched head of his as if to look at his delving paw, but instead he snouted at it, scenting at the earth it held. He slowly turned his paw and let its burden pour out all down his snout and face, down to the ground again.

Then he shook his great head and did what he had never done, never once in all the long days that Sedum had raised him. Humlock laughed.

And if that laugh sounded strange, from a voice that would never be normal, it was because he had never heard another laugh, and never would. But Humlock had delved his first deep delve and discovered in that place his own good laughter was to be found.

Glee did not pause a moment more before she was running back as fast as her paws could take her to where he was, to hug him, to hold him, to join her laughter to his own.

While Rooster turned to Drumlin and said gruffly, in a voice that was command rather than question, 'He's coming with us now, always and for ever. Humlock's with *us*.'

And whatmole could doubt that there is a season when the young take up the tasks of older moles, a season that is not defined by wind or rain or temperature, and that this great season came to the Charnel on that day?

Privet might have journeyed further into what she then knew of the rest of Rooster's story, had not her weary and stumbling paws pulled her past the last outcrops of dark grit through which she climbed, up on to the grassy undulations of Hilbert's Top itself.

Then she could think of nothing else but the fear and unease she felt, as she heard sounds of calling mole across bleak spaces, and saw the ruined portals of ancient tunnels from whence those sounds seemed to come.

'Dark Sound?' she whispered to herself.

She shivered; the sky was a slaty grey and the air cold, and she felt more alone than she ever had. Dark Sound without a doubt, and she knew enough to know she must get away. Yet her paws took her forward towards those fearsome tunnels, drawn by a yearning the calling wrought within her heart, and youthful faith as well that somewhere Rooster might be found at last.

'I'll go a little way . . .' she whispered to herself.

But a little way was far too far once the deep-delved tunnels in which she found herself – immeasurably more awesome than anything she had ever seen in Crowden – took her in. On she went, past portals beyond her imagining, through chambers with dark shining carvings that seemed to echo even her quiet breath, and turn it into the breathing of a frightened mole and one drawn into a darkness too great for her, and a danger that would destroy her very soul.

Lost, soon lost. Wandering, vagrant, frightened, her pawsteps became the pawsteps of the grikes who chased her, her gasps the screams of moles who died, until she began to run and run, not knowing where she went, but only that she was on the edge of a void of darkness wherein the Stone's Light was not known, nor its Silence ever heard.

Turning from it she cried out to the Stone for help, now, '*Now!*'

But the grikes in her soul were made manifest, and were running after her and before her and at her flanks and she was unable to escape, whichever way she turned, and the Stone too far to reach, its Light too . . .

Its Light. Far in the distance, tiny, a distant portal to the day, ahead where the grikes that seemed to be would not dare to go, ahead was the only way to look, the only way to go.

Silence; there, beyond the Light. A hint of it at least, an under-echo to all the fearful sounds of calling, fleeing, chasing, screaming moles she heard in those great delvings where she was lost.

'Silence, Stone, lead me to it.'

Never had she made so real a prayer as that.

'Lead me . . .' and her voice was echoed back to her in waves, some bearable, some not, as the portal of Light grew greater and she ran on and on, feeling the dark carvings, on to the portal, on into its blinding Light, out through its shining arches, to fall and roll and tumble into the void of nightmare sleep beyond, and beyond that still to wake, her limbs aching on warm grass, her snout scenting at good air, and her flank stilling to the touch of a great mole's paw.

She half turned, utterly unafraid, her long journey done. She opened her eyes and looked into the great frowning face of a rough-furred mole, his eyes were narrowed in his concern for her, gentle eyes, as gentle as his touch.

'Mole,' he said, his voice gruff and deep.

Rooster.

But she could not speak his name, hard though she tried, her mouth moving but not in her control, her paws struggling but too weak to move, her mind knowing, but too tired to think.

Rooster.

So she only stared into his eyes and slowly, a little fearfully perhaps, his eyes smiled into hers and Privet, sinking into peaceful sleep at last, knew that where she had come was where the Stone had wished her most to be.

'Rooster,' she whispered, as her eyes closed once more.

'Yes,' he said, at last.

Chapter Twenty-Five

When Privet awoke again, much refreshed, Rooster had gone, and in a way she felt relieved, for it gave her time to . . . to what? Catch up with herself perhaps. Scent his scent. Look about the place, and orientate herself, for all the Dark Sound had gone and she was herself again, not that beset and fleeing thing she had been before.

She found that the Top was elevated above the Moors, which stretched brown and bleak to east and south, which was the part she had crossed with Hamble and Sward on her way to the Dale. Hamble and Sward . . . she thought of them and then forgot them. That was the past and for now she was above all that, and not only literally, and wished to live in the present, and discover what she could of it.

Chieveley Dale lay westward on her left flank, and from that height, peering over the steep edge of the fissured scarp formed by the mill-stone grit, it looked like any other dale: flat, green where its stream ran down, broken up by a few outcrops of rock or boulders fallen from the Tops above, and finally inconsequential. Was down there where her life changed? She supposed it was, and looked northward.

There the undulations of the Top dipped finally away to reveal the blue mists of dim distance, and another rise of higher ground which must lead, she knew, to Whern. Well, that was not for her now, nor ever, she hoped. No no, such future as she had lay here and south of here, yes, to the south where civilized moledom lay. She and Rooster . . . and already she had started to dream.

She turned her attention to the Top itself. It was expansive and generally flat, the outcrops highest where she was, which was why the views were good. She realized with a start that in all her journeying so far she had never seen the Moors without their mists until now. She tried to retrace the route by which she had crossed them, but could not and did not try for long. It was a forbidding sight.

Since the soil seemed more wormful below the outcrop, and there were signs of delving there, she ventured downslope for a while, glad to get out of the wind. She found the soil lay in drifts between the outcrops and scattered boulders of a different rock, and stopped being wormful to the east, where the Top sloped away and changed to hags of peat and heather. There, she supposed, the Moors she knew began. She avoided the portals she saw, remembering the dangers entering them had led her into when she first came on to the Top, though whether that had been by night, or the previous day, she was not now sure. She had no wish to suffer Dark Sound again. Unless Rooster was with her.

She smiled to herself, feeling suddenly free and light-pawed, 'almost skittish!', as she said to herself, using a word she knew nomole in Crowden would ever have used of staid Privet, assistant librarian.

With a start she remembered the story her father Sward had told her of Wort's Testimony and how he had found it on Hilbert's Top, and left it where he found it. Should she look for it? She doubted it, and the idea drifted from her.

So Privet wandered, time of no consequence, comforted by the knowledge that Rooster was somewhere about the place, and certain in herself that when the time came he could find her again. It was the most secure and comfortable of feelings. She was meant to be here where Rooster was.

The grass shuddered with a colder wind, and she snouted about for an entrance below, sensing that she was clear of the ancient delvings now and nearer something more recent and domestic: Rooster's place. Feeling like a trespasser, she delved away some grass and mud and with a thrust of her back paws, ventured down, glad to escape the cold winds and lowering skies, and what she found took her breath away.

Broad, strong, superbly arched, the tunnel turned its splendid way; its air cool, its wind-sound subtle, its walls well made, no, *beautifully* made. But it was a rough beauty, a serviceable beauty and seeing it, and touching it, she felt herself in the presence of a Master of the Delve.

The tunnel echoed her pawsteps softly, and led her into the first of several chambers – 'burrow' was too mean a word – whose different uses she could not guess. The light filtered in from above, pale and soft, catching the entrances and exits just so, and making their curves and lines harmonious and deep. Then she paused, for there was some-thing *familiar* about the place, as if she had been there before.

She ventured on, and found what must be an eating burrow. Yet it was clean, and ordered, and comfortable, unlike so many she had seen in Crowden. Though her own had always been like this! But Hamble's! She smiled at the sudden and familiar memory of her friend's tunnels

312

and wondered coolly if she would ever see them, and him again. Of course she would! Back to the present!

She found nearby a smaller tunnel that led to a sleeping place, simple, peaceful, empty.

'Rooster's place,' she said in wonder to herself. 'Oh, he *can* delve.' But it was not its grandness, for it was not that, nor its snugness, for that is too little a word to describe what she experienced; nor its clarity of line, nor its subtlety – its beauty – of sound. It was all of these, and something more, much more. Something she had seen before, and *knew* . . .

In awe and wonder she wandered on, taking one of the several ways she could see back out of the burrows, emerging briefly on the surface again to find, to her astonishment, that she was much further downslope than she had expected. How he had achieved this effect she could not imagine, and so she went back down, exploring on, until, astonished by the cleverness of all the delving, she found herself back at his sleeping place once more.

Should she? Could she? Dare she?

Oh, yes she could! If only to stance down and find out what it felt like to be where Rooster had been. With her heart beating faster once more, she advanced into this most private secret place of his so that for a moment she might lie where once he had lain, and listen to how he had made the wind-sound and vibrations of the whole system centre on this spot.

Never in all her life had she stanced in a place so sensitive to sound, yet quiet in its effect, for all was carried here, and all absorbed here, and a shift to the right brought a whispering wall, and to the left another, and up above a ceiling, rough-hewn, yet, somehow, finished. She listened to the sounds of grass in wind, and trees whose leaves were shedding, and far, far off the roaring owls, all clear, all carried.

She reached out a paw to touch the wall that he had delved, and stretched out her body where he had lain, and closed her eyes, and knew that the Rooster she had known, that all the system knew, was not a real mole at all. This was Rooster, here was Rooster, and his form was beautiful, and the only thing that was grotesque was that he had been driven from this place, and it was – felt – bereft of him.

She closed her eyes, she thought of him, she slept, she dreamed.

'Mole! Mole!'

She woke quite terrified. Rooster was there and the tunnel was filled with strange bright light. She could not immediately tell what part of the day it was, nor how long she had been asleep. Then she knew. A whole night had passed, and new dawn had come. Time, on Hilbert's Top, seemed not its normal self.

'I . . . I . . .' she struggled to find words, to take a defensive stance, to, to . . .

'I'll not harm you, mole,' he said loudly, backing off as if it were he who was afraid. 'Didn't know you were here. Wondered where you'd gone. Don't *mind*. Anymole who gets this far into Hilbert's Top's not a harming mole.'

'I'm sorry, I —' but she could not speak. Never ever had she been so taken by surprise. Terror gave way to dismayed embarrassment. 'I came to ask you —'

'You from Crowden?' he said. He seemed to glower but perhaps it was his normal look. She noted that his front paws were different sizes, just as she'd heard. She noted too that there was something very solid about Rooster, gentle but solid.

'I'm Privet,' she said, 'of Crowden's Library.' At such a moment, and feeling vulnerable, she instinctively wanted to give herself the protection of her work.

He stared unhelpfully, seeming huger by the moment and more strange.

'I came to ask you a favour.'

'*Favour?*' It seemed not a word he knew.

Then words tumbled out of her, about Crowden, about what had happened at Chieveley Dale, about everything.

When she had done he made no comment about any of it at all, but said again, 'A favour?'

'I want you to come to Crowden,' she said.

Slowly he grimaced in what she thought might be a smile.

'Can't,' he said. 'Too late, too dangerous, no good.'

'The grikes?' she said.

He shook his great head. 'We'd never get across the Moors, not in time. Winter's come.'

Winter? She stared at him blankly. But it was only autumn!

He turned from her and without a word led her uptunnel to an entrance. He led her out and she found herself in the shadow of one of the great boulders and staring at a muted landscape of white snow. Not deep, not even covering all the Top. Beyond, the Moors were as yet untouched, just brown-black and dull.

'Soon now. Coming from the east. The Moors will be impassable. And anyway . . . I have delving to do.'

314

'Delving?' said Privet faintly.

He nodded, and peered vaguely about, his paws fretful among the snow on the ground.

'And I?' she said in sudden alarm.

He shrugged indifferently. 'There's worms, there's room, you'll survive,' he said. 'Stone decides all things. Stone brought you here.'

'Did it?' she asked.

He nodded gravely.

'And my friends, did the Stone let them survive?' she said with a sudden bitterness that took her by surprise.

'Some did,' he said. 'Saw them escape. They got away. Some will.'

She stared at him and suddenly felt tired, and yet relaxed. Stone decides all things, he had said.

'Rooster,' she said, 'do you mind if I stay here?'

He shook his head and looked away, and still looking away as if he could not meet her gaze, he said, 'Was alone too long. Can't delve well since Samphire went into Silence. Asked the Stone for help. You've come.'

Without saying more he ambled off, and she watched him go, as ungainly in his gait as his paw marks were irregular across the thin covering of snow.

'Rooster . . .' she whispered after him, breathing the chill air and staring at the snow-laden sky, and feeling that here and now, so strangely, her adult life had finally begun.

He turned as if he had heard her.

'Privet,' he said, speaking her name for the first time. Across the white layer of snow they stared at each other.

'Will you come back soon?' she asked.

'Will,' he said firmly.

'And talk?' she said.

He grinned lopsidedly. 'Want to,' he said.

'This evening?' she dared ask.

'Haven't delved for days and weeks and months,' he said. 'Can delve now you've come. Then we'll talk, Privet and Rooster. Talk till ravens sleep. Samphire used to say that. She was my mother.'

He turned and finally went off, and as Privet watched him go she felt she wanted to run after him, and hold him, and love him. She felt she wanted to cry out his name. She felt she wanted to become him.

'Rooster,' she whispered again, and for a moment he paused again, as if he heard, which surely he could not, and then was gone to delve.

It was night when he returned, and his paws and head were grubby with soil, his talons clogged.

'Have delved,' he said, and began to groom himself. She watched fascinated, almost hungering to help him groom, terrified of the power of what she felt. But she stanced still and staring, and not a single movement of eye or snout, of mouth or paw, of flank or tail, betrayed the passion that she felt as she wallowed in just watching him.

'Have delved well,' he said at last.

'Will you show me sometime?' she said, feeling suddenly stupid.

He grunted non-committally.

'Will talk now,' he said finally, as if hoping that was a good reply.

They stared at each other in silence and suddenly, for the first time since she was a growing pup, she felt her snout blush pink. Was he staring at her as she had at him, devouringly? No, no, no. No.

'Tell me,' she said impulsively with no idea what she wanted him to tell her until she said it, 'about the first time you went with Drumlin, Sedum and your mother, and the others, to see the secret delvings in the Charnel.'

'You know about me?' he said.

She nodded. 'Tell me what you want to, Rooster. Please.'

'That day my life began,' he said. 'That day the journey here began.'

'Today our journey on from here begins,' she said, again impulsively. Now why had she said that, and what did it mean? Oh, she knew, she knew what it meant!

Rooster blinked and his great paws fretted.

'Want to talk about it all,' he said.

Chapter Twenty-Six

The entrance into which Drumlin led Samphire, Rooster and the others, with Sedum taking up the rear, appeared at first as no more than a cleft among rocks, but once inside, they saw it continued steeply downward as a tunnel between narrow sloping walls. These came so close together that it was hard for the moles to progress without tripping over themselves, which most of them did; and it was made harder by the loose rocks and other obstructions which littered the tunnel's steep floor. It occurred to Samphire after only a short way that she would have already given up and turned back had not Drumlin, who had the advantage of familiarity with the place, been leading them on with such determination. But perhaps after all the tunnel was meant to be awkward, to discourage strangers from venturing down too far; and perhaps too this visit, which seemed so sudden and spontaneous, had long been planned.

After some initial nervous chatter they all fell silent as they continued to clamber steeply down, concentrating on where to put their paws. Twice they had to stop to catch up with each other and recover themselves, but at last the tunnel walls widened and the floor cleared and flattened into a more normal tunnel.

A short distance on the passage opened up, and they found themselves deep underground in a hushed, cool, cavernous chamber, across which, from fissures in the roof high above, great shafts of light shone down so brightly in the gloomy place that they obscured what lay at the furthest end, though some sense of sound and continuation came from that direction.

Those parts of the walls they *could* see, which ran back behind them to a gloomy end wall, were carved in deep and intricate patterns of an extent and beauty that quite took a mole's breath away. Their convolutions of spiral and incision seemed to shimmer and shine with the light from above, and when a mole stared at them they seemed to move as if they were alive, being sensuous and subtle in some places, stark and shocking in others.

'Was this *delved*?' asked Rooster in awe, going to the nearest wall

317

and reaching up to touch an area of the carvings. As he ran his paws over them a sound was emitted from the wall opposite, strange and wistful, then suddenly harsh, then fading into a cry from somewhere far away.

Rooster pulled his paw back in alarm, at which the sounds stopped as suddenly as they had begun, and he glowered first at the place he had touched, and then round at the far side of the chamber where the sound had seemed to come from.

Glee scampered after him to examine the wall, but when she touched it in her turn – and the carvings had a quality that invited a mole's paw to touch them – she did so more tentatively than he had; even so her touch brought forth similar echoing sounds from across the chamber, as of moles calling from the past. Once more, as she withdrew her paw, the sounds stopped.

Rooster stared upwards to where the carvings continued far out of reach of any mole, up so far indeed that they were lost in that bright part of the roof where the light came in.

'*Moles* delved these?' he asked again in wonder, pointing at the walls. He reached forward to touch the carvings yet again, but something in the awesome quality of the place stopped him, and anyway, from that part of the great chamber that lay beyond the light came a shuffling, dragging sound of mole, and they all turned that way in awed and silent expectation.

So absorbed had Rooster and Glee been by the sounds, and Drumlin, Sedum and Samphire by the effect they had on them, that it was only then, as they looked towards the light in the central part of the chamber, that they realized the dramatic effect the sounds had had on Humlock. Normally when Glee or Rooster took their paw from his to go and do something, as they had now gone to the wall, he hunched himself up protectively, head down, snout low, great shoulders massed and haunches held tight.

But now as they heard the shuffling sound and turned back from the walls towards it, they saw to their surprise that for once he had begun to move of his own volition. He held his head up and looked attentive, his great snout turned towards the light, and he began to move his head about most strangely, in such a way that a mole who did not know his disabilities might have thought he was trying to catch the sound of something amongst the odd echoes of the place.

A moment or two later, apparently satisfied that whatever he had 'heard' lay towards the light that flooded into the centre of the chamber, he set off in a shambling and tentative way towards it, pausing now and then as if uncertain, yet not once snouting round to his flanks as he so often did for Glee's and Rooster's support.

These two were about to go forward to him as they always did when Samphire said in a low voice, 'Leave the mole be, my dears, does he not seem to know what he's after?'

'But he never does anything for himself!' declared Glee, both puzzled and worried.

'I noticed him look up when you touched the wall,' said Samphire quietly. 'Perhaps he felt some vibration in the ground from the sounds . . .'

They watched in silence as he continued his slow and hesitant progress towards the light and in their different ways became conscious, as they had been out on the surface before he delved, that Humlock was in the process of discovering something for himself that moles could only direct him towards; the getting there he must do alone, and he was getting there now. But to where, and for what, none could guess.

The nearer he drew to the light the slower he became, and the more evidently in distress, so that the tension among his friends increased as the desire to let him discover life for himself conflicted with the growing urge to rush forward and help him. He began to stop more than he started, 'looking' round behind him as if hoping that his friends would come to his aid, and beginning to let his head drop down towards that posture of defence against a world that seemed to have given him so little.

'I must go to him,' said Glee anxiously at last, 'I *must*.' And so she might had not Rooster reached out a great paw to forestall her; with a thoughtful look furrowing his brow he turned back towards the wall, and watching Humlock closely, once more ran his talons over the carvings. He did so gently, and the resulting sounds were gentle in return, and in a way Humlock appeared to hear them, for he raised his head again for a moment, as hope seemed to come to his body, and he half turned towards the far side wall from where the sounds apparently came. But then he began to retreat into himself once more, and this time more quickly, as if he had lost the scent of something he had thought – he had hoped – might be somewhere there, and was now beginning to feel lost and in despair.

'It was *your* touching of the wall that affected him more,' said Samphire quietly to Glee.

Rooster pulled her to his flank and pointed silently at the carved wall and muttered, 'You do it now. *You*. It might help.'

319

Without looking at where she touched, for her eyes were on the mole she cared so much for, who now stanced alone near the light, all uncertain and lost in that mute and sightless world of his, Glee ran her talons gently along the wall. As she did so she whispered Humlock's name urgently, as a mother might purse her mouth in an effort to make a weaning pup begin to eat.

Her touching of the wall was no more than a caress; so light, so simple, that the sounds it made were soft and distant things, like whispered memories of once-loved moles whom others have lost touch with. These echoing sounds played wistfully and alluringly among them all, and after a moment Humlock seemed to hear them, and gain strength from them, and then find new inspiration, for he raised his head again, scented the air and went on to the centre of the chamber where the light was brightest.

As he paused there they heard quiet voices, barely more than whispers, which said, 'Welcome, mole! Welcome!' again and again. The light slowly faded, no doubt because cloud had crossed the sun in the sky they could not see out above the surface, and for the first time they were able to make out what was at the far end of the chamber – a great arched entrance, and a group of three or four moles, all grey and old and disabled. It was from these moles that the gentle greeting had come. As Humlock paused, and this group were able to see the newcomers as they themselves were seen, Drumlin started forward with an exclamation of pleasure and at the same time one of the far group broke free of his companions and came forward as well, both moving towards where Humlock now stanced.

Of the others none moved at all, as if they sensed that a certain formal propriety was needed for the greeting they were witnessing. Drumlin reached Humlock's flank long before the other, and a deep silence settled on the chamber, broken only by the sound of the dragging and shuffling paws of the advancing mole, and the whispered tremors of his painful breathing as he advanced ever nearer to Drumlin and Humlock.

At last he stopped before them both, nodded briefly to Drumlin, who seemed eager to go forward and greet him but held back out of respect, and fixed his eyes on Humlock. Then, in a gesture that combined welcome with reassurance, acknowledgement with blessing, the older mole reached out a paw to Humlock's and touched him. As he did so Samphire saw that the joints of his paws were swollen and bent, the talons crooked and useless, the fur almost all gone.

Then he spoke these words, and though his voice was but a painful

320

whisper they had about them the quality of a blessing ordained by the Stone itself.

'Be the grace of the Stone between thy two shoulders,
Protecting thee in thy coming and thy going;
Be the spirit of the Stone Mole in thine heart
Guiding thee in thy coming and thy going;
Be the love of the ancients ever with thee,
Their voice known for ever by thy going and thy coming.'

Then the old mole pulled back from Humlock, turned as best he could to Drumlin and said, 'Now, my dear, my beloved daughter, come and embrace me, show me the youngster of whom you're so proud, and her new friend . . .'

So this was Drumlin's father! She needed no further encouragement and happily went forward as he had asked, and embraced him warmly, saying how much she had missed him, and sniffling at some tears as she did so.

'It was too long to leave you, Father, your illness has hit you hard.'

'It was best you stayed away from here to have your pup, best for her to get fresh air, and for you to be free to help Sedum with her pup.' He nodded towards Humlock's abnormality. To this mole, it seemed, it was life that mattered, not normality. 'But you have found new friends . . . I knew your time of birthing would be propitious and it seems it was. Introduce me to them now.'

Samphire, Rooster and Glee came forward, while Sedum went immediately to Humlock's flank and put a proud paw to his, for had he not come forward of his volition and received a welcome on behalf of them all?

'This is my father,' said Drumlin. 'He prefers to be called simply by his name, which is Gaunt. This is Samphire, this Rooster her son, and *this* your granddaughter Glee.'

Gaunt smiled at them and bowed his head, looking piercingly at each.

'You'll find that moles hereabout call him Mentor,' explained Drumlin, 'because he's the Mentor of the Delvings, the one on whom the continuation of their traditions depends, and who teaches the others all he himself has learnt . . .'

'There has been a Mentor here ever since Hilbert himself first came,' whispered Gaunt, 'and that is many centuries ago, as no doubt you already know. But each of us hopes he is the last.'

'But if there was a last there would be no more, and that would

321

mean the traditions were at an end,' said Samphire. She spoke to him with a curious mixture of gentleness and familiarity, and Gaunt's face seemed to soften as he listened to her, as if her presence eased his pain. Indeed, watching the scene a mole might almost have thought the two had met before – though that, surely, was not possible.

'Yes, it might seem so,' he replied, 'but it is not so. You see, most traditions are bent on preserving the dead past from the living future, but ours has a very different purpose. We live in the hope that Hilbert's prophecy will be fulfilled, that one day a mole will come to the Charnel who will have the gifts and abilities to understand all that we have preserved here, and make it live again and take it forth into moledom. Such a mole will be a Master of the Delve and be the true successor to Hilbert and affirm the faith he had that better times would one day come to moledom. We here are simply intermediaries through time between two Masters, one past and one future, using our traditions to keep alive knowledge of the delving arts that moles of the Word so nearly destroyed.'

'Gaunt,' began Samphire, coming closer still and visibly having to restrain herself from reaching out to touch him, 'I feel that . . .' She shook her head, retreated a little in confusion, and in a vain attempt to hide it brought Rooster forward and said, 'I mean . . . Rooster, say hello.'

Rooster came forward awkwardly and touched Gaunt's paw formally.

'His greatest desire has always been to delve,' said Samphire.

Gaunt nodded pleasantly, but it was obvious that he was as affected by their meeting as she seemed to be, and all of them seemed to sense that there was something unfinished between the two moles, like a long-interrupted dialogue between moles who were separated which must now be finished before life between them could go on properly. Yet how could such a thing possibly be, between moles who had never met before?

'Drumlin,' whispered Gaunt, turning from this unspoken tension at his meeting with Samphire, yet speaking with roguish delight at this first sight of his granddaughter, 'your pup is albino and her fur is holy white!'

Glee giggled and darted a mischievous glance at Drumlin.

'Unholy white, *she* says,' said Glee. 'Makes me conspicuous, makes me vulnerable. Humlock and Glee are two of a kind in *that*. That's why Rooster was sent to protect us. *He* can see, and speak, and he's strong and he's dark! Aren't you, Rooster?'

Rooster frowned and muttered that he supposed he was, but all he wanted to do was delve.

'Ah! Delve! Yes, there's plenty of that for everymole, plenty of delving here!' said Gaunt, before turning back to Samphire, still confused by the sense she gave him of past knowledge.

'So you are Ratcher's consort! A unique accomplishment, I would say!'

'Former consort,' said Samphire firmly but respectfully.

'Quite so, Samphire,' smiled Gaunt.

Afterwards, when Rooster described these events to Privet at Hilbert's Top, he remembered well that particular moment when Gaunt spoke his mother's name. He had been staring at the delvings on the walls and listening to the subtle murmurs of echoes as the meeting with Gaunt continued. Was it Rooster's imagination that as Gaunt said 'Samphire', and the two looked into each other's eyes, the chamber seemed to tremble with discovered silence, as if some moment of past or future time had been touched, and sounded now in the whispers of the place?

'Come now, Drumlin, my dear, lead us on into the Delvings,' whispered Gaunt, breaking the moment as he had before, 'and speak for me, telling them all that I have taught you and what you have discovered for yourself, for my voice is weak today and painful. You Samphire, you stay near and help me if you will, and you Sedum, be proud of Humlock, for he has found a place to call a home and is welcome here. As *for* Humlock, and *you* two . . .' he half turned and nodded gently at Rooster and Glee, 'you listen, you learn, you act, for yours is moledom's future, to make as glorious as you will. There is so much for you to learn, and so little time to do it.'

The party turned out of the light and went on into that part of the chamber that had been obscured to them. There they were joined by the moles they had only glimpsed earlier, and whatever nervousness Glee and Rooster might have felt was gone in an instant before the shy friendliness of some, and the exuberant welcome of others as all followed on behind Gaunt and Samphire and entered into the lost Delvings of Charnel Clough.

The mysteries the young moles had encountered in the chamber where Gaunt met them – of strange delving, of old deformed moles, of haunting sound and strange prophecy – deepened the moment they accompanied him on into the Delvings. It was not that Gaunt or the others refused to explain or answer questions, but rather that they believed that the youngsters would understand the Charnel better if they saw and experienced things for themselves.

They did not know it, but this process of learning had already begun before they met Gaunt, and in the molemonths and years of summer, autumn and winter which now followed it continued more quickly. Some matters, like the organization of the Delvings and the moles who lived there, were easily understood; others, like the nature and purpose of delving, were matters of practice and increasing maturity which the three youngsters now became involved with.

One major issue – the extent of Rooster's special gifts, their development and their importance – was something which dawned only slowly on Gaunt and the others, and which he himself could not begin to guess at. All he sensed was, as he spoke of it so much later to Privet with increasing frustration, that he had a special role to play, a role that felt a burden to him, and was a source of confusion and, finally, distress.

Until they entered the Delvings that day Rooster, like his mother before him, had always assumed that the moles they occasionally saw out on the surface were the only moles who lived in the Charnel. In the main they were large slow moles, often partially deformed, but not so badly that they could not move about, find food, or delve simple tunnels in a slow way.

This body of moles, whom Samphire had first seen from the Reapside when she lived with Red Ratcher, she had thought, as the Ratcher moles did, *were* the Charnel system. The fact that some were diseased as well as deformed, and that they were seen sometimes to indulge in what seemed ritual sacrifice, or in journeys up-valley towards the Creeds with some vile deformity of a mole who had emerged from the tunnels and whom it seemed they were going to throw into the Reap, confirmed only that the Charnel moles, and their system, were little more than abominations. Since they appeared to be diseased as well, they were to be avoided, and really had only one possible use – to give the Ratcher moles the satisfaction of knowing that *they* were indubitably superior.

This perception, which Rooster had learned from his mother, and which Drumlin and Sedum had so far done nothing to deny, and which their own offspring if anything confirmed, had been upset by the meeting with Gaunt, and was quite overthrown by what they soon discovered. For what they found was a remarkable series of tunnels and chambers, each more beautiful, intricate, and complex than the last, in which even more remarkable moles lived and worked, for the most part unseen by the outside world.

The 'surface' moles were not the main body of the system at all, but rather the helpers of those who worked beneath. They were gentle, kindly moles, whose lives were dedicated to serving those whose only skill and purpose was delving, and the preservation of the delving arts. These strange moles, who lived almost perpetually underground, could not have survived at all without the helpers from above, who brought them food, cleared out their runs, and performed many services the delvers' infirmities and difficulties made necessary. It was, perhaps naturally, the delvers themselves whom Rooster and the others first took note of, since it was in amongst their tunnels and chambers that Gaunt first led them.

At first sight, to Samphire especially, they seemed shocking to behold. Most were deformed in some way, some grossly so. There were those who, like Drumlin and Sedum, were goitrous, one or two far more so, for their bald round excrescences hung bulbously from their necks, bigger than their heads, making delving with the paw on the flank on which they hung impossible, for it could not get past the growth.

Others were vilely hunchbacked, with horrific protrusions of joints and bone, and heads that looked as if they had been pulled off their necks and then put back at the wrong angle; others had limbs too small for their bodies and lay at their delving work on flanks or bellies, seeming able only to prod and poke and make no elegant delving strokes at all.

Others, worse to see, had skulls that were flat and cretinous, or snouts improperly formed so that the veins and mucus normally unseen was all too visible, moving and bubbling beneath a thin transparent skin, and it was hard to know where to look on such a mole for fear of showing horror or disgust.

There were a few who, at first sight, appeared to have no way of delving at all, since their front paws were so malformed that they were no more than stubs or flaps of useless skin. Yet, with caloused snout, or strange back paw, even such moles could make their mark, and did so, to contribute their delve to that lost place.

It was not long before Rooster and Glee understood how important the helpers were to them as moles who had the run of the tunnels, and wandered here and there as they were needed, bringing food, carrying helpless moles to their place of work, or shifting earth and stones which their weaker brethren could not move. It was with these moles that Rooster and Glee had their introduction to the system, being quartered, at Gaunt's wise suggestion, up near the surface and away from their respective parents, under the watchful eye of a ponderous male called Hume.

Recalling those days later for Privet, Rooster allowed a rare smile of affection and happiness to lighten his face when he mentioned Hume's name. From him the youngsters soon learned that though the whole purpose of the changes Hilbert's example brought to the Charnel was the preservation of the delving art for some future time, delvers and helpers held each other in equal regard. In the Charnel all had a place, for all were needed. Hilbert's genius, it seemed, had been to find for delving a home that had all the best qualities of true community, where moles subsumed their individual needs to those of others around them, and in which delving itself became through the decades and centuries the focal point for moles' dreams and desires, loves and hates, hopes and despairs.

When the youngsters arrived in the Delvings, and heard the continual roundel of sound about them, emanating from the delvings so many generations of lost moles had made, it was these whispered remembrances of past feeling they heard, the secret feelings and thoughts of individuals, struggling to find their special place in their community, and doing so with each other's help. Here, where life seemed so frail and so useless, life was the most valued thing of all.

Like all the other strange moles they met, Hume treated Humlock no differently from any other mole, understanding that touch was the only way he might communicate. Glee's natural over-protectiveness decreased as she saw Humlock relax among these new friends, and Hume quickly found a task that Humlock could perform, which was helping to shift some of the waste from the delvings below and thrust it out on to the surface.

It was not long before Humlock was happy to be left alone for long periods provided his task was made clear and others working near him came and made contact with him from time to time, so that Glee and Rooster were able to help the system in ways he could not – taking messages, feeding the more disabled, and, in Rooster's case, doing some heavier, more complex portage which a mole like Humlock could surely never do.

In this way the youngsters soon understood how the system worked and saw for themselves how it had evolved its unique methodology for the preservation of the delving arts long after Hilbert, the last Master of the Delve, had passed into Silence.

The delvers worked in different 'chambers' – a group of moles working together, their group names reflecting the fact that the territory of each was defined by a main chamber, and sometimes subsidiary tunnels and chambers.

There were five such chambers, and these formed the structure about which the days and nights of the Charnel's endless work revolved. Each was headed by a Senior Delver, and only slowly did Rooster and Glee understand that his name – or rather his or *her* name, since one was female – which was the name given generally to the Chamber whose work he watched over, was titular, real names having been subsumed to the position their appointment had placed them in.

So 'Prime Chamber' was headed by a dwarf mole called Prime, and his work, and that of the four who worked with him, was begun only as night changed to dawn. Then there was Terce, whose Chamber of the same name was a cheerful, joyous place, where the delvers hummed in the light of new morning, and joked with their helpers and made a mole feel glad to be alive.

Sext Chamber, and Sext its Senior Delver, was a slower, more contemplative place, with graceful sinewy delvings which calmed a mole and made him pause from the busyness of the morning that had gone before. Rooster liked going there, and enjoyed the measured quiet of Sext himself, who was thin and wasted with disease, and near the end of his delving days.

The fourth chamber, as the youngsters came to think of it, since its main period of activity was from mid-afternoon to dusk, was run by None, the only female amongst the Senior Delvers, and half-sister to Gaunt. Here things seemed to be completed rather than begun, here moles worked quietly together, advising each other, pondering, with occasional outbursts of annoyance that things were not quite right and that time was running out.

'Call None over! She'll advise!'

How Glee liked None, with her untidy fur and dusty snout, and her way of frowning with concentration as she snouted at a problem delve, and considered how best to deal with it.

'Give me a worm!' she would declare finally, and Glee would happily help her to one – she was goitrous and though she could delve she could barely feed herself – knowing that as she munched it None would find a solution to the problem that had baffled others. But if even she failed she would shake her head and say, 'It's one for Compline, and if *he* can't do it nomole but the Mentor himself can!'

Compline Chamber, and Compline! Last Chamber of the day, whose life saw out the daylight hours and welcomed in the night. Chamber of change and resolution, Chamber to which all moles went if it was peace they sought to soothe a troubled mind. Whilst Compline, a large fat-faced mole, though much younger than Gaunt, had the Mentor's same wise calm about him.

A hurrying helper, turning a corner and finding himself faced by Compline, always slowed, and looked a little meek, and tried to move quietly and with more grace, and though admonished by Compline's natural peacefulness yet felt cheered by it as well, and encouraged. Such were the five Chambers of the Delvings, and the five moles who watched over them, with whom Rooster, Glee and Humlock now found their lives inextricably entwined.

Although Gaunt had realized from the first that Rooster might be a mole of special delving quality he did not confide his hopes to Drumlin or Samphire, though no doubt the Senior Delvers knew something of his thoughts. He and they preferred to wait for the evidence to reveal itself. This it soon did, and it was Hume who noticed it, and reported it with some wonder and considerable excitement.

It seemed that the mystery of how the great chambers were delved in their higher parts, where the delvings stretched way out of reach of a mole's paws, was one which the delvers kept to themselves, not revealing its secret to newcomers until they had showed their devotion to the art, and a willingness to dedicate themselves to it.

Rooster knew nothing of that, and had no reason to know that his time with Hume was by way of an introduction to the system and that, when the time was judged right, he would be attached to Prime and so begin his years of study of the delving arts. He, no doubt, working with the Mentor himself, would guide him through a series of exercises of increasing difficulty, teaching him not only the techniques of delving, but the philosophy as well.

But from the first Rooster had stared in awe at the walls of the great chambers and asked how those high delvings were done. Gaunt had not answered him, and nor did the delvers, holding their secret back for a time. But Rooster was not satisfied, and in every moment he could spare from his tasks he found obscure places to try out delving for himself, and also pondered the secret of the chambers.

'How did they do it?' he asked Glee again and again when, tired from his extra-curricular delving practice, he joined Humlock and her in the quarters they had near the surface.

But Glee had no idea, and nor would Hume help, knowing as he did Gaunt's preferred way of teaching the arts. His frustration only increased when Gaunt refused to let him start learning delving formally until he had spent more time as a helper. That was the way it had always been done in the past, and the way it would be done now.

'But want to delve,' said Rooster. 'Feel the delving need.'

'Tell me about this need, mole,' whispered Gaunt.

'Like my paws know something's there waiting to be made.'

'Something?'

'Shape. Sound. In the walls. In the roofs. In the soil.'

'And the rocks, mole? Do you feel the need in the rocks?'

Gaunt's eyes narrowed as he waited for Rooster to reply, and watched the strange mole, his paws kneading at the air as he sought, in the desperate way he had, to find words adequate to express the feeling, the truth, he felt inside him.

'Rocks are part of it. Rocks are there for delving to go round. Rocks and stones are centres.'

'Centres of what?'

'Don't know!' shouted Rooster angrily, rearing up towards Gaunt, almost as if he felt the old mole was deliberately punishing him with questions that were impossible to answer. 'Like all is part of one. Can't be!'

Rooster stanced down again, angry, puzzled, confused, and frustrated.

'Know it,' he said at last.

'Mole,' said Gaunt, 'will you delve it for me, what you feel?'

Rooster looked startled, and afraid. 'Can't,' he said, staring malevolently at his paws. 'Hume won't say how high delvings made. Will you?'

Gaunt smiled softly. 'I have heard of your interest in that, Rooster. It pleases me. Natural delvers always want to know the answer.'

'Tell me!' said Rooster eagerly.

'You delve your feeling and think about the high delvings at the same time. Maybe one will lead to the other.'

'Will!' said Rooster suddenly. 'But have to be a helper as well. Delvers need my strength.'

'You're free to do whichever you like.'

'Will!' said Rooster again, thumping his bigger paw on the ground. 'Delve the feeling, mole. Do it!'

'Will do it!'

*

329

For a few days after that Rooster prevaricated, becoming even more assiduous in his helper duties, working all hours of day and night for others. Then, suddenly, he abandoned his tasks and was seldom seen for several days, occasionally glimpsed by one mole or another, wandering in a morose and pensive way about the chambers, staring and touching them, peering and snouting at them, seeking answers.

He found a small chamber high up and away from the main area, one abandoned decades before by some learner delver who, the story went, had died. There were a few crude delvings about those walls, and the sound they made was hardly anything at all. The place was light, secluded, and here Rooster began to try to delve his feeling as Gaunt had told him to. Others heard what he was about but left him to it, surprised that Gaunt had let him go off by himself without assigning a mentor to him from among the experienced delvers, nor even trying to explain what the Delvings were about.

But then . . .

'He's a bright one, that Rooster,' Hume reported to Gaunt and a few others one day, 'he's got the high delvings worked out.'

'He knows how they are made?' said Drumlin in surprise.

'He's beginning to *make* some, all of his own,' said Hume.

Gaunt wisely let him be, only hearing bits and pieces of what he did and how Rooster was beginning to plague the Senior Delvers and trying to run before he could even crawl.

'He's got Glee up there working for him now!' declared Hume, grumbling at this sudden loss of another promising helper.

'Have you been to the place where he delves?' asked Samphire, who like Gaunt felt it wisest to leave well alone, but like any mother was also curious to know what he was up to.

'More than my life's worth,' said Hume. 'But I'll tell you one thing – he's been about the place asking the delvers about this and that. He's discovered that some are good at one thing, and some good at another. It's like he knows what he wants to learn.'

'Aren't *you* curious, Gaunt?' asked Samphire with a smile. 'And the Senior Delvers?'

The easy way the two moles had had with each other from the start had continued. Indeed Samphire had become helper to Gaunt himself, a role Drumlin was especially happy to see fulfilled.

'Beauty and the beast!' she would say fondly to them both.

'There's no beast in Gaunt,' Samphire would confide. 'He's the gentlest mole I've ever known, except that his mind's so strong. All his power is in that.'

'You only say that because he's not teaching you to delve. How do you think he's got Rooster delving like he is? Now just you wait a short while longer and you'll see how tough my father Gaunt can be.'

She did not have to wait long. A few days later Hume brought the astonishing news that Humlock had joined Rooster and Glee in their endeavours in the chamber Rooster had found. They were using him to help transport material Rooster had delved, guiding him out to the surface and showing him how to dispose of it by touch.

'Hmmph!' said Gaunt, apparently displeased.

'But that's good, surely, getting Humlock involved,' said Samphire.

'Good in theory, fatal in practice. He'll get too big for his paws before long. I think the time's come for me to have a look, and I've a feeling that that's just what Rooster would like.'

Gaunt was right. Soon afterwards Prime came to see him and the two had a long and private consultation. Then the other Senior Delvers were called and all six moles went into a huddle which the whole system knew about. Then it dispersed, leaving only Prime and Gaunt to summon Drumlin and Samphire.

'We have come to a conclusion,' said Gaunt, 'which is that we will visit Rooster's delving. We understand . . . well . . . we shall see for ourselves. Come . . .'

'Aren't you going to warn him you're coming?' said Samphire. 'Rooster's a mole likes his privacy.'

'The Delvings are for allmole, not for one,' said Gaunt quietly.

It took them some time to climb the long way to where Rooster had made his delving, and at the steep last part Samphire helped Gaunt along, while Prime, his little paws scrabbling to heave him on, huffed and puffed and glowered as they went.

At last they came to a tunnel from which the noise of delving came, and entered it. There was a rough-hewn chamber used for spoil, in which Humlock, a begrimed and dusty Humlock, stanced in silent thought. Quietly the moles went on, until eventually an elegant and recently-delved archway led them into a medium-sized chamber whose walls were delved with all kinds of strange, stark indentations, whose sound was rough and cheerful, and whose light, cleverly using the fissures above, was both dark and bright, shifting and strange. Most astonishing of all, above them and some way out of reach of even the largest mole's paw, were delvings, high delvings.

Glee saw the visitors first and gave a warning shout to Rooster, who was busy at the far end of the place, his paws working powerfully at a bare part of the wall.

'Rooster! *Rooster!*'

The great mole, hearing the warning note in her voice, turned and saw Gaunt and Prime, and the two mothers, staring at him and all his work.

On Samphire's face was a look of pride, while on Drumlin's was one of wonder that youngsters such as these could have made anything so impressive, strange though it was.

'Didn't know you were coming,' said Rooster without pleasure.

'Didn't tell you,' said Gaunt.

'It's wonderful, all that you've done,' said Samphire, 'it's . . .'

'Yes, my dears, you've all—' continued Drumlin.

A frown from Gaunt, a wave of a paw from Prime, silenced them. Rooster came forward, his eyes on Gaunt and not on his mother.

'Wanted to delve the feeling. Wanted to . . .' He sounded defiant and wary at the same time.

'Silence, mole!' commanded Gaunt.

The Mentor signalled to Prime, and together the two slowly examined the chamber, peering up into its recesses, touching its walls and listening to its clumsy sound, shaking their heads in one place, nodding as they talked in whispers in another. The others awaited their verdict with bated breath. Rooster looked most uneasy, most unsettled.

'They'll like it!' whispered Glee. 'You'll see.'

At last the two came back.

'Well, mole?' said Gaunt.

Rooster stared, not knowing what was meant.

'I asked you to delve your feeling. Is this it?' He waved a paw dismissively about the great place.

'Tried,' said Rooster uncomfortably.

'But it's very—' began Samphire defensively.

'Madam, wordlessness is best on these occasions,' said Prime grimly. 'Words do not help.'

'Tried?' said Gaunt.

'The feeling. The delving need. Put it on the walls. Learned how to do the high delvings. Asked others to help. Only Glee would help. Only Humlock. Tried to make the delving true.'

Rooster spoke with increasing distress and anger.

'And has it worked, mole?' said Prime suddenly.

There was a long silence. Rooster looked about him, and at his work, and his breathing became rapid as he struggled with his feelings.

'You told me that in your delving need you felt all was one. Is this fragmented, noisy, ugly place, all one?' whispered Gaunt. His voice was filled with despair.

'It's . . . it's . . . it's me!' cried out Rooster, turning from them and barely knowing what to do with himself. He raised his paws and crashed them down on one of the walls he had so intricately delved, and his work fractured and broke where his paws had struck.

'It's me!' he shouted, turning to face them and raising his paws in despair as he looked wildly at his work. 'Tried to delve the feeling like you said. Tried and tried and tried.'

'And is this it?'

'ME!' bellowed Rooster, spit hanging from his mouth as he became utterly frustrated and enraged.

'Mole!' said Gaunt. 'It *is* you. The you I see. The you *we* see.'

'Not the feeling. Can't delve it. It's . . . it's . . .'

He bowed his great clumsy head in utter despair and Glee went to him and put her paws to his.

'Don't listen to him, Rooster. I can feel what it is you're trying to delve. I can, even if *they* can't.'

As she tried to protect her friend from the assaults that seemed to be coming at him, Humlock suddenly appeared at the archway and entered. Slowly he made his way towards the two of them, seeming to sense their distress and need. He reached out for them, and Glee went to him and led him to where Rooster wept. There, by the scarred wall, the three moles huddled.

'Humlock knows too,' said Glee.

But Gaunt's gaze was pitiless. 'And you, Rooster, what do you know?' he said.

Slowly Rooster raised his head and stared at the old mole. 'Know it's me but not me. Know I can delve better. Want to learn.'

Gaunt nodded and whispered. 'Yes, mole, I know you do. Now listen. You will go with Prime, Rooster, and he will teach what he knows. You, Glee, will go to None, for she has need of a female at her flank, and you will learn much from her that one day I think your friends will need from you.'

'What about Humlock?' said Glee, a little aggressively.

Gaunt smiled. 'Ah, yes. Take him to Compline. That mole will know what to do with him, for I have instructed him already. Now go! All of you, go! But for you, Samphire, I will have need of your help out from here. Go!'

When they were gone Samphire turned angrily to Gaunt.

'You are too harsh, Gaunt, far too harsh.'

'Am I, my dear?' he said, turning from her and looking about the chamber. 'Listen!'

He ran a paw over some delvings Rooster had made, and rough strange sounds echoed about the place, roarings and bellowings, breakings and fracturings.

'Listen!' he said more softly.

As the ugly sound died away, beyond it, for a short moment, they heard a quieter, gentler sound, peaceful, graceful, loving.

'That is your son,' he whispered.

'And this? Is it so bad?' said Samphire. 'Can it be so bad if there is a touch of something better in it?'

'Bad?' said Gaunt in astonishment, as if he could not understand why *she* could not understand. 'This chamber Rooster has made is the work of a Master of the Delve. In this beginning is our ending.'

'Then why . . . ?' said Samphire amazed.

'Because if he does not learn how to make as he truly feels he will be destroyed by the knowledge of what he cannot do. And he knows it, he knows it.' Gaunt said these last words in wonder. 'He knows he is not ready to delve the feeling he knows he has.'

'When will he be ready?'

Gaunt shook his head. 'It may take him a lifetime to discover it. But what he has made here already, a hundred lifetimes of Charnel delvers could not have made. Fear not, Samphire, for the Stone is with your son, and will protect him and guide him in ways beyond the capacity of moles like us. But we can set him on the path, now that he is ready to go down it.'

'Then why do you weep, Gaunt?' said Samphire coming close.

'For joy,' whispered Gaunt, 'that such a mole has come to my ken in my own lifetime. For joy and regret. The days of the Charnel are numbered and now moledom must prepare to take back what it once drove into secrecy here. The Charnel, and the moles in it, will soon be no more. A Master has come, as Hilbert said one day he would, and all will change, all be as a dream that was. The work of generations is nearly done.'

As if responding to what Gaunt said, the chamber whispered his voice back to him, rumbling, ugly, yet with whispers of beauty beyond. And where Rooster had crashed his talons into his own work and wept, a fragment of his delving fell down on to the floor, and after it a scatter of soil, and particles of rock.

Chapter Twenty-Seven

But again and again, no sooner had Rooster begun to tell her what really happened in the Delvings than Privet found there was a limit to what he would say about the world from which, miraculously as it increasingly seemed to her, he had escaped to live in isolation on Hilbert's Top. But it was a limit which gradually receded, for little by little in those days of deepening winter, when the two moles shared time together in such isolation from the rest of moledom, Rooster revealed more of himself.

Yet, telling of it so many moleyears later to her friends in Duncton Wood, she would pause and remind her listeners that her narrative was continuous and logical, whereas the story came from him only in strange fits and starts.

'There would be days and days when he would not speak at all,' she explained, 'or occasions when he would mention some detail to expand what he had said before, or tell me the name of a mole he had never mentioned but whom later he would come to.'

'It sounds frustrating and uncomfortable,' said Whillan, 'I mean . . . him not coming right out with it. All of it.'

'It was, my dear – at the beginning. Until a day came when he began to say he feared he wanted to hurt me, and the storm came, and winter really started. Oh, I wanted him then, all of him. But . . . we were not ready for that, and so we found another way forward, perhaps a deeper way, the most peaceful time of my life. You see, I understood him.'

'Understood him?' said Fieldfare, nudging Chater meaningfully. 'Well, you have to do that with a male who doesn't find it easy to talk about his feelings! If you want to get on with him that is. If—'

'If you want to love him,' said Privet, 'if . . . if you want *that*.'

How quietly she spoke, with what subdued passion and heartbreaking memory. She lowered her head and her voice quavered and tears came to her eyes such that several of them started towards her to comfort her, and Stour, not for the first time, said, 'If you would prefer . . . you don't have to talk . . . you are free . . .'

'No, no,' she replied, grateful for their sympathy but waving them away, 'I want to talk about that time now, I want you to understand, I *want* to talk.'

But Fieldfare, so loving, so caring, could not bear the tears that came to Privet now, and went to her and held her close, and let her cry; whilst the other moles, sensible of Privet's wish to share her past with them and, perhaps, aware that an understanding of it was important in some deep way to understanding Rooster, and all he might yet mean to moledom, stayed close and quiet and patient.

'These aren't tears of sorrow,' said Privet eventually, 'not really. Well, they are as *well*, but it's just that in the time that now began to come to Rooster and me up there so far from everything I felt as if I was awakening to life. And everything since has been . . . less intense, less *real*. I so often remember those days, and am grateful that I had something so few other moles had. I *would* like to talk about it if I may, because we touched something so near the Stone then. If I cry a little do not mind . . .'

'We don't mind, mole,' said old Drubbins, tears on his face, 'if you don't mind.'

They all nodded and murmured their agreement with that, for none of them were far from tears.

'Well,' began Privet, taking a deep breath and looking around appreciatively, 'I wish I could say exactly when our love began to be expressed, but I'm not sure that I can. Yet I suppose there was a day not long before Longest Night when suddenly we . . .'

The ice and snow that had appeared in November were not repeated, but the weather grew colder and the ground stayed white and grey. Chill winds blew off the Moors, carrying with them the dust and detritus of peat and dead heather, which dirtied the snow and, in moments of brief sunlight when the top thawed, settled down into it. Then when it re-froze, and the winds wore the surface ice smooth and shiny, the ground took on a dirty gleam. The rocks of the Top gained a verglas sheen which caught the grey evening light and gave Privet the feeling that they were in a great structure of dull ice from which they might never escape.

These were strange days, of the kind when Rooster disappeared for long spells into the tunnels where he delved, far beyond where Privet herself ever went. Until then the peace that had come over her on the Top, once she and Rooster had begun to talk, had not left her. But now, with winter set in, and the surface icy and uninviting, and the prospect of Longest Night approaching and the reality that she would be away from all she knew, she began to feel lonely and distressed.

She felt angry at Rooster for leaving her alone for so long, angry that when he was with her he would not or could not talk to her of the delvings he made, or continue his account of the Delvings in the Charnel; she suddenly began to miss Hamble, and the moles in Crowden, and texts. Texts!

It was then that her long reluctance to begin the search for Wort's Testimony, which her father Sward had found among the tunnels of the Top and had left behind only half-kenned, feeling he was trespassing into a world that was not his own, changed to an obsession to find it. All her frustration and anger began to focus on that search, and if Rooster would not talk to her, she would not talk to him. If he had delvings into which *he* could plunge his need for privacy, *she* had the hunt for a text meant only for her into which she could plunge hers. If he asked, she would not tell.

And ask he did. But the colder the weather grew, the harder the ice outside, the more sharp and shiny, impenetrably grey and slippery became her determination not to answer his questions.

He lingered near her more often, looking miserable and out of sorts, and in his monosyllabic way began to ask what was wrong.

'Nothing. I just want to be alone!'

How his great paws pawed the air in dismay.

'Looking for something. You are?' he said.

'I'm looking for nothing that's any of your business,' she said unpleasantly.

'You are angry!'

'I'm *not!*' she spat out at him, impervious to the hurt helplessness in his voice.

'Can't delve,' he said. 'Not with this.'

'Then don't,' she snapped, and set off again, up-tunnel and down-tunnel, day after day, into each night, looking, pushing, touching, trying to find a place the text might be. The sounds of the tunnels that had so confused her when she first arrived she hardly seemed to hear at all, her anger and rage and obsession to find all but blotting them out. When she slept, her sleep was deep and without dreams. When she woke it was to the need to eat quick, groom swift and be off.

'Rooster can help!' he said.

'Don't want your help.'

'Can't delve now.'

'And I don't care,' she thundered at him, as much as Privet ever thundered; but her eyes were like flashes of cold lightning.

The quarters they had taken up involved sharing a communal way and chamber, delved long ago by Rooster, though expanded by him since she had come so that, in quiet times, they could stance down in it together with enough space to be comfortable separately, but not so much that they were too far apart.

It had been here that Privet had first seen Rooster delve, and here that he had learnt to try to talk to her. But in those angry days she did not come to their shared chamber, but went to her own burrow, slept, woke, searched, slept again; and if she could not sleep she brooded, listening to the icy wind above, and the spatter of dust from off the Moors as it swirled about the Top, from one obstruction to another, or came down in its sudden way into their tunnels. She glowered at it, as she did when Rooster dared approach, as she did at everything – for everything it seemed conspired to stop her finding the text she was confident was still here.

She would have told Rooster about it, but that the last thing she wished in her present mood was to give him the opportunity of helping her; she did not wish her anger to be forced away by the need for gratitude. She liked her anger and the feeling of power it gave her, power over *him*.

She might well have, for Rooster remained miserable and confused, and if Privet understood why better than he himself did – because he had never in his strange and sheltered life experienced another mole's hostility, and did not yet understand that it had a language of its own, and was a cry to be heard – she did not care; she had turned down a tunnel of dark rage and there was no going back, only forward to its end.

So those hard days of cold passion went by, and might have continued a little longer if their end had not been signalled by a sudden and unexpected change in the weather over the Moors. It came by night, stealthily, a wind-shift westward, air that was warmer, and by dawn there came the drip, drip, drip of melting ice at the entrance, echoing down the tunnels.

'It's better,' tried Rooster that same day when they met in the tunnel. 'Isn't it, Privet?'

She watched him and his suffering face, and how his paws always reached out and nervously delved the air when he was unsure. She saw how he waited, no, how he *hung*, on the change he so needed to come over her, the change she did not want to make. She heard how his breathing was shallow and fast as his eyes, yes, his ugly eyes, watched her to gain a clue to what she would do.

And Privet felt power and control and hated him, and liked his suffering, and heard herself say, 'If it's getting better it means I can get away from this loathsome place. I hate it, Rooster, and I never want to come here again.'

He stared at her, eyes widening in dismay, and she felt herself go forward at him, felt herself bigger and stronger than him, felt herself powerful over him.

'I don't like being here with you and all this talk which never goes anywhere, and all this activity I never see, all this . . . this *delving*.' She spat out the word as if it were putrid food, and marvelled at the power and life she felt in herself as she did so, and how he stared at her, dumbfounded, unable to respond. Unable; *dis*abled.

'You . . .' He began to rear up, only dark and frowning at first. '. . . not . . .'

She backed a little, suddenly alarmed. His paws were beginning to rise over her, not nervously now, but fiercely . . . '. . . No.' . . . angrily, his huge paws rising as high as the tunnel's arch as his great chest heaved and he tried to speak but could not, for he was too angry, too outraged.

'No!' he roared, looming over her. 'No, cannot, must not . . .'

She tried to back away quickly, raising her own thin paws in self-defence, her anger giving way first to alarm and then almost instantly to fear as he brought one paw crashing to the floor before her.

'NO!' he roared, and more than roared, the whole tunnel shaking with his black anger, and the other paw beginning to descend, nightmare-like, slowly, hugely, down towards her snout, down at her. 'NO!'

She turned to escape, blundering into the wall, feeling his rage like talons on her, so frightened that her scream was mute as she reached a paw out towards the entrance, to escape, to get away, to . . .

'*CAN'T!*' he cried, and shouted and roared at her, his paws pushing her one way and another towards the entrance, lifting her, carrying her as it seemed, violently down the tunnel whose walls seemed to rush at her from each side as she tried to orientate herself. But his rage mounted even more, and the entrance rushed towards her, and the bright light outside, blinding, confusing, was on her, and she on it.

'Leave now. Go, now. Must not,' he shouted at her, almost inarticulate. 'Take you!'

'Where?' she cried out, desperate and frightened.

'Crowden!'

Such power as Privet had revelled in but moments before was all gone, replaced by terror and helplessness. His paw was at her rump, and she rushed and running, tripping and supported by him as the flat surface of the Top, with its hags and clear spaces, rocks and stones, dashed at her, and the light was still bright as they splashed and ran and hurried through the puddles the sudden thaw had left.

'Rooster!' she screamed, beginning to find her voice again as she realized he meant it, he *was* taking her, they were leaving, now. 'No!'

But her cry seemed only to strengthen his terrifying resolve to rid the Top of her, for suddenly they were among the fissures of the outcrop at the Top itself, hurrying through them, his grip on her so tight and powerful that she felt quite helpless.

'Rooster, I didn't mean—'

'Meant!' he roared. 'I mean! Always I mean. My words mean! You cannot do that!'

Then they were through the outcrop and beyond to that slope down across the Moors which led all that difficult and sullen way to distant Crowden.

'I can't,' she wailed, suddenly distraught with tears, and weak, and very, very frightened.

He stopped as suddenly as he had started, so suddenly indeed that had he not had so tight a grip of her she would have shot forward and tumbled down the slope ahead among the wet heather and black peat hags. He stopped, and ignoring all her cries and wails, stared through narrowed, furious eyes across the Moor.

There, coming towards them, even more massive than him, was a great wall of grey driving rain, and playing above and beyond it were flashes of lightning. He let go of her and went forward a short distance towards it. Shaking, crying, shocked, Privet stared as he raised his disproportioned paws in a gesture of defiance at the approaching storm. His huge dark form was black against the fast-approaching slate-grey clouds from which, in a great slant sweep across the Moors below, rain or hail seemed to fall.

As she watched the sound of thunder grew louder, the lightning flashes wilder, and she saw before she turned back towards the shelter of the outcrop the Moors turn white beneath the stormfall, though whether with water or hail she could not tell.

When she reached the outcrop once more, and turned to look back, the light growing more darkly menacing all the time, she saw that Rooster was returning as well. It seemed to her, watching him then, that he was the embodiment of the storm he preceded, and far from seeming dwarfed by its banking, driven clouds and slanting fall behind him, he controlled it; he *was* it.

He reached her, stared at her, and she saw horror in his eyes; horror that she knew came in some way from her, or from what she had done.

'Rooster . . .' she tried to say, reaching out to him.

'You stay. You shelter. You shelter now!'

He gesticulated ahead of him and she ran back the way they had come, the lightning crackling all about them and what had been bright day turned now to flashing night.

'Back to our tunnel!' he roared, his voice rising above the thunderstorm.

Lightning cracked, thunder crashed and she ran towards the entrance; her fear had rushed her through before she felt his paw on hers, guiding, gentle, firm, strong, powerful, and she heard him growling 'our tunnel' and felt at last that they might be one, they might, one day.

'Yes!' she cried ahead of him. 'Yes Rooster, yes!'

As they reached the entrance and dived down into it the first hail fell, heavy and stinging on their backs, scattering around their paws, and then they were safe again. She turned to him and looked at his huge dark shape where it loomed at the portal, as beyond it the dark sky was filled with lightning-lit hail.

He reached to her as she to him and he took her in his paws, tight and powerful, and she felt his huge body pressed to hers, and his strength, and heard him cry, 'Wanted to kill you, wanted to hurt you, wanted wanted wanted that!'

Then, breaking from her, he rushed past as if fleeing from the raging storm itself, and passed on down the tunnel, crying, roaring, raging, she did not know.

'Rooster!' she cried after him, but her voice was drowned by the storm sounds all about.

'Let him go, let him be, let him be . . .' she heard herself whispering, as she lowered herself slowly to the ground, back to the portal, the tunnel ahead lit up by recurrent flashes of lightning, as she gave herself up to tears and cries and knew that somewhere ahead, somewhere among his delvings, he was doing the same.

'Our' tunnel lay before her, and Privet knew she was not afraid of it now, or its darkness, or its light, for what was there was meant to be: she would play the games of anger and reproach no more, but strive to be as near like herself, as she felt herself to be.

'Stone, give me strength for it and for him; give me strength to love him. Help me, Stone.'

Help me, Stone – the prayer all moles must make if they are to turn from the narrow way of their past's forming, to the wide confusing plain of their personal discovery whose breadth only they, and they alone, can chart, The moments are few when historians can say that *there*, in that hour, something happened that changed the course of moledom's history. This was one of them.

Recovering herself, and as the storm continued, Privet followed Rooster down the tunnel, and turned the way he had gone, to those places beneath Hilbert's Top where she had never been. His ragings she could hear, and the crashings of his talons, and his cries and grunts. But she ventured on, for he was her destiny and she would shirk it no more.

How strange and striking the tunnels she found herself in, arched askew and carved with thin lines and stark embossments which harboured sound, and echoed it. Here and there were places where the walls were shiny, while in other spots the mole who delved the way had made use of outcropping rock to create great shadows across vast walls, from which, infrequently, there thrust out into the light some stone, or ancient root of a long-lost tree.

The meaning of it all defeated her, but she felt its presence and its beauty, and suspected from the feeling of age about the place that this was Hilbert's work. Beyond was Rooster's place, and when she came to it she knew that whatever it was he had made he was destroying in his rage.

The tunnels reverberated with the storm of thunder above, and with Rooster's sounds, but Privet was not afraid, only sorry for what she felt she had done, and anxious to make amends. How she would do so she did not know, but from the moment he had taken her to him, so briefly, so wildly, she had felt tenfold the aching need for him that she had felt in her fantasies before ever she had come to Hilbert's Top. It was this need, physical and emotional, that drove her on without thought of its real nature, or any understanding of what it might mean.

She turned a corner and his sounds grew louder, and as she did she saw that the carvings were all new, and the tunnel different; delicate, light, insinuating. She paused in wonder at what she knew he must have made. Then more crashes came, more sobs, and she started forward more quickly, understanding that in the rage she had put into him he was destroying something of what he had made. She turned another corner in time to see, amidst the dust and debris of a great chamber, Rooster stanced with his paws upraised towards the furthest wall.

She saw enough to cause her to cry out, 'No!' but it was too late. His taloned paws came down on what she knew was most beautiful.

'No!'

In those moments she had time to see, before it was destroyed, a carved wall and arch of complex beauty, all intricate and turned in and out, with light from above which shifted and played upon the place he had made. As she stared at it she realized too that the sound of storm and rage that echoed in the place came not from the tempest outside, but was reflected from the wall and all its subtle hollows and was the Dark Sound of Rooster himself.

Dark Sound! She had kenned it in the Crowden texts, but known it only to be something insupportable. Here, and Rooster's, it was not so much dark as muted, sad, the yearning call of a mole who knows not what to do. But beyond all that was the sense she had that what she saw in that last moment of its existence could not be replaced. The cracking, frightening sound in that chamber was the sound of a mole rending from something he could not bear to hold on to longer.

So when Privet cried out 'No!' she knew already it was too late and that her cry was as redundant to the life that was as a surviving mole's tears are to a mole that's gone. It was a sound she had heard before – the sound she had made inside herself, unheard by anymole, when she had found the body of her father Sward down in Chieveley Dale.

'Rooster!' she called, and went to him, and reached her paws up to his great rough back and touched him, even as he continued to raise his paws and pound them down to break and smash the lovely, intricate, detailed thing he had made.

'Rooster!'

The sound of dying began to fade, dust fell, fragments slipped, and only his heavy tired breathing remained, and her paws upon him, light and almost nothing to his strength.

'My dear,' she whispered, her head bowing to his flank; 'My darling' she wanted to say but dared not.

My dear.

He turned and stared down at her, his face-fur dark with dust, the creases about his eyes and forehead filthy with it, his chest heaving, his great mouth open.

'Rooster, I'm sorry,' she said, 'I'm . . . so . . . sorry,' she cried, 'I didn't understand.'

Understanding by her of him, and by him of her, was almost audible in the ruined, broken place, for even after all he had done the remnant carvings and delves held sound, and whispered it, and all was gentle, all quiet, all close. She reached out to him and he to her, and for a second time that day they held each other, and never in all her life, never in all her dreams, never among all her hopes, had there been such closeness as she now felt, such oneness.

So huge was his strength and yet so gentle his hold that Privet had the illusion – and not entirely an illusion, since her paws now barely touched the ground – that she was floating in a place of security and love such as she had sought all her life, had often missed, yet had never imagined what it might be like.

Indeed, so gentle did it seem, and so beautiful, that as he held her, and as she felt their need for each other begin to shine and ripple like early summer sunlight on a clear blue lake, she wept silent tears, and her sounds were the murmured sobs of one who has come home. But to Rooster it was not of his own strength that he was conscious, but the feel of her paws about him, and the warmth of her body, and all the love and passion he felt flowing from her, which made him feel wanted and desired, loved and cherished.

Which being so, when he opened his eyes after their long embrace – and held on to her lest she let him go – it was not ruin he saw about him, or broken walls, or delvings destroyed, but the wonder of a world which was suddenly his own, and a passion and a trust that was returned. In his own deep way he laughed, happy at what he saw beyond the destruction his rage had caused.

'Why do you laugh?' she whispered, pressing ever closer to him, and feeling shy and wanton, embarrassed and brazen, and beyond all that the sense that there was nowhere else in the whole of moledom that she would rather be than where she now was.

'Thinking that what I just did, here, is the best delving I ever did!'

'Oh, but you ruined it, Rooster. It was so beautiful.'

'Better now. Wasn't right before. Made me angry with myself . . .'

'I made you angry, not talking, not sharing . . .'

'Was angry before; have been angry a long time. Long time.'

They held each other close again and where earlier she had wept tears from the sense of wonder and beauty she felt, she now wept tears of release, and sorrow. Tears for that world which she had seen and to which she had heard him bid farewell.

'Want to talk,' he said. 'Want to tell. 'Bout Glee and Humlock. About my mother, about the Charnel. And . . . and . . .'

'And, my love?'

'Want to listen, want to learn, want to know about you and moledom.'

'Me and moledom?' she repeated with a gay laugh. 'Moledom and I? I'm not sure that moledom knows much about Privet yet!'

'Rooster knows less,' said Rooster. 'Want to know . . .'

So they touched and held and began to love, unwilling for a long time to let each other go. But finally they pulled apart, stared into each other's eyes in wonder, touched and touched again, and touching still as if to affirm that each was there they went back down the tunnel to their communal place.

On their way they turned back to the portal outside. The storm had passed, and in its place had come the heavy pure silence of a steady fall of snow, great and beautiful, as if to cut them off for ever from any world but their own.

But Rooster said, 'When spring comes, Privet, we'll be ready to go.'

'Until then we have each other to ourselves.'

'We have!' he said in wonder.

They turned and went back to the chamber they had shared for molemonths past and stanced in silence for a moment, unsure what to say.

'Feel like delving,' said Rooster before long. 'Feel like delving a place for us. Feel like delving something I never have before. *Will* delve.'

She looked at him with love. 'Does that mean I've got to go somewhere else?'

He grinned lopsidedly and shook his head slowly. 'Want you near. Want to talk.'

'Rooster?'

'Yes?'

'Do you know something? For the first time since I left Crowden I feel I want to scribe. All my life I've been with texts and studied them. Now I want to scribe, to make something. Like you want to delve.'

'The delving need,' he said, 'like that?'

'Yes,' she said happily, 'I'm sure it's like that.'

'We will,' he said.

345

He reached his paws to her and she came to him and he looked down at her and said, 'When I was angry, when you wouldn't talk, I wanted to hurt you. Wanted to *kill* you. But in the Delvings they said a mole must never feel that. Never. A Master of the Delve can never be a Master if he has hurt a mole. Never ever ever. But I wanted to hurt you.'

'I wanted to hurt *you*, Rooster.'

He grinned, relieved. 'Shall scribe, shall delve, shall talk: that's us. Not hurt.'

'And eat!' said Privet practically.

'And touch,' said Rooster with slight but delicious menace to his voice.

'When?' asked Privet breathlessly, her heart pounding, her body weakening towards his.

'When . . . ?' he mused.

His paws reached for her, massive and inexorable; her paws stretched out to his, timid and thrilled. Reaching, stretching, yearning wanting . . . how each generation of moles that hears their tale reaches with them, stretches to them, and yearns and aches that their consummation was there, and then, so much needing love, so unknowing that what they felt and needed was what all moles sometimes need.

'Afraid,' said Rooster, eyes wide and wild, afraid of the power he felt surging in himself, afraid of the great waves of desire that battled to overtake the fear and ignorance instilled into him in the Charnel.

Whilst Privet, unused to such a moment, not knowing that all she had to do was touch him now as she had touched him earlier by his delving, sensed his fear and was afraid herself. If only you will touch me, each said to themselves as their paws hovered, faltered, and fell back; if you wanted to you would, so as you don't you can't want to, not, not, not yet . . .

'Rooster?'

He stared, utterly confused.

'Will you hold me like you did before?'

'Will,' he said, and came to her and clumsily took her in his paws. She felt his strength, closed her eyes into his good scent, as hidden from his sight two tears coursed down her thin face. Not for herself entirely, but for him as well, for the pain she felt in him, and the remorse, and the guilt . . .

'Wanted to hurt you before,' he mumbled again, shocked.

Her tears came again, for she felt a sense of loss suddenly for something they had so nearly touched moments before, but which had now retreated before them, and might never come back again. He held her as a brother might and that power she had felt and for a moment seen, that open, raging sexuality – whose name she did not know, whose existence she had never before guessed – was repressed again.

The talons of his paws moved and kneaded into her back, and for a moment the thrill returned.

'Gone. Wanting to hurt you gone,' he said. 'Feel the delving need, feel it strong. But stronger still want to tell you, want to share.'

His voice sounded lighter and more excited by the moment, as if the burden of years was lifting from him.

Joy came back to her, but joy at a friend's call, not that of a lover.

He pulled her closer and she positively gasped, laughing at the same time.

'You are a strange mole, Rooster,' she said, not without disappointment.

He pulled away from her, grinning. They had been somewhere dangerous, they had touched things they were not yet ready to touch, and they had come back to the real world, still together, and closer still.

'Wanted to hurt you but didn't,' he said. 'Feel better. Can talk now.'

'About what?'

'About being Master of the Delve.'

She stared at his laughing eyes and saw the way his whole body was easier and in control once more. How could such a mole, so cumbersome, so heavy, so strong, seem to her so beautiful? It was the only word she knew.

'Master?' she said faintly.

He nodded, staring boldly and proudly at her.

She looked into his eyes, this mole she knew she loved and did not know how to reach as her innermost being desired that she should. She looked and seemed to see beyond him into time, and to know what he did not, which was that he was Master in the making and was not Master yet. Beyond him, stretching far into a distance of time and circumstance, was the way that he must go, which he could not see.

'Oh Rooster,' she said, tears welling up in her eyes.

He reached out to her again, his eyes troubled. As he took her close to him she said what she knew was truth, dreadful crushing truth, even as the words came to her.

347

'When you're Master, truly Master, *then* we'll love each other like moles should.'

Then, his strength about her, and his puzzlement too, she allowed herself to weep as she had never wept, knowing as his paws and talons held and held and held her, that one day his paws would know how to delve through her tears and find her where she laughed and played and ran. One day he would be there too.

'Oh Rooster!' she sighed, believing in the joy she felt. 'I don't mind how long it takes.'

But as she said those words aloud Privet said something else as well; a prayer to the Stone that it wouldn't be too long. Whilst beyond even that, beyond where her conscious thought went, was the knowledge that it would be long, too long perhaps to bear.

Chapter Twenty-Eight

Gaunt grew more pitilessly rigorous in his training of Rooster in the months following the confrontation with the younger moles in their high chamber. He had insisted that each major task that Prime set Rooster was adjudged by himself as well, and no judgement could have been harsher or more cruel. Try as Rooster did, it was never good enough for Gaunt, whose look of disapproval and impatience at the work he tried so hard to do well he grew to dread and hate.

Dawn after dawn poor Rooster rose, and, denied permission to eat or even groom before he had delved some more, he trekked the long way down into the gloomy Prime Chamber and began the tedious tasks of delving set for him. To begin what others would finish; to clear the mess that others had made; to clean out ancient dead delvings which seemed to have no more use; to wait patiently while others worked – these were his first tasks. Then, when Prime gave permission, to delve a little on his own account – though always under strict supervision – doing the best he could at delves he felt, he *knew*, had no real purpose or reason.

'It shows, mole – that you care not for it, nor heed what the Senior Delver says!' rasped Gaunt, drawing a talon across intricate work he had done and ruining it. 'Therefore, do it again.'

Again!

How he grew to loathe that word.

Again and yet again!

How his spirit wilted, and his paws ached before the relentless criticism of the mole he felt he had yielded his spirit to and who, it seemed to him now, abused that trust by destroying all he did.

'But Mentor . . .'

'Yes, mole?' said Gaunt sharply to Rooster, staring with distaste at new work he had done which Prime was showing him.

'I can't do better. *Cannot!*'

'No?' whispered Gaunt malevolently. 'Really, Prime? *Is* this the best the mole can do?'

Prime looked at the powerfully delineated work that Rooster had done.

'It is not suitable for Prime Chamber,' he sighed, looking at Rooster with a degree of sympathy. 'It is, as I said before the Mentor came, rather too strong. Its sound is not subtle enough for our time of the day. Prime Chamber is a place of dawning life, mole, and that is what your delving here must nurture and celebrate.'

Rooster looked miserably at what he had made. Other Prime delvers did too, sympathetically and with respect, for what the Mentor was dismissing was already better by far than most of them could ever have done.

'Do it again!' said Gaunt finally, ending the discussion.

'But . . .'

'Yes, mole?'

'Nothing.'

'It is well.'

It *was* well, and only Prime knew how much. For time after time following these too-public admonitions by Gaunt he had had to impose his will on the raging Rooster, telling him of the importance of obedience, and how if a delver cannot control his spirit he can hardly expect to control his paws.

'You will obey the Mentor and show him respect. He knows better than any of us.'

'He can't delve!' shouted Rooster, his voice booming around the great Chamber which had become his narrow cell. 'He can't even raise his paws any more.'

Prime fixed Rooster with a terrible gaze.

'The Mentor taught *me* to delve,' he said. 'The Mentor is the only living mole to have mastered three of the five Chambers, two of them the most difficult, which are Prime and Compline. In his day he was almost Master of the Delve.'

'Almost!' growled Rooster.

'Silence!'

'Almost!'

'Obedience, mole! Your unruliness and arrogance does me dishonour.'

'You, Senior Delver? Not you! You I like. You fair! But the Mentor . . .'

'The Mentor is the living Stone amongst us, mole. Learn to obey him and you will learn to obey life,' said Prime softly.

Rooster was silent for a long time before he turned and went away up to the surface. Next day he returned.

'Will try again,' he said.

But Rooster was not without friendship, support and love. For one thing he found it amongst the delvers in Prime Chamber, whose quiet presence and persistence at the tasks they voluntarily undertook was a comfort; their occasional nods and winks, whispered words of encouragement, and even compliments at work he did, gave him the will to continue.

'Never known Gaunt to be so hard on a mole in all my life!' he heard them say, and perhaps Rooster understood that if it were true it was a kind of compliment, as if Gaunt sensed that he could and would take the relentless criticism.

There was sympathy of a different kind from his mother Samphire and Drumlin. These two were now firm friends, and though they were rarely seen in the delvings, except on certain healing missions their skills enabled them to perform, Rooster saw them on or near the surface, and passed what few idle moments he was allowed with them.

Not that Samphire ever talked of delving to him. But her touch, her smile, her silent sharing of his pleasures of the freedom of the surface, with its distant unreachable skies, and the flying of the ravens amongst the fissures of the cliffs above, meant much to him.

So too did her evident new-found happiness, which was of a quality he had never known in her before. He was puzzled at its source, for she had seemed a worried mole when he was a pup, and one always remembering the distant past in Chieveley Dale, before Red Ratcher had taken her. Now she seemed immured in the present, and content to be so, but why he could not tell.

The explanation came from the third, and most potent, source of comfort to him – his two friends Glee and Humlock. Here, at least, normality had continued, since they were allowed to share the same tunnels and chambers as they had when they first came, and cheerful Hume continued to keep an eye on them, and offer them a consoling ear through the trials and tribulations of their introduction to the Charnel.

For Rooster was not the only one suffering at the paws of authority – Glee was as well. Attached as she now was to None, her role was more as personal helper to her Senior Delver, a female who, like Gaunt, suffered from a wasting disease, though her strength was more than his, as was her voice. Despite her handicaps she maintained the near-legendary good cheer of the None Chamber, executing delves of the brightest and most attractive kind and bringing, through sound and sight, the illusion of bright and happy light into the darkest of her

351

Chamber's corners. But woe betide poor Glee if she put a paw wrong, was late, was slovenly, or spoke out of turn, for then None's smile turned to disapproval, and her gentle voice to one of harsh disdain.

Glee's normally sharp and happy attitude changed for a long time to one of haunted gloom and self-doubt, which only increased Rooster's anger and confusion about the situation they found themselves in. Indeed, matters might have so provoked him that he would have been driven to abuse of those around him had not Hume, on the one paw, and Humlock, on the other, been sources of calm and restraint. Hume's good influence was already recognized, but Humlock's was as unexpected as it was welcome. For as time went by Humlock's emergence from his silent world continued, and under the benign authority of the mole Compline he seemed to blossom forth.

Not that he could talk, of course, that would never be; nor 'hear' as a normal mole could. But there was something about the Compline Chamber, where the quietest of the delvers saw day into dusk, and dusk into night, with delvings of a subtle and gentle kind, that caught some spirit locked inside Humlock's huge body, and brought it out. He found his confidence, and learnt to touch and snout about and find his way hither and yon in a system where none would harm him, or even try.

His interest was not in delving as such, for there the only task he fulfilled was clearing debris away to places others had only to guide him to once before he learned them, and, later as his confidence increased, to cleaning the dust from delvings already made, and moving about in his hulking silent way to tidy things up, and make all right.

To 'make all right' was indeed his strength, for at Compline's flank Humlock seemed to find a peacefulness that others recognized and were influenced by. His very existence, silent as it was, brought faith and hope and charity to the hearts of moles he went among, and the chambers he honoured with his presence.

Not least was this power felt by Rooster and Glee, suffering as they were the pressures of learning to delve, to whom he returned each day, bringing his calming influence. There was no doubt that with these two he was happiest – his frowning blinded face growing positively benign at Glee's loving touch, and at Rooster's, why, he actually smiled; even laughed indeed, though few moles who did not know him well would have recognized the strange grunting moans he made as sounds of pleasure and delight.

Though delving as such was not his skill, yet to say he was no delver would not have been quite right, for Humlock seemed to have a special understanding of the vibrations that delvings made. This had been plain enough from the time of his first meeting with Gaunt when he had seemed to 'hear' Glee's touch upon the delvings on the wall. Perhaps Gaunt had understood from the beginning how important Humlock's ability was, or would become, and certainly his decision to place the mole in the Compline Chamber, which most accepted held the subtlest and profoundest of the delves, was significant.

Compline himself soon understood this well, and so did his fellow-delvers, who were astounded by Humlock's ability to recognize them by their touch – not of himself, though that soon came, but of the walls and roofs they delved. More than that, Humlock had an unerring 'ear' for the delving balance of a Chamber, that elusive shifting place where the spiritual centre of a Chamber is, which changes with the slightest delve on wall or adjacent tunnel. Humlock, it seemed, could 'hear' more perfectly than anymole alive.

'But what of real Dark Sound?' asked Glee of Hume one day, as they talked with the old mole in their tunnels, her paw resting on Humlock's in the gentle friendly way he liked.

'Aye, 'tis a mystery, that!' said Hume, looking at Humlock. Dark Sound might not be a grave problem in the Charnel, where Hilbert had committed moles to the kenning of good sound through right delving, but all knew that the difference between proper delving and that which produced Dark Sound was slim, and the slightest mistake could produce sound that was uncomfortable. In addition to which it was part of the delving art to create Dark Sound to protect certain places from improperly prying moles, as in ancient days the Masters of the Delve were said to have protected the most holy sites of mole-dom by surrounding them with tunnels and chambers of Dark Sound, impenetrable to all but the most spiritually enlightened of moles.

Such Dark Sound existed here and there in the Charnel, and was not pleasant to any mole, and most hurried by, snouts low, praying aloud against the mounting confusions and doubts Dark Sound – which is no more nor less than the reflection of their darker selves – put into them.

But Humlock seemed nearly unaffected by such places and on occasion had been found happily resting and chewing a worm in places where no other mole would linger for long at all, not even the Mentor himself.

'Perhaps he's able to deafen that inner ear which "hears" the vibra-tions of the delvings and listen only with his outer, truly deaf ear,' said Hume.

'That's it!' said Glee.

'Or it's because he's perfect!' said Rooster gloomily. 'Eh, Humlock?' he added, digging his friend in the ribs. 'We're saying you're perfect!' Humlock grinned and pushed Rooster's great paw away with his own huge one, and then laughed in his strange disturbing way as if he understood – which perhaps he did.

'He's a mole and a half, *he* is!' said Hume. 'What he could tell us if he could talk!'

'He *can*, in his own way,' said Glee, ever defensive of the mole she loved so dearly.

But the comforts of intimacy are inclined, from time to time, to bring the discomforts of revelation, and to Rooster's already stressed world came the news, from Glee by way of her mother Drumlin, that Samphire had grown close to the mole he had come to dread and dislike, Gaunt. This was not something Samphire talked of, nor something a mole like Rooster would have been likely to notice; and nor was Glee's information passed on maliciously. Few moles were ever as innocent of such flaws as those three moles. No, in the spirit of curiosity combined with pleasure at what seemed Samphire's happiness, Glee cheerfully informed Rooster that his mother was, to all intents and purposes, sharing quarters with Gaunt.

The deeper implications of this were quite lost on Rooster; it was enough that she was intimate with his tormentor, or as Glee put it in the carelessly sharp way she sometimes had, his Tor-Mentor. Ha, ha!

Rooster sulked, and refused for a time to talk to Samphire, only going into his work more passionately and taking out his feelings of jealousy and rejection on the walls he was learning to delve. As for Gaunt's dismissal of his work, he positively revelled in it, and his disdain of rejection, his deep laughter at the words 'Do it again!' and the energy he found to do what would have caused lesser moles than he to sag and wilt, became the talking-point of the Charnel.

This response, natural as it was, underestimated the nature of Samphire and Gaunt's relationship. From the first there had been a natural accord between them, and a deep sense that they had been as one before and now fate had brought them together once again, in new lives and for different tasks. Perhaps they spoke of love, perhaps they were intimate in a way that Rooster was mercifully too innocent even to imagine. Perhaps.

It is enough to know that in Samphire, the Stone in its ineffable wisdom had provided for Gaunt that new spur to life and energy which with the youngsters' coming he needed, and without which he could not have done the work with them he did. For nomole understood better than he the nature of the task their coming set him, or guessed better its possible importance for moledom.

His harsh treatment of Rooster was at first a bone of contention between Samphire and himself, but as the weeks went by and he began to shape and mould the youngster's near-indomitable will to his own, that he might truly master his genius for delving and make it serve the Stone rather than himself, Samphire began to understand his purpose. She grieved to see her son oppressed, but was proud to see him survive, and excited that he might indeed become the Master Gaunt said he would surely be.

As for her feelings, her love, for Gaunt, they deepened as time went by until theirs was a sharing of minds such as neither could have dreamed was possible. Two moles, caught in a dreadful place, discovering a harmony of thought and spirit that freed them to travel where they might.

No wonder, then, that Samphire should share quarters with Gaunt, nor any wonder either that in so generous a system, with moles dedicated to life and celebrating it as best they could, those around them should be pleased for them, and give them privacy. If envy there was at first, Samphire soon dealt with it by the unstinting help she gave the ailing Gaunt, and the way she supported him, provided for him, and brought back to his kindly eyes and lined face that sparkle and glow for life that the older moles in the Charnel well remembered, and rejoiced to see again. None doubted that with Rooster's coming something important and most purposeful had come to the Charnel, and when moles saw Samphire's and Gaunt's deep love, they declared that whatever it was that had come must be blessed if it brought such happiness, and be of the Stone.

Yet where it was all going none but Gaunt himself could easily guess, and what its implications were he kept at first to himself. He had caught a glimpse of it and expressed his fears to Samphire when he had seen Rooster's delvings in the high chamber, warning her that the end to the world of the Charnel was imminent.

As the months and years of summer went by, and Samphire's closeness to Gaunt increased, even as Rooster's prodigious talent showed itself more, the old mole began to understand the grave and tragic nature of the task the Stone had set him. He had discovered love, but in the interests of the Charnel and for the preservation of the life of

355

the young Master who had come among them for training, he must put his love second; worse, he feared he might have to put it aside.

In late July, Gaunt was summoned once more to Prime Chamber to view Rooster's latest work – an extraordinary delve of sweet and gentle line, quite unlike the public character Rooster showed, a delve so elegant in its perfection that the delvers of Prime had already surreptitiously invited their peers in other Chambers to view the work, and marvel at it.

Indeed, the whole of the Charnel seemed to know of it before Gaunt himself, and all waited for his verdict, wondering how the Mentor could possibly fail to find something positive to say this time. As for Rooster, he was more tired than apprehensive, for the main thrust of the delve had been completed in one long night-time session, and its conclusion had run through the whole period of Prime, until, as the delvers of the Terce Chamber came slowly on duty as the first light of the full sun found its way into the deepest parts of the Charnel, Rooster reached a talon out and in one rapid final motion, delved the last mark of all.

His paw dropped to his flank, he stared at what he had done, grimacing and blinking with fatigue as one of the helpers, sensitive to the moment, had quietly come and offered him food. Rooster ate it absently as he continued to stare at what he had made.

'Are you not going to sound it, mole?' one of the delvers asked. For once a delve is done, as often during it, a delver will run his talons through it to hear its sound and check out its course.

But Rooster only shook his head and asked simply that Prime be called. Then Prime had come, and seen the work, and without sounding it had known that it was good: better indeed than any work he had ever seen done before in Prime Chamber.

'Have you sounded it, mole?'

But it was one of the other delvers who replied, for Rooster seemed almost dead to their ordinary world, only staring at his work, and seeing how the changing light played on it, and it played back the light; whispering in the recesses of what he had delved from depths he did not know he had, the sound waited, waited to be heard, already almost audible.

So Gaunt had been summoned, and all the system was abuzz, and if moles in other Chambers delved, it was but half-heartedly, for they waited on news of the Mentor's word.

Prime attended Gaunt to the new delve, which Rooster had made

356

not in the main Chamber itself, but in a side tunnel such as beginning delvers used, one which had links with other chambers more ancient; some so old, so ruinous, that their configurations were long since nearly lost, and their floors covered in debris and dust.

All work in Prime Chamber ended, not simply from the excitement moles felt at Gaunt's coming, but from a deeper sense that what Rooster had done somehow brought to an end in a rightful way all the work ever done in their Chamber. Try as they might they could not delve more, for their taloned paws hesitated before the walls at which they had been working all their lives, as if they knew that whatever was delved more would only detract from what had already been done.

Only two moles appeared unaffected by the excitement. One was Gaunt, who pulled himself slowly through the tunnels and chambers with no other expression than the now too-familiar look of doubt he always had about Rooster's work; the other was Rooster himself, who, having recovered from his earlier fatigue, now waited in an attitude of genuine humility, as if the efforts of the past hours had taken from him all the anger and frustration that he had so often shown and expressed, leaving only a mole who had done his best, and offered it humbly to his Mentor.

Gaunt came finally before the delve's central part, stared at it, cocked his head a little to one side to listen to the magical whispers the delve already made, and said, 'Well, mole, and is this the best you can do?'

A shudder of disappointment went among the moles who heard his words, and all eyes were fixed on Rooster who, surely, would now rise in just indignation, and what fellow-delver could blame him, whatmole would . . .

'It is the best, Mentor,' said Rooster. Astonishment.

'Yes . . .' sighed Gaunt gently. 'Sound it for us, mole; sound out the delving you have made.'

'Another mole should,' mumbled Rooster, his great head low. 'Prime said.'

'Did you, Prime?' said Gaunt.

'You taught me that yourself, Mentor Gaunt: the true test of a good delving is the sound another's touch makes upon it.'

'Yes, yes, so I did.'

How Gaunt's eyes shone.

'Would like you to,' said Rooster.

'It's your best is it, Rooster?' said Gaunt again, using Rooster's name for the first time any of them could remember, but ignoring his bold request that he should sound it.

Rooster nodded. 'Now it is,' he said. 'Can't do more, now. *You* sound it.'

'Mole, 'tis not for you to ask the Mentor that!' exclaimed Prime, concerned that Rooster should spoil such a moment.

But Gaunt smiled faintly and shook his head to indicate he did not mind. 'Well then,' he said, raising an arthritic paw with difficulty and pain, 'you shall help me, mole.'

Rooster advanced obediently and reached out his paws to support the Mentor. How huge he seemed, and how small was Gaunt; the one with life before him, the other with life nearly done. The one with dark bristling fur, the other with grey patchy skin, a symptom of his weakness and mortal malady.

'Just so!' said Gaunt, raised and propped by Rooster.

His paw reached out, and deep silence fell among the attendant moles; then, gentle as the lightest breeze, Gaunt touched the delving's central part, and ran his talons first one way and then another. Even at his first touch, the sounding began, gentle at first, but then burgeoning more powerfully, a sound that came not from where he touched, but from far off in an obscure recess of the Chamber, where dust and debris lay. There a delve made by a forgotten mole in ancient time found its long-silent moan in deepest night, when the primal dawn is no more than a momentary frown in sleep.

In black night it began and from there travelled on through time, first here, then there, all about them, re-discovering ancient echoes of the past, before the dawn when Prime starts, in that benighted hour which presages the light to mole who holds the faith that dawn will come. A time to say farewell to darkness past and turn a snout towards the time to come. That was where Rooster's delving began, its growing vibration casting off the dust from delvings so obscure that Prime himself did not know that they were there.

Then on it went, on about them all, finding new places to reverberate, places not of black but grey, where dawn light began, where hopes dared rise, where life quickened once again after the death of night. On and on through the Prime Chamber it went, as an echo travels up a fissure into light, touching one wall and then another, and each time making more joyous and more waking sound; on and on, and with it came the voices, the calls of moles long dead, the brethren of the Charnel whose memorial was here and now, here in the sounding of Rooster's delving, here when Prime Chamber reached its climax with the light, here where old Gaunt had touched the delving a young mole made, and touched an ending and beginning.

Here, where the sounding began to fade and silence to begin, greater by far than that which preceded it because it was touched by the living voices of the past, and showed by its depth and light the place where they had gone. From them and to them Rooster's delving took those awestruck moles.

Then silence only, and slow forgetting, for nomole can remember such sounding as was then, only the feeling of it and the joy, and the knowledge that it was, and is, and ever more will be so long as moles live on with ears to hear and hearts to feel such things. They had trained Rooster to make a delving to justify their lives; they had witnessed the true birth of a Master of the Delve.

'Prime,' whispered Gaunt when Rooster, humble and quiet, set him down and made him comfortable again, 'this mole honours the teaching you have given him. This mole honours thee. For now.'

A ripple of pleasure went among the listening moles. Gaunt was satisfied. But then, concern.

'"For now", Mentor?' said Prime, sharing the others' concern by repeating those last two ambiguous words.

'Well, Rooster?' said Gaunt.

'Could do better,' he admitted gruffly. 'Not best yet.'

'Not best yet'! What then would be 'better'?

'Well, then, mole, you'd best go on to the Terce Chamber this day and learn what more you can,' said Gaunt lightly.

A look of delight came to Rooster's eyes.

'But I thought . . . I was beginning here. I . . .'

'You are ready to move on,' said Gaunt, reaching a paw to touch him. 'You have learned much. Now, learn more. You may have little time.'

'But I have a lifetime—'

'Go, mole!' said Gaunt with mock severity. 'Go to Terce!'

It was after this incident that for the first time Gaunt laid bare to Samphire his fears and forebodings at what the future held for each of them.

'I said before that the coming of Rooster marked the end of the Charnel's usual life, and the beginning of something new. Today, when I heard the sounding of his delve, I knew that it would not be long before your son has done for the other Chambers what he has already done for Prime.'

Gaunt eased his aching limbs, and winced with the pain of them and with the effort of talking, and Samphire came closer to hold his head in her gentle paws. She knew how hard the time of Rooster's training had been for Gaunt, and how difficult it had sometimes been for him to be so relentless in his pressure for perfection on a mole who was from the first producing delving of a quality and depth far beyond that which any mole had produced in the Charnel before. Joy had vied with discipline, hope with fear that the dream of the coming of a Master could not last. Now there was foreboding.

'How little we have talked of matters close to ourselves,' whispered Gaunt, 'so close have we become there seemed no need for words. I, who am old and crippled, and close to dying now, could never for a moment have dreamt that so late in my life the Stone would send a mole to me I might love, and who might love me. But you came, Samphire, and your life and strength have prolonged mine, and made possible the last and most important part of my teaching life, which has been and is with Rooster, and, as well, with Glee and Humlock. For those two are part of his Mastership. Their love and friendship are the rock on which his paws are set.'

'The Stone will provide, my dear,' said Samphire. 'As it has brought us joy in this joyless place, so will it help Rooster and his friends.'

But Gaunt shook his head.

'No, Samphire, the Stone does not expect such passivity of mole. We must act, that is not only our right but our duty as well. Right action . . . it is the essence of life as it is at the heart of delving. The miracle of Rooster is that despite all, his sense of right action guides his paw, yes, despite "himself", whatever *that* might be! In Prime he has learned the techniques of delving, now in Terce he will begin to learn the sanctity of life; but he will not be a true Master until he knows himself.'

'He knows of the value of life at least, for I have taught it him myself. He knows my history, he knows of the savagery of his father Red Ratcher, he has learnt the gentle way. I know he rages, and fumes, but it is at himself and never at other mole.'

'Hmmph!' declared Gaunt. 'He is as near to violence as any delver I have ever known. It is the dangerous thing in him, and no doubt it comes from Ratcher's blood. I know not. But I know this: life is sacred. A Master of the Delve must never take it, never even think of taking it, or harming it. This Terce will begin to teach him, and None Chamber more so. But time is running out, and I fear for him. We must take him through all the five Chambers, you see, for then he will at least have glimpsed the ways in which he might master his natural wildness and savagery. Knowledge is all: the mastering can come later! I believe this is something Master Hilbert had to learn, and it was hard for him, very hard. Yet it is that very violence, or passion if you will, that makes a mole rise above the ordinary delver to *be* a Master.'

'You say there is little time, my love, and you frown and look away from me.'

Gaunt fell silent once again, staring sombrely before him, and occasionally squeezing Samphire's paw, in a way she knew must mean that he was thinking of them both, and their relationship, and that something troubled him greatly. She waited in silence, knowing he would speak of it when he was ready.

'Samphire,' he began at last, 'my Samphire. I never thought I would know such happiness, but if I had I would never have believed that I would be the one who had to end it.'

Samphire stiffened, suddenly much afraid.

'My love,' continued Gaunt, 'when the time is right we must find a way of getting Rooster out of here. I shall not be able to come, but you—'

'I will not!'

'You must, my love. You are the only one of us with experience of the other side, the only one who can find a way for Hilbert's prophecy to come true. If Rooster is a Master of the Delve he cannot, he must not, stay here. Moledom has need of him now, that is why the Stone sent him in our time. Through him our task shall be done. You must find a way of setting him free of the Charnel, you—'

'I cannot, I will not leave you, Gaunt!' said Samphire, hot tears coming from her eyes at the very thought of it.

'It must be,' said Gaunt gently. 'Until then . . .'

'It will not be!'

'Hold me close, my dear,' said the ailing mole, 'and let me tell you what being a Master of the Delve may mean for moledom. Against *that* burden our lives—'

'Our lives are as our love is, Gaunt, as valued by the Stone as all the Masters of this and Mistresses of that!'

Gaunt smiled at her passion, and nodded, wanting to agree.

'So tell me!' she said fiercely, holding him as if she would never ever let him go.

Chapter Twenty-Nine

Rooster's passage through the Chambers succeeding Prime moved apace as if he, like Gaunt, sensed that time was short and soon there would be none left.

While Glee remained with None, learning all manner of subsidiary skills to aid the delvers, and Humlock continued in Compline to learn to feel his way about by touch as, increasingly, he seemed to learn the meaning of the vibration of the delves, Rooster pressed on rapidly with the major delving skills. Prime had taught him the arts of the preparatory delve, of quarrying and scooping, and the rudiments of adapting present delves to harmonize with ancient forms that others had made before. He had always had a feeling for rock and stone, and now learnt to accommodate his delving to extant strata and rocks, and make the best of the exigencies of light.

In Terce he began to explore the subtle skills of tunnel formation, and appreciate how in a system of chambers, portals and tunnels a change in one part affects the balance through all the others, and as air flow changes so the nature and potential of sound, whether dark or light, changes as well.

As everymole knows, these are skills most learnt in only a rudimentary way, as much by absorption of the feel of their parents' tunnels as from any direct instruction. Indeed, most moles do not begin to think of the Terce or the possible harmony of things until they venture forth from their home burrow and begin to make a life on their own account. But then they are too busy with survival, and with protecting their own young, to do more than repeat what they can remember, and make up the rest as best they can.

But under Terce, Rooster was forced to ponder the relationship of things, and working in the looser soil that lay nearer the bank of the Reap he created tunnel after tunnel which, having made them, he had progressively to fill in once more, thus learning to make and unmake. It was only slowly that he understood that it was in the unmaking, in the filling-in, that he learnt best what he had failed to do before; and that what a delver does not do is as important as what he does. A non-delve, if properly pondered and decided upon, is just as powerful in its effect as a delve.

But July seemed barely to have advanced into a sultry August before Terce suddenly announced that Gaunt had decreed that Rooster move on to None Chamber, which, despite his protestations that he had not yet learnt enough, he was forced to do. His humour was not helped by discovering that the mole assigned to teach him was not Senior Delver None, but 'merely' Glee. Both found the role embarrassing, and for the first time in their friendship they quarrelled.

'It's not my fault, Rooster,' said Glee acidly, staring up at him fiercely through angry, narrowed eyes, her white fur seeming almost to shine with fury, 'and I don't like it any more than you do. Everymole knows you're a real delver and I'm not much more than a helper; *and* I don't pretend to be! But if None says I've got to show you how things are done round here then you can at least make it easier for me, instead of glowering and grumbling and making me feel *terrible*.'

'Want to *delve*,' said Rooster, 'not this . . .'

He had discovered that the delving in None was of a delicate kind, and by the standards of robust Prime and conceptual Terce its practitioners were somewhat airy-fairy in their activity, talking and joking, only occasionally making a dabbing delve in their half-hearted way (as it seemed to him) at the walls of the Chamber, and its light, simple tunnels.

'This,' said Glee, 'is *fun*. We're happy moles here. We enjoy life. We make friends of the soil, not carve it up like you're inclined to, and—'

'I—'

'. . . and what's more, I don't *believe* you can do half the things None can, despite her handicaps.'

'She's fat.'

'But her talons are delicate. Look at yours! Stumpy! Even stumpier than Humlock's. You'd have to work hard to achieve anything here with those.'

'Not working with you—'

'Huh! If I know None that'll mean you won't work at all. Stop being so proud, Rooster, in fact I suggest . . .'

As she went on and on at him, None and her fellow-delvers listened with a combination of surprise and amusement. Rooster's coming had been much heralded, and Gaunt's suggestion that it be Glee who tutored him at first was a considerable puzzlement to everymole.

'Trouble?' said a quiet voice.

How was it that Gaunt contrived to arrive at moments of crisis and drama in Rooster's life?

Rooster turned and stared at the artful Mentor, who seemed to know how to make him work, and when to drive him on. Rooster no longer hated him, nor feared him, but rather, felt awe and a kind of sinking dread that Gaunt was always ahead of him and understood him better than he did himself.

'She can't delve,' he said now, though with sinking heart. He had the feeling that Gaunt had expected this response.

Gaunt nodded slowly. 'No, mole, Glee is not a delver as you are. But she has another talent, and one you will do well not to underestimate. She is a helper, a facilitator.'

'Don't know what that is,' said Rooster.

'Quite so,' said Gaunt. 'You had best learn to know that though moles may not have your skills they may yet have much to teach you. Glee has won the admiration and respect of None. Your delving task in this Chamber is to learn why, Rooster: do that and it will be sufficient in the limited time we can allow you here. Watch, listen, respect, obey, and always remember that delving comes from the heart and not the paws, and to master its arts you must learn to listen and be humble with allmole. Therefore, follow Glee without complaint and learn all you can from her.'

Rooster did no more than growl.

Gaunt gave him a sympathetic smile.

'Come on, mole, 'tis not so hard to forget your pride with a mole you love.'

'Love?' said Rooster, staring uncomfortably at Glee, and her pale fur, her sharp black eyes, and her small compact body with its pink snout.

Glee grinned and nodded. 'Course you do, Rooster, you and me and Humlock are friends and that's the same as love. None said that. Love's a *good* word for what we've got.'

'Hmmph!' said Rooster.

'Leave him to me, Mentor Gaunt, he's not half as fierce as he looks; in fact he's not even one quarter or an eighth as fierce as that.'

'Could be twenty times more,' growled Rooster.

'Then let Glee teach you not to be,' said Gaunt amiably. 'The sanctity of life! That's the joy of None. A delver makes and does not destroy, never ever. Glee will lead you towards that, won't you, my dear?'

'Will I?' said Glee archly, glancing affectionately at Rooster. 'If he stops grumbling I might!'

Rooster did stop grumbling, and having learnt the lesson that Gaunt wished him to learn he began to see anew the wonders of the None Chamber, where the light was bright, the day always promising, and the best delves the simplest and lightest, like a mole's laughter on a summer morning when the darkness of preceding night and the greys of early dawn have fled, and the deeper hues of the day and coming dusk of Sext and Compline have yet to be.

Rooster proceeded with his training with a speed and application that astonished all who witnessed it, and though he did not intend to, and was unaware that he did so, he attracted the enthusiastic support of those delvers who worked alongside him; they learnt that though his manner was brusque and rude he was at heart a kindly mole whose appreciation of delving was so quick and intelligent that others slower than himself thought he was merely impatient and unwilling to talk. Such was the excitement his skills created, and the unaffected wonder that his successive delvings provoked, that few in the system noticed that the shadows that lengthened over the Charnel with the rapid passage of summer into autumn and an inclement rainy October, were rather more than seasonal.

For one thing, infectious murrain, the swiftest and most dreaded of the Charnel's fatal diseases, began a resurgence once more, and weaker brethren among the delvers suffered its vile death; whilst others, Samphire included, were displaying the tell-tale symptoms of its lesser form, where fur begins to patch, and eyes to ache, and haunches to become gaunt.

With this gathering shadow came another, which was the growing sense among the Senior Delvers, and a few other moles like Hume and Drumlin, that the notion of change that had seemed so exciting in the summer presaged an end to the Charnel as they knew it – which was just what Gaunt had privately predicted to Samphire. So a general restlessness came, and a feeling of purposelessness, as if moles sensed that time was in danger now of passing the Charnel by. The need for action had come, and the need was immediate.

Samphire had fought a long battle with herself against Gaunt's request that she think of a way of escape for Rooster, a battle made all the harder by the fact that Gaunt had not mentioned it again. She felt the onset of murrain in her body, and from Drumlin learnt its cause and its inevitable outcome, which would be a sudden decline into helplessness, and then a death that would be a merciful release.

Samphire took this prediction stoically, but along with the communal restlessness, it helped persuade her that Gaunt might be right, and that at the very least she should consider how the problem of escape he had set might be solved.

There were but two ways out. First, the forbidding Creeds, by which Hilbert had entered the Charnel and back up which, his prophecy said, a Master of the Delve would one day go. Rooster, perhaps? And the rest of them, what would happen to them? Samphire considered the idea and dismissed it: the fulfilment of prophecies was a matter for the Stone, not for mortal mole. If ever mole climbed the Creeds, and it seemed impossible that they would, then the Stone would decide the time, and the mole. Meanwhile, Stone forgive her, she would think of how to get Rooster out another way.

There was but one other possibility, and the more Samphire pondered it the less absurd it seemed, and the more her coming to the Charnel at this time seemed to make sense.

'The Span, Gaunt, that is the only way . . .'

There was excitement in her eyes when she finally told him, after days of stancing on the surface and gazing on the one place where Charnel moles habitually never looked, which was that spray-saturated hump of slippery rock and green vegetation over which, a lifetime before it seemed, she had come bearing her solitary surviving pup. There, beyond the spray, she sometimes caught a glimpse of the Ratcher moles, and wondered if Red Ratcher was there as well. The view was very hazy, the shadows long, the distant movement of mole hard to make out. That they stared she had no doubt, for once she had done the same.

But to cross it? With Rooster? And with others?

'Whatmoles can go?'

Gaunt studied her. 'Across the Span?' he said in disbelief.

'Have you never considered it?' she asked.

He slowly shook his head, his eyes widening in surprise at himself that he never had. None of them had. From birth it was always impressed upon them as a way they could not go, because the Ratcher moles would destroy them, and because they could not give up their task in the Charnel. It had taken an outsider to state the obvious, which generations of moles had ignored.

'I think it might work, my dear, though until you mentioned it I never considered it myself. We are all bound by the constraints of what we know and have been taught, and the assumption behind them. Well, now. You say the Reapside moles are afraid of the Charnel and its moles, especially of its disease. You think they might simply fear to touch us and let us out into freedom?'

'There is no other way.'

'What of the moles who cannot trek? Only some of us could go. I myself . . . must stay.'

She gazed into his eyes but did not move nearer. Her look was bleak.

'My son . . . I would see him to safety,' she said. 'You and I—'

'My time is near, Samphire, very near. And you have disease as well. Perhaps the Stone would wish us to part doing what we can for the future. I to serve out my days here until it is time for my trek to the Creeds, and you to serve us all by getting Rooster to safety. Perhaps if Red Ratcher sees you and seeks to confront you, or to stop you, you will find words to outface him. You will need to prepare for that.'

'We shall think about it, my love. We shall see.'

'Our thoughts run far ahead of what we dare say,' he whispered, shaking his head. 'We know this is the way.'

She nodded, certain of it, as certain as she knew how near he was to trekking to the Creeds.

'Only the preservation of Rooster's life, and other ambulant moles of the Charnel, could make me bear to part from you,' she whispered, coming close. But as she touched him, and he returned her touch, his so weak these days it was barely a caress, she knew the parting had already begun. Yet still Gaunt could surprise her with his continuing resolution.

'It must be done swiftly and boldly, like a just delve,' he said with sudden energy. 'Consult Hume and choose moles of sufficient number and sufficient strength to form the beginnings of a system. Males, females. Drumlin, Sedum . . . no, no, I will not think of their names. Theirs is the future, mine the fulfilment of the past. My dear, you must do it. And soon. *You* must lead them.'

'I know,' said Samphire softly. She continued to touch him, but already her gaze was far away, and a name whispered itself across the dream she saw.

'Chieveley Dale,' she said. 'That's where I shall lead them, my love.'

Perhaps she would, but Gaunt was drifting into sleep and only nodded his head vaguely, and made a noise to indicate he heard, or almost heard, before he slept.

If he dreamt, his dreams stopped at the Span, just as his life had always done. The greatest journeys of some moles begin only when they themselves have gone into Silence, and they are re-born in the tales and histories of others, whence they journey on beyond their mortal span to be known and loved even in the furthest and most obscure tunnels of moledom.

Perhaps Gaunt guessed the difficulties and disputes that would arise at even the first hint that some of the Charnel moles would, under Samphire's leadership, attempt to cross the Span to pastures new. Certainly, once the decision had been made he resisted all persuasion to become involved in its execution, saying only that as he would not be going it was up to moles who were to decide how and when the attempt would be made. As for which moles would go, well, others must decide, though he thought that the Stone would decide that in its own inimitable way.

In fact, Samphire and Hume conferred long and hard on which moles might go, and then they took the Senior Delvers into their confidence. To a mole they shared Gaunt's belief that the coming of Rooster had so changed matters in the Charnel that escape out into moledom was now the only way to carry its useful work on into the future. The time of hiding was over.

The arguments against, and there were no doubt many, Rooster himself did not dwell upon afterwards in his account to Privet, perhaps because his last days of study and meditation upon delving in Compline Chamber, which he had finally reached, absorbed him utterly, and brought him into a similar union of spirit with Humlock which he had already worked so hard to achieve with Glee in None Chamber.

Of the issues of change and escape that were now sweeping through the Charnel, he knew only that something great was apaw that would affect them all, and that it had to do with matters of delving, and his own undoubted skills in the greatest of moledom's arts.

By the time his training of Rooster was done Senior Delver Compline left him in no doubt as to the nature of the challenge his skills posed him. Perhaps at Gaunt's prompting, or perhaps of his own accord, Compline told him outright that his skill was such that he was the nearest the Charnel had ever come to a Master since Hilbert's day.

'Which means you have a responsibility greater than you know!' he said, using this as justification for the severity of his training of

Rooster's mind and paws concerning the deep delves of the end of day and dusk, and the approach of night, wherein a mole's greatest and most difficult journeys take place.

'These are the essence of what you have learned in Compline Chamber, and by now you will have understood that our Chambers here, as created by Master Hilbert, represent not just the journey through the hours of day and night back to day again, but the journey moles make through the days and nights of their lives. A delver touches these things in what he makes, and a Master of the Delve touches these things absolutely. It is a grave challenge, and one which I believe grows more difficult the nearer you get to achieving it. Learn from us all, and learn especially from Humlock!'

These were the lessons he learnt in those last days, which in later years he understood were the last days of his youth. In Compline, where many of the most crippled of the delvers worked out their lives, and willingly showed the young Master in the making all they could, and adjured him to learn from Humlock the art of being still and silent, Rooster saw most graphically how all the delvers' arts turn in the end towards a celebration of life. Compline ends the day, as it ends life itself, and offers a mole a time in which to reflect on what has been, and prepare for what is to come. If life, then let it be a better and more responsible one than heretofore; if death, then let a mole approach the Silence with joy for all he has known and made in his life, however brief, however long, for reality is what he brings to Silence.

'It is what the Delvings are all finally about,' explained Compline, 'and the whispers from the past, and the cries, and the calls that a sounding across delving resurrects, are the sounds of moles who once lived as you live, and left behind the best they had. A mole who does that may turn his snout to Silence with pride.'

'Like my Mentor Gaunt,' said Rooster sombrely.

'Yes, like Gaunt.'

The unpleasant weather of October eased for a time into milder days, when the sun cast russet rays out of a pale blue sky and lit up the cliffs across the Reap, and made more gentle the intimidating dark fissures of the Creeds. The tufts of heather and crowberry that grew among the scree had held their autumn colour well, and now shone in their final hour of glory before winter came and stole their brightness away. Even the ravens in the crumbling cliffs above the Charnel seemed more benign as they enjoyed leisurely flights off their sheer roosts, and tarried in the sun, their wings shining and their beaks glinting as they turned.

But the Reap was less benign, for the earlier rains had put it into minor spate, and some shift of the massive rocks in its gorge during the spring melt-spates meant that the spray was higher than mole ever remembered it, shooting over on to the Charnel's edge and beyond into puddles that sometimes spread dangerously near to floods, and up on to the Span itself, which at times was lost to sight.

'Come winter that'll freeze,' said Hume uneasily. 'I'd swear it's narrower than it was when I last had a good look at it. Ice would bring the whole lot down and then the Charnel would be lost to itself for all time and all our work a waste. If some of us are going to go across we'd better get it over and done with while we can!'

He tried to sound his normal cheerful self but even he was nervous at the prospect of crossing the Span.

'Well, the plans are well made and the Senior Delvers have drawn up their lists of the moles who are to come, and what their order is to be,' said Samphire. 'There's little now to hold us back but fear.'

Hume nodded, staring at the spray and straining his eyes to see beyond.

'What's moledom really like, do you think? I mean, is it so different from our home here?'

Samphire looked round at 'our home' – our enshadowed home – and remembered Chieveley Dale, *her* first home.

'Moledom's different,' she said, 'and warmer. There's places in moledom where the sun shines all day long and the rocks grow warm with it, and the soil as well. And the worms can be as long as a mole.'

'Long as a mole!' exclaimed Hume smiling. 'No, Samphire, that's just your memory as a pup. No worm could be *that* long!'

'You wait and see!'

Hume looked at her. 'When are we going then? Eh? When's the big day? Is it leaving Gaunt that's delaying you?'

She nodded. 'You're a perspicacious mole, Hume. You'll do well out there in moledom.'

'Now there's a word, "perspicacious"!' said Hume, grinning. His face grew serious. 'It'll be dangerous crossing the Span, more dangerous meeting the moles of the Reapside—'

'We'll do it,' said Samphire fiercely. 'Ratcher's moles only know the language of force.'

'There's not a mole among us will strike another mole, not even to save our life!' said Hume quickly. 'That's not the Charnel way.'

'No, I know,' she replied, 'but I believe there'll not be the need to. We'll look fierce, and we'll look odd, and they'll be afraid of our seeming strength and our appearance. But most of all they'll be afraid of the disease we carry. We'll be over and past them before they've time to recover from their surprise and decided what to do about it.'

'And then?'

'We'll go to Chieveley Dale!'

'Forgive me, Samphire, but after so long can you find the way?'

'I shall never forget it,' she said. 'I remember every rock Red Ratcher dragged me past, every stream we crossed, every patch of heather and grass, every peat hag over the high moor. Each one was one further from my home, where all my kin died. Get me beyond the Reapside, Hume, and Rooster at my flank and all his friends, and I'll not fail to lead you to a home you can only begin to dream of.'

'Well, we better get on with it while the weather's mild. Once winter comes . . .'

'Soon, we'll go.'

'And Glee and Humlock, are they on the lists the Senior Delvers have made? They'll be missed amongst the helpers.'

'Rooster would not go without them, though with Humlock's disabilities, and Glee's white fur, they're not a couple will ever find survival easy.'

'Aye, but you're right, Rooster'll never go without 'em. It's not for me to say it but I will: that mole may be a Master of the Delve one day but I'll swear he'll only be Master with Glee and Humlock at his flanks. They began in the Delvings together, they made their high chamber when they shouldn't have done, and I'll wager they'll finish up together. The Stone made them for each other, and anyway, do you think Masters in the old days worked alone? Not a bit of it! Delving's a communal art for communities, and a Master cannot delve alone without something in him dying.'

'Oh, but what of the ones we must leave behind, Hume?' she said sadly.

'Aye,' said Hume shaking his head, 'aye, that'll be hard.'

'Be bold and swift,' Gaunt had said, yet still Samphire hesitated, lingering out last days with Gaunt, though all knew now that the risky departure must be imminent. Days of adjustment, and of sadness, for friend must part with friend, as the system began to part from itself, and leave behind those moles and helpers who had no ability or wish to leave.

One thing only was a consolation to Samphire: there were few moles who were staying or going against their wishes, so few indeed that she could not but think that the Stone was giving them its blessing by timing the great event so that the least hurt was caused to the fewest moles.

The reason given for the delay was that Gaunt was preparing himself to speak to each in turn, following what moles understood to be his preparatory farewells to the Senior Delvers and Hume, who along with Samphire had taken the lead in organization. This seemed to be so, for Gaunt spoke quietly to moles like Rooster, Glee and Humlock, and wished them well in the world beyond. Other, ambulant delvers came, and those of the helpers who had not volunteered to stay behind, or *those*, the ones whom Samphire had decided would be needed in Chieveley Dale. These few were the unhappy ones, though wise Hume knew well that their reluctance to go arose less from the wish to help those staying behind than from a fear of what might come. It was an understandable weakness.

But Gaunt had got through his talks with no more than half the departing moles when one evening the weather worsened once again, the skies turned grey, and a drizzly rain began. It was nothing much at first, but as the night continued the drizzle turned to a downpour, and at dawn the downpour worsened towards a spate.

''Tis time, Samphire,' whispered Hume, coming to waken her.

'Yes,' she said blankly, awake already, her paws about the mole she loved.

'I must leave, Gaunt. If we delay we may not get across this side of winter. I must leave, my love.'

Hume retreated, tears in his eyes at the parting of two moles whom the Stone had brought together, but whom destiny and their own courage now pulled apart once more. He heard their moving words of love and faith and trust that one day, somewhere, they would meet again; heard but vowed never to repeat.

'Samphire, we—'

'A moment more, good Hume,' whispered old Gaunt, his paw lingering on Samphire's. As Hume went to retreat again Gaunt shook his head and called him to his flank.

'Guard her well, mole, for she is my joy, and all my strength. In her I live. Guard her as she will guard Rooster, and may the Stone be with you. You have been worthy, Hume, and your name will be remembered.'

Hume embraced his Mentor and with tears in his eyes turned from that beloved burrow in the Charnel, where so many moles had been privileged to hear Gaunt's words, and heard Gaunt say, 'Go, moles, go together, go, and finish the work that Hilbert began so many centuries ago and I was honoured to help continue. Go!'

Then he turned from them, unable to watch Samphire leave, and with her talons tight on Hume's paw, as if she otherwise could not have moved or even have supported herself, she left the chamber.

Chapter Thirty

At Hume's command the departing moles had assembled some little time before up near the surface, and their farewells were as Samphire's had been: tearful, unbelieving, and finally numb, as if they felt themselves entering a world of which they could not quite feel a part.

Rooster was there among the first group ready to cross, for he had grown now to his full size, and with his dark fur and furrowed, frowning face, he was as physically intimidating a mole as any there. Only Hume equalled him in size, excepting always Humlock, bigger than any mole, and no doubt just as capable of showing his strength if he had ever needed to. Others put in the first group of moles were Sedum and another goitrous female, for Samphire had frankly said that their appearance, so familiar and unremarkable to the Charnel moles, would put fear into the Ratcher clan. There too were moles with infectious murrain who though they had survived the disease had hanging skin and raw flesh enough to put off ignorant moles. Inspecting them all, Samphire could not but think they were a formidable vanguard.

Next after this were to follow some more vulnerable moles, those with poor sight or hearing who would need leading from the front, or pushing from behind. But everymole feared crossing the Span perhaps even more than what lay beyond, the more so because as dawn light came it was all too plain that the heavy rains of the night had put the Reap in such spate that the Span was close to being impassable, and if they did not cross it soon they never would this side of winter.

Yet their delay was not entirely due to fear or hesitation: Hume had long since said that the best time to cross would be in worsening rain when the Ratcher moles would least expect such a crossing, and might even be out of the way sheltering in their burrows.

'What I didn't realize was that the noise would be in our favour too, and that's a bonus!' he shouted to Samphire. 'But we had better begin, the rain is growing heavier still.'

They looked down towards the gorge and saw that the Reap's water was rushing ever faster and was filthy brown, its spume rising high and crashing on to the Span, while all along the gorge's edge up the valley spray and foam seemed to be spilling over and beginning to cause minor floods. Pity the moles who had tunnels near those places, though the Charnel moles never had, always fearing just such a flood as they were now witnessing.

'We go *now*!' cried Samphire, magnificent and purposeful, turning to the Span and leading the first group forward.

Once started there was no going back, nor desire to, for the group had a volition of its own, as each followed the other, and their paws ventured on to the narrow span of slippery rock and they looked ahead and not down into the void below.

'Go slowly and steadily,' Hume had said, 'and if spray buffets you, stance firm and do not falter. If one stops, others will be forced to pause and that's when courage fails.'

Rooster had wanted Humlock and Glee to travel with him, but Hume had decreed that Humlock must stay with the central group, with Glee at his flank to guide him, and Drumlin, whom he liked, just ahead.

Off they went into the rain, out of the shelter of the portal and across to the Span and then up to its narrowest and most treacherous point where the stone was barely a paw-width across, and the sodden rock dropped away to the terrifying rush of the Reap all turbulent below.

Samphire went first, as quick as she could so that Rooster and Hume could follow and not leave her vulnerable and alone on the far side for too long. As Rooster crossed the highest point a great plume of spray shot up to one side of him and then down again, just spattering his right flank. But as Hume followed on behind and reached the same place a second shot up, caught the wind and turned and flung itself on him, so that for a few moments none could see him at all. The moment of wild chaos seemed to last an age, before suddenly all cleared and they saw the last of the water running down on either side of the Span as the river below surged and heaved and seemed to seek to reach up once more, while Hume, blinking the water from his eyes, was steady where he was.

He heaved himself forward, ran the last few steps to safer ground, then turned with Rooster to help the others of the first group following behind, both of them almost pulling each mole that reached them off the Span so that others could follow on as fast as possible.

Meanwhile, Samphire was surveying the once-familiar terrace of the Reapside for sign of Ratcher mole and danger, but in the driving rain nomole was about at all.

'I'll signal the second group to start across,' said Hume, coming close to her, but still having to shout into her ear to be heard.

She nodded, still eyeing the ground ahead warily, and gathered each new arrival near, to form a defensive position in case the need arose. All had their instructions to look bold and unpleasant, and eyeing them now from the point of view of a Reapside mole, and seeing their strange looks, their goitres, their distortions of appearance and patched raw skin, Samphire could not help think with wry amusement that they had no need of instruction to look alien; any mole used to drab normality would find her group as fearsome as any clan. For a time at least. But then . . .

'Get the others over as quick as you can!' Samphire urged Rooster and Hume, sensing that the sooner they all got going the better. They had all the advantages for the moment, and once they were off and away from Reapside down Charnel Clough she would feel happier.

Rooster and Hume were already back at the Span urging the second group of moles across, and among them all the sense of urgency increased with the realization that separated as they now were they were at their most vulnerable. But then, as if wishing to add to their concern, violent winds began to drive the rain yet harder, so powerfully indeed that Rooster and Hume had to raise a paw to protect themselves from it, as it dashed into their eyes and stung their faces.

For oncoming moles, however, the direction of the wind was an advantage, since it almost seemed to bowl them across the narrow way, buffeting their rumps and keeping their snouts down as they did as they had been told to do, which was to peer down at where their paws went, and not dwell on the raging, roaring, frightening mass of water rushing below.

The leading moles of the second group were sturdy and careful and not one faltered or slowed, and as Hume had hoped, their example inspired the weaker ones who formed the bulk of the party. For a time even the torrent below seemed quieter, and its wilder eruptions and dangerous spouts of water were driven parallel with the Span and not across it.

'It's going too easily,' fretted Samphire, watching from the further side.

She was right; it was. Suddenly a mole recently ill with murrain and thus weaker than some faltered at the very highest point of the Span, and fatally raised his snout in fear as he froze to the spot, unable to go forward, unable to turn and go back. The mole behind was forced to stop on the precarious incline, whilst ahead Hume did his best to urge the mole forward. The torrent and the wind seemed to sense the mole's vulnerability, for suddenly the water rose, the wind shifted and a great wave bore down upon him.

Without a moment's thought Rooster and Hume reached out great paws to hold the mole steady as the water rushed into him and knocked his front paws flying. All on the Reapside could see the two moles' back paws strain as they clung on to the mole, just as they heard the shout, dreadful in its horror, of the moles back on the Charnel side as they saw what Rooster and Hume could not see.

As the water gushed away, and they pulled the faltering mole to safety, they saw that the mole who had been held up behind was slipping and sliding over the Span's edge, his talons unable to find a grip on the slippery rock, his eyes white with terror, and his mouth opening into a scream as he lost all grip and fell backwards down into the torrent of the Reap, nomole to help him, lost for ever in the rage of white water below.

It was Drumlin on the far side who now took action, realizing that unless those with her pressed on fast their confidence might go. For the moment the loss must be forgotten and the crossing continued as fast as possible. So she urged on the next mole, and the next, whilst Rooster stayed where he was and literally pulled one mole after another across.

It had been arranged long since that the last three of the second group would be Drumlin, followed by Humlock and then by Glee. That way he would know where he was, and could trust the mole at front and back, and if need be communicate quickly with them, for they were moles he knew better than any other, excepting Rooster himself. After them the last of the moles would come, encouraged by those of the Charnel who were staying behind, but felt strong enough to brave the elements and watch this historic exodus of moles from their ancient system.

So now Drumlin started, and as she did the rain suddenly eased, and the air cleared but for the spray that drifted sometimes with the wind from the gorge. It was not that the Reap's flow had lessened, but rather that its nature had changed from being wild and rushing to something deeper, more angry, more powerful, and far more deadly.

'Come on, Humlock, follow me!' she said, as much to get herself started as to speak to Humlock, who could not hear her words, but only responded to her urgent touch. Then off she set, as did Humlock too after only a moment's hesitation. Drumlin paused frequently so that Humlock did not lose touch with her for more than a moment, whilst behind, Glee prodded him occasionally just to show that she was there.

Though the rain had stopped the thundering sound of the torrent now increased ominously, and as the three moles reached the Span and began their slow passage over it, the attention of those watching them so anxiously was drawn by an abrupt if distant roaring sound that came from far up-valley, right at the head of the gorge where the three Creeds rose darkly to the skies.

At first nomole could make out what had made the sound, but then one by one they saw its cause, and gasped in awe and fear. The central and biggest of the Creeds was turning white before their eyes as, from off the Moors above, the ancient and forgotten gully that had once fed a stream to carve the great fissure, seemed to have flooded and now directed its waters over the edge and down the Creed's dark channel.

The re-born waterfall gathered momentum as it fell, fed by water from above, and dark grey chutes of water massed and shot ahead and at the sides as it thundered down into the gorge below, and thence joined the Reap. Even as moles took this horror in they realized its implications, for what must already be coming down-gorge towards them would make the present torrent seem but a tiny stream. Worse, since the Reap was already near to overflowing it was plain that its banks would soon flood.

Even as the moles realized this, and the sudden danger they were in, Hume and Samphire began to order the moles on their side to escape from the bank and head for high ground; while on the far side some of the helpers did the same for the watchers, and had forcibly to push back those still waiting to cross, their hopes of escaping now all gone.

But this left Drumlin nearly at the centre of the Span, with the unseeing and unhearing Humlock behind her, and Glee behind him, and two more moles waiting near her who, perhaps unaware of the danger they were in, stayed close by. The roaring increased and suddenly, up-valley of them, those who dared to look saw an ominous and angry wall of water shoot massively up from the gorge, distant at first but growing ever nearer and ever louder.

With a roar Rooster surged forward up the Span and reached a paw towards Drumlin on the far side of the rise. As he did so Samphire turned from the higher ground a little way off and cried out to him to come back; if he was lost, all might be lost.

At the same time Drumlin, until then only partly aware of the change in the noise, neard the ugly sound of the roaring wave that was descending the gorge towards her; more ominously, the wind suddenly died completely and all was still. Feeling Drumlin stop, Humlock stopped, and half turned and reached out a paw to Glee behind. For her part she had seen what was happening, and the disaster that seemed certain to be about to engulf them, and had quickly turned and ordered the other two moles back. They, after stancing in numb fear for a moment, now turned and fled back to the Charnel side where willing paws pulled them upslope into the portal, and thence out of sight, to retreat up-tunnel to high ground.

'Quick, Drumlin!' roared Rooster as she strove to turn back and then, unable to because Humlock was there, turned forward again. She looked up-valley and saw the huge risen wave smoking and thundering massively towards them all, and stanced suddenly still, unable to think, unable to move, unable to do anything at all.

Glee meanwhile was first pushing, then pulling, and then pushing at Humlock, wanting him to do one thing or another, *anything* but stance still. She screamed at him to move, but he seemed not to understand.

'Run!' cried out Drumlin to Glee. Though herself in panic, she seemed yet to have a mother's instinct to save her kin. Glee's desperate face told more than words ever could. She clung to Humlock, and would not leave him, come what might. So there the three stanced, doomed by their uncertainty as the great wave of water roared nearer with each moment.

Then Rooster reared up, looked past the panic-stricken Drumlin to Humlock and with a great cry brought one of his paws down on to the Span, and thumped it several times in rapid succession. What it meant nomole could tell, but that it was a signal, and one meant for Humlock too.

'Yes!' roared Rooster as Humlock, calm in the storm of chaos and danger all about him, turned a blind head towards Rooster, who thumped the Span once more. 'Do it, mole!'

Then Humlock turned and seemed to stare up-valley, his head bent to one side into the stancing he habitually made when he was listening to vibrations; his paws lightly touched the Span ahead of him and then behind. Then, with a strange primeval bellow, as of a creature that is emerging into light after a lifetime in the dark, he turned massively to Drumlin in front of him, reached out his paws to her, heaved her

379

from the rocks to which she clung so obsessively and hurled her bodily towards where Rooster had struck the ground.

As she flew through the air, and Rooster strained forward to catch her and pull her to safety, Humlock turned on his back paws precariously, and reached out towards Glee.

Already the level of the Reap had risen, and now the water that flowed under the Span was smooth and yellow, and treacherously fast, while where it touched the edges of the gorge that confined it great splashes of water shot this way and that, and fell back into themselves. Rooster saw this, and caught a glimpse of a great shining wall of water bearing down upon the Span, before he took Drumlin up as Humlock had done and threw himself back to the Reapside, scrabbling desperately up the slope that Samphire and the others had already run up in the hope of escaping the oncoming flood.

As the great wave struck the Span with a thunderous roar, Rooster thrust Drumlin ahead, and Hume reached down to pull her up to safety. Then, disdaining the security of the high ground and the peril of the flooding water that was surging up towards him Rooster turned, not to run back to the Span – that was too dangerous now – but to watch in desperation as the waters descended upon his friends.

But he was too late, too late to see, that is. Already the flooding wave was breaking over the Span, and spray and raging water and driving yellow foam were over it and over them. There was vague movement in the racing broken water, a great paw reaching desperately out, a white-furred haunch among the foam, black talons thrusting helplessly from out of yellow water, as on and on the flooding came.

Rooster stared; the water drove up towards where he was, right over him, and he pushed upslope to fall and flounder amongst his friends, so that for a moment he thought they were all going to be drowned. But no sooner had he struggled to hold his stancing than he was buffeted half off balance by the water's return as it rushed back downslope, and he found himself struggling to help others hold their place, and not be swept past him downslope into the raging torrent of the Reap.

The moment passed, the water eased, and all were safe. He turned in hope that he might yet help his friends upon the Span, turned to hear a growling, cracking roar, turned to see the Span's highest point shudder and twist, crack and break, and then, a sight that mocked the earth's great strength, he saw the Span begin to slide and fall, water crashing over it as it collapsed down into the raging Reap.

Once more water rushed up towards him, once more he was forced to hold his place and help others do the same, once more the flow came back again, this time pushing him downslope as Samphire screamed behind him. Only with resolution did he hold himself, every muscle straining as the water drove on by and cascaded down to where the Span had been and thundered over into the gorge below.

He raised his head and looked in numbed disbelief across the gap, and saw that on the far side water rushed over the gorge's edge as it did below where he now stanced. He looked desperately for his friends in the broken water, but saw only jags of protruding rock, and tumbling waves, and wild nothingness. Gone, gone into that horror that flowed angrily past, gone. All gone.

A scream, faint in the water's roar. A strange, muted, bellowed shout. Desperately his eyes searched the water and the rocks, and he rose, ready even then to try to go to the aid of whatever mole it was that called. Then he saw them, not down in the gorge itself, but clinging on to the edge of the far side, the back of a great mole, the left paw of a great mole, reaching, heaving, pulling, whilst its right paw held on for dear life, life that was most dear to it.

It was Humlock who clung and Glee he held, his strength pulling them now up on to the bank with one paw, his blind mute love driving him on far past the point where mere brute force would have failed him. How small she was, how hard to see amongst all that white water that still cascaded over them; but he had her, and held her, and with those strange bellowings he heaved her up to safety through the dying waters of the flood, and pulled himself to safety as well.

Only then did the Charnel moles above them see where they were and that they were safe, and several helpers came timidly down and took the half-drowned Glee in their paws.

Then Humlock turned and snouted out across the impassable gorge, stancing up as Rooster did, two friends, two great moles, who for a moment of terrible despair seemed to reach across a void nomole could ever hope to cross again. Rooster opened his mouth in a silent cry, and raised his paws, but it was Glee who screamed on one side and Drumlin and Sedum from the other, before Glee shook herself free of the protection of those who held her to go back to Humlock's flank and stance with him and stare and reach to mothers and a friend they could surely never reach again.

It was Humlock who turned first, perhaps sensing a resurgence of the Reap's torrent, and he reached out and took Glee towards the Charnel's entrance upslope among the scree. The last thing Rooster saw before the returning wind threw spray across the gorge and obscured all view, was Glee, eyes wild, mouth open in grief, and a thin white paw raised in a solitary gesture of farewell and benediction towards him: he to go on into life now on their behalf as well, and they to stay for ever where they had been born, never to know what might have been.

Then they were lost in the driving spray, and when it passed on by all Rooster could see were the wet grey rocks of the Charnel's surface, the ragged tufts of vegetation, and looming over them all the great dark cliffs which had been the boundary of his puphood, and was now the prison of his dearest friends.

Yet one more thing occurred before he turned away from his loss, and he ever after believed it to be significant. Samphire had often told him of the raven that had stooped down into the gorge on the day she had taken him to the Reap's edge to hurl him in at Red Ratcher's command. Now another stooped down, a great ragged thing that turned and twisted in the violent wind and hovered for a time over where the Span had been, unaware it seemed of the danger it was in, or defying it.

Then a great fountain of spray rose up and was driven by the wind on to it, and for a moment it was lost in white. Yet it seemed undaunted, for the water fell away and the raven opened its bedraggled wings and sent forth a dark raucous cry, before wheeling round into the wind and over the Charnel once more. It rose slowly up the cliff's face, higher and higher, gyring sometimes in the eddies there most purposefully before, with a last thrust, it powered its way above the cliff's highest edge, turned for a moment as if to survey the Charnel Clough a final time, and then was gone across the unseen Moor.

As Rooster turned blindly from his grief to find Samphire and begin the now reluctant flight from all he knew, he heard her cry out to him to beware, and come quick, come now, or it would be too late. Was it the waters she feared, or that he would turn back and hurl himself into the gorge for loss of the friends who were his life, his limbs, his normality? Or was there something more in her cry than that?

Certainly some warning note made him instinctively stiffen his body as if for assault as he looked up, and was brought immediately to an appalled stop by what stanced directly in his path.

For there reared a great mole, his taloned paws outstretched, and as Rooster stared at him it seemed he saw the embodiment of the wild elements that had seemed to bring such disaster so early in their escape. The mole was massive, his fur as rough and dark as Rooster's own, and russet in places just as his was; his face too was furrowed and lined, like Rooster's. Only his eyes were different. They were piggish and deep-set and rimmed in red, ignorant and cruel.

Rooster stared into the eyes of his own father.

Even so many moleyears later, when Rooster reached this part of his tale as he told it to Privet up in Hilbert's Top, he had seemed to regress to the moment he described. He had reared up, he had raised his talons, and as he stared ahead it was not the blank wall of their communal chamber he saw, and nor was it before the presence of Privet that his breathing grew more rapid as his great chest heaved and he sought to control himself.

'Wanted to hurt him,' he gasped, 'wanted to kill him. *Want* to!'

It was not lost on Privet that he spoke this last in the present, nor, now he had explained how essential to his training was the idea of not harming life *ever*, did she find it hard to understand the terrible conflict she saw in him there before her eyes.

'He could hurt, I couldn't. He could kill, I can't. Hated him. He hurt Samphire. It was like he was the Reap. He was the waters down the Creed that broke the Span. He was all darkness to me. Want to hurt him. Could have killed him. He was first evil I knew. He is darkness in my Dark Sound.'

But he had not attacked his father, and thereby his anger had stayed alive, and grown, and deepened, and Privet saw he was still savage with it.

'Samphire saw I would hurt him and cried out to me to behave as a Master must. Didn't . . .' Rooster bowed his head and began to slump down in their chamber at the memory of it. 'Didn't want to *be* Master, don't want to be Master, 'cos then I can't be mole. Not fair. Want to be mole. Want to be me. He was him. He made me. Then I saw the me in him. Same, same, same . . .'

Rooster cried like a pup at the remembered agony of seeing from whatmole he had come, and of wanting to kill Red Ratcher who had made him, of knowing he could, and yet of knowing he must not even try, not even *think* of it, but behave 'as a Master should'.

That, Privet saw, was his agony, that the Stone had played a cruel trick upon him, putting the spirit of a Master of the Delve into the body of a fighting, killing mole. This was the tragedy only Gaunt had seen at first, and which, in the short time he knew was left to him, he had tried to train poor Rooster to contain and triumph over.

383

'Didn't want to tell you this, not today of days,' said Rooster, 'tonight of nights. Wanted peace.'

Privet smiled, and went to him and touched him and held him as in the past days she had learned to dare to do. That there was passion between them none knowing their story could doubt, but they had turned from it before, as being too frightening and too like 'hurting', as Rooster put it, and though their touches were deep and full of trust they had not again become physically passionate. Time and the Stone would tell them when if it ever did. So now Privet held him and shook her head at his regret for talking as he had *that* night.

For it was Longest Night, the first Rooster had shared with another mole, a normal mole, and had he not found the courage to talk they would have long since eaten the food that Privet had prepared, and spoken the quiet rituals she had learned in Crowden, the like of which he had never shared.

'Would like to eat, would like the prayers,' he said. 'Will you still?'

She nodded silently, feeling her love for him great about them both.

'Will,' she said.

And so she did, there in their chamber, and then up on the surface amongst the icy rocks near the Top, quiet beneath the stars before she spoke the prayers all moles repeat that night, which speak of darkness past, and the light to come with the new cycle of seasons whose turning begins that Night of nights.

'What do we do now?' he said when it was done.

'We go down to where we live. We tell tales. We sing. And if there were more of us we would dance.'

'Dance?' said Rooster, wondering what that was.

She laughed at his disquiet as she danced a little about him, as once, so long ago it seemed, her friend Hamble had tried to make her do.

'Dance!' she said.

He shook his great head. 'Will tell you to the end now,' he said.

'Tonight? Below?'

He nodded.

'But won't you at least try to dance afterwards?' she said.

He raised his head to the sky and stared at the stars. He raised a paw and looked at its silhouette and saw how, as he moved it, some stars disappeared, and others came into sight again.

'Afterwards I'll make a delve.'

'What of, my dear?' she asked.

His paw came down and fretted at the icy ground. His face furrowed into deep black lines. His eyes were lost in dark shadows as he stared at her.

'What of? Not sure, but it's strong. It's good. It's . . . it's . . . it's for us, Privet. A delve to help us. Nearly can do that now.'

'To help us what?' she said. These days she dared press him, for now he would respond.

His voice grew almost gentle, and his touch nearly casual. 'Powerful this delving need. To help us be, be always one day.'

'Be always one day!' She wondered if Masters of the Delve were always so inarticulate as Rooster. For the sake of moles who had loved them, as she knew she loved him, she prayed they were not. How could a thing 'be always one day'?

'Come on,' she said, tugging at his paw. 'The best bit of Longest Night is after the prayers and rituals.'

Together they moved among the starlit rocks of the Top towards the entrance to their tunnels, and had others seen how they crossed the shining icy ground they might almost have said that Rooster and Privet danced.

Chapter Thirty-One

It was not only Red Ratcher that Rooster found himself facing, but a good number of Ratcher's clan as well, which meant that among them, though he did not know it, were some of his brothers, all older, all as big as . . . all much like himself.

Great though his instinct to attack was, his training was greater still, but had he been alone or even out of sight of Samphire and Hume and the others of the Charnel, who stared at him now in dismay, for they guessed what was in his mind, he might well have tried to kill his father.

If Ratcher had been alone he might well have succeeded too, for Red Ratcher had aged, and he was, as Samphire had predicted should he see them there, both surprised and afraid of what had so suddenly appeared from the Charnel side. Rooster's evident anger and lack of fear of him helped too, for fearlessness is a most fearsome thing to a mole who rules by fear and Ratcher was not used to the kind of disgust and frowning disdain that Rooster showed him as he pushed past and joined his mother.

'Well!' said Ratcher, not recognizing his own likeness in Rooster or guessing who he might be. 'Damn me, but it's Samphire herself, came back from the diseased dead. Ha!'

'*With* the diseased dead,' mocked one of the largest of Ratcher's sons. Ratcher came closer, sneering and peering, and some of his aides grouped close behind. He stared intently at his former mate.

'Thin, ugly, old,' he said, spitting out each word at Samphire through yellow stumpy teeth, and grinning in a half-mad way. 'That's what you are. When I had you, you were worth having. Now you're disgusting.'

'And diseased,' said Samphire, finding her courage to be bold and approaching him. 'Like all my friends.'

Ratcher backed away.

'We can force the buggers into the Reap,' said the mole who had spoken before.

Samphire stared at him and wondered if it was one of her sons.

Most of the Clan stanced like ancient rocks, dark and forbidding and slow. Had she been of them once? Had this disgusting mole 'loved' her? Had she suckled these great things?

'We go,' said Rooster firmly, and Hume, recognizing the moment was right and they still held the advantage of surprise, herded the others together and turned the way Samphire had already pointed out as leading from Charnel Clough.

'I said we can drown the filthy scum in the Reap,' said the mole who had spoken before.

'Shut up, Grear,' snarled Ratcher, turning round dubiously and thrusting a stubby paw without warning straight at Grear's eyes. The big mole seemed used to this treatment, for he ducked quickly, rose up again, and thrust out an insolent paw in response, pushing the stolid Ratcher off balance.

A fight might then have ensued which would have taken them all down a path they could not return from, but in the midst of their angry exchange two grubby females appeared suddenly from a portal some way across the Reapside shouting about flooding and needing help.

The clan moles turned as one and deserted the escapers to go to the rescue of their kin, except for Red Ratcher and Grear; the one because he was old and slow and the other because alone of all the moles he seemed to understand that the sudden emergence of moles from across the Span might have implications the clan should deal with. But the cries for help increased and could not be ignored. Red Ratcher swore, and Grear stanced hesitating, looking first at Rooster and Samphire and the others, then back the way he should go.

Suddenly he came forward powerfully, raised a paw towards Rooster, who did not flinch, and then, so swiftly it was over and he was gone before they saw what he had done, he spitefully talon-thrust Samphire in the flank, hard and deadly.

'Mother?' he said, in a voice of utter hatred and contempt.

Red Ratcher looked surprised, his pig eyes widened, and then he laughed, a vile mocking laugh, before clapping Grear on the shoulder and turning towards where the others had gone, leaving Samphire half-collapsed among her friends. Only Hume's firm paw on Rooster's shoulder prevented him from chasing after the two moles.

'Come!' said Samphire urgently, her voice full of pain as she clutched where she had been taloned. 'We must go before they return. Now is our chance.'

'Aye, Samphire,' began Hume, worried for her.

'Leave them be, Rooster,' said Samphire. 'You'll find worse provocations than that in moledom when we get to it. Now, moles, the Stone has given us a chance and we shall take it.'

Rooster stared with shock and dislike at the retreating rumps of his brother, as he now knew Grear to be, and his father.

'I go last!' he declared, herding the rest ahead of him down the narrow path that led out of the Reapside, and none there doubted that whatever his training, if the Ratcher clan came after them Rooster would be happy to break his vows and use his talons on them; nor did any doubt, which was comforting, that Rooster would win the struggle too.

But they were not followed, nor did they see the Ratcher moles again that day. They went on steadily down the Clough led by Samphire, despite the blood that came from her wound. Down through the narrow gorge, with the crashing Reap off to their left flank and all their lives left behind in that shadowed lost place which just occasionally, they turned back to look up at, and shuddered.

Until at last the Clough opened out, and for the first time for all but Samphire the moles saw a view that was not confined by sheer cliffs, and crashing water, nor made hazy by driving spray. A view across a valley, with hints of green and the reflections of flooding water, and beyond, further than they could have imagined eyes could ever see, a clearing October sky that arced across a great wide world which they had heard was moledom, and was theirs.

For a short time they paused and caught their breath as Hume attended to Samphire's injury; though the blood had stopped flowing, she felt a deeper pain that augured ill.

'You must rest, my dear!' said Hume, as Rooster stanced by, fretting and worried, and angry.

'No, I shall not rest until I have led you all to Chieveley Dale,' she said, eyeing the way ahead. She snouted about a little, and finally decided the course to take. 'It's a long way for moles like us who have never travelled far, but we'll get there! The sooner we start the more likely we are to stay clear of Ratcher's lot. Now, give me your support, Rooster, and the rest of you follow me!'

With a final look back at the shadowed, narrow passage between bluffs of dark rock which marked the entrance to Charnel Clough, they were gone.

Few escapes are so stirring as this fabled exodus of Samphire and the moles of Charnel Clough, and many are the accounts that have been left behind. None better known perhaps than that which Privet later scribed from Hume's own words, which describes so graphically how Samphire led the moles up on to the Moors and thence by slow degrees, successfully avoiding all contact with Ratcher's clan who came out in pursuit the following day; and how finally she led them to her birthplace, Chieveley Dale, where Rooster directed the others to create their extraordinary system of false tunnels and misleading chambers, protected by Dark Sound, and so made them safe from Red Ratcher for a time.

Of these things Rooster spoke deep into that Longest Night, and at the end of how his mother Samphire never recovered from the blow Grear, her own son, had struck her near the Span. Weakened already by murrain, bereft without her Gaunt, she saw the little group she had led delve itself into safety in the Dale she loved. She saw life return to her old home-place, and in the molemonths following she watched her friends gradually recover from the loss each felt, finding enough in the future to recompense them for the losses of the past. In the clean air, and the good soil, and with worms as long as moles – just as she had said – Samphire had time to see that there was a possibility that some of them would survive.

She saw how Rooster, though grieved at losing all hope of contacting Glee and Humlock again, shook off his pain, controlled his anger, and began to lead moles she herself had not strength to lead more. His energy and skills created their defences, and his restraint prevented anymole from seeking to confront the Ratcher moles when they came snooping. All this she saw, and had time to do one thing more before she died.

'Climb to Hilbert's Top, my love, and see what is there. It is your right and your duty to do it, for there you may find comfort for the pain you bear in the former Master's delvings, and guidance too. Go, my dear . . .'

So Rooster had gone, up to that mysterious place, in amongst its strange delvings, and sounded them, and heard their distant familiar cries – of mole calling from the past, or mole urging to the future, and of the rudiments of Prime, and Terce, and None, and Sext and Compline. All there, nascent, as yet unformed, a place where a Master found himself and his great task. Strange its sounding as he turned to leave like the final valediction of a mole hidden amongst delvings, an old mole, a wise mole, a mole Rooster had learned to love.

'Mentor Gaunt,' he murmured, for it seemed it was his voice amongst the whisperers, saying his last farewell.

Back down to the Dale went Rooster then, fearing long before he reached home that he was not the only mole who heard Gaunt's voice that day.

Aye, his mother Samphire seemed to have heard it too, and had turned her snout from life, looked into the Silence where her love had gone, and followed him, knowing perhaps that she had done enough. Others would have to carry on the task of bringing Rooster forward, and making him the Master of the Delve that moledom surely needed once again.

'She might have waited to say goodbye,' whispered Rooster when he told the tale to Privet, angry that she had not, and knowing his anger to be unreasonable, yet feeling it all the same.

From that day forth Rooster was not of their world, nor able in his loss and loneliness to service the tunnels. Hume's account tells how at last disease quite overtook them, and they became unable to maintain the specially delved tunnels they had made. Ratcher's moles began attacking them, making incursions into their modest territory, torturing and killing the moles they caught. So were they forced to flee over the Moor to Crowden, and alert those sturdy moles to their plight, which first brought Hamble, Sward and Privet out in search of Rooster.

'And you, my dear, did you not think of going too?' asked Privet at the end.

Rooster shook his head. 'Not the time. Was learning. Hilbert's delvings spoke to me. Waiting.'

'For what?'

'Your coming, Privet. Longest Night. Things. Had to delve my way out of darkness of Glee and Humlock not coming. Stone decided, I fought it. This is hard.'

'At least . . .' she began, thinking to say something consoling. But no words came. What consolation was there in thinking Glee and Humlock safe if they were so unreachable that they might as well be dead.

'Couldn't delve without them,' said Rooster, 'before you came. Now . . . can delve a bit, but differently.'

They were silent and sombre for a time.

'This is Longest Night!' Privet suddenly declared.

He nodded slowly. 'Said I had the delving need!'

'And . . . ?'

'It's a Compline delving, a sounding of the future.'

She nodded, only half understanding what he meant.

'Where will you do it?'

'Here,' he said, looking around their shared chamber, whose subtle walls and elegant portal he had made with such skill and love. 'On our walls, somewhere.'

'When?'

'Now,' he said, frowning, and reached out a paw to touch the wall.

Privet shrank back into the darkest shadows to give him privacy, feeling almost that she should leave, but he sensed that she might go and turned and said he wanted her to stay.

'For us!'

More than that he did not say, but became still and quiet, his only movement at first being an occasional touch of the walls, now here and now there, sometimes with both paws at once, as if trying to find something he knew was there but could not see.

Occasionally he let out a slight groan or sigh, and even a 'Hmmph!', but after that he retreated to a low stance, and for a time Privet thought he had given up altogether in disgust. But then he started up again, raised his talons to the wall and made some sudden swift jabs, and a sweeping delve as well, before stopping as suddenly as he had started, and stancing quite still to stare in a most malevolent way at what he had so far done.

Worse, he looked round at her, the unpleasantness still in his gaze, and she was about to say something when she realized that he did not see her at all, but something else far away in a distance of time and space. He seemed to be awaiting a call.

The call must have come, for he turned back to the wall, and reaching forward sounded the few delves he had already made, which emitted a broken kind of sound, pained and disturbing.

'Ha!' muttered Rooster to himself, not at all displeased, hunching purposefully over the wall and seeming suddenly to have gained control of something he had struggled with.

'Yes!' he cried out.

Then his delving truly began, strong and purposeful, mark after mark, delve after delve, the thinner talon followed by the blunt, the scratch followed by the score, the score by the finishing touch. As he did so the chamber was filled with sound, though it was muffled and muted, as if it came from beyond an obstruction.

'Portal!' he whispered to himself. 'Must remember. Will! Ha!'

As she watched him delve, Privet saw and heard a Rooster she had not known before, and felt him too, for the Chamber was filled with a growing sense of ease and confidence. This was not an inarticulate mole struggling to find speech, which when it came was usually mono-syllabic, at best only stilted. This was a mole in communion with himself and allmole, a mole speaking his language at its highest level, a mole of power and absolute clarity.

'Yes! Yes! Yes!' he declared suddenly, stancing back from the wall, peering round at the chamber's only portal, and then back at the vast and elegant pattern he had made, which now slowly revealed itself in the dawning light.

'Is it . . . ?' she began.

'Nearly!' he said sharply, silencing her. He fell into thought again, peering at his work, and then round at the portal that seemed to worry him so much. He reached out a paw and sounded part of the delving, and though it was still muffled and strained, Privet thought she could hear a voice calling, or voices.

'You!' he said turning on her. 'You delve now?'

'Me?' she said faintly. 'What? And where? I can't delve, Rooster.'

'All moles delve all the time. It doesn't matter. It's your mark, your touch that counts. Now, before you think too much! NOW, PRIVET!'

His voice was suddenly urgent, and his great paw pulled her forward and almost hurled her at the wall.

'But what?' she said.

'Your mark!'

She turned, raised a paw, and paused as he had done at first, and as she always did before she began a scribing. Her eyes travelled over the wall, she saw a space that summoned her talons, and there, impulsively, she began to scribe her name. She stopped when she had done so, not because she did not know what she wanted to scribe next, but because the space that followed did not seem right.

She stanced back from the wall, watching the light shimmering on its protrusions, dark in its recesses, brighter elsewhere, and impulsively once more she went to a different place and scribed again. When she had finished she pulled back, and felt sudden fatigue come to her paws and body as if she had scribed a great thing.

'Done?' said Rooster.

She nodded, vaguely.

'You delved good.'

'I only scribed,' she said.

'Same,' he declared appreciatively, going to the two places she had scribed and touching them.

'What?' he asked.

'That's my name,' she said pointing to her first mark, 'and that's yours, my dear,' pointing to the second. 'Rooster.'

'So far away, one from other.'

'Felt right,' she said.

He chuckled in his warmest, nicest way.

'Was right,' he said. 'Far, far apart. We've made a delve to make us one again.'

'Have we? Can I sound it?'

'Not properly. Portal's involved and must be sealed and then broken, *then* will sound like it should.'

'When?'

He shook his head. 'Longest Night over. Must sleep, both together.'

'Yes,' she sighed. 'I love you, Rooster.'

'Know it,' he said matter-of-factly, 'it's in your delving.'

They slept, paws about each other, deep, deep, trusting sleep.

When they awoke the burrow was filled with light and they both wanted to go out on to the surface and see the new day.

But before they went through the portal out of the chamber Privet asked, 'What is the delving of? Can't I sound it just a little?'

For once Rooster looked gentle, his familiar frowns giving way to an unwonted smile, the menace of his form lightening into something more approachable.

'A bit, you can,' he said, evidently pleased with himself, like a pup who wants to show off something he has found, or made.

She touched it lightly, and the chamber was filled with the muted call she had heard before, but of two moles, far in the distance, in different places, muffled, lonely; sounds whose full strength could not yet be heard because they had not yet been made.

'What is it?' she whispered.

As she spoke Rooster reached up to her paw and, touching it, drew it across the delving again or, rather, drew it down and *through* it, following some line that he had made among the many, and which he knew and wished her to know too.

As he did so she felt the line like the touch of a forgotten friend or the scent of some long-forgotten place where she had once loved to be. With these feelings came a fuller richer sound amongst the others, sudden and powerful, sweet and overwhelming in its effect, such that she gasped before it, and turned to him and looked into his eyes, as he into hers.

'What is it?' she whispered. To him? To herself? Or of the sound? The question was for all these things.

393

'That is the sound of Silence,' he said, 'which I was taught to make, though I have never made it until now, not like that, not for another mole. Made it for us, for you. Masters don't do that!' He grinned as the sound faded about them, and restrained her paw when, almost instinctively she tried to sound the delve again. He shook his head.

'No,' he said, 'not yet for us. But don't forget. One day might help. Had need to show you.'

'I will never forget,' she said.

As their paws withdrew from the delved wall together they brushed some other part of the great delve, and another sound came then, far off, heavy, dragging, like shadows of mole across a vale, striving to reach something beyond their easy reach.

'It's the sound of us, one day,' he said sombrely.

'It's so sad,' she said, suddenly clinging to him.

'Us . . .' he said. 'We will need help, Privet, we will. This delving will show a mole how. Don't know why, or how; don't know where sense comes from. But felt it, and my paws delved it, *had* to delve it, would die if I could not. This is my delving need.'

'When will mole find it?'

'Long after we've gone.'

'To the Silence?' she whispered, afraid.

'No, no, no!' he said, laughing. 'When we're gone from here.'

'We're going?'

He touched the delving he had made again.

'All's finished here, have no more need here. When snow goes, we'll go.'

'Where to?' she said faintly.

He grinned. 'Your home system, of course. Crowden! Rooster's ready to try to be a Master now.'

Sudden excitement came to her. They were leaving Hilbert's Top! When spring came they could travel. Relief flooded into Privet as she sensed that their test here was over. They were ready to move on.

'Come on,' she cried, 'let's go to the surface. Let's look at the Moors. Let's guess how long before the snows will thaw.'

'Too long!' said Rooster. 'Want to go *now*!'

Privet laughed aloud, almost for the first time during her telling of her tale in Fieldfare's chamber in Duncton Wood.

'He was so impatient you see, a wise mole in some things, a pup with everything to learn in others. And spring took a long time coming over the Moors, longer probably than anywhere else in all moledom!

But there we were, and there we stayed until the rooks winged their way over the thawing snow, and settled again on the black grit outcrop of the Top to tell us it was almost time to go.

'I finished my scribing of the long time we had had together, and Rooster visited the tunnels and finished things off he had been unable to do before. We spent long hours together and talked of the days in the future when we might make tunnels together and have young.

'Yes, we talked like that. Talked, but did nothing more. Sometimes he wanted more; sometimes I did. Spring was coming after all!'

'And . . . ?' said Fieldfare, ever curious about such things, and liking mole to find happiness through having young, as she and Chater had.

Privet shook her head. 'I'm sorry, Fieldfare,' she said with a smile, 'but we never did express our . . . passion. It was there all right! But the time wasn't right, it was too soon. Rooster was still angry, and the loss of Glee and Humlock seemed to hold him back from many things, including that, though he never talked of it. And he still feared the feelings he had had of wanting to "hurt" his father Red Ratcher, for he knew he would have done if he had had to defend the Charnel moles against attack. And then, where would his responsibilities as Master of the Delve be? He knew a Master must *never* hurt another.

'As for love . . . he seemed to think that wanting me, loving me with all of him, was so powerful and dangerous that it felt like wanting to hurt me. He knew no different, and how could I, so innocent, so young, explain? I was almost as ignorant of such things as he was.'

'So you never knew him, never made love, and never pupped?'

A dark look went across Privet's face. 'No, I never knew him, as you put it, Fieldfare. But I *did* have pups. I did!'

There was an astonished silence in the burrow at this late and unexpected revelation. The dawn wind rattled vegetation at the tunnel portals, and somewhere across the Wood something crashed down.

Privet's friends were still, and silent, as she began the last part of her tale.

Despite its frustrations, the period following Longest Night on Hilbert's Top before they felt it was safe to set off for Crowden was one of relief and happiness for Privet and Rooster. From the moment his delving for the future of them both had been made and they had gone on to the surface it seemed that a great weight had been lifted from his mind.

An important and original delving had come to him, and he had no doubt it had the blessing of the Stone, and that made him believe that the loss of his friends in the Charnel, and his guilt at not being able to return to see if they were safe, or could be reached, was something he need no longer feel. The Stone would watch over them better than he could, and its purpose was something he could not question or comprehend. He believed that they were still alive, and had the consolation of knowing that they were for ever safe from the world of trouble and danger into which the escape had led him – and which had already claimed the lives of so many others from the Charnel.

Perhaps, after all, such moles as they, the one so disabled and the other so distinctive in appearance and vulnerable, were never meant for the real world and could not long have survived in it. At least they had each other, and their companionship and love was more than most moles had, as he understood from all that Privet had told him.

Stirring in him too was something he had not felt so powerfully before, because of the dark seclusion of the place he had been in: spring. As the snows melted away from the Top, and all across the Moors the white gave way to sodden greys, and then in late February to brighter colours of renewing heather and green bilberry shoots here and there amongst the hags, Rooster felt the mysterious stirring of the new season.

The rooks had begun to arrive, and down in Chieveley Dale they saw the stream run white and then blue, and grass began to turn a brighter shade of green as other birds, too far off to identify, began to flock down there, and the striving sun to lighten all before its weak rays.

It was on such a bright day that scurrying about, their paws restless and their minds full of the coming journey over the Moors, Rooster suddenly found the text that Privet had sought when she first came, hidden in some obscure spot beneath one of Hilbert's delvings. What it was she had no doubt, and even before she opened its old cover, and reached out a paw to touch its small, neat scribing, she knew that what she touched was meant for her, just as her father Sward had told her.

Its first words were just as he had remembered them, and as she had in her turn learnt. Her grandmother Wort, once the Eldrene Wort, had scribed, 'I have found the sanctuary of the Stones again and I am thinking what it is I must say to you. You whose name I do not know, you whose life was all my purpose, you for whom my little life was meant . . .'

So Privet began to ken Wort's Last Testimony, a text surely meant especially for her, to tell her of a love that came back from beyond the Silence, a love Wort had wanted to give her daughter Shire but which was denied to her, and so a love that lived on only in scribing, awaiting the moment when it might be kenned and known.

Rooster watched her begin that kenning and then quietly left her alone as the first tears came, knowing that there are some griefs, some discoveries, a mole best experiences alone. He stanced up near the Top, and watched the hours of that day through, as the sky lightened and became pale blue, and the wind shifted, and warmth began to spread all across the Moors.

'Time,' he muttered to himself, 'time to leave.'

Only later was he aware that Privet had crept to his flank and was stanced quietly down, her eyes red from crying, her paw wanting to be held.

'I want to go from here now,' she said.

'The text . . . ?'

'I'll leave it in the chamber you made. Also what I've scribed about us since I've been here. Just us will do for travel; we'll leave all our past behind.'

'Can go *now*,' he said.

The warm wind rustled at the Moor's edge.

'Good,' she whispered.

They turned together and went back down to the chamber.

'Where's your scribing and the Testimony?' he said.

'Buried it in the wall,' she said. 'Your delving will protect it.'

'Won't, Privet. But I'm going to seal up this chamber and protect it with Dark Sound.'

'What about the mole . . . ?'

'That mole'll be all right. Will have strength to break the seal and go through Dark Sound. *Must.*'

'And then?'

'Will hear the delving we made for us. Hear all of me and some of you. Will know what to do then. But . . .'

Before she could ask what his hesitation might mean he went to the wall, peered at the place where she had buried the texts and vainly tried to conceal her delving, turned to her with a grin, and with a few fast delves concealed the place properly beneath more delving.

'No mole will ever find that place again!' she said, staring at the convolutions he had made and becoming unsure where it was herself.

'Mole who comes will. Delving tells him!' said Rooster with mischievous glee. 'Delving can be fun! That's what Glee said!' A dark look briefly crossed his face. 'We'll go,' he said sombrely. 'You first, then I'll seal behind me.'

She took one last look, and then turned and left, going up slowly to the surface as he did his mysterious work, and running the last part, for she heard a grim confusing sound which made her want to flee to the fresh air above.

'That's the Dark Sound he's making,' she said, shuddering, and wondering at the complexity of the mole she loved, who could be so gentle, and yet had it in him to create such savage sound. 'May the Stone protect him from himself if he ever loses control of the anger and loss he still feels!' she whispered, staring at the dark rocks of the Top, and at the raven that hovered there and turned on its back in the wind, all strange, and then was gone.

'Rooster!' she cried out, suddenly afraid. 'I want to go. Now!'

'Rooster too!' he said, emerging from the portal for the last time. 'We go now!'

His paw was gentle on her flank, as they wended their way through the outcrop on the Top, and then emerged into the balmy airs of spring, and pointed their snouts southward.

A sudden gust of wind rushed at the entrances to Fieldfare's tunnels. Then wind-sound through trees, and the crack of branches across the Wood.

'Listen! Moles!' said Maple, stancing into alertness. 'Silence!'

At first they could hear nothing, but then there came what sounded like a distant call of a mole. Then even before Maple was up and through the portal, they heard the drag of paw, and the call again, and they realized that what had seemed distant was simply muted because it was weak.

Weak, and desperate, and not far off. The sound of an injured mole calling out for help with his last breath before losing consciousness.

Maple signalled to Chater and Whillan to come with him, and together they went out swiftly.

All waited in silence, listening, and Privet looked in despair. They heard talking and then a pause, and after that the sound of the moles coming slowly down the tunnel helping a mole along.

Then in they came, Maple in front supporting Pumpkin, who at first was hard to recognize. His fur was wet and in disarray and there was blood about his face, and a nasty injury in his shoulder. He was only half-conscious, yet trying to speak, and his paws and belly were muddied and torn, as if he had crawled right across the Wood.

'Where's Husk?' said Privet with sudden urgency, trying to run out of the tunnel and up into the Wood. 'He's in trouble at Rolls and Rhymes, he needs our help.'

Maple held her to stop her rushing off.

'Let him recover himself and talk, mole, you'll gain nothing floundering about the wood distraught. Now, Pumpkin, can you tell us what happened?'

'Whatever it was it was while I was talking,' whispered Privet, much distressed, 'and I should have been there, not here. I should not have left Husk alone!'

'What's apaw, Pumpkin? Whatmole did this to you? Where's Husk?'

'Dying,' whispered Pumpkin at last, wincing as he shifted to try to ease the pain.

'Try to tell us what happened,' said Maple.

It took Pumpkin some time more to find strength enough to talk, and when he did what he had to say was grim indeed.

'Newborns came to Rolls and Rhymes,' he gasped. 'Texts all broken and destroyed. Husk . . . dying where I left him.'

'Where did you leave him, mole?' asked Chater urgently.

'Where he asked me to take him: at the Stone.'

'You've come from there, *now*?' said Stour.

Pumpkin nodded wearily, close to tears. 'They just came. Six of them. Too many for us. I tried to dissuade them, and even offered to fight them, me! Keeper Husk said not. They hit him. They began to destroy his tunnels to let the storm and rain do the rest. When they were gone there was nothing we could do and he asked me to take him to the Stone and then do my best to come here . . . I'm sorry, I could not do more.'

'You did more than many moles did, Pumpkin,' said Stour. 'This night we have seen how history turns, and turns again and now a long night has begun, and we are of it, all of us. Now listen each one of you, for this is what we each must do. Drubbins and I will go to the Library, for that is where I should be. You, Maple, will accompany us, to protect us if need be. You, Pumpkin, shall stay here with Fieldfare, who will tend to your injuries until we are ready to decide what we should do with you.

'You, Privet, will go to the Stone with Chater and Whillan, and find out what state Husk is in. We must hope that he is not in as bad a state as Pumpkin seems to think – injuries can seem worse than they are. Then you will go to Rolls and Rhymes and having done that with all due caution, join me in the Library.

399

'Now we have work to do this dawn and we must do it fast. But when we come together in the Library I shall tell you what tasks – what great tasks – I believe await us all, and how it may be that the tale Privet has told us, of delving and of Rooster, may have prepared for what may soon begin, unless this night's Newborn destruction of Rolls and Rhymes means it has begun already. Of the rest of her story, for good and ill, we must await the telling until times are more propitious. Away!'

PART IV

The Sound of Silence

Chapter Thirty-Two

It was as well that Stour insisted on Whillan and Chater accompanying Privet across the Wood to the Stone to find Husk, for she herself was in no mood to go cautiously, and think of the dangers along the way.

Her mind raced with doubt and grief, and was filled with apprehension of what she would find at the Stone, even as her innermost being succumbed to the growing realization that the darkness she had in earlier years found so troubling and insupportable in moledom had finally caught up with her in the one place she had hoped she might for ever avoid it.

Of these things, and many others too no doubt, she thought, and tormented herself with them as she hurried across-slope towards the Stone. Only the presence of Whillan and Chater kept her from erring off course, or turning and turning again as the troubles of her mind sought to confuse her. Indeed, more than once Whillan had to put a forceful paw to her flank to guide her into safer and more shadowed ways, and it was left to Chater, so long used to travelling through danger, to stay close by them both, eyes narrowed and head hunched forward, ready at any moment to call out a warning and stance still and protect two moles he regarded as his wards.

Certainly Chater showed no fear, nor felt any, for Pumpkin's terrible story had angered him, and affirmed the doubts he had felt for some time about the Newborns, and it seemed to him now as if a long struggle was beginning for which he had been as long prepared. Indeed, he felt relief that its time had come, and that surge of energy and purpose a strong mole always feels when the waiting is over was on him, and so his mind was clear.

He noted with approval the calm and reassuring way Whillan took charge of Privet; for a scholar, the youngster was doing well, and it was increasingly obvious that he might have more about him than his thin and gawky appearance at first suggested. For in its mysterious way, the Stone somehow brought moles forward in each generation and prepared them for the time when they would have to take up the challenges of the day, and find words and courage and the will for deeds in order to preserve the light of moledom from the threatening darkness.

Privet herself said not a word; her mouth set, her eyes frightening in their blank intensity as she stared ahead, she seemed not to notice when briar tore her flank, and bramble lacerated her face. It was at the Stone she wanted to be, with Husk, who might yet have survived and need their help. So anxious was Privet to get to the Stone and do what she could for Husk – if only to whisper a melancholy goodbye over his broken body and ask that the Stone accept him to its Silence – and so much were Whillan and Chater concentrating on their self-appointed task of watching over her, that the sudden lightening of the Wood ahead beyond the great leafless beeches that confronted them took them all by surprise, and the little party stopped in its tracks.

'We're almost at the Stone clearing already,' said Whillan, and indeed they were, for their minds had been so preoccupied with what they might find when they got there that their journey seemed to have taken no time at all.

Chater quickly quartered the ground all about for signs of danger and ambush, while poor Privet, who had been carried this far across the Wood by the strength of her concern for Husk, suddenly faltered and looked thin and weak, and full of fear at what they would shortly find before the Stone.

Until then, none of them had paid much heed to the winds and wet that beset the Wood, but now they had paused in their grim journey, the wild threshing of the high branches of the trees above came to their notice. Now and then wet brown leaves turned and flew through the air above their heads, while off across the High Wood, scurries of wind, like pups playing at the flanks of a parent looming high above, scattered leaves among the beech roots, and caused the branches of holly and the briars of bramble to shake and shudder with their passing.

The immediate way ahead was blocked by the fallen litter of broken branches and bark, and the only thing that seemed permanent in all about them was the presence of the great, dark, grey-green trunks of the beech trees, which rose up and up above them, their sinuous, smooth lines belying their strength. It was westward beyond the biggest of these, their ancient roots spread gnarled and knobbly across the ground, that the Stone clearing lay, and as they stared through the wind-loud Wood towards it, they could just make out part of the Stone itself, grey and shiny like the wet trunks that obscured it, its top blunt and very slightly angled one way.

For a moment Chater allowed himself to take his eyes off the shadows about and the dangers they might hide, and looked in his rough and unsentimental way towards the Stone itself.

'Should have come up here more often than I have,' he muttered. 'Shouldn't have had to wait until all *this* happened . . . Stone knows, a mole forgets where his centre lies and when he does, a little bit of the system forgets as well.'

Privet glanced at Chater with a sudden bleak smile and nodded her understanding before reaching out a paw to Whillan and touching him.

'You lead us on, my dear,' she said, 'for our generation is beginning to need the strength of younger minds and hearts and paws. Stay as close as you have been, for I may need you. Husk is most dear to me.'

Husk *is* . . . for Privet, then, he was still alive, still a mole to revere and turn to, still waiting in his wisdom and kindliness, still . . .

Whillan led them on, head up and eyes alert, breaking through the obstruction and then skirting the roots of the last great beech before entering the clearing and gaining full sight of the risen Stone. They paused again as each of them quickly scanned the surface of the clearing ahead, beginning with the area near the base of the Stone, and then in ever-widening circles among the leaves and litter and indentations of bare chalk and grass which formed the clearing. Chater was concerned still to look for enemies and signs of threat, but Privet and Whillan were looking for Husk; but at first none of them saw anything at all. Just the Stone and the wan expanse of the clearing, and the shifting trunks and branches of the trees.

Then one of those swirling eddies of wind that had lifted leaves over the surface around them in the time just past, came noisily from behind, and went rushing in a mêlée of leaves into the clearing and across to the edge opposite them, where it paused, turned, lifted leaves once more, and was gone. To there it was their gaze shifted, and there they saw, with a mounting realization that soon had Privet hastening across after it, tell-tale dark movement among the wet leaves. As they got nearer they saw a limp paw, half hidden by leaves, then a thin and wizened snout, and a face bloodied, its wrinkles marked out by dried blood and pain, its eyes but half open as they stared, or sought to stare, up towards the Stone. It was Husk, half buried by leaves driven by the wind. Chater stretched out a paw to hold Whillan back so that Privet might go on alone to find out for herself what the Newborns had done to her mentor and friend.

Whether he had been alive or dead, she would have done as she did then, going swiftly forward, speaking his name gently and with love and reaching out her paws to take up his light old head and cuddle it, and snout at it, and say that she had come.

She found Husk alive, but only just. As she held him close he seemed to sigh, and the look of pain on his face eased to one of comfort and content. For a moment Chater and Whillan thought he had just then passed on to the Stone, for his body, which had been shivering beneath its covering of leaves, stilled and went limp. But his eyes opened and half smiled, and turned to look into Privet's, and then, in a whisper that was like the final rustles of last autumn's leaves before the winds of new times and seasons, he said, 'Memories of old friends, old stories, kept me alive until you came. Knew you would come. Yes, yes, knew that.'

'I didn't want ever to leave you, Keeper Husk,' said Privet. 'I thought you'd be safe, and now you and Pumpkin –'

'He's safe?' asked Husk, his face darkening until he sensed from Privet's touch that Pumpkin *was* safe. His face lightened with a soft smile. 'Good mole, he is. Would have fought for me. Pumpkin! But against them . . . against those moles he couldn't . . . and I said he mustn't. All my work, all my scribing, my thoughts –'

'Oh, Husk,' interrupted Privet, 'have they destroyed them? Pumpkin said –'

'No, no, my dear, I did not mean that. Paws cannot destroy what a mind thinks and dreams and knows. No, no . . . I was just trying to say that all my work has been towards not hurting others. The Stone Mole said that violence is not the way. I would not have another hurt on my account. Pumpkin cried when they hit me but when I ordered him not to hit back he was still. Yes, they have destroyed the books, and broken the tunnels down to let the wind and rain add to the destruction of their paws.'

'Oh, Husk!'

Privet bent her head and wept her tears into his frail body and Whillan watched helpless and much moved as Husk's paw feebly tried to pat and caress her shoulder, as if, even when he was so near death, his thoughts were for her.

'My dear, it's not as it seems, at all, it's not . . .' His breathing became more difficult and Privet pulled away, sniffed, and with Chater coming forward to help, tenderly examined the wounds that Husk had suffered. In truth they were less severe than they had seemed at first, being deep cuts and lacerations to his head and left flank from talon thrusts, rather than anything worse.

But from the amount of blood, and the way that his skin and fur had broken and folded back, it was easy to see how Pumpkin had been convinced that it was from his wounds that he was dying. To Privet, looking at him now, it was all too plain that what ailed him was the shock of these recent events on his frail body, and exposure to the elements all night long. The assault he had suffered had been less than it seemed, and perhaps the Newborns who had come to his burrows had intended to do no more than frighten him, their true objective being to destroy his books.

Had his wounds been deeper, and his body less frail, there might have been something they could have done, if only to remove him from the clearing to somewhere safer and warmer. But it was all too plain that rather than delaying his death, such a move would more likely hasten it, and anyway, as if understanding that moving him might be half in their minds, he whispered; 'Leave me be: here, where I can see the Stone; here, where others of Duncton have come to die, or have sacrificed their lives. I feel their great spirits with me now, and am content to end my time in such companionship. My life has been devoted to the scholarship of memory, and I have come to see that I am part, as we all are, of something greater and wiser than I knew.'

He indicated to Privet to have Whillan hold him a little more upright, that he might speak to them the easier. His breathing was coming with increasing difficulty.

'Privet, my dear, and you, Whillan . . . and your friend, whom I don't think I know, listen now, for there are some things I wish to say. It seems that Pumpkin has told you most of what happened – of how the Newborns crept up on us in the night with such a force of moles as would have defeated a whole community, not just two bookish moles like us. Then they began destroying my tunnels in frustration.'

'Frustration' repeated Privet.

'Oh yes! They seemed to think they might find something special in your Collection, something they would not name.'

'The Book of Silence,' whispered Husk with a smile, *'that's* what they came looking for.'

'But surely, Keeper Husk . . . !' began Privet in astonishment.

'Surely nothing!,' said Husk, with something of his old impatience. 'I told them I had no such Book, only a Collection of texts from which, through many decades, I had made up a modest and thoroughly unsatisfactory Book of Tales. They did not believe me and, like all moles who do not understand the nature of a question they have asked, and distrust the answer they receive, being unsatisfied they tried to destroy what they did not understand. But in doing that they made *me* understand . . .'

He shifted his body a little as if to ease himself from pain, but instead went suddenly breathless, and all he could do for a time was cling on to their paws and stare at the Stone while he struggled for normality once more.

'Do not try to talk to us any more now,' said Whillan, 'it can wait till later.'

'W . . . w . . . wait?' gasped Husk. 'Won't say much when I'm dead, that's for sure! No, mole, you remember that it's now or never in life, now or never. Where was I?'

'They made you understand . . . ?' said Privet softly.

'Yes, Privet, yes, my dear. They did. Of course they couldn't find the Book of Silence but when they started to destroy the tunnels, and bring out my books into the open which I had tried to preserve so long . . . do you know, after the first shock I felt relief, such relief to see all that clutter go and there at last I saw a tale I had searched for for so long. The one I always said would be the last tale, you *know*, my dear, I told you.'

'You mean the tale you called "The Sound of Silence"?'

'That's the one! It was *there*, waiting in the clutter. There all the time, amongst the folios *you* dealt with, you. I had passed it over, but you . . . it's your tale to make and tell, Privet. That's why I couldn't find it, and Cobbett couldn't, and scholars have never found it. It was not made, *it was waiting to be made*.'

'I don't understand, Keeper Husk,' said Privet urgently. 'Please try to explain because it's hard, it feels hard . . .'

'Oh it is hard, very very hard,' said Husk. 'As for explaining . . . but you'll find the courage to find it. Don't you remember what I said about that tale when you first came to me . . . ?'

'You said that all that was known of the tale of the Sound of Silence was a fragment that said "in its beginning is its ending, and in its ending is its beginning" and that you did not understand . . .'

'Today I understood, Privet, I understood at last and I believe that in the past others have understood as well, yet not said what it was they knew. But you know the sound of silence, Privet, you *know* . . .'

'No!' cried out Privet, staring where Husk stared blindly, at the Stone.

'Yes, my dear, and now you must go forward towards it and I shall

408

die content knowing that I have known the mole who will complete the Book of Tales and in that ending find a beginning greater by far than all we could have hoped for.'

'I am not worthy!' whispered Privet, as Whillan and Chater, not understanding at all what Husk was really getting at, or why it should have made Privet so distressed, looked at each other in wonderment.

'Yet,' whispered Husk weakly, for now it was plain he was sinking lower, and what strength he had had was all but gone, 'yet the one thing all my researches showed beyond a shadow of a doubt was that the sound of silence had to do with a Master of the Delve. I wish . . .'

'But, Keeper Husk,' said Whillan impetuously, and before Privet could stop him, 'there *is* mole others call a Master of the Delve, there is . . .'

'A Master of the Delve has come?' whispered Husk, awe on his face, reverence in his voice. 'This mole Rooster, whom Privet would not talk about?'

'Aye, that's the one!' said Chater, studiously ignoring Privet's silent pleas for them not to disturb Husk more.

'Well, of course,' said Husk after a moment, '*of course* Privet wouldn't have told me. Too frightened to, don't you see! Too afraid of what it meant. *I* would have been too. Well, it's out in the open now, isn't it, and you can't pretend it's not, Privet! So! I did get as far with my Book of Tales as I could have done. Privet, I let you take most of it up to the Library, and some remnants too, so it's safe even if the sources it came from have been destroyed. Promise me this: you'll scribe the last tale of the Book before you do anything else, scribe it for me. Tell me that and I'll die content, my work accomplished. Tell me . . .'

'Keeper Husk, I cannot . . .'

'Mole, I ask you to do it!' said Husk, turning to her and reaching a feeble paw desperately up towards her face.

'Privet . . .' said Chater warningly, 'you can't run from things always.'

'It's but a tale to scribe, Privet,' said Whillan, 'you can surely promise Keeper Husk that!'

It was Husk smiled and shook his head.

''Tis not just a tale, young mole, and nor can Privet be blamed for running from something that most moles cannot even contemplate facing,' he said, as if Privet was not there. 'It's because she knows how formidable the task is that she's tried to escape from it. 'Twas wrong of me to ask her to promise such a thing . . . but *you*, Privet, it must be you. You who sought to run from life, you are the one to see my work to its conclusion. Yet not my work alone. Many many moles' work, allmoles' work; you, my dear, you must try to scribe and continue even when you fail. Continue then and you will discover what I could not.'

'But, Keeper, I cannot, I am—'

'You shall find the way in contemplation of what I have left behind, and in contemplation of the Silence of the Stone. Others will help, for nomole is alone in any task, least of all this great one towards the Book, the last Book . . . It was so near to me all those long years, so very near and now, at the end, I am blessed to know a little of what will surely be.'

'Stay to guide me,' whispered Privet, her paws encircling him, her voice weak and shaking.

'No strength for that, my dear, and I have done all that I can. My task is almost over now.' Then turning to Whillan he said, 'Tell me that *you*'ll help her, Whillan.'

Whillan could only nod his promise that he would, for tears coursed down his face and such words as he had could not then have been clearly spoken.

Husk nodded, and looked down at his old paws, smiling, then up to the Stone once more, and back at last to the listening moles.

'Whillan, you must travel as your adopted mother has. Only through a journey of experience is a true scribe made. Therefore, journey forth, discover, question, seek out, always remembering that your roots are here, like these great beeches, and you must one day return here and help her as you have promised to do. The Book is incomplete, the last tale must be lived before it can be told. Therefore . . .' But here he coughed, a weak, racking cough, and for a time could hardly catch his breath.

'You, mole,' he said at last, turning to Chater.

'I'm Chater, sir, a journeymole.'

'Fieldfare's mate . . .'

Chater looked surprised that Husk knew, and the old mole suddenly chuckled and said, 'The Wood whispers much to moles who listen. Well, mole, see that Privet is watched over. She's not a strong mole, and needs others about.'

'She does, sir. We . . . value her. We'll watch over her.'

'Yes, yes,' said Husk, turning from Chater back to the Stone. 'Now, help me, for I would touch the Duncton Stone one last time; help me . . .'

410

So Chater went to Husk's other flank as Privet and Whillan continued to support him, and then all three lifted the old mole across the clearing towards the Stone.

'Oh yes,' whispered Husk, striving to reach out before them, his eyes full of the Stone's Light, and joy in the last words he spoke: 'Yes! *Now* I hear the Sound of Silence, Privet, you can surely hear it too . . .'

And they knew, even as they carried him to the base of the Stone, that old Husk had found his strength again, and now journeyed on ahead of them, purposeful, joyful, certain, fulfilled, into the Light and the Silence of the Stone.

They laid him where he died, and even as they backed away from him and Privet spoke the ancient liturgy of farewell, the winds stirred again, the branches threshed and the wet leaves swirled, half covering Husk where he lay. It seemed that he was already fading into the memories of earth and time, to be reborn in a tale yet to be told.

'Yet to be told . . .' whispered Privet. 'He said the last Book had to be lived before it could be told. But he *is* part of that last tale; he was trying to tell us that here, now, what has just been, what will be, are all parts of the great Book of Silence. Do you see, Whillan? *We* are the last Book.'

But Whillan's snout was low, and his head bowed down, and he wept for the death, the first death of a mole he loved.

Whilst Chater, suddenly aware of how exposed they were, began to look about at the lengthening shadows beyond the clearing, then stanced up restlessly and broke into their grief to warn that they must go before others saw them. Their task here was surely done.

'Yes,' said Privet vaguely, 'yes, it is. Come, Whillan, there is no more we can do for Keeper Husk, and we have other work to do.'

Whillan wiped his eyes with both paws, coughed, nodded, sniffled at the air, and said as bravely as he could, 'So! We're the Book that's yet untold, are we! We better make it worth the telling then, hadn't we, Chater? Hadn't we, Privet?'

His sudden good humour was what they all needed, and Chater said, 'There's no sadness in a life well lived, and Keeper Husk seemed to have done that. Of his Book of Tales and all of that I know nothing, and can say nothing. And as for that task of scribing his last tale, which he called the Sound of Silence, I can't for the life of me see why you couldn't undertake to do it. But despite your failings I swear by our great Stone that I shall do my best to watch over you, Privet, as Husk

411

bade me do. And I'll warrant that Whillan here will always do the same.'

'I swear it,' said Whillan impetuously. 'Over Husk's body I swear it.'

The clouds darkened as Privet said gladly, 'I know you will, my dear, and you, Chater, as your Fieldfare has always done, from the day I came to Duncton Wood. It is a comfort to have such friends. Now: we must go across-slope to Husk's burrows, for there may be texts there that can be saved and taken to the Library. I would like to go there now, before darkness comes, and more rain.'

'Well . . .' began Chater dubiously, furrowing his brow and contemplating the possible dangers.

'Come on!' said Whillan suddenly, all eagerness and energy, anxious to get away from the clearing. 'We'll survive better than any texts! You're always so cautious, Chater!'

'Caution got me where I am – here, alive and in one piece!' said the journeymole stoutly. 'And I dare say caution got Privet here where she is! You come back here in twenty moleyears as alive and well as we are and I'll hazard you'll declare caution saw *you* through. Now, let's get going.'

As Chater led them out of the clearing, growling and grumbling about caution and hot-heads, Privet smiled, and Whillan, winking at her, grinned and let her pass. With one last look back at the Stone, and at Husk's little body that lay so near it, now almost obscured by leaves, Whillan raised a paw in salute and farewell, and turned to follow the other two.

Just as Chater watched protectively over Privet and Whillan on their journeys through the Wood that day, Maple had to do the same for Stour and Drubbins on their journey upslope to the Library, and his courage and strength had been needed, and not found wanting.

They had left a short time after Chater and his group, leaving Pumpkin safely behind in Fieldfare's burrow for her to attend to whilst he recovered from the shock of the night attack, which it seemed it would take him some time to do. Maple had insisted that Fieldfare take poor Pumpkin to the quietest and more obscure part of her tunnels, and so she chose a place that Chater had prudently delved the previous summer as one of safe retreat in case troubled times came to Duncton.

Thus satisfied that the two were safe, and leaving them with strict orders not to move even into adjacent tunnels until Chater or he himself came calling her name, Maple went out on to the surface to lead his elderly charges up to the Library.

It was his wish to travel by as obscure a route as he could find, but Stour and Drubbins were not prepared to journey through their own system like fugitives hurriedly seeking sanctuary and so they travelled along the major communal route that runs from the Eastside up to the edge of the High Wood, much of which uses labyrinthine surface runs amidst the roots of the ash and beeches in those parts. Overhung and shadowed as it is, in places so hemmed in that moles can only go along in single file, conscious that they can be watched unseen or their passage easily blocked, it is not a route to make a fearful mole feel secure, and Maple was not happy taking it. The more so because the Wood was shaken still by the wild winds of the night's storm, and their progress was slowed by drifts of wet leaves and the detritus of dead twigs and branches that had fallen in the night.

But if Stour was aware of how vulnerable they were to attack, he did not show it in the least; on the contrary, he dawdled along, chattering to his old friend Drubbins about great storms of the past and other such irrelevancies (as they seemed to the increasingly impatient Maple).

But Master Librarians are not to be hurried, and if Maple was at first somewhat brusque in his anxiety to get Stour over and round the more awkward places and obstacles his mood soon gave way to one similar to that of Drubbins, who showed a more kindly appreciation that this journey through the Wood might well be Stour's last before his self-imposed incarceration in the lost tunnels of the Ancient System, and he might therefore wish to prolong and enjoy it.

So it was that Maple's impatience gave way to something more philosophical, and whilst remaining watchful he suppressed his fears and enjoyed instead the old mole's cheerful discourse about the history of the Wood about them, and those who had lived there long ago.

'I don't suppose you've ever even noticed that tree there!' said Stour, turning suddenly to Maple and pointing to a sterile trunk from which most of the bark had long since fallen, leaving only a thick pale shaft with a moss-covered base. The main part of the tree had rotted and collapsed into itself where it had fallen decades before, and was covered now in ivy and the fronds of withywind.

'I'd hardly call it a tree now, Master,' declared Maple, 'and what remains needs only a blast of wind from the right direction to topple it for ever.'

'Well, we'll all be like that one day, Maple, just remnants of what we were, even you! But I'll tell you something about that tree. Look at its topmost part, where the trunk broke off. What do you see?'

Maple peered upwards and saw that the highest edge was all rough and blackened, except where some bird, a rook perhaps, had used it as a staging-post and stained it grey. Maple shrugged his shoulders, uncertain what the Master was getting at.

'You see, Maple, coming from the Westside as you do, you would have no reason to know that this tree marks the highest point to which the great fire of Bracken's day reached. At the base of this very tree a party of moles, stricken by fire and half suffocated by smoke, unable and unwilling to progress further because an elderly member of their party was too weak to continue, crouched together in expectation of death. The fire came roaring up to them and they prayed to the Stone for a miracle of deliverance. Out of the High Wood came a mighty and wrathful wind, sent no doubt by the Stone, and it confronted the fire and fought with it, and after a tremendous struggle over the very heads of those good and faithful moles, when sparks flew, and fires roared and flaming branches fell all about them, the fire was stopped and came no further, and so they were saved.'

All thought of the present danger they might be in fled from Maple's mind as the old mole deftly recounted this nearly-forgotten incident from the legendary days of Bracken and Rebecca, and he stared among the roots of the old tree, and then up again at the last evidence of the fire.

'There are many such reminders of the past throughout our beloved system,' said Stour, 'whose meaning and memory are passed down from parents to pup, from old mole to young, as testimony that ours is not the only generation, ours not the only task, and that many have gone before us, living and feeling, hoping and loving, longing and finally dying, as we must do.

'Remember this tree, Maple, and that its old dead trunk, which seems to have nothing left to give, can still tell a tale worth remembering to the mole who knows what language it speaks. And though the names of the moles who once sheltered here may be forgotten – and certainly none could remember them when I first heard the tale on this very spot from my father's mouth – their courage and their faith lives on. Our heritage is something we all need at some time to remind us of our origin and identity. Remember that, Maple, always remember it.'

Maple stared down at the old mole and saw as it seemed for the first time how solid his paws were upon the ground, for all their pale frailty. Before such wisdom, and such truth to the past, all present troubles seemed as nothing.

'Master . . .' began Maple, for he sensed suddenly that such another chance as this to talk to moledom's greatest scholar and librarian might never come his way, and he felt time was running out and that all his years of waiting as a warrior in the side tunnels of life were over, and great things, dangerous things, were on them now and that here, right here before him, was the making of memory he might one day need. So . . .

'Master,' he began, wondering what it was he sought.

'I see you need reassurance, Maple,' said Stour. 'Fear not, for though I myself have never been as close to the Stone as I would wish since doubts get in my way, I know it is there for all to find and trust. It will give you no task you have not strength and courage to fulfil, nor place you before any enemy you cannot overcome, so long as its Light and Silence are in what you seek to do.'

'And you, Master? Will you be safe?'

Old Stour smiled, his pale eyes clear, his gaze on Maple like that of a father upon a son: 'No, no, I shall not be safe. None of us are ever "safe". But loved in the Stone I shall be, even I who have so many doubts of faith and whom some have called an unbeliever! The Stone's Silence is my destination now and I shall be safer in retreat trying to find it than if an army of the greatest Siabod moles that ever lived came to look after me.

'But now the Wood trembles for itself, the winds fret, and this old librarian grows cold and hungry and tired. Lead me on, Maple, deliver me up to where I would be "safe"! And remember that I loved this system, and value more highly a single morning in its company than all the honours and the power that my years of scholarship and work with moledom's greatest texts might bring.'

'I will, Master, always!' said Maple fervently.

Soon after that their route grew clearer and they passed into the High Wood, so that a journey that had seemed so slow to Maple at first, was suddenly and regretfully over. The entrance down into the Library loomed and Stour paused one last time to look about the leafless beeches of the High Wood, and through the windswept dells that stretched into the distance to east and to west, over to the south, and back downslope to the north.

Stour's face grew grim, as did Drubbins' beside him, and when in later years Maple recounted that historic moment, he would say that though he had no sense then that moledom's history was turning there in the wood that day with them, yet something made him look around as well, as if it felt important that he should remember the Wood as Stour then saw it.

'Remember!' the Master had said, and looking around him Maple knew he always would, and that one day when time had given perspective to that moment and that day, he would understand better what it was he had been party to. He moved a little way from his charges the better to look about.

He was brought out of this moment of reverie by the sound of movement, and looking back to Stour and Drubbins once more he found they had turned from the scene about them, ducked their heads, and were halfway through the entrance of the tunnel that led into the Library, and their pawsteps were already echoing ahead of them into a dark future nomole could foresee.

Chapter Thirty-Three

But the future was already happening, and bringing discomfort and dismay to the moles who might have seemed the least endangered of all: Fieldfare and Pumpkin.

After the others had set out on their risky treks across the Wood, Pumpkin had lain meekly enough for a time, recovering from the battering and shock he had received, first with fitful sleep, then with the food and tender loving care that Fieldfare was so adept at providing to anymole that needed looking after, and then with a time of deeper sleep. But then he woke, and he felt refreshed and restless and was up on his paws and eager to be doing.

'Doing what, Pumpkin? Our orders are to stay here and stay here we shall,' said Fieldfare.

'Doing *something*,' he replied, 'that's what. Why, a library aide can't just lie about with the day advanced, the Master on the way to the Library, with scholars needing help all over the wood and with Rolls, Rhymes and Tales in ruins and awaiting attention. Why, this is a *crisis*, Fieldfare, and nomole is going to say that old Pumpkin failed to serve when he was most needed!'

With this he looked about the chamber for a way out on to the surface, and seeing it, struggled to raise himself up and head towards it. But seeing his intention, and wishing to thwart it, Fieldfare placed her ample frame in front of the only exit and looked determined.

'Maple said we were to stay here until he or Chater came back and that's what we'll do –'

'Is that the way out?' interrupted Pumpkin, pointing over her plump shoulder, then trying ineffectually to squeeze by.

'It doesn't matter if it is, we must stay here, my dear,' said Fieldfare. 'Have another worm and *rest*, you can do no good out there.'

'I can do no good in here!' declared Pumpkin, too polite to try to push his way past, even if he could have managed to shift her, and so dancing about from paw to paw. 'There's *work* to do, Fieldfare. Dear me, I can't just *stay* here.'

'You must, Pumpkin.'

'Let me by!' said Pumpkin, suddenly making a dive for a gap a quarter his size between her rounded flank and the portal's side. They locked in a reluctant embrace which after only a few moments left Pumpkin breathless and dazed. He was not made for fighting, nor even tussling, and never had been.

'Dear oh dear, this is unseemly and quite unnecessary!' he sighed at last, falling back and pawing at his patchy fur to get it straight again. 'How can I persuade you to let me go and do my duty?'

'I'm only doing mine,' said Fieldfare amiably, 'and I must say you are making it very difficult . . .'

But, if she had been about to say more, or Pumpkin about to continue the argument, neither did so, but instead fell silent. From somewhere above them, out on the surface, came a shout and the patter of solid, stealthy paws. Then more such sounds, and the gathering of three or four moles right above their heads.

Fieldfare backed away from the entrance she had been defending, her eyes suddenly afraid.

'They're Newborns, Pumpkin,' she whispered, 'I *know* they are.' Anger, despair, fear and apprehension were in her face.

The pawsteps ran about above them, there was another shout, and the sounds went away, beyond the chamber's roof.

'They've found the eastern entrance,' whispered poor Fieldfare, coming clear of the portal and stancing close to Pumpkin.

For a moment the library aide saw his way was clear to escape, and indeed he considered doing so. But only for a moment, for his sense of duty to the Library was quite overcome by the need, most unfamiliar to such a mole as he who until the night before had never been in trouble in his life, but who now once more . . . by the need . . . to defend Fieldfare. Redoubtable she might be, but despite her protestations the night before about having lost all fear, a sense of horror came over her as the stealthy pawsteps and voices began to echo about her tunnels reminding her of her time in the Marsh End and then, horror compounded with horror, to come closer. And with them voices . . .

'This way!'

'It goes on down here!'

'I'm sure these are the tunnels where Sister Fieldfare and her consort in sin the journeymole Chater live!'

Sister Fieldfare?

It was enough to freeze Fieldfare into a stance of despairing hopeless fear, in which her kindly face, her generous flanks, her gentle paws, seemed to shrink and wither before Pumpkin's eyes.

418

'The Stone will protect us!' he said fiercely, outraged that anything or anymole could have such an effect on good Fieldfare.

'They've come for me,' whispered Fieldfare, 'as they said they would!'

'The Stone will not have this!' declared Pumpkin stoutly, Fieldfare's terrible fear his sudden strength. 'Stay still and say not a single word!' he ordered. 'Leave things to me!'

'To you?' said Fieldfare, looking wildly around the chamber as if in hope of finding something or somemole more substantial than Pumpkin.

'Sister Fieldfare!' came the Newborn call again, insinuating itself down the nearby tunnel and into the chamber where they now stanced in dismay and fear. Hearing it Fieldfare wilted still further, and all her normal resolve was gone, as with one last vestige of courage and concern for others she said hopelessly, 'I must go to them and perhaps they'll not find you . . .'

'Yes, me!' cried out Pumpkin, brushing busily at his flanks and sleeking his meek face-fur down as if in hope of making himself more presentably fierce. 'Leave things to me. Certainly you must.'

It was as feeble a war-cry as ever moledom heard, yet war-cry it was, if only for an army of one, and with it, and with no thought of his own safety at all, Pumpkin turned towards the portal which until then had been denied him by the very mole he was now seeking to protect, and went out into the tunnel to face their Newborn adversaries.

When he was gone Fieldfare sank down to the earthen floor, head low, snout abject, eyes half closed as her spirit began to die. And so she stayed, even when voices drifted down to her, the first being Pumpkin's.

'Looking for Sister Fieldfare?' he called out.

'We are!' cried out several purposeful voices.

'Well, you'll not find her here. Wrong tunnel, wrong burrow.'

'And who are *you?*' a cold voice asked. Young, strong and zealous.

'Library Aide Pumpkin and you're in my tunnels.'

'Brother, would you not welcome us?'

'Welcome you? Me? Old Pumpkin's glad to see anymole, of course. Ha, ha, ha.' Pumpkin's cracked laugh was the laugh of nervousness and fear.

'Any other moles down there with you, Brother?'

'Hundreds!' said Pumpkin. 'Oh yes, they all flock to Pumpkin's flank! Pumpkin's so incredibly popular! Ha, ha, ha! Come and see for yourself!'

419

There was a dreadful pause, and then these nightmare words from another mole, a female mole, a mole Fieldfare knew.

'We will,' said Bantam, and pawsteps came nearer, and long shadows and the acrid scent of zealots played at the portal beside which Fieldfare crouched. Her fur was spiky with the sweat of terror, her eyes staring, her chest tight, and heaving with the gulping, shallow breaths of panic.

'I thought these were Fieldfare's tunnels,' said Bantam.

'They were,' piped Pumpkin, 'but she consorts now with Chater the journeymole and lives upslope of here.'

'Hmmph!' muttered Bantam, pausing but moments from the portal, her fierce shadow falling upon the floor of the chamber.

Bantam's snout appeared at the portal; then a glimpse of a paw, then a flank, and in Fieldfare's chest her heart beat again and again and again, faster and faster, such that it must surely be heard. And she wanted to cry out, 'I am here, take me! Release me from this doubt!'

'Here,' said Fieldfare to the portal at last, 'I am here!'

But her terror was too complete for her voice to carry far, and before her whispered declaration could be heard Bantam turned and was gone.

Fieldfare could not afterwards remember what happened next, except for some dim sense that she had been rushed out through the tunnels, and out on to the surface to a place of safety, away from the Newborns.

However it had been, she 'woke' from a state of shock to the urgent bidding of Pumpkin's voice, and found herself in the rough shelter of a tangled bramble bush out on the slopes far enough away from her burrow not to recognize the place.

'Come on, Fieldfare, you've got to move, more might come. You must *try* because I haven't got the strength to take you any further. More Newborns might come, or the others might come back.'

So, in response to his urgent pleas, she came out of the fear she had been in.

'Where are we?' she began.

'As far from your burrows as I could get you before you collapsed,' said Pumpkin, somewhat ruefully. If *her* chest had been thumping earlier from fear, *his* was heaving in and out now from the unaccustomed and unwelcome effort of pushing and shoving a female mole twice his size through the Wood.

'I didn't go upslope towards the Library,' he explained, 'because that's the way they went, thinking they'd find you there. I didn't go east because that would have brought us to the Wood's edge and with nowhere left to go. I didn't go north downslope because that's where they came from. So I brought you westward. And anyway . . .'

As he explained himself in his roundabout and pedantic way, Fieldfare had time to catch up with herself, realize she was all right and they were both safe; having passed through the death of extreme fear she was beginning to feel the surging courage of rediscovered life.

As this welcome change came over her, Pumpkin had looked slowly westward, and interrupted himself in a strange voice and with those words: 'And anyway . . .'

His breathing slowed, light came to his eyes and with it a look of purpose quite different from that which had overtaken him when Fieldfare had been in such peril. Now another kind of strength entered him, and he stanced up, mouth half open with his unfinished thought and sentence, looking like a mole who has caught sight of something among distant trees, something he cannot see clearly but for which he has searched for a long time.

'What is it, Pumpkin?' asked Fieldfare.

'It's Rolls and Rhymes, yes, it's there. We must go there. It'll be all right if we go there.'

'Then let's go there!' said Fieldfare, now quite ready to do whatever the brave and courageous and most purposeful Pumpkin advised her. He had been right thus far and she had no reason to think that the Stone would not see him right to the end.

'Work to do . . .' he muttered, 'lots of work . . .' and away he busily led her, out of the temporary shelter he had found and on through the Wood towards where once old Husk had lived.

But they had hardly started before scattered drops of rain came down, now before them, now behind them, now to their right and left. Then the rain stopped and wind flurried by. Then a few drops of rain fell once more, and the sky darkened with heavy clouds that were the tide of time.

'Must get there quickly, Fieldfare, to save what texts we can,' said Pumpkin, and Fieldfare saw that his eyes still held the light of a task ahead.

It was that same rain which woke Privet, Whillan and Chater from the strange sleep they had fallen into.

They had left the clearing after Husk's death and final passage to the Stone's Silence, but their plan of going to Rolls and Rhymes had soon faltered, and it was not Privet who slowed them down, but Chater.

Just as, unknown to each other, Pumpkin in one place, and Maple in another, had had revealed to them a glimpse of the Stone's Light and need for their support, so Chater had as well. The strongest had weakened, for not long after leaving the clearing he had paused and said he felt . . . Well, he knew not what he felt: strange; tired; sick.

But to Privet it seemed that the light in his eyes was more alive than anything she had seen there before, and to Whillan this sudden faltering of Chater was all of a piece with the mystery of that morning, when the Stone rather than themselves seemed to be directing them.

'Can't go on, Privet, must rest for a bit,' Chater had said, astonished at his own feebleness, and wishing to reach out for something that lay ahead of him at the same time as he wanted to find a temporary burrow and close his eyes and yield up to the heavy tiredness that inexplicably beset him. It was Whillan who took charge, finding a scrape that would serve to give them shelter from the adversities of the day, where they might rest until Chater was recovered.

But what began as rest for Chater drifted in no time at all into sleep for all of them, and huddled together in fatigue they slid into a dreamless darkness, and the Stone watched over them.

Until, towards midday, the plop! plop! plop! of rain on the leaf-litter just above their heads woke them with a start, and they knew as one that they must go to Rolls and Rhymes immediately. It was just that they had needed time to pause.

So it was that by the time they arrived at the ruins of Rolls and Rhymes, Pumpkin and Fieldfare had been there all morning, and long since discovered that there was little left to save but the few broken fragments of texts and folios which had by chance found shelter from the torrential storm under some fallen branch or projecting root when the Newborns had done their destructive work. But almost all the precious material had been scattered out on to the open surface, and exposed to wind and rain the long night through, and was now sodden, broken, indecipherable – lost to moledom for ever.

When he had first seen the ruined tunnels of the place, and the destruction the Newborns had so effectively wrought, the light of hope that had shone in Pumpkin's eyes had faded, and he had wept. But then his long training in the care of texts had reasserted itself, and he had wandered here and there, sifting out the few remnants that made sense to him, while Fieldfare kept watch, and encouraged him as best she could in his work.

'They knew what they were doing, Deputy Keeper Privet,' he said sombrely. When he heard of Husk's death he openly broke down and cried, as much for what seemed the death of a lifetime of work as for Husk. 'They made sure the rain got to everything, and even waited to see that it did, pulling out texts which were protected by others so that all suffered the same fate,' he said, his normally cheerful and positive voice as near to bitterness as any of them ever heard him get. 'But at least Keeper Husk is in the Silence of the Stone, which is a blessing in such a troubled time as this seems to be. We have that to be thankful for.'

But it was cold comfort, as he and Privet wandered miserably around the site, while Whillan peered here and there in the hope of finding something that had been overlooked and might still be preserved, and Fieldfare and Chater watched over them all, together again, one ever the comfort of the other.

'I shouldn't have left you, my beloved,' said Chater miserably, alternately punishing himself by insisting that Fieldfare repeat what had happened and tell of the narrow escape she had had, and congratulating Pumpkin on his bold fooling of the Newborns and 'that bloody Bantam'.

The Newborns had done their work of destruction so well that it was at first quite difficult to work out the line of tunnels that both Privet and Whillan had once known so well, but they persisted in clambering over the open exposed ground in the hope that they might at least find that the Newborns had not penetrated into Husk's inner sanctum, and found and destroyed his Book of Tales.

'If we could just find that,' said Privet, 'then his work will not have been in vain. Nomole but he knew what was in that great work, except for those few of us honoured to hear him tell a tale or two. If only we could find . . .'

But though at last they worked out where his scribing place had been – now just a heap of rutted earth and a mess of obliterated texts – nothing more seemed to be there at all.

'All gone,' whispered Privet at last, 'all but the few things you found, Pumpkin, before the later rains came and finished off the work.'

But what were they? Nothing of consequence at all.

'We could try delving in the spoil in the hope that a few texts have been covered up,' said Pumpkin, and they did, but nothing did they find.

Or almost nothing.

For just as Whillan and Privet were giving up, and Chater was suggesting that they should make their way to the Library before darkness came, Pumpkin unearthed the first complete unbroken folio they had found.

'Why, it's one of the discards from his Book of Tales,' said Privet in astonishment, smiling ruefully, and explaining that these were things she herself had specially preserved, and of all things to survive . . .

'At least they are in Husk's paw, and a relic worth keeping if only for that!' she said.

'And the text he's scored out is clear enough,' said Whillan, running his snout and then his paw over the folio.

'Perhaps there are some more where you found this,' said Privet.

'Aye,' said Whillan, going forward to delve, 'perhaps there are some more.'

Then, most uncharacteristically, Pumpkin grew quite fierce, reaching out a paw to hold Whillan back and saying in a voice that was both warning and plea, 'No, Whillan, that's my task!'

It was not only Privet who saw the light of purpose come to Pumpkin's mild eyes, for Fieldfare saw it too and instinctively grasped Chater's paw with her own as if she sensed as well that something was apaw now in that place, and it was more than mole.

'Let Pumpkin delve, Whillan,' said Privet quietly. And delve he did, and found the discarded folios from Husk's great work all but complete, neat, dry, as good as when Privet herself had set them to one side. Pumpkin took them up carefully and laid them out for Privet to examine.

The wind had died, and a still, pale afternoon was on them before Pumpkin came back with the last of the discarded folios. He was tired and needed a rest and the food they gave. Then, paw-weary though he was, he bravely said, 'I've strength enough in my old paws for one last trek this day! If you're in front, Chater, and Whillan's behind, and the rest of you around, I'll get there!'

'And where would that be, mole?' asked Chater jocularly, respect in his voice.

'Why, the Library of course!' said Pumpkin. 'That's where we must go! And if you don't mind indulging an old Library aide I'll carry these folios myself. There's a right way of doing even the humblest tasks!'

'The Library it is!' said Chater, and off they went through the gloom of the still, damp afternoon.

Chapter Thirty-Four

'The Master is in his scribing cell,' said Keeper Sturne impassively when they arrived in the Main Chamber of the Library. 'He instructed me to inform you that you are to ascend to consult with him. Even you, Library Aide Pumpkin. Even you. He needs me not it seems!'

There was bitterness and defeat in his voice, and hearing it, and believing that he knew its cause, Whillan thought it a pity that some moles seemed never quite to fulfil their ambitions, and so lived perpetually dissatisfied. Sturne held his gaze as if he knew his thoughts, and Whillan looked down discomfited, hoping that if ever the day came when he reached a point in his life when hope declined and ambitions seemed all spoiled, he would not be as bitter as this mole Sturne.

'Deputy Master Snyde has been sent for and will be here before long,' continued Sturne. 'The Master wishes to see you now.' Then as they mounted the ramp he added tersely, 'The mole Maple and Elder Drubbins are there already . . .'

'Why is the Library so empty of mole?' asked Privet, pausing for a moment and turning back to look down at Sturne. 'Where are all the aides and scholars?'

'When he came today the Master ordered that they go to Barrow Vale for the Meeting on the morrow.'

'And you, Sturne?' said Privet. She had always regarded him with respect, if not with affection, for though he had little to say to moles as mole, he was a true scholar and lover of texts, and the truth was all he cared for.

Sturne shrugged. 'The Master wished it, and Meetings are only a place where moles talk, not a place to think.'

'Are they, Sturne?' she asked.

He stared up at her impassively, frowned, pursed his mouth and turned back to his text.

'You will call us when the Deputy Master comes?'

Sturne looked back and nodded brusquely before turning his back on them.

They found Stour talking quietly to Drubbins, with Maple deployed near the entrance through which they came, as watcher perhaps, though when they arrived he appeared to be dozing, his powerful head extended comfortably along his paws, his eyes closed. Though there were now so many moles crammed into the study cell, somehow its habitual hush imposed itself so that when Stour finished talking to Drubbins, a deep silence fell and they all waited expectantly for him to speak again.

At first, but for the occasional stir of Sturne in the Main Chamber below, there seemed no sound at all. But then there came to them the distant but awesome wind-sound of the Ancient System, whispering, harsh, a call from distant time, and the occasional warning vibration of Dark Sound.

''Tis always worse after a storm,' observed Stour.

The portal leading into that almost forgotten place was directly behind him, and it seemed to Privet, and the others too perhaps, that stancing there he looked at once its guardian and its victim, and she did not know whether to feel awe or sympathy.

Each knew that soon now he would turn from them and go into a final retreat to guard the six great Books of Moledom, and to pray that the Seventh might come soon that all moledom might know that its harmony and Silence had returned to ground. None believed that if he ever emerged from his retreat he would be the same mole they saw before them now. But the truth was that Stour was about to remove himself from life, and it was a prospect which each of them there regarded in a different way.

He seemed to sense their sympathy and understanding, for he looked around at them and smiling gently, nodded his head, and half sighed. He seemed about to speak, but something stopped him and he glanced down at his paws, and then round at all of them, as if he knew it was the last time he would see them in the way he now could.

Then, in a silence that deepened with each second that went by, but by the ominous wind-sound that seemed to threaten them all from beyond the chamber, the Master slowly approached them one by one, reached a paw to them and gazed into their eyes in a way that suggested he knew their innermost thoughts at that historic moment. It was to Fieldfare that he turned first.

She, like many others in Duncton, had come to regard Stour as the living symbol of the system's moral strengths and purpose; but now the Master looked old and lonely, and she began to cry. A part of her world was ending and she felt that this was a sad and incomprehensible way for it to go. Yet as he held her paw she felt her devotion towards him deepen further still, and knew that when he spoke to them all, as it seemed likely he would shortly do, she would abide by all he said, and seek hard to believe that there was sense behind the confusion and terrors of the present change.

At her flank even Chater was forced to clench his mouth and fight back his tears, for though he understood a little more of all that Stour had told them the previous evening, now he saw only a mole alone, who must face things whose terror was beyond imagining. It was not a way *he* would like to go.

For Pumpkin's part, he could only stare, and wonder at how events could so quickly change his life: that it *was* changed he had no doubt, and that it was to Privet he owed his loyalty and devotion the Stone had made clear to him. As for the Master, Pumpkin understood the inevitability of what he did, and knew enough of scribing and of history to know that where Stour was about to go other great scribes and thinkers had gone in times past.

Even the great and mysterious Boswell, White Mole, had his time of retreat. But *he* had survived it, and Pumpkin had the comfort of that scrap of history to fall back on, and the consolation of knowing moledom's battles on behalf of the Stone were fought in many ways, and perhaps its greatest warriors were those with the courage *not* to raise their paws in attack, or even defence, nor even to speak, but to take to themselves something of the Stone's Silence, and by example lead others towards that difficult but greatest of ways.

Already Pumpkin knew, or believed, that the Stone was with them in all of this. When Privet had earlier commanded him to hide the folios discarded by Husk and the cover of the Book of Tales, and when he had seen the last words Husk had scribed, he had felt that it was the Stone that spoke and so he trusted what was happening, and did not feel sad now in the presence of Stour.

Drubbins also understood something of this, and in truth he looked positively benign, comforted perhaps by the private talk he had had with the Master, and made easy with the equanimity that comes to some moles with growing age. His eyes were a little restless, for old though he was he had work to do outside – the Library was not and never had been his place, and he trusted absolutely in Stour's judgement about what he should do within it.

There were no tears in Whillan's eyes either, and he too was restless, but the reasons were rather different from Drubbins'. Though he was sensitive enough to the nature of the moment he was witnessing, perhaps more so than anymole there except Privet, he was still too young to make sense of the great tide and current of historic change he had felt massing in the system through these extraordinary hours. He was caught up in a wash of change, and turned and turned again by it with nothing solid in reach of his paws to touch and hold himself still by, while he made sense of it. More than that, he began to realize that what Husk had told him by the Stone as he lay dying, was true, *his* destiny lay beyond Duncton's familiar system, with moles and in places whose names he did not yet know or guess, where he must fulfil tasks which only the Stone could foresee or understand. For Whillan then, this moment of the Master's retreat was a farewell to his youth, and the beginning of the necessary acceptance, frightening and hard to believe, that the hour had come when he must turn his snout towards the life of adulthood, for which there was surely no time left for further training or preparation.

Perhaps Maple had similar feelings, though he was a full cycle of seasons older than Whillan. His own conviction of what he wished to be and do had been formed long since and was well known – he was a warrior, and thus far had been a warrior without a cause. But, with Pumpkin's help, he had learnt enough of scribing to wade through the great military texts of the past, and to live, again and again, the campaigns of ancient and modern times. Now he knew his hour had come, but he was no longer a hot-head, nor likely to be cruel or tyrannical in his discovery of might and power. The system's inherent good nature, and its Stone-loving moles, with Drubbins and Stour at their head, had prepared him well for the burden that he suspected, and hoped, was soon to come his way. When Stour had paused out on the surface earlier that day, and talked of the past, Maple had felt a great surge of love and faith in the system that had reared him, whose values then, now and for all his life he felt the Stone had given him special strengths and talents to defend. His time had come, and he was ready for it.

Last of all there was Privet, and on her old Stour's gaze lingered longest and most intently, as hers on him. She understood that where he was going was beyond mole's help – to that place of Silence where a mole's only friend is himself, his only strength his own courage, and his only hope in the dark night of his soul must be his faith in the Stone. So she stared at Stour now without tears in her eyes, but with a prayer in her heart for a mole who had nurtured her in her adopted system from the first, but who now had a task before him different from that of watching over and guiding others.

'He is our spiritual father and mother,' she said to herself, 'but now he can give us no more. The time for being taught is done, and the time for doing has begun. And he . . . he is about to begin his final and greatest trial of doubt in the Stone's power and if he is to survive it in spirit, if not in body, he must know that we are here, always here . . .'

So Privet understood, and did what none of them had, which was to reach her second paw to the Master's so that she had his between her own. And Whillan, who was watching all, saw that only before her did the Master's gaze falter, as if he saw something he could not bear to see; or, perhaps, sensed a strength beyond his own, which all of them, and especially he himself, would need.

'Yes,' Whillan whispered to himself, beginning to articulate those thoughts, 'it is Privet who must . . .'

But then the Master took his paw from Privet's and went back to his former stance by the portal into the Ancient System, and spoke to them all at last, saying, 'My friends, last moles that I shall know, you may be eager to tell me what happened this day out in the wood. To Husk, to Rolls and Rhymes, and to you, Fieldfare and Pumpkin . . .'

He raised a paw slightly as they all broke into a babble of talk to answer what seemed his questions, and they fell silent again.

'No, no, such matters are your concern now and I trust you to deal with them as you will. My world lies in the darkness of retreat beyond this place and I must let all past history go. Even matters which remain so far unresolved I must let be, trusting that others will find confidence in the Stone to do what they may to help and give support as they must. You, Privet, whose full tale I do not yet know, must find time and faith in the future to tell moles you can trust – your friends here, perhaps – what they will need to know if they are to help you in your tasks, for though you have told us of Rooster, of yourself, and all that happened since you left the Moors, you have said nothing, and hinted at little. Well, mole, you must choose your time and place to tell . . . but not now, not to me, that history is not mine. You others are its guardians now and it is a task I relinquish for ever, not entirely gladly, for there is much that I would know and shall miss. Yet I leave it with satisfaction, for you shall be abler guardians than I in the time of strife to come.

'Listen now, and remember. I am able now to leave you because you, Pumpkin, found the strength to join us, and make up the seven when I am gone. For seven shall be needed, to match the seven Stillstones, and the seven Books. Seven shall be needed to help recover the last Book, which is of Silence.'

'But Master,' said Chater, ever practical, ever blunt, 'what if one of us does not survive until the coming of the last Book?'

429

'What if the circle is broken?' said Stour softly. 'Well, now, the Stone will provide . . . or, at least, that is what I am meant to say. The Stone, the Stone – you all know my doubts. You all know that I have toiled all my life to believe its Silence and to have faith.'

'We know, Master,' said Privet. 'You have become the embodiment of the struggle against doubt across all moledom – your honesty is known.'

Stour nodded with genuine humility and then gave one of his rare and mischievous smiles.

'I have thought about the problem Chater raises, that one of you might not survive, and I have made provision for it. There is another mole –'

'Another?' said Whillan immediately. 'Tell us his name.'

'Or *her* name, Whillan. If you look around you, you will see that males do not have the sole prerogative in such things!'

'Female, then?' said Maple. 'It would be helpful to know.'

'The mole or moles concerned, whether male or female, or female or male, will make themselves known when they need to – I hope! If not then you'll know my doubts were justified. But enough of that; let the Stone sort out its own Seven Stancings. We have little time now before Deputy Master Snyde comes, and I wish to have all done by then, and be gone.

'I have a few short observations to make, and my last instructions as Master – though I prefer that you take them as no more than suggestions, to reject or modify as circumstances dictate. Last night I told you of my concerns about the system and moledom, and Privet informed us of matters of recent history, and of Rooster, Master of the Delve. Only Pumpkin here was not privy to those matters then, but I have asked Drubbins to inform him fully of them. I therefore have no more to say of that, except that I have little doubt that what Privet was moved to tell us of her past, and of the Master of the Delve, shall play its part in the events that are now beginning to unfold.

'Now, I have no doubt that moles who openly resist the Newborn way will soon find their life intolerable here in Duncton Wood, as Fieldfare's recent experience in the Marsh End shows. For this reason I believe that discretion is the better part of valour now, and that most of you should leave the system for a time. This has been the way of its defenders in the past who, when danger has threatened, have found support and wisdom in travelling out into moledom, and there discovering a way to return and see the system through into the ways of the Stone once more.'

The seven had fallen silent again, very silent, almost as if each awaited the sentence of an elder after some wrongdoing.

'I mentioned your recent experience, Fieldfare, so let me deal with you first –'

'I'm not going to leave my Chater, and that's flat!' declared Fieldfare. 'Not me, not ever again. When I was almost caught by those Newborns and he and Maple here rescued me I decided then and there never ever to leave him, whatever the circumstances! As for leaving the system, a mole like me? At my time of life?'

Stour raised a paw to silence her.

'I was about to say, Fieldfare, that I have no intention of suggesting you and your beloved Chater part company. If the Stone did not already want you to be together I am sure you would see that it did! No; but what I shall ask of you will be hard and difficult, and you will need a mole of experience in journeying at your flank. In short, you will need Chater.'

Fieldfare looked at once relieved and puzzled.

'But certainly you cannot stay here now in safety, and the sooner you go the better. Now, there is a system that long ago provided us with a mole who brought back love and security to Duncton Wood. I speak of Mistle, and her system of Avebury. You've taken texts there once before, I believe, Chater . . .'

'I have Master, and it's not a hard journey but for the crossing of the Ridge.'

'You could get Fieldfare there in safety?'

'I could,' said Chater with determination, 'and will do so gladly if it will make her safe. But there are Newborns there too, Master.'

'Aye, that I know. But I believe that great system's Stones are likely to be the harbingers of moles who will have the spirit to resist the Newborn threat. They are moles glad to have bred Mistle in decades past, and they will surely know how to protect refugees from Duncton and give support when it is needed in the future. But it is not just to escape that you will go there, Fieldfare. For you, more than any of us except good Pumpkin here, are of the very essence of our system. You know its ways, its lore, its traditions, its character.'

'But I'm not a scribemole, Master!' declared Fieldfare.

'You're something more important than that, my dear – you're a true mole, whose paws have been rooted firmly where you were born, whose values are of the essence of all that is good and true in the moledom of the Stone. Let Chater guide you to Avebury, or at least to moles in those parts if the Newborns make it impossible to enter

Avebury safely. Find a scribe there unaffected by the Newborns who will scribe down all you know of Duncton, and much that you do not know you know. Make a Book for all our pups, Fieldfare, and their pups, and their pups after them. Give through that Book to future generations what daily you have given to all who have known you through your life.'

'Me make a Book?' whispered Fieldfare in awe, eyes wide and looking at Privet for support. '*Me*?'

'You, my dear,' said Stour with a smile. 'It shall be a Book of Duncton more loved by moles than any scholar's work. And when a scholar's day is done he, or she, will turn to the Book that Fieldfare made and know what it is to be true mole.'

'Yes, Master!' said Fieldfare faintly.

'I'll get her over that way and find a scribe if I have to push her the whole way!' said Chater purposefully, and for once his sweet, his beloved, the mole he loved and who loved him more than any other in the world, responded not a word.

'Next,' Stour continued, 'the question of the Convocation in Caer Caradoc summoned by Thripp of Blagrove Slide. You already know my doubts of that and it is with trepidation that I speak the name of those who should represent us there. I wish to condemn no mole to travel to a place of danger, deceit and death, which is what I believe Caer Caradoc could become.' He looked gravely now on Privet. 'Yet, it could also be a place of opportunity, the last we may have if we are to avoid a repetition of a war such as that between Stone and Word. It is you, Privet, who must represent our interests, which is to say the interests of the Stone, at the Convocation. I shall travel with you in spirit as I would have done in body had I been younger – as I travelled once to the Conclave of Cannock so many decades ago.' He smiled wryly and continued, 'Of course, whilst it is not my wish to mislead anymole, perhaps a mole of my professed doubts may be allowed a certain casuistry regarding my journey with you, Privet.'

'Your journey, Master?'

'It will do no harm if Deputy Master Snyde were to think I *have* travelled with you. It may serve most usefully to confuse the issue . . .'

His wry smiled changed to one of kindly mischievousness and then his voice quickened and became more urgent.

'In short, it will be put about that I am of the party to the Convocation, and that we have gone by the shorter and more usual route of Rollright. But unless Chater disagrees, I think the better route is the obscure one which, if my memory of history serves, was once used very effectively by moles in Tryfan's day.'

'You mean Swinford?'

'That's it, Chater. You will lead Privet and Fieldfare that way, and once Privet is across the Thames, you can turn south to Avebury with Fieldfare.'

'But, Master,' interposed Maple, 'Privet cannot travel alone.'

'Indeed not, Maple. Whillan will go with her, and you as well, Maple, to give them protection along the way, and learn what I think you will need to learn about moledom and the moles who live in it before you are needed for a task of greater protection.'

A look of satisfaction came over Maple's face, and determination too. None there could doubt that Privet and Whillan could have no better protection than he would provide.

'That way is somewhat obscure, Master,' observed Chater.

'An advantage I think,' said Stour. 'The larger systems will already be quite overrun with Newborns and I am sure that Privet's party will find more interest, and more education, in the smaller, humbler systems, where the spirit of the Stone will still be strong, and which may as yet be untainted by the Newborns. But I do not advise you to travel covertly – say whatmoles you are and that you are the Duncton delegation to Caer Caradoc.'

'But the Newborns will soon hear of us!' said Maple.

'I wish them to. For I have no doubt that Deputy Master Snyde, on learning that I am myself on the journey and therefore out of harm's way, will choose to follow "us" and join the delegation. You see, the Newborns are poised to attempt the destruction of the Library as we know it, and it will be convenient for all concerned if Snyde is out of the way and so not tainted by blame for the destruction by any inquisitions that may follow. I have no doubt that nomole will have expected an old fool like me to travel abroad so far, and that therefore I am expected to stay behind and appoint him my representative, rather than go myself and leave him in charge. Yes, yes, we must confuse them as best we can.

'But doubt it not, Privet, Snyde will follow you, and catch you up, and on discovering (to his seeming dismay but enormous satisfaction) that I died along the way and ended up as owl fodder, he will assume command of the delegation, and lead you all with due pomp to Caer Caradoc to win the approval of Thripp.'

There was a murmur of surprise that the Master could be so devious as this.

'Meanwhile, none shall know that I am all the time where I should be, here, near our greatest texts, with unseen work to do in peace and anonymity to protect the holiest of them all. Which leaves you, Drubbins, and you, Pumpkin. Drubbins I have spoken with already, and it is best his tasks remain known to him alone. You, Pumpkin, will stay here and simply be what you have always been – until this night. A worthy aide, who obeys without question the Master's edict. It will not be an easy task. When I have gone into my retreat Snyde will be your Master until such time as he leaves in pursuit of myself and Privet, and I would not wish that on anymole, but there it is. If, as I expect, he follows Privet to Caer Caradoc then Keeper Sturne will be acting Master for a time and you, Pumpkin, Stone bless you, will be as meek and mild with him, and as obedient, as you always were with me.

'He is not an easy mole, I know, and one cannot predict how well or ill he will resist the Newborns' pressure, which will be considerable. I rather fear that a taste of power will go to his head, and if supporting the Newborns means he can hold on to power then no doubt he will do so. The study of history makes a mole realistic.'

'Master!' cried out poor Pumpkin, who did not like at all the role he was being assigned or this overt criticism of a mole he had so often defended against the censures of others. 'I can't say I like Snyde much, but Keeper Sturne has always been fair to me and the other aides, and considerate, but pretending to be Newborn . . . ?'

'Obedience, mole!' said Stour sharply, though with a slight gleam to his eye. 'The Stone will not mind a little exploration of other sects by its followers, and if this pretence saves your miserable and humble life so that you can later perform the far greater tasks that I believe it has in store for you, then being a Newborn for a time is a small sacrifice to make.'

For a moment Pumpkin was about to expostulate further, but then he remembered his position, and he saw that the covert task he was being given now was all of a piece with that. He! Pumpkin! So trusted! Well, then, let him be obedient and let his strength be the knowledge that his Master Stour so trusted him that he was of this seven.

'Yes, Master,' he said meekly.

'That's better, Pumpkin. Now, go and summon Keeper Sturne. I must give him a duty to take him from here to allow time for us all to go our separate ways. For now the moment has come when we must part and begin these great tasks which our lives have been leading us towards.'

Sturne was soon fetched and ordered to some obscure part of the Library on an even more obscure task, well out of the Main Chamber and away from the route to the surface. From the sharp way in which Stour spoke to him, and the irritated way in which Keeper Sturne obeyed, none could have guessed the most secret trust the Master had earlier placed in him. But so it was, and so that time of change continued. Once Sturne was gone it was plain that Stour felt there was little need, or time, for further talk.

'We must shortly go our separate ways and may the Stone be with us all, in its Light and in its Silence. For my part I feel the same apprehension and excitement I felt the very first time I came into this great Library. Now my task has changed and I turn from this life with gratitude that my work here is done and that what remains, great as it will be, is in the paws of seven moles such as yourselves. You are all worthy of the Stone's trust, and of that great tradition of service before self for which our system is famed. I believe that when each one of you is tested, and you will be, you will find strength in the remembrance of our stancing here together. In community is strength. Now, I pray you, accompany me to the start of my journey.'

He turned from them, and ducking through the portal, led them into the tunnels which none of them had ever entered before. Dark, arched, sonorous with wind-sound strange and beautiful; but from beyond came those darker sounds that chilled a mole's blood, and filled his mind with confusion and his heart with fear.

'Be not afraid . . .' whispered Stour as one by one they went forward, snouts low, eyes only on the rumps and back paws ahead, pawsteps echoing about them, before mounting like great shadows that held sound, giant sound, fearsome, dark, far beyond their strength to bear for long.

They went on long enough to feel that they had passed with Stour from an outer to an inner place, when the tunnel opened out into a chamber where on a few racks and shelves and in untidy piles, books and texts had been placed. They were of many kinds, representative of the library's great collection and Whillan and Privet had time to see many were originals of familiar texts such as a scholar might choose to Ken to call himself a scholoar.

'Place those discarded folios you have brought *here*,' said Stour to Pumpkin, pointing to a place in the middle of the collection of texts. They saw that where he pointed was the Book of Tales that Privet had commanded Pumpkin to deliver up to the library while she had been with Husk. As he did so the others became aware that there was a group of six, texts of differing sizes and age, which judging from their battered covers and loose folios were originals.

435

'The Books of Moledom,' whispered Master Stour, looking at them.

'The *Books*?' declared Pumpkin, astonished and awed and peering more closely, but not daring to touch them. 'Indeed there *are* six of them, as there would be since the seventh is lost. Bless me, but they look as if they could do with a bit of tender attention!'

Stour laughed. 'Well, mole, I doubt that there are any books in moledom's history that have had more attention than those, or journeyed more – buffeted and battered by the changes of history, and the forces of darkness and light. Yet here they are, together, in a system that has honoured the ideals they represent. But they cannot stay *here* in this chamber much longer, for I believe that it will not be long before the Newborns seek to take them for themselves. I fancy that Thripp of Blagrove would like nothing more than to hold these books himself, as evidence that his way to the Stone is the only one.'

'Why are they here,' asked Whillan, staring at them with awe, 'where they can be so easily reached by others? Why have they not already been placed somewhere safer, as the Stillstones were placed beneath the Duncton Stone decades ago?'

'We have been awaiting the discovery of the last Book, the Book of Silence,' explained Stour. 'We, and by we I mean Masters of the Library past and present, had thought that the last Book should come to ground before we tried to move these texts. You see, they are not easy to move.'

'But they're just texts,' said Whillan, going forward and reaching out to touch one of them.

He did so despite Privet reaching out a paw to stop him, but as he touched it he started back, as if his paw had been burnt, and Dark Sound flared up about them for a moment, like flames in a fatal fire.

'You see,' said Stour, philosophically. 'But now . . . I am no longer certain that the last Book can be found. I fear it may be too late, and that moledom has not been able to trust itself to go on into the Light of the Stone's Silence enough, before the ever-present forces of darkness engulf it once more. So I have taken it upon myself to try to move at least these six Books and Husk's Book of Tales, to take them into the Ancient System and with the Stone's help place them far from prying eyes and paws, and there stance in retreat over them as best I may.'

As he talked Dark Sound rumbled angrily about the chamber.

'Before we part I wanted you to see these books, and know something of what it is the life of our system has been dedicated to for so long,' said Stour. 'Pumpkin, you can help me take them down.'

'*Me?*' said Pumpkin in alarm, staring at the Books with trepidation.

'You,' said Stour firmly. 'Are you not a Library aide? Are these not books? Am I not your Master here?'

'Well, yes, you are,' said Pumpkin, 'but –'

'Help me!' said Stour.

It was then that one by one the Master Librarian, with Pumpkin's help, reached up to the shelves nearby and took down the six great Books of Moledom. Poor Pumpkin! How he struggled with each one, as if it were the heaviest thing he had ever carried, as indeed each felt to him: heavy, powerful, burdensome beyond belief. He panted with exertion and sweat glistened in his fur as he struggled to move the texts to positions indicated by Stour on the floor of the chamber.

'Master,' he gasped, struggling with the last but one, which either eluded his grasp, or was simply too heavy for him – small though it looked. 'I cannot, I *cannot* do more. These texts are not normal texts at all!'

'Indeed they are not, Pumpkin. Many lifetimes of experience lie between the folios of each one, and the one you are struggling with now is perhaps especially difficult to move, let alone carry. That is the Book of Healing. You see, with each of these Books, a mole who is not of the Silence of the Stone will feel the sufferings which first drove moles to scribe them . . . all in all I feel you have done quite well!'

He took the Book from Pumpkin's trembling paws and holding it carefully, repeated the names of the Books he had already begun to lay out in a circle on the ground before them.

'Seven books made . . . of Earth, of Suffering, of Fighting, of Darkness, this of Healing . . .'

It was plain that he too found the Book hard to hold for long, and as if struggling with a great boulder that a delving mole must lift to one side if he is to continue his work, Stour placed the book down in its rightful place to continue creating the circle.

He turned to the only book that now remained on the shelves and waved Pumpkin back as the aide loyally, though with considerable trepidation, came forward once more to try to help. He stared at the Book and its scratched, worn cover as if preparing himself for a great effort – as indeed he was.

'This last is the Book of Light, but it is not easy . . .'

Without more ado he reached up and with a struggle took it down, and as he did so the chamber seemed to glimmer towards a greater gloom and darkness, and the rumbling and roaring of Dark Sound grew louder again, like the first growls of thunder far beyond a wood where a mole waits for a coming storm.

Gasping as Pumpkin had before him, he carried the Book to the others and placed it thankfully with them to almost complete the circle. A gap for only one book, the seventh and last, remained.

> 'Now we wait on
> For the last Stone
> Without which the circle gapes;
> And the Seventh
> Lost and last Book
> By whose words we may be blessed.'

His voice was shaky as he quoted the famous poem of holy prophecy whose striving for fulfilment the modern history of moledom had been about.

'Well, the last Stillstone came back to Duncton Wood a century ago, and all the Books but the last are here. The time is coming when we must risk all in striving to complete the circle, and discover and bring home the missing Book of Silence.'

They all stared at the patch of earth where the circle was incomplete.

'You cannot leave them here, Master,' said Privet, 'hard though they are to carry. Let us stay here in the Ancient System with you to help.'

As she spoke the rumbling of Dark Sound grew louder still, seeming like a tidal wave that was already gathering in the unvisited tunnels of the Ancient System that lay darkly beyond the chamber.

'No, Privet, that is not your task but mine. Now moles, place your paws in turn on the ground where the circle gapes, and vow in your different ways to give what you can of yourself towards the discovery of the Book of Silence. There is little time – begin!'

Then one by one they came forward to the gap, and placed their paws in the dusty earth, each paw making a print that melded with the previous one so that the paw mark they made together seemed to grow bigger and ever more powerful, though each found it hard to keep a paw there for more than a moment, and the Dark Sound began to surge and mount in the very chamber itself.

'Maple . . . Fieldfare . . . Chater . . .' cried Stour as in turn they filled the gap with their right paws; 'Pumpkin . . . Whillan . . . good Drubbins . . .'

Only Privet hesitated, eyes wild and looking round in fear as the Dark Sound came on them, dangerous and seeking to sweep them up and batter them against the walls of the chamber, and subsume them.

'Privet!' ordered Stour. 'Do it now, it is your turn. Place your paw where the others placed theirs. Do it, mole!'

Gasping, sobbing, her whole body seeming to be struggling to stay on the ground against the terror all about, Privet reached her paw out and fought to place it on the earthen floor. Then she screamed, a desolate scream, which was taken up into the sound and twisted and turned into a thousand screams.

'I cannot touch the ground!' she cried out.

'Mole, you must!' cried old Stour still louder.

With another scream she tried again and as she did the first of them turned and began to run from the place, the sound unbearable in their ears, its pain and suffering and confusion overtaking all else they felt.

'Help me,' she cried out. 'Help me, Stone!'

Then for a moment, brief as first light of dawn, there came from beyond the Dark Sound something different. A cry as of a mole that sought to help, deep and inarticulate, distant, beyond giving help yet striving to come nearer; then beyond even that, and briefer still, a moment of pure Silence, the voice of the Stone.

The effect on all of them of this moment of soundless sound was great, but on Privet it was the greatest of all. While the others suddenly stilled into quietness, she seemed almost to become pale or light, as if caught by some errant ray of the sun across a way that had until then been dark. More than that, it seemed to those around her as if she danced, or moved with a grace that was Stone-given.

As they watched she went from one Book to another, touching each as if to take in what they were and pass on to the next. Their names she whispered wonderingly.

'Earth . . . Suffering . . . Fighting . . . Darkness . . . Healing . . . Light . . .'

But the last, Silence, greatest of all, she could not say, but hovered in that strange light that was an aura about her and held them all so still before the gap where that lost Book should have been.

Then, from out of the place to which the sound of Silence had removed her, so near to them and yet so far, she called their names, much as she had spoken the names of the Books. It was a call for help.

'Fieldfare, Chater, Maple . . .' so that their names seemed to echo and meld into one name, the name of allmole, of which each of them was one part of the greater whole, essential yet not entire, while she was beyond them, on the way towards the Stone. It was no longer Master Librarian Stour who was apart from the Seven Stancing, and she who was of it, but he who was of it, and she apart.

439

Yet she called out from the Silence for their help, like a mole with courage and strength and purpose but who yet needs help from others who have not quite the strength and grace she has.

'Help me,' she called, as her dance in the light began to falter, and the sound of Silence terribly to fade. 'Help me now . . .'

Which one moved first to help her? Which next? Which last?

Nomole knows for certain, though historians have argued, most convincingly, for one, or yet another of the moles who were there, so that all of them have followers.

One thing is certain, one thing most appropriate: it was good Pumpkin, Library aide, who, prompted perhaps by one or all the others, and stirred out of the stillness into which the Silence had cast, turned from the circle, took up the broken fragments and folios of the rescued Book of Tales, and placed them before Privet most reverently.

Then she spoke, and though it was softly her words carried a compelling authority.

'Now,' she said, '*now* is not the time for us to leave. In that moment we heard the sound of Silence, and I heard in it a warning against leaving before my task here is complete. Now I must begin . . .'

She seemed then to lull into a half sleep, a half stare, as they stared in awe at her and she, seeming not to know they were there, began to go through the Book of Tales, bit by bit.

As she did so the last moment of the Silence faded away and the Dark Sound returned, louder and more virulent than before. Yet, perhaps because they too had been touched by Silence and had now in their hearts a memory of its sound, they were able to withstand it better than before.

Master Stour, who understood better than the others that the Stone's power was profound among them then, signalled to Fieldfare to come and watch over her, while Pumpkin, understanding that Privet might have need of him as aide, stanced before her, ready to help with the folios. Whillan watched nearby, still affected it seemed by the Silence they had heard, and glancing sometimes, half in awe, half in fascination, towards the arched entrance to the tunnel that ran deep into the Ancient System from where the sound had come.

While they did so Stour quietly ordered Maple and Chater to go back through the tunnels to his study cell and look down into the Library to see if there was sign of danger there. This they quickly did, and on their return reported that they had been able to see from the secret gallery tunnel that ran from it across the high end of the Library's Main Chamber a great mass of Newborns, waiting and watching.

'But they seemed afraid to come up the slipway to the study cell, Master, though we could not tell why,' they whispered, their voices quiet because of the sense of awe and reverence surrounding Privet where she stanced. 'We saw Snyde there, looking as hateful as only he can, and that mole Bantam who terrorized Fieldfare, she's there too; and with them is a third more powerful, more dangerous-looking mole, one of their Senior Brothers perhaps. Then behind them there's more, as if they're massing ready for assault. We feel we should go back in case they summon up courage to ascend and attack. They . . .'

'Moles,' said Stour, 'your thoughts are worthy but I doubt if you can defend us as well as the Stone is already doing! Perhaps it was the power of the Seven Stancing, perhaps the Dark Sound delved so many generations before in this ancient place to protect moles whose tasks are for the Stone against such forces of darkness as now linger and hesitate beneath the portal of my Study cell.

'Stay here quietly, do not disturb Privet, and if the Dark Sound begins to fade, and our protection to weaken, then go back to the portal, see what you can see, and let me know if the Newborns come closer, and endanger all we do. I sense there is but little time for Privet to complete her task.'

As he gave his quiet instructions, and Maple and Chater took up a discreet stance near the entrance to the chamber, Privet ended her examination of the Book of Tales, if so ragged a thing could be called 'book' at all, and asked Pumpkin to put out the cleanest folios from amongst the discards that he held separately.

'They're all scored and marked, just as you picked them up,' he said.

'Find the clearest ones you can. Hurry, mole, hurry while I have the strength for this . . .'

Quickly he found a half-used folio and proffered it to her, and she nodded her thanks, and indicated he should sort the rest into what order of possible usage he thought best. Then without more ado she placed the folio before her and began to scribe the last tale of Husk's great work, the lost tale called 'The Sound of Silence'.

For those who witnessed that great scribing, there in the presence of the six Books of Moledom, with the ever-present roar and shattering, fading and swelling, calling and screaming, pattering and sliding of Dark Sound from the Ancient System, there could be no forgetting.

Here was the making of a final tale of Tales, a tale which told of Husk, and Husk's father's father's making of a collection of tales; a tale whose tunnels and labyrinths explored the laughter and the tears of a generation of moles who had lived in the long shadows, and the new discovered light, after the war of Word and Stone.

Not only Husk was there, young once, eager, determined, growing old as his great Collection grew more jumbled and chaotic, but Cobbett too, whom Privet herself had once known. He was there, and looming near but not yet come, the shadow of Rooster, Master of the Delve, for in that tale there were beginnings in the endings, just as in the seasons' turn at Longest Night, the distant call of spring may be heard beyond the approaching thunder of the winter.

Of these things Privet scribed, and something, too, of the moles who gathered round her in the chamber as she fulfilled her promise to Husk, and her task. Of Fieldfare and her life in Duncton Wood, of Chater, and the love he had for the mole who was his home; of Drubbins, wise old mole, and Maple, whose destiny was yet to come. Of all their story.

Of the Master Stour she scribed, for his tale wound its way amidst the others, leading them all towards that sound of Silence which Husk had sought so long, and then seen just beyond his living grasp.

Until, as she took up the very last folio of those discards Pumpkin had offered her one after another with increasing doubt, for he wondered how she could find space to scribe at all so great a theme on so ruined a set of folios, she turned by that infallible instinct all scribe-moles possess to the last and most mysterious part of her tale, which would – though she could not yet guess how – take it to its ending, and a beginning once again. She began to scribe of Whillan.

Of him she scribed, of what she knew of his coming, and of his puphood, and his first exploration of the wood alone which took him – truly, how tales encircle on themselves and like the seasons come back to where they first began, beginnings, endings, and beginnings once again! – to Husk's tunnels, and his discovery of the mysteries of Rolls, and Rhymes, but most of all of Tales.

'Whillan, my dear . . .' whispered Privet, looking up at him as if to help with this last effort she must make.

But if Whillan was there a moment before, he was not there a moment after. For while the others in the chamber has found their tasks, Whillan had stayed in a state of seeming quiet, unnoticed by the others, or ignored.

Yet when Privet came near the end of her scribing and began to recount his part in the last tale, he grew suddenly alert and restless, his eyes first on her and her scribing paw as if he felt in pain that she might try to put him into the ordered eternal place of a told-tale, out of which he had first come.

Then, 'Whillan . . . ?' she whispered, and on impulse, as it seemed to Stour who was watching, he was suddenly gone through the portal at the end of the chamber and into the tunnels of the ancient system.

'No, mole, not there . . . no!' cried out Stour, disturbing the strange quiet that had survived amidst the sound about them.

His cry echoed harshly all about, breaking the fragile peace and bringing forth a renewal of Dark Sound such that all of them but Privet and himself cowered once more, distraught.

The fearful sound swelled, and thundered, so that the chamber they were in seemed to shake and threaten them; but then the thunder became the sound of distraught running paws, and the crying of a mole, a mole in mortal danger, a mole whose cry Privet knew as that of a pup, long before, called Whillan.

A pup who ran back down the south-eastern slopes beyond the wood towards the place of darkness from which Stour had rescued him, a pup whose Dark Sound was the beating rooks' wings, and the pointing and the tearing of rooks' beaks and the shadows of a cross-under, where no hope was, where no light could be, where death was when a mother began to die, and a father was not.

Up and up around them the Dark Sound mounted, and somewhere beyond the dark portal, not far but too far for them to reach, Whillan cried out he was lost again, lost as he had seemed to be at birth, lost as, at some time in their lives, some soon, some late, all moles are; lost in the darkness from which they reach out blindly to touch the Stone and know that they are safe to be that part of themselves that lives on still, at peace beyond the dark sound of it all.

Then, threatening, sensing weakness and distress, the Newborns found their courage and their cries, mounted up the nearby slipway towards the Master's study cell and so towards where the moles tried to hold on to their Seven Stancing, and see a way, if only for a time, to fill the gap that broke the circle of the great Books of Moledom.

Strength magnificent and courageous – is it only when moles are tried their farthest that their greater selves are found, touched, never quite lost again?

Maple rose through the Dark Sound to turn towards his task, putting out a great paw to pull Chater with him, that together they might go and face the Newborns and stop them, or hold them, or merely slow them for a time, time before which the Dark Sound was taking Whillan into death.

443

While in the chamber where the Books lay still, and Fieldfare was huddled and mute, and Pumpkin dumb, and Drubbins' paws could not move themselves . . . there in the swirl of pain and loss that once was long before, and was now a pup's nightmare once again, an old mole slowly moved.

Master Stour, Librarian, doubter, scholar, friend, put a brave paw forward into the darkness about them, and then another, and so on until he reached poor Privet's flank, where she stared at the dark portal, her scribing forgotten, the last folio of the ruined folios incomplete, hearing her Whillan's dark flounder into death.

'Come,' commanded Stour, 'together we shall find the strength.'

Then, as Maple had taken Chater from the Chamber towards the world of day and physical danger, so Stour took Privet through the portal into night and the void of spiritual death, where moles see their own weakness and know not where to go.

Into the Dark Sound they went, down a tunnel of delved carvings and indentations, all ugly and strange, to a mole who floundered now, blinded by sound, deafened by dark light, his paws reaching vainly across the walls in panic and desperation as with his last strength he sought a way back out of the darkness into which his own fear, his own birth, had put him.

Towards him they struggled, each holding the other knowing that if they let go of each other perhaps their last touch on the world beyond themselves would slip away and they too . . .

'He's searching for something,' cried out Stour as they neared Whillan's wild form, though Stour's cry seemed no more than a whisper.

'Do not lose touch with me, Master Stour,' Privet sobbed, reaching to the walls as Whillan wildly reached, searching amongst their dark delvings as he searched, and then, with a cry, finding what he did not find.

'I cannot keep in touch with you more,' cried Stour as she moved beyond his paw as if she saw the beginning of something high, high up in the deep-delved wall, a line, a hint of light, the merest scratch of a talon in that place that so long before only a Master of the Delve could have made.

As Stour, unable to hold on to her, himself began to fall into the void of Dark Sound, and Whillan uttered his last despairing cry, as he had once before beneath the cross-under beneath the slopes south-east of Duncton Wood, Privet put the talons of her right paw to the beginning that she found, and began to find again the line, gentle and soft, sinuous and subtle, that a Master had made that another mole might find. A line made centuries before for this moment.

With increasing certainty, and with another cry as if to welcome once again the touch of a mole she had loved and lost, Privet began to sound out the delving just as Rooster had so long before showed her against just such a moment as this, and about them all the sound of Silence sounded out again.

Light was there! The void in retreat! The shadows in disarray . . . and Stour stanced down and staring, not at Whillan who had turned back to them and was safe again; nor at Privet, whose kenning of the delve was nearly done and the sound continuing to swell magically about them, healing and good; oh no, not at them did wise Stour stare.

But beyond further down the tunnel, to where the shadows fled far away, and where too, turning and staring for a moment, was the form of a great mole who once had been and might yet be again: a Master of the Delve. His brow was furrowed, his eyes askew, his head nearly monstrous, and his paws both huge, yet one more huge than the other, whilst his roar, like his tears, was silent. Then, as Stour reached for him, almost it felt to help him, he was gone . . .

'How did you know?' whispered Stour as, together, the three retraced their steps through the new-found light back through the dark portal. 'How did you know where the delve might be?'

'He taught me,' Privet whispered with joy, 'Rooster taught me, forced me to learn though I did not want to, because he knew one day, one day . . . yet, how did Whillan know what to search for?'

'*This* is the beginning of the Book of Silence' said Stour, ignoring her last question. 'It is now shown to you that you may have example and faith to rise up from the fear in which you have lived so long, and go and seek the Book that is not yet. That is your task, Privet.'

Very tired, at peace, she nodded and said, 'It is begun, Master Librarian, begun already, but not only I, but all of us shall finish it.'

Then they went through the portal and Privet led them to the Books, and touched Pumpkin, and Drubbins and Fieldfare, and called for Maple and Chater to come.

'The Newborns almost entered,' they said when they came back, 'but when the Silence began again, they fell back without us having to raise a paw, almost all of them fell back . . .'

But their words faltered and stopped as Privet turned to the last folio, on which she had only partly scribed, in which the last tale was therefore unfinished, or seemed to be; or was it only just begun?

445

Then, with reverence, but with no difficulty, she took it up and there, where she had failed to put a paw before, where the gap between the Six Books of Moledom waited to be filled, she placed the old, worn, scribed, scored and over-scribed folio down, which was the sum, the total, of so many moles' lives and tales, and made this holy dedication and offering: 'In your ending, Keeper Husk, who had faith in all the tales, and sought to honour them, is this beginning to the Book of Silence. We will seek the rest of it out and we shall find it, so that we may bring the last Book home to ground; the seventh lost and last Book . . .'

Then she placed the solitary ragged folio on the ground and completed the circle, the sound of Silence was all about as, at her command, each one of the moles placed their paw on hers to mark their acceptance of their part in the coming task.

'Come now,' said Maple at last, and boldly. 'Come while the Silence protects us and the Newborns are confused . . .'

'Aye, go now, moles. Go as I have commanded you, for I have strength now to fulfil my task, as you have,' said Stour.

With last embraces, each whispered their farewell to the Master Librarian who had given them, and moledom, all his life. Then each through the portal back towards the Library went, with Whillan at the last. He looked back one last time, as he had up in the clearing, to see where Husk lay. What he saw there he never forgot.

Just an old mole, pale of fur, wizened with age, who looked smaller still for the dark light that engulfed him, and the huge portal that rose above him into the ancient system. Whillan watched as Stour bent down painfully, and with enormous effort he turned towards it and took up the completed Book of Tales and began, step by slow step, breath by panting breath, to seek a place where nomole could find it, and where it would be for ever safe. But that was just the first: how could anymole survive more, let alone carry The Six Books of Moledom?

'Stone, protect him, give him all thy love,' whispered Whillan, as the returning Dark Sound reached out to claw him into itself and a paw reached from the portal at which he had paused and pulled him out of that wild darkness to safety once more.

There at least, and in the study cell beyond, the sound of Silence lingered on, gentle and balmy, safe as summer air.

'Look!' warned Maple, still hidden with the others inside the portal and pointing down the slipway to where, amazed, dumbfounded, nearly frightened, a mass of Newborns stanced uncertain still. At their head and coming up the slipway, was Snyde on the side near the wall, and Bantam on the other, near where the slipway fell sheer to the Library below; leading them was a dark mole, purposeful.

'What mole is that?' asked Privet.

'It's the one they call Chervil,' whispered Fieldfare.

'Come!' said Privet.

Even as their forms darkened the portal, substantial but not yet identifiable, the Newborns saw them, and seemed to see monsters. For theirs was a cry of alarm, a turning of panicked moles, for after the Dark Sound, after the Silence, came forth moles touched by Silence, and the Newborns were afraid.

Snyde turned first, hiding his face in the indentations made by generations on the slipway and covering his distorted ears; the mass below turned next, on each other, terrified, clawing and stampeding to escape through the Main Chamber and beyond to the Small, and thence, in a thunder of paws, and with books and texts flying all about, up and out into the Wood and downslope away as far as they could get from the Ancient System.

Finally Sister Bantam, in panic, turned into space, reached out a paw for support, and screaming fell down on to the hard ground below, her snout crushing, that scream the last of many that vile mole made through her destructive life, whether of perverse ecstasy, of gloating triumph or, as now, of fear of the dark void which had taken her at last.

Only Chervil did not move in fear, and one other mole, below, watching and still: Keeper Sturne.

'Come!' cried Privet again, and led the seven moles forth from the Master's cell, down past Senior Brother Chervil without a word, out of the Main Chamber and through the Small Chamber to go out into the Wood.

There, with the great beech trees of the High Wood silent about them, Drubbins and Pumpkin took leave of the other five. Their farewells were brief, for what can moles say who have lived through darkness and heard Silence? Nothing, but wish each other the blessings of the Stone, and the final blessings all moles make when they set off on a quest in the Stone's name.

'May you return home safeguarded!' said Pumpkin, as cheerfully as he could, running a little after them as they wended their way through the High Wood towards the south-eastern pastures.

'They'll go down there and then through the cross-under,' said Pumpkin quietly when he had gone back to where Drubbins stanced solidly down staring after their friends.

'Aye, mole.'

'And then their journey will begin, won't it, Drubbins?'

'It will, mole.'

'I'll . . . m . . . miss them,' said Pumpkin. 'Hard times are coming and I'm afraid. But the Master . . .'

'The Master's safe now, mole, safer than we are! But the Stone will watch out for us all.'

'We better not linger,' said Pumpkin. 'Had we?'

Nor did they, though the sound of Silence did, about the High Wood, about them both, too, as they went off to begin their task.

The Silence lingered also, longest of all perhaps, in the Library itself, where Chervil stanced still on the slipway and Snyde, looking up at last, took one final fearful look and crept away.

'Mole,' said Senior Brother Chervil, turning his head and looking down at where Keeper Sturne stanced. 'Are you Newborn of the Stone?'

Sturne stared up at the Senior Brother and pondered the question, his face impenetrable.

'I think perhaps I am,' he said without expression, and in view of what he had heard and seen in the hours just past he thought that perhaps he *was* 'new' born, and he told no lie. He hoped that following the Master's instructions might continue to prove easy as this first lie!

'Come here then, mole,' said Chervil.

Sturne mounted the slipway and stared into the cold dark eyes of the Senior Brother.

'Was Master Librarian Stour among those who passed me just now and left the Library?'

'"Just now!"' thought Sturne to himself. 'Why, it was an age ago and afternoon has come, and the Brother's been stanced there utterly bemused. He doesn't know if it's day or night. Silence, it seems, does not agree with Newborns!'

'Well, mole?'

Now the Silence was almost gone and Chervil's eye was growing brighter by the second.

'The Master was among them,' said Sturne, thinking to himself that in spirit the Master surely *was* and, too, for a dreadful moment that this had been a test for him by Chervil. But it seemed it was not, and that the Senior Brother had been as confused as the other Newborns by the Dark Sound and the sound of Silence. Yet he alone of all of them had had the strength to stay which, thought Sturne, scholar that he was, was most interesting.

'Well, mole, there's no need to linger more, is there?' said Chervil irritably. 'So seal it up, seal it up.'

'Seal what up, Senior Brother?'

'That study cell, or whatever they call it. Seal it up such that nomole may go there more!'

He turned suddenly from Sturne back down the slipway, saw Bantam lying dead, and, as if she was mere pile of rubbish left in an old tunnel waiting to be cleared, commanded Sturne in the cold Newborn way to 'rid the Library of her'.

He stared about the Library, narrowed his eyes and, to Sturne's surprise, his face broke into a strange bleak smile.

'Keeper Sturne! On the morrow the Brother Inquisitors, will come to the Library. You will assist them, will you not?'

'As far as the Stone enables me, Senior Brother, I will,' said Sturne, with an ambiguity he was beginning to enjoy. He wondered why he had no fear that Privet and the others would be caught, or Stour's retreat detected, but he did not. Sturne was beginning to wonder at many things.

'Good,' said Chervil and, thankfully it seemed, he too was gone, leaving Sturne alone in the Library.

'So,' he said, his eyes narrowing, his body calm, 'my task has truly begun at last. Stone, give me strength for it.' He stared up towards the Master's study cell and whispered to himself, 'I must start as the Master bid me start and, Senior Brother Chervil, too. In retreat it seems we and the Newborns can all agree!' He mounted on up the ramp towards the cell.

'Stone, let him always know thy Silence and see thy Light,' he said as he passed through the portal and entered. Then, his short prayer done, and with a muttered and reluctant, 'Now . . .' Sturne turned to the further portal which led from the Master's cell into the Ancient System beyond, and methodically and with measured delves, began to seal it up.

Epilogue

Epilogue

Mole, I think I've grown to love you, for you've listened well and almost silently! That's rare!

With shy Privet I began and told how she first came to Duncton Wood, a mole shrivelled up with loss, and with the desire to hide from life.

No hiding for her now! Nor any desire to!

But me? I'm tired and need to doze a little, and ponder on the things the telling of this tale has stirred inside me: memories of friends and places, memories of ideas won, and held, which I had thought had slipped away again.

And what of you? You came to Duncton Wood with nothing but hope and faith in your heart, and now, through listening to the tale I've told of Privet and the Book of Tales, perhaps you've begun to guess whatmole you really are. You've said little, and never once spoken out your name. We don't even know where you're from, or what you already knew before you came.

No, no, don't tell me yet. I've a wish to pray before this old Stone of ours, which knows so much and has seen much more. No need to clutter me up with names, other histories, and more concerns. I'll leave your name with you for now!

Aye, let me be awhile, let me think; go and find a younger Duncton mole to take you about our lovely Wood, which is at its best of a summer evening such as this. Go over to the Eastside, stare over the pastures the way, as you now know, Privet and her friends went to start their long journey, which was perhaps the greatest moles ever made. Yes, perhaps it was. . .

Then linger for a time in the High Wood, as Pumpkin often did, and Drubbins, too. If you're lucky you'll find a mole to show you where Rolls and Rhymes once was, and then guide you, by way of the Westside (always a most wormful place) to Barrow Vale. Now *there* you'll hear some tales! More dramatic than any I can tell you, more full of action and fighting and all that kind of thing. If you've any sense you'll stay the night in Barrow Vale, and eat, talk and be merry!

And *don't* look so worried – tomorrow I won't die! Come back up here and you'll find me dozing in the shade if the sun's too hot, or stretched out in its rays if it's shining just right. I won't be far off, you'll snout me out. But bring me some food again, flatter me, tell me you never heard such a tale as the one I've told you before the Stone this lovely day, encourage me . . . ! Then, and if I'm in the mood – and only if! – I'll tell you the true tale of how it was that the Book of Silence came to ground. The real version, as it happened to moles I near-enough knew myself, and not as you might ken it from some book scribed by some scribe who was not there. Tales told from experience, and from one heart to another, as I tell my tales to you, are the only tales worth hearing!

Aye, I've a mind to speak of the Book of Silence and its coming, one more time. For here in the Ancient System was its beginning, as you've heard, and here too was its ending, here right where we stance now by the Duncton Stone. . . .

To learn the final truth about the Book of Silence . . .

DUNCTON STONE

William Horwood

As Privet, scholar and scribemole, and her adopted son Whillan, escape from Duncton Wood in search of the Book of Silence, the Newborn Inquisitors seek to take over the system.

Only old Stour, Master Librarian, and the timid aide Pumpkin can defend Duncton and the precious holy Books of Moledom against the Newborn moles. But time is running out as Privet journeys in search of the lost and last Book. To find it, she and her friends must go to Caer Caradoc, centre of the Newborns' power, and face Thripp himself; there, too, she must reveal the secrets of her past and give up all hope of reconciliation with the only mole she has ever truly loved: Rooster, Master of the Delve.

Yet always the light and Silence of Duncton's fabled Stone beckons, offering hope to all moles with the courage to confront their faith, and a last chance to discover the truth of the Book of Silence.

Duncton Stone is the last tale of moles whose task is the discovery of truth, but whose hope is only that one day they may return home safeguarded.

Duncton Stone will be published by HarperCollins*Publishers* in Spring 1992.